LEGEND
OF THE
DINOSAUR TAIL

PART I

ARLENE COTTERELL AND
PHILIP OLONZO HITE

BLUEPRINT PRESS
INTERNATIONALE

Legend of the Dinosaur Tail
Copyright © 2023 by Arlene Cotterell and Philip Olonzo Hite

ISBN
978-1-959365-71-6 (Paperback)
978-1-959365-72-3 (eBook)
978-1-959365-70-9 (Hardcover)

TABLE OF CONTENTS

CHAPTER ONE

The year was 2925, a time when our planet was barely conversant as everyone dwelt amid technology. People did not have identification cards or numbers anymore. Now at birth, a chip was implanted in the back of the neck and all information on that person would be found there by simply scanning it with a small hand-held device that used laser technology. That person's information was read right on the scanner. In the late 1990s, people had started to build smart houses in preparation for the end of days to withstand the harsh environment and stocked up on goods for preparedness. Only the wealthy could do this. For further preparation, those people took college classes in medicine, computer technology, and electronics for autos and household appliances. Those skills were taught to younger generations by the older generations. Now there was no cooking or cleaning up like in the old days. In fact, everything was replicated—food, water, clothing, medicine, household items, and so on.

There were not even real doctor visits anymore. The doctor was a hologram that could perform all medical diagnosing and procedures at the person's home. It was known as the holodoc. All the adults carried the knowledge of what used to be a registered nurse practitioner. Even the police were nonhuman; they were complex robots. Occupations, television, and music were things of the past. However, television shows and music archived in their computers could be retrieved and enjoyed. As for occupations, they were now extinct. Everyone was technologically gifted and passed this gift from generation to generation as previously mentioned. The community worked together as a whole to keep the homes and transportation up and running smoothly. In fact, paychecks were also a thing of the past; money had no bearing on the functionality of society anymore. Automobiles as we knew them were extinct; now there was the use of the hovercraft. The hovercraft was a motorcycle-type vessel that had no wheels; it simply hovered, flew, and was much faster than any automobile that was ever made.

In the western part of the United States, there was a town named Las Vegas, population approximately one thousand and rapidly diminishing. Las Vegas was often called the "land of the lost wages" because it was illustrious of places called casinos; they were the state's primary income. Visionaries had never fathomed the fall of Rome nor the fall of the gaming industry. The buildings still stood but were run-down and inhabited by people who needed to be isolated from society due to deadly contagious flesh-eating illnesses; it was worse than the leprosy outbreak described in history. The population around the world was declining quickly also due to the lack of natural and man-made resources. For those who were surviving, it was just a matter of time before the elements or sickness struck them and they would perish. Due to an age-old legend, no one dared to move there, and poverty kept residents from relocating. The wicked sandstorms, radioactive air, and intense smog kept people indoors, in their smart houses, most of the time. Most modes of transportation and all homes were hi-tech, computerized, and airtight. It was required to wear a face mask with filters and a protective outerwear if one needed to be in the elements. Each home was surrounded with a dome to protect the house and allowed some minimal outdoor time safely without the protective outerwear as the dome was airtight. One could say that the survival of humanity relied heavily on the coddling of technology, more so now than ever.

In Las Vegas, there was a fifteen-year-old girl that did not let the griefs of society bother her. She spent many hours sitting in her bedroom twirling her long wavy brown hair while she pondered the legend that tormented the town. Her large green almond-shaped eyes glazed as she daydreamed of what lay ahead soon; the new school year was to start tomorrow. She was five feet and a half inches and weighed one hundred and fifteen pounds but did not let her stature stop her from challenging life's calamities. Her name was Camillia, and this is her story. Now that the summer was over and she had reached the first year of high school, the only thing that crowned hpper curiosity was the strange jay-shaped patch of green that was surrounded by extinct foliage found near Dobbins Memorial school, which was a K-to-12 school. That lustrous jay-shaped patch was known as the Dinosaur Tail, as it looked like the tail of a dinosaur. Dobbins Memorial was the only school the children could attend since there were so few of them.

Camillia remembered the legend of the dinosaur tail being introduced to her during kindergarten. As it was to all kindergartners, it stirred the imaginations of all the children, young and old. At first, this was simply construed as the average childhood boogeyman; but little by little, it evolved into twisted dark stories of child abductions and torturous murders carried out by an anonymous individual in the community with a suspect in mind but not proven. You see, it appeared that all the adults were too afraid to converse about it with much detail, so every year children learned of more and more macabre details from the school district's officials as if it was part of the curriculum—kind of how driver's education was part of the curriculum in the old days.

Camillia used to interrogate herself in silence if this was supposed to be a warning, a scare tactic, method of control, or a form of some sick adult entertainment. Some of the kids took the stories seriously, and others laughed it off as an addition to Grimm's fairy tales. She tried not to believe in the stories but was unable to shake the possibility of some truthfulness. She thought bluntly then concluded that all legends bloomed from some truth and became over exaggerated as time went by. The tail was estimated to sit approximately four miles away from the path along the side of the road by the old tunnel between Camillia's home and school. It was said to stretch the length of at least thirteen miles, but no one really knew for sure. The rich glistening emerald green angel-wing-shaped leaves were extremely mesmerizing. There must be millions upon millions of them huddled together in perfect symmetrical order. The field used to be easily seen, but now the land there was surrounded by a large thick metal electrical border that had a four-foot-tall blackened force field. Going there was forbidden, and it was protected by the police. It was monitored 24-7 by the nearby military installation called area 54 as well. At one time, there was an installation called area 51 that denied its existence; it was now just another military station along with areas 52 and 53. The station was manned by high-tech computers and lifelike robots. They were armed and programmed to shoot for the kill upon trespassers, no interrogation necessary.

Last school year, each school day, as she and her best friends—also simply called "the girls"—Melanie, Michelle, and Bridgette rode their hover bikes past the tail, they heard a strange song, like that of a sailor's siren, coming across the crisp morning air. Every time Camillia heard this "song," she would pause for a moment to listen if she might be able to decipher some sort of message. Melanie, a fifteen-year-old five-foot-two and one-hundred-and-twenty-pound girl with blond hair and wide blue eyes, was rather reserved and did not say much. Michelle, also fifteen years old, had black hair. She was the shortest of the girls at only five feet with dark Asian eyes and weighing one hundred pounds. She had the talent of debating. As for Bridgette, she was the tallest at five feet and six inches. She had luxurious red curly hair that stretched to her buttocks with piercing green eyes and weighed one hundred and thirty pounds. She would be fifteen by the start of school. She was also the most opinionated one of the group. Together, the group of four made a well-balanced team.

According to the legend, in the year 1922, a six-year-old boy named Lloyd was teased and scrutinized every day, in and out of school, by all the other kids at Dobbins Memorial. None of the adults would dare step in to protect Lloyd for fear of retaliation from the older teen bullies. He was always being called offensive names, pushed to the ground, shoved into the walls, locked in small rooms, and so on. He was only about three feet four inches and walked with his head down so that his appearance was not identifiable beyond his hooded cloak. Yes! He wore a cloak. The only obvious deformities were the hump on his back and his twisted, mangled face. Because his parents Deanna and Darren were brother and sister—identical twins of about five foot two, blond hair, fair complexion, and ice-blue eyes—Lloyd had deformities so grotesque that he wore that hooded cloak to hide behind; only his parents really knew what he looked like. In fear of being harmed by passing school kids, their boy was unable to play outside after school. Lloyd's physical abnormalities were much more immersed than just skin deep. They hindered his physical agility and stamina as well. He would hibernate in his bedroom and daydream of permanent ways to defend himself: poisonings, cutting of throats, execution-style shootings, torturing to death, and much more.

After a while, the only solution he apparently came up with was to eliminate all the problem children once and for all then move on to naive children, but how to do so was never determined, as far as anyone knew for sure. In fact, it was never officially said to be Lloyd who committed those child abductions, and the children had never been found so it was not known for sure whether they were dead or alive. However, per legend, it was the day after Lloyd concluded he had to end his torment that he began his silent killing sprees, methodically plucking the children from one family at a time. His parents were said to have even been additional suspects, but again, nothing was ever substantiated. This case was, and remained to be, very perplexing to officials.

It was theorized that Lloyd lured those children into the field near the school by asking them if they wanted to see what he looked like then carried out his bloodthirsty plot. He would quickly bury the body, change clothes, and wait for the next inquisitive victim. It was said that for each body buried, a set of leafy wings would appear in the field. No one thought of linking Lloyd to the most current murders at that time until his eighteenth year, when the community suspected that he committed suicide in the same field. At that point, his parents were never seen or heard from again. There was no explanation for their disappearances. Maybe they too committed suicide over the grief of the loss of their only son, or maybe they went underground due to some sort of illness. This was when the foliage around the graves died, never again to flourish, exposing the dinosaur tail. The traveling songlike sound from there was said to be the voices of the souls of all the departed children; this was how in Lloyd's supposed death most parents believed he still lured inquisitive Dobbins high school children to the field. No one knew how he still managed to kill because anyone who had gotten past the forcefield and gone there had never returned, but like before, a new set of wings would magically appear. Even if he didn't commit suicide, he was sure to have passed away by now due to complications from his deformities. The authorities had never caught anyone behind the force field, so no one has faded that way.

Over a century later, Dobbins Memorial was remodeled several times over, the tail continued to grow, and teenagers on the way to school continued to disappear in groups of up to six. Camillia often wondered if Lloyd really died or if he had simply started an underground operation of some sort, maybe a cult. She was sure the police a century ago worked on the case of the missing children because she knew they were working with resistance now to find out where the current missing children were. She felt within herself that those disappearances had and continued to have something to do with Lloyd somehow. One day she would like to visit the tail although the girls—Melanie, Michelle, and Bridgette—continued to try to talk her out of it. Even though Camillia was not fully persuaded of the legend's veracity, she tried to convince the girls that the stories they had been told were just legends and that if they went together they would be fine.

How could one robot person overpower four healthy humans, even if they were just young girls? She also knew that they were as inquisitive as she was; they just would not admit it. It was Camillia's goal this freshman year to secretly uncover the facts from fiction of the legend of the dinosaur tail and possibly overcome the barrier to the field and visit the alleged grave sites.

It was the first day of school, and the four girls were motivated to go so they could see the field and hopefully hear the whispering song of childlike sirens. Maybe today would be the day to explore the song. The girls all lived on the same street. They would be meeting before school at six thirty in the morning at the end of the street by the decaying stop sign so they could travel together for safety. It was a three-mile ride to school and took only five minutes. This left time to have breakfast at the school cafeteria and catch up on the latest happenings from acquaintances and teachers. Classes started at seven and went until four with a half-of-an-hour lunch. The food was not bad; it was replicated just like at home. Moving on, it was now time to leave for the meeting place and travel to Dobbins Memorial. Like clockwork, everyone arrived at the same time.

CHAPTER TWO

The first two miles of the ride were uneventful; however, the next half mile became intense. It was the tail—it was much more extensive than it was at the end of the school year last year, and the song was so much more roaring and more mesmerizing than last remembered. Camillia and the girls stopped to listen and peered over the force field from their hover bikes.

They were in awe as they saw a faint movement of one set of leafy wings. It was a miniangel; it fluttered for a second then landed on the rest and nestled into position, fitting in as though to fill a void to maintain the perfect symmetrical formation.

Did something move, or was it an anticipated over imaginary response to the excitement of the first day of school? The girls quickly peeked at one another in amazement. Their hearts pounded practically out of their chests. Camillia took one more look to see if she really saw movement, and to her uncanny surprise, she did. Another set of green angel wings fluttered above the rest. She urged the girls to look, and they hesitantly did. They all agreed they were not imagining this but now questioned what this admiration could possibly be. It could not be a leaf; maybe it was an entity of some kind. Another pair of wings rose and fluttered above the rest. The girls froze in fear.

In silence, they all inquired the purpose of this phenomenon. The girls struggled to move, passed through it with no effects from the electricity. Once through, those emerald green leaflike structures transformed into iridescent angelic beings with beautiful faces. They were about four inches tall with a wingspan of eight inches. Their voices had a perfect soft soprano tone that but they could not. It was like someone had placed a mold over their bodies and was holding them in midair. The flitting leaves began to move closer and closer to the barrier until they seemed made by God himself. The girls' minds were cleared of all thoughts, and they began to relax; their trepidation and prompt to flee was gone.

Suddenly the girls understood what the angelic beings wanted to say: "It will be okay." This message propelled the girls to reach a hand out to the flitting angels before them, and the angels palpated their hands in return. Then in a flash, the beings were gone. There was something happening there, but it was not quite clear as to what that might be.

The girls realized they were free to move. Prodigiously they looked at one another. The girls decided to land their hover bikes and walk the rest of the way to school. None of them understood why they decided to do this, but they just knew it would be okay, regardless of the school's forewarnings not to challenge such heedless odds.

The girls parked their hover bikes by the side of the road and checked one another's oxygen tanks to warrant enough oxygen to get to school, and they thought they did.

Camillia was startled at how different things looked while walking compared to riding at a slow speed of seventy-five miles per hour. There was so much to perceive that she had not espied before. The old-style town from the year 2000 had buildings for everything—church, medical care, various shopping, leisure time, and other services. All those services were now provided in everyone's home holographically. Current homes were all computerized and interactive by voice command. Due to the Earth's mortal state of existence, homes had to be protected by specialized airtight domes so people did not have to live in space-like suits and could still have some outdoor time in the small yardage that was also under their domes.

Still slowly walking, the girls noticed that there was now only one obstacle between them and the school—a short tunnel. Out of curiosity, the girls decided to poke about the tunnel to see what else they may have previously neglected to mark. The tunnel was only one quarter of a mile long, but it was as thick as it was long and said to be hollow; no one had confirmed nor could deny that. With expressions of deduction, the girls stared at the tunnel for a few moments then turned to one another and agreed that the only harm that could come to them would be from one end of the tunnel or the other, not inside. Normally, the girls would ride their hover bikes around the tunnel, as part of the legend has it that children ought to steer clear of the tunnel without explanation. There were a few people that sensed children coming up missing in the tunnel though it was unclear as to how Cautiously, Camillia led the group into the head of the tunnel with Melanie bringing up the rear. The intensity was so heightened that each girl could hear the silence of the rest of the girls holding their breaths. Bridgette began to hesitate to move much farther when Michelle jabbed her to move on and keep up with Camillia; after all, the deal was for all of them to check out the tunnel together. The sounds of crunching pebbles under their feet and the whispering wind whooshing through the tunnel added to the thought of hysteria.

This whole legend thing hit close to home for Bridgette because her boyfriend Matthew was one of the latest abductees;

there were four other male students that went missing that day. Whoever overpowered him either had help or scored a lucky blow. Matthew was a healthy young lad of fifteen years; he weighed one hundred and fifty pounds and was five feet seven inches, with brown hair and brown eyes. He always found time to exercise and lift weights; he was very agile. It was hard to understand why anyone would want Matthew gone; he was a good student, a humanitarian to everyone, and well respected.

As the girls moved deeper into the tunnel, they could sense water oozing from the side of the tunnel just above their heads; that did not make any sense since there was no water source nearby. As Camillia and Bridgette reached up to touch the area where the water was coming out, the girls heard a creaking sound like that of a squeaky door. The girls jumped in horror and expeditiously turned about as if to see someone or something behind them; however, no one and nothing was there and the squeak stopped abruptly. Once again, the girls turned their attention to the water leak on the tunnel wall, and again, they heard the awful squeal of stone being dragged on stone; it was reminiscent of fingernails being dragged down a chalkboard. Again, the girls gyrated, expecting to see someone or something; but all they saw were some small rocks falling from the ceiling area of the tunnel from which they heard the noise. The water from the tunnel wall and rocks from the ceiling were both peculiar; Camillia could not help but try to contemplate what it meant. Was it connected to the dinosaur tail, or worse, the missing students? The girls looked back and forth between both ends of the tunnel and concluded that there was no immediate threat; they were just letting their paranoia get to them.

In a final assent to move on and finish walking the tunnel, the girls started to walk when they heard the creaking noise again. Camillia had finally had it! Girls or no girls, she was going back to where the small rocks fell and investigate it further. In fear and frustration, Michelle, Melanie, and Bridgette followed her. The girls were closely examining the wall of the tunnel where the rocks fell for cracks or splits, and sure enough, Camillia found a large crack in the wall that ran from the ceiling, as high as they could see, to the floor. Bridgette found another split in the side of the tunnel about as far apart from Camillia's split as a doorway would be. With this new discovery, Camillia called for a meeting of the minds.

The girls huddled in a half circle with their backs to the wall having the cracks in it. The meeting was about deciding if enough was enough and they should run from the tunnel or walk on slowly and scout the rest of the tunnel. Before the girls could come to a decision, the tunnel wall behind them opened swiftly and suddenly, and many pale arms reached out, grabbing the girls. As quick as the wall opened, it shut, and the girls found themselves in a world of darkness. Were the angelic beings the girls previously encountered honest in representing that all would be okay, and if so, how could the girls be sure because the situation was surely not okay? Were they even part of their abduction somehow? All the girls could do was see what these strangely pale people wanted of them and find a way to escape. Though escape had never been heard of, there was always a first time for everything.

Now having been abducted, the girls could understand how Matthew was abducted—he was overpowered by many pale ones, as well as the rest of the boys with him. There had been many stories of the pale ones' existence over the years, but until now, they were only old wives' tales. Not much had been said about them except that they were a peaceful people who could withstand the elements and survive on very little. The pale ones were the least likely suspects in the disappearances of the schoolchildren.

Still being groped at, the girls tried hard to see what the pale ones looked like up close and where they were being directed to. That part of the abduction seemed to be uncoordinated and chaotic. The girls had been minimally separated among the pale ones in a small area headed down some brick-laden stairs. Deeper and deeper down below the ground they all went. There were twists, turns, and a lot of loose stones to fumble through. Even though the girls seemed to be prisoners to the pale ones, they seemed to care for the girls' safety, gently helping them through the tunnel and keeping them from slipping. This part of the journey was more orchestrated and orderly the land had evened out with a dirt foundation and an occasional pebble. It was very damp and smelled of wet wood; they could hear the water seeping down the sides of the tunnel. At that point, the tunnel appeared to have widened more and more. There was now a dim light to the area, but it was not obvious where it was coming from.

The evident leader of the pale ones had stopped and enlightened everyone to rest their feet and lungs. Until now, the girls did not think of their oxygen tanks and what would become of them once the tanks were empty. How were they going to check their tanks when they could not envision their own tanks and they had been kept a short distance apart, which kept them from checking one another's tanks? Unknown to them, their tanks had been empty for quite some time now and they had been breathing tunnel air.

In a state of alarm, all four girls tried to observe one another for some sort of answer to that question. The pale ones were also telepathic, which was not in any of the old wives' tales, nor known to humans, so the chief of the pale ones not only noted the panic on the girls' faces but also knew what was unsettling them.

He approached Camillia gingerly, put his left hand on top of her head and his right hand on the right side of her head, and with a breakneck snap of a motion ripped her helmet right off. She gasped as she was taken back in astonishment and fright. Melanie, Michelle, and Bridgette tried to plunge for Camillia's side but were held back by other pale ones. The girls waited for Camillia to take in the effects of toxic radioactive air and suffer a strangulation type of death, but nothing happened. The foremost of the pale ones instructed Camillia to take long deep breaths and let it out slowly to adapt to the thinness of the air.

CHAPTER THREE

B y this time, all four girls were gripping their chests, all as an anticipatory caution. Everything was okay though Camillia's lungs felt dense and slack. The other three girls removed their hands from their chests and breathed an extensive sigh of alleviation. The pale one who was in charge instructed the rest of the girls to remove their helmets, saying that they had been out of oxygen for a while now and that just like their friend, all would be fine. Slowly the other three girls reached for their helmets and, with caution, removed their helmets. They had some fear of what would happen if they did not follow instructions. Although the pale ones were said to be a peaceable people and they did handle the girls with concern thus far, it was still unpredictable if they would turn fierce if they were to get angry. As with Camillia's lungs, the girls' lungs felt dense and slack, but they were okay. It felt like the girls had been in their suits and helmets for days, so it was an alleviation to take off the helmets as they were oversized and thick. Carrying all that weight made the girls feel like they had been walking for days.

In all actuality, the group had only been walking for four hours and resting for half an hour. However, there was still a long way to travel and would take about six more hours until they reached what was called the land of grandeur. That place was spoken of in the old wives' tale; it was supposed to be a place of clean air, streams, forests, and presumed to be plentiful of fruits, vegetables, nuts, and grains. It was also said to be a world for beasts and critters of all kinds, but nothing had been mentioned about angel-like creatures such as the ones the girls had previously encountered. It sounded otherworldly, and that was just what this part of the tale was taken as—a fantasy.

Once they were to reach the land of grandeur, the girls' family and friends would miss them and start to worry, hopefully sending out a search party and finding them alive and well. Now without helmets, the girls wished to shed their suits as well, and the chieftain bid them to do so. Now that the girls' lungs had acclimated to the air and everyone had unwound, it was time to walk some more. The foremost pale one requested that everyone get up and start on their lengthy journey. With having so much land to cover and the amount of time it would take them to travel, one would have had the rationale as to why the small groups of children that were taken only occurred once a week.

The walk was uneventful and long. Several hours passed, and the girls started to wonder if their destination, the land of grandeur, was as astounding as it was said to be. Camillia tried to use small talk to strike up a conversation with the pale ones, but the followers said nothing the whole trip thus far and the leader was not a man of many words. All she wanted to do was find out more about them and what their plans were. They were, however, interesting to look at. Now without helmets, the girls could see more clearly.

Their hair was the same as humans, but their eyes were yellow and gleaming, for they could see in the dark easily, much like that of a cat. Their skin was a pale bluish color; you could almost see their veins laid out like an old road map. They held the same stature and variety in body size as humans; they seemed to be rather athletic with a well-defined musculature.

Their personalities seemed to be more tranquil and merciful than that of a composed human although it seemed that they were not much for verbalization due to their telepathic abilities. Their voices were nothing special except that they were very indulgent.

The path that had been expanding was now as wide as the eye could see; there was now a beauteous shade of green grass on the ground. The lighting was blinding and came from lightning bugs; there had to be billions of them above their heads. You could hear bubbling brooks; there was even a gorgeous pond just off to the right side of the group. Up ahead, there was a lush forest with trees taller than the mind could imagine. Off in the distance, you could hear the birds' songs being carried by the moderate breeze. The girls were in complete amazement to see such beauty for the first time in their lives and to hear the various noises. Besides the brooks and birds, the girls heard noises they could not explain as they were new and to them had no names; they were simply noises made by other animals.

Another four hours passed by, and everyone seemed exhausted. They came upon what looked like a good place to rest; there was only another hour and a half until they would arrive at the compound. As the girls rested, they spotted deer, rabbits, lions, zebras, and many other animal life-forms. They knew of these animals because they were in history books at school, but they were supposed to all be extinct due to the tragedy that civilization created above ground. Who would have thought the underground could thrive like this?

The compound was just as astonishing. Instead of being a prison-type building as one would expect, it was built like an old-day castle. Each brick and stone was meticulously placed to make the structure look authentic; the girls had no clue of what structural amazement awaited them. All the pale ones stood up and awaited the girls' positions to follow suit; the half-an-hour respite had gone by expeditiously. The girls were exhausted, their muscles were cramping, and they were very thirsty as well as somewhat hungry. The pale ones were very aware of this so a few of them reached into pouch-like bags they carried over their shoulders and pulled out large strips of dried meat, much like a beef jerky treat they used to replicate and eat at home after school each day. They would be coming up to the lakeline area in about a half an hour and could acquire water at that time. Like the last time, this walk was uneventful and without conversation. Now at the water's edge, the lead pale one simply said to drink as he pointed at the water, and the girls moved to the water's edge to do as commanded. This was the first time since the abduction that the girls could be near one another.

Once their thirsts were quenched, they realized that they were not separated and simply stared at each other in silence. The girls began to huddle for a group hug, but the pale ones stepped in between them and separated them once again. The girls had only fought for their emancipation at the time of the initial abduction; since then they have been cooperative and sympathetic so they could not apprehend why they were not allowed to be together. All they wanted to do was feel self-possessed and advocate for one another, but the pale ones felt that might lead the girls to return to the tunnel wall and escape. The girls were not missing family or friends yet, but they would begin to soon enough and the pale ones knew this. They also knew that missing loved ones would cause the girls to behave irrationally, but that too would be addressed. There was only one more hour left to walk until they would reach the compound, but it was within sight. Again, the rest of the walk was without incident and dialogue.

Now, an hour later, at the door to the towering brick wall enclosing the compound, the pale ones placed the girls together and encircled them. The girls became fearful as to what was going to become of them. They grasped one another's hands and began to tear up. They started to reflect on friends and family.

Would they ever see them again? Camillia started to plead for their lives when the lead pale one quietly said to be silent and cheer up, for today would be the day of a regeneration for all the girls. The pale one then turned toward the great wall and raised up both hands as if to offer up an invisible offering to some strange god. The wall began to open wider and wider, giving out a great rumble until it was visible, the land of grandeur. It was beautiful with all sorts of colors and everything seemed to be tipped in gold glitter. There were small angelic beings fluttering about, just like the ones the girls saw at the dinosaur tail. This was beyond what any fairy tale could conjure up.

Meanwhile, back at the girls' homes, friends and family were missing them. The remaining children were instructed to stay home for safety reasons while the adults would suit up and backtrack the girls' route to the school and check to see if they even made it there. The adults seemed to be rather stoic when they were apprehensive about going out. Nonetheless, the search must occur. The girls' parents tried to rally other adults, but out of fear, they gave their condolences and declined to join them. The search party only consisted of the girls' parents. They went out and onward. Each parent traced the steps of their daughter until all the adults met at the old scabrous stop sign. Riding a slow forty-five miles an hour, everyone scanned for signs of the girls, but there was nothing.

Finally, at the area of the dinosaur tail, there were the girls' hover bikes parked carefully along the side of the old trail that led into the tunnel. The adults stopped and looked around as far as the eye could see and were unable to spot the girls. Finally, Camillia's mother looked down and noticed a large number of footprints in the soft parts of the gravel, and she pointed down to them. Everyone else looked, and they visually traced the tracks to the tunnel. Heavy Heartedly, everyone knew it was time to turn back and summon the robot police, for no one dared to enter the tunnel. Everyone drove to Camillia's home to discuss the findings with the authorities. The parents' report was immediately called out to other robopolice near the area to be checked out. They could only report that the girls' tracks led into the tunnel, but they could not enter the tunnel. All the parents could do was, like all the other parents of the lost children, wait for them to return—though none ever did return when it came to the dinosaur tail or tunnel. Most of the parents assumed the girls were dead, as all the children had to be. The girls' parents just knew in their hearts that they had to be alive.

As for the girls, they just stepped into the land of grandeur past the great wall. The wall began to close behind them with a clamorous gnashing of rocks. There were many pale ones with each seeming to have a purpose. They all buzzed about like an ant colony. Some females were picking fruits, vegetables, grain, and seeds; and some were planting more, with the assistance of younger children. The male pale ones were out hunting for meat to eat, furs for clothing, and bones for weapons; they used every part of the animal for something. The girls noticed that the grass there was like that of the dinosaur tail by their home.

Upon a more careful look, they noticed that there were angelic entities flitting just above the grass line; they were beautiful and vivacious. It was unclear as to what they were doing and what their purpose was, but it was apparent that they were magical creatures much like that of unicorns or mermaids in the old tales.

The girls wondered if there were any other magical-like creatures in this land of grandeur. This whole place was a mini society run with precision. The lead pale one ordered the girls to walk, and without hesitation, they followed him. They started to walk along a brick-laden path toward the castle-type building. It was about a twenty-minute walk until they came to the door of the majestic building, and the doors began to open leisurely.

The girls could tell that the doors were heavy, they stood the height of three normal doors by the width of two normal doors. The doors were fully opened, and the pale ones stepped to the side of the doors pointing inward; the girls knew this meant to enter alone. They did as motioned, and all at once, more of them swarmed the girls from both sides. These pale ones were pawing and grasping at them. The girls panicked. The girls were swarmed from all sides now and being held in place. They could not continue to walk as instructed.

Each girl cowered down and rolled into a fetal position on the ground. A single pale one grabbed Camillia's hand and held it tight then extended the thumb. Camillia felt a prick on her thumb and looked between the other pale ones to see what it was. It was a pale one holding her hand injecting something blue into her thumb. The prick was not too bad, but the stuff being injected was thick and burned tremendously. After injecting Camillia, he moved on to the other girls one by one, injecting them also. The burning sensation crept from their thumbs to their arms and into the rest of their bodies.

It was excruciating. The pale ones let go of the girls as they lay on the ground disabled and took several steps back. The girls' bodies began to turn blue, and it felt like they could not catch their breaths. They wondered what was happening to them. Their bodies started to get a vibrant blue plastic-like coating. All but four pale ones left the girls' sides, and the chief stepped toward them. He looked at them with an expression of concern then knelt beside them. Though the girls could not see the leader's mouth move, they all thought they heard him say not to fight the transformation and it would be less painful. The girls cried out in pain, begging for the pale ones to stop it from hurting.

After about fifteen minutes, the burning stopped and their lungs started to function fine again. They were completely consumed by a fiery blue coating, and it was beginning to loosen on them. The girls sat up on their buttocks from the fetal position and looked at one another as well as themselves with curiosity. What had happened, and what was going to happen? The blue fluid was a vaccination against the earth and its deadly elements. As for the blue coating around the girls' bodies, it would shed and leave their skin a pale bluish color. They too now had telepathic abilities; that was why they heard the leader speak without seeing his mouth move. They just did not know it yet. The blue coats they grew were tight all over, including the neckline, and made it difficult to breathe. The pale ones reached one hand down to the girls to help them up from the sitting position. The girls reached up with one hand to meet theirs for help, standing erect.

With all this movement, the blue skin began to tear around the neck and stretch out everywhere else. The pale ones took the skin from behind the girls' heads and pulled it over their heads and off their faces. They were free to breathe once more. The pale ones then walked around to the girls' backs and tore the skin in a semi straight line down their backs so all the girls had to do was step out of the skin like a spacesuit. The girls did just that. The girls stared at one another with amazement at the transformation that had taken place; they now looked just like the pale ones. They then began to examine their own arms and torsos; they noticed that their veins showed road maps just like the pale ones.

The girls were thinking of comments, concerns, and family when they started to feel one another's emotions and practically hear their thoughts as well. They realized this was phenomenal and wondered how this could be. One of the pale ones thought of the answer to their question of how it could be, and the girls swore they could hear him through his mouth and did not move. Again, he thought of their telepathic abilities and how that was part of their transformation as all pale ones were telepathic. The girls then understood and accepted that logic.

CHAPTER FOUR

Everyone in the compound had to undergo the same transformation. The vaccine was developed by Lloyd's parents Deanna and Darin. They had started to work on it when Lloyd was fourteen years old. It was designed to extend his life and help safeguard him against the various diseases that plagued the town. The lifespan on average was about forty-five, but the vaccine extended it to about two hundred and fifty. His parents had no idea that the vaccine would provide protection from the earth's calamities and turn him a pale blue color or turn his eyes yellow and allow sight in the dark. They certainly did not realize that the change would be so painful. They finished their project when he was eighteen. The vaccine was made of all-natural ingredients so his parents presumed that if it did not work, it could not hurt him.

By this time, Lloyd was on the brink of death with organ failure and speedy aging due to his severe deformities. Once the vaccine was given, his parents noted that his aging process slowed and his damaged organs had regenerated. His parents also noticed that he was immune to the effects of the radioactive air and allowed for communication to be telepathic rather than verbal. After this, they decided to take the vaccine themselves, and it had the same effects. However, it was suspected that the vaccine made people sterile. Now that they were different, they had to flee to the underground land. They did not know what to expect down there, but to their surprise, it was a wonderland. It flourished with plant and animal life and had plenty of clean water. It also offered much for building materials; it was Lloyd and his parents alone that built the castle-like compound and surrounding wall. Lloyd would lure the kids into the tunnel, and his parents would overpower them and inject them with the transformation serum.

At that point, there were about two hundred pale ones living in the compound, all willfully. Although they were abducted and missed their loved ones that remained above ground, they chose to stay and be loyal to the cause of repopulating the earth with a new breed of people. That story was conveyed to the girls as it was to all the new pale ones. The only difference now was that Lloyd no longer lured people to the tunnel; they were simply snatched by many pale ones after the angelic beings led them there. Lloyd had since passed away of old age, as did his parents. Now the vaccine was made by a pale one with knowledge in medicine, and the formula was passed down to the younger hopefuls for the job.

The girls were still in disbelief and figured they would try that telepathic thing out for themselves. Before the girls could try out their new ability, more of the pale ones approached them, and they were bombarded with greetings and wishes of good health, whatever good health meant. The girls looked at Camillia and Bridgette gasped. Behind Camillia stood Matthew; he was alive and well. However, just like them, he had been turned into a pale one. Camillia felt Bridgette's surprise and amazement so she turned around to see what Bridgette saw. It was Matthew! Behind him were the four boys that went missing on the same day.

Camillia could never forget who came up missing that day because one of the other boys, Andrew, was Camillia's secret love.

Her best friends don't even know about that. Camillia felt a warm affectionate sensation coming from the crowd of pale ones, but she did not pay any attention to it.

Little did she know, it was coming from Andrew for he felt toward her what she felt for him; they just never expressed it. The leader of the pale ones came back to the girls and commanded the crowd to disperse apart from Matthew and Andrew. Now it was just the two boys, the four girls, two other male pale ones, and the chief. They started to walk to the doors of the actual compound building. It took eighteen minutes to reach the doors from just inside the great wall where they were. The two strange pale ones extended an appendage out for the doors and began to open them. The girls could not help but try to peer through the doors for what awaited them. They thought that if the outside was so luxurious, the inside had to be extravagant. Once again, Camillia felt the warm affectionate sensation and seemed to hear some words of love. She shockingly looked at Andrew and held eye contact for a few minutes. With even more excitement, she grabbed Andrew around the neck and gave him a long passionate hug then thought of words of love in return to him. The other girls were shocked to see that display of love for Camillia never spoke of having feelings for Andrew. Andrew had also kept his feelings for Camillia a secret.

The chief was proud of their actions and compatibility. The chief then asked for Bridgette and Matthew to pair up as a couple, and they gladly did so. Their feelings for one another were no secret. Now the doors to the compound were open as wide as they would go, and the leader told the girls to enter and follow the strange pale ones that tagged along. One couple was to follow one pale one while the other couple followed the other strange pale one. The leader was to return to his domicile for a rest from the long journey they had just finished. The strange pale ones took the couples to their new accommodations for a resting period. The quarters did not seem very large from the outside, but they were like small houses once you were inside. Each home was fully furnished and stocked with plenty of food and water.

The couples found their bedrooms, kicked off their shoes, and lay down on their beds for a resting period as advised. The other two girls were just as well off and happy about their accommodations but had no one to share it with. Melanie and Michelle wondered if they would be spouseless for the rest of their lives or if they too would meet someone and settle down. Only time would tell. They had their own little homes to themselves for now. The walls were decorated with bone set into the hieroglyphic-carved stone. The bedding and furniture covers were made from soft furs. The floor was a spongy fine sand-like substance that massages your feet as you walk on it barefooted.

As they lay on the bed, Camillia told Andrew about her most profound feelings toward him, how she loved him since the seventh grade. Before that, he was her fancied friend since at that age, kids thought the other sex had cooties or something. Although they had grown up together, she had observed him as something special at first in kindergarten. Andrew sat up and took Camillia into his arms and embraced her closely. He agreed that they should be together, for he had fallen in love with her around seventh grade as well. Camillia could feel Andrew's heartbeat; it was so swift and rhythmic. She reached her left hand up to his hair and caressed it gently. He tilted his head into her hand so gently. Their faces were slowly drawn together until their lips pressed together gently; this was their first kiss.

After the kiss, they snuggled down into the bed and rested together with Camillia in Andrew's arms. As for Bridgette and Matthew, they had been an item since the sixth grade and best buddies since kindergarten. They too had grown up together. Most of the kids in the human society had grown up together; their parents were all friends and helpers to one another. Two hours passed since the kids had been left in their quarters when suddenly, they were roused by a knock at their doors. They were being summoned by the lead pale one through regular pale ones. This was a relief to the girls since they were accustomed to eating dinner about that time that they could now ask the pale ones for nourishment. The boys already knew it was dinnertime, but they did not know that tonight was going to be different than usual.

Usually, dinner was held in a large dining hall and served by other pale ones who would eat later. Every pale one held a purpose in their society, whether it be indoors or outdoors. This was much like the way the human society above ground ran. However, the pale ones' society was much more complicated as they ran things without all the up-to-date technology. There were no holographic doctors, but there was a medicine man simply called doctor with runners up. A runner up was a trained individual in line for a job in the event the job holder died or had to be euthanized. If the runner up were to be utilized, another individual would become a runner up and trained for that job.

There were no robo police, only pale ones called scouts whose job it was to uphold the laws and the chief who oversaw them. Their mode of transportation besides being on foot was horse-drawn carriages or ox-drawn plows, no hovercrafts or cars. Their food was not replicated, but hunted or harvested then hand prepared and replaced through animal breeding or planting. Clothing was handmade of animal hides instead of replicated and made of synthetic materials; the styles were even different.

Upon opening their doors, the kids were surprised to see a female pale one standing outside of each one's door. The females came in and took measuring tapes from their pouches. They began to measure the girls, twisting and turning them about from position to position. It became quite personal as the pale ones measured the girls' crotches, hips, breasts, and so on. Matthew and Andrew chuckled at their women, as the boys had already been through that process when they first arrived to get their clothing fitted for comfort and functionality.

When the female pale ones were done, they nodded their heads in an up-and-down motion then left the rooms silently, shutting the doors behind them. Not a word was spoken or sensed from the pale females; the girls felt that was a quick yet simple task they were supposed to cooperate with, so they did. The boys agreed with Camillia and Bridgette; the other two girls were left to assume. The girls started to think about dinner once again, and an hour and a half passed by when there was another knock at their doors. It was the same pale females as before; this time they had something in their arms. The girls invited them in and marveled at what they had. They had lavish floor-length dresses made of fur, leather, and intricate beadwork for Camillia and Bridgette and fur and leather knee-length less-luxuriant dresses for Michelle and Melanie, but each girl did not know what the other had yet. The females instructed the girls to put on the dresses, and they apprehensively started to do so. The girls were not happy about changing clothes in front of the female pale ones; Camillia and Bridgette paused and requested that their men step into another room.

The boys did as they were asked, and all four girls had finally changed. Camillia and Bridgette called their men to ask what their opinions were on their new attire. The men were astounded at how beautiful the girls looked in their dresses.

The other two girls were complimented by the female pale ones that were in their presence. The pale ones tugged and twisted at their dresses to assure endurance and to inspect for any fitting problems; everything fit okay and passed the endurance test. The females requested that the girls give up their old clothing to them so they could burn them as they were hazardous due to exposure from outside of the compound walls. The girls curiously gave their old clothing to the females as asked. The pale ones gave a simple thanks to the girls and hurried off, closing their doors behind them. The girls felt this was odd since they were told the air was fine and they survived breathing it. What kind of contamination could it have been?

Now that all the clothing issues were done, the girls turned their minds to dinner. They were ready to go in search of food themselves. After all, what else could be more important at that point that could not wait until after dinner? Before the girls could go into action, there was another knock at their doors; that knocking was becoming redundant. It was a female and male pale one at each door; they told the girls that they were part of the clergy. They paired up in husband-and-wife teams, and there were ten couples with runner-ups. They were there for them for spiritual support and would guide them through the "ins and outs" of their society since the girls were newcomers. The rules and regulations were simple and easy to follow; it was basically "do unto others as you would have done unto you" and follow the Ten Commandments that the Bible spoke of. The Ten Commandments were laid out in its simplest form, leaving no room for questions by the male pale clergyman. The pale ones explained to the girls that everyone held a place in this society and that they would also. They went on to assure two of the boys that because they were no longer single, their status would be changed to a higher status by the chief. Camillia and Bridgette would hold a higher status than Michelle and Melanie because they were not going to be single anymore. Camillia and Bridgette were to be married that day, then after the wedding ceremony, the medicine man would bless the union; the leader of the pale ones would then reveal their duties. The clergy explained their spiritual beliefs as being like that of a fundamental Bible-believing Baptist church, just like that of the late 1900. The space age Camillia and the rest of the kids grew up in put no emphasis on religion, so spirituality really did not exist above ground.

CHAPTER FIVE

Although their religious concept was new, it intrigued the girls, and they were willing to follow its teachings; it fit right in with their personal feelings and how things should be done. The boys were pleased that the girls made that life-altering decision. The clergymen gave a sermon to the kids and explained who Jesus was and what his purpose was and what the plan of salvation was. The girls accepted Jesus into their hearts and vowed to follow Jesus's examples, as well as the laws of the land. Each girl was given a brand-new Bible and advised to read daily and bring it to the Wednesday and Sunday sermon gathering. It was required that every pale one attend those sermons. The girls wondered if there was a punishment for not accepting the pale ones' religion. With that interrogation, the pale females looked away and the male pale ones answered yes. The clergymen told the girls that every newcomer was given that option without knowing the outcome of either decision, and if they were not willing to accept the ways of the pale ones, they were euthanized before they could become the downfall of their society. That life-altering detail was never revealed until it was the only option because the pale ones wanted the newcomers to follow their hearts, no matter how corrupt they may be.

The female pale ones interrupted and announced that dinner was next and it was time for them to leave; they said that someone else would summon them for dinner. The pale ones exchanged hugs with the kids and left their domains. Now alone in their domains, Camillia and Deanna want to discuss marriage with Andrew and Matthew.

The thought of marriage was frightening when taken into a perspective of a forever union. What if they became incompatible, or something happened to one of them? They were only fifteen years old and knew very little about life; there was a lot of maturing for them to do. They decided they needed to let their love grow and to let their hearts guide them and not be stagnant in work or love. The wedding was going to occur soon. Deanna and Michelle sat quietly in their rooms with thoughts of how their futures would be in this new world. All four girls knew somehow that this new life would be better for them and hold promise for all pale ones. The girls began to miss their families again. It would be nice for their parents to give last-minute advice and be present at their wedding, but they assumed that they would never see their parents again. They realized at that moment that they may see some of their friends if they were abducted and safely processed as they were.

The girls' thoughts were interrupted by a knock at their doors. Outside of each door stood a female pale one who was there to summon the kids for dinner. This was a relief for the girls since they were famished. The kids were to follow the females to the dining hall, and they did. Once in the dining hall, the boys knew that it was more than a regular evening of eating and socializing. The hall was beautifully decorated, and pale ones were seated in an organized fashion by hierarchy instead of the usual chaotically mixed for the luxury of conversation. The clergy sat in the front of the hall, and the chief, who usually ate alone, was at the head of the clergy. Also by the clergy and chief was an empty table for the kids to sit at; they were obviously the guests of honor for no one is placed near the chief without good reason. Camillia and Bridgette realized that their attire was much more elegant than anyone there, including Melanie and Michelle. The two girls noticed that many of the pale ones were pointing, smiling, and whispering among themselves; they felt like they were on display.

Finally, they were seated at their table, and things settled down among the pale ones. The chief stood up behind his table and introduced the kids then announced the marriage of Camillia to Andrew and Bridgette to Matthew. Michelle and Melanie were in shock over the imminent marital union of their friends.

The two couples were asked to stand before the pale chief and present themselves. The two girls felt their legs and hands start to tremble; could they do this without fainting? The two boys held their girls tight and guided them to the altar. The boys had attended a previous wedding, so they knew what to expect of the leader and that the clergy would leave the room with the new couple after the union. What exactly the clergy would do once they were in private quarters remained a mystery. The girls were only familiar with human weddings and had no idea that the wedding had a second part that does not occur in human weddings. The chief did what a human clergy would do, and the clergy would perform a second secret part. The boys did not know what the second part consisted of because it was done in private while the guests were entertained.

After the clergy was finished, the couples came out and dinner was served. The pale chief began to talk, saying the things that are said in a human wedding, all the way to "do you take this woman" and "do you take this man." Both couples' answers were that they did. At that moment, two clergymen and their wives stood up, went down to the new couples, and grabbed them by the arms and whisked them off to a back room. The two couples were separated and sat into chairs, and there they were told of a prophecy and how it would affect them should it come to pass. This legend was not to be known by any single individual, so after their conversation and upon leaving the small room, it was not to be spoken of under any circumstances.

The legend was that the only pale ones able to reproduce were Lloyd's parents, but due to their relation, it would cause birth defects as in Lloyd's case. The scrutiny caused Darren and Deanna to move underground and start a new society of peace and true freedom. That involved the making of the vaccine, but what was not understood about it was how it affected the gene pool. Everyone had the same number of chromosomes and at an even amount. Legend said that there would come a male and a female with an odd number of chromosomes, an extra half if you would. It was said that if these two individuals found each other and united, they could produce a child. This child would have abilities that would far surpass any pale one or human. The union of two such people was not difficult; it was in them finding each other by chance. Since all pale ones had become sterile with the vaccine, that remained a legend.

With that, the kids were asked if there were any questions, and Camillia came up with one: what would happen to the parents of that miracle baby? The pale man simply responded that the parents would become breeders; their only job would be to produce children unless the chief decided differently. Camillia was glad that she was never lucky to win or exceed at anything. With that subject now closed, everyone stood up to exit the room and join the guests. The boys started to open the doors, and the male pale one put his hand on it and held it closed. There was one piece of business to address before letting the kids go. If they were the chosen ones, could they perform the duty of bearing child after child? After a few moments of silence, they all answered yes. This was good because had the answer been no, they would have been euthanized. The punishment of death for breaking the rules or not being willing to perform accordingly seemed harsh, but that kept the society crime-free and in working order. There had been some euthanizations in the past so the people knew that the leader was true to his word in that matter because not only had it been done, but it also was a public process.

As the two couples stepped back out with the guests, they all stood up and clapped and whistled. You see, there were not a lot of marriages, and each marriage was known to be special though the details were not widely known. The couples were sitting back at their table, and on the table in front of them were folded pieces of paper that contained their job title with a list of duties. Also in front of the boys were sets of wedding rings to be placed on their new wives' left ring finger and one for their left ring finger as well. The rings were placed on each couple's fingers, then they each took a glimpse at their job title; they left reading the duties of their jobs for later. Andrew was listed as clergy along with Camillia; her job was to support him and address the females where appropriate. Matthew's title was a livestock doctor, better known as a veterinarian. His wife, Bridgette, would be his assistant. She was to help with procedures and keep records of all the animal vaccinations and procedures if there were any. Both jobs were well respected and hard to be placed into. Both couples had some education to undergo prior to being able to perform their duties alone; they all looked forward to that.

Melanie was to work as a maid for clergy members, and Michelle was to work as a public records keeper; that job entailed things such as keeping a roster of the people, updating it as more members arrived and noting essential information about them.

There would be no honeymoon, the kids' education where to start first thing in the next morning. All four kids were pleased with the jobs bestowed upon them, and they had planned to do their utmost best. As for the absence of a honeymoon, they figured that with such a long life ahead of them, they could devote a small part of their day each day to a honeymoon moment. The pale leader quieted everyone down then proposed a toast to good fortune for the four kids and a healthy marriage for the two couples. Everyone drank and then the guests took their seats.

Now for the moment the girls had been waiting for—dinner. Since this was a special occasion, the meal was more extravagant than usual. The dishes were made of real crystal, and the flatware was made of gold; both had designs carved into them. The homemade food was much better than that of a replicated meal. The girls could smell all the different smells of all the different foods; at home, the food all smelled the same. The girls thought dinner was a real treat; then came dessert. The wedding cake was three feet tall and had tiers; it was covered in an angel theme. The girls never knew that food could be so good and so beautiful. Once dinner was over the guests socialized some, and the kids were asked to return to their homes so they could finish settling in. Unbeknown to them, they had a lot of clothes to try on then either return for alterations or hang up in their closets. While most everyone was at the wedding there was a large group of seamstresses working hard to put together an appropriate wardrobe for the kids and their new positions. The girls could not believe their eyes when they saw all the vigorous work.

The kids tried on all their new clothes in front of the seamstresses, and everything fit perfectly so they hung the clothing up in the closets. Now it was time to relax, and the rest of the night was theirs to do whatever they wanted, within reason. The compound did have a curfew of ten o'clock at night; that was when everyone had to be in their homes. The businesses closed at six o'clock at night, but started at six o'clock in the morning. The twelve-hour shifts were only five days a week for they had Wednesdays and Sundays off. Those two days were devoted to religion and socialization. Breakfast call was at five in the morning, lunch call was at one in the afternoon, and dinner was at seven in the evening.

It was now nine at night, and the girls have had a full day being abducted, changed, getting married, and gaining a lot of additional information. The boys had a quite exciting day also, definitely different than any other day they have had since being turned. Melanie and Michelle climbed into bed and fell fast asleep. Camillia and Bridgette decided to start their first moment of a honeymoon. The two girls spoke to their husbands about their new jobs. They could not wait to start their jobs after the schooling was done; they felt confident that they would be good at what they would be doing. The conversations came to a premature end, and the two couples went to bed. Bridgette and Matthew fell asleep quickly.

Camillia and Andrew lay in bed and caressed each other's bodies, exploring every part of each other. Their hearts started to pound, and Camillia started to quiver. Andrew questioned her as to whether she wanted him to stop. She said she was fine and nestled into him. They continued to caress each other gently, paying special attention to the erogenous zones. Things continued to get hot, and they started to kiss passionately. Things moved on, and they made love for the first time ever. Camillia felt different somehow; it was indescribable. She had a heavy feeling in her abdomen. Afterward, they spent the rest of their awake time just holding each other and finally fell asleep in each other's arms. The night went by in a flash. It was time to get up and prepare for the new day, but it felt like they had just fallen asleep.

It was nearly five in the morning; that meant it was time to get to the dining hall for breakfast. Each girl planned to find the rest and sit together so they could catch up on things and compare notes on what had been happening to them; the girls did not realize that they all had the same idea because they were not close enough to one another to sense one another's thoughts. Melanie and Michelle found each other right away; together they found Bridgette then Camillia, along with the boys, of course. The girls left it to the boys to find a space with enough chairs for them all, and they did immediately. Everyone sat down, and their conversation began with comparing notes on their transformations.

The transformation was just as painful for one as it was for the rest, and they agreed that the walk was dreadful. The boys even recalled their abduction and transformation and agreed with the girls' notions of how dreadful it was. Next, they revealed to one another what their jobs were and what each job entailed. They could not say much more because their breakfast had come and it was time to eat. There was so much more to discuss, but nutrition was more important at this moment in time. The smell of the food was wonderful, but for some reason, it turned Camillia's stomach upside down; this was not normal for her. She tried to eat anyway, but found that her appetite had suddenly left. After Andrew finished his food, he picked at Camillia's food and discovered that there was nothing wrong with it. He urged her to eat, but she said she had an overwhelming feeling of nausea. This was concerning to Andrew and the other girls because pale ones do not get sick; they were immune to these things. Breakfast was now over, and it was time for everyone to report to their duties for training. The girls gave one another hugs, the guys shook hands, and everyone went their own way.

CHAPTER SIX

Andrew and Camillia were at the meeting place for clergy and ready for instruction before anyone else showed up. There were supposed to be nine other clergy couples and two hopeful couples. Andrew was eager to start his new job, and Camillia was more than ready to support her husband's work. The rest of the clergy arrived and instruction began, but it was hard for Camillia to focus on the lesson at hand. The lead clergyman sensed that and summoned his wife to take Camillia out of the room for interrogation. This greatly concerned Andrew for his wife's safety could be at risk; he pleaded with the clergyman that she was just fine and to please let her stay in the room. The clergyman's wife took Camillia's hand into hers, assured Andrew she would be okay, and started to gently tug on Camillia's hand.

When Camillia stood up, she immediately fainted and fell to the ground. Andrew slid off his chair down to his wife's seemingly lifeless side and held her in his arms. Knowing this was highly abnormal for she was now a pale one and things like that were not supposed to be able to occur, the clergyman requested that his wife summon the doctor. Right after the clergyman's wife left the room to get the doctor, Camillia regained consciousness. Everyone in the room told her to stay where she was, not to try to get up. The doctor finally arrived; it seemed like it took an hour when in all actuality, it only took six minutes. Everyone remained in their seats and Andrew got back in his seat so the doctor could get to Camillia. The doctor noted that her pale blue color was paler than it should be, her heartbeat was abnormally high, her blood pressure was slightly low, her temperature was slightly elevated, and her blood sugar was on the low side of normal. He asked her if she felt okay that morning, and she told him how the smell of breakfast turned her stomach and trying to eat made her feel like she was going to throw up so she skipped breakfast.

The doctor told the clergyman that she needed to be in the hospital for some testing and observation. The clergyman sent his wife to the chief to tell him of this new development and get authorization for Camillia to miss class time and have Andrew take the lessons to her in the hospital and spend personal time keeping her up to date on the lessons. The leader came back with the clergyman's wife to see this phenomenon for himself. After speaking with the doctor and examining Camillia for himself, the chief agreed that she needed to be in the hospital and approved for Andrew to keep her up to date on the lessons during their personal time. The doctor summoned for a horse-drawn medical transport. Andrew had to stay behind to receive the lesson so he could learn his trade and teach it to Camillia. She grabbed her husband's hand and assured him that she would be okay and that she would be waiting to see him during free time. During the ride to the hospital, Camillia started to feel better; she assumed it was the fresh air Andrew paid close attention to the lesson given so he could adequately instruct his wife; he wanted her to have the best of everything.

Now at the hospital, the doctor asked Camillia how she felt. She said she felt normal again. A hospital attendant brought out a gurney for Camillia to lie on; the doctor did not want her to do any walking for she might faint again. She assured the doctor that she could transfer from the wagon bed to the gurney on her own safely. He allowed it, and she was just fine. The doctor had the attendant take Camillia straight to a room where she would be staying until her discharge, and he followed behind closely. Camillia was ready to transfer from the gurney to her bed when she detected the smell of lunch on the way. Again, it smelled good, but it turned her stomach upside down. The doctor noticed the change in her demeanor and questioned if she was okay. She replied by saying not really. She explained that she could smell lunch close by and although it smelled good, it was making her nauseated.

While talking to the doctor, she was scooting close to the edge of the gurney so she could plop into the bed, but she was feeling wobbly sitting up. The doctor ordered the attendant to put her into the bed and he would step out to retrieve a nurse to change her into hospital attire. The attendant did as he was ordered and stood by Camillia to make sure she was fine until the nurse arrived. A nurse saw the doctor and asked him if he needed assistance; he said yes and to follow him. They got back to Camillia's room, and the nurse changed Camillia's clothing. The doctor told the nurse that he wanted to speak with the nurse who oversaw that room; the nurse told him it was her and asked what he needed. He ordered her to establish an intravenous line and that he needed to check Camillia out further before ordering tests but she should go ahead and draw some blood for testing. The doctor told the nurse Camillia's symptoms and what happened to her in class. The nurse agreed that this was an unusual set of symptoms, especially for a pale one.

While the doctor was gone, he got a handheld ultrasound machine and the nurse established a line and got six tubes of blood. The doctor returned so the nurse left the room. The doctor laid the bed flat and began to poke at Camillia's lower belly. It did not hurt, but the doctor found that her uterus seemed to be inflamed and he could not feel either ovary. It was usually the other way around, swollen ovaries and not being able to detect the uterus. The doctor used the ultrasound machine. With a quick glimpse, his eyes grew large, and he ran out of the room after gasping that he would be back. He located the nurse and told her to get the chief there as quickly as possible and to get the blood to the lab for stat results. The doctor wanted an HCG level, and that took priority over everyone in the hospital.

About the time the chief arrived, the doctor got the blood work results; that was perfect timing if what he suspected was wrong with Camillia really was the problem. The doctor noticed that everything was within normal limits except one thing—her HCG levels were higher than normal. That meant she was possibly pregnant.

The doctor saw the chief and requested to go into a private office to discuss the possible affliction; the chief agreed that it could be an affliction. The doctor explained what the blood tests were looking for and what HCG was along with the normal limits for a nonpregnant woman; then he showed the leader the HCG results. The chief advised the doctor to let Camillia and Andrew in on the news, but no one else other than the couple and themselves only until further notice and to repeat the one blood test weekly to see if it continues to go higher. The chief also wanted the couple to understand the importance in not telling anyone and to report to the doctor weekly until further notice. The doctor agreed to follow instructions. Per the tests Camillia did not need to stay in the hospital; she just needed bed rest at home. The chief agreed with that also so he would have arrangements made for Camillia and Andrew that day so she could go home when her husband came by.

It was finally six o'clock in the evening so Andrew was free to go see Camillia in the hospital. Many scenarios ran through his mind, but they all ended the same way—not good. The doctor was waiting impatiently at the hospital doors for Andrew, and suddenly there they were face-to-face. The doctor took Andrew by the arm, and as he was dragging the boy, he said that they needed to talk in private; that really concerned Andrew. The doctor took Andrew into the same office that he took the chief into and laid out all the facts to Andrew. Andrew was in shock and told the doctor that they were both virgins until the previous evening. The doctor responded that it only took one incident at the right time of the month. Andrew agreed not to tell anyone, and he would make sure that Camillia was there for her blood tests until further notice. Together, Andrew and the doctor went to see Camillia and break the exciting yet shocking news to her.

Now in Camillia's room, the doctor told her that she was blessed. Andrew approached her bedside and held her hand and kissed it tenderly. The doctor proceeded to tell her about her HCG levels and results of other tests being normal, her having to return weekly until told otherwise and not to mention the possibility of being pregnant to anyone. Camillia took all this in and agreed to keep everything a secret and do what was required of her. The doctor then told the couple that the pale leader planned for her to go home and be on bed rest while keeping up with her occupational lessons. This was fantastic! Camillia's release papers were written out, and she was transferred from the bed to a wheelchair and taken to their horse-drawn buggy where she transferred from the wheelchair up to the buggy. Andrew drove them home and, just like Camillia, had no idea of what to expect there.

Now back at home, Camillia and Andrew were greeted by a clergy servant, who were always single females. Andrew got off the wagon front and helped Camillia down. Together they all three walked into the house. The servant went on to escort Camillia to her room to get changed into bedclothes and lay down. Andrew stayed behind to close the door, but there was some resistance. He opened the door a little bit and realized that the lead clergy, his wife, and the chief were standing there. Andrew invited them in, and they all went to the bedroom to speak with Camillia about special privileges and the help she would receive. The chief also had something else about the legend to discuss with the kids, in private. Andrew knew that as a rule, the chief did not go to people's homes; he would summon the people through his personal runners and the people would meet with him in an office-type room. Andrew explained that to Camillia so she could understand the significance of his arrival. Camillia's servant got chairs for everyone to sit in and stood at the head of her bed awaiting further orders. The clergyman and his wife started out the conversation wondering how she was. It was difficult to hold a conversation on that matter when they wanted an explanation of what happened earlier and she could not say anything about the diagnosis. They pressed her for information, but she did not say anything.

Finally, the leader stepped in and told the clergyman and his wife that she was pregnant. They were ecstatic; the legend had come to pass. The maid heard this and gave an expression of shock for she did not know of a legend of this sort; until now it was understood that no pale one could reproduce. The maid was told that this was why she was summoned for that unusual job. Each clergy member already had maids, but all they did was clean the quarters, stock up on food and water, then leave. No clergy member had ever had a private maid that was to assist them in bathing and doing activities of daily living, care for any pet they may have, and so on. That Sunday, which was tomorrow at their religious meeting where everyone was to attend, the leader wanted the clergyman to make the announcement of Camillia's pregnancy to the people and preach on the legend behind it.

The maid was told to keep that to herself until the announcement was made, and she replied with "as you wish." The chief then asked for everyone to leave the room so he could talk to the kids in private; everyone did as they were asked. The chief told the kids that the legend did not tell all; it left a lot to the imagination.

However, from what was known about it, each pregnancy could be different for Camillia. The gestation period was forty-eight weeks instead of forty, but the deliveries would all be easy and quick. He told the kids that if they had any questions or concerns at any time, they should not hesitate to call the doctor or himself. The goal was to keep her as stress-free as possible. He also told the kids that the main castle where he resided would be doubled in size and they would transfer there. They must have rooms for the children. He then told the others it was okay to return to the room, and then he excused himself from the home. The clergy couple wished the kids a good night and left also. The maid went into the spare bedroom and went to bed. The couple nestled down for a good night's rest as well.

The next morning, Sunday, the girls and Matthew heard about Camillia being sick, so they knew when she and Andrew did not show up for breakfast that it must be true. It was not like Andrew to miss a meal. No one realized that the young couple had eaten in their quarters due to her condition. Other pale ones at the dining hall were talking about Camillia being sick and had been worried for their own health as well. They were not sure what was wrong, but hopefully it was not contagious. The news had spread fast due to a lack of understanding. She was not sick at all; she was pregnant. The other girls and Matthew were distressed for the new couple, but they ate breakfast then headed for the religious hall. Andrew and Camillia were on the stage to the right of the pulpit, and the chief was at the pulpit. The clergyman was standing to the left of him with his wife at his left side. The rest of the clergy and their wives sat in the center front seat in the congregation. When people walked in and saw the couple on the stage, they knew that the sermon was going to be different; they just did not know how.

The girls and Matthew walked in and noticed their friends cheerily sitting up on the stage and were concerned for them. Camillia slipped them a quick thumbs-up, and they relaxed then sat down together in the center aisle toward the front. You see, there had never been guest speakers, only an occasional word from the leader if something was to be announced to the people. The rest of the pale ones were taken by surprise to see the couple up on the stage; nobody ever got up there besides the preacher, his wife, and occasionally the chief. The religious hall was full, and you could hear a low roar of voices as everyone talked among themselves about what to expect from that day's sermon.

The leader raised his right hand and motioned for the crowd to be still. Eventually, everyone was quiet and waiting to hear what the leader had to say. He put his arm down to his side then started to explain the legend of the pale ones; then he announced that it had come to pass. He explained that Camillia was not sick at all, but she was with the child and Andrew had sired the child. Practically all the pale ones in the audience gasped at what was said—this was wonderful news. The chief took his seat to the left of the stage. The clergyman and his wife approached the pulpit, and he began his sermon about the legend. With that sermon, it would elaborate on the details about how the couple would fit into their society, what the children would be like, their special abilities beyond that of a regular pale one, and much more. The sermon was about over so the chief and kids were escorted off the stage; they sat at the exit doorway to greet people as they left. Normally, everyone piled out by the bunch full, almost like they were in a hurry.

CHAPTER SEVEN

That day, everyone stopped to shake hands and congratulate the young couple, and they exited just a couple at a time.

When it came time for the girls and Matthew to exit, they hugged and congratulated their friends. Once everyone was gone, the preacher, his wife, and the chief congratulated the couple as they shook hands. The sermon lasted so long that there was no free time before lunch like usual, so after practically everyone was in the dining hall, the couple joined them. Camillia and Andrew looked for their friends to sit with them and finally found them in a group of their own. They had not bonded with any other groups yet as others had. This was not due to their status or being shunned by others; it was due to their newness and shyness. The couple sat with their friends and began to catch up on what had been going on with them and the miracle of the pregnancy. Andrew and Camillia were excited about the baby and felt blessed that they could reproduce; they just were not expecting to have a large family as was being asked of them. Camillia felt that two or three children was a good-sized family, and Andrew agreed.

From the sounds of it, Camillia would spend the rest of her days being pregnant, and Andrew, like livestock, would be placed into an imaginary pasture and used simply for breeding. That was sort of nice because they would have more time together than other couples in the clan. What was not nice was the pressure to perform a task that was supposed to be sacred and enjoyable, a time to share each other intimately in a way no one else could do. They did decide to not let the pressures of their elders interfere with the expression of love during their sexual encounters. The kids got all caught up on one another's happenings and were hopeful for one another's private, social, and occupational lives. They decided it was also time to reach out to other pale ones socially for the benefit of being a part of the society. Who knew, they might even be able to rub elbows with some of the individuals that were higher up in the society. They knew there was much to learn and a lot of room for growth, and it would take the influence of other pale ones to give aid in this. The kids' conversation was about to end when lunch was set before them. They ate and it was time to return to the spiritual hall. Sundays were different from Wednesdays. On Sundays, there were two sessions of preaching, one after breakfast and one after lunch. There was then a bit of free time before dinner and free time after dinner until curfew. On Wednesdays, there was preaching after lunch until dinner. Free time was the rest of the day before preaching and after.

On the way to the spiritual hall, Camillia and Andrew were pulled aside by the head clergy and told that the chief wanted to see them. As the couple was ready to separate from their friends, the clergy told their friends to follow along as he had a splendid idea. Now in a small room, the couple stood in front of the chief while the rest of the kids stood outside of the room awaiting further instruction. The chief announced that their new home was ready to move into and that it was ready to be staffed, as he was. They would have several maids; several nannies; cooks; gardeners to harvest fruits, grains, and vegetables; hunters to furnish meats and furs; their own personal clergy for private sermons so they did not have to attend regular sermons if Camillia was feeling ill;

security for them and their home, with the doctor becoming their personal doctor, as well as someone for any other service needed or wanted within reason.

The clergyman requested to intervene in the conversation, and he was granted permission. He suggested that their friends hold a position in the couple's home for extra social and personal support since they were so close. The leader felt that was a clever idea for Camillia's condition and said to bring those children before him at once. The preacher thought that the chief would go for this so that was why he had them waiting outside; he did not want the chief to have to wait long.

He told the chief that the kids were just outside of the room, and the chief had his guard escort them in. The kids had no idea why they were there, but they were about to find out. They did know it was a privilege to sit before the chief privately as it seemed that their two friends had done a lot of. The leader appointed Matthew to be a personal security guard for the couple; he was never to be far from them at any time. He appointed Melanie to be Camillia's personal maid. Bridgette was to be the head nanny, and Michelle was to be the dietitian and oversee the cooks. Everyone was happy with their new positions and ecstatic about being put together. The group would all live in the same home and have a chance for socializing more. The chief would find other pale ones to fill in the rest of the positions; a few would live there, but most would have their own homes to go back to. The kids were dismissed from the chief's presence and had to hustle to the spiritual hall for they were already late and that was where they were supposed to be.

The service was inspirational and enlightening as usual. The preacher was so good that even though he was preaching to the group, it seemed like he was preaching to everyone directly.

Everyone got something personal from it. Now it was time to make the big move; every one of the kids had to get their personal belongings to the new house. There were other pale ones offering to help, and of course, the kids accepted. It was nice to see the community step in to help, for the chief did not have to volunteer anyone. With everyone pulling together, the move was made within half an hour. Now the rest of the help was beginning to arrive, all bringing an individualized touch to the home. The house had more rooms than one could count and was all basically decorated and set up for children. Everyone that was to live there was settled in by the end of the second half the hour. The kids even made some new acquaintances.

It was now free time, and there were many knocks on the door of the couple's new home. It was other members of the community coming to bear housewarming gifts and baby supplies that were handmade. This was a warm surprise and made Camillia feel a sense of sentiment. It was not very long before the door became quiet since it was nearing curfew time and everyone was scurrying to their homes.

Each day of the week was about the same as the next. Andrew and Camillia filled their days with outings since they technically did not have jobs. They enjoyed some beautiful sights and picnics. However, they were never alone since the security, a maid, a runner, and the doctor all followed close behind. The couple did not allow this to bother them; they still made it out to picnics, laughed at each other's humor, and discussed serious matters.

The week went by so quickly, and it was time for Camillia to go back to the hospital for her blood test. Camillia and her husband arrived at the hospital, and the head doctor, her personal doctor, was anxiously awaiting their arrival. He took Camillia by the arm and swiftly whisked her away, Andrew could barely keep up. Once the doctor drew her blood, he requested the test be done immediately and wanted the results stat. Twenty minutes later, the results were ready to be read, and just as the doctor suspected, the HCG level was higher than before. That was just as it was supposed to be. He gave her a basic physical and deemed all to be well with her. Although the smell of food still made Camillia somewhat nauseated, she could eat with ease. The doctor summoned a courier to send written word of Camillia's health status to the chief. Upon receipt of the news, the chief was very pleased. This went on for weeks. Camillia was now halfway through her pregnancy at twenty-four weeks, her stomach was huge, and she was beginning to have difficulty getting around. She was no longer experiencing nausea though. Everyone in the community was now getting excited about the arrival of the baby; people were giving boy and girl baby names for ideas. So far, there had been no complications. Camillia wanted a daughter and had a name picked out already—Armellya. Andrew wanted a son but had no name picked out yet; he was leaving that task to his wife.

It was a new day, and the couple planned to go on an unusual outing before tending to their doctor's appointment. They wanted to go just outside the court's edge after breakfast. The court's edge was the wall that surrounded the pale ones' community, which consisted of their homes, the leader's castle, the secondary castle that the kids lived in prior to moving into the main newly remodeled castle, the dining hall, the religious hall, the social hall, fruit patch, grain patch and a patch of vegetation, and a few other leisure halls. Only the hunters went beyond the court's edge and into the woods to hunt for food and furs regularly. Occasionally, some females would go beyond the wall to the forest's edge to pick elaborate flowers for dedicated events like weddings, prominent birthdays, funerals, and so on. No one else was to go outside of the commune walls for any reason, but Andrew and Camillia didn't see anything wrong with going out there since other pale ones with reason could go out there. It seemed safe when they were out there walking from the tunnel to the compound.

However, there were many dangers such as confrontational wild beasts, poisonous fruits, vegetables, and flowers that could be harmful just by the touch, just to name two of the dangers. As the couple had seen it, they only had one obstacle, and that was to get rid of all the observing help so they could truly be alone and share some sentimental and romantic moments. Andrew had an idea of how to get out of the home unseen, but that could only occur if they could get their friend Melanie the maid to stay out of the room for a few minutes and somehow get their friend Matthew the security guard that was at their door preoccupied elsewhere. The couple had to be able to get to the hallway right next to their bedroom.

At the end of the hall was a door that led outside. It was an emergency exit in the event there was the need for a quick way out from the back of the house. The couple decided that Camillia would find something for the maid to do elsewhere and Andrew would find somewhere to send the security guard for a few minutes. Camillia asked the maid to go to the kitchen to get her a snack of fresh milk and cracker bread, which was a bread dough made so thin that when baked, it came out with a cracker texture. The request for fresh milk meant that someone had to milk a cow immediately to serve while still warm. Had she simply asked for milk, the maid could have brought some milk that was in storage for future use and kept cold. Andrew asked the security guard to attend to the windows throughout the house and make sure they were all shut and locked for they did have them open earlier in the day. Both Matthew the guard and Melanie the maid left their posts to do as their superiors and friends Camillia and Andrew had asked.

Quickly, the couple quietly walked out of their room and headed for the hallway just to the right of their room. Now there, they turned the corner just in time to miss the security guard returning to his post right outside of their bedroom door. It was close, but they did evade him. The couple had just exited the hall door when they heard the maid greet the guard and open the bedroom door. She stepped in softly so she would not disturb the couple then screamed in horror as she noticed that Camillia and Andrew were no longer there. Matthew rushed into the room to see what the screaming was all about. When he took note of Camillia and Andrew missing, he knew he was in a lot of trouble. This event could even cost him his life though the couple did not know it or they would not have run off. The security guard rushed to the bedroom window and looked out; he could see the couple dashing toward the doors of the compound wall. Matthew ran for the hallway door to get out of the house quickly and follow the couple; he had to bring them back at once. Melanie followed closely behind Matthew because she knew that Camillia was headstrong and that it might take both to convince her to return to her home before she was noticed outside. All pale ones knew this rule and knew who Camillia and Andrew were.

Now at the wall doors, Andrew worked on trying to convince the gate guards to open the doors for himself and Camillia. The conversation went back and forth between one gate guard and the couple while the other guard fled to summon the leader. The guards had not received any word that it was okay to let the couple out and needed confirmation of their request to exit. Melanie and Matthew caught up to the couple and told the gate guard that they would handle Andrew and Camillia themselves and get them back home safely. Matthew started out by telling the couple that their running off could cost him his life. He could be euthanized for allowing such risky behavior. Melanie did not have a chance to say anything before noticing that the other guard was absent. She grabbed the guard that was there by the arm and demanded to know where the other guard went. The guard told her and the rest of the kids that the other guard went to retrieve the leader for permission for the couple to be let out of the commune. Everyone but the kids knew that no one was to leave the compound unless they had a purpose for doing so such as the hunters, field workers, and harvesters. The guard then sharply jerked his arm from Melanie's hand.

The other guard and the chief were rapidly approaching, and it was obvious that the chief was unhappy about the situation Camillia and Andrew created with the maid and personal security. He was also enraged over how many people the couple had involved in their plot to escape for the day. Besides involving their personal workers, they involved public workers and made a small scene by the great gate doors as onlookers were beginning to accumulate. All this was unacceptable. The rule for who went out of the great wall was mainly set for the protection of the people from dangers in the area and somewhat from trying to return to the tunnel and jeopardizing the community if word of their existence and well-being should become known to human adults. The chief looked at Camillia and Andrew then locked eyes with Andrew. Andrew started to beg forgiveness for himself and Camillia and asked the chief to spare Camillia from any punishment, to let him take the full responsibility of their foolish actions. He apologized to the gate guards and to Matthew and Michelle for indirectly involving them in their scheme of temporarily escaping for the day. Everyone but the chief verbally accepted the couple's apology. Matthew and Michelle went back to the young couple's quarters where they belonged. The chief looked away from Andrew and said that he had a soft spot for Andrew and was getting one for Camillia; they were like the children he never had.

CHAPTER EIGHT

The chief went on to say that he would forget that the incident occurred, but if the couple wanted something out of the ordinary such as leaving the compound, they should ask and if it is possible to fulfill the request, he would. The chief went on to say that they could go out of the commune walls for the day, but they would absolutely have to take a few hunters with them to protect them from some of the wildlife out there that was known for attacking with no reason or warning. The couple explained that they wanted some alone time together and that they wanted to spend it outside of the house. The chief suggested that they go to the orchard area behind the castle; it was safe from wild beasts for it was within the compound walls and he could have the workers take the afternoon off. There would be no need for security because the only way into the orchard was through the castle. Andrew looked at Camillia with a satisfied look, and she spoke for both when she asked the chief if he would please make the arrangements for that as soon as possible. The chief said it would be done that day, within fifteen minutes. That would give the couple time to get lunch in a basket and some other picnic stuff rounded up. Everyone was pleased and would be safe.

Back at the kids' castle, Matthew was posted at attention just outside of their main doorway. Michelle had gone from the kitchen to the living room; she had gotten things ready to bombard them with—their picnic supplies and everything they could possibly need for a romantic meal. The leader was going to go back to his castle to resume what he had been doing after having a messenger tell the orchard workers to take the rest of the day off and go out for leisure time or go home. Camillia and Andrew were on their way back to their home. It only took seven minutes to go from home to the compound doors because they were essentially trying to temporarily escape, but it took eleven minutes to get back home because they were walking leisurely.

Upon approaching their domain, they could see Matthew outside of their door. As they got closer, he broke his composure to open the door for the couple. Once inside, Michelle came toward them rather swiftly with all the picnic supplies they would need to have a romantic lunch. Andrew took the food and supply basket while Camillia took the fur blanket they would be sitting on. The couple then headed for the chief's emergency exit to pass through to get to the orchard. Other than the chief's servants, no one had been in his castle so that was surely a special privilege. That was also the first time that the orchard workers got to leave early since no one ever got sick and the orchard had never been used for leisure time. It was now lunchtime for everyone so they would all be going to the dining hall while the couple looked for a good spot to have their picnic and some romantic time away from home and other people.

The couple found a plush secluded area under a peach tree, so Camillia spread out the blanket and sat down. Andrew sat close beside her and began to unload the picnic basket. Camillia decided to help empty the basket, but when she reached in, she grabbed Andrew's hand instead of a supply or food. They both giggled, and Andrew took her hand into his and put it up to his lips and kissed it sensuously. They held hands and spoke words of love and appreciation to each other. They also shared their excitement for the family they would be producing, starting with the baby that was on the way.

After a brief time of this, they turned their attention to eating. Melanie had the cooks prepare an assortment of fruits cut into bite-sized pieces, vegetable chunks with dip, fresh juice to drink along with some water and wine, dried peppered beef strips, small chunks of cheese, and a fresh wheat bread loaf with butter. The couple was amazed to see such an elaborate selection of food for a simple lunch, but it was refreshing and impressive. The kids decided to feed each other slowly as they discussed their future together. Andrew brought up the fact that from here on out she would practically stay pregnant. She replied that she did not mind if he was the father. She stated that although she was afraid of the birthing process and that she was not sure she could handle it, she would continue to reproduce. Andrew promised that he would be there to support her through it. That made Camillia feel much more relaxed. They stared into each other's eyes for a few moments as their faces drew closer and closer until their lips met, then they passionately kissed each other for several minutes. The couple went back to eating their meal, that time of feeding themselves and each other. It was not too long before the couple had both taken in so much food that their bellies were uncomfortable. Camillia scooted herself to the base of the peach tree and lay back against it. Meanwhile, Andrew packed up the picnic basket. Once the basket was packed, Andrew scooted next to Camillia and sat with her.

It was nearing the time for her to be at the doctor's office for a checkup and blood draw. Today was a special checkup day because she was far enough in her pregnancy to be able to find out the sex of the baby if so desired and the kids desired. Matthew moved the basket to the side of the blanket and helped Camillia to her feet so they could prepare to leave. She moved aside by the basket so Andrew could shake out the blanket and fold it back up. Their picnic was an enormous success. The couple entered the chief's home to pass through to the front door so they could go about their business. Along the way, they were greeted by many of his servants whose duties varied. The kids made it a point to thank them for their assistance in the picnic and asked them to thank the leader for them.

Now at the section of their home again, the couple checked on their own servants and freshened up for their doctor's appointment. Before leaving again to go see the doctor, Camillia and Andrew thanked Michelle and Matthew for their loyalty and apologized for the trouble they caused them. Since the commune was like a small town, it was too far to walk to the hospital, so Andrew had the stable boy hitch up a team of horses so the couple could make it to the hospital safely and on time. Camillia was not supposed to be up and about and has already far exceeded her activity limit by going to the edge of the great wall on foot and back again. She should not have even been on the picnic either. That alone made the appointment imperative to attend. The pregnancy was a joyous event for the couple but was taken as a serious part of the pale ones' history and evolution by the chief and community.

Now up in the seat of the buggy and on the way to the hospital, Camillia felt a sensation of the baby kicking strongly. She had felt the baby kick before, but this sensation was different, much stronger and lower. She felt a sense of alarm and told Andrew how something did not feel right with the baby. Matthew then snapped the reins on the horses, which made them go from a slow walk to a fast trot. He felt that if anything was wrong with Camillia or the baby, it would be his fault for not insisting that she stay in bed as the doctor had advised. The picnic was just a honeymoon moment, a moment in time, but the two lives that Andrew was responsible for was a lifetime commitment. Andrew knew that the baby was not close enough to its due date for a successful live delivery; he secretly felt that if anything happened to that baby, he would never forgive himself.

Camillia felt the change in Andrew's demeanor and the urgency of his actions were obvious so she took it upon herself to calm him down. She assured him that she was not in any real discomfort so she could not be in labor. At that point, they pulled up to the hospital front doors, and Andrew jumped off the buggy before the horses came to a complete halt. He hitched the horses to the pole in front of the hospital doors and went around to help Camillia down so he could carry her into the room where she would be placed in for her examination. Although she was uncomfortable and felt that there might be something wrong with the baby, she tried to get Andrew to let her walk. He stood his ground and carried her anyway. Andrew followed the nurse to the room that was to be Camillia's for the time being and then told the nurse how Camillia was feeling. With that information, the nurse said she would summon the doctor immediately. She told Andrew to put the hospital attire on Camillia and get her comfortable in the bed then to relax in the chair next to the bed and the doctor would be in shortly.

The doctor just happened to be looking up the hall and saw Matthew carrying Camillia to her room. He felt that it could have been an emergency crisis so he went straight to her room without the nurse having to tell him anything. He walked into her room happy and bubbly as usual so he did not let on that he was deeply concerned that something was wrong with the baby. Camillia explained that she had felt a heavy feeling in her lower abdomen and that the baby was periodically kicking extra hard, but that she was in no pain; she just had new and exaggerated sensations. The doctor was concerned that she may be in preterm labor. He did an ultrasound to see the baby's position, umbilical cord placement, sex, and the amount of fluid surrounding the baby. The baby was now positioned head down, which was not the case on the previous visit. The cord was free floating, which was good and as it had always been.

The doctor could see the sex of the baby and asked if they wanted to know what it was. They both said yes so the doctor replied that it was a girl. The fluid surrounding the baby was within normal limits so the doctor checked to see if Camillia was losing any fluid, and that test came back negative. So far everything looked good, but the next test was the most important at that point. The doctor had a nurse put a halter around Camillia's belly that would measure for any contractions and if there were to be any, how strong they were. The doctor sat in Camillia's room for a half hour watching for contractions and observing Camillia for anything out of the ordinary.

CHAPTER NINE

There did not seem to be any contractions, and Camillia was resting peacefully. Andrew noticed that the doctor was not alarmed so he began to relax also. The doctor had the nurse come back into the room to remove the halter and help Camillia change.

During that time, the doctor spoke to the couple and assured them all was well, that Camillia was probably sensitive to the baby and the feeling she felt was probably the baby flipping upside down and positioning into the birth canal. The doctor went on to say that it was extremely imperative that Camillia stay in bed or she would surely go into premature labor, which could lead to the death of the child. The nurse added that the bed rest may seem to go by slowly but in fact would go by quickly if she had things to occupy herself while staying in bed. The couple was overjoyed that all was well with the baby and Camillia. They were excited to know that it was a girl; they could now start planning for the specifics that made a difference like clothing and decor for the bedroom. They also made a vow to the doctor and nurse that she would stay in bed unless she had to utilize the restroom. The doctor told the couple that the rest of the checkups would be performed by house calls so Camillia would not be jostled around in the buggy, and on that note, the doctor added that visits would be biweekly instead of monthly.

The couple walked out of the hospital and got back into the buggy to go home. Matthew kept the horses at a slow walking pace so he could cut down on the amount of jostling that would be placed on Camillia. She was comfortable on the way home; it was an eventless ride. Now back at home, Andrew helped Camillia down from the buggy at their front door so she could go inside their home and nestle down in bed after changing into some bedclothes. All the couple's servants were curious about how the doctor's appointment went and how she was. Andrew sent Camillia into her room to get ready for bed and climb in while he updated the servants.

Michelle and Matthew were especially happy for the couple since they were personal friends and had been for all their lives. Bridgette was getting excited since she was set to be the nanny of the child. This was all becoming real for Bridgette little by little; starting now, she had much to do with helping with the child's specific bedroom decor and in making sure the room was set up for functionality. She had not seen much of Camillia since she got pregnant, but that was about to change that very day for she was to move into the castle immediately. As the nanny, it was up to Bridgette to have the dressmakers make whatever was needed for the baby or her room, have the child's laundry kept up on as the diapers were washed separate from all clothing, work with Melanie the dietitian once the child starts to eat real food, educate her on a basic level until it became obvious what her talent would be then nurture that, take the child to its mother for nursing times—those were just a few things Bridgette would be doing for the child. Bridgette was not living in the kids' castle, but it was now time for her to move in and start her preparatory duties. The kids were overjoyed that their duties brought them together the way they did; it would have been a shame for one of them to be left out or for none of them to be together.

The chief heard about the doctor's appointment through the doctor and went by the kids' castle to visit them. He spoke to Andrew and Camillia alone first. He congratulated them on the news of a girl on the way and told them how proud of them he was and that they were special to him personally as well as to the community. He then spoke to all six of the kids together and explained that fate put them together, not him. Except for Andrew and Camillia, he had placed them into the position that best suited everyone involved. He wished them all prosperity and left to go about his own business.

Now it was time for everyone to get to their duties. Matthew posted himself outside of the couple's room and stood at attention, guarding Camillia. Michelle went to see the nutritionist Melanie and cooks about retrieving a snack for Camillia and Andrew. Bridgette went to the dressmakers to start giving orders for the baby's room decor and diapers as well as a couple of first outfits. Andrew and Camillia sat together in the bedroom and spoke about the baby, her name, her hopeful future, all the brothers and sisters she would have, and about what her special abilities might be that were beyond that of a human and a pale one. The couple discussed whether to ask the chief about those abilities. Would it be better to go through the abilities as the child exhibits them, or should they be aware of what they were as they could be developmental milestones?

The couple decided to summon the leader to come at his convenience to discuss the child's special abilities. The couple summoned the chief through a runner. He was instructed to tell the chief that it was not urgent, to come at his leisure. They just wanted to discuss the legend in relation to the child's extra abilities. The messenger left and went to the chief's side of the castle to pass the message to his personal messenger, who said he would tell the chief as soon as he saw him. That was satisfactory. The kids' messenger returned to them and relayed that the message was left, but there was no telling how soon the leader would get it or respond to it. The fact that the message was left was sufficient, the leader was usually quick to respond to the kids, and his servants knew better than to not do their job.

The chief got the message immediately upon returning home from visiting other pale ones he had business with for that day. The leader left as quickly as he had entered to go see the couple and discuss the baby's special abilities. Since the couple's castle was built in conjunction with the chief's, it took no time for him to get there and report to the door security outside on who he was there for and why he was there. The guard opened the door and announced his arrival; a butler came and escorted him to the bedroom where the couple was. Andrew stood up and welcomed the chief into their home. The chief told Camillia not to get up; in her condition, she would be excused. Camillia did have Michelle prop her pillows so she could comfortably sit up to talk to the chief. She wanted to show some respect by not just lying there and speaking to him. Michelle offered the chief a chair to sit in, he did sit and asked the couple what they wanted to know. Andrew started out by asking if it would be best if they knew of the baby's abilities ahead of time, or just learned of them as they developed.

Without hesitation, the chief replied that it would be best to know ahead of time for watching the child's milestones, and ensuring that they were appropriately reached. However, the legend was not specific on some things and did not provide a full list. The couple looked at each other with an expression of defeat then looked back at the leader. He told the kids not to be discouraged, he would look deeper into the legend and try to find some specifics for them. He had a book that had been handed down from the beginning of their existence to date. Keeping that book updated and recording the important things that came up in their colony was one of the many duties of every chief. Camillia asked the leader if he would tell them what he knew so far, and he agreed to do so.

He said that first, the child would look human; she would not have a pale bluish-colored skin that revealed all her arteries and veins. The eye color and hair color would be whatever the dominant color was between the parents before being turned into pale ones. The child would see in the dark just like the pale ones. She would have strength and speed beyond that of anything ever known of. Her intelligence would surpass any genius, and she would have a superior charisma. This child's physical growth would be rationed like that of a human child. She would be telepathic, as all pale ones were. These were the only things the chief knew at that point in time. He said he would update the couple if he found out anything new. The couple was glad to get that much information and agreed to wait patiently for an update. All the kids knew there was a special purpose to the child's life and that it would be life altering to them and the rest of the community, but what it could possibly be was the question on their minds now. The chief stood up from his chair and excused himself; he had a lot of research to do among other things.

It was near the end of that day, and things had settled down so Camillia summoned Bridgette. When she arrived in the room, Camillia told her they needed to talk about the baby. Bridgette knew that it was something serious because her tone of voice and body language were direct and she failed to smile as usual.

Bridgette was standing next to the bed, and Camillia told her to sit in the chair next to them; she did as she was asked. Camillia proceeded to tell Bridgette what the chief said about the baby's milestones and added that she did not know at what age each thing was supposed to develop, but she would let her know when she found out. Bridgette was amazed at the things the baby would be able to do and that she was chosen to be the nanny of such a precious individual. She promised Camillia that she would take the best care of the child that she knew how.

Camillia gave a soft smile and thanked Bridgette for responding so fast and for listening then told her she was excused from the room and to please go back to what she was doing. Bridgette left the room promptly and went back to the dressmakers to continue ordering baby clothes, diapers, and room decor. As Bridgette left the room, Melanie entered to find out what the couple wanted for a snack. Neither Camillia nor Andrew wanted anything to eat so she went back to the kitchen to plan dinner. Michelle came close to the bed from across the room and offered to lay the pillows down and help Camillia settle into bed. Camillia okayed that and settled down in bed. Andrew then pulled the chair into view of Camillia and sat down to talk and comfort her from the stress of the day and excitement about the baby. The day seemed quite long and took all of Camillia's energy; she was ready to go to sleep.

Twenty-four weeks went by, and all Camillia had done was sit in the chair next to her bed or lie in her bed. Andrew stayed at her bedside the entire time and made sure all her needs and wants were met. The only time either of them moved from their spots was to use the toilet or shower. Michelle would assist Camillia in the shower; afterward, Camillia would sit down in a chair at the vanity in her bathroom and brush her hair. During this time, Michelle would change Camillia's bedding. Matthew stayed posted outside of her room at attention, ready to announce anyone who came by and keep the inside of the castle secure; there were other guards positioned outside of the castle. The doctor came by every two weeks, and today was a day he was supposed to show up for a quick checkup. Camillia would have to ask the doctor if he knew if her future pregnancies would leave her bedridden also. Camillia felt love and compassion for the baby she carried, but hoped the delivery would be soon so she would not be bedridden any longer. The good news was that if she went into labor, the baby would be ready and the doctor would let her have it. She also hoped her next pregnancies would not have her bed bound; she was not sure if she could continuously stay in that bed again.

However, the monotony of the bed rest was broken by people in the community for the last two weeks. They brought her baby gifts, gifts for her, and even gifts for Andrew, and they all would stay and talk for a half hour or so. The couple thought it was fabulous that the community came together and supported them like that. Suddenly, Camillia noticed that although she was not in any pain, she kept feeling a strange intermittent sensation around her vagina; this had been occurring for close to an hour. The doctor was due to arrive at any time so Camillia saw no reason to withhold the information from Andrew. Hopefully he would not become alarmed and panic. Camillia told Andrew she had something to tell him, but he had to stay seated and not panic; she wanted him to promise. He promised to stay calm and do as he was told so she told him about the sensation and how long it had been occurring. He asked her if she was in any pain, and just then, the doctor arrived at the bedroom door. The doctor asked what pain they were talking about. Camillia explained to the doctor that she was experiencing a strange sensation around her vagina but that she was in no pain and it had been occurring for about an hour.

The doctor said that she could be dilating in preparation for the delivery. The doctor checked her and said she was completely dilated and ready to have the baby at any time. Andrew asked if he had ever delivered a baby before, and he said no. However, as a doctor, he had been trained; before he was changed, he had just become a doctor. The pale ones were abducting adults at that time to build their society with the necessary adults needed for a stable society. Nothing about adults being missing was ever spoken about above ground; maybe that was why the adults were so scared and took the legend of the dinosaur tail so seriously.

CHAPTER TEN

The couple was somewhat unsettled by having a doctor who had never delivered a baby. What if something went wrong, would he know what to do? Because of their telepathy, the doctor knew what the couple was thinking so he verbally told them not to worry as he was prepared for anything that could possibly happen. Camillia interrupted the doctor to tell him she had just started experiencing some light cramping and the baby felt like it was coming out. Andrew grabbed her hand and held it tenderly while the doctor checked for the baby's head to crown. Sure enough, the baby's head and shoulders were out.

He told the couple that the baby was practically out and added that the worst was over. The doctor told Bridgette to have a blanket ready, and she already did. The doctor reached down and picked the baby girl up with his bare hands and handed her to Bridgette, lastly cutting the umbilical cord and making sure the airway was clear. Bridgette swaddled the baby in a fur blanket and placed the child into Camillia's arms. Camillia moved the baby to her side that was closest to Andrew so he could get a good look at his new daughter.

Together, Camillia and Andrew unwrapped the child to check and make sure that there were no obvious deformities, and there were not. The new parents agreed that the child's name would be Armellya. She was so tiny, but normal sized for a newborn. Her coloring was like a normal human, and as all newborns, she had blue eyes. The infant started to cry so Camellia placed the bare baby to her chest facedown on her breast and started to nurse her. The baby was again content, and Camillia pulled her blanket over herself and the baby to keep warm.

It was time to get the leader there to greet the young one. It was important for him to know of the birth as soon as possible and to know that everything went well. Together, Bridgette and Michelle got Camillia and the baby cleaned up and then moved them to a chair to clean the bedding. By that time, the chief arrived and he came bearing gifts. Andrew immediately stood up and shook hands with the leader, and the leader grabbed Andrew and hugged him. The chief then walked to the chair and gave Camillia a big hug. He had suits for Andrew, nursing dresses for Camillia, and outfits for the baby. He set all the clothing by the foot of the bed and asked if he could hold the child, and both kids said absolutely. Camillia held her out for the chief to take, and he gently took her into his arms. He asked what they were going to call her and Camillia replied, "Armellya." This was a combination of Andrew's mother's name of Arlene and her name of Camillia. The baby was born with brown hair, and the eye color would not be evident for some time. All babies were born with blue-colored eyes.

The chief told the kids that he needed to discuss something important with them in private, right away if possible. Due to the seriousness of his tone, the kids knew that it must be something significant. Andrew excused the help then offered the chief a chair next to the bed, and he sat down. Andrew sat on the edge of the bed facing the chief. Camillia scooted her chair closer to the leader's chair so she could give him her undivided attention. The chief started out by saying that he was nearing the end of his life, and he needed someone to replace him that was strong and reliable. Someone who could run the society as he would. Although there were four people in line and trained to take on the position, he did not trust them to keep things as they were. He was afraid that too many things would be changed and so much would not be adhered to. The people in line for the job were too young and full of ideas of implementing more useless technology.

The kids were surprised at what they were hearing. Things seemed to run great the way they were, and the kids believed that if something was not broken, do not try to fix it. Camellia asked the leader if there was anything they could do to help, and the chief said that was why he was there. He said he wanted them to run the society as he had and to pass it down to their children when it was time. He said if he adopted the kids, they would be in line for the chief's position ahead of the four people who were trained and waiting. He added that he could train them himself. The chief liked that the kids appreciated the way things were in the commune and saw what kind of damage major technology could do to a society. Andrew asked what would be involved in the adoption process and how soon would this have to take place. The leader told Andrew that the adoption was a ceremony followed by a reception, much like a wedding, and that the sooner it took place, the better off he and the kids would be.

The couple looked at each other, and Camillia slightly nodded her head in a yes motion, so Andrew told the chief they would be honored to succeed him. The chief said they would do the adoption ceremony the next day in place of lunch, but for now, it was nearing dinnertime and they would be presenting the baby to everyone. The couple agreed that would be the best way to do things. Andrew told the chief that he was worried about hard feelings toward himself and Camillia for getting the chief's position when it would be time and jumping ahead of the four pale ones who had been waiting. The chief told the couple not to worry; pale ones were forgiving and loving people and did not turn to negative actions or reactions.

It was now time for everyone to gather at the dining hall. Andrew carried Armellya, the baby, and Camillia was held steady by Michelle. Matthew, Melanie, and Bridgette followed closely behind the new parents. The chief led the way. Now at the dining hall, the leader took his place in front of the podium, Camillia sat next to the chief, and Andrew gave Armellya to her then took a seat next to her. By the time the kids and the chief were seated, every pale one was in the dining hall and seated. They all noticed Camillia holding the baby and became silent. Before the meal was to be served, the leader was going to introduce baby Armellya and allow some time for congratulations to be offered to the new parents, as well as a warm welcome to the child. The chief stood up and spoke of the legend about a couple who were pale ones that could reproduce and how special it was, as well as what it meant for their society. Most of the pale ones had heard of the legend but did not know any details of the legend of the pale ones; they only knew it existed and took it for a legend that was nothing more than a tall tale—everyone knew pale ones were sterile. Sterility was a side effect of the injection given that was responsible for being turned from a regular human to a pale one. The chief finished his speech then announced that the next dinnertime was to be a banquet following an adoption.

With that announcement, practically everyone gasped. The chief then said that anyone wanting to welcome the child or congratulate the new parents was welcome to do so at that time; he then took his seat. Everyone stood up and formed a line to take their turn to go up to the podium and take care of their business with the new family. Everyone was kind and loving toward the couple and their child; in fact, they promised gifts for the following day and asked what they needed. Bridgette took over in telling everyone what they needed for the new mom and baby. The dad did not really have any needs, so Bridgette gave a list of his desires. The whole procession took at least two hours, but dinner was finally served.

During dinner, everyone was discussing the legend of the pale ones and wondering who was going to be adopted and by whom; they also discussed how beautiful Armellya was. Once the chief was finished eating, he leaned over toward the couple and told them to meet him in his castle after dinner; they agreed to do so. The chief then went to his own home and waited anxiously for the couple to arrive. Once the couple had finished eating, Camillia handed little Armellya to Bridgette so she could take her home while they were at the chief's home. Bridgette left the dining hall immediately to take the baby to her home to bathe her and get her ready for her next feeding. Andrew and Camillia left the dining hall just moments later to head straight for the chief's home. Now at their destination, the chief himself invited the couple into his home. This was the first time the chief answered his own door; this was what he had a butler for. The leader excused his help and asked the couple to take a seat on his couch, and the kids quietly and promptly did as he asked.

He sat down in a chair across from them and began to speak to them in a low tone of voice so the help could not hear in the event he had any eavesdroppers.

The leader started out by saying how he favored only them; he knew there was something special about them. He just did not realize how special they would be. He continued with telling them that it was an honor to him for them agreeing to being adopted by him. He went on with saying that his time was limited; he was already two hundred years old and ready to retire. He wanted to live out his last days being able to mingle with the commoners freely. He wanted their titles to be king and queen, for this was the first time a leader would have a wife. He then picked up a box from the floor next to the chair, opened it, and took out two crowns that he had just made. One being masculine for Andrew and the other being feminine for Camillia, both were made of 24-karat gold and jewels. He showed them to the couple and then put them back away until the proper time to present them.

Andrew asked the chief if he would be interested in being the adviser to the king so he would still have a purpose in the community, and the chief accepted the offer. The chief went to stand up, so as a proper gesture, the couple stood up and the leader gave the kids a big hug. He advised the kids to go home and get some good sleep because the next day was going to be a big one, and all their days after that would be extremely busy.

On the way home, the couple quietly discussed what had been happening to them since being abducted. Andrew started first with his abduction. He said it was swift and very organized. He and four other boys were overpowered in the tunnel. They knew not to go in there, but they were curious about some noises coming from there. The tunnel wall had a large hidden door that sprang open when the boys got right in front of it. Each boy was grabbed by several pale ones, and as quick as the door opened, it was shut fast behind them. The boys were afraid of what was going to become of them. Only one pale one spoke, and he did not say much—that was the chief. They were forced to walk a long way, but they were given some jerky like meat along the way and water when they came to a beautiful lake. They could take several breaks and rest their feet and lungs. The boys were in a state of shock when they found out that they could survive without their suits and helmets. They were surprised when they got to the compound gate and it was opened for them; there were so many pale ones, and they had an organized society. No one seemed surprised to see them; the boys figured this was a normal activity for the pale ones.

Camillia interrupted and said that was the same thing that had happened to her and the girls. She went on to say that once inside the great wall, they were changed by the blue serum created by Lloyd's parents. She spoke of how painful the change was, but that it did not last too long. They were shown their quarters and brought new clothes; the pale one who brought the new clothing said that the original clothes they were wearing would be burned. Andrew agreed that the same thing had happened to him and the boys. Andrew continued that after all that, they were given daily responsibilities to carry out. Next, the chief paired up Bridgette with Matthew and himself with Camillia. They both agreed that they were blessed with having each other. Neither one of them dreamed that they would fulfill the legend, but they were ecstatic about having little Armellya. Andrew and Camillia did not mind being part of the clergy, but that had to change when it became obvious that they could produce children. Now the chief wanted to adopt the couple and make them head of their society. The couple agreed that all this happened so quickly that it was exhausting. They were approaching their front door, so all talk about the next day had to stop because there were small bits of confidential information being discussed.

Once inside, Camillia had to nurse the baby before going to bed herself. Andrew stayed up with her to keep her company and admire his new daughter. Soon, Armellya was done nursing so Camillia handed her to Bridgette to be put to bed until the middle of the night's feeding.

Camillia and Andrew went directly to bed and fell fast asleep. A brief time later, Andrew was awakened by the light that illuminated his room from the hallway when Bridgette opened the bedroom door to rouse Camillia for Armellya's middle-of-the-night feeding.

It seemed to Andrew that only a few hours had passed, and when he checked his clock, it had indeed only been a few hours. Andrew rolled over in the bed toward Camillia to awaken her gently, but it was not an easy task. Andrew whispered in Camillia's ear that it was time to feed the baby, and she woke right up. Andrew stayed awake with his wife; he was amazed at the way nature gave females in most all species a way to directly feed their babies. He told Camillia that he was proud of her for being such a good mother even though it had not been for very long. Bridgette went to Camillia and handed her the baby. Camillia nursed Armellya until she fell asleep again then handed the sleeping baby back to Bridgette to be returned to her bed. Bridgette took the baby and quickly left the couple's room; she was headed for the baby's room. Armellya was returned to bed, and Bridgette went to her room and climbed into her bed; she was asleep when her head hit the pillow. Andrew and Camillia slid down in their bed, got comfortable, and drifted back to sleep.

The next morning arrived so quickly, the couple got out of bed feeling drained of energy. They had been having such busy days and evenings, and now they must get up in the middle of the night until the baby slept through it. The couple would also be going through some intense training while doing the job they would be training for. This was also a twenty-four-hour job, and they would be summoned at odd hours because everyone works from six in the morning until six in the evening, and they were devoted workers. That meant that the couple's private time, leisure time, and sleep time would be interrupted by others seeking wisdom. The couple discussed how the job would be possible at times as Andrew laid out Camillia's clothing and grooming items then got himself dressed and groomed while Camillia fed Armellya. Once Camillia was finished feeding the baby, Andrew took her for a brief time while Camillia got dressed and groomed. It was time to head out for the dining hall, and on the way, the new parents stopped at Bridgette's room to give the baby to her.

At the dining hall, the couple looked for their friends to sit with, but they could not find them. Suddenly, Andrew felt a hand grab his shoulder. Alarmed, Andrew turned around quickly and was ready to defend his wife and himself. When Andrew looked, he realized it was Matthew's hand, and the rest of his friends were there also. Everyone said hello and laughed as they proceeded to get a table where they would all have a chair together. Breakfast was enjoyable as everyone congratulated one another on their job positions, personal strengths, and in surviving the change. They then ate and discussed their short-term and long-term goals. Upon the end of that discussion, breakfast was over, and it was time to part ways. Camillia and Andrew went to see the chief at his castle to start their training, and the rest of the group went to their own jobs. Once with the leader, he asked the couple to sit for a while because there were some things to be discussed before starting the training. He said it was about the legend of the dinosaur tail and the legend of the pale ones. This intrigued the couple very much. The leader sat down before the couple, shifted around in his seat to get comfortable, and began to talk. He started with the legend of the dinosaur tail.

CHAPTER ELEVEN

With that said, Andrew became nervous about becoming chief. Camillia picked up on Andrew's nervousness so she told him he would be a great leader. She also told him that he would be the reason that the town would be complete and everyone would truly be happy. Camillia reminded Andrew that she would be right by his side throughout that task as well as the rest of his tasks throughout his command. Andrew gently smiled at Camillia and simply told her he loved her and that she was the most wonderful and important person in his life after their child. The chief smiled warmly at the young couple and wholeheartedly assured them that they were the right choice for the job. The chief continued about the legend of the dinosaur tail. Once everyone, adult and child alike, were in the compound in the land of grandeur, all the miniangels would return to the lands forests. Once that mass migration was over, there would be much to do, such as enlarging the compound perimeters, doing a large number of buildings to accommodate all the people, and creating more jobs that were necessary at that time but did not have enough people to fill the positions.

The couple took each other's hand and squeezed firmly then told the leader that they would not let him down. The leader told

Camillia and Andrew that they now had the basic overview of the legend of the dinosaur tail, and now it was time to get the details on the legend of the pale ones. He continued by saying that they got the basics on how the parents of Lloyd made the injectable potion for the transformation of all humans. He reminded the couple that the transformation was meant to unite the population and to offer a defense mechanism to withstand the harmful effects of the earth's tragic changes, such as toxic radiation, lack of food, drinkable water, and so on. The chief said that even though the transformation would leave everyone except the couple barren, their lives would be extended by hundreds of years, that would offer not only an extended quantity of life but quality of life as well.

He reminded them that it would be up to the couple to produce as many children as possible that would keep their bloodline alive. They were now viewed as royalty so the governmental aspect of their society would function as such, meaning leadership of these people would come from Camillia and Andrew's family as in the old days of kings and queens. It was foreseen that hundreds of years in the future the bloodline would most likely go dry. That would be the time that the governmental leader would have to be chosen as it had been prior to the couple's arrival. The last of the bloodline would have some runners up in a fashion of hierarchy to stand by as the next leader.

The chief said that there was a group of pale ones that were scientifically inclined; they were working on the potion to enhance the side effects of longevity, telepathy, and immunity, but most important to reverse the side effects of sterility so the race did not die out and the people could enjoy the blessings of parenthood. The chief told the couple that he would take them around to formally meet the people in prominent positions and at that time the people could inform them of where they were at their job improvements. He added that that would take several days and they would start the next day after the baby's morning feeding. They could take a break for Armellya's lunch feeding then get right back to the introductions. He concluded by saying that each day they would be done by dinner and would have the evening time for personal family time. Now it was time for the baby's feeding followed by lunch. With nothing left to say, they parted ways; the couple headed for their home to feed the baby, and the chief went out and about to see how things were running as well as to make sure no one needed anything.

Andrew and Camillia noticed how accepting the community was of them for on the way home, everyone looked up from their duties and waved; they also said hello. The couple smiled big, waved back, and said hello. Now at the door of their home, the couple could hear Armellya fussing for a feeding. They quickly entered, and Camillia took the baby from Bridgette. Andrew went on to see how things were running in the house; all was well. After checking on the home, Andrew went to check on the baby and his wife. He noticed that Camillia looked paler than her usual bluish-pale like color. He asked her how she was feeling, and she admitted she felt somewhat nauseated and lightheaded. Andrew told her he was going to call for the doctor whether she wanted him to or not; this was not a normal state for her or any pale one. He had his own suspicion on what the issue was, but he wanted the doctor to confirm or deny that hunch. The doctor arrived and checked Camillia over; he said that he was sure of what was going on, but he would need a simple blood test to confirm it. The doctor did not want to give his suspicion to the couple until the blood work was done. Camillia handed the baby to Bridgette then together the doctor, Camillia, and Andrew went over to the hospital. The nurse took the blood sample; then she sent it off to the lab for immediate results. The doctor sat and conversed with the couple while they were awaiting the test results.

Within twenty minutes, the results were in, and the doctor looked at them. It was just as he and Andrew suspected—Camillia was pregnant again. This was cause for celebration; the chief was to be notified immediately. The doctor hailed a runner who was sent out into the community to seek out the chief. The runner shortly found him and summoned him to the hospital for some important news. It was a short trip to the hospital, and once there, the doctor told the chief that Camillia was pregnant and that she should take things easy. She and Andrew were very excited as well as the doctor and chief. The chief agreed with the doctor that the news was cause for celebration so they would have a special dinner, make the announcement to the community, and hold a party celebration right after dinner.

The whole community would be there. The chief said that there was no time to lose; he had to get to the chefs, bakers, and party planners immediately so they could have as much time as possible to arrange for the celebratory meal and party. He wanted everything to be perfect. He was quickly out of the room and on his way.

The couple had no clue that there was to be a special dinner followed by a party for them. Andrew and Camillia left the hospital to go back home. Out of excitement, they wanted to start on the new baby's bedroom immediately. They were extremely excited and overjoyed about the arrival of another child. It was a tough pregnancy with Armellya, but an easy delivery. Armellya and Andrew were hoping for a better pregnancy and another easy delivery. The couple did not tell their friends who were their staff about the good news because they knew this was the chief's pleasure. With that, the couple had to just envision what they would like to do with the new baby's room. If they were to do anything in the room or start to order furniture and necessities, it would make their staff suspicious.

It was now time for the couple and their staff to leave the home and go to the dining hall. As they stepped out of the home, they noticed others leaving their homes and jobs to head to the dining hall as well. As always, everyone was in a cheerful mood and conversed about their day. Tight friends Camillia, Andrew, Bridgette, Matthew, Melanie, Michelle, and of course, Armellya all slipped into the crowd and blended right in with their cheerful dispositions. Once in the building, the group looked for a place to sit where they could be together, and it was quickly spotted by Matthew. There was a spot just for them across the room so they dashed over and swiftly took their seats. After everyone was seated, a runner arrived and handed an envelope to Andrew then disappeared back into the crowd. Andrew opened the envelope and read the paper from inside it; it simply requested that the couple meet with the chief at his home after dinner to discuss some upcoming business. There was no further explanation.

The group of friends spoke about how they loved their jobs, how they were coming along with personal goals, and simple chatter. The group noticed that the food servers were lined up to bring out dinner but were not moving; this was not normal. Suddenly, they saw the chief stand up from his chair, still behind his table, and he was using a microphone to address the small population. He was asking for everyone to give him their attention. The room became quiet, and the leader said he had an announcement to make. Now having everyone's undivided attention, the chief asked for Camillia and Andrew to please stand. The couple nervously pushed their chairs back and slowly stood up. The chief started out by saying that everyone would be having a special dinner followed by a celebratory party due to the expectancy of another child from Camillia and Andrew. Everyone clapped and congratulated them. The couple said thank you and took their seats. The food servers began to bring everyone's meals out to them, and people began to eat and converse.

It was not long before dinner was over and dishes were being removed from the tables. Upon the completion of all tables being cleared, more servers began to bring out party foods and wine. Behind the party servers was a small group of people with various musical instruments playing party music. Everyone was in the spirit of cheer and goodwill. Members of the community went by the couple's table to give hugs and words of joy. They all asked what the couple needed for the new baby's room as well as for the baby so they could share in the joyous event by contributing needs and desires. The couple said that they would have to get back to the people with what the new baby would need when the pregnancy was further along and the doctor could tell if the baby was a boy or a girl. The party came to an end so everyone except the couple went home. Camillia and Andrew had to go to the chief's home to discuss something important that remained unknown to them.

Once there, the chief had the couple take a seat and made sure they were comfortable. He bluntly told them that it was time for another child abduction from above ground. Camillia did not know what to think or say, so she stayed quiet, hoping her husband would address that. Andrew knew this was for their benefit and well-being, but as an abductee, it was traumatic at first; he was sort of speechless. Before Andrew or Camillia could say anything, the chief spoke. He told them that Camillia did not have to participate in the abductions; she would just take care of things solo in the compound while Andrew was away. He also said that Andrew would be accompanied by him for the first time, but in the future, as the new leader, he would be on his own with the abduction crew. The chief explained how it worked; the crew did the abducting, and he would show his authority over the scouts. Although the resting places were preset and when to do the change was also preset, he would make the command known, and the crew would follow through. Those things never changed, so when it appeared that there was disorganization, there was organization and control.

Andrew agreed that this was a good tactic, but still felt uncomfortable doing it. The chief assured him that the first time was always hard, but once those people acclimated, the reward would begin. He told them to remember back to when they were abducted and compare life above ground to life in the land of grandeur. They both agreed that although they missed their adult friends and family, they were much happier. Before, life was a struggle, but now it was like being in a utopia. He also reminded the couple that in time, the adults would be part of their society also. Camillia also reminded Andrew that she would be there to support him through anything and everything. He gave her a loving hug and told her that because of her, he could do anything. The chief told Andrew that they would be leaving in the morning before anyone else got up. Andrew agreed and Camillia said that she would be there to see them off. The chief was pleased to hear that. The chief and the couple stood up to say their farewells. Andrew and the chief shook hands, and Camillia gave the chief a big warm hug. Andrew and Camillia left the leaders home and returned to their home. Everyone called it a night and went to sleep.

The next morning, Andrew and Camillia awoke early and had their nutritionist, Melanie, prepare a knapsack full of jerky, dried fruits, and nuts. Melanie also filled a clean canteen full of fresh springwater. Michelle got up with Armellya and fed her with warmed-up mother's milk previously excreted by Camillia and kept in the refrigerator. Andrew spoke with Matthew, their personal security guard, and told him to keep a close eye on Camillia and to keep her safe. Matthew agreed and the two shook hands. As Andrew turned his back to walk away, Matthew told Andrew to keep safe and return soon. Andrew gave no response. The couple was nervous about temporarily parting ways, for this would be the first time for them to be apart since they had been married.

Andrew then went to the baby's nursery and peeked in on Armellya. He told Bridgette to take loving care of the baby and he would return as soon as possible; she agreed to do so. Andrew went back out into the main living quarters and scooped Camillia up in his arms and reminded her to take it easy and to take care of herself and their unborn child; she agreed. The couple kissed passionately then Andrew put Camillia down. Andrew then took his satchel and canteen from Melanie and put them over his shoulder. He slowly walked to the front door, opened the door, then disappeared into the early morning light.

CHAPTER TWELVE

Suddenly, Camillia felt alone and afraid. Michelle noticed Camillia's state of abandonment and consoled her by telling her that Andrew would return safe and sound and that the time would go by quickly. As the chief was gradually turning over leadership to Andrew, it was becoming his job to run the compound. In Andrew's absence, it would be Camillia's job to take over until his return; that would help time go by quicker.

Once outside, Andrew walked quickly toward the chief's home so as not to be late. As he got closer to his destination, Andrew could see that the leader was coming out of his door. The two met up at the point where the walkways meet the street. As the two greeted each other, Andrew got a sick feeling in the pit of his stomach. He felt like the abductions were a major crime although it was for the best interests of the abductees. Andrew knew he just needed to get over the shock of the task at hand and remember the difference between living above ground versus underground. He would not wish anyone to remain above ground; the land of grandeur was just as it sounded. Now both men were headed to the church hall to meet up with the scouts that were responsible for grabbing the humans that were to be abducted. The scouts consisted of twelve strong youngsters. That allowed for two scouts per human for a human count of up to six. The pale ones had never taken more than six children or adults at a time, and they hopefully never would. Now all together, the chief introduced the scouts to Andrew. That excursion would take no more than twenty-four hours. It was about ten and a half hours' one way to a total of twenty-one hours' round trip. In the final three hours of that twenty-four-hour period was when the transformation occurred and the settling into a home and other tasks to assure the new pale ones would be comfortable and know what their resources were for various needs. The scouts were not involved in the final three hours of settlement; only the chief was.

Now on their way, the group would walk for three hours then rest for a half hour then walk another three hours followed by another half-hour break and walk three more hours for the last half-hour break at the abduction site followed by the abductions. Once the scouts had the people, the walk and break schedule would start all over again in reverse. The first break was after the tunnel widened out into a field. The second break was by the lake that sat along the way. Finally, the third break was just outside of the compound wall. It was important to let the humans rest before entering the compound because right after passing the wall, they would be injected with the serum and changed. The change took a lot out of them, and they needed some strength to undergo the change.

Andrew questioned how the children were lured to the tunnel since it was an off-limits area for them. The leader said it was simple—the fairies from the dinosaur tail lured them there. Once the children got comfortable in the tunnel, they would inspect the walls and find the water leak. Discovery of the water leak would put the humans into a proper position for the pale ones to quickly open the tunnel door and grab them.

Although the abduction plan was not foolproof, the pale ones never had a problem thus far. As Andrew, the chief, and the scouts continued their way, Andrew found that he could not get his mind off his wife and children. He could not wait to get back to them.

The journey was a quiet one until the first break when the scouts stirred up some conversation with Andrew and the leader. The conversation was very interesting and helped time to fly by quickly. The topic of conversation was life above ground versus life underground. It was amazing; all of them held the same view. They were no longer tied down to rely on technology, lack of freedom due to the need of spacesuits and domes, the threat of sickness and imminent death, the lack of leisure activities and facilities, the loss of social experiences under a variety of conditions, and so much more. They all agreed that although the change was painful, the transition was a blessing. The walk from the compound to the tunnel was a long one, but the rest periods came just in time, and by the time the rest period was over, everyone was well rested. Andrew now realized that this was a very important task and they would be back home within twenty-four hours.

Now everyone was just behind the tunnel door. Andrew was reminded that it was crucial to remain as quiet as possible from here on out. The scouts were positioned at the door from shortest to tallest so it would be easier to grab around one another. The chief, and now Andrew, would stand a short distance back to observe the event. Once the scouts have the humans and the tunnel door is closed behind them, the only pale one to speak would be the chief. That was to express who was the dominant abductor and to keep conversation controlled and at a minimum. The chief's main job was to keep things under control as well as to keep the humans calm and obedient so no one would get accidentally hurt. Soon the chief would resign, and Andrew would be king of the land of grandeur; the chief's position with the scouts would be his, and he would go with them alone. The scouts began to use hand motions to reveal that they could hear the voices of children and they were about to find the water leak on the other side of the wall. The chief quickly perked to attention as did Andrew.

Suddenly, Andrew could hear the children's voices then the scouts swiftly opened the tunnel door and started to grab the small humans. As quick as the door was opened, the scouts had it shut again. The scouts had all the children that were there. There were five of them. Three girls and two boys. The abduction was now throwing Andrew into a déjà vu when he was abducted. At that point, it was Andrew's job to observe and learn from the leader. The chief would take charge for the last time, and the scouts would continue to do as taught. Now that the main part of the abduction was over, it was time to start the divided nine-hour walk with one and a half hours' of rest divided three times. The scouts moved about the children so they were subdivided from one another; this was to aid in controlling the group of humans with ease. Everyone walked for four hours until they reached a spot where the tunnel opened into a field. There they would take a half-hour break.

During the break, the chief nodded his head at the scouts; that was the scout's cue to grab the children's helmets with no warning and swiftly pull them off. The element of surprise was so alarming that once the helmets were removed, the kids went from sitting positions to lying-down positions. The pale ones silently held out a hand in hopes of showing the children that they were okay and to help them up to their feet. It worked and the children realized that they were temporarily stunned, but fine. Upon the chief's word, they all started to walk again. The chief did not sense fear in these kids as he did in the others, instead he sensed an urge to please. Instead of trying to engage in small talk, these children just went with the flow.

This was a pleasant change for the chief; it decreased his level of guilt for behaving with such haste in the abduction.

As the long walk continued, the children appeared to enjoy the changing view and different sounds. This pleased the chief and helped Andrew to condone his involvement in abducting the children. Now that Andrew was relaxed and able to face his conscience head-on, his mind started to wonder how his wife was doing. With them being so far apart, he was unable to connect with her empathetically. He tried to figure out what was worse, leaving his wife for up to twenty-four hours or dealing with the idea of capturing humans for the change. He failed to come up with a conclusion. The chief understood what Andrew was experiencing; at first, he had suffered the dilemma of dealing with his conscience also. Although Andrew kept his composure, the chief kept in tune with Andrew's thoughts and feelings empathetically to ensure he would be able to handle this part of his job in the future. At that point in time, the chief was sure Andrew would adapt; after all, it was for the betterment of mankind.

With all the observations and the monitoring of thoughts and feelings, the walk seemed to go by fast for Andrew and the chief. The second stopping spot, the lake, was in nearby sight. For the first time since being in the pale ones' custody, the humans spoke. They commented to one another on how beautiful the area was. The chief verbally commanded that they take a break by the lake. Everyone was ready to stop for a spell. The pale ones refilled their canteens in the lake while the humans appreciated the sight and sounds. After getting water, the pale ones took some jerky out of their satchels and gave some to the children. The children hesitantly took it and cautiously ate it once they saw the pale ones eating some. In every abduction, the humans were offered food to keep up their strength and to assure a happy tummy; the pale ones knew that hunger was a very uncomfortable feeling. It was about a half hour later and everyone was fed, watered, and rested so it was time to travel once more. The next stop would be just outside of the compound wall; there the humans would be injected with the serum then immediately would undergo the change from humans to pale ones. Being just four hours away from the compound, Andrew was forced to recall the extreme discomfort of the change.

The journey was nearly over, and the children continued to be amazed by the sights and sounds. Just like all the other abductees, the children were seeing animals that they had only seen in school books that were thought to be extinct. They passed by the outskirts of the plush forest. There were so many assorted colors, and everything seemed to be tipped with gold. The children even recognized the miniangels fluttering about; there were so many of them. The children were amazed to see so many different animal species thrive together in peace and harmony. Per school books, some of the animals were not known to be able to get along due to being natural carnivores versus herbivores. Either human history had that wrong or the land was more magical than was obvious. Either way, the children were amazed.

Now that the tip of the compound and the great wall was in sight, the children started to become overcome with curiosity. Although the structures were beautiful, that meant the end of the line for the children, and they knew that. With the apparent city in sight, the children wondered what was to become of them. The unknown frightened the children. They were taught about the legend of the dinosaur tail to an extent, but nothing prepared them for what was to come after being abducted. So far, they have experienced many things—fear, shock, admiration for beauty beyond comparison, and kindness. Now feeling intimidated, the children tried to speak with the leader to find out what was to happen to them next. The chief nor Andrew entertained conversation. The last stretch went by like a flash. The scouts were tightening the space between themselves and the children in preparation for the serum injection. The group had finally reached the compound wall. Each child had two pale scouts guarding them during the trip. Now at the end of the trip, one pale scout expeditiously held the child they guarded while the other pale scout gave the injection into the thumb of the child they were responsible for guarding.

As soon as the injection was given, the child was eased to the ground by both pale scouts to undergo the transformation safely. The children's peachy skin began to turn pale, almost white, and they began to sweat profusely. Their breathing became shallow and rapid, almost nonexistent. Their eyes turned white and rolled into the back of their heads. Their bodies were limp and numb, unresponsive to willful movement. The children would not be able to move if they were to try due to the numbness and pain. Everything seemed to pause for several seconds; this was the halfway mark of the change. Finally, their skin became cold, they stopped sweating, and they started to turn a pale blue. They started to breathe deeper and slower. Their eyes turned back into the front of their heads and then turned yellow. The children started to jerk uncontrollably; then they finally had purposeful movement, and the numbness went away. A few more seconds passed then they started to get up. The scouts helped the new pale ones to their feet.

The transformation was quick; after about six seconds of being injected, the changing process began. After about fifteen minutes, the process was complete and the humans were now pale ones. Although the change was extremely uncomfortable, the discomfort, like childbirth, would be remembered but would not seem to be so bad after the fact. It took fifteen minutes for the five humans to become pale ones. Once they stood upright on their feet, they became ready to enter the compound. The scouts allowed the group to check on one another and speak freely. The chief welcomed the group to their new home and apologized for the harsh way that he and the others had acted. He assured the pale children that it was for their best interest, and he hoped they would be happy. The chief concluded by telling them that if they had any needs or desires, they should let Andrew know. They agreed. As the compound doors were opened and they started to walk in, the chief told the new citizens that there would be other pale ones to greet them and show them around; they would explain how things worked and let them know what their duties would be. That was where they were headed at that time. The chief asked if there were any questions so far; the children had none. Then the chief asked the children if there were more children above ground; they all responded, saying that they were the last of the children. The children questioned why he needed that information, and the chief continued with his introduction by giving the schedule from the time of awakening to the time of turning in. Andrew and the chief turned the children over to the welcoming committee and allowed everyone to introduce themselves to one another.

Now that they had returned and the new pale ones were in good hands, it was time for Andrew and the chief to go back to their homes and settle down so they could prepare for the next day's routine and the unborn baby.

The excitement soon rallied up some concern and questions for Andrew about his friend the chief. Andrew and the chief already parted ways, but Andrew's heart was heavy for the chief. He knew the chief was headed for home so instead of going home himself, he went to see the chief first. Andrew walked at a superfast pace and could catch up with the chief before he reached his house. Still walking, the chief sensed some distress from Andrew and asked if everything was okay. Continuing to walk, Andrew replied affirmatively and went on to tell him that he was concerned for him. The leader told Andrew that there was no reason for concern. Andrew asked if he could speak to him privately.

They arrived at the chief's home; he invited Andrew inside and told him to make himself comfortable. The chief sat next to Andrew and asked what the problem was, telling him to be blunt and to the point. Andrew told him that he was concerned for him for being lonely or possibly grieving. The chief, having no clue what Andrew was talking about, asked for him to be more specific. Andrew said that he must be lonely having no wife or possibly grieving the loss of a wife. The leader chuckled a bit then told Andrew that he had never had a wife or girlfriend. He explained that he was just a young boy when he was abducted and changed and that it was a bit over two hundred years ago. He continued by telling Andrew that when it was time for him to become the chief, he just did not have the time to be exclusive with anyone. He never regretted it because everyone in the whole community became his child in a sense, so he had an enormous family. The chief reminded Andrew that in their community, unlike above ground, everyone took care of everyone. Andrew now saw the brighter side of things, and his heart was no longer ailing. The chief also told Andrew that being chief was really for a single person due to the lengthy time demands as well as the occasional round-the-clock duty.

CHAPTER THIRTEEN

The chief said that the view was going to change for the first time because he and Camillia were the chosen ones. The chief continued by telling Andrew that his reign was to be over as soon as the chosen ones arrived; that was a foreseen legend that came to pass. There would be no more chiefs; now there would be a king and queen. He went on to tell Andrew that he would be honored to be the king's adviser. Andrew was relieved to know that the leader was okay. They both sat there in silence for about five minutes then finally the chief broke the silence by telling Andrew to go home to his wife. Andrew gave the chief a big bear hug and told the chief he was proud to have him as a close family and adviser. Both men sentimentally waved goodbye as Andrew walked out of the leader's door. The chief's door closed, and Andrew practically ran all the way home. Within five minutes, Andrew made it to his part of the castle. He was anxious to see Camillia and Armellya and to check on the status of his unborn child.

Stepping onto the porch, he noticed an oddity—there was a horse and carriage outside with no driver. Since there was no one with the carriage and the horse was not tied up, Andrew rushed inside. When Andrew got inside and shut the door, he noticed that no one was there to greet him. He called out for Camillia and got no answer. Becoming more concerned, he headed for their bedroom. Matthew cut him off at the beginning of the hallway. He grabbed Andrew's arms and told him to remain calm. That made Andrew more nervous, so nervous that he froze, he was speechless, and all he could do was stare right through Matthew. Matthew knew that Andrew's state of petrification would not allow him to listen clearly. No one was in the home except Matthew; he was to wait for Andrew. Matthew's job was to take Andrew to Camillia. She had fallen ill and was in the hospital. Matthew did not have any details on what the ailment was, if she was going to stay at the hospital, or what the status of the unborn child was. Bridgette had Armellya and was on an outing with the baby.

She took the baby out, hoping the fresh air and a relaxing walk would take her mind off Camillia's current situation even though she did not know the exact ailment or condition of Camillia and the unborn baby. The walk was not working so Bridgette decided to walk to the hospital with Armellya; she was just a few minutes away. Matthew, Andrew, Bridgette, and Armellya made it to the hospital about the same time. Bridgette was relieved to see Andrew until she saw that he was in a state of shock. They all four entered the hospital together. Bridgette took Armellya and Andrew to sit down in a waiting area while Matthew went to the nurse's desk to inquire about Camillia. The emergency room nurse could verify that Camillia was there, but she was not able to give Matthew any information. He let the nurse know that Camillia's husband was there; the nurse cut him off and told him that she knew who they were and that the doctor would find them when he could. Matthew grabbed the nurse's hand gently and asked if the unborn baby was okay. The nurse simply said to take a seat. Matthew was extremely worried about mom and baby and scared for Andrew.

After a long painstaking wait, the doctor appeared and asked if they were waiting for Camillia. Andrew, Matthew, and Bridgette looked up speechlessly. The doctor asked them to follow him, that they needed to speak in private. Once in a small room, the doctor closed the door behind them then asked them to take a seat. Camillia's two friends and husband took a seat while the doctor stood over them. He began to speak, telling them that per several witnesses, Camillia was involved in a serious accident. Everyone sitting down silently stood up at attention. There was about ten minutes of silence before the doctor continued. Knowing who Camillia was and that she was pregnant made it hard to talk to her friends and husband. The doctor's eyes were fixed on Armellya as he told them that her accident was a serious one. He said that Camillia was hitching up a horse to a small buggy when the horse got spooked and reared. Camillia tried to grab the horse's bridle to calm it down when it knocked her down and stomped on her head and torso repeatedly. Some pale ones were passing by and saw what happened. They rushed over, scooped her up, and took her to the emergency room. The doctor concluded by telling them that she was in a coma and there was no telling when she would wake or if she even would. Andrew asked the doctor if the unborn child was okay and if they could go see Camillia. The doctor told them that the unborn baby was fine at that time and that they could go to see her, but not to have any expectations of her awakening. The doctor took Camillia's husband and friends to her hospital room.

Camillia was on life support. There were tubes and wires everywhere that the whole scene looked like something from a television show with Dr. Jekyll and Mr. Hyde. Andrew finally cracked and started to cry hysterically.

As he walked from her bedroom door to her bedside, it became obvious that she had been through something traumatic. Her bumps, bruises, and cuts were very visible. It looked like she was beaten and left for dead. Matthew and Bridgette were still standing at Camillia's hospital room door, both in tears but maintaining some composure. It was tough to see Camillia lying there in such a state and Andrew torn up like he was. Matthew and Bridgette slowly walked past the doorway to console Andrew.

As they laid their hands onto Andrew's back and started to rub, before they could say anything, Camillia's body started to shake violently all over. The bells on Camillia's machines started to sound very loudly as she began to lose all color. In shock, Matthew and Bridgette took their hands from Andrew's back. Andrew and his friends took a step back as several nurses and the doctor went rushing in. As the doctor started to expeditiously shout commands, the nurses started to move at the speed of light. Andrew noticed one nurse putting some medicine from a syringe into Camillia's intravenous line. A few seconds later, Camillia stopped shaking. The doctor was pleased as Camillia started to regain her normal pale-bluish color. The doctor excused the nurses then turned to Andrew and his friends to speak. Facing Andrew, he put his right hand on Andrew's left shoulder and began to speak freely. The doctor said that Camillia had only one major injury that was responsible for her sickly state. He went on to say that her brain was swollen due to the severity of the head trauma from the horse repeatedly stomping on her head. The doctor went on to tell them that he had put a pressure monitor on her brain to monitor the swelling. The swelling was increasing, thus the seizures as they had just witnessed. That seizure was just one of many that have already occurred.

With that traumatic news, Andrew dropped to his knees and held his face in his hands. The doctor stood there speechlessly as Andrew's friends bent over him to help him to his feet. Matthew and Bridgette were just as devastated as Andrew but had to hold up their composure for Andrew to help him deal with the tragedy. That was extremely difficult for them, but necessary. They would both save their crying and state of panic for a private moment when they would be alone. Finally, having gotten Andrew to his feet, they spoke words of sympathy and strength. They told Andrew that he had to be strong for Camillia and the unborn baby. They went on to say that although she was in a coma, she should still sense their presence and state of emotion. Andrew pulled himself together, wiped his eyes off with his shirt sleeve, and hesitantly walked to Camillia's bedside. Matthew and Bridgette were right behind him and kept one of their hands on one side of his shoulder each.

Andrew took one of Camillia's hands into his hands and began to speak to her. He was telling her that he loved her deeply and that he could not function without her. He continued by telling her to fight and get better because Armellya needed her and so did the unborn child. There was no response from Camillia; that just continued to break Andrew's heart. Andrew bent over Camillia and took her into his arms and began to rock her gently and lovingly. Matthew and Bridgette both went to the opposite side of the bed from Andrew and touched Camillia's limp arm. They began to sob; their hearts went out to Andrew and Armellya. After holding Camillia for ten minutes or so, Andrew put her down, recomposed himself, and said he needed to find her doctor. Andrew walked out of the room, leaving Matthew and Bridgette to watch over Camillia. They stayed at Camillia's bedside and continued to hold her arm.

In Andrew's absence, Matthew and Bridgette broke their composure and began to cry insanely. Meanwhile, Andrew approached the nurse's desk and requested to speak with Camillia's doctor. The charge nurse stepped forward lend said she diwould get the doctor for him immediately; she told him to stay put, then she swiftly walked away. The doctor must have been nearby because it only took a few minutes before the charge nurse came back with the doctor. As the doctor approached Andrew, he asked what he could do for him. Andrew, knowing that Camillia's condition was grim, asked to speak to the doctor in private. He did not want anyone to know how serious her condition was because he wanted everyone to keep hope that she would recover. The doctor commanded Andrew to follow him then led him into a small room. The doctor stopped at the doorway as Andrew proceeded to fully enter the room.

After shutting the door behind them, the doctor turned to Andrew and asked him what he could do for him. Andrew told the doctor that he wanted full details on Camillia's condition, how serious it was, what her chances of recovery were, and if there was anything he or his friends could do to help.

Andrew told the doctor to be straightforward. The doctor then took Andrew by the shoulders and told him that he would be completely honest—her prognosis was not very good. He reminded Andrew that getting sick was not something that occurred in pale ones. He continued in saying that the healing process from a sickness in pale ones was assumed to be speedy, but that it had never been tested. The doctor added that the assumption was just that, an assumption. No pale one had ever been injured that severely before. The doctor continued to tell Andrew that it surprised him that Camillia was sickly during her pregnancy with Armellya. He reminded Andrew that having a pale one who could conceive was only a legend until he and Camillia came along.

Once again, Andrew asked the doctor for details on Camillia's condition and if there was anything they could do to improve her chances of survival. The doctor bluntly told Andrew that her survival was not likely, and the only thing they could do was to be by her bedside if she may be able to have any awareness of her surroundings. Although the news was not what Andrew was hoping to hear, he was satisfied with the doctor's explanation. Andrew thanked the doctor for his time and headed for the door.

Just before Andrew opened the door, the doctor blurted out that he would do everything possible to save her life and the life of the unborn child. Andrew stopped dead in his tracks and turned in the doctor's direction then asked him, if Camillia were to become brain-dead, would there be a way to save the baby? The doctor told Andrew that he had already thought about that. He would simply keep Camillia on life support until the baby was at full term then deliver the child by cesarean section. Andrew simply nodded as if to say okay then exited the room, leaving the doctor to stand there alone.

Andrew went back to Camillia's hospital room. When he got back, Bridgette said she needed to leave to go back home and take care of Armellya. It was her feeding time, and it was important to keep her on a regular schedule of walks, naps, playtime, and so on. Andrew strongly agreed. Bridgette leaned over Camillia and kissed her on the forehead. So far, the only people that knew of the state that Camillia was in were Matthew, Andrew, Bridgette, and the couple of pale ones who rescued her from the horse attack. Matthew told Andrew that he felt it would be a promising idea to summon the chief; in fact, it was truly important. Andrew agreed so Matthew left at top speed. Andrew stayed at Camillia's bedside and held her hand firmly. He spoke to her about how he and Armellya needed her, how he loved her with all his heart, and how he could not imagine his life without her. He commanded her to recover and go home with him. He kissed her hand and held it to his lips as he sobbed.

Just then, the chief and Matthew entered her hospital room. They walked over to Andrew, and the chief put his hand on Andrew's shoulder. The chief told Andrew that she had to pull through because she was a fighter and mentally strong. He concluded by saying that if she had any choice at all, she would come back to them. The chief told Matthew to resume his duties and that if there were to be any breaking news, he would be sure to let them know. Matthew nodded and silently left the hospital room. The chief took his hand off Andrew's shoulder and walked to the other side of Camillia's bed to hold her other hand. The chief held Camillia's hand to his cheek and told her to come back to them. About that time, the machines she was wired to showed that her pulse had risen. The chief noticed that and with anticipation told Andrew to keep talking to her. Andrew had not noticed the machine reading since his back was turned to all the machines, but he did as the chief suggested. Andrew continued to tell Camillia that he loved her and got specific in telling her all the things he loved about her.

The chief, watching the machines, noticed that now not only was her pulse rising, but her respiration was increasing also. The chief felt that the increase of Camillia's pulse and respiration was a good sign. Not knowing that Camillia's machines could be monitored at the nurse's desk, the chief told Andrew that he needed to excuse himself for a second. He did not tell Andrew about his observations because he did not want to falsely get Andrew's hopes up, but he did want to tell the doctor in case this was a sign of hope. About the time the chief put Camillia's hand down at her side, the doctor and several nurses rushed into the room. Once they got near to her bedside, they pushed the chief out of the way. The doctor observed Andrew at her bedside and sharply asked what they were doing to her. Andrew took that defensively; he put Camillia's hand on the bed then abruptly asked the doctor what he meant by the statement he had made. Between how the doctor asked what they were doing to her, followed by an order for the chief to move aside, Andrew became enraged.

Suddenly the doctor noticed Andrew's negative disposition. He apologized for being such a brute. He quickly told Andrew that they noticed some sort of possible response from Camillia by the monitor screen at the nurse's desk. The chief moved to sit on a chair that was next to him against a wall so he could stay but not be in the way. Andrew stood up then stumbled a few steps back. Without pause, the doctor moved to the side of the bed that Andrew was on then compressed his body in front of Andrew's. In a bent-over position, he proceeded to check Armellya's eyes for pupillary response and her arms and legs for neurological responses, which both had been absent. He then wanted to check the cranial pressure for any change. The nurses stood back on standby for any commands given by the doctor; they held their hands together tightly in hopes that the possible responses would turn out to be confirmed as a voluntary response. Andrew steadied his stance and awaited word from the doctor. The chief, just as anxious to hear a good report from the doctor, stood up and went to stand beside Andrew. All together they watched the doctor intently. After the doctor finished holding both of Camillia's eyes open and shining a small light into them several times, he moved to her legs and used a small hammer-like tool to thump her legs. He then moved to her arms and did the same thing that he did with her legs to her arms, and finally, he checked her cranial pressure monitor. The doctor slowly stood upright and turned toward Andrew and the chief; he had a strange look on his face.

After a prolonged period of silence, it became obvious that the doctor's expression was not a negative one; it was more like an expression of curiosity. The doctor ordered the nurses to stay with Camillia then started to move past Andrew and the chief. As he did so, he asked for them to follow him. Just past the threshold of the room, the doctor stopped and turned to the chief and Andrew. The doctor sighed and wiped his forehead. He said that the rise of Camillia's pulse and respiration were possibly in response to their presence and that her cranial pressure was down. It was conceivable that she was starting to heal, thus becoming aware of her environment.

CHAPTER FOURTEEN

Andrew knew that the good news from the doctor was nothing short of a miracle, and the chief felt the same. Now that there was a glimmer of hope, Andrew's body language relaxed a bit and revealed his physical and mental exhaustion. Once the chief and Andrew returned to the compound from the abduction of some more children, the chief could go home to rest a bit. Upon returning home, Andrew immediately realized that his wife's life was in serious jeopardy so he went to the hospital where she had been ever since he left for the abduction. As Andrew started to turn to reenter Camillia's hospital room, the chief grabbed him by the shoulder and demanded that he go home to get some rest before his mind wore down and his thinking became irrational.

That was not what he wanted to do; staying with his wife was more important to him than living his own life. If she were to die, he was not sure he could raise Armellya and possibly the unborn baby by himself, nor would he want to. The chief told Andrew to go and update Matthew and Bridgette then go directly to bed for some sleep and to eat when he awakened.

After all that, he would accept Andrew back, and if there were any significant changes, he would alert him immediately. Andrew agreed that this was probably the best thing to do, but prior to leaving, he had to see Camillia once more. The chief agreed. Andrew and the chief walked the rest of the way into the hospital room together. The chief sat down in the same chair he had previously sat in while Andrew continued to the other side of the bed. Andrew took Camillia's hand in his and bent over her then whispered in her ear. He told her that he loved her very much and missed having her at home and finally that he had to go rest but would be back shortly. He kissed her ear then stood up and placed her hand across her stomach. After releasing her hand, he placed his hand onto her stomach next to hers and said he loved the baby too. He slowly removed his hand from Camillia's body and put it to his side. He looked at the chief and told him to watch over and protect her as he would his own wife. The chief assured Andrew that he would and for him to rest easy.

Andrew left the hospital room and was almost out of the main hospital doors when the doctor caught up with him and stopped him to talk. Before the doctor could speak, Andrew told him he was going home as he needed some rest before he became physically and mentally incapacitated. The doctor barked back at Andrew, telling him he could not leave no matter what the circumstance. Andrew was taken aback and told the doctor in no uncertain terms that he was going back as he was going home to rest and would be back shortly. The doctor asked Andrew to hear him out. He was going to make some changes to Camillia's treatment, and the outcome could be dramatic; it could very well go for the better, but there was a chance that she could make a turn for the worse. This caught Andrew's full undivided attention. Andrew immediately warned the doctor that he had not slept for over twenty-four hours, and the lack of sleep could lead to him being unreasonable and temperamental. The doctor said that he could arrange for Andrew to get some rest in Camillia's hospital room by placing a cot in the room next to her bed. Andrew said that the sleeping arrangement was sufficient; then he wanted to know what changes the doctor had planned to do to Camillia's treatment. The doctor asked that before he explained the changes, he wanted Andrew to arrange for someone to be in the hospital room with him always so that when he was sleeping, they could keep an eye on Camillia and while he was awake, they could be there to support him. Andrew said he would discuss the arrangement with the chief, and together they would come up with something. The doctor said that was reasonable and to call for him once arrangements were made, and he would explain the changes, their risks, and the hopes. Andrew started to walk away toward Camillia's hospital room when the doctor called out to him, saying that he would be at the nurse's desk. Andrew just waved one hand in the air and silently continued to walk.

As Andrew entered Camillia's hospital room, with complete surprise, the chief flew out of his chair and rushed to the doorway to head off Andrew. Before the chief could utter a word, Andrew explained that the doctor caught him at the main hospital doors and requested him to stay. The chief gave an awkward look and stood there in silence. Andrew was about to start talking to the chief when two porters arrived with Andrew's cot, a pillow, and some bedding. The two men stood aside so the porters could enter Camillia's hospital room and set up the bed. While the porters were making up the cot, Andrew took the chief by the shoulder and guided him to the chair he had been sitting in.

The chief sat down then asked Andrew what was going on. Andrew silently stood in front of the chief, up against Camillia's bed. He took Camillia's hand then looked the chief dead in his eyes and told him that the doctor was going to make some enormous changes to Camillia's treatment. The chief's face showed signs of grave concern. Andrew went on to tell the chief that the changes would cause Camillia to get a little better or put her in more danger. The chief's jaw dropped open, and he was left speechless.

Andrew walked to the doorway and called out toward the nurse's desk that he was ready for the doctor.

Without waiting for the doctor to show, Andrew walked back into the hospital room and stood by Camillia's bedside again. While they were waiting for the doctor to arrive, Andrew told the chief that the doctor requested for someone to be with him always. The chief immediately responded; he told Andrew that he would stay around the clock just as Andrew had to. The chief's solution to the dilemma of needing someone there around the clock caused Andrew to have a puzzled look on his face. The chief told Andrew there was a simple solution. They would both stay and take turns sleeping on the cot and watching over Camillia. Andrew agreed that the solution was simple and that he would be honored to have the chief stay. The chief and Andrew sat in silence for fifteen minutes and the doctor still had not come in so Andrew let go of Camillia's hand and decided to go to the nurse's desk to retrieve him. As Andrew started across the hospital room, the doctor walked into Camillia's room. The doctor asked Andrew to take a seat on the cot and waited for him to get across the room. The doctor followed Andrew in but stopped at the foot of Camillia's bed then folded his arms.

After taking a couple of deep breaths, the doctor told Andrew and the chief that Camillia was at a point where the medical treatment needed to be changed. He warned that the changes would mean that Camillia had to fight a little harder to recover and support her pregnancy. That meant that she would either improve and the treatment could continue to slowly dinasge, or she would not be able to adjust and her condition would worsen, possibly killing her. The doctor said this was why he wanted Andrew to stay and to have someone there for support twenty-four seven. The doctor concluded by saying that there was a fifty-fifty gamble. The changes were to begin immediately, and he would explain to them what he would be doing as he did things. The doctor turned and walked toward the hospital room door. Just as he walked over the threshold, he told them not to be afraid to ask questions if they did not understand something. That last bit of news had the chief and Andrew deeply concerned.

The doctor left the room to retrieve some nurses to aid in the changes that were to be made with Camillia's care. It took him ten minutes to find the specific nurses he wanted to help him and to continue helping with Camillia's care. When the doctor walked into the hospital room with his nurses, Andrew asked him to answer one question before doing anything to Camillia.

The doctor asked what the question was and said he would answer it the best he could. Andrew asked him why the community had a hospital if pale ones did not get sick. The doctor said that due to Camillia's pregnancies being so risky and now the accident, it was a good thing they had a hospital. He went further to say that although pale ones do not get sick, that's not to say they do not get hurt on the job. He added that a pale one heals ten times faster than a human, and hopefully, being a pale one will be an asset to Camillia. This surprised Andrew because pale ones had a heightened speed, strength, and agility over humans. Andrew's mind was quickly taken off that question when the doctor asked Andrew if he and the chief were ready to start the treatment changes. They both answered yes.

Andrew stood up and walked to Camillia's bedside then gently took her right hand into his hands. At the same time, Andrew stood up and so did the chief. The chief also went to Camillia's bedside, and he took her left hand into his hands then held on to it firmly. The doctor said that the first thing they were going to do was to stop sedating her. Because of being intubated and in enormous amounts of pain, she was sedated to keep her from feeling the pain and pulling at the breathing tube. He also said that the sedation kept Camillia from fighting the respirator. However, they would have to keep the hand restraints on her to prevent her from pulling the tube out since it is an automatic response. Next, they were going to reduce the amount of work the respirator did and give her body a chance to take over her breathing. The doctor said that when she could breathe adequately on her own, they would remove the respirator tubing and the restraints. The doctor said that by the time they would be ready to take out the breathing tube, the sedation would be worn off and she would be alert. The doctor also said that her cranial pressure was under control so they would be able to remove that equipment. There would still be a lot of healing needed, but if all that flew without complication, she would heal with ease. On the other hand, when they stop sedating her, the pain may contribute to some setbacks. When they decide to give her a chance to breathe on her own, she could crash and succumb to respiratory distress. The doctor was no longer concerned that the cranial pressure would increase, but it would be wise to keep it monitored for a bit longer. The doctor asked if they understood what was about to occur. They both answered affirmatively.

The doctor moved to the foot of Camillia's bed, folded his arms, and started to give the nurses orders. A registered nurse took away the medicine pump that had sedation medicine in it. Then the intensive care unit nurse changed the settings of the ventilator. Finally, as a last-minute decision, the doctor took away the cranial pressure monitor and closed her head. To Andrew and the chief, those changes did not seem to be many, but they knew the results might be dramatic one way or another. The doctor and nurses waited for fifteen minutes and watched Camillia's vital signs and the respiratory effort she was exhibiting. Everything appeared to be going well. Satisfied with how things were going, the doctor released the nurses and headed out right behind them. The chief told Andrew to get some sleep and that he would watch over Camillia. Hesitantly, Andrew let go of Camillia's hand and went to the cot, lay down, and fell fast asleep.

After Andrew fell asleep, the chief stood at Camillia's bedside for two hours holding her hand. His feet and legs became tired so he decided to let go of Camillia's hand for a moment to pull the chair he had sat in over to the bedside. Once he sat down, he took Camillia's left hand into his right hand again and bowed his head down as if to pray. Another couple of hours went by, and the chief felt his eyes getting heavy so he decided to talk to Camillia to stay awake since it was not near time to wake Andrew.

He was not sure if she could hear him or not, but just in case she could, he wanted to be truthful and sentimental. He spoke about how he felt toward her, that she seemed special when she first got abducted, but he never fathomed that she was the chosen one. He told her how beautiful her family was and that she was very loved by everyone in the community. He asked her to fight for her life and the life of her unborn child. He was about to say something else when he felt her hand lightly squeeze his. That was cause for great excitement and celebration. The chief called out to Andrew to wake up after an insufficient amount of sleep.

Andrew bounced to his feet as he opened his eyes and asked what was wrong. The chief answered with joy that Camillia had squeezed his hand while he was talking to her. Andrew could not believe his ears. He shuffled to her bedside and grabbed her right hand with his right hand. As he gently squeezed her hand, he told her he was there and to please squeeze his hand if she could hear him. It took a couple of minutes, but she did squeeze Andrew's hand. The chief told Andrew to continue to try and get her to rouse more while he went to go get the doctor. Andrew continued to hold her right hand in his right hand and used his left hand to caress her left temple. He asked her to open her eyes if she could. Andrew continued to caress her head and repeated the command for her to open her eyes.

Five minutes passed and finally the chief and doctor arrived at Camillia's hospital room. As the doctor drew nearer to Camillia's bed, Andrew told him that she had squeezed his hand. The doctor stood next to Camillia and took her left hand into his right hand then commanded her to squeeze his hand. She did not squeeze the doctor's hand. After several failed attempts to get her to squeeze his hand, he said it must have been an involuntary movement, a twitch of sorts. Andrew started crying loudly; his tears were falling on her hand. The chief walked over to Andrew and put his hand on Andrew's shoulder then told him that they knew different. The doctor was ready to leave the hospital room but looked down at her prior to letting go of her hand. As the doctor looked down, he was startled to see two eyes looking up at him. His reaction got the chief and Andrew's attention. They looked at Camillia and were amazed to see her golden yellow eyes opened. Andrew moved his face above hers and told her he loved her; she tried to smile the best she could.

The doctor put a damper on things when he said that even though Camillia was stable, she was not out of the woods yet. Andrew stood erect and told the doctor she would be just fine, that she was beginning her recovery. The doctor acted as though he did not hear Andrew. He leaned over Camillia and told her to blink twice for a no response and three times for a yes response. She held eye contact with the doctor as he asked a few questions. He asked her if she was in any pain, and she responded with no answer. He asked her if she knew where she was at the current time; her eyes answered yes. He then asked her if she knew who everyone in the room was, and she again answered yes. The doctor straightened back up and exclaimed how miraculous her status was.

The doctor told Andrew and the chief that it was now time to push the odds again by taking the breathing tube out of her. The doctor said that he needed to get a couple of nurses to assist him, especially if Camillia stopped breathing soon after the tube was pulled. He left the chief and Andrew to watch over her while he went to retrieve some nurses from the nursing desk. Again, Andrew and the chief took one of Camillia's hands and held them lovingly. Andrew bent over Camillia and kissed her on her forehead then told her he would be with her forever then stood back up. The chief took the opportunity to tell Camillia that she was the daughter he never had and that he loved her as such; then he bent over her and kissed her forehead.

Just as the chief stood upright, the doctor stormed in with several nurses. The doctor told Andrew and the chief to step back so everyone that was to be needed to extubate Camillia could get in to her and be prepared to intubate her if needed. The two men went to the foot of the bed and waited for the doctor to do what he needed to do then move away so they could get back to her.

CHAPTER FIFTEEN

The extubation process was done at a high rate of speed. It made Camillia gag a bit, and her eyes started to water a lot, but so far, she was breathing on her own. Now that the tube was out, the doctor removed the hand restraints, and Camillia could move in bed freely. The doctor told one of the nurses to stay in the room for about a half hour to monitor her breathing on room air. He wanted to make sure that Camillia would continue to breathe on her own and not need any oxygen supplementation due to low oxygen saturation in her blood. Finally, everyone was out of the way so Andrew and the chief could stand back at the bedside. A nurse stayed standing at the foot of the bed. Andrew told the chief to go get something to eat so that afterward he could take a short nap. Andrew said he would be fine during that time. The chief was not too keen on leaving Andrew alone because he was so exhausted and had not eaten or drank anything in close to two days, but the chief was not going to fight a lost cause.

As the chief was leaving the hospital room, he told Andrew that he would bring him back something to eat and a drink. Just as the chief turned the corner of the hospital door into the hallway, he heard a loud crash that sounded like it came from Camillia's room. The chief rushed back into the room to check things out, and he immediately noticed Andrew on the floor with the nurse standing over him; Camillia was trying to sit up to check on Andrew. The chief started to dash over to Andrew and the nurse when she ordered him to immediately call for the doctor and extra help. The chief did as he was asked. The doctor and a few nurses came running over thinking there was something wrong with Camillia. When they got to the room, it took a few seconds for them to realize that the crisis was not Camillia; it was Andrew.

The nurse that had been in the room said that Andrew was standing one minute then collapsing to the floor unresponsive the next minute. The doctor checked the first things that were in order—the airway, breathing, and circulation. The chief told the doctor that Andrew had not gotten adequate sleep for two days and had not eaten or drank anything for two days. The doctor told one of the nurses to get a couple of porters to put Andrew in the cot; she left the room posthaste. He told another nurse to put intravenous access in Andrew and to get blood samples while she was at a good vein; she began to act on her orders. The doctor told the third nurse to draw up a sedative to give to Andrew in his intravenous line. The first nurse made it back with two porters before the second nurse started to look for a good vein on Andrew so they went ahead and put Andrew on the cot before anything else was done. The doctor ordered that nurse to get a bag of saline solution for Andrew's intravenous therapy and to also get a syringe of dextrose to inject into the saline to be distributed evenly over several hours.

The chief asked if all that was necessary, and the doctor said absolutely. The doctor explained that Andrew, in a state such as this, was of no use to his wife. He was neglecting his body by depriving it of sleep and nourishment; it finally led to him collapsing and being unresponsive to pain as well as ammonia packets. The chief told the doctor that he did not understand how

Andrew, a pale one, could get sick. The doctor's reply was that it was true pale ones did not get sick, but they were not immune to death due to neglect such as this. The nurses had finished their duties, the intravenous access had been achieved, the fluid therapy had been started, the blood samples were on the way to the laboratory, and the sedative had been given.

Now it was time for Andrew to receive some much-needed rest and nourishment at the same time. The doctor told one of the nurses to remain in the room until further notice from him. The doctor then told the chief to go get food and beverage for himself and to take his time for afterward it would be his turn to get some rest. The doctor added that the chief could do this the uncomplicated way, on his own or that he could do it for him as he had to do for Andrew. The chief agreed to take care of those things himself.

The chief went to the hospital cafeteria for nourishment. He had a four-course meal with water for rehydration. While eating his meal, the chief remembered that he promised to tell Bridgette and Matthew about any changes in Camillia's condition, good or bad. The chief realized that sharing the good news created a dilemma; he could not leave Andrew at the hospital alone, not to mention the situation Andrew had gotten himself into—he was heavily sedated and under the doctor's care.

Once he was done eating, the chief decided to express his authority, which he seldom had to do. While heading back to Camillia's room, the chief stopped at the nurse's desk and made a request for two runners to run an errand for him. He would have one runner retrieve Bridgette and Armellya and take them to the waiting room and have the second runner retrieve Matthew and take him to the same waiting room. Once they were both there, they could go to see for themselves that Camillia was doing much better. That would bring a boundless joy to their hearts. However, when they happened to see Andrew, they may be led to think he was suffering from a serious medical ailment. The chief knew he would have to be quick on his toes to explain the situation before they panicked; that was why he was having Bridgette, Armellya, and Matthew brought to the waiting room. The chief finished his meal and left the cafeteria and headed straight for the nurse's desk. He found the head nurse and made the request for two runners to be at his service. The nurse said it would be no problem then immediately made a rather brief phone call.

As she hung up the receiver, she told the chief that the runners were on their way posthaste. The chief thanked her then went to the hospital doorway of Camillia's room and waited. Within minutes, the runners reported to the chief for their service requests. The chief told them that they were to retrieve someone; one was to get Bridgette with Armellya, and the other was to get Matthew. He told them where to find their targets and demanded that they be brought to the waiting room where he would be waiting. The runners went on their way like a bat out of hell, so the chief decided to check on Camillia and Andrew before going to the waiting room. As the chief came around the corner of Camillia's hospital doorway, he could see Camillia sitting up in bed with a warm smile on her face. He continued through the room to the other side of Camillia's bed so he could get a visual on Andrew. Andrew was still sleeping soundly. Camillia held out her hand toward the chief to have him go to her bedside and take her hand; he did just that. The chief held his other hand up to her mouth and put one finger over her lips and told her not to try to speak yet.

He told her he had to leave the room for a short time, but he would bring back a surprise for her. He left the room heading straight for the waiting room where he would await Bridgett, Armellya, and Matthew's arrival.

Ten minutes later, both runners arrived with their targets. The chief quickly spoke up, telling them to sit down and ask no questions until he was done speaking. They sat down and, with overly concerned looks on their faces, gave the chief their undivided attention. The chief decided to save the best news for last, so he started to tell them about Andrew. He told them that Andrew was severely sleep deprived, grimly dehydrated, and very nutritionally deficient. Continuing, he told them that after falling to the ground unconscious, the doctor had to sedate him and put lines in him to hydrate him as well as infuse nutrition. Matthew and Bridgette's mouths dropped open, but before they could utter a word, the chief simply said to wait. The chief told them that there was something they had to see, and they needed to follow him. He gave a suspicious smile as he started to walk toward Camillia's hospital room.

They went around the slight corner and came to the threshold of Camillia's hospital door. The chief barreled right in, but Matthew and Bridgette were so shocked by what they saw that their bodies just froze. Without any pause, the chief walked up to Camillia's bedside, took her hand into his, and said that there was her surprise. Camillia was so happy to see her friends that she practically started to glow. She held out her free hand toward them and waved it in a motion as if to say come in. Bridgette and Matthew walked up to her bedside and began to sob tears of joy. Camillia pulled her one hand free from the chief's hand and thrust herself forward to give her friends a group hug. After the group hug was over, Camillia reached up to Bridgette's arms to touch Armellya. Bridgette held Armellya out toward Camillia so she could hold her, and she did. Camillia looked at the chief and tried to tell him she was thankful, but the words would not come out. Her throat was sore and raw. The chief understood what she was trying to say.

Camillia, Bridgette, Matthew, and the chief were pulled from their sentimental moment back to a sobering reality by a few groans given off by Andrew. He was starting to wake up.

The chief told Matthew to keep an eye on Andrew and not to let him get off the cot while he went to retrieve the doctor.

Matthew said he would do his best. Camillia felt that Andrew would listen to her over anyone else, so she handed Armellya back to Bridgette in case she needed to try to get out of bed to be at his side to coax him into cooperating. The chief was scrambling to find the doctor to get him into the room on the double. He feared that Andrew might be somewhat confused upon fully awakening and possibly angry at what was done to him. Andrew managed to swing his legs off the cot and sit up. Matthew told him to take it easy, to just sit there for a few minutes. Before Andrew became fully aware of what had happened and what was done to him, the chief returned with the doctor. Camillia was relieved to see the doctor, she wanted to know when she and Andrew could go home. The chief stood at the foot of Camillia's hospital bed while the doctor knelt in front of Andrew. The doctor asked Andrew how he felt. He said he felt rejuvenated, like he had just awakened from hibernation. The doctor asked him if he was aware of what happened to him. He said he suddenly felt dizzy then everything turned black, but he could still hear what was going on around him for a few minutes and then he woke up.

The doctor asked him when he last ate, drank, and rested. Andrew said he got a couple of hours of sleep there at the hospital, but the last time he ate or drank was on the way back from the abduction journey, probably two days ago. The doctor explained that he had fainted from his blood sugar being lethally low from not eating, his electrolytes being highly abnormal due to severe dehydration, and finally serious fatigue due to insufficient rest. He told Andrew that his body just could not take any more abuse, so it gave out. If left unattended, he could have slipped into a coma and possibly not have come back. The doctor told Andrew that he gave him a sedative to induce the proper amount of sleep that he needed; then he had to do intravenous therapy to get him hydrated and stabilize his blood sugar levels. Andrew apologized to the doctor as well as everyone in the room. The doctor gave a short reply of welcome back. As soon as the doctor finished speaking, Camillia started to wave both hands about, trying to get the doctor's attention.

Once he stood up and turned to leave, he noticed her waving her arms about wildly. He walked to the side of her bed, gently took hold of one of her hands, and asked what he could do for her. Camillia put her free hand on the doctor's cheek, gave an innocent type of smile, then used telepathy to ask when she and Andrew could go home. The doctor chuckled and verbally said that it was strange that every pale one was telepathic but seldom used it. He told her that she was resourceful to think of using telepathy until her throat was feeling better. He finally answered her question aloud and said as far as she was concerned, providing things stay good, she could go home the next day and he would do daily visits with her at her home. Then he verbalized that Andrew would be free to go home as soon as they took the intravenous setup out of him. Camillia took her hand off the doctor's face and placed it into her lap then nodded her head as if to say okay. Andrew told Camillia that he would stay with her since Armellya was in good hands with Bridgette and he had the chief to cover their responsibilities. Camillia smiled a big smile. The chief agreed to take care of things until Andrew was ready to resume his duties. The doctor said he would have a nurse come in to take out the intravenous line as expeditiously as possible and that he no longer required someone to stay with him, but it was fine for them to stay if they would like, but not overnight. The doctor left the room and headed straight for the nurse's desk to give an order to discontinue Andrew's line. Andrew thanked Bridgette and Matthew for being such good friends and for being there for them. Andrew told them that even though they work for him and Camillia, they were family first and always would be. Once it was established what Matthew and Bridgette meant to Camillia and Andrew, the nurse for Andrew arrived to remove his intravenous line.

The intravenous line was removed, Andrew was free to move about, and he did. He went over to Camillia's bedside and held her hand and told her how happy he was that she pulled through. He said he was frightened for a while that she and the unborn baby might not have made it.

The sentimental ambiance in the room was disturbed by some arguing in the hallway by the nurse's desk. The chief decided to check out the situation to see if he could help in resolving the issue at hand. He observed two pale ones arguing with the charge nurse. After standing there for several minutes without being acknowledged, he decided to interrupt by asking the pale ones if he could be of any assistance. They stopped talking, turned toward him, and started to yell at him but suddenly realized who he was. They apologized deeply for yelling then the two pale ones just stood there with blank faces now speechless. The charge nurse proceeded to tell him that they were inquiring about the patient who got trampled by the horse. She told the chief that those two people were the ones that rescued her and got her to the hospital. She told the chief that it was against the hospital policy for her to confirm or deny someone being there. The chief told the nurse that he was thankful she followed the law and that he would handle the two pale ones. The charge nurse walked away with relief and went back to her duties.

Meanwhile, the chief asked the two pale ones for their names. They gave him their names. The chief then asked them why they were there. They told him that they had rescued the upcoming queen from a brutal horse attack and brought her to the hospital. The chief thanked them and asked what it was that they wanted. They told the chief that they only wanted to see how she was doing and to offer to shoot the horse for its disobedience. The chief smiled appreciatively at the pale ones and told them their services would not be needed, but if they wanted to see for themselves that the upcoming queen was doing well, thanks to them, that he would take them to her. Both pale ones thought that was splendid and promised to behave themselves. The chief started to walk away and motioned with his hand for them to follow him. Everyone looked toward the hospital door when the chief returned. They were extremely surprised to see that he brought some strangers back with him. They surpassed the chief and walked to Camillia's hospital bedside. They told her that she may not remember them, but they were the two men that got her out from beneath the horse's hooves and directly to the hospital. Using telepathy, Camillia told them that she could not speak yet, but she was thankful for their brave act of kindness. She revealed that she did not remember anything from that evening and that she was overjoyed that they came to see her. They verbally told her that they only did the right thing and now that they could see their efforts were not in vain, they could move on. Camillia let them know that they could visit her any time; the community was one large family and that they were part of that family too.

CHAPTER SIXTEEN

As they went to shake her hand, she pulled them in closer and gave them a hug. The chief thanked them again and walked them to the hospital door. They continued to walk on while the chief turned back around and reentered the room. Armellya was starting to get antsy and whiny so Bridgette announced that she had to leave so she could lay Armellya down for her nap. Everyone said their goodbyes to Bridgette and Armellya, then they left to go home. The chief said he needed to get himself back on schedule so he could balance work and recovery time. He leaned over Camillia's bed and gave her a tender kiss on the forehead. As he was headed for the hospital door, he advised Andrew to get himself back on schedule also. Andrew acknowledged. Matthew asked Andrew if he was going to stay with Camillia or go home. Andrew said he was going to stay with his wife and suggested that Matthew go back to his duties and get back on schedule. Matthew acknowledged, said his goodbyes to Camillia, then promptly left for his designated duties.

Now it was just Andrew and Camillia left at the hospital. Andrew felt that they would have a quiet and relaxing evening together, but the doctor shattered that assumption when he entered the room. Just like the chief, the doctor advised Andrew to go home and resume a normal schedule. He stated that it would be the best thing everyone could do for Camillia. He also reminded Andrew that he had to get the home resituated to fit Camillia's needs since she would be on bed rest for quite some time. Andrew questioned the doctor's order by wondering why she needed bed rest if the only healing left was for her trachea to heal so she could speak once again. The doctor reminded him that Camillia was carrying a high-risk pregnancy with Armellya, which automatically made this pregnancy elevated risk. Andrew asked how he figured that this pregnancy was dangerous since there had not been any problems yet. The doctor told Andrew that the pregnancy was already threatened by the horse attack. She had some major healing to do, and he was concerned that her body may shun the pregnancy to focus on a rapid healing process. The doctor strongly warned him that the chances of that happening were far higher than not. Andrew dropped his head and slowly shook it back and forth as if to say no.

Again, the doctor advised him to go home and get things ready for Camillia and to take care of himself. Camillia sharply cut into the conversation and promised that the baby would be fine and that she would carry to full term then deliver a healthy infant naturally. She told Andrew to go home and do whatever it was that he needed to do, not to worry, and she would be home the next day. Andrew finally agreed to go home. He went over to Camillia's hospital bed, bent over her, and gently kissed her lips. Before he could straighten up, Camillia wrapped her arms around his neck and held him close for a few minutes. She finally let go of him and allowed him to stand erect. They gazed into each other's eyes for a few seconds, then Andrew broke off the eye contact by sharply turning around. Without hesitation, he walked out of the hospital room. He felt like he had just lost his only friend in the world, but he knew that feeling would pass on the next day.

While Andrew was walking up the pathway from the main street to his front door, he noticed that someone was at his door. He was still too far away to recognize who it was. Because it would take a few minutes for Andrew to reach the door, he was fearful that the visitor might assume no one was home and leave. He hollered at the person, but he did not appear to hear him. He hollered out again even louder while he kept walking, and this time the person responded. It was the chief. He thought Andrew might have been home already. He went by to see if Andrew needed any help getting the house ready for Camillia to come home. The chief figured that with two people working on the preparations, it would get done faster and more efficiently. This meant Andrew would have a bit more time to wind down. Andrew felt it was important for the chief to help because as he verbalized before, he viewed Camillia as the daughter he never had. He believed that allowing the chief to help would be therapeutic for the chief. It was exceptionally important that everything be perfect for Camillia.

They went into the house together and divided up the list of things to do as evenly as possible. Once they knew who was doing what, they separated and started to complete the items on their lists. It only took two hours to complete all but one thing on Andrew's list. That last item was for Andrew to get all the help together in one room and discuss their specific duties and new specialized duties that they would temporarily have. Once Camillia was off bed rest and back to normal, the temporary specialized duties would no longer be necessary. The chief offered to help round up everyone to meet in the family room so Andrew could address his staff. The chief told Andrew to wait in the family room and he would send everyone in to him. Andrew sat in the family room for five minutes; then one by one the staff arrived. Melanie the family dietitian was there, Michelle who was Camillia's personal caretaker was there, Bridgette the personal nanny for Armellya and soon the unborn baby was there, Matthew the house security was there, the temporary home health nurse was there, the ranch hands were there, and some other staff was there along with the chief. The chief had everyone sat down and silent, including himself.

Now it was time for Andrew to address them with the doctor's instructions. Camillia had to be on a special diet and build up to normal eating habits slowly, so Melanie was spoken to with the specifics of her job. Michelle was told that Camillia had to have help with certain things, supervised with some things, and other things that had to be done for her; all the specifics were given to her.

Bridgette was told that Armellya's schedule would have to change a bit to fit Camillia's schedule, and that Camillia would not be able to nurse Armellya anymore. Andrew gave her the specifics of her job. Matthew was given specifics for his job and told he would no longer guard the whole house and bedroom. He was now to guard only Camillia in the bedroom; there would be another guard to come in to guard the rest of the house and yet another guard to watch the property outside.

Andrew knew that the home health nurse knew the specifics of her job, but he went over it out loud so everyone else knew her job and that she would only be there while Camillia needed her. Andrew covered the specifics of the ranch hands' jobs as well as the rest of the staff as he had done for everyone else. He felt it was necessary for everyone to know everyone else's job so they could respect one another's space now that there was at least double the normal number of staff. Andrew reminded everyone that these arrangements would only be for a brief period. Andrew excused everyone except the chief and ranch hands. He inquired about the whereabouts and status of the horse that injured Camillia. The ranch hands told him that the horse was in a stall and uninjured. They went on to say that the horse was the newest addition to their herd, and they had not had the chance to break it yet. Now the chief and Andrew understood why Camillia was attacked and injured so badly. It became obvious that Camillia was not aware of the horse's training status. Andrew fell deep into thought. Because of telepathy, the ranch hands and chief knew what Andrew was so deeply pondering. It was a debate on whether to keep the horse and try to break it or let it lose to run with the wild horses in the area. The issue with letting it loose was if someone else caught it and could not break it, they may be injured beyond their survival threshold. The ranch hands asked if they could offer their suggestion. Andrew said he would accept any solution they had to offer since their specialty was to handle the livestock as well as the capture and breaking of horses. They suggested keeping the horse and trying to break it, and if that became impossible, they would put the horse down.

That way, if it was impossible to break it, it would not be able to hurt anyone else. Andrew looked at the chief as if to request his thoughts on the ranch hands' solution to the horse issue. It was obvious that Andrew's real dilemma was not in trying to break the horse versus letting it rejoin the wild herd; it was in putting down an animal that was just behaving out of fear and instinct. The chief noticed Andrew's look of uncertainty so he spoke up on Andrew's behalf. He instructed the ranch hands to work on breaking the horse and if it proved to be impossible, they would deal with that at that time. The chief told Andrew that he had the best ranch hands in the community and that they would succeed in breaking that horse. Andrew agreed to do as the chief suggested. Andrew told the ranch hands that they were the best there was and wished them luck. They promised the chief and Andrew that the horse would be broken and become timid enough for a proper lady to ride the side saddle with ease. Now that the chore list was complete, the chief suggested that everyone get some shut-eye. Andrew agreed so he excused the ranch hands, said his goodbyes to the chief, said good night to his staff, and went to bed.

The next morning arrived, and Andrew slept in. The staff awoke on time and tended to their duties quietly so as not to awake the master of the house. Upon awakening, Andrew realized he had slept in and began to panic. The doctor did not give a specific time that Camillia would be released from the hospital, but he wanted to arrive at the hospital early in hopes of having a morning release. He began to rush about to prepare himself for the day. Once Andrew got himself put together, he darted through the house checking with all the staff to make sure everything was ready for Camillia's return. Everything was in order so Andrew left at top speed to get to the hospital by horse and buggy to be with his wife.

As he entered the hospital, Andrew was headed off by the doctor. He informed Andrew that he needed to add another person to his temporary staff. Andrew became alarmed, thinking something had gone awry while he was at home. The doctor quickly told Andrew that everything was fine, but that Camillia was unable to walk without assistance. It seemed that because of the amount of time she had spent in the hospital bed, her muscles had deteriorated some. The doctor continued to say that he was going to send a physical therapist home with them to work with her on building up her muscle tone. He told Andrew that Camillia would slowly regain her strength and eventually be just as strong as she was before the accident, but in the meantime, they needed to do everything possible to assure her safety and the safety of the unborn child. Andrew relaxed and thanked the doctor for being so good to him and Camillia.

Together, they walked to Camillia's hospital room. The doctor was ready to release her to go home but wanted to check on her one last time. As they entered the hospital room, Camillia started to glow. She had read their minds and knew that she would be home within the hour. She motioned for them both to come close; they responded to her desire. Once they got to her bedside, she took each one's hand in hers and sent a message of appreciation. The doctor told her how special she was to him and that he did not want to see her injured again. He wished her a speedy recovery and said that soon he only wanted to see her for her prenatal appointments. He put his free hand on her abdomen and said he was looking forward to welcoming a beautiful full-term infant with her. She promised him that it would come to pass in due time. The doctor asked her if she was ready to go home; she excitedly nodded her head in an affirmative motion. He said he would go put in the order for release; he would see her daily until she was back to full function and check the fetus on regular intervals unless there was reason to do differently. She nodded in a yes motion. The doctor released her hand and took his other hand off her abdomen then turned and walked out of the room. Camillia pulled Andrew close and gave him a passionate kiss on the lips then wrapped her arms around his neck, holding him for several minutes.

Their intimate encounter was interrupted by a porter. It took a few seconds for the porter to realize that Andrew and Camillia were having a personal moment. He told them he could return when they were ready to be escorted to their buggy. Andrew and Camillia immediately broke their love lock and gave the porter their attention. Andrew speedily told the porter that they were ready when he was. He said he would need Andrew's help getting Camillia into the wheelchair. Andrew told him that would be no problem. Together, they supported Camillia's weight as she did her best to help them move her. She could swing her legs off the bed so she was in a sitting position; then she scooted to the edge of the bed. Andrew and the porter each took an arm to help Camillia stand up. They got her turned around and pulled the wheelchair up to her legs for her to sit down. It was a short way to get outside.

Out at the horse and buggy, a stable boy held the horse steady while Andrew stepped up into the buggy. The porter scooped Camillia up in his arms then handed her off to Andrew. He sat her next to him then turned and assumed the proper position necessary to drive the horse-drawn carriage. The porter called out wishes of good health as Andrew and Camillia drove off; then he went back inside the hospital to resume his duties. As Andrew pulled up to the house, Camillia became overwhelmed with joy to see such a large welcoming party outside their home. Andrew stopped the buggy where they were to get out; the chief told the stable boy to join the welcoming group, and he would hold the horse steady. Everyone was waving and calling out words of warm welcomes.

It was now time to get Camillia inside and tucked into bed. The chief continued to hold the horse steady as Matthew walked up to the buggy to help Andrew transfer Camillia from the buggy to bed. Andrew scooped her up into his arms then handed her down to Matthew. Andrew jumped down off the buggy, and together he and Matthew took Camillia into the house. Andrew walked a bit ahead to pull down the bedding so Camillia could be easily tucked in. Just as Andrew was done and turned toward the door, Matthew entered the room with Camillia. He placed Camillia on the bed, and Andrew tucked her in. Everyone else that was outside followed Andrew and Matthew in then scrambled to get to their posts so they could resume their duties. The chief took the horse and buggy to the stable so the stable boy could store the buggy then unhitch the horse and continue with his duties. The chief made his way into the house and headed for Camillia's bedroom.

Once there, he patted Andrew on the back and made a comment that it was nice to have Camillia back home. Andrew agreed and patted the chief on his back. Andrew thanked the chief for all that he had done. Andrew went on to say that he would not have been able to get through the challenging time without his support. The chief responded that he was pleased to be of assistance and not just in the way. The chief told Andrew that word had gotten around the community that Camillia had an accident. He said that the people were concerned for her and the unborn baby's well-being. He said that now she was stable and home, he needed to address the population over this matter. Andrew stayed silent; there was a long pause because he did not know if the chief needed his attendance when he addressed the public. The chief's words and body language seemed to be suggesting that Andrew's attendance was needed. The silence went on for a few more minutes before Andrew began to speak. Andrew was straightforward with the chief and asked if he needed him to be there. The chief said that it might be an excellent idea to make an appearance. Andrew said he would be there; he just needed to know where and when. The chief said that the sooner that was done, the better the situation would be. Andrew suggested that we hold a public conference that evening. The chief said he would plan to hold the conference right after dinner in the dining hall since everyone would be there.

Andrew said he would have dinner with Camillia and arrive at the dining hall when it would be time to address the public. The chief felt that it was an excellent idea for him to wait and show up at the last minute so everyone could be addressed at once instead of him being questioned repeatedly by many individuals. Andrew asked the chief to send a runner after him to assure that he would be there at the right time. No sooner and no later. The chief said that was a clever idea and that he would comply.

The chief looked over at Camillia and told her that he would stay close by. He turned back to Andrew and said that if they needed anything to let him know, it did not matter what time of day or night. Andrew thanked the chief then told him that he would see him after dinner. The chief acknowledged Andrew then turned to leave. The chief went back to his duties. Andrew explained to Camillia that he had to tend to his duties as well. Andrew practically ordered Camillia to send a runner for him if she needed him for anything; he added that no matter where he was or what he was doing, he would respond immediately. Camillia agreed to do so. Andrew went to the chief's house to continue learning his new trade. The chief was surprised to see Andrew so soon. Andrew noticed the surprise in the chief's face, so before he could say anything, Andrew started to explain his presence. He told the chief that no matter what happened to someone in his household, no matter who it may be, the community continued to function.

CHAPTER SEVENTEEN

In fact, with that fact brought to light, Andrew said that unless the tragedy incapacitated him, he still needed to be there for the people. The chief said that although that was true, he needed to stay close to Camillia and that there were others who could act on his behalf. Andrew got frank with the chief. He told the chief that Camillia understood and that he needed to continue with his duties and hold the community together. He continued and said that every issue needed to be addressed immediately before it had the ability to become a larger problem than necessary. Even though there were others in line for his job, he did not plan to ever leave the position of king until there were no other choices and his oldest son, if he had any, could take reign. The chief was proud of Andrew for his dedication to his position in the land of grandeur. The chief told Andrew that his own judgment and outlook of things had been clouded by sentiment and personal attachment. Andrew told the chief that it was a natural response, and he was glad to find that he had concluded this without anyone having to step in. Andrew added that under no circumstances could they allow that to occur again. The chief concurred. The chief restarted Andrew's training by picking up where they left off. Meanwhile, back at home, Camillia was taking a much-needed nap. All the movement she had tried to do coupled with the excitement of arriving at home to a welcoming party took a toll on her emotionally and slightly physically.

The chief told Andrew that now that they were back to work, they needed to deal with the newest pale ones, the ones they had just abducted. Each pale one was to receive a visit from him and Andrew to welcome them to the community, find out what their needs were from their perspective, set them up with the necessities, provide some desires, discuss how things were run, the few basic rules, and how their change would affect them from then on out. The individual visitations would allow them to handle any questions or concerns that someone may have. Although the chief said the visitations would be completed within that day, prior to dinner, Andrew could not see how it would be possible. The two men left the chief's house at once. As Andrew accompanied the chief in the visitations, it appeared that the children were over the shock of being abducted. He remembered that he got over the shock right away when he was abducted, but he could not imagine that everyone would. Andrew was also amazed that no one had concerns and they were only asked a few questions by the new pale ones.

The visitations were now done, and it was an hour and a half until dinner. Andrew suggested that he and the chief pop in on Camillia. The chief thought that was a lovely idea so the two of them headed for Andrew's home. Along the way, the chief told Andrew that the children said they were the last of the children above ground. Andrew was not surprised since their whole community was made up of children of all ages. He asked the chief if he had any idea on how the adults might handle the abduction and changing process. The chief told Andrew that he was thinking of questioning how well the adults would fit in and adjust to being a part of the community. Andrew replied that fitting in and adjusting would be the easiest part. The chief questioned why he thought that. Andrew's explanation made sense; once they were there, they would see their children again and notice how happy they were. The people were there by will after their welcome visitation. The adults would know for sure that if they decided to leave, they would never see their children, friends, and other family members again. The chief and Andrew were arriving at Andrew's house so the chief said they would finish the conversation later; Andrew agreed.

When they walked into the house, they were surprised to see Camillia in the living room sitting in one of the plush chairs, the physical therapist right next to her. She turned her head and looked at them then gave the biggest grin she could as if she was proud of herself for getting up. Andrew and the chief dashed over to her and told her how proud they were that she was out of the bed. Andrew asked the physical therapist how he got her there. He told Andrew that with assistance, she could walk short distances. Andrew bent over and gave her a kiss and a hug. He told her he was proud of her. The chief told her she would be back to normal in no time. The physical therapist said that she wanted to get out of bed to eat dinner, but he would be helping her back to bed after dinner. As the chief waved goodbye to Camillia, he told Andrew that he needed to get to the dining hall. Andrew told him he understood and that he would be there shortly.

Andrew ate dinner with Camillia. During dinner, he told her he had to eat fast if he wanted to finish his meal. She gave him a look of concern and made sure he saw it. He told her that he had to go to the main dining hall for a meeting about her accident and status. He said that word spread through the community about the accident and everyone was concerned. Because the whole community had expressed concern and who knew what had been said, he and the chief needed to address the people before rumors started. As soon as he finished telling her what was going on, there was a knock at the door. Andrew knew what it was about so he said his goodbyes to Camillia then headed toward the door.

The butler opened the door; the guest identified himself as a runner sent by the chief and said he was there to retrieve Andrew. Right as the butler turned to summon Andrew, he was already standing there. He thanked the butler and pushed on to walk through the threshold of the door. Camillia settled back into the chair then proceeded to finish her dinner. Andrew and the runner went directly to the main dining hall. Finally, at the dining hall, the runner went his own way to find his place at the table where he was eating. He sat down and awaited the chief's address, as was everyone else. As Andrew went to the stage where the chief was and took his place at the chief's side, people started to change the subject of conversation to gossip about Camillia and the situation that nearly killed her.

While the tables were being cleared off, the chief leaned over to Andrew and consulted on the best way to handle the people. The chief told Andrew that he decided he would give the factual details of the accident from when it started to her being rescued then taken to the hospital. He also decided to give a short synapse of her stay at the hospital. In conclusion, he would let the community know that she was home and continuing to heal.

Andrew told the chief that it sounded good to him. The chief stood up and requested for the crowd to quiet down several times. The room finally fell silent. The chief took a few steps forward then started to speak. He told the community that Camillia was in the process of hitching a horse to a buggy when the horse seemingly became spooked.

Without pause, he went on to say that the horse was in fact still wild; it was recently captured and the farm hands had not broken the horse yet, but Camillia was not aware of that. He told them that when the horse started to act wild, she innocently got in front of it and tried to calm it down. Continuing, he said that the horse knocked her to the ground and proceeded to stomp on her repeatedly, and that was when two men spotted her in trouble. They went to her rescue and immediately took her to the hospital. The people were on the edge of their seats trying to assure that they did not miss any details that the chief offered. He told them that due to the traumatic head injury from the horse stomping on her head, her brain swelled up and caused her to slip into a coma. He stated that the doctor was not sure she would pull through the coma. He said that she was on life support also, but she woke up and got off the life support. The chief concluded by telling them that she was currently home where she would continue to recover, which would take some time. Many people raised their hands; they either had something to say or had a question.

The chief told one of them to speak; the person stood up and asked if Camillia was receiving guests. The chief's response was a simple affirmative. As that person sat back down, all the hands that were up went down also. Apparently, everyone had the same question, and there were no comments to be given. The chief told everyone to have a good night and to be as they were prior to his public address. The chief told Andrew that he needed to turn in early due to major fatigue. He stood up and started to walk away; Andrew called out to him that he would see the chief bright and early the next morning. The chief acknowledged Andrew as he kept walking away. Andrew was anxious to be back with Camillia so he stood up and headed for the dining hall doors. Everyone was stopping Andrew to give their condolences, words of good health, and requests to visit Camillia. Andrew felt like a repetitive tape recorder as he told people, one by one, thank you for the kind thoughts and that they were welcome to visit Camillia. Andrew finally got out of the door to the outside where he would climb in his buggy and head for home. It was late when Andrew headed for home so the dining hall was empty and tightly shut.

Once he got home, he got out of the buggy and turned it and the horse pulled it over to the stable boy. He was so anxious to see Camillia that he rushed with all his might to get into the house. He glanced at the chair that Camillia had been sitting in when he left for the dining hall, but she was not there. Andrew darted for their bedroom to see if she was there; she was not. Andrew panicked and asked all the staff if they had seen her; no one had. Andrew then found the occupational therapist and asked him what he did with her. He told Andrew that when she was ready to leave the chair, he helped her back to bed. Andrew told him that she was not there; he began to panic with Andrew. The physical therapist told Andrew that Camillia knew she was not to walk without assistance, but it became apparent that she did just that. Andrew told the physical therapist to stay inside and wait for her possible return. Andrew said that he was going to go outside and look around the yard and check with the outside guard for a possible sighting. Inside the house, the physical therapist put the entire staff on alert to watch for Camillia while doing their duties. He asked them to let everyone else know if she turned up; they all agreed without hesitation. Meanwhile, outside, Andrew was not finding Camillia in the yard, front or back, and the guard said he never saw her leave. Andrew decided to get the chief so he could look beyond their yard. Maybe she made it off their property, and someone in the community had spotted her; the chief could go around and ask. With pale ones being such peaceful people, he could not imagine anyone taking her from home.

Andrew was already halfway to the chief's house when he decided to get his help so Andrew ran the rest of the way until he got to the chief's front door. Andrew loudly banged on the front door until it started to open. The chief's butler answered the door so Andrew pushed his way by the butler and proceeded to look for the chief. Andrew ran around the chief's house and called out to him for what seemed to be an eternity. Andrew was about to go past the chief's bedroom door when the chief unexpectedly stepped out of the room. Both men jumped and took a step back. The chief snapped at Andrew and asked what all the noise was about. Andrew tried to tell the chief that Camillia was missing, but he was speaking so fast that the chief had to tell him several times to slow down and try again.

Andrew finally got himself under control and could tell the chief that Camillia was missing. The chief asked what he meant by missing. Andrew replied that she was not in the house anywhere nor was she outside on their property. The chief said it was not likely that anyone took her; pale ones do not commit crimes like humans.

For no specific reason other than desperation, Andrew asked the chief to help him check his property. The chief told Andrew that it was unlikely that she would be there, but if it would help him feel better, then they had better do it. Andrew made the request that he and the chief stay together while they were on his property searching for her; the chief said very well, and they began to search. The chief decided that they would start the search in the front of the property and work their way around until they got back to the front. They checked the front to no avail. They went to the side next to Andrew and Camillia's house and saw what looked like a large log in the tall grass. The chief knew he did not have logs lying about in his yard so they walked closer to see what it was. Lo and behold, the log-looking thing was Camillia. She must have walked out the door of her home unseen and made it partway to the chief's house then collapsed. There was no telling what kind of shape she was in or how long she had been there. As Andrew scooped her up in his arms, the chief said he would get the doctor. Andrew started to walk home with her.

Before Andrew got on his own property, the chief was riding bareback off his property toward the doctor's house. Right as Andrew got to his front door, the chief and doctor came riding up hard. With the nature of the emergency, the doctor did not even take the time to saddle up either. The doctor opened the front door so Andrew could take Camillia to her bed. The doctor and chief followed close behind. Andrew finally got Camillia onto the bed then moved back so the doctor could get in there and do his job. As he was checking her vital signs, he got a strange look on his face that concerned Andrew. The chief held a great poker face. The good thing was that she was conscious and alert. All three men had a lot of questions for Camillia, but first thing was first, making sure that she and the unborn baby were okay. The doctor pulled a small portable ultrasound machine out of his black bag; it was time to check on the baby. Camillia pulled her shirt up above her belly so the doctor could do the ultrasound, and Andrew noticed major bruises on her belly and ribs that shocked him. He suddenly realized that he had not understood the real damage that the horse had done.

The doctor caught Andrew's expression from his peripheral vision. As he was looking at the image on the portable ultrasound machine, he told Andrew that her remaining injuries were not as bad as they looked. Andrew remained speechless. The doctor cleaned the ultrasound gel off the portable ultrasound machine while Camillia cleaned the gel off her belly. As he was putting the portable machine back into his black bag, he told Andrew that the baby looked good and that he could not foresee any issues with the pregnancy at that time. The chief asked if Camillia was still doing good or if he had found any setbacks. The doctor was speaking to Andrew and the chief when he said there were no setbacks that he could identify; in fact, she should be walking and talking within the next couple of days.

The doctor was ready to leave, he said that he would show himself out. As he exited the room, the chief and Andrew rushed over to her side to hound her for answers to their questions.

Before they could start, Andrew needed to get her paper and pencil so she could answer them in writing while the chief needed to get a porter to go around and inform everyone that Camillia was safe and back in her bed. Now that Andrew was calmed down about Camillia's whereabouts, he found himself holding some anger toward his security people for not watching Camillia better. Andrew also held some guilt for not being there for Camillia at a time of apparent need. She should have never been able to slip by the guards. He decided that he would deal with them after getting an explanation from Camillia about where she was going and why. The chief felt Andrew's anger and frustration; he advised Andrew to handle Camillia tenderly and to deal with his security rationally and with a clear conscience, or he would just be contributing negativity to the incident that was not necessary.

CHAPTER EIGHTEEN

Andrew thanked the chief for his advice; he said that it was helpful that he had been able to keep focused on the whole picture and not pin fault on any one person or people. Andrew handed Camillia a pad of paper and a pencil. She already knew what he was going to ask so she started to write immediately before he could ask anything. She explained everything in a series of short sentences. She wrote that she was headed for the chief's house to be with him and the chief. She was hoping to resume as many of her duties as possible while on bed rest because she did not feel that it was appropriate to leave her husband to take care of her responsibilities also.

As Andrew slipped into deep thought, he handed the letter to the chief so he could understand what was going on. The chief read it then tuned in on Andrew's thoughts telepathically. The chief smiled at Camillia sentimentally then told her that he and Andrew would find a way to allow her to help without going against the doctor's orders for bed rest. Camillia was very pleased to hear that. Andrew told her that if it was that important to her, he would comply; but if it started to prove to be too much, he would put a stop to her helping. He did not want anything to happen to her or the unborn baby.

The two men agreed to ponder potential duties for Camillia over the evening and negotiate her duties in the morning. The chief went home and went to bed right away. Andrew sat next to Camillia's bed until she fell asleep; then he went to bed himself. The next morning arrived at top speed. The chief sprang out of bed and, with double speed, got dressed and ready to go out. He went to Andrew's home to negotiate Camillia's duties. Andrew and Camillia were awakened by the chief's arrival. Michelle moved at the speed of light to get Camillia ready to receive visitors while Melanie prepared her breakfast. Andrew stumbled around trying to get presentable for receiving guests.

Finally, Andrew greeted the chief, and the chief returned the greeting with a chuckle. Andrew showed the chief to the living room where they sat and began to discuss their ideas on the duties that they came up with for Camillia to do while on bed rest. There were not many options because the duties were physical in nature. The two men bounce ideas off each other but came to no conclusive ones. As they continued to try to come up with appropriate ideas, Camillia worked her way out to the living room where they were. She stood there for several minutes listening to the men's conversation; they failed to notice her and continued to speak freely. Camillia began to feel sad. She made herself apparent and told them that she could not stay in bed doing nothing much longer. With expressions of surprise, both men looked up at Camillia. Andrew suggested having the doctor over so they could talk over some leniency in the bed rest order. Camillia and the chief agreed

Andrew sent for a runner to bring the doctor back to the house; he left instantaneously.

Camillia took a seat next to Andrew and apprehensively awaited the doctor's arrival. They sat in silence for fifteen long minutes before the doctor got there; they all sighed in relief. As the doctor entered the living room, Camillia got up from her seat and met him halfway. She gave him a bighearted hub and spoke for the first time since the accident; she said hello. Everyone shockingly stared at her, unable to respond. Camillia turned, went back to her seat, sat down, and remained silent. Andrew invited the doctor to take a seat so he silently made his way to an empty seat and sat down. Because there was much to do that day, the chief figured he would break the stillness and start the conversation. He explained to the doctor that Camillia wanted to start to work from her bed but that there was not anything they could find for her to do since the job required her to be out of the house and on her feet for many hours. The doctor said he would consult with the physical therapist to see where she was with her strength and ability to walk steadily. The doctor asked Andrew how her speech was coming along. He said that her saying hello to him was the first word he had heard her speak since being home. The doctor was not concerned about her vocal ability because he knew within the day or at least on the next day she would be talking just fine. He was concerned about her stamina in walking. Andrew told him that she was walking short distances without aid, but he was not exactly sure how far she could walk before becoming overexerted. The doctor requested that the physical therapist be brought into the room. Camillia stood up and said she would go get him. She expected the guys to stop her, but to her surprise, they were supportive of her need to show them that she could walk. Camillia returned within five minutes with the physical therapist. She returned to her seat while the therapist stood next to the living room entrance. The doctor bluntly asked him how Camillia was doing with her strength and endurance. The therapist told the doctor that her strength was just about back to normal, but her endurance still needed some work.

Andrew jumped into the conversation with a question. He asked the doctor, if her job only required her to walk in short bursts, since her strength was back, could she work outside the home with constant supervision? The doctor and physical therapist consulted with each other and concluded that it would be fine. Camillia was bursting at the seams with joy. She sprang from her seat, grabbed Andrew's hand, then told him she was ready to go out and resume her duties. The doctor stood up, put his hand on Camillia's shoulder, then told her that she no longer needed the home health nurse, the physical therapist, or daily visits from him. He told her that when he got to the hospital, he would discontinue those services and that she could go to his office for her prenatal checkups. She verbally agreed then pulled Andrew up out of his seat. The doctor showed himself out and headed straight for the hospital. Andrew asked the chief if he was going to discontinue the extra security that he had put on his and Camillia's premises. The chief told Andrew that because he and Camillia would soon become rulers of the land of grandeur, the heavy security would be staying. He told Andrew that the one in command was always heavily guarded; although there was no crime in their society, it looked official and proper. Andrew acknowledged the chief's response. The chief told Andrew and Camillia that he would be seeing them at his home as soon as they could get there. They both told the chief that they would be there on the double. The chief went out their front door and disappeared like a flash. They were about to go out the door behind the chief when Melanie stopped them and told Camillia that she could not go anywhere without feeding the unborn baby. Melanie looked at Andrew and reminded him that if he was to care for Camillia all day, out and about, he needed his nutrition also. They both headed for the private dining room, sat down next to each other, and began to eat.

Right before they were finished eating, Melanie set two packed lunches on the dining table right between Andrew and Camillia; then she warned them that she expected them to be obedient in consuming their lunchtime nutrition. They both thanked her and agreed to do as she command

They finished eating, grabbed their lunches, then headed for the front door. Bridgette was there by the door with Armellya to see them off. She inquired as to when they would like to spend time with the baby so she could make sure that Armellya was fed, changed, and past her naptime. Camillia told Bridgette that it probably would not be until that evening after work because there was a lot to catch up on. Andrew and Camillia disappeared out the door so Bridgette shut the door and resumed her duties with Armellya. Andrew and Camillia arrive at the chief's house soon after he had gotten home.

The chief told them that they were going to spend the day going over all their new responsibilities. This was the step in their training that Andrew and Camillia were waiting for because the next step was going to be that they would start to perform their duties, but the chief would be observing them and being there if they needed guidance. His in-depth guidance would only be for a brief time because once Andrew and Camillia took over, the chief would become the official adviser to the king and queen. Up to now, their training consisted of the explanations of various proceedings such as wedding ceremonies, funerals, information meetings, celebratory parties, abductions, and the settling in of new ones, among other official plans of action. During that time, Andrew and Camillia only took their place beside the chief to make their upcoming positions in the land known to the people and to allow the couple to observe firsthand those events.

The chief wasted no time; he first asked if there were any questions or concerns about what they had learned and observed so far. Andrew and Camillia told the chief that they were confident that they could handle the duties they had been shown. They said they had no questions or concerns. The chief moved on; he told Andrew and Camillia that it was going to be their job to know every one's business, both professionally and personally. He warned them that the people would go to them for personal advice and direction in their lives and that they had the responsibility of pointing out the diverse options that might be available. They were not to tell the people what to do; they were only to show them the whole picture from an outsider point of view, and the people were to make their own deductions. He told them that it would also be their job to visit the many shops and community services in the compound to assure everyone has the products necessary to function, and if not it would also be their job to help solve the problem with the shopkeeper. This was the professional aspect of their job. The chief took a break to make sure that Andrew and Camillia were still following him. They assured him that they understood so far. The chief told them that the most important and tough job they would have was to balance the economy. That meant that they would need to assure that there was an appropriate number of people in each line of work and that their jobs were being conducted as safely as possible.

Andrew and Camillia agreed, commenting that the balancing of the economy would be the most challenging task. The chief changed the subject slightly. He bluntly told them that he would be stepping down on that day. He told the couple that due to them becoming king and queen that evening, they would each be given a personal runner as part of their staff. He suggested that they have their runners with them everywhere they go. Lunchtime rolled up on them rather speedily, so the chief and the young couple took a break to eat. Everyone focused on eating and finishing their meal at top speed without acting like wild animals scavenging on a carcass; there was not even any conversation. Everyone finished about the same time so the chief said it was time to go over the last detail, and that was the changing of reign. There was a ceremony for that also; it would mark the end of the chief's rule and welcome the new king and queen.

Although it may seem to be a sad time with the chief stepping down, it was a long-awaited turning point for the community. The legend of the chosen ones had come to light. The chosen ones were said to be a fertile couple among a community of barren individuals that would bear many children. They would rule the land and help it to flourish and rescue all the humans from the earth's surface. When Andrew and Camillia officially take reign, it would be a historical moment for the land of grandeur and its citizens.

The chief was inspired when he unveiled to Andrew and Camillia that the changing-of-reign ceremony would occur that day right after dinner. The young couple suddenly felt nervous. The changes were all happening so fast. They knew that the chief had reigned for many, many years and the people adorned him. They knew that they were going to have to do a lot to fulfill the chief's duties as well as he had and work their way into the people's hearts. Andrew and Camillia were concerned that the people would have a tough time adjusting to their reign. They were ready to earn their position and expected to have to do no less. That was acceptable to Andrew and Camillia; if they were in the position of the people, they realized that they might require a new leader to prove him or herself as well, so they could not expect the public to be any different from them. The chief was aware of their thoughts and feelings. He told them not to worry so much; the public had already accepted them as the chosen ones and knew about the legend. The legend not only told of the ability to reproduce but included them to govern the land.

Again, he asked them if they had any questions or concerns. They both denied having either. The chief told Andrew and Camillia to go home and prepare for dinner, and while they were doing that, he would get their runners and send them to their house for introduction. The chief told them that their runners would start their job upon arrival and be available to them around the clock.

Andrew and Camillia said that they would be expecting the runners and would welcome them in with open arms. The chief headed for the front door, opened it, then said his goodbyes to the couple. As they walked out of the chief's house, they said their goodbyes to him and hurried home. When Andrew and Camillia got home, they went in search of Bridgette so they could visit with Armellya for a brief time. After searching the house and not being able to find Bridgette or Armellya, they asked the rest of the staff if they knew where she and the baby were. The roaming house security could help; he told Andrew and Camillia that she took Armellya for a walk in the baby buggy and would go to the dining hall on foot. Andrew could sense that Camillia was missing Armellya; he assured her that she would be seeing her baby at the dining hall during dinner. They went to their bedroom to change clothes, and they prepared for the changing-of-reign ceremony. As soon as they were finished getting ready to go, they checked the time and found that they needed to leave immediately for the dining hall, but their runners had not shown up yet. They were not sure if they should wait a few more minutes to give the runners time to arrive and cut their time short or just go without having to hurry. Andrew made the decision for them—they would go ahead and leave. Everyone was to be at the dining hall for dinner anyway so they could search for their new runners there. Andrew and Camillia went to the front door, opened it up, and were about to exit when two men popped into sight. They started to apologize for being late, but Andrew interrupted them and asked who they were even though he suspected that they were the runners he and Camillia had been waiting for. They confirmed that they were the runners and were ready for duty.

With that settled, they all four walked off the porch and approached the horse and buggy that would be taking them to the dining hall.

They all stepped up and got seated. Due to being late leaving, the driver had to run the horse hard to make up for lost time, but they all got there just in time to take their seats up on the podium, next to the chief, without becoming a distraction. While their dinner was being served, Camillia nervously looked over the crowd of people in front of her. When she spotted her friends and servants, as well as Armellya, she began to relax a bit; she did not like to be the center of attention. Being up in front of everyone did not seem to bother Andrew though. Of course, prior to them being changed, Andrew was the popular kid at school, and she was just the wallflower. Dinner had been served and the crowd combined eating with conversation. The people seemed to be in high spirits and looking forward to the change of reign. Dinner was coming to an end; the dining hall servants were picking up the dishes for the kitchen crew to wash. There would be a break between chores to allow time for the change-of-reign ceremony.

Now that the tables were cleared, the chief stood up and took several steps forward. As people started to notice the chief's stance, they became quiet, little by little the noise level lowered, and the dining hall eventually became completely silent. First, the chief spoke of the legend of the chosen ones then announced that Camillia was with child again. Everyone clapped and whistled. Once they became quiet again, the chief announced that he would be stepping down to being the personal adviser to the king. Everyone stayed quiet so the chief could continue; he stated that as of the morning, the land would be run by a king and queen instead of a chief. The crowd stood up and clapped. The chief motioned for everyone to sit and silence themselves. Eventually they did so, and finally the chief could formally announce King Andrew and Queen Camillia. The chief spoke his last words and said that the people could now greet their royal leaders. The people were already forming a line before the chief could get to his seat and sit down. Andrew, Camillia, and the chief were all happy with the public's response. The couple was surprisingly very relaxed while they greeted everyone; the line seemed to go swiftly. Now that everyone had piled out of the dining hall, the kitchen staff would be able to take care of the dirty dishes then go home. Outside of the dining hall, Andrew, Camillia, and the chief shared a group hug then went their own ways.

Camillia, Andrew, and their runners got back into the buggy and headed home. Once there, the runners went to their quarters and the new king and queen spent time with their daughter, Armellya. While they played with Armellya, Camillia felt the unborn baby move for the first time. She grabbed Andrew's hand and placed it on her belly for him to feel the fetus move. It took a couple of minutes, but he also got to feel the fetus move; it excited him very much. Although Andrew and Camillia had a short encounter with Armellya before having to hand her back to Bridgette, the night needed to come to an end. It was vital to get a good night's sleep because they had to rise extra early to meet with the chief and abduction crew, also known as scouts, after they checked on the status of the new ones. If they were to be settled and stable, it would be time to start to make the plans for the abduction of the adults. If for some reason the new ones were not settled and stable, then the couple would have to address that first. Andrew and Camillia climbed into bed and wasted no time falling asleep.

CHAPTER NINETEEN

The next day, they awoke earlier than usual, which was what they had hoped they would do. They crawled out of bed and fumbled their way around to prepare themselves for a long day's work. Once they were ready to start their day, Camillia rounded up Melanie for their morning nutrition and the runners for the new day's work. Andrew called for Bridgette to bring Armellya so they could have a few minutes with her before leaving and the stable boy to have a horse and buggy ready.

Michelle awoke from all the hustle and bustle so she got up and started to tend to her duties as Camillia and Andrew's personal maid. After Camillia and Andrew spent some time with Armellya, Andrew and Camillia went to their private dining hall at home and ate the first meal of the day. Everything at home was under control so Andrew, Camillia, and their runners left home to go to the chief's house.

Upon arriving at the chief's house, the couple noticed that the abduction crew, known as scouts, were already there so they went in prepared to get down to business. The chief and crew welcomed the couple and their runners. Everyone took a seat around a large round table and waited for Andrew to begin the meeting. It took a few minutes, but Andrew finally realized that everyone was waiting on him to start the meeting, and he finally did. He looked at the chief and asked him if he knew how the new ones were doing, if they were settled in or not. The chief told Andrew that they had obtained their place in the community, but he did not know if they were settled in. Andrew announced that their first task would be to check on the new ones and help them if needed. He then turned his head toward the scouts and commanded them to be on standby because if the new ones were settled in, they would be getting back together immediately to plan an adult abduction.

Andrew, the chief, and the scouts would have to formulate a slightly different plan for abducting the adults above ground because they would be larger and stronger. Andrew had excused the scouts and told everyone else that they would be with him. Because of the high number of people in their group that would be traveling, the chief told his runner to go out to the stable boy and have him hitch a team of horses to a large buggy. The runner moved like the wind. As swiftly as the runner left, he reappeared and everyone leisurely headed out of the chief's house trying to give the stable boy time to hitch the horses to the buggy. When they got out there, the horses were almost hitched. It was only a couple of minutes before their transportation was ready to go. They headed for the spiritual hall where the king, queen, and chief would wait for the arrival of the new ones. The king's runner, queen's runner, and chief's runner went out into the community to recover the new ones so they would be able to convene with the king, queen, and chief. The chief knew that it would take some time to collect every new one so he wanted to chat with King Andrew and Queen Camillia until the runners got back there with their targets. The chief was interested in knowing of the changes that Andrew wanted to make with the abduction process since the current way worked just fine, so he simply asked. Andrew told the chief that they had to take into consideration that they would now be trying to snatch humans that had escaped their traps in the past; most of them were children when the abductions originally started. The adults were bigger, faster, stronger, and more leery about where they went. Camillia added that it might be an excellent idea to ensure that the last abduction was truly the last of the children above ground.

Andrew said that was an excellent idea then added that they were going to have to go after the adults instead of waiting for them to come to them. He intuitively felt that they would not be successful in luring them in. The human adults would only draw back in fear and spread the word to the other adults to be on alert. The chief admitted that he had not taken those things into consideration. Andrew had some questions for the chief about the process of the child abductions. For instance, were the children always taken from the tunnel, and how exactly did they get lured to their abduction sites? The chief answered Andrew's questions without hesitation. He said that the children were always taken through the tunnel door but had to be lured in there by the miniangels.

He said that the angels knew when it was time to act, and there were never any problems getting the children into the tunnel because of their inquisitive nature.

Andrew butted in to tell the chief that the adults were much more reserved. They were far more frightened than inquisitive. He was not sure how the adults would react to seeing the angels. It seemed to him that they would have to have more scouts than usual go on the retrieval of humans so they could break into smaller groups and abduct adults from a few homes at a time while they slept. Andrew added that the pale ones would have to take as many humans at a time as possible because they would catch on to them quickly and possibly start sleeping on opposite schedules so some could rest while others stood watch then switched off. That made full sense to the chief. He told Andrew that he was amazed at how he was still able to think like a human after being a pale one for so long. Andrew sharply responded that it was not that he thought like a human, he was just speaking from a strategic point of view and doing his job as the king to ensure that a task was carried out in the safest way possible. Their conversation abruptly ended when the runners and new ones arrived.

Before diving into any of the business at hand, Andrew wanted everyone to get comfortably seated and relaxed. Now that everyone had given Andrew their undivided attention, he welcomed the new ones and asked how they were getting along in their new environments. All five of them pretty much had the same answers. They thought that the land of grandeur was beautiful and peaceful. Their homes were more than sufficient. They were pleased that the community instantaneously accepted them like close family. They said that their jobs fit their skills perfectly and that they enjoyed their work. They completed their point of view by thanking him and the chief for abducting them and allowing them to live without all the restrictions placed upon them above ground due to Earth's destruction. Andrew, Camillia, and the chief were all pleased with the new one's responses. Camillia told them that if they needed anything, no matter how insignificant, to call on her or Andrew. Everyone stood up, and the new ones started to shake hands but Camillia said there would be none of the formal stuff there; then she pulled everyone together for a group hug and said they were a family. The runners were ordered to take the new ones back to where they needed to be at that time, so they all left at once. Andrew told the chief and scouts to sit back down; it was time to discuss the assurance that there were no more children above ground, and how they were going to abduct the adults.

Before Andrew had a chance to say anything, the chief spoke up and said that he liked Andrew's ideas on how to get the adults, but they still needed to work on getting them to cooperate during the long walk back to the compound. Andrew's answer to that was for the scouts to abduct them from bed, take them straight to the tunnel, then turn them into pale ones immediately. One of the scouts spoke up and asked what they were supposed to do if the humans decided to be difficult after being turned and chose to resist following them for the long walk. Andrew said that he had no solution for that yet. Camillia jumped forward in her seat and said that she had an idea. She said that 99 percent of those adults would still be grieving the loss of their child or children so they should use the children as the lure. Everyone in the room stayed quiet for a while so Camillia broke the silence by asking if everyone followed her idea or not. The chief said he understood the concept but was not sure how they could fine-tune the idea into a fail-safe plan. Andrew suggested that he should have a specific min speech memorized to entice the adults to follow them.

The scouts agreed that the new abduction plan had the capability to run smoothly, but that they needed a backup plan to get the adults to still follow them in case they do not buy into the child-lure plan Camillia assured the scouts that the child-lure plan would work because the parental instinct was a natural uncontrollable drive; all parents would do anything to get a missing or deceased child back. The scouts asked Andrew how soon he wanted to take the abduction journey. Andrew in turn asked if they were rested from the last child abduction and how much time would they need to prepare for the next journey. Camillia swiftly jumped into the conversation before the scouts could answer and asked how they were going to assure that there were no more children on the earth's surface. Andrew replied that the scouts would check all the domed homes then report back to him prior to abducting any adults. That way, several scouts could go out and look, covering more ground in less time; and by meeting prior to abducting any adults, it would reassure everyone that they were working together and safely. The chief wanted to know how soon Andrew wanted to start abducting the human adults, but before he could ask, the scouts said that they were well rested and could be ready to travel within a couple of hours. The scouts just needed to wrap up things with their staff and spouses, for those who had a spouse, and pack their satchels. Andrew made everyone aware that he would be quadrupling the number of scouts that usually went so they could compensate for the adult's strength, size, indisposition, and awareness. That would also allow the scouts to take twice the number of humans than before.

Then Andrew answered the chief's question before he had a chance to ask it. Andrew told the scouts to take the rest of the day to rest and plan to leave bright and early the next morning. The scouts answered affirmatively then left the spiritual hall to go to their homes to rest, pack, and tie up their loose ends. The chief was concerned with the number of humans they would be taking and questioned Andrew's judgment. Andrew told him that they might only get one shot at abducting the adults before they found a way to compensate, for instance, sleeping in shifts. Having no more questions or concerns, the chief spoke with Andrew and Camillia about how impressed he was with the way they solved the abduction of human adults and in making sure that there were not any children left on the earth's surface. The chief said to Andrew that he was anxious to hear his speech at dinner about the adult abductions. Andrew said he would be ready. Then the couple thanked him for the compliment. The chief gave them a hug then headed for his home to await the time to leave for the dining hall or if he should be summoned for service to the king and queen. Andrew and Camillia went straight home to make their announcement speech about the adult abductions. They had to work at top speed if they were to make it to the dining hall on time.

Andrew told Camillia that he wanted her opinion about the adult abduction that was about to occur. She welcomed his request. Andrew said that he was concerned that if they did not take all the adults at one time, they might compensate by sleeping in shifts. If that were to occur, then they could lose the element of surprise, which was their only asset. Camillia agreed then asked him if there was an estimate of how many humans were left on the earth's surface. Andrew told Camillia no, but that they could find out from the record keeper from her census book. Camillia sharply cut back into the conversation, suggesting that they do that even though it would delay the abduction by a day or so. She said that by doing that, they would know what they were up against beforehand. Andrew saw the sense in what she had suggested so he decided to delay the next morning's abduction by a day or two. Andrew hollered to the driver to stop at the chief's front door. The driver confirmed the request then complied.

As they approached the chief's door, Andrew jumped off the buggy before the driver got the horses completely stopped. Camillia waited in the buggy while Andrew ran to the chief's door and banged on it until the butler answered it; then he burst by the butler and went to the living room where he sternly requested to see the chief.

The butler shut the door and said he would get the chief. The chief was walking toward the living room and heard Andrew's voice. He recognized the voice so he went directly to the living room. Once there, the chief asked what he could do for him. Andrew explained that he wanted to get the census count to estimate how many adults were still on the planet's surface. He said that with that knowledge, he would know if he could take all of them in one swipe or if he would have to break the abductions into smaller groups, which meant doing several abductions. Andrew told the chief that if there were to be several abductions, it would be more difficult because they would have to assume that the humans had compensated by sleeping in shifts. He asked the chief if he had any advice as to how they could handle both scenarios. The chief sat down then thought about both situations for a few moments.

Finally, the chief spoke. He said that if there were enough scouts to handle the number of humans left on the surface, there could be one sweep and that it sounded like the most logical thing to do. Andrew agreed. Then the chief said that if there were too many humans to handle in one sweep, there would be no other choice but to somehow find out if they have compensated or not then take the situation from there. Andrew told the chief that he had come to the same conclusion. Andrew then requested to borrow the chief runners so along with his own runners they could alert all the scouts before dinner that the next morning's abduction had been canceled. The chief said that it would be no problem then summoned his runners; Andrew's runners were already there. Together, the two sets of runners went out to find their targets and pass on the message of the delaying of the abduction before dinner.

As Andrew got ready to leave the chief's house, he asked where Camillia was. Andrew told him that she was outside in the buggy. The chief decided to walk Andrew out so he could give his regards to her. As they headed outside, the chief got another idea that he felt would be helpful to Andrew. The chief told Andrew that he could have the census counter look up how many runners there were in the compound because next to everyone's names was their community responsibility. Andrew told the chief that he had a wonderful idea with that suggestion. He said he would do that and have the counter give him a list of names so he could track down all of them. Now that the chief and Andrew made it out to the buggy, the chief said hello to Camillia and engaged in some small talk. He was pleased to see that her pregnancy was going smoothly and that she was feeling well.

It was time to head for the dining hall so Andrew invited the chief to go with them; he proudly took Andrew up on his offer. The chief sat next to Camillia then off they went. As they got to the dining hall, the chief and Andrew saw their runners waiting for them outside of the hall. While everyone got off the buggy, the runners approached them and told them that all the scouts had been alerted of the change of plans. Everyone went into the dining hall to eat. Andrew and Camillia could not sit among the commoners so they missed out on the opportunity to catch up on things with their friends. Camillia missed that experience very much and commented to Andrew that she wished that they could arrange for them to sit together. Andrew felt the void in Camillia's heart so he told her that he would see what he could do to change that situation. The chief overheard Camillia's comment and Andrew's response. He told Andrew that he had a possible solution. Andrew was pleased and asked what he had in mind. The chief chivalrously smiled then told him that since all his friends worked for him, he should schedule for family time where they all could get together and catch up on things and possibly do some sort of activity together. Camillia heard the entire conversation and became fired up about the suggestion. Andrew noticed the change in Camillia's demeanor and felt the heaviness lift from her heart so he agreed that the chief's idea was a splendid one and that they would follow through with his plan.

CHAPTER TWENTY

The couple ate their dinner double quick, hoping dinner would end on the double so they could hold a meeting with their staff at home to make the family time arrangements. Camillia was so thrilled that she hardly ate her dinner. Finally, dinner was over and everyone piled out of the dining hall to go home. The chief was dropped off at his door. He said his goodbyes and went into his home. The couple went to the other side of the castle where their doorway to their side of the castle was and got off the buggy. The stable boy took the horse and buggy to the barn. Andrew and Camillia entered their home and immediately had Matthew gather everyone into the family room. Andrew instructed Matthew to return with the other staff.

Once everyone was accounted for and seated, Andrew wasted no time getting to the point. He started out by telling everyone that they had been friends practically all their lives and that since he and Camillia had taken on the role of king and queen, they had not gotten to have leisure time together. He told the group that the lack of time together was bothering Camillia and affecting her in many negative ways. He said it bothered him as well. Camillia and Andrew's friends butted in on Andrew's talk and said that it was affecting them also. Andrew continued to say that the meeting was to find a time that was good for everyone so they could have family time together during work time. Andrew explained that he wanted the family time to be during work hours so it did not interfere with their personal time. He informed them that the family time would be for catching up with one another and doing some activities together.

Everyone became thrilled. Bridgette asked if the time could be scheduled around Armellya's naptime and feedings so she could be part of the group also. With that, Andrew and Camillia could have some time with their daughter as well. Matthew said his schedule was easy because he had to be where Camillia was so any time would work for him. Michelle said that she could participate whenever Camillia chose because as her personal maid, she only worked hard when Camillia was home. Melanie said she could work family time into her schedule also; she just needed a time frame so she could keep the cooks and bakers on track and that would not be hard. Camillia took over the conversation and asked everyone if they could handle lunchtime plus two hours after to commit to family time there at the castle or wherever an activity may be. Matthew said that was feasible for him. Bridgette said it worked for her and Armellya. Michelle said that it would fit into her schedule. Melanie said that it was perfect timing for her and her staff. Andrew popped up out of his seat and said that it was settled—lunch plus two hours after was for family time and activities and that it would start the next day. Everyone was delighted with that arrangement. Andrew excused everyone then sat next to Camillia and declared his love to her. She vocalized her love for him in return.

After a small sentimental moment, Andrew emerged from his chair and said it was time to get back to work. Camillia said that she needed to get some rest because she was feeling depleted. Andrew followed Camillia to their bedroom and helped her get into some bedclothes then tucked her into bed. They gave each other a kiss and hug; then Andrew turned and exited the room. Camillia fell asleep before Andrew could reach the end of the hall to the living room. He bypassed the living room and went straight for the front door. Once outside, he asked the stable boy to saddle up a horse for him pronto. The stable boy saddled up Andrew's favorite horse right away, and no sooner had the boy brought the horse out of the stable than Andrew was on its back and riding off. He went to try to talk to the census girl about getting an estimate of how many humans were still above ground and how many scouts there were in the community as well as their names. Andrew arrived at the census hall and saw the census worker moving about so he went rushing inside to see her. He was in such a hurry that he did not even hitch his horse.

As soon as Andrew approached the desk, a young girl looked up and told him that the census hall was closed for the day; then she realized who he was and apologized to him then asked him if she could help him with something.

He told her he needed a count of the number of human adults that were still on the earth's surface and a count with names of all the scouts in the commune. She told him to return the next morning and she would have all his information ready. He thanked her then whisked out of the census hall. When Andrew got back outside, he realized he had not hitched his horse but was grateful that the horse was right where he left it. Andrew was glad that the census girl lived in the census hall or his request would have had to wait until it reopened the next day. Now back on his horse, he headed for home. When he got home, he noticed that everyone was in bed for the night except the butler; he waited up for Andrew to return home. Now Andrew and the butler could go to bed.

The next day, everyone awakened ready for the new day. Andrew could not wait to get his information from the census hall. He could feel the joy in everyone's heart because they were motivated by the arrival of the first of many family times. It was time for Camillia to feed Armellya while Bridgette changed the baby's bedding, Melanie was having the kitchen crew prepare an early morning snack for Camillia, Michelle was on standby to help Camillia prepare for the new day, and Matthew had just shown up for security duty outside of Camillia's bedroom door. The morning was running smoothly, so before anyone knew it, the time to leave for the dining hall for breakfast had come along. Everybody went to the dining hall and found their seats, the meal was served and eaten, and finally, everyone left for their jobs in the community. After Andrew and Camillia showed their love to their child and told Bridgette goodbye, she took Armellya for her morning walk. Camillia and Andrew went to the census hall to pick up the information that Andrew requested the night before. They got there right as the census girl was unlocking the door. Andrew jumped off the buggy, hitched the horse to the post, then helped Camillia down. Together they went into the census hall.

The census girl saw them walk in and remembered Andrew. She told him that she had all the information he requested then handed a small stack of papers to him. As Camillia and Andrew turned to leave, the girl congratulated the couple for becoming the new rulers of the land of grandeur and on their second pregnancy. Camillia walked back to the girl and gave her a hug then said thank you as she rejoined Andrew. The couple got back onto the buggy and headed for home, where Andrew could review the information he had just received. Arriving back at home, Andrew helped Camillia down from the buggy, and they went inside of their home. Andrew headed directly to his study room while Camillia checked on things around their home just to make sure everything was running okay. Andrew was in his study room for ten minutes looking at the paperwork he had just gotten; then he abruptly barraged out of the room bellowing for his runners. Camillia made her way to Andrew's study room to find out what the apparent emergency was. As she curiously approached the study room, she heard Andrew commanding his runners to get the chief over right away. Once the runners bolted out of the castle's main door, Camillia asked Andrew if there was a problem. Andrew declared that the census report had delivered some promising news—the next abduction could very well be the last one. Camillia was wordless; she practically froze where she stood. Andrew sensed her astonishment then told her that if they could get all the adult humans at one time, then there would be no issues in the community with some children having their parents while other children questioned when or if they would get their parents. It would also solve the issue of the humans possibly compensating after one abduction.

Before she could say anything else, the runners entered the living room with the chief. Andrew took Camillia by the hand and led her to the living room. Everyone sat down, and Andrew spoke right away.

He told the chief that there were eighteen human adults above ground and twenty pale ones that specialize in abductions, but they had sixteen pale ones that were runner ups. The runner ups had businesses in the community so their shops would have to be closed for the day if they went on an abduction trip. Andrew had the idea to have all shops closed that day so the child pale ones could welcome their parents. The only question he had for the chief was, could the community handle a large number of new pale ones to be placed in homes and jobs? The chief said that closing all the shops that day was a clever idea. He also suggested that the parents stay with their children until they get more homes built. The last thing to be addressed was jobs; they would have to wing it. Camillia asked, if they were to take eighteen adults, would that upset the balance of things in the community? Andrew and the chief both sat there in silence contemplating. Andrew broke the silence by confirming that it would probably be better for the children to bring all the adults at one time so there would not be any questions, plus the community could settle down once and for all. The chief said it would take a lot of laborious work, but he concurred.

With all that said, Camillia asked Andrew when he planned to do the abduction trip. Andrew told Camillia that they were going to hold a meeting with the scouts right after lunch, and the runners would start immediately telling the scouts to arrive at that time. Then Andrew and the chief called for their two runners and instructed them to alert the thirty-six scouts about the meeting that was to be held directly after lunch. Each runner had nine scouts to find so they would have enough time to reach their targets and still make it to lunch with time to spare. Andrew told the chief and Camillia that the abduction trip would probably be in two days from that day; they needed a day to prepare then they could leave on the next afternoon. Andrew told the chief that he needed to put together his abduction speech for the community as well as one for the humans above ground. The chief agreed then excused himself; he said he would show himself out. Camillia asked if there was anything she could do to help him. Andrew told her that there was nothing except to have fun at family time. Camillia asked him if there was any way he could participate in family time. His answer was that if he could finish the speeches beforehand, then he could participate in family time. Camillia said that she would leave him to prepare his speeches and expected his presence at family time. She gave him a quick peck on the cheek; then Andrew left for his study room and Camillia left to go to the chief's garden area.

As she left her and Andrew's part of the castle, she told Matthew where she would be if Andrew needed her. Camillia walked out of their front door and went around to the chief's front door. She knocked on the door until the butler answered and she requested to see the chief. The butler turned and began to walk away as he instructed her to follow him. He led her into the chief's study room where he was going over the history of the pale ones in hopes of correctly speculating how the community would change once there were no more humans above ground. He was hoping to get an idea of how to accommodate so many pale ones. It appeared that Andrew had not entirely thought that through. The chief's intent was to help King Andrew with the monumental task ahead of them; as the king's adviser, that was part of his job. Camillia poked her head into the room and asked the chief if she could speak with him briefly. He did not answer her so she softly walked into the room and stood over his shoulder. She could not help but see all the paperwork in front of him and what was on them. She asked if there was anything she could do to help him. He leisurely looked up at her and murmured that he could use another person's view of the situation that he was in the process of pondering. She pulled a chair from across the room up next to him then sat down.

The chief told her that there were eighteen adult humans that they had to find jobs and proper housing for. He said that the housing was an easy solution; they could stay with their children until their homes were built. Furnishing the homes and stocking them up with food and other supplies would be a slow process but also easy to do. It was placing so many new pale ones into community services that would be difficult to do. There was the possibility of creating new services for the community thus requiring more building and stocking; then there was the issue of finding out what the professional strengths were for everyone and all the while keeping the community's business world balanced. Camillia intervened and told the chief that it might be an innovative idea to write a list of businesses that the community did not have that were needed and some that they did not have that would be for leisure. Camillia continued to speak; she told the chief that he could use the list as a guide. He could put names next to the positions that fit together as they came up; that would help keep things organized.

The chief sat back in his chair then stated that she had an incredible idea, and he would start writing the list of necessary businesses that they did not have yet and some services that would be nice to offer the community. Now relaxed, the chief realized that he had not inquired as to why Camillia was there so he apologized to her and asked if there was anything he could do for her.

She replied that she was there for permission to admire the garden area while listening to the birds so she could release some tension. The chief said absolutely; he added that he would leave orders with his staff for her to go there as she wished, and she would have the ability to relieve the garden workers so she could enjoy the garden fully and privately if need be. It was getting near lunchtime so Camillia thanked the chief for giving her unlimited privileges to the garden area then left his study room to go home. As she was leaving, she offered to help the chief with the business lists if needed. The chief thanked Camillia then went back to his work. Camillia went back to her side of the castle and entered Andrew's study room. She asked Andrew how he was doing in his speeches. He told her that he had just finished them so he could participate in family time. She was delighted to hear that.

It was now lunchtime, and that was the beginning of family time. Instead of eating at the dining hall, Camillia, Andrew, Matthew, Bridgette, Armellya, Melanie, and Michelle would eat at home together so they could catch up on what had been going on with them. Melanie arranged for the kitchen staff to prepare their meal, serve it, then collect the dishes when they were done eating. They all gathered together and got a seat at the round table in their castle's dining hall and began to discuss their latest news. Lunch was brought out to them so they began to eat while talking. There was so much to say that they took longer to eat than usual. Once they finished eating, the dishes were cleared by the kitchen staff, but there was still so much to discuss. The group ended up gathering together in the family room to finish sharing their latest happenings and expressing their familiar love for one another instead of doing an activity. Andrew and Camillia had a tough time keeping the news of the next abduction trip to themselves although they and the rest of the pale ones would find out at dinnertime. Andrew and Camillia knew that having everyone's whole families together again would be exceptionally pleasing to everyone. Family time had come to an end, so everyone went back to their duties. Andrew stayed in the family room because his next matter of business was to be held there. Andrew had to meet with and prepare the scouts for the final abduction. He called for his runner to retrieve the chief at once. The runner went to the chief's side of the castle and could get the butler to send the chief to him so he could guide the chief to Andrew. The chief seized his list of businesses that they did not have but needed and the list of current businesses that could use another employee then followed the runner to the king's side of the castle. As soon as he got in front of Andrew, he told Andrew that he had something to share. Andrew said okay then told the chief that he needed to use his runners with his own runners to get all the scouts together before them as soon as possible. The chief was fine with that. Andrew gave a paper to each runner then told the four runners to retrieve the nine individuals on each of their lists.

Without hesitation, the runners scurried out of the castle into the community to do their jobs. While Andrew was waiting for the runners to return with all the scouts, the chief started to tell Andrew about Camillia's brilliant idea of making a list of shops that they needed and a list of shops that could use another pale one to make things run with ease. Andrew was extremely interested in the chief's preparatory lists so he asked to hear about them. The chief explained the lists as quickly and simply as possible because he knew that there was not much time before the scouts would be arriving, and he was right. Just as the chief finished sharing his work, the runners returned with the thirty-six scouts. Andrew quickly told the chief to write a copy of his work so he would be able to adhere to the outline; the chief said he would comply. Andrew then turned his attention to the scouts; he told them to sit and listen carefully because they were about to engage in the largest abduction in their history and for them the first one with adult humans.

All the scouts soundlessly sat down and got comfortable. Andrew revealed that there were eighteen adult humans on the earth's surface and no children; he instructed them to work in teams of two pale ones per human. He warned them that the current abduction would be the largest group of people that they had ever had to keep control of and that the humans may be more resistant than the children were.

Andrew continued in telling them that they would use their children as a lure. He explained that they were to go into their homes while they slept, wake them, then get them to the tunnel door. Once all eighteen adults were there, they would change them immediately. All thirty-six scouts had a look of horror on their faces. When Andrew noticed their expressions, he reminded them that not only was abducting humans their job but that they were excellent at what they did and he knew that they could do the job before them. Andrew's confidence in the scouts relaxed them a little bit. He asked if there were any questions or comments, and everyone shook their heads as if to say no. He then announced that they would be leaving in the afternoon of the following day. Everyone acknowledged Andrew. Then he dismissed the scouts and they piled out of his family room one by one.

CHAPTER TWENTY ONE

Once all the scouts were gone, Andrew asked the chief if he would take care of Camillia while he was gone on the abduction trip. The chief promised Andrew that Camillia would be in good hands. As the chief turned to exit, Andrew reminded him to get the written lists of new occupations as well as current shops needing extra help. The chief assured him that the lists would be in his hands before dinner; then he headed home to work on duplicating the lists. Andrew sent one of his runners to seek out Camillia and bring her to him. Within five minutes, the runner had brought Camillia to Andrew. Camillia rushed into Andrew's arms, and they embraced each other for quite some time. As she started to pull away, Andrew asked her if she was okay. She told him that she was better than okay now that they were back in sight of each other. Andrew affectionately rubbed Camillia's belly and asked how the baby was doing. She placed her hand atop of his hand and told him that their baby was doing good. They giggled for a few seconds; then Andrew told Camillia that he was leaving her in the chief's hands while he was on the abduction trip. Camillia accepted that and said she and the unborn baby would be fine while he was gone.

The dinner hour had arrived, and it was time to get to the dining hall. Andrew got his notes for his public address from his study hall while Camillia waited for him in the castle's foyer. The stable boy already had their horse and buggy ready for travel so when they got outside they could leave immediately. Andrew was excited for the community because everyone still had family on the earth's surface that they missed. Once the abduction trip was completed, they would all finally be filled with the ultimate joy. He was also somewhat nervous about the community knowing about the abduction because he feared that they might want to go above ground to help and just get into the way or make matters impossible to control.

Andrew and Camillia were on their way to the dining hall, and Andrew was unusually silent and it concerned Camillia. She inquired as to what he was so deep in thought about. He asked her if she felt that it would be better for the abduction trip to be kept under wraps and surprise the community children with their parents when they got back so things could be calm and run as usual in the compound while they were gone. Camillia ordered the driver to stop the wagon then she asked Andrew if he foresaw a potential problem in letting the children know about the plan to bring their parents to the land of grandeur to be with them. He said he was afraid that the community would be overanxious and possibly want to help bring their parents underground, and that would create a problem for the scouts. Andrew told the driver to continue to the dining hall; then he told Camillia that if the children went, it would likely make it impossible to control the crowd.

Camillia suggested that the abduction trip be kept still and to worry about one thing at a time—first getting the adults, then housing them, then placing them into a profession. She

concluded that the adults would most likely settle in quicker than the kids did because they would have their children to fall back on. Andrew said that sounded like the safest way to do things and that he was going to forego the speech. They finally approached the dining hall, and Andrew jumped off the wagon and rushed into the building leaving Camillia behind so he could find the chief and let him know the new plan. The driver helped Camillia off the wagon, and she went in and headed for her seat on the stage. Whether Andrew gave his speech was of no importance to the scouts because it did not reflect on their job; either way, they were going on the abduction trip and rounding up all the adults, changing them, then bringing them back to the compound. Andrew found the chief and informed him that he was not going to make any speech because he felt that it would have a negative effect on the community.

As the two men found their seats on the stage next to Camillia the chief acknowledged Andrew, and dinner was being served. Like usual, everyone ate and conversed, the time flew by, and the next thing everyone knew, dinner dishes were being picked up by the kitchen staff. Andrew and Camillia went back outside, got into their buggy, and were on their way home. The chief mounted his horse and was not far behind Andrew and Camillia. He was also headed to their home; he needed to give the job lists to Andrew for review right away. With all the excitement of the speech, the chief forgot that he had the job lists with him. As soon as Andrew and Camillia arrived at home, the chief caught up to them before they got off their buggy and could hand Andrew the job lists. The chief went on to go home and settle down for the evening. Andrew and Camillia got off their buggy and went into their home. Andrew went to his study to review the job lists in case he wanted to revise them at all. Camillia got ready to go to bed then settled down into the bed. She was tired but could not get to sleep because she was getting excited thinking about seeing her parents again when Andrew and the scouts returned. Camillia knew that it was going to be a long night. Andrew was going to be up later than usual because he needed to analyze the job lists and possibly make some changes. He was up only three hours later than normal and made minimal changes to the job lists. Now it was bedtime for him, but when he got changed into bedclothes and climbed into the bed with Camillia, he realized that she was still awake, which was out of character for her. Andrew asked her if she was feeling okay, and she said yes. Because of telepathy, he knew what was on her mind and that reuniting with her parents was what had her awake. He told her not to worry about her parents' arrival and to control her excitement until the right moment because he did not want anyone else to know what was about to happen by reading her mind due to her behaving very peculiarly compared to normal. Camillia said she would try to keep her thoughts buried so no one could read her mind and then know the secret of their parents being changed and brought into the community. Andrew stressed the importance of keeping her mind clear once again. She told him again that she would do what was necessary for the good of the community of pale ones. They snuggled up to each other, kissed each other, then started to relax to go to sleep. After thirty minutes, they were both asleep.

Morning came rapidly. Camillia got out of bed slowly so she would not wake Andrew up. Camillia moved about the bedroom as quiet as a mouse and got herself changed from bedclothes into day clothes. She went into the bathroom that was connected to their bedroom and got her hair styled, brushed her teeth, and washed her face, and Andrew was still asleep. Camillia slipped out of the bedroom, closing the door behind her, then headed to the living room where she would await breakfast hour. Time seemed to go by more leisurely than usual. She knew it was just because she was anticipating the reunion with her beloved parents. There was so much to share with them both good and bad to make it as if they had been there the whole time.

The most important thing was now she would have some extended family in Andrew's parents. The adults had gained an in-law, and they were grandparents. Camillia's thoughts were starting to surface to her forebrain so she had to stop thinking about the addition of the adults before her staff read her mind or someone out in the community did. She changed her thoughts to Armellya and the unborn baby. In fact, she had just remembered that she had a prenatal checkup on that day; and because it would be in the late afternoon, the chief would probably have to go with her. She also realized that if the doctor could get a good look at the baby's genitals, he would be able to tell her the sex of the baby. Camillia figured that she could find out right away and surprise Andrew with the news when he returned. She started to think about getting the new baby's bedroom ready and all the things that would need to be done.

As she slipped deeper and deeper into thought about baby stuff, she suddenly felt a hand on one of her shoulders; it frightened her, and she looked up hastily. It was Andrew; he had awakened and at top speed gotten himself ready to go to breakfast with Camillia. He bent over her and kissed her passionately. As he sat down next to her, she reminded him of the doctor's appointment that day. Andrew apologized and told her he would have to leave before the appointment for the abduction trip but that the chief would accompany her. She understood and said it would be fine for the chief to be there. About that time, there was a knock at their door; it was the chief. He told them that he thought they could ride together to the dining hall; Andrew said that they would appreciate the lift. The chief informed them that it was time to leave so they all went to the front door.

While walking to the buggy, Andrew reminded the chief that Camillia had her checkup that day and asked him if he would mind going with her in his place. The chief said if Camillia did not mind, it would be his honor. Camillia spoke up immediately and told the chief that she would love to have him accompany her. Andrew told them that it was settled; the chief would go in his place. Everyone was in the buggy, and off they went to the dining hall. Having gotten to the dining hall, everyone piled off the buggy, went inside, and sat at their seats on the stage. Breakfast was served, everyone ate and chatted as usual, then left the dining hall to go to their places of work. Camillia and Andrew went back home and the chief accompanied them. Once they were in the privacy of the castle, the chief made a request to speak to Andrew in private. Andrew took the chief to his office room; they both sat down then the chief began to tell Andrew that he would take appropriate care of Camillia in his absence. He also praised Andrew's ability of being king then gave Andrew some tips on handling the abductions that he had to learn over time through trial and error. Andrew listened intently then thanked the chief for the much-needed tips, taking care of Camillia in his absence, and the compliment of being a great king.

The two men stood up to leave, then Andrew turned to the chief and gave him a friendly hug and told him that he was a great man himself and that his strength to run the commune came from him and Camillia. Andrew and the chief recomposed themselves and exited the office room to reunite with Camillia. When they got to Camillia, she could feel their sentiment so she gave an observant smile to both. Knowing that the last of the business before Andrew had to leave was done with, Camillia asked the chief if he would like to participate in family time. He told her that family time was supposed to be for her and her closest friends to get some undisturbed quality time together, and he did not want to intrude. Camillia sternly told the chief that his participation would not be an intrusion and that he was a part of their inner family and that the others would agree. She finished scolding the chief by telling him that she did not want to hear such negative talk again.

He was somewhat drawn back by her motherly concern for his welfare, but he knew he meant a lot to her. The chief answered her request for him to participate in family time by telling her that he would love to be a part of her special gathering and activities. Camillia replied that it was settled and proceeded to tell him that family time would start with having lunch there at the castle's private dining hall. She continued to tell him that there would be a lot of verbal sharing and catching up while they ate, then they would transfer to the living room to either talk some more or do an activity, unless the activity were to be done outside of the castle. She concluded the family time information by telling the chief that they still had so much to catch up on that they were still in the conversation phase. The chief revealed that he had some valuable talk to contribute to their conversation. Andrew stood with the chief and Camillia in silence; he was humbled by the sentiment that the chief had put out. Andrew jumped into the conversation and told the chief that he wanted him to be present for all the future family gatherings. It was now time for Andrew to turn Camillia over to the chief's hands so he could go and prepare to leave on the abduction trip, and it was time for Camillia to get ready for her doctor's appointment. Andrew summoned Melanie to prepare his satchel with the appropriate foods and fill his canteen with water. While Andrew was dealing with Melanie, Camillia summoned the stable boy so she could have the horse and carriage ready for her and the chief to go to the hospital.

Andrew and Camillia excused themselves from the living room to go to their bedroom to spend some last-minute time together before they would be forced to temporarily go their separate ways. Camillia was frightened for Andrew's safety as well as excited for him to return with their parents. Andrew did not like to be so far away from Camillia and to not be able to be accessible to her. They held each other in their arms and kissed zealously for quite some time. Andrew finally pulled his face from Camillia's face and softly told her that the time for him to meet with the scouts had come. She tenderly professed her love to him and him to her; then they let go of each other. After a small pause and last look, they departed from the bedroom and returned to the living room. Andrew received his satchel and canteen from Melanie and put them over his shoulder then moved into the chief and Camillia for a group hug. After the group hug, the chief told Andrew to be safe and to handle the adults with caution. Camillia told Andrew to return as quickly as possible. Andrew told them that he would be safe and return in due time. Andrew walked out of the castle door and headed for the spiritual hall to meet up with the scouts so they could leave instantaneously. Camillia and the chief walked out of the castle right behind Andrew so they could get onto the buggy and go to the hospital for her prenatal appointment.

Upon Andrew's arrival to the spiritual hall, the scouts all had the same question for Andrew, why did he not give his speech the previous night? He answered them with a simple and basic answer; he said that it may have a negative effect on the whole operation. That was enough of an answer so they then left the spiritual hall for their journey. Meanwhile, Camillia and the chief got to the hospital and made their way in. The nurse they had checked in with instantly took them to a room where they would wait for the doctor to come in and examine her. Within a few seconds of being in the hospital room, the doctor went in. Camillia lay back on the examination table and pulled up her shirt while the doctor grabbed the ultrasound machine. The examination was brief. As the doctor cleaned off the machine and Camillia cleaned off her belly, the doctor asked her if she wanted to know the sex of the baby. With enthusiasm, Camillia said absolutely. The doctor announced that she was having another girl. The appointment had come to an end so Camillia and the chief made their way back out to the buggy and went back home. Now that she knew for sure that she was having another girl, she could start to get the new baby's room ready.

After arriving at Camillia's castle, the chief uttered that it was time for family time to begin. Camillia took the chief by the hand and led him into their private dining hall then announced to everyone that the chief was going to participate in family time from there on out. Everybody was overjoyed to have him there and showed their acceptance by individually giving him a hug and verbally welcoming him.

The chief told them that it meant a lot to him to be involved in their personal time as a close family member because he had not had family since he was just a boy; both of his parents passed away a long time ago, and he was an only child. Everyone sat down around the round dining table, and Melanie had her staff serve lunch while everybody shared the latest news to one another; the chief even had a lot to contribute. They continued to share while eating, and just as the day before, lunch took twice the amount of time to complete because they were busy talking at the same time as eating. Once lunch had been consumed, the kitchen staff took the dishes from the table and everyone retired to the family room to carry on their discussion. Everyone took turns playing with Armellya. Time went by speedily, and now it was time for Armellya's nap and for everyone to return to their duties. The chief even had responsibilities to attend to. Everyone went their separate ways, and Camillia was left alone. She could not help but think about where Andrew was on his travels and if he was okay. She knew she was not to think about those things in case someone was close enough to read her mind, but it was so difficult to do. Camillia decided to try to stay secluded without making anyone concerned or suspicious so she could try to control her thoughts so she left to go to the chief's garden area and let the help take the rest of the day off so she could be alone.

In the meantime, Andrew continued to travel toward the tunnel wall. He and the scouts had passed the lake and the widest part of land that extended from the tunnel wall. All they had left was to travel through the tunnel area to where it got to its smallest area, which was where the tunnel door was located. Because of the scouts' excitement and his own excitement of seeing their parents again, they did not stop at the lake to rest as was usually done. By not taking the lake break, they were a half hour ahead of schedule. As they were walking, Andrew reminded the scouts that they were to visit their indicated homes and check for children then return to the tunnel to report back. Once all the scouts were back and it was determined that there were no more children, they would all go out together and abduct their targeted adults. Andrew and the scouts had gone through the tunnel with ease and were now at the tunnel door. Because they had traveled faster than usual and had skipped the lake break, they had to wait at the tunnel door for it to be time for the humans to go to sleep. After nearly two hours of waiting, it was time for the scouts to go out and check for children then check in and if there were no signs of children, go back to get their designated adults.

CHAPTER TWENTY TWO

It took about twenty-five minutes for all the scouts to return after checking for children; they all reported that there were no signs of children. Now it was time for them to go back out to their same homes and abduct their human targets while he stayed waiting just behind the tunnel door. It had been about thirty minutes since the scouts left for their targets, and no one had returned yet; Andrew was starting to get a bit nervous. Andrew forgot to allow time for the adults to suit up, and that was a process. About the time that Andrew was starting to really worry that something had gone wrong, the scouts began to arrive with their human targets. It took a total of forty-five minutes for all the pale ones to return from the earth's surface. The adults were concerned with what the pale ones wanted with them, but they were complying with the orders that were given to them.

Without wasting any time, the scouts got into their satchels and pulled out their syringes with the serum in them and without delay injected the humans in their thumbs. The humans were then eased to the ground by their pale ones, and the change started to occur. After ten minutes, the changes were complete and all the humans were now pale ones. The scouts helped them to their feet, and they began to walk out of the tunnel toward the field, the lake, and the commune.

So far, the new pale ones were quiet and obedient so Andrew was not going to entice them to conform by using their children as bait until he would need to. The adults were traveling much faster than the children had so they were even more ahead of schedule than they were when they got to the tunnel door. They had reached the first resting place along the way, the field, so Andrew ordered everyone to stop. Halfway through the rest, Andrew gave the cue for the scouts to pull off the new ones' helmets so they would know that they did not need them anymore. With super speed, the scouts grabbed their chosen helmets and with a breakneck motion removed the humans' helmets.

The adults were stunned but did not panic as the children had. They realized very rapidly that they had sufficient oxygen.

It was time to move on to the next resting spot, the lake. Again, the adults moved faster than the children had so they were even more ahead of where Andrew thought they would be. That was pleasing to Andrew and the scouts as they were wanting to get back to the compound as soon as possible to be paired up with their parents. Andrew wanted to be back with Camillia and present her parents to her. The scouts were really wanting to be with their parents as well. Andrew was surprised that his and the scouts' parents had not recognized them yet. They continued to get more and more ahead of schedule as they were already at the next resting place, the lake. The scouts reached into their knapsacks and pulled out some jerky for themselves and the adults.

After finishing their jerky, Andrew told everyone to get water from the lake. The scouts filled their canteens while the adults drank with their hands. Since the next break was at the compound door, Andrew decided to explain their change to them before going any farther; he would also tell them that their children were safe and sound and that they would be seeing them after the next break. After his speech, Andrew asked if there were any questions or concerns. All at once, many of the adults verbally admitted to recognizing their child among the scouts; they just did not say anything because of the possibility of negative repercussions. Andrew announced that the next stop would be at the compound doors in which they would be living in with their children. The adults got excited; they could not wait to start a new life with their children. Andrew told them that they would travel at the pace of the adults and could skip the rest period that was usually taken just outside of the commune doors. Everyone agreed to going as fast as possible and skipping the final break. Andrew led the way, and they started walking again.

Twenty minutes later, the group was at the compound doors. Andrew turned and told everyone that when they entered the community, they should stay put and the scouts would round up all the children then everyone could reconcile. After reuniting, they would stay by their child until the welcoming committee visited them for individual information. Andrew gave the commune door security the command to open the doors, and they did. Everyone entered and stayed where they were to await their child. Andrew sent the scouts throughout the community to have all the children come to the commune doors except for Camillia and the chief. It took a total of thirty minutes to get everyone at the doors. The children could not believe their eyes; they were so thrilled to see the adults. Each child looked for their parents, and each parent looked for their child. It only took forty-five minutes for all the parents to be reunited with their children. All the children took their parents to their place of work so they could close the shops until further notice; then they took their parents home with them to start catching up on all the lost time. Andrew had his parents with him as well as Camillia's parents. He told them that he and Camillia were married and living in the same castle so he was bringing them to the castle now.

Camillia had planned to spend the day alone, but the chief picked up on her saddened yet excited emotions as she passed by him to go to his home garden so they spent the day together in the house garden. They thought that together they could keep each other calm and content, and they did to some degree. Neither of them slept the night Andrew was gone so they were beyond exhausted and felt closed in. The chief and Camillia worked on the new baby's room all night to pass some time and do what needed to be done anyway; they had it completed by morning.

Finally, they decided that they needed to get out of the castle so instead of eating breakfast, they agreed to take a stroll. They had walked through the chief's side of the castle to Camillia's side and had gotten to Camillia's front door when they opened it to see Andrew getting ready to enter.

That surprised her because he was back in half the time than usual. She greeted him with a big long hug and a lot of kisses; then suddenly, she noticed their parents standing behind him. She was shocked, speechless, and her body felt like it was frozen in place. Their parents squeezed by Andrew and went to Camillia to give her a hug; she hugged them back and told them that it was a dream come true that they were finally there. Her parents told her that they missed her every day she was gone and that they never stopped looking for her. Andrew's parents did not know Camillia too well, but they told her that they were pleased to have her as a daughter-in-law. Everyone, including the chief, went into the living room to sit down and talk about what had been going on in Andrew and Camillia's lives. Camillia summoned Bridgette to leave her parents long enough to bring Armellya to her so that she and Andrew's parents could see her for the first time.

While waiting for Armellya's arrival, both sets of parents inquired about Camillia's current pregnancy. Camillia told them that she did not have long to go until delivery time.

She took one of Andrew's hands into her hands and announced that they were having another girl, and she had just found out when Andrew was leaving to get them from the earth's surface. Andrew and both of their parents were elated to hear that the pregnancy was going well and that it was another girl. Just then, Bridgette and her parents showed up with Armellya. She handed the baby to Camillia, and Camillia excused Bridgette to be with her parents. It was nearing lunchtime so Camillia explained that they would be having family time during lunch plus two more hours. It was arranged so that they and their closest friends could get together and catch up on how each one was doing and to do fun things together. Andrew told them that they were not sure that they would continue to have family time as it was because now everyone had their parents and would probably want to have family time with them. He finished with what he had to say by adding that they would take a census on the subject during that day's lunch at home because he knew that they would all be there. It was time to head to the castle's private dining hall for lunch and family time.

By the time Andrew, Camillia, and the chief got to the dining hall, everyone was there and seated. There were twelve people not including Andrew, Camillia, and their parents or the chief at the table; that would make nineteen people total. After everyone was seated, the kitchen staff brought out lunch. Andrew started the group conversation by asking if everybody wanted to still have family time as before and add their parents to the group, or if everyone had family time with themselves and their parents. Andrew said that they were going to take a vote. Everyone voted to keep family time as it was and to add their parents. The chief was proud of the children's decision to keep what they had with the family time gatherings. All the children agreed that their parents needed to bond with one another as they had and that they would still be one happy family, just larger than before. They all finished their lunch, and the kitchen staff picked up the dirty dishes. Everyone decided to remain at the gigantic round table to converse. They started with introductions. They were to say their names, who their child was, and what their job specialty was when they were above ground.

After the introductions were over, Andrew explained that as they and all the adults knew, no one was to separate from their child until the welcoming crew visited them. Andrew said that as king, he and Camillia could be their welcoming crew. He continued by telling them that during the introductions, revealing their above-ground specialty would help in placing them into a position in their new community that best fitted their desires and functionality.

The chief spoke up and made the proposal of trying to have their friend's parents added to the castle's employee list. Everyone there got motivated over the chief's suggestion because that would keep the adults close to their children. Andrew said that after family time, he would retire to his office room and start to work on the employee arrangements. There were a lot of people to try to make a placement for and that would be a challenge, but Andrew knew that his friends were counting on him to keep their parents close by. Family time seemed to last a lot longer than usual, but it was not nearly long enough to completely catch up on things. Everyone discussed their abduction process and being turned. They shared their trip experience of being transferred from the tunnel to the land of grandeur and how everything was done with precision and care.

When family time was over, it was time for the children to get back to work and the adults to tag along with their child. Before everyone could scatter, Andrew told the adults that he would be meeting with them individually to find out where to properly place them among his staff and to let them know what their duties were and, finally, to give them their job descriptions. Andrew's announcement was over so the children went their own separate ways and took their parents to tag along while they carried out their responsibilities. Andrew went to his office room to start the tedious task of finding a placement among his staff for all the parents. He recruited the help of the chief and his wife. After a long hard look at his current list of staff and comparing it to a list of open positions, Andrew found a placement for most of the adults. Andrew would have to create positions for the rest of the adults because the list was not long enough to accommodate every one of the adults.

Now it was time to start to create positions. He would use Camillia's and the chief's ideas for creating new jobs. The chief and Camillia had a lot of ideas; they shared them with Andrew. Their ideas for more positions were more than sufficient so after writing them down, he was ready to start to call the parents and their children into the office room one family at a time. Andrew started with Melanie. She was his and Camillia's dietitian; she planned all the meals. He would make her mother head baker and her father head chef. He gave them their new job descriptions, and they were all pleased. Andrew excused them and told them that their jobs would start immediately; they thanked him and went to work. Next Andrew called in Michelle, who was Camillia's personal maid. He made her head maid, which meant that she was to oversee all the maid service people. He made her mother Camillia's personal maid and made her father Andrew's personal manservant. He gave them their job descriptions, and they were all pleased with their jobs. They thanked him and Camillia; then Andrew told them that their jobs would start immediately and excused them to begin their duties.

Now it was Bridgette's turn so he called her and her parents in. She was Armellya's personal nanny. Andrew left Bridgette as Armellya's nanny then made her mother the nanny for the unborn child. Her duties would not start until the baby was born, but that was not far away. Andrew had Bridgette's father on standby to be the male nanny of their firstborn son, whenever that would be. In the meantime, if Bridgette or her mother needed any help, he would assist them. Andrew also told them that their duties would start immediately. They thanked him; then he excused them to go about their duties. Andrew called for Matthew and his parents. He was Camillia's personal security guard. Andrew made Matthew head of the castle security, his father his personal guard, and her mother Camillia's personal security guard. He gave them their job description, and they were thrilled. After thanking him, he excused them to get to work.

Now that everyone was dealt with and very happy with their positions, the chief told Andrew that he did a wonderful job of adding everyone's parents to his staff and shifting the children's positions to still be the head of their departments.

Camillia and Andrew were pleased with the new job arrangements. Andrew still had one more duty to do regarding his employees; he had to write up a list of names with their job positions for the census hall so they could record it. Camillia and the chief left the office hall so Andrew could work without distractions. The chief went to his side of the castle, and Camillia went to her bedroom to take a small nap before dinner time arrived. Shortly after getting in bed, Camillia fell asleep; and right after she fell asleep, Andrew finished his list for the census hall.

Once everything was completed in the castle's positions, there was a knock on the front door. The butler answered it, and it was a courier delivering a note for Andrew. It said that all the parents were settled in their new positions and had already started to work. Andrew was pleased that all went smoothly and had gotten done so quickly. The census hall would be busy for a few days trying to catch up on all their new records, but that was to be expected.

Now that Andrew had some free time before dinner, he went to find Camillia so he could spend some quality time with her. As he walked up the main hallway of the castle, he got near to his and Camillia's bedroom and heard some whimpering; it sounded like something was wrong with Camillia. He hurriedly went to the bedroom door to check on her, and when he got there, he saw her holding her stomach while she lay on her side in a near fetal position. That alarmed Andrew so he walked up to her and knelt so he could speak to her. He asked her if she needed the doctor, and she replied that she felt like it was time to deliver the new baby. Andrew became horrified because as far as he knew, the baby was not due for another couple of months. Andrew told her that he would get Matthew and together they would get her onto the buggy and take her to the hospital. She said that it would be a clever idea, so together Andrew and Matthew got her onto the buggy and off they went to the hospital. They rode fast and hard so they got to the hospital in just a few minutes. Andrew left Camillia with Matthew and went inside to have some porters bring out a gurney. He went directly to the nurse's desk and told the charge nurse that Camillia was in labor; she instantly called for some porters to get Camillia into a room as speedily as possible. The porters were at the nurse's desk in no time so Andrew took them out to the buggy and they got Camillia onto the gurney. They took her into the hospital and a nurse was waiting on them. Upon contact, the charge nurse directed Andrew and the porters to a private room. The charge nurse ordered a nursing assistant to retrieve the doctor without delay while she got Camillia changed into hospital attire.

CHAPTER TWENTY THREE

While waiting for the doctor, the charge nurse hooked up a fetal monitor to her; they needed to track the contractions. Right after the charge nurse hooked up the fetal monitor, the doctor walked into the room. He greeted Andrew and Camillia then looked at the printout from the fetal monitor. He told Andrew that Camillia was definitely in labor. Andrew sent for Matthew to come to the room so he could speak to him without missing anything with Camillia and the new baby. Matthew responded with the speed of light. Andrew told him to go and get both of their parents and to bring them into the hospital bedroom and to make it quick. As Matthew was walking out of the room, Andrew asked the doctor if there would be enough time for their parents to arrive before the baby was born. The doctor told Andrew that if the delivery process did not speed up, they would have enough time for their parents to arrive and share the experience with them. The doctor also told Andrew that he was a bit concerned for the baby's well-being because it was two months early. Andrew asked the doctor if the baby would still be healthy and strong. The doctor was honest with Andrew and told him that the only thing they would have to worry about was the development of the baby's lungs. He added that if the lungs were not developed enough, they could work with that by placing the baby into an incubator with oxygen supplementation and the administration of medicines.

Andrew could hear his and Camillia's parents coming up the hallway to the hospital room so he silenced the conversation with the doctor because he did not want them to worry about anything. Andrew and the doctor went to the doorway of the room to greet their parents.

As they went around the corner of the room to go inside, the doctor continued to walk out of the room while Andrew hugged them and told them that it was nearing time for the new baby to arrive. Camillia's mother went over to her and asked her how she was doing as Andrew and his mother went to the other side of the hospital bed. Andrew placed his hand on her abdomen then told her he was there for her. She answered her mother by telling her that the contractions were very strong and painful. Andrew could feel her stomach tighten with every contraction. Both of their fathers stood at the foot of her bed. After an hour went by without being sought out by Camillia's family or the charge nurse, the doctor returned to Camillia's room to check on how close she was to delivering the new baby. The doctor announced to everyone that it was time for the delivery. He got Camillia into the proper position on her back and took his position at the foot of her bed. Both fathers went to the head of the bed. Andrew's father stood with him and his mother while Camillia's father stood with her mother.

Suddenly, Camillia let out a small cry, and the doctor immediately told her to push. This was the moment everyone was looking forward to. Within seconds, the doctor had the baby in his hands, and it began to give out healthy cries. As the doctor began to double-check for a clear airway and doing the clipping of the umbilical cord, Camillia let out another cry. The doctor checked Camillia and was surprised to see another baby crowning. He handed the first baby to Andrew and received the second infant. The ultrasound never showed a second baby. The doctor made sure the airway was clear then cut the umbilical cord, and the baby started to cry. Camillia was finally able to relax, and the doctor handed her new baby to her and Andrew handed the first baby to her as well. Sure enough, one was a girl and the second was a boy.

Andrew and Camillia named the girl Kaylina and the boy Kevin. Andrew sent one of his runners to find the chief and bring him to the hospital as soon as possible so he could see the new babies at once because the doctor had decided to keep Camillia and the babies in the hospital overnight just for observation. Twenty-five minutes after Andrew sent his runner to get the chief, he showed up at Camillia's hospital room with the chief. As he admired the twins, Andrew asked him if he would announce the births at the beginning of dinner. The chief said he would be proud to do that. It would now be time for Bridgette's mother to assure that they had everything necessary for Kaylina and if not, to get it; her bedroom was already ready. Bridgette's father would have to quickly get Kevin's room ready for him and assure that there was everything in the room that the baby would need. Because of the lack of notice of his arrival, there would be a lot of pressure to have the large task done in such an abbreviated period.

Camillia was still exhausted from the lack of sleep from the prior night, and the delivery took everything she had left so she handed Kevin and Kaylina to Andrew. He admired his new daughter and son then passed them around the room for everyone else to adore. After everyone had the chance to hold the twins, a neonatal nurse entered the room to take them to the baby nursery. The hospital had just added the nursery on to the building after Armellya's arrival because it was foreseen that Andrew and Camillia would be producing many children. Andrew and Camillia's parents left to go back to the castle to wrap things up with their jobs before the dinner hour so they could enjoy being with their own children during free time and before going to bed for the night. The chief stayed until it was time to leave for the dining hall, and Andrew skipped dinner at the dining hall to be with Camillia.

The dining hour arrived rapidly, and the chief made it to the dining hall to make the announcement of the twins' birth. Everyone was pleased and definitely astonished. A kitchenaid brought dinner to Camillia and Andrew at the hospital and stood close by in case they needed something about dinner and to take their dishes back to the dining hall when they were done. Andrew ate his dinner in regular time, but Camillia took a lot longer to eat because she was still exhausted and now weak from the birthing process. Eventually they both finished their dinner and the kitchenaid took their dishes back to the kitchen. Camillia lay back down to get comfortable and rest. Andrew told her that he would stay until she fell asleep then he would leave for home, but he would be back in the morning to get her and the twins and take them home. It took a while for Camillia to get comfortable, but once she did get comfortable, she fell asleep right away. Andrew bent over her and kissed her forehead then stood upright and left the hospital room. He went to the baby nursery to check on the twins before going home. The babies were fine, and the nursery nurse told Andrew that they would be able to go home the next day because both babies were doing exquisitely. Andrew thanked the nurses there for caring for the babies so well then turned to go home. He got home, changed into bedclothes, then got into bed, and fell fast asleep. He found it difficult to stay asleep without Camillia being there, but he did eventually fall into a deep sleep.

Andrew woke up earlier than usual the next morning because he was eager to get Camillia and the twins home. He was shocked to see Bridgette's father up and working already. He told Andrew that he had some last-minute touches to do to Kevin's bedroom prior to him coming home from the hospital. He also said that there were still a lot of things he had to go out to get for the baby and his bedroom. After speaking to Bridgette's father who was baby Kevin's male nanny, there was a knock at the castle's front door. The butler answered the door, and it was the first person in a lengthy line of people who came bearing gifts for the twins prior to going to the dining hall for breakfast. It was a good thing Andrew woke up early or the people bearing gifts would have awakened him and he would not have been able to dress on time to receive guests prior to having to go to the door. He accepted all the gifts and wholeheartedly thanked everyone individually as they dropped off their gift. Andrew and Bridgette's father felt that the gifts were a blessing because many of them were items that were still needed for the baby and his bedroom; other items were things that one could never have enough of. The gift giving was over just in time for everyone to get to the dining hall in the nick of time.

Andrew and his staff were a bit late to the dining hall but were still able to finish their meals before the kitchen staff came back out to collect the dirty dishes. The chief asked Andrew how Camillia and the twins were doing. Andrew told him that they were supposed to go home that day but that he had not been at the hospital since the prior evening, but everyone was doing well when he left the hospital. The chief asked if there was anything he could do to help them get home and settled in. Andrew said there was nothing needed but that he could tag along if he wanted. The chief appreciated the offer and agreed to go with Andrew to the hospital to ensure that everything went smoothly. Everyone was leaving the dining hall to go to work; Andrew and the chief left also to go to the hospital. The chief would ride on the buggy with Andrew, and they would tie the chief's horse to the back of the buggy.

The ride was a short one, and when they got to the hospital and went inside, everyone was congratulating Andrew on the miracle of having twins. The chief and Andrew got to Camillia's hospital room, and Camillia was up and dressed in her outside clothes. She told the men that the nurse was watching for Andrew to arrive so they could have the babies ready to go home. Camillia was not tired anymore; she caught up on sleep the night before. She was still a bit sore, but the doctor said she would be, especially after giving birth to twins.

Andrew, the chief, and Camillia sat in the hospital room chatting for a few minutes; then finally two nurses arrived with the twins. They handed the twins to Camillia, and she told the chief to take one of the babies so he took Kevin. Camillia was unsure about holding both babies at the same time much less trying to walk with both in her arms. Once outside, Andrew held Kaylina so Camillia could get on the buggy; then he handed her up to Camillia then he held Kevin so the chief could get on the buggy; then he handed Kevin up to the chief and finally Andrew got on the buggy and they headed for home.

On the way home, Andrew told Camillia about the community getting together and bringing gifts for the twins. Camillia was pleased and thankful; she agreed that the gifts were a blessing. They finally got home, and Bridgett's mother was there to receive Kaylina from Camillia and her father was there to receive Kevin from the chief; then finally, the chief, Andrew, and Camillia got off the buggy and everyone went into the castle. Everyone at the castle was standing in the living room waiting to greet the twins and fuss over them. When Bridgette's parents walked into the living room, they were swarmed by all the castle staff members; it was a wonderful experience. It took an hour for things to settle down, but once they did, everyone went back to their business and the nannies took the children and went about their business of feeding, changing, playing, and napping. Andrew even had to get back to work; he took the chief with him to help him in place of Camillia because she was still not strong enough to support Andrew with his duties. He had to go to every shop in the community to check on how things were running now that the adults had been added to the community and possibly having to fix an issue or two. Andrew also had to go by the census hall to find out where they were in documenting the latest changes and arrangements. He had to deal with the building crews to start the building of houses for the children's parents; then he would have to deal with the supply crews about making sure the new homes were furnished and stocked up with food, water, and other supplies. While Andrew and the chief would be gone, Camillia would be in bed resting up for family time at the lunch hour. Andrew and the chief would have to divide their duties into two sections so that they would be able to participate in family time; they would check the businesses before the lunch hour then meet with the building crews, census hall, and supply crews after family time. Everyone was so involved in their duties that the day seemed to fly by like the wind.

It was already time for lunch, and everyone but Camillia was gathered at the castle's private dining hall. Andrew went to his and Camillia's bedroom to wake her up so she could join in on family time, but when he got there, she could not be awakened and she was lying on the bed in an extensive puddle of blood. Andrew knew that it was not normal to have so much blood loss, and it was very terrifying that she would not wake up. Andrew had been missing long enough for everyone to miss him so the chief went to go to his bedroom to check on him. When the chief got to Andrew and Camillia's bedroom and saw Andrew standing at the doorway gazing at Camillia without expression, the chief looked in on Camillia and right away he too noticed the extensive amount of blood surrounding her on the bed. He pressed past Andrew and went into the room and then tried to awaken Camillia, but it was impossible. Reacting at top speed, the chief ran back to the castle's private dining hall where everyone was gathered so he could get Matthew and a runner. The chief sent the runner after the doctor with the news that she was unconscious and bleeding out profusely and that they needed him to come to the castle.

He got Matthew to retrieve Andrew and get him to the castle's private dining hall with others who could help him through the horrific emergency. The chief stayed with Camillia. Matthew announced to everyone that Camillia was in a crisis, that she was unconscious and bleeding heavily. Matthew made the request that everyone help pull Andrew out of shock and stay with him. Everyone was concerned about Camillia but focused their efforts on Andrew as asked. Twelve minutes after sending the runner for the doctor, they both appeared at Camillia's bedside. The doctor stayed to care for Camillia, and the runner went back on standby, out of the way. The doctor told the chief that he needed to get Camillia to the hospital on the spot. Because Andrew was still out of commission, the chief called for Matthew to get Camillia to the buggy for an emergency transport. It was difficult for Matthew to see Camillia in the shape that she was in, but he held himself together for her sake and swept her up in his arms, carried her to the buggy, and placed her on the buggy. The doctor and the chief jumped on the buggy, and they left for the hospital. The chief ran the horses at full pace so they got to the hospital in four minutes.

The doctor left Camillia with the chief while he went inside to get two porters with a gurney. The doctor was back in a flash with two porters and a gurney. The porters transferred Camillia from the buggy to the gurney with ease just like Matthew did; then they whisked her off with the doctor in tow. The chief jumped off the buggy and tried to keep up with the doctor and porters. They suddenly turned into a room and transferred Camillia from the gurney onto a bed swiftly. The chief made it into the hospital room and found several nurses and another doctor with her personal doctor. They were buzzing around Camillia like bees on honey. The nurses got two large-bore intravenous lines in her, attached a medium-sized machine to keep track of her blood pressure and pulse, and another smaller machine to keep track of her oxygen saturation. Her blood pressure was dangerously low; the nurses could not even get a diastolic pressure, and that was due to the amount of blood loss that she had. The doctor needed to give her a blood transfusion, but they did not have a blood bank because pale ones never got ill. Camillia had been the first and only pale one to need such services. The only other thing the doctor could think of doing was to find another few pale ones with her blood type to donate blood. That meant that they would have to type her blood then type the other pale ones who volunteered to give blood for compatibility, and it would take some time, time they did not have. To shorten the process, they would not test it for any impurities however since blood coming from a pale one would be safe as pale ones were immune to disease. The doctor ordered a bolus of fluids to be given while he worked on getting some volunteers to be possible donors. The doctor remembered that there were many pale ones, friends and family alike, congregating at Camillia's home so he sent word of his need with the chief to get those pale ones to the hospital posthaste.

The chief left the hospital and got back to the castle where he made the announcement of the need for blood donors, which brought everyone on their way out to their mode of transportation whether it be on horseback or by buggy. Andrew was now alert but in no shape to see his wife in the condition that she was in, so the chief stayed at the castle with him. Back at the hospital, all the pale ones were there to be tested for compatibility to Camillia. There were so many that the doctor had to call in extra nurses to help draw blood and label tubes for the lab to test. That part was not hard nor did it take very long. Unfortunately, it was the actual testing that would take some time, so for now, the doctor was having the nurses push the fluids into Camillia to try to keep her blood pressure from falling any more than it had already. The doctor kept a close eye on Camillia; she was not getting any better, but she was not getting any worse either.

Finally, all the test results were in so the doctor got everyone's attention and told them that if he called their names, they were to go directly to the waiting room to donate blood. The doctor called Melanie, Matthew, Camillia's father, Bridgette's mother, and Andrew's mother. Those five pale ones were set up for the collection of blood while everyone else except Camillia's parents and Andrew's parents was sent back to the castle so they would not be in the way at the hospital. The doctor went to the waiting room and explained to Camillia's and Andrew's parents that he was going to do a dilation and curettage on her to remove any abnormal tissue that he suspected was in her uterus thus causing her to hemorrhage, but it would have to wait until her blood pressure was stabilized. Both sets of parents understood and asked how soon the doctor would be able to stabilize her blood pressure. He said most likely after two pints of blood was infused into her. Before walking away, he told them that her blood loss had slowed down immensely. The doctor left her and Andrew's parents to go check on where they were in the blood donation process, and to his surprise, they had just finished and the blood was ready to be infused. He wrote the order for two pints of the blood to be infused right away and for a nurse to monitor her for an increase of blood loss.

The nurse that had been sitting with Camillia walked out of the hospital room and into the hallway, and she bumped into Andrew and the chief. Andrew had pulled himself together with the aid of his friend the chief, and they managed to get to the hospital where Andrew promised to stay calm and supportive. Andrew and the chief went into the room to be with Camillia as the nurse was going out to get the doctor with fair news. After the bolus of fluids and two pints of blood, Camillia was somewhat alert and her blood pressure increased and became stabilized and finally, the blood loss had stopped; however, Camillia said she was cramping in her stomach and back. The doctor was very happy to hear the news of her alertness and the lack of blood loss, but he was concerned that the cramping was going to lead to more blood loss so he instructed the nurse to prepare her for surgery right away; he said he would be ready within the next five minutes.

The nurse went back into Camillia's room and cleaned her up then got her off the bloody bed and onto a clean gurney then transported her to the operating room. Andrew waited in the hospital room for the nurse to bring Camillia back from her surgical procedure, and the chief went to the waiting room. The doctor went into the operating room before the nurse could get out so he asked her to assist him. With the nurse's help, the doctor completed the dilation and curettage speedily and safely. As he predicted, there was a lot of abnormal tissue in her uterus, but now that everything was finally as it should have been, the bleeding had stopped immediately, her blood pressure was back to normal, and she was somewhat alert. Once the anesthesia wore off completely, she would be exhausted, but alert and sore. The nurse took Camillia back to her hospital room, and Andrew sat next to her as she became more and more alert.

Andrew took Camillia's right hand into his hands and told her that he loved her. Just then, she turned her head toward him and smiled at him then told him that she loved him too. Camillia asked how the twins were doing, and Andrew told her that they were just fine. The nurse got Andrew's and Camillia's parents from the waiting room to go see Camillia and how well she was doing.

The chief went home so the visitation would be with immediate family; he knew he would be seeing her at the castle. Andrew's parents stood next to him, and Camillia's parents stood on the other side of the bed. Her mother held her other hand and told her she was very relieved that she was doing so well. Camillia was now fully alert and wanted to finish resting up at home; she would even approve a home health nurse's presence. Andrew said he would find the doctor to inquire about sending her home with home health services. Andrew found the doctor at the nurse's desk and explained that he and Camillia would like for her to recover at home with home health services in place.

CHAPTER TWENTY FOUR

The doctor said that he would do that on one condition, and that was if Camillia stayed in bed until he said otherwise, not even to go to the bathroom. The doctor said that he would have a nurse place a Foley catheter in her to address the issue of having to get up to urinate. He then said that he wanted bed pads on her bed in case of a fecal accident, and she was to use a bedpan to have a bowel movement in and that he would be there to check on her daily. Andrew agreed and so the doctor gave the order, and the nurse carried out the order. She placed a Foley catheter in Camillia and got a bedpan to send home with Camillia. Andrew went back to Camillia's hospital room and gave her the good news. When he told her that they would be going home that day, she was elated. Once Andrew got back in the room, the nurse had already explained to Camillia why she had a Foley catheter and that she was to use a bedpan, and she agreed to it. Their parents were delighted that she was going home also; they all four cared for her dearly, Andrew's parents had even accepted her as their own child. Two porters went into the room with a gurney to transfer Camillia to her buggy, and that went smoothly. Andrew had the driver keep the horses at a very slow walk to try to keep from jostling Camillia around on the buggy too much.

They finally got to the castle, and Andrew scooped Camillia up into his arms and carried her to her bed. Once he got her situated in her bed, Andrew went to talk to his runners. He told the runners to find everyone that participated in their family time and tell them that at the beginning of the next hour, he wanted everyone to be in the family room pronto then went back to sitting with Camillia. The next hour arrived, and just as Andrew had requested, everyone that was part of the family that participated in family time every day was there. Everyone was sitting and conversing in a muffled voice, but when Andrew walked into the family room, everyone shut up. No one knew why they were asked to be there all together, and no one knew that Camillia was home yet. Andrew told everyone that they were there to get the whole story on what had happened to Camillia up to that moment, but first he wanted to thank everyone for their help, support, and for being the best family a couple could have.

After giving a short sentimental speech and bringing tears of sentiment to everyone's eyes, Andrew went on to tell of what happened to Camillia. Andrew said that what happened to Camillia was quite simple. After giving birth to the twins, her body did not expel everything it was supposed to, and that caused her to hemorrhage. The doctor could fix that but not until her blood volume was replaced so she would be stable for the surgical procedure. Andrew took the next few minutes to thank everyone for offering their blood for Camillia. Then he moved on to tell everyone that she got some blood, then she stabilized enough for the procedure to be done and now she was home, so if anyone wanted to visit with her, they were welcome to do so. Andrew completed his talk by telling everyone that she was on bed rest until the doctor said something different, so the more visitors she had, the swifter time may go for her.

Everyone had something to say to Andrew so they all waited their turn then said their piece. Everyone gave Andrew words of love and happiness; they offered to be there for him and Camillia whenever they needed them. They finished by telling Andrew that they were family and that family stayed together and supported one another no matter what. Everyone visited Camillia regularly, and before she knew it, the doctor was allowing her to get up for short periods of time to sit in her chair in her bedroom and she no longer had to have the Foley catheter or use the bedpan; she could use the regular bathroom and shower. The doctor was still checking on her daily, and the family was still visiting regularly.

The days were going by fast for Camillia, and the next thing she knew, the doctor gave her full privileges as tolerated; and instead of family visiting her, she participated in family time each day. Gradually, Camillia was getting her strength back. She had been home for four weeks now and was back to assisting Andrew with daily tasks. Some were rather easy and some were exceptionally difficult, but she was up for the challenges.

Camillia's mother had a challenge for her daughter and Andrew; she was not sure if it would be easy or difficult, but it did need to be addressed. She was normally laid-back and easygoing, but she had a grave concern that she had not shared with anyone, so she went to Andrew and Camillia and addressed them as king and queen of the community instead of daughter and son-in-law. Because of the way she got their attention, Andrew knew that she was very serious about something and that it meant a lot to her. Andrew led her and Camillia into his office room to have some privacy and to show her the same respect he would any other pale one with business for the king and queen. They all took a seat, and Andrew asked her what was bothering her. Camillia's mother did not believe in beating around the bush so she just blurted out her response to him. She told him that there were still humans, adults and children of all ages, above ground and that she wanted to know what would become of them.

Andrew was beside himself for he had not known that there were other humans on the earth's surface. Camillia stayed quiet. Andrew told Camillia's mother that he needed to consult with the chief but to stay put while he sent a runner to retrieve him. Andrew called for one of his runners and commanded him to get the chief over to him at once. While waiting on the chief, Andrew went on to telling Camillia's mother that he had no idea that there were more humans and that he was under the impression that she and the rest of the adults that were taken with her were the last of the humans. Andrew told her that prior to him becoming king, the chief was ruler of the land of grandeur. He was hoping that the chief would be able to shed some light on the situation.

Just then, the runner showed back up with the chief. Andrew thanked the runner for producing the chief on the double. Andrew rashly told the chief to come the rest of the way into his office room, close the door behind him, then have a seat next to Camillia's mother. The chief knew what Andrew was so agitated about because he had read Andrew's mind upon entering the office room. The chief rapidly shut the door behind himself and sat next to Camillia's mother. Right as the chief was about to sit down, Andrew started to speak. He bluntly told the chief to tell him about the humans that were still on the earth's surface; he wanted to know why the scouts never admitted to seeing them. Andrew said that when he sent the scouts out to speculate the number of humans left prior to the last abduction, they reported that the ones that were taken were the last of them. Camillia's mother felt that she may have caused a problem between two friends but that she had to do what she felt was the right thing to do; she wanted to save every one that could be saved.

The chief began to tell Andrew and Camillia that he knew of those people above ground, and he explained that they were called the walking dead. Andrew, Camillia, and Camillia's mother remained quiet while the chief continued to tell the reason that the existence of those people was withheld from him. The chief said that he would start from the beginning of the humans' troubles and finish with where they were at the current moment in time. The chief said that prior to the release of the nuclear bombs, people were preparing for a nuclear fallout because everyone knew that eventually there would be a world war, so those who were of a wealthy status made what they called smart houses. The chief told Andrew and Camillia that the safe houses were the domed homes from where the adults were abducted. He went on to say that the humans that had survived the bombings and did not have the resources to build safe houses were left to deal with the effects of the radiation and eventually lethal diseases created by viruses and bacteria that had mutated due to the radiation.

The chief hastily stopped there and heedlessly told Andrew that Camillia's mother could fill in the rest of the blanks then he would reveal why they were not spoken of. Camillia's mother embarrassingly told Andrew that those people were deathly ill and contagious so the healthy adults shunned them and forced them to be cast out to the broken-down old casino buildings so that they were far away from the healthy people. Then she looked over to the chief as if to pass the rest of the story to him so he took over to finish giving Andrew and Camillia the rest of the information that Andrew was wanting. The chief said that at the beginning of the abductions, the pale ones targeted the sick humans first, trying to save them from deteriorating any further; but when they tried to turn them, they were not strong enough to withstand the effects of the serum. They died a horribly painful death. Because of their health status, they became known as the walking dead, and the pale ones started to focus on saving the healthy people before they succumbed to the effects of the earth's surface.

Andrew cut into the chief's response and asked him why that had not been revealed to him upon becoming king and being responsible for the rest of the abductions. He stated that he felt like he was deliberately lied to when the scouts came to him telling him there were no more humans on the surface and when the situation had not been revealed to him upon taking charge of the community's well-being. The chief took full blame for the deception and said that he would accept any punishment deemed appropriate for the crime. Camillia's mother begged forgiveness on the chief's behalf. She said that now she heard the whole story and that there was an attempt to save those humans, she was no longer holding the lack of attempting to save everyone against Andrew. Andrew asked Camillia how she felt about the situation; she told Andrew that since the chief did try to save the walking dead, there was not a crime committed, but there was the issue of withholding information. Andrew asked Camillia's mother if she was satisfied with what had been said so far; she said that she had not known that the chief already tried to save the walking dead, and it seemed to be a horrible death sentence for them and that it might be easier on them if they died from the disease process instead.

Since Camillia's mother was satisfied and no longer haunted by the walking dead's welfare, Andrew excused her from the office room. Andrew and Camillia still had to deal with the chief's deceit. Andrew asked Camillia how she felt they should deal with the chief. Camillia suggested that he and the chief have a discussion to ensure that there was not anything else he forgot to tell Andrew. Camillia felt that if there was nothing else to reveal, he should simply remind the chief of his duties as the king's adviser and leave him to perform his duties. She said that if there was more to be revealed, the chief had better come clean or he would change the possibility of receiving a harsh punishment. The chief said that there was nothing else that was held back so Andrew explicitly reminded him of his duties as the king's personal adviser then excused him from the office room to go about his business. Andrew and Camillia felt like they had treated the chief as though he was a criminal, but they knew that they had to take charge and act as the king and queen that they were. They had to put aside the fact that they were friends; those were the moments that forced them to take charge and show no partiality.

Family time was getting close so everyone was starting to arrive in the family room. Camillia's mother ran into the chief and pulled him aside to speak to him somewhat privately. She apologized to him for putting him on the spot and creating some tension between him and Andrew; she said that she thought she was trying to help other humans get the gift she had been blessed with by being brought down to the land of grandeur. The chief told her that it was not a problem; he and Andrew were still good friends

He told her that Andrew was in the right when he conducted their business as king and not as a friend; business was business, and under those circumstances, a person had to be able to take things from the appropriate perspective. The chief gave Camillia's mother a hug and told her that he was proud to have a selfless individual like her as a friend.

Now everyone who participated in family time was there. Andrew rushed over to the chief and gave him a hug and told him he was happy to have such a good friend and adviser. The chief told Andrew that he was proud of him for being the great king he was and for putting his kingdom before himself. At that point, everyone realized that they were all there so they headed to the castle's private dining room for lunch. Everyone was in their seats so the kitchen staff brought out lunch. Everyone shared how their day had gone and what they would be doing the rest of the day. Everyone talked about how they loved their job and were willing to go the extra mile for whatever task was at hand. Camillia and Andrew were exceptionally pleased that their friends were so close to them during their workday. Because the group of close friends all worked in the castle, they could briefly chat periodically throughout the day, and that helped the day go by faster and more pleasantly.

The lunch hour plus the two-hour family time went by like the speed of light. When it was time for everyone to go their separate ways, everyone hugged everyone then moved on to their responsibilities. Just before Andrew and Camillia could go very far, Camillia's mother asked for Andrew to call the chief into his office room so she could speak with them along with the chief. She felt awkward about the meeting that was held earlier. Andrew obliged her request and got the chief before he could leave the family room then led him to his office room. Camillia and her mother followed closely behind. Camillia and Andrew had heard her request, but the chief had no idea what the meeting could be about.

Once everyone was in the office room, Andrew sat at his desk, and the rest of them sat on the chairs provided across the room from Andrew. Andrew gave the floor to Camillia's mother by announcing that she called for the meeting. Camillia's mother started out with an apology. She said that she needed to know that the chief was still the friend to Andrew and Camillia that he was prior to the meeting about the walking dead. Andrew chuckled, stood up, walked around his desk to her, and pulled her by the hand into a standing position. While pulling on Camillia's mother, he requested that Camillia and the chief stand also; they did. Andrew called for a group hug then told everyone to sit back down as he went back to his seat.

Andrew told Camillia's mother that the whole community was like a large extended family but that those who participated in their family time were like immediate family and would always be. Camillia's mother sighed in relief and relaxed her posture. Andrew went on to tell her that although they were family, his job as king was taken very seriously and came first. He said that business was business, and during that time, everyone was treated equally and fairly but that he had to step away from being family and be professional by acting as the king and do what was best for the community. Camillia's mother said that she understood, and his ability to separate his job from pleasure was an ultimate responsibility and that she admired his ability to separate himself like that. Andrew thanked her and told her that if she ever had anything to say, she should do so. He also told her that if there were to be a concern or problem, she should not think of it as getting someone in trouble because if there was to be wrongdoing, then those responsible got themselves in trouble, not the individual who brought it to his attention.

Now that they all had the same understanding of the day's event, everyone involved could relax and have no hard feelings or concerns. Everyone stood up to leave the office room and shared another group hug before exiting. Camillia's mother went back to her job. The chief went to his side of the castle where he would be until needed. Andrew and Camillia needed to go to the census hall to ensure that the addition of adults with their professions was getting documented and done correctly. Camillia felt the motherly urge to check on her children, so while she was doing that, Andrew had the stable boy saddle up two horses for their travel to the census hall. While Camillia checked on Armellya in her bedroom with Bridgette, she felt a strange tickle in her abdomen. Camillia ignored the funny sensation, and after giving Armellya a kiss on the head, she moved on to Kaylina's bedroom where she briefly spoke to Bridgette's mother about how the six-week-old twin was doing. Camillia also kissed Kaylina on the head, and in doing so, she got the same funny feeling in her abdomen.

She again ignored the strange sensation and proceeded to Kevin's bedroom to check in on him.

While there, she spoke with Bridgette's father, and he said that the twin was doing good. Camillia went over to the baby and gave him a kiss on the head, and for the third time, she got the same sensation in her abdomen. That time, she had a challenging time ignoring the sensation; it was not painful, just strangely indescribable. Camillia went to meet with Andrew so they could get their errand done and spend some personal time together. Andrew was outside with the stable boy and horses; Camillia went out there and mounted her horse while the stable boy held the horse steady. The stable boy then held Andrew's horse steady while he mounted up. Together they rode off to the census hall. They got to the census hall quickly because they rode hard, they dismounted, tied their horses to the post provided, and entered the census hall. In speaking to the recorder, Andrew and Camillia realized that there was still a lot of work to do, and even though she had help, it was not enough to speed up her job. She had gotten a good amount done, so Andrew told her she was doing an excellent job and not to lose hope in getting to the end of recording. She thanked him and Camillia for checking in on her and trying to make her job easier. There was nothing more they could do there so Andrew and Camillia left the census hall.

On the way back home, Andrew and Camillia walked the horses slowly to give them a chance to catch up on their day. The census hall was close to the castle so it was a short trip home and did not allow Andrew and Camillia to discuss much. They decided to finish their day's encounters with each other after they got home and retired to their bedroom. The stable boy held the horses steady while Andrew and Camillia dismounted. The couple went into the castle and headed straight for their bedroom where they would spend some quality time together.

CHAPTER TWENTY FIVE

Now in their bedroom and dressed for bed, Andrew asked Camillia how her day had been. She told him that her day went by rather quickly and that there was only one event that stuck with her. The mention of an event piqued Andrew's interest. He knew that it had nothing to do with the meeting with her mother and the chief because he had tried to read her mind, but all he got was the impression of a peculiar feeling. He started to get the impression of peculiarity when they were on their way to the census hall. Camillia started to get sentimental with Andrew over their children, how beautiful they were, and how proud of them she was.

Suddenly, Camillia teared up and got emotional for no apparent reason. She apologized to Andrew for her behavior, saying that she did not understand where it was all coming from. Andrew was all too familiar with the short bursts of mixed emotions that she was exhibiting. Camillia asked Andrew if she could tell him something, and he said she could talk to him anytime about anything; she told him about the strange sensations she got when kissing the children on their heads.

She explained that it only happened when she had some sort of physical contact with the children and that it was an odd sensation—it was not ticklish or painful; it was indescribable. Andrew believed her when she said that she had no clue what was happening to her, but he had an idea and to confirm or deny his conclusion would involve the doctor's assistance. Andrew told Camillia that he felt it would be a promising idea to visit the doctor in the morning to run some tests on her. She questioned the necessity, saying she was not sick; pale ones do not get sick. He bluntly told her that he felt that she was pregnant again because the twins were six weeks old, and there would have been a window of opportunity and they would have done nothing to prevent another conception.

Camillia was surprised to hear Andrew's explanation of what she was going through. She told him that her body had not completely healed and had enough time to support another pregnancy. Andrew's concern was that eventually a pregnancy would kill her because so far, all the pregnancies and deliveries had been risky, which did not seem right, being she was a pale one and pale ones were supposed to be immune from human ailments. Andrew asked her if she would go into the hospital to visit the doctor the next day, and she said only if he went with her. He agreed then they went to sleep for the night. Camillia had trouble staying asleep. Every time she fell asleep, she dreamed that she was dying due to a pregnancy, but she never got to see if the baby survived or not due to waking up too soon. Finally, it was time to get out of bed and prepare for the new day. Camillia was exhausted from lack of sleep and worried about her well-being; it was almost like her nightmares were premonitions. Camillia had a feeling of great doom, and Andrew was sensing it from her. They both started to mention going to the hospital right away and having something to eat when they finished and returned home. It was common for them to think alike and to think of the same thing at the same time so it did not surprise them when they came to the same conclusion at that moment about going to the hospital right away.

Being they both had the same suggestion, they decided that it was the best way to handle that situation. They both got into day clothes and went outside to have the stable boy hitch a horse to a buggy. The stable boy worked at a high rate of speed to get the horse and buggy out to Andrew and Camillia. When the stable boy brought the horse and buggy out, Andrew said that they did not need a driver because he was going to drive. The couple got up on the buggy, and Andrew drove the horse hard to get to the hospital as soon as they could. Once there, they had the hospital's stable boy take their horse and buggy to tie up and watch over. They jumped down and went into the hospital. They headed straight to the nurse's desk and requested to see the doctor. The nurse asked what the nature of the emergency was, and Andrew told her that it was for the doctor to determine. The nurse gave a look of confusion then left the desk to get the doctor.

As she was walking away, she told them to stay at the nursing desk. About ten minutes later, the nurse returned with their doctor. He asked Camillia and Andrew what the problem was and added that he had to hurry because someone had an accident at work and needed surgery to have two fingers reattached. Andrew told the doctor that Camillia was exhibiting some signs of being pregnant again and that he wanted her tested right away to confirm or deny their theory. They knew the doctor had something more pressing to take care of so they told him they could wait until he was free. The doctor told them that the nurse could draw the blood and send it to the lab, and when the results were back, she could send a runner to them with a letter of confirmation or negative results. The doctor advised them that if the results were positive, he would be seeing Camillia as soon as possible. The doctor left to perform surgery, and the charge nurse took Camillia and Andrew to the waiting room, drew her blood, sent it to the lab, then told them she would send word of the results.

Andrew asked how long it would take to get the results back, and the nurse told him that it would be twenty minutes. Andrew told the nurse that they would just wait in the waiting room and stay if it was positive to see the doctor at his convenience or leave at that time if the results were negative. The nurse agreed to let them stay and told them she would watch for the results and get back to them as soon as possible. The twenty minutes went by like a flash, and the nurse went into the waiting room with a gigantic smile and told Andrew and Camillia congratulations.

With that news, Camillia got visibly upset. She started to shake and cry hysterically. Andrew remained under control so he could try to calm Camillia down, but he wanted to panic as well. The nurse's demeanor changed as she saw how badly Camillia panicked. She told Andrew she was sorry for upsetting the queen and to please forgive her. She moved in front of Camillia and got on her knees and told Camillia that she could put her into a private room to wait for the doctor. She also told Camillia that she could talk to her woman to woman and she would do her best to help her with whatever it was that had her upset. Camillia looked up at the nurse and told her that her offer was appreciated and that she would take her up on her offer. Everyone stood up, and the nurse took the couple to a private room to wait for the doctor, and she sat in a chair and gave Camillia her undivided attention. Camillia told the nurse about the nightmares and how she felt that they were premonitions. Andrew told the nurse that he had been able to sense her panic and fear. Andrew added that all her pregnancies had been elevated risk and she had almost died with the twins. He told the nurse that the twins were only six weeks old and that there had not been enough time for her body to heal and to support another pregnancy.

Now the nurse understood why they were so upset by a positive test. She said that she would check on the status of the doctor and have him in the room as soon as possible; then she left the room and checked the surgical suite to see if he was done or not. It appeared that he was finishing up so she watched impatiently for him to come out of the surgical room. Fifteen minutes later, the doctor finished with his patient and he came out of the surgical suite. The nurse caught the doctor before he could do anything else. She told him that Camillia's pregnancy test was positive and that she was terrified about being pregnant so soon after giving birth to the twins and that Andrew had the same concerns as Camillia. The doctor asked where the couple was, and the nurse told him that she put them into a private room then led him to the room.

Camillia was still shaking, but she had her crying under control; now she was only sobbing. Andrew was holding Camillia around the shoulders and trying to keep his composure. The doctor started to talk to them as soon as he entered the room. He told them that Camillia was stronger than they thought and that if she were human, he would be concerned; but as a pale one, her body healed double quick. Andrew told the doctor about the nightmares Camillia had been having and how she died in them and would always awaken before knowing if the baby even survived and how it seemed that this was more of a premonition than an ordinary nightmare. The doctor said that it was certainly an unusual thing to have repeating dreams, but they were in good hands and he would do everything possible to assure a good pregnancy with a safe delivery. Andrew asked the doctor what he was going to do differently from what he had not done in previous pregnancies to ensure the safety of mother and baby. The doctor said he was going to check her weekly instead of monthly and biweekly at the end. There was nothing else he could say or do to help, so Andrew and Camillia went back to their buggy to go home.

Andrew and Camillia were gone so long at the hospital that it was nearing the time for family time so they did not have the snack they had planned on having; they were going to wait for lunch. Besides, neither one of them was in the mood to eat. They were going to go to their bedroom to recompose themselves, but the family was already gathering in the family room to have family time.

Andrew and Camillia stayed in the family room so they could join in on family time also. It was not very long before everyone was there and they all headed for the castle's private dining hall. They all got seated, and lunch was served. Everyone ate and shared their day as usual, but when it came to Andrew and Camillia's turn to share their day, Andrew had to tell everyone about it because Camillia started to sob again, which made everyone deeply concerned. Andrew told them that Camillia had been exhibiting some signs of being pregnant so they went to the doctor and he could confirm that she was pregnant again, but that they were concerned about this pregnancy because it was so soon after having the twins and she was a high-risk pregnancy anyway. Andrew revealed that Camillia had been having repetitive nightmares of dying from a pregnancy but awakening before she could tell if the baby had survived or not. Everyone was happy that there was going to be another baby but concerned for Camillia's emotional well-being. They all said that they would keep an eye out for her and be there for her to talk to at any time of the day or night.

Camillia and Andrew thanked everyone for their concern and offered to help. Camillia had decided not to let the pregnancy take her away from her normal upbeat self, so they went about their next two hours of family time having fun. At the end of family time, Camillia gave everyone a hug and told them that she would be fine and not to worry. Andrew was amazed at how she seemed to turn her emotions off and replace them with a seemingly false sense of security. Now that family time was over and everyone was back to their duties, Andrew took Camillia into their bedroom and had a talk with her while reading her mind to ensure that what she was saying correlated with what was in her head and heart. It was not that he did not trust her to tell him the truth; it was that he did not trust her to tell herself the truth. Andrew outright asked Camillia what made her fears go away. She told him that she had to accept that if it was meant for her to have a healthy baby, she would; and if it was meant for her to survive the pregnancy, then she would. She told him that she refused to live in fear for the next eight months or so.

Camillia asked Andrew to do something for her then took a long pause; he felt as though it was a last request. He hesitantly asked her what that request was, and she told him that if something happened to her, she should not be sad, and if he found someone else to be queen and that if he was happy with that individual, he should do what he felt was in the best interest of the land of grandeur. Andrew stopped her there and told her to quit speaking with such negativity as he did not want to deal with those things and he wanted her to live as if she had an eternity with him. He finished speaking his peace by telling her that she would be the only queen for him and that he wanted every day to be a happy and productive day for them together. Camillia said she would speak no more of those things and that she was content with her life and with him and the babies. They lay on their bed and cuddled for a while.

Eventually, Camillia fell asleep and Andrew lay there watching her sleep and caressing her hair. He thought about how happy he was with her and about the beautiful children they had together and how he was looking forward to another two hundred years with her and many more children. With those thoughts, Andrew suddenly got an idea. Everyone in the community went through the same changing process, but the serum did not work on her and himself as it had everyone else. It made everyone but them barren. He was thinking if their scientists who produced the serum that had been used to change humans to pale ones could come up with something to give to Camillia and himself, maybe it would help against the minute human qualities that they exhibited without making them barren and then Camillia could have normal pregnancies with good deliveries and could withstand getting pregnant repeatedly in such a brief period. Andrew decided that he would discuss that with Camillia when she awoke and maybe go to the science hall and together they could consult the idea with them. Camillia slept nightmare free for three hours due to her fatigue from the night before.

When she woke up, he told her that an idea had popped into his head while he watched her sleep. Camillia felt the excitement in Andrew, and that made her eager to hear his idea. He started out by telling her not to interrupt him and revealed that his idea was a long shot but that it could be possible. She agreed not to interrupt as she was getting closer to Andrew's side. She was feeling sentimental as if she was falling in love with Andrew more and more. Andrew reminded her that they had the same serum to turn them into pale ones as the rest of the community, but it seemed to leave them with some human quality that allowed them to reproduce, which it had not done with anyone else. He suggested that maybe the scientists that worked on reproducing the serum that turned humans into pale ones could make a serum just for them to make them stronger without making them barren. Andrew asked Camillia what she thought of that idea. Camillia silently thought about it for a few moments then said it could be promising, but the only way to test the new serum would be on one of them, and what if it caused a mutation of some kind or killed them? Andrew suggested that the scientists find someone who was willing to be a test subject; they would not be able to tell if it would make them barren being that the test subject would already be barren but the scientists could keep track of any other changes. Andrew's suggestion made Camillia excited as well.

Science was not Andrew's or Camillia's specialty, but since the idea was within their grasp, they felt that the scientists might be able to do something with their theory. Camillia thought about it sensibly and concluded that the new serum would be a simplified version of the original serum, which they had mastered. Andrew took the theory even further by having the idea that the scientists might even be able to come up with an appropriate serum to turn the walking dead into pale ones. They could always abduct them one at a time to test it, and if it killed them, then it was just a faster death than what they would have had and the scientists would know based on the walking dead's reaction how to change the serum. Maybe they could come up with a vaccine for them first that would heal them then use the regular serum to turn them once the vaccine did its job.

CHAPTER TWENTY SIX

Now that Andrew and Camillia were thinking about the serum and making another serum, all kinds of ideas started to come to them. First things first, going to the science hall and discussing the production of something that would help themselves. They got up out of bed and straightened themselves up so they could go out and about without looking like they had just crawled out of bed, even though they had. It was getting close to dinnertime, but the couple had already considered missing dinner and getting a simple snack when they returned from the science hall. They knew that the scientists would be at the community's dining hall soon, so they had to get to the science hall before they left and have them come to the castle for dinner then they could discuss business. Andrew and Camillia told Melanie that they would be having dinner a bit late and that they would be bringing dinner guests home with them and to have it ready. Melanie assured them that there would be enough to go around, and it would be ready upon their arrival.

The young couple got out of the door in a flash and got their horses without waiting on the stable boy. They rode bareback and pushed the horses to go as fast as they could go. Andrew and Camillia got to the science hall just as the scientists were getting ready to leave for the community dining hall. Andrew slid off his horse and approached the scientists. He asked them to join him and the queen for dinner at the castle's private dining hall so they could discuss some possible business. They all agreed to join the king and queen at their private dining hall and were very interested to hear what the king's proposal was. Camillia was extremely excited that they could catch the science team before they left for dinner. The science team mounted their horses and leisurely followed Camillia and Andrew back to the castle.

When everyone arrived at the castle, the stable boy was ready to take the horses. Everyone went inside and gathered at the round table in the private dining hall. Melanie had dinner ready to serve, and she had the kitchen staff carry everyone's dinner out to them. It was a wonderful-looking meal. Andrew and Camillia spent the dinner hour getting to know the science team and letting the team get to know them as they ate.

Once everyone was done eating, the kitchen staff cleared the table and stayed in the kitchen to do cleanup. By now, the dinner hour was done for the community so Andrew sent one of his runners to bring the chief over for the meeting; the runner moved at top speed. While waiting for the chief's arrival, Andrew told the science team to address himself and Camillia on a first-name basis, not as king and queen. Andrew told them that the community was a big family, an extension of their immediate family. They agreed that the community was a big family. The runner and the chief showed up at that time so Andrew thanked his runner and asked the chief to sit at the table with them. The chief obliged; then Andrew told everyone that they were there because he had an idea that might save Camillia's life as well as an unborn child. Andrew reminded everyone about how risky Camillia's pregnancies were then announced that she was pregnant again. The group intervened to congratulate the couple. Andrew and Camillia thanked them; then Andrew continued. Andrew told the chief to just listen and, as the king's adviser, add what idea may pop into his head; the chief acknowledged Andrew. Andrew told the science crew that their intelligence far surpassed what they had been doing so he had a project for them. They all leaned into the table so as not to miss a word, and Camillia got a large smile on her face. The chief could feel the couple's excitement and anticipation, not to mention that he noticed her encouraging smile. Andrew told the scientists that he felt that they may be able to make a new serum that extended off the original one. He suggested a serum that they could give to him and Camillia that would strengthen them and allow for the minuscule amounts of human traits left in them to be gone without making them sterile.

The science team gasped, they had never thought to do such a thing. Andrew said that they may even come up with a vaccine to help the walking dead overcome their diseases so that they could be successfully changed without killing them. The science team started to think about what Andrew was saying. Up to now, their purpose was to keep enough serum on hand to assure the changing of the humans above ground, but now that there were no more humans above ground to change, they could be useful in other endeavors. Coming up with a serum for Camillia was a fabulous idea, and working on a way to help the walking dead was just as good of an idea. The walking dead were someone's family member, why not try to unite them with their colony member if possible? The chief even stated that the ideas were great; they would keep the science team busy, and it could be beneficial if they produced a serum that worked.

The science team spoke up and told Andrew that they could see making these ideas become a reality. The scientists said that they would get on it right away and that they would divide the team in half. One group would work on the serum for the queen, and the other half would work on the vaccine for the walking dead. Andrew and Camillia were very thankful, and the team was eager to leave and get started. Andrew excused them, and they left in a hurry to get back to the lab. The chief was amazed that Andrew and Camillia were able to come up with such ideas, but he was still impressed and very supportive. The chief asked Andrew and Camillia to keep him up to date on how the science team was getting along, and they said they would. Everyone was excited to get some positive results.

Once the scientists got back to their lab, they called in the rest of the scientists that worked with them occasionally. When the surplus of scientists got to the lab, the original team told them that there were two projects to be accomplished and that they wanted the work to be done around the clock. There were enough pale ones to separate into four groups so the head scientist divided the group into smaller groups of four. He told them that they were to work in twelve-hour shifts, two shifts per project. He pulled the first two groups aside and told them that they were to work on a serum for the queen and king that would make them stronger by combating the minuscule amounts of human traits left in them, but it had to leave them capable of reproducing. He finished with them by telling them that by working in twelve-hour shifts, they could work on the serum around the clock. One group would be updated and start where the previous group left off and continue the pattern until they had a successful serum. He told the groups that they would worry about finding test subjects later when they got to that point. He went to the second two groups and said the work pattern would be the same, only they were working on a vaccine to heal the walking dead of their ailments if not completely, at least to the point of being able to turn them into pale ones safely. If they were no longer suffering or contagious, they would become a part of the community and could have the same opportunities as any other pale one.

Both teams saw the challenge of their projects and knew it was going to take some time, but they would not stop trying until they succeeded or got old and died of natural causes, and the latter of the two was a long time away. Knowing that the queen was pregnant, the teams working on a serum for her and the king hoped that they could come up with something to help them before she ran into complications with the current pregnancy, if she should have issues. Each group knew what to do—two groups, one from each team went home to sleep and the two remaining teams got to work immediately. The head scientist would keep track of both projects' advances and make sure that all four teams were doing their jobs and getting proper sleep because there was no room for mistakes or wasted time. He would also report back to the king and queen on the progression of both projects.

It was nearing bedtime so Andrew and Camillia went to their bedroom early so they could spend some private time together before it was time to go to sleep for the night. They were so excited that they knew that they would have trouble going to sleep so they agreed that when it was time for lights out, they would cuddle and talk about the possibilities. They got into their bedclothes and lay down in bed to cuddle and discuss the projects. Camillia asked Andrew if he had any walking dead that were friends or family, and he said yes. He had several childhood friends that were not able to withstand the earth's toxins; they were exposed by faulty suits. Camillia felt bad for him and his friends.

Andrew asked her if she had any attachments to any of the walking dead; she said she had a couple of family members that could not afford to build safe houses and her parents would not extend a helping hand to them, but she did not know why. Andrew thought that was odd and selfish on her parents' part. He asked her if she ever inquired as to why they refused to help the family; he could understand if it were a stranger, but that was family.

Camillia said it had been bothering her ever since the tragedy, but she was too afraid of questioning their judgment. Andrew understood the position she was in, but he still felt it was the wrong thing to do. They were both saddened by reminiscing about their loved ones that were affected by the earth's devastation. Camillia and Andrew were hopeful that the scientists would come up with a vaccine to help the walking dead so their loved ones would be able to join them in the land of grandeur.

Camillia sort of changed the subject. She told Andrew that she was really hoping and praying that the scientists would be able to come up with a serum to help them, especially her. She said that it might have been selfish for her to say she hoped for the serum for specially herself over the walking dead and even him, but sometimes she still found herself fearing the effects of the pregnancy and the possible loss of the baby. Andrew told her that everything would work its way out, not to fear the unknown. Andrew and Camillia scooted closer to each other in the bed and cuddled for a while in silence. Several hours later, they were both still awake; they knew that they would be dragging their feet the next day, but their efforts to fall asleep were in vain. Camillia called for Melanie to get them some fresh milk from their cow so they could have warm milk. They were hoping that the enzymes from the warm milk would help them to fall asleep. It worked when they were much younger. Melanie went out to the barn and milked their cow for just enough milk for Andrew and Camillia to have a full glass each. They thanked Melanie for the milk and her time; then she went back to bed. Shortly after drinking their warm milk, Andrew and Camillia fell asleep also.

The new morning arrived, and Andrew and Camillia were in such a deep sleep that they woke up extremely late. They found that they had missed the entire breakfast hour, and no one had tried to get them up out of bed. They jumped out of bed and rushed to get dressed and put together before going out to the public. Before going anywhere, they were going to stop at the castle's private dining hall to ask Melanie to fix them a heavy snack. After eating something, they planned on popping in on the children and giving them some loving hugs and kisses and holding them for a bit. That way, the nannies could take a few minutes to do whatever they wished. After loving on the children, Andrew and Camillia had to get the chief and discuss some possible test subjects and how to get volunteers so that when the lab was ready, they would not have to wait for that process. Camillia was going to do whatever it took to help the lab succeed, and Andrew knew that.

After pulling themselves together, the couple said good morning to each other, gave each other hugs and kisses, then went to the dining hall where they asked Melanie for a heavy snack. Melanie had planned on letting them sleep for another five minutes then take breakfast to them to eat in bed together in private so they could get going at an easy pace without rushing, but they had already awakened on their own. Melanie told Andrew and Camillia to have a seat at the round table, and she would have their breakfast brought out to them. She was a wonderful dietitian and was always able to work around the couple's busy schedule when necessary. They relaxed during breakfast and enjoyed each other's company. It seemed that Camillia had a new outlook on her condition and was ready for whatever challenges may come her way. Andrew's idea for the science crew was brilliant if he might say so himself. It gave Camillia a whole new outlook on things. They were full before finishing their entire meal so the kitchen staff retrieved their dishes and put the leftover food into a bucket in the corner of the kitchen that once full by the evening would be fed to the hogs.

Andrew and Camillia proceeded to go to Armellya's bedroom and hold her and give her a lot of hugs and kisses. They spent fifteen minutes with her then went on to Kaylina's bedroom to do the same. After fifteen minutes, they went to Kevin's bedroom and repeated what they had done with the other two children. After fifteen minutes, they left him with his nanny as they did with the other two children and went to start their day's business. Now it was time to meet up with the chief and discuss finding adequate test subjects. Andrew and Camillia went to the chief's side of the castle and knocked on his door. His butler answered and led them to him. He was pleasantly surprised to see them so soon; he figured they would see him after making rounds through the town checking on the businesses and then dropping in on the census hall to get an idea of their progress. Andrew and Camillia greeted the chief with a hug then sat down beside him to talk.

The chief abruptly said that he had something to say, and he did not want any arguments about what he had to propose. The couple was becoming nervous about what the chief had to say because in trying to read his mind, he had blocked them from doing so, but they did pick up some mild tension from him. He told the couple that he had been up all night thinking things over about the new serum that the science hall was to make for them, and he knew that they would need a good test subject that had no ties but was healthy so that ruled out the walking dead and most of the community. Andrew was about to interrupt the chief when the chief suddenly blurted out not to interrupt him because he was not done yet. He went on to tell them that he felt that he was the best choice for being the test subject—he had no ties, and he was healthy. He also stated that he was nearing two hundred and fifty years old so he was nearing the end of the estimated lifespan of a pale one. No one knew for sure how long a pale one would live for because so far, everyone that had ever been turned was still alive, but he was the oldest and most logical choice.

Camillia was appreciative of what the chief was ready to sacrifice for them but was unable to accept his offering. They felt that the chief was the most important cornerstone of the community and that there was still a lot to be learned from him. He was a walking, talking history book for the entire history of the pale ones, thus the name chief. No one knew what the chief's real name was because from day one, he went by chief due to his position over every one of the pale ones; it was even questionable if he remembered his actual name himself after close to two hundred and fifty years of not using it. Camillia told the chief that they would most likely need many volunteers for the science hall to perfect the serum. The chief told Camillia that there was nothing he would not do for her because she was the daughter he never got to have naturally. Andrew told him that all in all, he and Camillia were his children because he adopted them to make them head of the society if he remembered correctly. The chief said he remembered that day very clearly because it was one of the few special things that had occurred in his life as a human and a pale one.

The three of them shared a sentimental moment then hugged again and decided to move on with their day. They did discuss the search for volunteer test subjects and concluded that they would make a public announcement that evening about the making of a serum for the couple but to keep the vaccination attempt for the walking dead a secret and hope some pale ones received a personal conviction to volunteer; the couple did not want anyone to be forced to be a test subject. The couple was getting ready to go out among the town and do shop checks to make sure all was running smoothly and that no one needed anything or if they did that they received whatever it was that they needed within reason. The chief was going to wander about the town on foot just for a long relaxing walk with a view and maybe some small talk with the shop workers and others who were simply passing by.

About the time they were getting ready to part ways, Camillia suddenly remembered that she had a prenatal appointment with her doctor, and she could not miss that. Andrew had a long trip to take care of traveling the entire town to check on things, so the chief offered to go with her if Andrew did not mind. Andrew and Camillia both agreed that it would make Andrew's day a bit shorter, and Camillia would have some support from the chief in the event the appointment did not go very well; and if it went exceptionally well, she would have someone to share that with as well. Either way, Camillia would have good company. Andrew walked back to his side of the castle and had the stable boy saddle a horse for him so he could start his rounds right away. The stable boy left to get the king's horse and was back in a flash so the king mounted his horse and left for his duty.

CHAPTER TWENTY SEVEN

Camillia and the chief went to her side of the castle to have the stable boy hitch a horse to a buggy so she could go to the hospital for her prenatal checkup. The stable boy got the horse and buggy for the queen and the chief. The chief told the driver that he did not need him because he would drive the horse. He and Camillia got up on the buggy and left for the hospital. At the hospital, the chief turned the horse and buggy over to the stable boy there, and he and Camillia walked into the hospital. The doctor was waiting for her to show up so he took her and the chief to a private room and asked her how she had been feeling. She said that she had been feeling fine; she had no sickness or discomfort. The doctor got the ultrasound machine out and looked at the baby. He looked carefully to try to ensure that there was only one baby in there. The doctor got another small handheld machine that she had never seen before and used it to hear the baby's heartbeat; that would also help them to know how many babies were in there. The doctor reported that he only heard one heartbeat, and it sounded great. The doctor gave her and the baby a clean bill of health. He did want her to go by the nurse's desk and have another blood drawn to keep track of her pregnancy hormone to assure that it continued to rise as it should and that it stayed within normal limits for the stage of pregnancy that she was in.

He wanted to do everything every time she came in to help assure a healthy baby with a good delivery and a strong healthy mom. Camillia was very pleased with how the doctor's appointment went, and so was the chief.

Before they left the doctor, he reminded Camillia that she was to be back on the same day of the next week at the same time. She said she would be there with whistles and bells. The doctor chuckled and said his farewells until the following week. Camillia and the chief got back on the buggy and were ready to head for her home when they ran into Andrew. He knew what time Camillia's doctor's appointment was and tried to plan his route through the colony to allow him to meet up with her along the way so he could find out how the appointment went. When asked, Camillia told Andrew that the appointment went well; she and the baby got clean bills of health. Andrew had to move on so he told Camillia that he loved her, and she blew kisses back at Andrew; then they went their separate ways. The next time he would see her would be at lunchtime. The chief got the horse moving and got her home in no time. Camillia invited the chief in to keep her company until family time when they would be joining the group of friends. The chief agreed to stay and visit; then he asked her what was on her mind. She said she was curious about how the science team was coming along with her and Andrew's serum. The chief told Camillia that he knew that it was going to take some time for the scientists to perfect the serum, but that when they did, it would probably be the best experience of her life. Camillia agreed, saying up to that point, her being turned to a pale one was the best experience so far. She told the chief that life as a pale one had far outweighed the ten minutes of excruciating pain that was experienced upon being turned.

The lunch hour arrived, and Andrew made it home just in time to participate with everyone without missing out on anything. Everyone was starting to gather in the family room so it took

Andrew a few minutes to find Camillia, but he finally did. The chief was right next to her so Andrew walked over to them, and he told the chief that he really appreciated him taking time out of his day to go to the hospital with Camillia. The chief told Andrew that it was his pleasure, and as her father, it was his job to be there for her. Camillia's birth father and mother were close enough to her and the chief and had heard the chief's comment about being her father, and they felt a sense of curiosity toward the unknown situation. Camillia's parents pulled the chief aside to ask what he meant about being her father. The chief told them that he had held an adoption ceremony between himself and the young couple in front of the whole community, and the reason was to allow them to be his successor and be the leaders of the land of grandeur prior to the runners up and to keep the rein in their family since they could reproduce.

The chief explained that they were the chosen ones spoken of in the legend of the pale ones. The chief told her parents that he meant no disrespect toward them and that he was not trying to take their place in her life. He was simply making them rulers of the land of grandeur with the assurance that no one could question the legality of them being the new leaders.

Andrew's parents were close enough to hear the full conversation between the chief and Camillia's parents; they thought that the chief was acting per legend, and they were proud to be the parents of the community's leader. They walked over to the chief and thanked him for taking their son under his wing in their absence and making him such an important part of the community. They said that they felt their boy had enormous potential, and they were glad that he saw it also. When Andrew's parents were done speaking to the chief, Camillia's parents suddenly saw the whole situation for what it was worth, and they thanked the chief as well. Andrew's parents, Camillia's parents, and the chief shared a group hug, and everyone agreed that their children would get the things they worked for and that the parents would not get in the way; they made it official among them by verbally handing their parental rights over to the chief.

The entire family had arrived at the family room so they transferred to the castle's dining hall and sat at the massive round table. Melanie had the cooks and bakers prepare a special lunch to celebrate her appreciation and love for her family. Everyone thought the gesture was fantastic. As usual, they went around the table and shared their day so far with one another; then they would tell what the rest of their day held for them all while eating lunch. At the end of lunch, as the dirty dishes were being picked up by the kitchen staff, everyone told Melanie what a wonderful job she had done and that they appreciated it. Melanie responded appropriately; then everyone transferred to the family room to finish enjoying one another's company. The two hours went by too fast, and when it was time for everyone to return to their duties, things felt gloomy suddenly. Everyone gave hugs to everyone before going their separate ways. During that family time, Andrew's and Camillia's parents bonded on a personal level, and they had the chief to thank for that, and they did thank him. He was the one who brought them together. The chief felt that the family time that day was a productive one. Andrew and Camillia kept the chief in their family room to speak with him after everyone was gone. They wanted to thank him for bringing their parents together, and they told him that no matter what, they were still his children, and they loved him very much.

Camillia wanted to change the subject so Andrew and the chief waited to hear what she had to say. Knowing that Andrew was going to make a public announcement for the need of volunteer test subjects that evening, she asked when they would be checking in on the science hall to see where they were with the serum and vaccine. Camillia could not get the serum out of her thoughts and wanted it done right away although she knew that it would take more time than she would like.

Andrew told her that if it would make her happy, they could go by the science hall before dinner. Andrew asked the chief if he wanted to accompany them to the science hall, and he told Andrew that it might prove to be interesting. They decided not to wait to go because they wanted the scientists to be able to slowly walk them through what they had at that moment and to answer any questions that they might have. They went out to get on their horses and make their way to the science hall.

They got there, got off their horses, tied them to a pole, went inside of the building, announced themselves, then asked where they stood with the serum that they were making for the king and queen. The lead scientist just happened to be there at the time that Andrew, Camillia, and the chief got there. That was good because no one had to stop working to give them the tour with explanations. The lead scientist told them that they were not going to develop a serum as they knew it to be; they would be producing more of a booster shot. They had broken down the original serum to individual ingredients then found out which ingredient was responsible for what reaction in a human. They could pick a few ingredients that were obvious necessities to the booster shot for the king and queen. They went on to tell Andrew that the product would be more like a booster shot and had the potential to be uncomfortable but not as painful as the original injection. The scientist looked at Camillia and told her that they were making sure it would be safe for her and her unborn child. The scientist told them that they were ready for their first test subject and that the booster would be either too weak to make any changes or just about right to combat the human trait that appeared to be left in Andrew and Camillia. The science team knew that the reason Andrew and Camillia were still able to reproduce after receiving the original serum was due to them both having extra chromosomes and an odd number at that; it was like a never-seen natural mutation. The scientists theorized that the booster shot would not affect the reproduction process because the chemicals being used did not target the reproductive system as to where the original serum had chemicals that affected the reproductive system, and it may have killed some of the normal chromosomes but could not kill the mutated chromosomes. The scientist did add that the first test subject would have to be either the king or queen because the booster would not affect the community pale ones. Their change was complete, but Andrew and Camillia's change was not complete as they knew because they had blatantly shown some human traits. Camillia and Andrew told the chief scientist that they would both try the booster shot because if it were to kill one, the other would not want to be left behind to be lonely.

The chief did not like the idea of them both being the test subject, but he understood where they were coming from. The chief asked the scientist how soon they would be ready to give the booster, and he replied that it could be done whenever the king and queen were ready. They said they were ready at that time so the scientist told them to lie on the floor for their protection; he did not want them to fall if the effect were to cause them to briefly weaken at the knees as the original serum had done. They did as they were asked, told each other they loved the other, grabbed each other's hand, shut their eyes, then told the scientist to inject them. The chief was extremely nervous; he did not want to lose his son, daughter, or his unborn grandchild. The injection was given, and all the scientists gathered around to watch intently. The king and queen started to exhibit seizure-like activity, but the lead scientist knew it was not a seizure—it was the vaccine spreading throughout their bodies. The severe shaking stopped after three minutes. Everyone was watching with anticipation. Andrew and Camillia lay there lifelessly for another two minutes.

Suddenly, they both gasped for air and slowly opened their eyes. They looked around as if they were confused about where they were. They sat up slowly then looked at each other and smiled at each other. They had survived the booster shot, but did it combat the human traits, and how would they know? The scientist was sure that if the booster shot worked, the couple would be stronger and faster than other pale ones. They would also have their five senses more sensitive than any other pale one or animal for that matter. The chief asked them how they felt, and they both told him that they felt great so he helped them up off the floor. Camillia could feel the baby inside her even though the pregnancy was not far enough to normally feel the baby. The lead scientist asked Andrew and Camillia a series of questions and had them both perform some specific tasks, and with the results they got, it appeared that the booster shot did better than just remove their human traits. Another good thing was that it did not appear to harm the pregnancy, but the lead scientist suggested that he and the king and queen go to the hospital to get checked out with the baby just to be sure. The couple agreed to see the doctor. The chief asked if they would mind if he tagged along; the couple told him to please come along for at least moral support; after all, he was the child's grandparent.

The scientist, the chief, Andrew, and Camillia went to the hospital unannounced. They found the doctor at the nurse's desk so they approached him all at once. When the doctor saw everyone going at him all at once, he started to feel a bit overwhelmed. When they got closer to the doctor, he could read their minds and realized that it was just an unplanned early prenatal visit. He began to relax and became curious as to why Camillia was going in so early. They were standing at the nurse's desk, and Camillia spoke up and told the doctor that she needed an early prenatal visit. He asked her if something was wrong. She told him that it was his job to determine that. Camillia explained that she and

Andrew had gotten a booster shot from the head scientist to get rid of their human traits, and she just needed to know if it had affected the baby and if so how. The doctor was happy to be a part of her completely being turned into a pale one because he knew how much it meant to her and that he believed that it would help Camillia have easier pregnancies with quicker deliveries and to be healthy all the way through the experience. He also hoped that she and her body would be able to handle being pregnant all the time.

The doctor led them into a private room. He got out the ultrasound machine and looked at the baby; it looked good. Like before, the doctor asked if she felt okay, and she said that she felt great and that she could feel the unborn baby, which she could not feel previously. The doctor then listened to the baby's heartbeat and that sounded good, and as it was on the last visit, she appeared to have only one baby inside her womb. The doctor told everyone that mom and baby seemed to have a good bill of health so far. Everyone went outside to go their diverse ways; the scientist would go back to the science hall while the chief would go to his side of the castle, and Camillia and Andrew would go to their home. They all mounted their horses, and just before the scientist headed back to the science hall, he told Andrew and Camillia to check in with him periodically. He wanted to find out if the vaccination gave them any extra abilities and to monitor how it affected the abilities that they already had, if it did. The couple agreed to check in once a week on the same day that they would be going to the doctor, and everyone went their separate ways.

Before the chief could get too far ahead of them, Andrew and Camillia invited him over to their side of the castle. He appreciated the offer, and after careful thought, he agreed to go with them to their home. Andrew and Camillia asked the chief if he would do something for them; he said of course, he would do anything for them, they were his only children. Andrew asked for him to monitor their every thought and action for any signs of change from the vaccine. Camillia told them that she had noticed some changes already.

She had a telepathic link with the unborn child; it was just as if it had a conscience already. She could feel the child growing stage by stage; she even told Andrew and the chief that she knew for sure that the unborn child was another girl and an only child in the womb. After talking for a few moments, they got the horses moving at a slow pace and headed back to their side of the castle.

Andrew and Camillia were picking up on everyone's thoughts as they passed by. This was unusual because normally they had to be within arm's reach or closer to pick up on other thoughts, and if someone did not want their minds read, they could block the reading. The couple found out that no one could block their minds from being read by them, but they could tell when they tried. They hoped that it would not be a problem for them to constantly be hearing everyone's thoughts. They also realized that they could see farther than a normal pale one and in greater detail. They had more energy and could move faster than before. They also noticed that their hearing was more acute; they were hearing things before they could visually focus on them. They could even hear their blood pumping through their veins.

While they were riding home, they shared that information with the chief, and he was more and more amazed at what they were telling him. The chief, Camillia, and Andrew made it to Andrew and Camillia's home so they let the stable boy take the horses while they went inside of the home. Once inside, they realized how late it was. It was practically dinnertime so they went to the castle's private dining hall and got settled. As usual, Melanie provided them with a fabulous meal. They ate until they were stuffed to the gills then retired to the family room. While the castle's workers were finishing up with their chores for the evening, the chief, Andrew, and Camillia visited with one another and discussed the vaccine some more. The chief was fascinated by the vaccine and relieved that it did not harm or kill them or the unborn baby. Andrew and Camillia could not wait for family time the next day so they could share the news of the vaccine; only the chief knew that the science hall was working on something of that nature for them so they certainly did not have any knowledge of the vaccine being administered. The chief cut the conversation short because it was getting a bit late and he wanted to leave some time for the couple to spend together prior to turning in for the evening. The couple appreciated his gesture and told him that they would be seeing him the next day for family time if not before. The chief went home and went directly to bed.

Andrew and Camillia took some time to go to each one of their children's bedrooms and give them some good night love. After visiting with their children, the couple went to their bedroom and got ready for bed. They lay down to relax and cuddle together. Andrew had one of his arms around Camillia and rested his hand on her abdomen. She had a small baby bump, and he loved to rub her belly when she was pregnant. Camillia got excited when Andrew put his hand on her stomach because she could feel that the baby knew that her daddy was there. Andrew told Camillia that he could feel what the baby was feeling; he could even detect the baby's heartbeat. The couple was excited that upon physical contact, Andrew could get a telepathic link with the baby; that appeared to be a new bonus from getting the vaccine. The couple realized at that moment that they got so involved with themselves and the vaccine that they had not checked with the scientists to see where they were with the vaccine for the walking dead. They agreed that after breakfast, they would return to the science hall so they could get updated on the status of that vaccine. Andrew and Camillia got comfortable in bed and went to sleep.

CHAPTER TWENTY EIGHT

The next morning, Andrew and Camillia woke up feeling great. They were well rested and full of physical energy. Their minds were picking up on everyone's thoughts and feelings in the castle. The couple found it to be a good asset; it did not overwhelm them.

They got their day clothes on and went out to the private dining hall to have breakfast while the rest of the community went to the community dining hall. Camillia and Andrew ate a rather small amount of their breakfast; they were in somewhat of a hurry to get their day started. Their first stop would be at the science hall; the couple wanted to be there when the scientists first arrived there. Andrew sent word for the stable boy to saddle two horses while Camillia briefly visited with Melanie and her parents. Her parents reported that they loved their work and that they had a lot of fun creating meals and desserts for her and Andrew. Melanie was proud of her parents for the work they did, and they did not mind working under their daughter. Camillia was proud of all her staff and was very thankful that all her friends were close to her. Not everyone was able to work with their family or friends. Camillia was also thankful that her friends could keep their parents close to them.

Andrew cut Camillia's time with Melanie short by calling to her, saying that the horses were ready. Camillia hugged Melanie and her parents and told them that she could not wait to see them for family time then walked over to Andrew. Together, Andrew and Camillia walked out of the front door of the castle and mounted their horses and headed to the science hall. As the couple approached the science hall, they saw the scientists going into the building. They quickly closed the gap between them and the science hall, slid off their horses, tied them to the pole that was provided, then went into the building. The head scientist was there and would be for a short while. Andrew asked the lead scientist for a report on their progress with the vaccine for the walking dead. He walked Andrew and Camillia through the lab and showed them the different combinations of plant extracts and explained what the combinations would most likely do to a walking dead individual.

The lead scientist told them that it was difficult to make a complete single vaccine because they did not know what viruses and bacterias they would be dealing with other than the obvious radiation poisoning. Each combination of plant extract would target a specific virus or bacteria, but the science team wanted to make a single vaccine that would target everything. So far, they had a series of vaccinations that would only target one thing. They also said that there was another difficulty—not every walking dead would be in the same stage of the disease process so the vaccine may help some, kill some, or do absolutely nothing for others. They theorized that they may have to inject some of the walking dead multiple times because they would be worse off than the rest of those that may have the potential of being helped. They figured some may be suffering minimal effects from the earth's surface and may only require a single injection. Finally, there may be no hope for some of the walking dead.

The scientist then told Andrew and Camillia that there was the issue of examining them and speaking with them prior to giving any injection so they could estimate who would require what treatment, if any. Andrew knew that there would be an issue with abducting the walking dead because there were so many of them and they slept together in the same old run-down casino building. It would be difficult to abduct a small group of the walking dead without being noticed by the other walking dead. There would also be an issue with getting them to walk a medium distance from the old building to the tunnel wall; they may not be able to make it. Andrew already knew that once the scouts got them behind the tunnel wall, they would be injected there. That way, the location and existence of the pale ones' colony would not be compromised. If the vaccine worked, then they would give them the serum to turn them and could take them to the compound, but there was the question of what to do to those whom the vaccine did not work on or kill. The vaccination project for the walking dead was obviously going to be a trial-by-error project.

To Camillia, the walking dead project seemed to be too risky for the scouts and Andrew. Andrew told the scientist that he would deal with getting small groups of the walking dead just behind the tunnel wall so that the scientists could do their job, but unlike before, the scientists would have to be part of the abduction crew. Andrew also told the scientist that he would figure out what to do with the walking dead that the vaccination would not work for and did not kill. The head scientist told Andrew that it would be no problem to join them. Camillia asked the scientist if he could estimate how much longer it would be until the vaccine was ready. He told her that they were trying to make a single vaccine to where it would combat all known viruses and bacterias as well as reversing the effects of radiation poisoning. The scientist told Andrew and Camillia that it was definitely going to take more time and that he could not give an estimation as to when the vaccine would be ready. Andrew and Camillia knew that the scientists were working hard on the walking dead's vaccine and that they had a lot of barriers to break, but they all had hope;

they liked a good challenge and, so far, have overcome all their challenges. The scientists believed that the walking dead vaccine challenge would be overcome also.

Camillia and Andrew thanked the science team for their time and told them to stay in touch. As they were walking out of the building, Andrew looked back and told the head scientist that he would take care of getting them to the earth's surface and back so they could do their job. The head scientist thanked Andrew as Andrew continued to walk out. Camillia and Andrew got back on their horses and headed for home; they had spent all morning at the science hall getting the grand tour, looking at what vaccines were made, discussing the ultimate vaccine to be made, and briefly talking about the abduction trip. By the time they got home, it would be time to go to the living room to meet up with their friends and go to the castle's private dining hall. Camillia could not wait for family time so she could tell her friends about the vaccine that she and Andrew had received. Andrew could feel Camillia's excitement growing as they got closer and closer to home.

Finally, Camillia and Andrew got home and gave their horses' reins to the stable boy. They wasted no time getting inside of the castle, and just as they thought, people were starting to gather in their family room for family time. Camillia could hardly wait for everyone to start sharing their day so she could share her and Andrew's exciting news. Camillia and Andrew were not going to say anything about the vaccine for the walking dead that was being made because it was not known yet if it would work on any of them or just some of them or maybe even kill them. There was also the issue of abducting them in small groups without being caught by the rest of the walking dead. Besides, just as they kept the adults' abduction a secret because the chief wanted everyone in the colony to be able to focus on their duties and themselves, Andrew and Camillia wanted the same with the situation of the walking dead.

Everyone finally got to the family room so together they shifted to the castle's private dining hall and took their seats. Melanie had lunch served immediately, and it was a wonderful-looking meal as usual. Everyone started to eat, and the sharing time was to begin. Camillia was sure that hers and Andrew's news might take up most, if not all the lunch hour between telling them what she had to say and answering questions that her friends might have so she asked everyone if she and Andrew could share their day first. Everyone could feel her excitement and was eager to find out what it was all about so they all said for her to please share first. Andrew was just as excited as Camillia and wanted to share their experience as well, but he wanted his wife to share everything because he knew what it meant to her to be able to reveal their scientific endeavor. Camillia shifted in her seat to get comfortable, which had everyone else on the edge of their seats and leaning into the large round dining table. Things were so intense that everyone stopped eating at that moment.

Camillia broke the silence and started to tell of her and Andrew's adventure-like experience. She said that she and Andrew had put in a request with the head scientist at the science hall to produce a serum to take away the small amount of human qualities left in them so they would be completely pale ones. She said that they were not ashamed to still have human traits, but it seemed to affect her pregnancies in that she was at such an elevated risk. She was sure it was because of still having the human traits. Everyone had a look of curiosity on their faces and remained quiet, waiting to hear more. Camillia said that she would try to make the long story shorter. The group told her not to worry about making her experience shorter because they did not want to miss out on anything. They all said that they were willing to give up their sharing time to hear of her and Andrew's wonderful day. Camillia thanked the group then went on with telling them of her and Andrew's day. She said that the scientists were very happy to work on a serum to change their human traits and that the lead scientist called in all the scientists and divided them into groups so that they could work around the clock. She continued and told her friends that the next day, she was anxious to see how far the science hall had come in the project so Andrew took her to the science hall to check on their progress. Camillia told them that to her surprise, the scientists were ready to try out a vaccine. She explained that per the lead scientist, a serum would have probably killed them so the scientists came up with the lesser of the strengths of injection by producing a basic vaccine. She explained that the serum would have targeted all their body systems and the vaccine only targeted the systems that were still humanlike.

Everyone understood what she was saying about the difference between the serum and the vaccine. She told her friends that the scientists were keeping in mind that she was pregnant so they made sure that the vaccine was not too strong in targeting the reproductive system so it did not harm or terminate the pregnancy. She told them that the scientists used the original serum to break it down to each individual ingredient and to know what system of the human body that it targeted and how. She said that then they took the ingredients that targeted the systems that she and Andrew still had human qualities in and combined them to make the vaccine; it was quite simple. Camillia paused for a moment to catch her breath, and the group of friends told her to hurry and continue because they could not wait to hear the rest of the event. Camillia started to speak again; she told her friends that when they went to the science hall, the scientists gave her and Andrew a tour as they explained specifically what they had done, and then they explained in detail about their vaccine for the couple and Camillia just happened to ask the scientist if they had any idea when they would be ready to test the vaccine. Camillia revealed that the scientists said that they were ready to test the vaccine at that point in time.

Everyone gasped and moved yet closer into the round table to make sure they did not miss out on any details. She continued and told them that the head scientist told her and Andrew that they could not test the vaccine out on anyone but them. The scientist felt that the vaccine would do nothing for a pure pale one, and it was definitely not strong enough to turn a human, besides there were no humans to use as test subjects. The scientist even thought of using a walking dead but realized that a walking dead would be an inappropriate test subject; they needed a healthy individual as a test subject. The only obvious choice for a test subject was her and Andrew. It was a high-risk gamble in what it would do to them if anything, but the couple made the split-second decision to go ahead with it being tested on themselves. Everyone was stunned to hear that she and Andrew were willing to be the test subjects and risk their lives as well as the life of the unborn baby.

Camillia told them that they were aware of the risks but that they felt that if it killed her, it would be quick and painless because the way that her pregnancies were going and having already coming close to killing her, it would be better to die quickly from the vaccine than slowly from the pregnancies. Andrew spoke up and told their friends that the reason he decided to be a test subject at the same time as Camillia was to live or die with his beloved. He said that if it killed Camillia, he could not imagine his life without her. Everyone thought that the gesture was a romantic one. Camillia told her friends that they then lay on the floor in the science lab, held hands, then told the head scientist to inject them together. Camillia told her friends that the vaccine was not painful. It was more like having an out-of-body experience for about ten minutes; then they felt like they were overly aware of their surroundings, and the next thing they knew, they were being helped off the floor. She said that the vaccine seemed to work.

Their friends asked how they knew that the vaccine did something for them. Camillia told them that their telepathy was stronger, they were faster than before, their eyesight and hearing was stronger, their sense of smell was stronger, they had much more energy, and they were even able to have a telepathic link with the unborn child. Their friends were amazed at the results and relieved that they did not die from the vaccine. Their friends asked them why they did not say anything about the vaccine prior to now. Andrew spoke up and told them that it all happened so fast; it started after the prior day's family time and was completed by that evening. He added that Camillia had been so anxious for the current family time so she could fill everyone in on the whole experience. It was now time for the kitchen crew to gather the dishes from the table, but when they got out to the table, they noticed that no one had eaten much of their meal. Melanie knew why no one had eaten much so she told the kitchen crew to come back for the dishes a while later so everyone could finish eating. Everyone began to eat again as they shared their thoughts of the vaccine endeavor with Andrew and Camillia. They all expressed their relief of the couple's survival and were extremely pleased that the vaccine worked.

Camillia informed them that although the vaccine did not negatively affect the current pregnancy, they would have to wait to see if she and Andrew would still be able to reproduce. Everyone was shocked by that revelation. Camillia told her friends that the scientist theorized that she would still be able to reproduce due to the current pregnancy surviving the final change. As everyone finished their meals, they told Camillia and Andrew that they would be in their prayers for the ability to reproduce. Camillia's friends knew that having children pleased Camillia and Andrew beyond what words could describe, and it would break their hearts if they lost that ability. The kitchen crew started to gather up the dishes from the dining table while everyone continued to discuss Andrew and Camillia's experience. Camillia reminded her friends that the vaccine gave her the ability to have a telepathic link to the unborn baby and that she could physically feel the unborn child grow in her uterus. Andrew intervened and told their friends that upon contact with Camillia's abdomen, he could feel the unborn baby's feelings and growth also. Camillia went on to tell them that she knew for a fact that the unborn child was another girl so she wanted her friends to help her with coming up with a girl's name for the baby. Her friends questioned her as to how she knew she was carrying a girl since it was still too early for the doctor to even tell. Camillia told them that the telepathic link along with the new ability to feel the baby's growth left her with that information.

Andrew interrupted and told their friends that he got the same impression from the unborn child also. Everyone was amazed at the couple's deduction and agreed to help with some baby girl names. Camillia revealed that the baby could hear outside of the womb at that point of her pregnancy. They asked how she knew that, and she replied that the baby responded to their voices specifically and positively; she was already aware of who was who. She said that the baby did not respond to strangers' voices individually; she simply responded to them as just another outside noise. The group was surprised that the baby already had a relationship of some sorts with them. They asked Camillia if she would mind if they greeted and spoke to the baby while touching her abdomen. She said that she would not mind at all and that it would even be a clever idea; the baby just like the rest of her children needed to be shown love also. Family time was about over so everyone went into the living room and lined up for their turn to interact with the unborn baby. After everyone was done paying attention to the baby, Camillia told them that it was a positive and wonderful experience and that the baby liked it too. Everyone agreed that when they dealt with Camillia individually throughout the day, they would at least tell the baby hello.

CHAPTER TWENTY NINE

Everyone finished with their goodbyes and went their own way. Andrew and Camillia had to have a meeting with the chief about how to deal with the Walking Dead's abductions. Andrew believed that speaking to the chief for general advice would be the best resource at that time. The chief had an extensive amount of experience abducting humans, and Andrew needed all the tips and tricks that the chief could offer. Andrew and Camillia knew that abducting the walking dead was going to be tricky only because they all stayed together always and there was no way that Andrew and the scouts could abduct them all at one time; there were too many of them. It was also important to keep the scouts safe. The abduction of the walking dead was starting to prove practically impossible.

Andrew and Camillia were at the chief's side of the castle and knocked on the door. The butler answered and knew that they were there to see the chief, so without question, he simply led them to the chief's office where he was documenting the additional happenings of the week up to the point that they were at. The chief greeted them and the baby then asked what he could do for them. Andrew told him that he needed some firsthand insight on the art of abducting humans. The chief told Andrew that there were no more humans left above ground and asked what a firsthand insight could do for them now. Andrew informed the chief that the science team was working around the clock to develop a vaccine for the walking dead. They were hoping to heal them from disease then turn them into pale ones and bring them to the land of grandeur. Andrew told the chief that those individuals were someone's family member or friend that was already a pale one. It seemed to Andrew that if he could unite the entire living family, things might be even better for their community because down inside, the pale ones knew that they still had family and friends missing from their lives due to the diseases.

Even though the chief did not know of the history behind the walking dead and how they got the way they were, Andrew and Camillia did. The chief asked Andrew if he would mind telling the story behind the walking dead, and Andrew told him he would explain how the walking dead came about. The chief showed Andrew and Camillia to the family room, and they all sat, got comfortable, and Andrew began to speak. Andrew told him that many of the humans prepared for the nuclear war but that it only consisted of the wealthy humans. He told the chief that it was quite simple, really; once the nuclear bombs went off, many of the people died right away. Those that did not die succumbed to the effects of the bombs' radiation and fell gravely ill. Those that survived without any effects acclimated to a new lifestyle inside the safe houses and learned how to protect themselves from the radiation in transport to and from the school.

Andrew went on to tell the chief that those who were ill were forced to live together in one of the town's old run-down casino buildings. It became a law for them to keep to themselves. If any of the ill humans were caught near the colony of the healthy humans, they were shot dead by the robo security and their bodies would be taken back to their area. Andrew told the chief that many of the humans begged their friends and loved ones to let them into their safe house after the bombs had done their damage, but the healthy humans refused to help the exposed humans because they were already sick from the radiation and the healthy humans did not want to chance being affected also.

It was a tough decision for the wealthy humans to make and even tougher for the sick humans to accept. The chief told Andrew that the story of the walking dead was unfortunate and that if he could help in any way he would. The chief was curious if Andrew and Camillia had any relatives or friends that were among the walking dead, and they both answered yes. Andrew had some friends and so did Camillia, but neither had any family members among them. Andrew told the chief that the scientists were sworn to secrecy because just like preparing for the adult abductions, he wanted the community to function as normal and be surprised when they brought them, but in case they could not get the adults, he did not want the community to be affected by such a huge loss. The chief swore his secrecy and said he would start to think of ideas on how the scouts could retrieve the walking dead safely. Andrew and Camillia thanked the chief for his silence about the project as well as his input and advice. The chief told Andrew and Camillia that prior to abducting any humans, he had to send out all the scouts to get an idea of how many humans they were going to have to deal with. The scouts went back and reported how many children there were and how many adults there were. The chief said that during that trip, the scouts had to familiarize themselves on how to get into the smart houses without being detected. He continued and told Andrew that at first, they were going to abduct the children from home but later realized it was too dangerous, so they then devised a plan to lure the children to the tunnel wall.

Just then Andrew had an idea, and he wanted to speak to the head scientist to see if his idea was feasible. Camillia knew what Andrew was thinking so when he stood up to leave, she did too. The chief asked what was going on, and Andrew told him to follow him and that they were going to the science hall and he would explain to everyone at once. Everyone went outside, and the chief asked his stable boy to saddle up three horses so they could travel fast. Since Andrew and Camillia walked to the chief's house, they needed horses too. The stable boy brought out the saddled horses, and the chief, Andrew, and Camillia mounted a horse and left for the science hall. They had to work swiftly because dinner was approaching rapidly.

Everyone got to the science hall and made it inside. Andrew immediately asked for the head scientist. One of the regular scientists got the lead scientist for him, and everyone greeted everyone. Andrew asked the scientist if they could use long-distance dart guns that could hold multiple darts each. Andrew suggested that the scouts could use the dart guns to knock out all the walking dead then vaccinate them, and if it was a successful vaccination, they could then bring them to the land of grandeur. The only thing they needed the scientists' help with was in how to tell that the vaccine had worked. The scientist told Andrew that the sores on their bodies would heal right before their eyes, and their skin color would go from a gray color to a fleshy pink color then to a pale blue. The scientist told Andrew that his idea was a grand one and may very well work.

Camillia had a concern about the new idea. Once they had put all the walking dead to sleep and gave them the vaccine while they were knocked out, how would they separate the new pale ones from those who were alive but not turned? Andrew said that it might be possible to try a second vaccine right away if the original dose was not strong enough. The chief suggested that Andrew do what he had done and have the scouts go out and find out how many walking dead they would be dealing with and divide the number into adults and children. The chief's idea was a good one;

it would help the scouts in knowing how many individuals they would have to keep control of, and they could use the children to control the adults. The scientist reminded Andrew that the vaccine may not be strong enough for the lesser-affected walking dead, and then it may even kill the walking dead that may be very sick and ready to die. The scientist told Andrew that the walking dead were getting repeated exposure so the quicker they could act, the more walking dead they would likely save. Andrew decided that he and the scouts would make a trip of observation with the possibility of turning into an abduction trip the following night. They needed to find out how many walking dead there might be because Andrew knew that they could handle a total of one hundred walking dead at one time. Andrew told the chief that he wanted him to get their runners to get all the scouts together in his living room immediately.

The chief acted right away on his orders. The chief left the science hall to get his and Andrew's runners to get all the scouts gathered together in Andrew's living room. Andrew asked the scientist if he could put together some tranquilizers for a dart gun, and the scientist told Andrew that it would be an easy task and that he and the other scientists would start getting them ready. The head scientist told Andrew that they would produce the tranquilizer darts as fast as they could and when he got back the next morning they would make sure that they produced two darts per walking dead in case it was not strong enough for some or if they missed their target. Andrew told the scientist that he would take what they had made by the time it was time for them to leave. Andrew could not believe that there would be more than one hundred of the walking dead total so that would be two hundred tranquilizer darts and two hundred vaccine injections. Andrew thanked the head scientist and told him that he would be back the following day; then he and Camillia left the science hall to get home to receive the scouts. Andrew got back to his home and instructed his stable boy to return the two horses to the chief's stable boy then get back in a hurry because they would be getting company at any time. The stable boy wasted no time and barely made it back home to start receiving guests' horses.

Twenty minutes after the first scout arrived, the last scout walked through the door. The scouts were standing in the front room talking about their day's events and their families. Andrew loudly interrupted them and asked them to sit down and give him their attention. Everyone sat down and got quiet. Andrew started to tell the scouts that they would be leaving the next evening for an observation journey possibly turned into an abduction journey. He told the scouts that he needed a head count of how many adult walking dead and child walking dead there were. Andrew told the scouts that he wanted to tranquilize all the walking dead at once using dart guns then vaccinate all of them and bring back the ones that not only responded to the vaccine but also survived the change that the vaccine would cause. The scouts were surprised to hear that there were walking dead on the earth's surface. The scouts had heard of the walking dead and of their story of existence but never realized the story was true; they had never seen one in all the times they went above ground to get the humans.

Andrew told the scouts that unlike usual, he would be going out to the old run-down casino for several reasons. One reason was to show the scouts where they were located; the next reason was to determine whether to do the abduction right then. The scouts questioned doing the mass abduction on an observation journey. Andrew explained that if they could handle all the walking dead on the current trip planned, then they should because all the walking dead would know that something strange had happened to them. Andrew reminded them that like all the other abductions, they needed the element of surprise. Without that, they would most likely fail to succeed in their abduction operation. Everyone agreed that they needed the element of surprise. Andrew asked if everyone was good with the plan and if not to speak up and give their reason so he could address the situation. Everyone said that they were good with the plan. Andrew asked everyone if there were any ideas or alterations for the plan that no one else had noticed. Again, everyone said that they were good with the plan on hand. Andrew said everyone could go home and that they would meet right after dinner there at his family room.

Everyone was gone so Andrew went to find Camillia. She was in their bedroom resting in a chair and waiting for him to finish with the scouts. Camillia stood up from the bedroom chair when Andrew walked in, and she met him halfway through the bedroom. They stood at the foot of their bed and held each other for a short while. While Andrew was holding Camillia, he had his right hand on her abdomen and was talking to the unborn baby. Both Andrew and Camillia could feel what seemed to be a response from the infant. The baby was moving all about in Camillia's womb, and they both were picking up on telepathic messages. It was apparent that the child knew that Andrew was her father and she wanted to share the love he was giving with him.

It came time for dinner so Andrew and Camillia kissed each other and then let go of each other to go to the castle's private dining hall. Bridgette and her parents were at the dining table with the children next to them. It was not often that they could join the couple for dinner because they held a different schedule with the children, but it was nice when they could. Melanie got dinner on the table for the adults and had a small snack for Armellya and warm milk for the twins, Kaylina and Kevin. Everyone had a fabulous meal, and Andrew and Camillia could have an adult conversation with Bridgette and her parents about how the children were growing and the milestones that they had reached. Bridgette told the couple that Armellya had some talents that were unbelievable. Not only was her telepathy extra strong but that she was also telekinetic. Andrew and Camillia were both beyond belief because that ability had not been spoken of, but the chief did say that there was not a full list of abilities for the offspring of the chosen ones. The conversation with Bridgette was very helpful to her parents because now they had an idea of what to watch for in the twins. Dinner soon was over, and Bridgette and her parents needed to get the children bathed and ready for bed. Andrew needed to get to bed early so he could go to the science hall before leaving for the observation and possible abduction journey. Andrew and Camillia went to their bedroom and changed into their bed clothes then went to bed and cuddled together to fall asleep.

The morning hour arrived, and it was time for Andrew and Camillia to get out of bed. Camillia had to go to the census hall to make sure the census girl was finished with documenting the new arrivals with their professions next to their names, especially since there was to possibly be another mass abduction. Andrew had to get to the science hall to make sure they were done with the tranquilizer darts and vaccine for the walking dead and that they had two hundred of each. The chief wanted to catch up with Andrew before he got to the science hall. The chief had a demanding time sleeping because he had been thinking about how the walking dead had been turned away by their family and friends after the nuclear bombs landed. He was afraid that the issue of being turned away might harbor some negative feelings in the hearts of the walking dead, and he wondered how that would go over between them and their family or friends once they were all at the commune.

The chief was having his breakfast at his private dining hall, and Andrew and Camillia had their breakfast at their private dining hall as well. The chief finished his meal ten minutes before Andrew and Camillia so he made it to their home before either of them left for the day. They could feel the intensity of his thoughts so Andrew asked him what was bothering him so much. The chief told Andrew that there may be a problem if he and the scouts bring the walking dead back. Andrew and Camillia could still feel the chief's feelings being in an uproar, but they could not fathom why. As far as Andrew could see, he was doing a good thing for the rest of the surviving individuals and their pale one friends and relatives.

Finally, to get Andrew to see things from his perspective, he bluntly told Andrew that there were many of the walking dead that begged for help from friends and family in the domed houses and they were turned away and exiled. After that incident, the healthy humans continued to thrive, and the walking dead suffered immensely. It was the suffering and being forgotten about that may have hardened the hearts of the walking dead. The chief asked Andrew, suppose they came to the land of grandeur and confronted their loved ones and it led to a negative situation? The chief wanted to know who was supposed to keep them from fighting. The chief reminded Andrew that the commune was for people who were kind and forgiving. He asked Andrew, what if the walking dead could not find it in their hearts to forgive? Andrew and Camillia were quite astonished to see the issue through the chief's eyes. Everything the chief said was definitely possible.

CHAPTER THIRTY

Andrew needed some time to think about bringing the walking dead to the compound, and he had to conclude by the time the scouts arrived. Andrew and Camillia could feel that the chief felt some relief for getting his thoughts out in the open, but there was still a great concern for how Andrew was going to handle the situation. Andrew felt trapped between keeping the commune mentally stable and saving as many of the walking dead as possible. This decision was the hardest thing Andrew has had to deal with as king of the land of grandeur. Andrew felt that he needed to discuss the pros and cons of both sides of the situation with Camillia and the chief. The discussion was to happen immediately. Camillia was going to have to visit the census hall later, and Andrew would have to see the scientists before leaving on the journey, if he was even to go. In their discussion, they came up with a lot of small pros and a lot of small cons that could be overcome with both the pale ones' cooperation and the walking dead's cooperation. The cooperation was where they got stuck in the conversation because they had no way of knowing how the pale ones and the walking dead would react with one another.

Camillia said she had two ideas. Andrew and the chief looked at her inquisitively. One of her ideas was to speak to the public and let them know that there was a plan to bring the walking dead that can be turned healthily back to the compound and remind the people that the ones who would be brought back would be someone's friend or family member.

After the announcement, the people should be allowed to speak and explain how they feel about the idea. With that idea comes the second idea. If it were to be decided that it would be best not to bring the walking dead to the compound or the public opposes, then the walking dead could still all be tranquilized and changed then left at the empty domed houses to live with some dignity. Andrew and the chief thought that both ideas were good, and it seemed that making the announcement to the pale ones before lunchtime would be the thing to do then take the situation from there. Also, having the announcement prior to lunchtime would allow for the friends to still have their family time if everyone was still up to it. Andrew and the chief sent their runners out into the small town to have everyone gather at the spiritual hall for the announcement.

The chief, Andrew, and Camillia went to the spiritual hall to await the townspeople. Everyone started to trickle in faster and faster until eventually, everyone was there and very curious of what was so important to have a town meeting in the middle of everyone's workday. Andrew started to speak. He told the townspeople that there were walking dead above ground that they could heal and turn. Everyone suddenly seriously focused on Andrew. He continued by telling them that he knew those people were friends or family to some of the pale ones already there, and he wanted to give everyone a chance at a good and productive life. Andrew asked the public for their input on whether to bring the walking dead to the compound.

Nearly everyone raised their hand with something to say or ask. Andrew called on someone, and they had a question. They wanted to assure that the walking dead would be completely healed and turned. Andrew told the public that they were going to vaccinate all the walking dead, and for those who were strong enough to survive the complete change, they would be brought to the commune. Andrew added that those who did not survive would be given a proper burial on the earth's surface. Andrew asked the community if they felt that they could work through the possible hard feelings associated with turning their family member or friend away when they lived in their safe houses on the earth's surface. It was unanimous that everyone felt guilty for turning their loved ones away, but they had no choice if they wanted to remain healthy themselves; their friends and family members had already been exposed to the radiation. They were diseased and contagious.

At that point, Andrew knew that it was important to know if the walking dead would be ready to work through the possible hard feelings from being turned away. Andrew told everyone that he would do his best to get their loved ones home to them. Everyone was excited about the possibility of having the rest of their loved ones there with them. They all disbanded and went back to their shops so Andrew, Camillia, and the chief went directly to the science hall.

Andrew, Camillia, and the chief got to the science hall when the scientists were getting there. Everyone went inside together, and Andrew asked about the difference in how the original serum that was used to turn the healthy humans and the vaccine that they would be using to turn the walking dead were different as far as their effects on brain function, specifically with reasoning. The scientists believed that they knew what Andrew was trying to ask since they too were in the community meeting. The lead scientist asked Andrew if he wanted to know how the walking dead's brain chemistry would change in that they could turn violent in any way whether it be physical, mental, or verbal. Andrew told the scientist that he would like to know just that information prior to bringing them to the commune and finding out the hard way that they were angry and willing to seek revenge on their loved ones.

The scientist explained that the original serum did massively increase the human intelligence quotient and that the vaccine would do the same for the walking dead. The brain was the largest target to both the serum and the vaccine. Andrew bluntly asked the lead scientist if that meant the walking dead would not be capable of harboring negative feelings and thoughts against the already pale ones. The lead scientist simply replied yes; they too would be peaceful people. Andrew asked the scientist if he was sure about the vaccine leading the walking dead to being peaceful. The scientist told Andrew that it would not wipe out their memory, but it would make it insignificant; everything would be put into the past and stay there. Andrew felt a sense of relief over the possibility of war in the land of grandeur. The chief then moved on to asking the scientist how he and his team were coming along with the tranquilizer darts and the vaccine. The scientist told the chief that there were two shifts working in the lab so they could prepare all two hundred of the tranquilizer darts and two hundred doses of the vaccine; it was all ready to be picked up by the scouts. Andrew, Camillia and the chief were very pleased with the scientists. They thanked the scientists and told them that they would be back after dinner to pick everything up. The lead scientist told Andrew that they would be ready for him and the scouts.

Everyone said their farewells for now, and Andrew, Camillia, and the chief left for the census hall to see if the job there was complete. Once they got to the census hall, Andrew and the chief waited outside with the horses while only Camillia went in. Camillia spoke to the head census worker and asked her if the new residents and their job positions had been recorded yet. The head census worker told Camillia that her workers had just finished that task. The census worker showed Camillia the document books and how they went from one book to three, and she speculated that there would be another full book once the walking dead got there. Camillia agreed and then told her that she had done an excellent job and good luck with the rest of the work. The census worker hugged Camillia then Camillia went back outside to report to Andrew. Andrew asked his wife how things were going for the census hall, and she told him that the records were up to date until the mass abduction. Andrew was pleased that the census hall had everything caught up.

It was close to family time so Andrew, Camillia, and the chief headed back to the couple's side of the castle to start to receive guests for that day's family time. There was so much for Camillia and Andrew to share during the day before family time that no one else had the opportunity to share their day so the couple planned on letting their friends take up the three hours of family time on the current day. When Andrew and Camillia got home with the chief, there were already pale ones gathered in their living room. Right after Camillia and Andrew walked into their home, the rest of the pale ones arrived. Everyone went into the castle's private dining hall to eat lunch and catch up on the latest gossip. Everyone wanted to interrogate Andrew about the abduction of the walking dead. They wanted to know when he would be leaving, when he would arrive at the old run-down casinos, and when he would be back to the community with their loved ones. Andrew answered their questions then asked some of his own questions. Everyone ate while they were asking and answering questions. Andrew told his friends that he and the scouts would be leaving after dinner and would return about twenty-four hours later. He asked his friends if they had ever rejected anyone after the nuclear bombs hit. They all said yes, that they were already exposed and sick as well as contagious, so they had no choice if they wanted to survive. They all hoped that their loved ones understood. Andrew told them that he would address that with them on the trip back to the commune.

The lunch hour came to an end and everyone was finished eating, so they relocated to the living room to finish with the two hours left with one another; they all spent some time talking to the unborn baby while rubbing Camillia's abdomen and the kitchen crew cleared and cleaned the round table. At that point, the conversation shifted to everyone cheerfully sharing their memories, thoughts, and plans regarding their walking dead loved ones. They could not wait to see their loved ones and hoped that they would survive the change although they stayed realistic and knew that it was a fifty-fifty chance that their loved ones would come back to them. The two-hour family time came to an end so everyone said their farewells then got back to work.

Before Andrew and Camillia could leave their living room, there was a knock at the front door. The butler answered the door and saw that it was the chief so the butler welcomed the chief to enter the couple's residence; then he led the chief to the family room to speak with Andrew and Camillia. The chief told the couple that he had eaten in the community dining hall so he could hear how the community was dealing with the walking dead situation. Andrew and Camillia perked up to listen closely to what the chief had to report. He told them that everyone was eager to see their loved ones but kept the situation realistic by keeping in mind that not all the walking dead would survive the change. Everyone remained upbeat, hopeful, and ready to focus on their community responsibilities. Andrew was thankful that everyone was ready to go to work and would be able to focus on their jobs.

Camillia reminded Andrew of her doctor's appointment for her weekly prenatal checkup in just a few hours so Andrew went to their bedroom to nap until the doctor's appointment. Andrew wanted to accompany Camillia to the hospital so he left strict words with Camillia to wake him a half hour before the appointment; she promised that she would. They kissed each other then Andrew told the unborn baby that he loved her while rubbing Camillia's belly. Camillia could feel the baby physically responding by moving about hard and quick. She and Andrew sensed a telepathic message of love from the baby. They spoke out loud and told the baby that they loved her also. After tucking Andrew into bed, Camillia went back out to the family room where the chief awaited her return. Camillia told the chief about her prenatal checkup and invited him to go with her and Andrew so he could see his granddaughter on the ultrasound machine. The chief was overjoyed about the invitation and sentimentally accepted the offer. The chief gave her a hug then rubbed her abdomen while telling the baby hello and speaking words of love to the unborn child. Camillia told the chief that the baby had a positive reaction to his touch and wanted to share words of love for her papa chief. The chief was thrilled that the vaccine Camillia and Andrew received was a success; it made her completely aware of her pregnancy and able to communicate with the unborn child, which he felt was truly a blessing. The chief hoped and prayed that the couple would still be able to conceive and that the pregnancies would all be a pleasant experience for the couple, and when it came time to deliver, the chief hoped that it would be a breeze.

Camillia took some time out to relax in the family room and have a cup of hot tea. She asked the chief to sit with her and offered him a cup of hot tea. The chief accepted the offer and sat with her. Camillia and the chief ended up having several cups of hot tea while discussing all the changes to the commune and with the pale ones since she and Andrew became the leaders of the land of grandeur. The chief complimented Camillia on how wonderful things had been and how well Andrew had solved so many difficult issues. He was very proud of them.

The time to wake Andrew had come so Camillia left the chief in the family room while she went to her bedroom to get Andrew up out of bed. When Camillia went to touch Andrew's shoulder to wake him, he was already somewhat awake so he grabbed her arm and pulled her into the bed next to himself. They both giggled and kissed. Andrew put his right hand on Camillia's belly and spoke to their unborn child. As usual, the child responded to her daddy; she moved about in excitement and telepathically shared her feelings of safety and love. Camillia sat up in the bed and told Andrew that they had to leave for the hospital soon and that she had invited the chief to go with them so he could see his grandchild on the ultrasound monitor. Andrew thought that was a very clever idea.

The couple got off the bed and straightened their clothing and fixed their hair then went out to the family room. The chief asked Andrew if he got enough rest for the upcoming journey, and Andrew told the chief that he did. They went outside and asked the stable boy for three saddled horses, and he got them ready and out to them in no time flat. The three of them headed for the hospital for Camillia's prenatal appointment with the doctor. They got to the hospital just on time to give their horses to the hospital stable boy and get inside. The doctor had been waiting for them for a few minutes. Camillia apologized for being a bit late, and the doctor told her that it was not a problem. The doctor led Andrew, Camillia, and the chief to a private room where Camillia got onto the hospital bed and lifted her shirt. The doctor got the ultrasound machine and placed it on her belly.

Right away, the baby turned so the doctor could determine the sex of the child. He asked the couple if they wanted to know if it was a boy or girl, and Camillia told the doctor that she knew it was a girl but to go ahead and confirm it. The doctor told them that they were right; the baby was a girl. He continued with the ultrasound to check the size of the baby, how much amniotic fluid appeared to surround the baby, and the position of the baby. Andrew and the chief were astonished at how much the doctor could tell with that small machine, and they watched the screen and saw the baby; they both thought it was incredible. The doctor used a different small handheld machine that allowed him and everyone else to hear the heartbeat. The doctor said that it sounded good as he was gently pushing around the outside of Camillia's belly. He asked her if anything was uncomfortable or hurting, and she denied any type of pain or discomfort.

While Camillia was readjusting her clothes and the doctor was putting away his tools, the doctor reported to the group that the baby was growing well; she had a nice strong and healthy heartbeat, the amount of amniotic fluid looked normal, and the umbilical cord was free floating, which was excellent. The doctor told Camillia that her other pregnancies were risky but that this one appeared to be as wonderful as it got and that he was looking forward to the delivery; it should be fast and essentially painless. Everyone thanked the doctor then left the room headed for the front door. On the way out of the hospital, several nurses that had heard about Camillia's baby being gifted in that she was responsive to the world outside of the womb and had a strong telepathic link with her mother wanted to rub Camillia's belly and talk to the baby. The group stopped to speak to the nurses, and Camillia allowed the nurses to rub her belly.

The baby loved the attention and responded positively to the nurses. Camillia told the nurses that they made the baby happy and thanked them. The group needed to get back on their horses and get home because it was getting near the time for the journey to begin for Andrew and the scouts; plus, they needed to stop by the science hall to get the dart guns, tranquilizers, and vaccine. The three of them made it back to the couple's side of the castle and left their horses with the stable boy while heading for the castle's front door.

CHAPTER THIRTY ONE

As they were about to enter through the door, the scouts started to trickle in. While waiting for the rest of the scouts to arrive in their living room, Andrew and Camillia verbalized their love for each other and told each other to be careful. Camillia told Andrew that she would be waiting diligently for his safe return. The chief even got a chance to speak his piece and told Andrew to have a safe journey and good luck handling the walking dead. Andrew gave Camillia a hug and rubbed her belly while telling the baby how much he loved her. Then he hugged the chief and asked him to look after Camillia while he was gone and that he would be back as soon as possible. The chief told Andrew that he would always look out for him and Camillia always, not just in one or the other's absence. The scouts were all in Andrew and Camillia's family room raring to go. Andrew got their attention then announced that they had to stop by the science hall before leaving to get their supplies. Everyone was looking forward to getting as many of the walking dead as possible healthy and changed so they could bring them home. Camillia and the chief stood behind the group of pale ones so they would not get trampled in all the excitement of everyone's hope and desire. Andrew worked his way to the front door, opened it, and everyone piled out like a herd of cattle. They would be traveling by foot so the chief and Camillia knew that it would be the next day before they got back with the newly turned pale ones. That made Camillia sad because she started to miss Andrew right after he left for the science hall. She started to sob so the chief tried to console her, but the only thing that would cheer her up would be seeing Andrew home again.

Andrew and the scouts made it to the science hall quite rapidly, and they got their dart guns, tranquilizers, and vaccine. It was time to head outside of the great wall and up to the earth's surface. As everyone was passing through the great wall, Andrew asked the scouts if they were well rested, and they all said yes. Andrew's next question for the scouts was if they wanted to make their time a bit shorter and they again said yes. Andrew suggested that they skip the rest periods on the way to the surface and skip a couple of the rest periods on the way back. The scouts agreed and said that they were up to it. As Andrew and the scouts walked toward the lake, which was one of their resting places, they sped up their pace. Once they got to the lake, they topped off their canteens and moved on. Everyone was in good spirits but a bit afraid of what to expect when they reached the walking dead. They got to their next resting place, the field where the tunnel begins. Andrew checked with the scouts to find out if anyone needed a break, and everyone said that they were ready to push on.

They finally reached the tunnel, and as they traveled through the narrow space with ease, they were extremely nervous because they did not know what to expect once they were on the earth's surface. They passed through the tunnel door and shut it behind them to keep it from possibly being discovered by any kind of individual. Now the scouts were following Andrew because only he knew where the old run-down casinos were. Andrew made sure that they left the commune at a certain time so that they would get to the walking dead during their sleep time. Andrew got them to the few run-down casinos that there were, and the scouts checked all of them then reported back to Andrew. Per the scout's reports, all the walking dead slept in one casino together; the other two casinos were empty. There were men, women, and children of all ages. The scouts counted their people, and Andrew added all the scouts' counts together but it was not divided into adults and children. Andrew was happy to hear the report that the walking dead were all in one space; it would make the scouts' job easier. All thirty-six scouts got into position to tranquilize the walking dead.

Fortunately, the dart guns were quiet and everyone slept in an orderly fashion. The scouts divided the walking dead into small groups, and there would be a scout for every small group of sleeping walking dead. Within fifteen minutes, all the walking dead were tranquilized so now the scouts could go through the group and vaccinate them. Again, they were divided into small groups for each scout to have one group to deal with. It took a half hour to get every walking dead individual vaccinated. Andrew and the scouts watched every walking dead person for signs of changing or passing on.

After twenty minutes, all the scouts got together with Andrew and reported the number of changes and deaths. To Andrew's surprise, there were no deaths; but in total, there were one hundred and forty-four new pale ones to get back to the commune. That meant that each scout had four individuals to keep control of, but they knew that they could do it. Fortunately, the tranquilizer was short acting because otherwise the scouts and Andrew would have to wait a long time for it to wear off before heading back to the commune. The new pale ones were waking up and looking around with fear. Their surroundings looked familiar, but they did not look the same and they were not sure what became of them or how they were changed.

Ten minutes after the first new pale one awoke, the last of the new pale ones awoke. Andrew stood up where they could all see him and explained that their lives were changed for the better; they were now healthy and immune to the earth's nuclear waste, diseases, and viruses. He told them that there was a place where many people, their friends and family members, had undergone a change just like them, and they lived in a community together and he wanted them to join their friends and family. Andrew told them that if they wanted to go with him and the scouts, they should come and stand by them. Little by little, the new pale ones slowly walked over to Andrew and the scouts. It seemed that a few were apprehensive but went because everyone else had.

Finally having everyone ready to go, they started their journey. Andrew led the way while the scouts were mixed among the new pale ones. They walked from the old broken-down casino to the tunnel door. The last individual through the tunnel door was a scout, and he shut the tunnel door behind himself. The large group of pale ones got through the tunnel to the area where the tunnel ended and the golden field began. That was where the first resting period was supposed to occur, but everyone was still going strong so Andrew deliberately skipped that breaktime. Everyone continued and the new pale ones were observing the scenery and how it was changing; it was becoming more and more beautiful. They finally came upon the lake, and the scouts needed to refill their canteens so they did while the new pale ones drank from the lake using their hands.

After everyone got their drink, the scouts pulled out some jerky from their satchels and split it with all the new pale ones to keep everyone's strength up. Andrew asked the new pale ones if they would like to stay by the lake for another ten minutes or so to admire the surroundings or rest up some. They all agreed that they wanted to move on so they could see their friends and family; the closer they seemed to get, the more excited they became. Andrew was ready to leave, but he decided to speak to the group of new pale ones before leaving the lake. Andrew stood aside of the group and requested their attention.

When everyone was quiet, Andrew announced that he needed to address a situation before getting to the compound. Everyone became curious and drew closer to Andrew. Andrew told the new pale ones that he had a concern that there would be some confrontation between them and the community over them being turned away after the nuclear bomb hit. Everyone began to say no, and Andrew put a stop to the new pale ones speaking out of turn. He told them that their family and friends knew that if they helped them, their lives might be compromised also. The new pale ones told Andrew that they never held that against them. They also told Andrew that they were thankful for the scouts helping them and for their community coming up with a way to help them in the first place. At that point, Andrew knew that there would not be any issues in the community over any hard feelings, so it was time to move on. Everyone was ready to move on and get to the compound so Andrew led the way and the new pale ones followed.

CHAPTER THIRTY TWO

The walk went by swiftly, but everyone was walking at top speed. Everyone found themselves at the compound wall. Andrew gave the command for the gate security to open the wall doors so the group could enter. They all made it back before lunch, which was good because the travelers could rest up a bit then have a full meal. Andrew instructed the scouts to go to every shop and close it for the day then have the employees go to the community dining hall. Andrew took the new pale ones to the community dining hall to wait for everyone else to get there. The scouts had gone to all the businesses so they stopped at all the houses along the way if someone was there and not at work for some reason. The scouts knew to go to the chief's house and Camillia's house so when they did, the chief and Camillia were both surprised that Andrew was back.

Camillia wondered if Andrew and the scouts brought anyone back with them because they should not have been back until late evening. As Camillia was walking out of her front door, the chief found her. Camillia asked the chief if there could be something wrong with the journey because of Andrew getting back so soon. The chief told her that by getting back so soon, that would tell him that the group did not take the usual breaks at the designated spots. As they spoke, they walked to the public dining hall since everyone was supposed to be there. By the time Camillia and the chief got to the public dining hall, everyone else was already there.

Andrew stood up at the podium and told the community that the new pale ones had arrived. Camillia and the chief joined Andrew at the podium. Andrew asked the new pale ones to stand against the walls of the dining hall. Andrew asked the original pale ones to look for family among the new ones and, if they found a family member or more, to bring them off the wall and go into the middle of the room. All the original pale ones went around the room looking at the new pale ones and found family members. They got together and moved to the center of the room. All the new pale ones were spoken of as being family to an original pale one. Andrew spoke to the groups all at once and asked them to provide a room and nutrition to their new family member until the community could get them their own home built. Every old pale one agreed, and every new pale one was thankful. Andrew told the community that a welcome committee would be going around to meet with all the newcomers to make sure that all their needs would get met and to establish their occupational placement in the community; then everyone was excused from the public dining hall to go home. Andrew, Camillia, and the chief were the last ones out of the public dining hall, and like everyone else, they were headed for home.

There was still a lot of work to be done besides building more new homes. Andrew and Camillia had to find a place of work for most of the new pale ones, hopefully with their loved ones, if possible. Andrew felt that it was very probable that the community would have to build some new businesses to offer work to everyone. There were a lot of nanny positions needed because approximately half of the new pale ones were small children who needed supervision and teaching. Camillia had decided that she would make the mothers the nannies for their children and the husband could go to work outside of the home. That would take care of filling those positions without having to make new businesses to suffice a working position. The one good thing that came out of the whole situation was that the pale ones knew that there were no more humans or walking dead left on the surface of the earth. Andrew, Camillia, and the chief were proud of the fact that they got everyone that was still alive healthy and together again.

However, Andrew and a few scouts needed to go back to the surface to visit the dinosaur tail. Although there were no more humans of any status on the earth's surface, the robocops were still there and fully functioning. They were still guarding the area of the dinosaur tail known as area 54, and there was the issue of getting over the tall blackened metal electric wall. It would be a dangerous journey, but it had to be done—the lives of the miniangels there were at stake. There were not many angels left because every time a human or walking dead was taken, one angel for everyone followed and returned to the grand forest. There were extra angels left because they were there for individuals who were supposed to go to the land of grandeur but passed away before the pale ones could save them.

On the way home, Andrew spoke to Camillia and the chief about expanding the commune wall to allow for the large number of buildings that they would have to do and where to place the new pale ones in their community where they would be needed and be happy. Andrew also spoke to the chief and Camillia about the next and final journey above ground to get the miniangels. He was highly concerned about the robocops killing him and the scouts. Camillia could feel the heaviness on Andrew's mind. The chief told Andrew to worry about one thing at a time. He suggested that Andrew think about getting the commune put together first then worry about retrieving the angels. Andrew felt that the chief's idea was a good one. The community just practically doubled in population so it was going to take some time to build that many homes and possibly a few community buildings to suffice a workplace for some of the new pale ones that would be beneficial for everyone.

The most important thing with the mass building projects was the breaking down of the great wall so they could expand the land to allow more building and leave an appropriate amount of space for travel in between buildings and getting the wall rebuilt for safety reasons. Camillia told Andrew that she could help with the expansion project. Andrew appreciated the chief's and Camillia's concern for him, and he told both that he would keep an open mind and welcome their opinions and suggestions. Camillia assured Andrew that together they would keep the commune spectacular and functional. They made it back to the castle so Andrew and Camillia said their goodbyes to the chief, and they parted ways until family time.

On the way to the castle, Andrew asked Camillia to go with him to the office room. She followed him, and once inside the office room, he shut the door. She sat down in the chair opposite of Andrew's chair. Andrew sat in his chair and told Camillia that he had an idea of something for the scientists to work on. Camillia could not imagine what they could possibly need so she sat forward in her chair to listen to Andrew closely. Andrew told her that he was concerned about the pale ones dying out in time. Camillia could tell that the thought of going extinct had really bothered him, but before she could say anything, he started to speak again. He asked her what her opinion would be of having the scientists work on an injectable formula that when given would allow a couple to reproduce. He was not sure if it would be possible or not, but it would give the scientists something to work on. Camillia thought that was a splendid idea, and she told Andrew so. Andrew told Camillia that he was going to focus on the building that needed to be done first along with placing the new pale ones into their occupation. That way, he would know if it would be necessary to build new businesses or not. Camillia told Andrew that his thought of how to handle getting things done seemed to be the best way to go.

She told him to outline how he wanted things done and she would help things along where she could. Before Andrew or Camillia could say anything else, there was a knock on the door; it was the chief. He went to see if the couple was going to participate in family time. They did not realize that so much time had passed and told the chief that they would be out soon. Andrew told his wife that they would start work after family time and move on things as fast as the situation allowed. Camillia agreed; then they both left the office room and went to the family room to meet with everyone else.

By the time the couple got to their living room, their friends were all there and waiting for them. Everyone went to the castle's private dining hall and prepared to eat while sharing their day. Everyone wanted to hear about what Andrew planned to do with the community now that it had doubled in population. Andrew told them that the solution was easier said than done, but that the plan was quite simple. Andrew got quiet and waited for someone else to talk, but it seemed that everyone was more interested in finding out what the king had in mind for uniting the new pale ones with the old pale ones. Andrew told them that the first thing he was going to take care of was housing them; they needed to build thirty-six more homes and furnish them. He said that while building the homes, he was going to see what their personal assets were to help place them into an occupation that they would like and be good at. Andrew briefly mentioned that they might have to build some shops for public services to open some occupational options. The group wanted more detail on what kind of shops he had in mind, but he said he was still working on that and it would only happen if it was necessary. He was keeping the conception project he had for the scientists a secret. The chief did not even know; only Camillia knew.

The kitchen staff started to bring lunch out so Andrew got quiet. He did not want a whole lot of individuals knowing what he was thinking because he was still figuring things out as he went along. Andrew did tell his friends that he was going to start the housing construction that day. He was also going to split the workers into two groups so the construction could go on around the clock and get done faster. He did tell his friends that by dinnertime he would know what everyone's prime choice for employment would be. Everyone was surprised that he would have that information so soon. Lunch had come to an end so the welcoming committee was out interviewing the new pale ones for their work potential.

There were still two hours of family time left, and the group continued to ask Andrew and Camillia questions about upcoming changes and the new pale ones. The couple answered the questions the best they could but with caution as to keep secrets a secret. Time went by faster than usual, and it was time for everyone to return to work so that was what they did. Andrew and Camillia figured that the welcoming committee would not be at their door for a couple of hours, but right after everyone went their way, there was a knock at their front door. It was the welcoming committee, every one of them. They dropped off their written notes of who the new pale ones were and what their occupation should be. Andrew thanked all the welcoming committee members then told Camillia to join him in his office room.

Once the office room door was shut, Andrew and Camillia got to work in finding out who was to have what position in what occupation. It took a few hours to organize the papers and to get an overview of the information given to them, but they could call the welcoming committee back in to give them a copy of the notes for every new pale one that stated what their occupation would be. It was much easier than Andrew thought it would be. Andrew called for his runners to retrieve the entire welcoming committee so each new pale one could be notified immediately and start their jobs the next morning. The runners were told that after they notified the entire welcoming committee to show up at the castle, they were then to go and retrieve the entire construction crew to report to him. Andrew's runners did not waste time getting out the door. About a half hour after they left, the welcoming committee started to show up. Once all the committee members were in front of Andrew, he gave them their occupational orders and off they went to deliver the hopefully good news to the new pale ones. Right after the committee members left, the construction crew started to show up. Once the entire building crew was there, Andrew split them into two groups and explained that there were thirty-six homes to be built but that they would have to rebuild the great wall because they would need more land to accommodate the houses and still leave a good amount of land between the homes so children would have some play space and wagons could fit through there. Andrew also explained that he split the personnel into two groups so the construction could go around the clock and get done faster.

The head crew member told Andrew that by doing the construction his way, they would have the entire project done in about two weeks. Andrew was pleased to hear that. The head crew member asked Andrew if there would be any businesses that needed to be built, and Andrew told him no but that the existing businesses may need their stable space expanded and the various halls might need to be expanded also. Andrew said that he would have to track the activities of each business and hall for ample room to handle the guests and ease of access and for their stables' ability to handle their guests' horses as well as horse and buggy so that was something he would have to get back with him on. Andrew told the head crew member to start working immediately, and the crew member said he would do as instructed. Andrew thanked him for his loyalty, and the building crew left Andrew's office room to go straight to work.

Now that Andrew was done with the face-to-face part of things to be done, he needed to get the notes of names and occupations of new pale ones to the census hall to be recorded in the official book of records. Camillia was put in charge of visiting all the new pale ones and finding out what set of parents had which child so it could be turned into the census hall for proper recording. Camillia planned to tackle that task the following morning and have it ready to turn into the census hall by that evening. In the meantime, Andrew wanted to discuss the conception project with Camillia. She told Andrew that there was no reason to hold back on getting the science crew started on that project; they had nothing going on at that moment. Andrew agreed and asked if she would go with him to the science hall and be an active part of the project. She told him that as his partner, she would be honored.

To get the conception project started immediately, Andrew and Camillia had to rush over to the science hall to catch the scientists before the scientists closed the science hall for the night and left for dinner. The couple made it to the science hall just in time to catch the scientists and spoke to the head scientist about creating a medicine that could be given to the commoners that would allow them to conceive children. The scientist told the couple that it was a grand idea but that nothing like that had ever been attempted. Andrew told him that before Lloyd's parents, there was never an attempt to save the lives of humans, but it was achieved. The scientist agreed that it was worth a try; the science team had also been aware of the possibility of them going extinct, and it was disturbing to them also. The head scientist told the couple that like the last project, they would divide into groups so the project could be worked on around the clock. Andrew said he appreciated that and that he would be checking in periodically to see how things were going.

Now that things with the science hall were squared away, the couple said their goodbyes and went home to get ready for the dinner hour. On the way home, Andrew spoke to Camillia about the need to go on another journey above ground. Camillia told him that there were no more humans and no more walking dead on the earth's surface so she did not understand why he needed to go back up there. He told her that there were miniangels that got left at the dinosaur tail, and he needed to retrieve them so they did not perish. Camillia asked how they were forgotten, and Andrew told her that they were for the walking dead that were supposed to come to the land of grandeur but that they had passed away before he and the scouts got up there. That made sense to Camillia, but she was concerned about him and the scouts being murdered by the robocops. Not only did they have to worry about the robocops seeing them, but they also had to try to get past the four-foot darkened steel electric wall around area 54.

Camillia understood that the need was urgent and that there was no way that he could send someone else, but she was deeply worried. Andrew told Camillia that he could not go until the commune was settled with the house building and job placement, and in the meantime, he could devise a plan to overcome the obvious hurdles as well as a plan for anything that was not obvious but possible. Andrew said he would consult with the chief and the scouts before going anywhere. Camillia told him that she would help as an individual looking at the situation from an outside view, and maybe as she listened to everyone, she may be able to contribute an idea or two. Andrew told Camillia that she was more than welcome to help; any suggestion would be welcomed.

CHAPTER THIRTY THREE

With all the work that had been done and in a fleeting period, the couple seemed to lose track of time, and they found that they were late for dinner so they were not at the castle's private dining hall on time and that was rare. Andrew and Camillia were reminded that it was time to have dinner by Melanie. The couple stopped their conversation and followed Melanie to the round table. As soon as they got seated, there was a knock at the front door. The butler answered the door, and it was the chief; he wanted to spend some down time with Andrew and Camillia, and he also did not want to eat alone. The couple invited him in to eat with them, and Melanie happily got a plate of food for him.

The chief did not want dinnertime to be about business, but he was curious about where Andrew was with getting things settled for the new pale ones. Andrew did not mind discussing things with the chief so he and Camillia told the chief where they were with things. Andrew gave the chief the brief explanation; he said that everyone had their profession and would start the following morning, the thirty-six homes that were needed would be done in about two weeks, he needed to check the various halls for the proper amount of room to handle everyone as well as the stables around town, and when all that was done, he would be planning another journey to the earth's surface to retrieve the last of the miniangels. The chief was amazed at how fast Andrew was at getting things done and how thorough he was. Andrew told the chief that he could not do it without the help of his wife. Andrew told the chief that he had a project for the science team and he would discuss it after dinner in private, but that it was big and would solve a major issue. The chief said he was very interested to hear what he was doing.

Dinner went by fast, but there was still dessert and Melanie always had something that satisfied the sweet tooth. It was not long before dessert was over and Andrew took the chief to his office room. Camillia tagged along so she could hear what the chief had to say about the conception project. They all got in the office room, and Andrew shut the door behind them then took his seat. Camillia and the chief took their seats, and Andrew started to talk. He told the chief that he gave the scientists what he called the conception project. It was for them to develop a medicine that would allow those who take it to be able to have children. The chief told Andrew that it was a long shot, but it would keep the scientists busy. Andrew told the chief that if that became possible, it would solve the issue of the pale ones' extinction in due time. The chief thought that it would be wonderful if the species could grow and evolve. Andrew told him that was the prime objective. The time was getting late, and Andrew was exhausted from the journey and Camillia needed to get her rest due to the pregnancy. The chief said his goodbyes and went back to his side of the castle to go to bed.

The couple went to their bedroom and changed into their bed clothes then lay in their bed and caressed each other. Andrew rubbed Camillia's tummy and spoke to the unborn baby. Suddenly, he thought he felt the baby kick so he spoke some more to the baby and sure enough the baby kicked again; that was so exciting to Andrew. Andrew and Camillia fell asleep without even knowing it; they slept through the night then woke up bright and early the next day. The new day was going to be just as busy as the day before. Camillia had to find out who the parents were for every child that was just abducted so she could give the information to the census hall for proper documentation, and that would take most of the day. Andrew had to check on the construction crew's progress then ride through the community to see how things were going for the new pale ones in their new jobs as well as checking the various halls for adequate room and the community stables for the ability to hold all the horses and buggies, and that would most likely take all day. The couple got themselves ready for the new day then went to the castle's private dining hall for breakfast.

After eating a full heavy breakfast, the couple hugged, kissed, then went their separate ways. The stable boy had their horses ready for them when they were ready to leave. Andrew made his way to where the new homes and wall extension was. Over the night, the construction crew had knocked down the original compound wall and put up the new wall, making more room for the houses to be built and securing the community from the wild man-eating beasts that wandered the forest. The construction crew had one house built so Andrew needed to put the chief in charge of making sure the new houses were furnished and stocked. Camillia was going from home to home trying to find out what child went to which parents. After going from home to home, she would have to go from shop to shop to make sure she got every one of the children accounted for. Andrew got halfway through checking the various shops to see how the new pale ones were doing by the time the lunch hour had come. Camillia had just finished checking all the houses and shops to find out who the parents were for each child by the time lunch hour came.

Both Andrew and Camillia headed for home for family time and lunch. By the time they got home, the couple found that everyone was waiting for their arrival to start lunch. Upon entering the door, everyone went to the castle's private dining hall, and Melanie had lunch already on the round table. Andrew and Camillia's friends asked to know how things had been going for the new arrivals. Andrew told them that he had only gotten half of the shops visited, but so far things were great; the newcomers seemed to like their work. Andrew told the group that the construction crew was making satisfactory progress; it would only be approximately two weeks until all the houses were built. Camillia told their friends that she got every child matched up to his or her parents and that all she had to do now was drop that information off to the census hall for documentation. Everyone was glad to hear that so much had been done.

By the time the couple shared their reports of their duties for that day, lunch was over and now there was two hours left of family time so the couple could hear how their friends' day had gone so far. Everyone got to share their day just in time for family time to end. Everybody was happy about how family time had gone; it had been a while since everyone could share.

Everybody hugged everybody then the group stopped at Camillia's side to talk to the unborn baby while rubbing her tummy; eventually, everyone returned to their duties. The chief offered to take the census information to the census hall for Camillia, and she let him and told him she appreciated his help, and he left right away. With that, Andrew told the stable boy to take Camillia's and his horses and then hitch up a fresh team to a buggy so Camillia could go with him for the last of his duty. As usual, the stable boy got their ride out to them in a hurry. The last of the shops had been visited, and it appeared that all the new pale ones were happy with their community duties.

Andrew turned the buggy around and started for home, and on the way, Andrew told Camillia that he wanted to go to the community dining hall for dinner to make sure that there was enough room for everyone. Camillia agreed that it was something they needed to do. She commented that if the public dining hall needed to be expanded on, so would all the other community halls. Andrew saw her point and agreed. Andrew and Camillia decided to go to the chief's home to get him for dinner so he could be aware of the number of individuals in the dining hall and help them to determine if they needed to make an expansion.

By the time the couple got to the chief's front door, it was time to head out for the community dining hall. Andrew got down from the buggy and knocked on the chief's door; his butler answered and took Andrew to the chief. Andrew told the chief that they were there for his opinion on whether to expand the community dining hall, but that they needed to visit the building while it was in use. The chief understood and agreed so he joined them.

Andrew, Camillia, and the chief got to the community dining hall just on time for dinner to be served. Before touching his dinner, Andrew looked around the dining hall to see if there were enough seats for everyone. The chief and Camillia scanned the large room also before touching their dinner. Andrew was not pleased with what he saw; he told his wife and the chief to go to his office room right away then got up to leave. Andrew charged like a bull for his office room; what he saw suppressed his appetite completely. He decided that he and his wife and the chief could eat at the castle's private dining hall after they discussed the issue he had with the community dining hall. Camillia had never seen Andrew so upset; neither had the chief for that matter. Camillia and the chief had to practically jog to keep up with Andrew because he walked so fast.

They all three made it to the office room where Camillia and the chief sat down. Andrew shut the door behind them rather hard then took his seat at the head of the office room. As soon as Andrew sat, he asked Camillia and the chief if they had seen the same thing he saw. Camillia and the chief glanced at each other with expressions of confusion then told Andrew that they saw what he saw. Andrew spoke harshly when he told Camillia and the chief that he could not believe how their people were being forced to eat and that it was not right. Camillia spoke up to her husband and told him that what they saw was parents having to hold their children in their laps to eat due to there not being enough seating therefore the kitchen served one plate of food per adult and the children had to share their parent's food. The kitchen workers were not paying attention to the fact that some of the adults were holding children so the children accidentally got skipped for plates of food. Andrew declared that in his kingdom, no one was to go hungry or be forced to be uncomfortable in their community and that he wanted the situation remedied right away. Andrew barked orders to the chief to stop the building of the houses and for the construction crews to focus on enlarging the community dining hall. Andrew told Camillia that while the construction crew was fixing the issue of not having enough room in the dining hall, she should oversee, making sure that the woodworkers built some baby chairs so the parents could eat with ease and feed their child comfortably, and the kitchen would recognize the children as individuals and serve them their own plates of food. Camillia and the chief both told Andrew that they would get right on it.

Everyone stood up to go to the castle's private dining hall, and before Andrew opened the door for them to go out, he apologized for his negative attitude and verbal abuse. He said that he should have treated them respectfully. Camillia and the chief told him that they accepted his apology and that they were just as disturbed about the situation and would address it right away. Andrew gave the chief and his wife a hug and thanked them for their support and understanding. The three of them went to the castle's private dining hall and ate their dinner then got ready to take care of business. The chief went home and sent one of his runners out to get the construction crew and have them report to him at once. Camillia sent one of her runners to get the wood shop workers to report to her on the spot. The construction crew reported to the chief as fast as they could; they knew if they were being pulled off their house-building job, it must be something important.

The chief told them that they needed to stop work on the houses and expand the community dining hall to fit everyone comfortably with much room to move about. The chief told them that after they did that, they could resume work on the houses; then after the houses were built, they needed to expand the rest of the community halls. The construction crew acknowledged the chief then said they would get right on it and work hard around the clock. The chief thanked them then excused them from his presence. Meanwhile, Camillia was speaking to the wood shop workers about making approximately thirty-six baby chairs so the mothers of young children did not have to hold their child on their laps. She told them that with the chairs, the mothers would be able to enjoy their meals and the kitchen staff would start to bring out separate meals for the children instead of the mothers having to share their food with the children. The head wood shop worker told Camillia that they could have all the chairs done by breakfast time. Camillia thought that was great and told them so; she thanked them for their willingness to help their community then excused them to start work instantly.

After dealing with the construction crew, the chief went to his bedroom to relax and go to sleep. It finally got late enough for Andrew and Camillia to go to their bedroom and change into bedclothes. The couple lay on their bed so Andrew could spend some time with his wife and unborn baby. Andrew was gently rubbing Camillia's belly and enjoying feeling the baby move. Camillia was getting more and more relaxed as Andrew rubbed her belly; she fell asleep fast. Andrew watched his wife sleep for a while and felt sentimental toward her. After a short while, Andrew laid his head on his pillow, scooted closer to Camillia, then fell asleep.

After a good night's sleep, the morning hour rolled around and Andrew woke up well rested. He woke up Camillia with a low loving voice telling her he loved her and giving her kisses on her cheek. Camillia woke up to Andrew's kind gestures, and in response to his loving disposition, she picked up his right hand and placed it on her abdomen so he could get the baby up and moving with sweet words and a loving touch. Andrew and Camillia focused on the baby for a short while as they kept feeling her move about in the womb. Breakfast was drawing near, and the couple had so much to do that day, and because of that, they were not sure if they would make the last two hours of family time; it would depend on how much they accomplished beforehand. The couple got up and got their day clothes on, groomed themselves, and got out to the castle's private dining hall for breakfast. While the couple ate their meal, they discussed who would do what to get all their tasks completed for the day. Andrew and Camillia finished their breakfast then said their farewells to go out to the community and take care of their business. Andrew went to the community dining hall to see how the expansion project was going.

To his surprise, the construction crew had the dining hall done, and it was more beautiful than before; plus, it had more than enough room for the people to enjoy their meals in. Camillia went to the woodworkers' shop to check on the production of the baby chairs. To her surprise, the woodworkers worked through the night and got all thirty-six baby chairs done and placed into the community dining hall. Camillia went to the dining hall to see the chairs and ran into Andrew; they were both very pleased with the work that they had seen. Together, they went to see what kind of progress the construction workers had made on the houses. When they finished with the community dining hall, they went back to working on the housing project. They were getting things done by leaps and bounds.

There was still quite a bit of time before family time so Andrew and Camillia went to the science hall to get an idea of where the scientists were with the conception project. The lead scientist was not very pleased with where they were in the project. They were still trying to figure out what in the original serum was making humans sterile so they could focus on what may reverse the effects of that ingredient. Andrew and Camillia were fascinated with the scientists' talent to work with Mother Nature. There was nothing new with the science hall at that point in time, so the couple left and went to their home to prepare to greet family as they arrived for family time. Andrew and Camillia were home for only ten minutes when the family started to arrive in their front room.

CHAPTER THIRTY FOUR

By the end of ten more minutes, the last of the family was showing up so everyone transferred to the castle's private dining hall to have lunch and share their day. Andrew and Camillia would share their day last because everyone would have questions, and it would take longer to discuss their day than anyone else. Bridgette and her parents went first so Andrew and Camillia could hear how their children were doing. The children were down for naps during family time so that allowed Bridgette and her parents to join in on family time. The nannies all say that the children are doing well and growing so fast. Bridgette said that Armellya had fully developed her telekinesis so she had to be watched very closely. Andrew and Camillia were very proud of their daughter. Everyone else expeditiously ran through their day so far so they could all hear how things were going for Andrew and Camillia in the community.

Now being the couple's turn, Andrew spoke first. He said that the new community dining hall was built and that it looked fabulous, and thanks to Camillia's vigorous work, the woodworkers made baby chairs so the mothers of small children could put them into a chair and make their meals more enjoyable for both mom and baby, not to mention that way, the kitchen gives a plate to the children so the mother does not have to share her meal and no one goes home hungry. Camillia told her friends that the census hall had gotten all the information to appropriately record the new pale ones' full names, positions, and children's names. Andrew spoke again and told everyone that the construction crew was back to building houses for the new pale ones, and at the rate that they were going, they would be done before the two weeks was up. Everyone thought that was amazing; they did not think the houses could be done in two weeks much less before the two weeks was up. Camillia told everyone that after family time, she had a doctor's appointment for her prenatal checkup.

Andrew had to put a damper on all the good talk by revealing that he had to take one more journey to the earth's surface to rescue some miniangels that got left behind at the dinosaur tail. The group was concerned about the same things that Camillia was concerned about. The robocops were programmed to protect that area and to shoot to kill upon seeing someone near the wall in area 54. There was also the problem of getting over the four-foot darkened metallic electrical wall. Matthew suggested that he and Andrew go alone. They had been able to get to the wall many times without being spotted by the robocops when they lived above ground, and if they should be seen, they knew how to ditch them. Bridgette was not very happy about her husband offering to go when it was not his job, and it was too dangerous. Andrew told Matthew that he might have the best idea of how to handle getting the miniangels back. They were best buddies on the earth's surface and knew each other's silent cues, and now that they had telepathy, they would definitely have an advantage. Matthew went on to say that the scouts were not familiar with the surface like they were, and they could utilize the hover bikes left near the wall by the girls just before they were abducted to get around on and, if necessary, they could take cover inside one of the safe houses because the robocops would not go inside a home without an invite. Camillia and Bridgette were both concerned about how they were going to get over the wall without being electrocuted. Andrew told the girls that they would not have to go in to get the miniangels; the miniangels would come to them. Andrew reminded Camillia that the miniangels could travel through the electricity without being affected. The only thing they would need was a basket for the angels to gather into for travel, and once they got to the great golden forest, they would flit from the basket to the wildflowers that grew in the forest and join the rest of the miniangels.

Andrew and Matthew looked at each other and said in unison that just the two of them going was the best way to handle the situation. Andrew told Matthew to take the rest of the day off and rest up for the trip and to spend some time with his wife, Bridgette. Andrew said that he would get another nanny to keep Armellya from then until they left, and once they were gone, Bridgette could go back to her responsibilities with Armellya. Bridgette's mother suggested that since she had Kaylina and her husband had Kevin, maybe they should stay together and share the responsibility of keeping Armellya. That way, she would be with people she knew as well as her twin siblings. Bridgette's father said that they could all share one of the spare nursery rooms and have it set up to occupy three babies instead of just one baby. Camillia said that the plan sounded good. She agreed that if anyone could accomplish the task of going to the earth's surface to retrieve anything, then it would be Andrew and Matthew. Then she asked when they planned on leaving.

Andrew asked Matthew if leaving right after family time the next day sounded good to him, and he said yes. Andrew announced that they were going to leave right after family time on the next day. Michelle, the personal maid for Camillia, and her parents; Bridgette, Armellya's nanny, and her parents; Matthew, the king and queen's personal security, and his parents, all got together to fix up one of the spare baby nurseries. Once the nursery was done,

Matthew and Bridgette went to their bedroom, put on their night clothes, and would be staying there until dinnertime. Everyone else returned to their duties. Andrew and Camillia had to go to the hospital for her prenatal doctor's appointment. The couple got in their buggy and left early so they could go by and pick up the chief so Andrew could speak to him about the journey. While heading to the chief's home, Andrew asked Camillia if she had a basket around the castle somewhere. She said that she did not have one but that she could go to the community dedicated events decorators and get a basket of any size; she just needed to know what size he needed. Andrew told her that he needed one that was about sixteen inches around and not too deep. She told him to consider it done. Camillia told Andrew to stop by the dedicated events hall on the way home, and she would go in to talk to the girls and be back out with the basket. Andrew agreed to do so.

They were at the chief's house so Andrew got down from the buggy and went to the door. He knocked and the butler answered the door; he invited Andrew in, but Andrew told him that he was there to pick up the chief and that they were in a hurry. The butler went to get the chief and told him that the couple was outside waiting on him and that they were in a hurry. The chief made it outside and asked Andrew what was going on. Andrew told him that they were on their way to the hospital for a prenatal checkup and wanted him to come along so they could talk about some business. The chief said okay and jumped on their buggy and sat down. Andrew got the horses moving, and he told the chief that he had the journey of going to the earth's surface to get the miniangels that were stuck there to bring them back to the great forest garden and return them to their home. The chief thought that his heart was in the right place but that he was going to be on a fruitless journey due to the heavy security around where the miniangels were. Andrew told the chief that was why he was teaming up with Matthew; they were in tune with each other without telepathy, and now that they could read each other's minds, they had unspoken communication as an asset. Andrew told the chief that they had some prearranged tactics for avoiding the robocops.

The chief told Andrew that he was not comfortable with the boys going on the journey, but he also knew that no one would be able to talk them out of it. Andrew reminded the chief that the angels were their friends, and they deserved the same chance as the humans and the walking dead had gotten. As Andrew drove the buggy up to the front door of the hospital, the chief finished the conversation by telling Andrew that he was there for him and would do anything that he asked of him. Everyone got off the buggy and went into the hospital; they walked up to the nurse's desk and told the charge nurse why they were there and that they needed Camillia's personal doctor. The nurse took them to a private room for her to get ready for her exam, and the doctor walked in as the nurse was walking out. The doctor did the ultrasound and listened to the baby's heartbeat then he poked and pushed on Camillia's abdomen while asking her if there was any pain or discomfort, and Camillia told him no. The doctor announced that the baby looked good and the heartbeat sounded perfect. The doctor made sure that Andrew and Camillia understood that the current pregnancy was very healthy, and he did not foresee any problems. Andrew, Camillia, and the chief were very happy to hear another good report.

While the doctor was putting his tools away, Camillia was getting off the bed and straightening her clothes. As they were all ready to walk out, Camillia hugged the doctor and thanked him for his care. Andrew, Camillia, and the chief went back to their buggy and got on it to head to the dedicated events decorator's hall for the basket. They got there, and Camillia went in to get a basket. A few minutes later, she came back out with the perfect basket. Camillia got back on the buggy, and they headed for the couple's home. But before they got too close to home, Camillia asked the chief if he would like to join her and Andrew for dinner. The chief said that he would enjoy that. They got to the castle, and everyone got off the buggy. The stable boy took the horses and buggy to be unhitched and put away.

Andrew, Camillia, and the chief went to the castle's private dining hall for dinner. Everyone was rather quiet during dinner so the time seemed to go by fast. Everyone finished about the same time, and when it was time to leave the round table, the chief excused himself to go home and go to bed for the night. Andrew and Camillia went to their bedroom and got into bed clothes then went to bed also. The couple slept soundly and woke up the next morning just on time to get ready for the day and get to the castle's private dining hall. Melanie had breakfast on the table waiting for them; they ate leisurely then went out to get on their horses to start their errands. The couple went to see the community's construction crew about the houses being built. Right as Andrew and Camillia rode up to the house that the crew was working on, they put the finishing touch on the house. That was the thirty-sixth and final home to be built. It was now time to send in the decorating crew that would be furnishing the homes and the welcoming crew that would be stocking up the homes with necessities like food, water, and the likes. The occupants should be able to move in by that evening. Andrew and Camillia complimented the entire crew for a job well done; then they turned their horses around and headed for the census hall.

When the couple got to the census hall and walked in, it appeared that everyone was working hard. Camillia asked for the head of the department, and a worker got her. Andrew was looking through some of the documents to assure that the work was getting done correctly. Camillia and the census worker spoke about the mass documentation of the new pale ones, and the worker said that they were close to done. They got every adult's name in the book, and next to their name was their occupation; all they had left to do was to document the children with their parents. Andrew and Camillia were pleased to know that so much had been done; they were ahead of schedule, but it was because the workers were broken down into small groups and followed a continuous schedule so work had been getting done throughout the night as well as during the day. Camillia complimented the census workers for a job well done, then she hugged the girls that worked there and said her goodbyes. Camillia and Andrew needed to stop at one last place for the day, and that was the science hall; they saved the most interesting errand for last.

The couple rode up to the science hall with excitement to see what they had come up with so far. The couple went inside the science hall and saw a man walking around poking his nose in everyone's business. Andrew asked him if he was the lead scientist, and he said yes. Andrew asked him to take a break for a few moments so he walked to the front of the hall, and the couple followed him; he finally stopped walking and asked what they needed. He was a bit rude and did not seem to know who they were. Andrew asked him how often he worked at the hall, and he said that generally he did not work at the hall; he worked out of his home. Andrew informed him that the project was submitted by himself, and just so he knew, he was the king of the land of grandeur. The scientist apologized and told Andrew that he would tell him anything he needed or wanted to know about the project. Andrew put his hand on Camillia's shoulder and told the scientist that he could tell the queen also. He bent his head down and begged the queen for her forgiveness for his poor behavior. Camillia told him to always hold his head high, and she hugged him; he was relieved that he was not going to be punished for his inhospitable behavior.

Andrew asked how they were doing on the conception project. He told them that they had successfully broken down the original serum to all its single ingredients, which they had done once before but they were familiar with only a few of the ingredients and they were having trouble finding out what ingredient targeted what body system. He assured the couple that they were working around the clock to get it figured out. Andrew thanked the scientist for his time and wished them luck on their work. The couple left the science hall a little let down, but they saw hope in the scientist's eyes so they did not give up hope either. The couple mounted their horses and headed toward home.

Andrew and Camillia reached home and gave their horses to the stable boy then went inside their castle. When they entered, they did not hear anything or anyone, which was not normal. Andrew told Camillia to stay behind him and to follow him while he snuck around to find out what was going on. Bridgette had Matthew in Armellya's nursery; Andrew and Camillia found them but not anyone else. All four stayed in the nursery room for some sense of security. It was close to family time, but no one was showing up—that was strange and had not happened before. The two couples waited to hear someone but never did so. Once they were about ten minutes late for lunch, they went out of the nursery room toward the castle's private dining hall. Andrew led the way with Camillia followed by Bridgette and finally Matthew bringing up the rear.

They had just entered the dining room when suddenly, everyone jumped out at them from nowhere. Everyone yelled "Surprise!" and laughed. Melanie and the rest of the kitchen group had a special party meal for Andrew and Matthew for their journey. The party was to celebrate the coming home of the angels. Bridgette and Camillia would like to believe that the current journey would be the last of them, but for some reason, Camillia did not think so; and based on Camillia's feeling, Bridgette could not believe that it would be the last journey either. The girls decided that they would deal with that later if it should occur.

In the meantime, the group of friends enjoyed each other's company and ate some finger lunch foods and miniature desserts. Melanie and the kitchen crew definitely went out of their way to prepare such a wonderfully fun meal. The group of friends spent the whole family time eating and reminiscing about life together above ground. They realized that although they had no responsibilities before becoming a pale one, their lives were much better now especially since they had their complete families and they were strong and healthy. Family time was coming to an end, and everyone had to get back to work. The first thing to do was to get the spare baby nursery emptied while everyone was still there. Everyone pitched in, and all the children's belongings were back in their own rooms and Bridgette went back to caring for Armellya. Camillia was planning her day because she had to keep things running as usual in Andrew's absence. Andrew and Matthew were planning to leave within minutes.

At the last moment, Andrew sent one of his runners to bring the chief to him. About five minutes later, the runner reappeared with the chief. The chief asked if the trip was still on, and Andrew told him yes but he wanted the chief's help. Andrew told the chief and Matthew that he had another idea for making the trip go by faster, which could get them back in ten hours. Both men were very interested to hear his idea because the fastest trip was twenty hours. Andrew told the chief that if they rode their horses to the tunnel opening and had someone to care for the horses while he and Matthew went the rest of the way on foot, get done with their business, and get back to the horses, they could travel twice as fast. Matthew told Andrew that the idea to travel by horse was the best idea for the journey he had heard yet; the chief agreed. Andrew asked the chief if he was up to the ride and willing to wait with the horses. The chief told Andrew that he was not for the trip because of the danger involved, but that he understood why he had to do it. The chief told Andrew he would stand behind his king until the day he died as the king's orders were not to be questioned, they were to be faithfully followed through, and that he would be proud to go on the trip with him and Matthew.

Andrew said that it was settled then. He told Andrew and the chief that they would meet out front with their horses in five minutes so if there was anything to take care of at the last minute, they should do so now. Andrew went and told Camillia that they would be back in about ten hours and asked her if there was anything she wanted or needed from her smart house that he could bring back. Camillia told him not to push his luck, to just come back to her and their children safely. Matthew went to tell Bridgette that they would be back in about ten hours and that he loved her. They kissed each other and hugged then Matthew went outside to wait on Andrew; the chief was already there. Andrew went out front and saw the chief and Matthew all ready to go, so he took his horse from the stable boy and everyone mounted their horses and off they went.

Right after the men left for the earth's surface, Camillia had one of her runners go find the head of construction to give him a written order from the queen of the land of grandeur for him and his crew to expand the rest of the community halls as they did for the community dining hall. Camillia would wait to receive written word from the construction crew's boss about the order of the halls to be done and approximately when they would be done. While waiting for the runner to get back with written word from the construction crew boss, Camillia sent her second runner to the head of the welcoming crew to find out if the homes were ready to be moved into, and the runner would bring back a verbal report from the head of the welcoming committee.

CHAPTER THIRTY FIVE

Once Camillia got her runners out, she sat back in her chair and relaxed. She was feeling a slight ache in her lower back, which she figured might have been due to all the weight she carried in front due to the pregnancy. Camillia stayed in the office room until the runners got back. The second runner returned first with word that the new homes were ready to be occupied. Camillia got into the desk and pulled out a list of new pale families so she could make a new list of the thirty-six heads of household's names. Once the list was finished, she would give it to a team of runners so they could go out and notify those families of their home being ready and which home was to be theirs. Camillia knew that their move would be completed before the lunch hour.

Right when Camillia finished her list of new homeowners, the first runner got back with a list from the head of construction showing the order of the community halls to be expanded on and an approximate date of when they would be done. There was a note at the end of the list that informed Camillia that the expected finish dates of each hall were set at the maximum time estimate; they would most likely be done sooner. The construction was to be started on that day, and they would be working in shifts to enable the work to go on day and night, therefore getting finished sooner than the estimated dates given; Camillia was happy with that. Camillia called her two runners into the office room and instructed them to get five more runners each then all of them to return to the office room. The two runners left on the double and returned fifteen minutes later with five other runners each. Camillia gave all twelve runners three names with which house those families would belong to and instructed them to seek out their individuals and let them know which house they would belong to and that they were to start their move immediately, to be done by the lunch hour.

Now that the office work was finished, Camillia had to visit the science hall to get an update on how the conception project was going and the census hall to see how close the girls were to finishing their documents. Camillia knew that she needed to get up out of the chair to leave the castle to finish with her day's duties, but due to the back pain that she was experiencing, she felt that she needed to lie down for a short while even though there was no time for that. Before getting up, Camillia rubbed her belly and verbally asked the unborn baby what was going on. Camillia felt the baby moving, but it was different than usual; it felt like the baby was pressing on her lower abdomen and giving off a sense of slight stress. Camillia somehow knew something was different with the baby, but she could not pinpoint what it was. Camillia decided to go ahead and run her visitation runs to the science hall and the census hall, but she was going to get Michelle, her personal maid, to accompany her. That way, if she needed help, Michelle could go and get it.

Camillia sent one of her runners out to the stable boy to get him to saddle up two horses; then she sent her second runner to bring Michelle to the office room. Ten minutes after sending out the first runner, he got back to his queen and reported that the stable boy was getting the horses ready to go. Right after the first runner checked back in, the second runner got back with Michelle. Michelle was watching Camillia because she looked paler than what a pale one usually looked, and she noticed Camillia running a hand across her back. Michelle could not help herself; she had to ask the queen if she felt okay. Camillia replied that she just felt a bit strange, like something was different but not wrong, if that made any sense. Michelle understood and told Camillia that maybe they should go and see the doctor just to be on the safe side. Camillia told her that they had two errands to take care of, then if she felt that the strangeness had progressed, she would check in with her doctor. Michelle was not exactly happy with that answer but had to be obedient; at least if there was to be an emergency, she could go for help.

Together, Michelle and Camillia left the office room and went outside to mount their horses and get to the science hall. On the way to the science hall, Camillia told Michelle that she needed her to stay outside with the horses because she had to address some personal business. Michelle said that she did not mind. Now at the science hall, Camillia left her horse with Michelle and went inside. She requested to see the head scientist, and he noticed Camillia standing in front of the building so he went over to her. She asked him how the conception project was going, and he said he was afraid that it was going a lot slower than he had hoped. He told her that it was not hard to isolate each individual ingredient in the original turning serum because they had done it recently to make the walking dead's vaccine, and they kept detailed records of every step in the process. He explained that with the vaccine, they just needed to alter the strength of most of the ingredients and make sure that everything was still balanced between opposing factors.

The scientist went on to tell Camillia that the problem was in deciphering Deanna and Darren's notes from ages ago. They know what some of the ingredients target and how, but most of the ingredients they do not have a clue about; in fact, there were a couple of ingredients they believed could only be gotten from the earth's surface because they knew for a fact that they could not be obtained in the land of grandeur or the nearby forest. Camillia sadly said she understood, and the head scientist told her not to lose hope because they knew that the conception project was going to be challenging and they liked challenges. He told Camillia that there had not been a challenge yet that they had not figured out, and in time, they would figure this one out also.

Just then, Camillia's knees buckled due to a sharp pain that shot from her back down into her legs. The scientist caught her halfway down to the floor and asked her if she was okay as he helped her straighten back up. She told the scientist that she just had a spell of weakness but she would be just fine. Camillia left the science hall and went back to Michelle and her horse; now they would head for the census hall. Michelle noticed that Camillia was not riding her horse too well; it seemed to take all she had just to stay on her horse. The girls finally got to the census hall so Camillia got off her horse and went inside. Camillia asked to speak with the head census worker so one of the workers went to the back of the hall and got her.

When she got to Camillia, she told her that the job was done. Camillia could not believe that they had finished so soon because it took them so long to do the records when they added the abducted human adults and now they had double or more individuals to add this time and managed to finish in half of the time; it just did not seem right. Camillia asked if they got each child registered with the right parents, if they documented who was head of household, and noted their home location. The head census worker admitted that they had not documented the housing information because they had not gotten that information yet. Camillia told her that she would make sure that they get the information. The census worker told Camillia that once they get the information, they could have their records all up to date and complete within one business day. Camillia was happy with the honesty of not having complete documents and for the woman's word that it would be completed so soon. Camillia turned and walked away, went outside, got on her horse, and rode toward home with Michelle.

When the girls got back to the castle, the head of the welcoming committee was there waiting for Camillia to let her know that all the new families had successfully moved into their homes and the men were back at work. Camillia thanked the welcoming committee member for the information then asked her to please document who was where so the census hall could copy it into their books. The woman said that she would be happy to help and that she would have the list within half an hour and drop it off at the census hall. Camillia thanked her as she was getting off her horse. Michelle was off her horse also, and the stable boy took the horses back toward the barn. The girls went inside the castle; Michelle went back to her original job. Camillia was suddenly taken by a surge of fatigue so she decided to get into her bedclothes and lie down for a while. She would be able to rest for a long time if she needed to because there was not going to be family time during lunch since Andrew and Matthew were gone. Camillia stayed in her bed instead of going to the castle's private dining hall for lunch. Camillia could not help but worry about Andrew and Matthew; she hoped that they were okay. She missed having Andrew around, and since she was not feeling well, she wished that he was there to comfort her. She had been keeping track of time so she knew that he was on the earth's surface already.

Andrew and Matthew had just gotten on the earth's surface and were headed straight to area 54. They had the wall in sight and could not see any robocops so they headed for the wall. The boys walked along the wall as close as they could get without getting shocked. The angels knew that the boys were there and that they were going there for them. Matthew was going to be the lookout for the operation while Andrew would retrieve the miniangels. The miniangels were starting to flit about. Once they got off the ground, they moved as a single unit toward the basket that Andrew was holding up. Andrew was starting to get a bit nervous because they had been there for ten minutes already. Matthew told him that they were still in the clear so far. The miniangels were just passing through the electrical force field so Andrew had to stay there even if a robocop was to show up because the angels had to have a safe landing place. The angels were weak and close to death because they did not have a human or walking dead individual to share a mental link with; they survived off the human or walking dead as if they were hosts, but not in a physical way. The miniangels finally settled into the basket, and Andrew lowered his arm, bringing the basket to chest level. He glanced into the basket at the angels and could not believe how beautiful they were.

Matthew told Andrew to hurry because he saw a robocop coming their way and he believed that it had not spotted them yet. The boys started to run for the hovercraft that was left by the girls the day they were abducted. They each got on a hovercraft and made a run for the tunnel. Right as they turned into the tunnel, they knew that the robocop had spotted them because it started to dart for them. The boys ditched the hovercraft and ran through the tunnel to where the door was and got it open, just as the robocop got to the edge of the tunnel. For some reason, the robocops would not go into the tunnel so the boys knew they had a slim chance to escape. They had to quickly get the door open, get inside, and shut the door back up. Even though the robocop would not go into the tunnel, that did not mean that they would not shoot into the tunnel at them. The boys managed to get through the door and shut it safely. They ran through the narrow space of the tunnel toward where the tunnel widened into a field, which was where the chief was waiting for them.

Andrew and Matthew finally got to where the chief was and took their horses from him. They mounted and began the ride back home. The boys and the chief were getting near home on the double. Andrew started to feel an overwhelming sense of pressure in his back and abdomen that he could not understand why. The closer they got to home, the worse the pressure was in Andrew's abdomen. Matthew and the chief noticed that something was wrong with Andrew because he started to lose what color he had and his riding posture was sloppy; those things were not normal for Andrew. The group was going to stop at the lake to water the horses then mosey the rest of the way home, but due to what the chief and Matthew saw in Andrew, the chief suggested that they ride straight through and keep it at a fast pace. It became obvious that they needed to get Andrew to the hospital to be checked out by the doctor and Matthew could ride on and get Camillia and bring her to Andrew's side.

The chief told Andrew that he was going to take him to the hospital, but Andrew refused to go until after he had taken care of the miniangels and seen Camillia so the chief told Matthew to ride on home with Andrew and get him settled in his bed while he went for the doctor and he would bring him to the castle, Matthew acknowledged the chief's order. Matthew knew how urgent it was for the miniangels to be returned to the forest, so the boys stopped at the edge of the golden forest and let the miniangels go into their natural habitat, which was a spectacular sight to see. Right after setting the miniangels free, the boys got to the castle and Matthew practically carried Andrew into the castle and to his bedroom; they were both shocked to see Camillia in bed with the same symptoms as Andrew. Matthew got Andrew into the bed next to his wife and stayed there waiting for the chief to show up with the doctor.

Camillia was excited to see Andrew; she told him that she was not feeling well; then she told him that she had a heaviness in her lower abdomen and some low back pain. Andrew told Camillia that her symptoms were the same symptoms that he had. Just then, the chief walked into the couple's bedroom, and he had the doctor with him. The doctor asked Camillia what her symptoms were and she told him; then he asked Andrew what his symptoms were, and he told him. The doctor chuckled and told the chief that there was nothing wrong with Andrew; he was just having sympathy pains for Camillia. The doctor said that he needed to check Camillia to see if she was dilated for childbirth. The doctor checked Camillia, and sure enough, she was dilated five centimeters. The doctor told the chief to get a horse and buggy ready because they needed to get Camillia to the hospital. Then he turned to Andrew and told him that he needed to break his mental link with Camillia so he could feel normal again and be of some use during the delivery of their child. Andrew could break his mental link with Camillia, and sure enough, he felt normal again and realized that the symptoms were sympathy pains for Camillia and he was beside himself when he suddenly realized that Camillia was about to deliver the baby at home and what if something went wrong. The chief came back in and told the doctor that the buggy was ready. The doctor asked Andrew if he could carry Camillia to the buggy, and he said yes.

Andrew got off the bed and walked around to Camillia's side of the bed and picked her up off the bed. He took her to the buggy and laid her in the back then got on in front. The chief got on the buggy next to Andrew, and Matthew stayed behind so he could see his wife and let her know that he was back from the journey. The doctor got on his horse and headed for the hospital. The buggy followed him to the hospital; it took a bit longer to get to the hospital than usual because everyone in the community was headed for the community dining hall. When they finally got to the hospital, Andrew got off the buggy and went to the back to pick up Camillia. The chief followed the doctor as he showed Andrew where to take Camillia. When they got to a room, Andrew laid Camillia on the bed and stood beside her and held her hand while the chief found a chair at the head of the bed to sit on. The doctor left the room to get a couple of nurses to aid in the delivery, to get a delivery kit, and to wash up.

When the doctor got back into Camillia's room, he checked her to see how dilated she was and found that the baby's head and shoulders had already been delivered. The doctor finished delivering the rest of the baby then handed her to one of the nurses. The doctor congratulated Andrew and told him and Camillia that the baby was a healthy girl. The doctor asked Camillia how she felt, and she told him that she felt great at that point; she said she was not feeling so great a few minutes ago. Camillia asked the doctor when the baby could go home with her and Andrew, and he told her that the baby could go home in about an hour and so could she. Andrew and Camillia were excited and started to discuss what the baby would be named; they decided to name her Jaquelina. Once the chief heard the doctor tell Andrew and Camillia that they could take the baby and go home in an hour and that everyone was healthy, he decided to leave at top speed so he could go to the community dining hall where everyone in the community would be to announce the birth of Jaquelina.

CHAPTER THIRTY SIX

Dinner was about to end and many of the pale ones were ready to go home, but the chief got there just on time to stop them from leaving so he could make his announcement. The chief went to the podium and announced that the king and queen just welcomed a beautiful baby girl and that they had named her Jaquelina. When the community heard that announcement, they cheered and everyone hugged everyone. Eventually, everyone went home and the chief left the dining hall also. The chief went back to the hospital to see if Andrew and Camillia were still there so he could help them get home, and when he went inside to the room she was in, he found her and Andrew still there. In fact, the nurse was giving Jacquelina to Camillia. Andrew saw the chief at the door and called out to him to go in and see the newest addition to their family. The chief walked up to Camillia to see Jacquelina, and Camillia handed the baby to the chief so he could admire her. The nurse told the proud parents that they were good to go.

Camillia and Andrew got on the buggy, and the chief handed Jacquelina up to Camillia then he got on his horse and followed them home. When the couple got home, the chief followed them inside, and as soon as they walked into their home, everyone in the castle standing near the door became ecstatic. Once Camillia and Andrew were all the way inside their home, they took a seat in the family room and gave baby Jacquelina to her nanny who passed her around for everyone to hold and admire. After an hour of passing the new baby around, she became fussy; it was time for her to sleep so her nanny took her into her new nursery room and laid her down for the evening. Everyone in the family room dispersed and went to wrap things up with their jobs so they could have the rest of the evening to themselves. Andrew and Camillia changed into their bed clothes and lay in bed. Together they shared details of their time apart and shared sentimental feelings toward each other. Andrew and Camillia discussed getting pregnant again; they agreed that they wanted to try as soon as bodily possible because they wanted to have a lot of children and they needed to find out if the vaccine that they were given to have their few human traits turned to pale one traits made them sterile or not. Camillia and Andrew cuddled and went to sleep in each other's arms.

The next morning rolled around. Andrew and Camillia got out of bed and changed their clothes into day clothing. They went to the castle's private dining hall for breakfast. They had to go to the census hall and the science hall after breakfast; they also needed to speak with the construction crew about how the expansion projects were going with the various community halls. The couple ate slowly and enjoyed each other's company. They laughed together and got sentimental with each other; their day had started out great. They tried to stretch out their breakfast time because they were having so much fun with each other. They thanked Melanie for another wonderful meal and headed for the front door to start addressing their responsibilities. When the couple got outside, Andrew asked the stable boy to saddle up two horses so he ran to the stable, saddled two horses, and ran back out with the horses. Andrew and Camillia were headed to the census hall. When the couple got to the census hall, they went inside and spoke to the head census worker and asked her for an update on where they were on documenting information about the newest pale ones. The head census worker told Andrew and Camillia that they had finished the documentation of everyone. She said that she even documented information on Jaquelina already. The couple was pleased to hear that all the work had been done. The couple thanked the census worker for their promptness then excused themselves to tackle the next errand.

Andrew and Camillia left the census hall and headed for the science hall to see how they were coming along with the conception project. It did not take long to get there; they got off their horses, tied them to the pole in front, and walked into the science hall. Camillia asked for the head scientist, and one of the workers went to get the head scientist. He walked across the hall rather urgently, and when he got to Andrew and Camillia, he seemed to be a little excited about something. Camillia asked how the conception project was going, and the scientist smiled widely and said that they had gotten a hair further. Not only had they gotten every ingredient isolated, but they had also found out what most of the ingredients targeted and in which body system. There were still a few ingredients that they did not know anything about or if it was even available in the forest because when the original serum was made, some ingredients came from the forest and some from the earth's surface.

The scientist told the couple that they made a giant discovery; they found two ingredients that targeted the reproductive system and that they were in the process of breaking down dhosoe two ingredients to their purest raw form to see if they were available in the forest or from the earth's surface. The scientist said that they wanted to gather those specific ingredients so that they could perform some experiments with them. Camillia sprang into the scientist's arms and gave him a big hug and told him she was excited and that he had a job well done. Andrew asked the scientist to stay in close contact with them and that he would assign a runner to him so he could send word of the various stages of the project to them. The scientist said that would be great because they were looking forward to having some grand results. The scientist jokingly told Andrew that he may want to have a runner for the original runner because the information to send would be coming at them in double time. Andrew and Camillia laughed at what the scientist had said; then Andrew got serious and told the scientist that it would be a clever idea to have a second runner for them. With two runners, no information would be missed and it would be easier on the runners in case they needed to have a snack, go to the restroom, or just take a break.

The scientist thanked the couple and turned to go back to his work. Camillia and Andrew left very pleased and anxious to hear more. They decided to head for home so they could assign two runners to the head scientist as quickly as possible. They were going to call for the head construction worker to go to them for a report on their progress instead of going to the community hall that they were currently working on to get an update. The couple got home just in time to see the chief getting off his horse in front of their home. They rode up and met him outside, and he was overjoyed to see them. They got off their horses and walked up to the chief and greeted him. The stable boy took their horses to the stable while they stood outside and talked for a few minutes.

The chief was there for a few reasons. First, he wanted to check on mom and new baby to see how they were doing. Camillia told the chief that she felt great and that Jaquelina was a wonderful baby. Camillia told the chief that she had the mom's intuition that Jaquelina was more gifted than the other children. She said that Armellya and the twins were born when she still had some human traits so that was a disadvantage for those children, but Armellya was more gifted than the twins for some reason. She went on to tell the chief that even though the new baby was so young, she was already showing signs of her gifts. Camillia reminded the chief that Jaquelina was exhibiting her gifts from within the womb. The chief asked Camillia if she thought that Armellya and the twins had human traits or if they were completely pale ones. Andrew answered and told the chief that if Camillia was not a complete pale one during the pregnancy through birth, then he could not see how the child would be complete. Camillia told Andrew that maybe the science hall would be able to tell. The chief came up with an idea; he told the couple that they were not completely pale ones during the pregnancy with Jaquelina but that they were changed the rest of the way during the pregnancy so she would most likely be complete. The couple still did not see where the chief was headed with the comparisons. The chief finished his idea and told the couple that maybe the vaccine given to them during the pregnancy would be perfect for Armellya and the twins. Camillia thought about it for a few minutes then said it was logical. Andrew told the chief that what he said was a great deduction and maybe they should consult the doctor and see what he had to say.

Camillia agreed and told Andrew that if the doctor agreed with the theory that they could then turn to the science hall for the solution. Camillia thought about it further while the chief and Andrew were talking and told them that they may have to wait until they see if it caused them to become sterile or not. Andrew agreed because then they would know if the children would have to be treated with what the scientists were trying to produce at the current moment or not. Andrew and Camillia needed to get inside so they could take care of the last of their business so they invited the chief to go in with them and said that they would get to him right after dealing with the runners. The chief said that was fine and that he would wait. Andrew went straight for his office room to get the first runner while Camillia sat with the chief. Andrew told the runner to bring the head of construction to him, and the runner acknowledged him and left pronto. Andrew got the second runner and instructed him to be on call for the head scientist; he acknowledged Andrew and left right away to go to the science hall. Andrew went out to the living room with Camillia and the chief and sat down next to Camillia then asked the chief what he needed to speak to them about.

The chief told the couple that he would like for them and the babies with their nannies to accompany him to dinner at his private dining hall. The couple said that they would love to and asked what the occasion was. The chief told them that there was no real occasion, it was just to appreciate them and celebrate being a real family and share the love that goes with being a family. Right then, the first runner got back with the head of construction. Andrew instructed that runner to join the other runner at the science hall; he left immediately and headed for the science hall. Andrew asked the head of construction how they were coming with the expansion project. He told Andrew that they would be finished with the last hall that day and that when it was finished, he would report back. Andrew told him that he and his crew had done an excellent job and that he would be waiting for the report. The head construction worker thanked Andrew for the compliment and said he would be in contact later then left to go back to the job site.

It was just a few minutes until the family would be gathering in Andrew and Camillia's family room for family time so the couple and the chief stayed there to wait for everyone to show up. Five minutes went by, then there was a knock at the front door. The couple thought it was family starting to arrive, but it was one of the runners from the science hall with a message. The butler let him in and took him to Andrew. Andrew asked Camillia and the chief to join him and the runner in the office room. Everyone went inside the office room, and Andrew closed the door behind them. Everyone sat down, and Andrew asked the runner what he had for them. The runner handed a note to Andrew and told him he had no verbal explanation for his visit, only a written statement. Andrew read the letter silently then asked the runner to step out into the hallway and wait until further notice. The runner stepped out and closed the door behind him.

Andrew told the chief and his wife that the science hall was focusing on the two ingredients they found that targeted the reproductive system and found that one was female-organ specific and the other was male-organ specific. That meant that there would have to be two separate vaccines made, and they would be gender specific. The science hall noted that there was one problem—to get more of the ingredients in their raw form, they would have to go to the earth's surface. The chief told Andrew that going to the earth's surface was dangerous, and if they did go, how would they know what to look for? Andrew told the chief that it would be easy to work out a plan of action, but it would involve both going as well as Matthew. Andrew said that they would have to basically escort two scientists above ground and guard them. Andrew told the chief that if danger did find them, he and Matthew would have to stay as a diversion so the scientists could make it back with the ingredients. He concluded his thought by telling the chief that he would be there just as before, to watch the horses. The chief told Andrew that it was a risk that everyone would have to think about long and hard.

Camillia had an idea. She asked if there would be any way to find ingredients that were in the forest that would work just as well. It would take some extra research, but it was safer for everyone involved. Andrew stood up and went to the door and opened it; he told the runner to go back to the science hall and tell the head scientist that the three of them would be arriving two hours after the lunch hour to discuss the note. The runner said okay and left. Andrew went back into the office room and told Camillia and the chief that after family time, they were going to the science hall to give the head scientist Camillia's idea. Everyone was good with that plan and went back out to the family room to receive their family members.

By the time that Andrew and Camillia and the chief got to the family room, everyone was waiting on them, which was nothing new. Everyone went to the castle's private dining hall for lunch where Melanie had all the food laid out on the table. She decided to do a buffet-style lunch instead of serving everyone the same thing. Everyone served themselves as they spoke about how wonderful Camillia and Andrew's children were. They made a comment about how they wished they could produce children. Only the chief, Andrew, and Camillia were aware that the science hall was working on the conception project. Camillia wanted to tell them that there may come a chance if the science hall was to be successful in producing a vaccine, but it had to remain a secret. During the lunch hour, no one really spoke; they were so engrossed in the wonderful food that Melanie and her parents had prepared that they could not stop putting food into their mouths long enough to get a word out.

The lunch hour did seem to go by fast, and before they knew it, they were in the family room conversing about the children. Everyone wanted to see the children and love them so Camillia went to Bridgette and asked her to get her parents and the children and bring them out to the family room; she happily acknowledged Camillia and did as she was asked. Everyone got quiet waiting on Bridgette and her parents. When they got to the family room with the children, everyone held their arms up for the babies. The family decided to sit in a circle and spend some time with each child then pass the children to the next family member. Eventually, everyone had a turn and Bridgette and her parents took the children back to their nurseries. Family time was over, and it was time for everyone to get back to their duties. Andrew and Camillia as well as the chief needed to go to the science hall. Once the last person left, the couple and chief asked the stable boy to saddle up three horses; and as usual, he had three horses ready in twelve minutes. The couple did not know how the boy could get their rides to them so quickly, but they were very pleased with him. Camillia told Andrew that she wanted to do something special for him, and Andrew agreed that it was important to do so. Andrew, Camillia, and the chief mounted their horses and headed for the science hall.

When the chief and the young couple got to the science hall, the head scientist was eagerly awaiting them. Andrew told him that he got the note and that they needed to talk. The scientist told Andrew that the two ingredients came from the earth's surface. One ingredient was male specific and the other was female specific. Andrew asked the scientist if there were two ingredients from the forest that could be substituted and still have the same effect they were looking for. The scientist had not thought about that and said he could look for something that would be an equivalent, but that it would extend the time for achieving the vaccine. Andrew said it would be worth it because traveling to the earth's surface was dangerous. Andrew added that to get the ingredients meant that two scientists would have to go along and that was two more lives at risk. The scientist understood the risk and was willing to do everything possible to avoid having to go to the earth's surface. Andrew told him that if there was no other way, then they would travel above ground; after all, it was for the benefit of saving their species. The scientist told Andrew that he would put together a team to send out to the forest right away. Andrew told him to keep in contact, and the scientist said he would. Andrew and Camillia were done with the science hall for now so they took a ride to the hospital. They were going to consult with the doctor about their theory of the first three of their children having some human qualities and the fourth being complete. Right when the couple got to the hospital, the head construction crew member noticed that they were there. He had to ride by the hospital from where his last job was to get to the castle. He detoured to the hospital to catch Andrew and Camillia and report that all the halls had been completed and were ready to occupy.

Andrew and Camillia were relieved that the expansion project was complete. Now the community could utilize each hall for what it was intended for and have the proper environment for what they were there to do. The couple said goodbye to the head construction worker and went on into the hospital. They walked to the nurse's desk and asked if their doctor was available. The nurse told them that he was around somewhere and she would find him for them and in the meantime they should wait in the waiting room. Camillia and Andrew went to the waiting room and sat down. Camillia was commenting that it was certainly different to go into the hospital without needing care. Just as Andrew was about to comment, the doctor came around the corner and greeted them. The doctor took them to his office room and offered for them to sit down. They sat down and started to get to business.

CHAPTER THIRTY SEVEN

Camillia asked the doctor, if she had some human qualities when she had the children, would they also have human qualities? The doctor said he had never had to work with humans and that the couple was the closest to humans that he got before they had the vaccine. He told Camillia that the first three children probably did, but that she had the vaccine during her third pregnancy so it was a fair guess that it affected the baby also. Andrew asked the doctor if the vaccine that had been given to Camillia during her pregnancy to remove her human traits would be appropriate for the first three children. The doctor said that it would work, but that the dose had to be altered because there was an enormous difference between an adult and an infant. The couple said that they would run the idea past the scientists and find out if they felt it was possible to be done without negative results or side effects. The doctor agreed that the scientists were the best individuals to speak to about the vaccine. The couple thanked the doctor for his honesty and time. The couple wanted to stop back at the science hall before going home while the subject was fresh on their minds. Andrew and Camillia went outside, got their horses from the hospital's stable boy, mounted, and rode off. They got back to the science hall in no time. The couple entered the hall and looked to see if they could see the head scientist, but he spotted them first and raced to the front of the hall. The head scientist greeted Andrew and Camillia then asked them how he could help them. They told him that they wanted to discuss the vaccine that he had given to them to remove any human traits that they had left. The scientist asked if it appeared to fail or if it caused negative side effects. Camillia told him that it seemed to work and that there were no negative side effects except the possibility of making them barren, but that had yet to be determined. The scientist asked what they needed to know about the vaccine and why.

Andrew told them that their first three children may have some human traits since they were conceived and birthed prior to them receiving the vaccine. Andrew went on to say that they got the vaccine during their last pregnancy, and it appeared that that child was a pure pale one. The scientist told the couple that he guessed that they were thinking of having their first three children vaccinated against human traits. Camillia told him that he guessed right then asked, if the dose was appropriate, would it work without harming them? The scientist told them that they had perfected the vaccine before giving it to them, and they recorded the instructions on how to reproduce it in their official books so that they or anyone that may take their place down the road could produce it so yes, they could give the children the vaccine. The scientist told them that he would want to do it in the hospital with the doctor on standby because it was uncomfortable to undergo the transformation and it would stop the children from breathing for a few minutes, and if something went wrong and they did not start breathing like they should, the doctor would be there to intervene.

Andrew and Camillia fully understood the risks and benefits and asked when they could do it. The scientist said they could do it on that day, but it would have to be after dinner. The scientists would need from the current moment to dinnertime to produce the vaccines then they would go to dinner and then get the vaccines from the science hall and head to the hospital.

Andrew and Camillia said that they could meet him at the hospital with the children and their nannies. The scientist said that it was a date. Andrew and Camillia thanked him then turned to walk out. The scientist pulled a few science workers from the conception project to work on the anti human vaccine. They had to produce enough for three babies. Andrew and Camillia got on their horses and headed for the chief's house to tell him of the latest news.

When they got to the chief's home, he was outside getting ready to go somewhere. The couple rode up to the chief and asked him where he was going; he told them that he was on his way to their home to check on how the various projects they had going were doing. The chief asked them why they were there at his house. Andrew told him that he had some news for him and that he may want to be a part of it. Of course, the chief was curious so he asked what the big news was. Andrew told him that they should go inside and talk. The chief okayed the suggestion. The couple got off their horses and gave them to the chief's stable boy then followed the chief inside. The chief took Andrew and Camillia into his family room where they all sat down and got comfortable. Andrew told the chief that Armellya, Kaylina, and Kevin had human traits in them because Camillia had them and was not vaccinated yet. The chief was listening attentively. Andrew told the chief that the vaccine that he and Camillia had gotten during her last pregnancy was safe for the babies and that after dinner, the nannies were to bring the babies to the hospital to meet with the doctor and scientist to get their vaccine. Camillia reminded the chief that Jaquelina basically got the vaccine because she was pregnant with her when she got the vaccine. The chief was surprised that they would do their vaccines with them as young as they were. Camillia and Andrew wanted all their children to be pure and have all the assets that go with being pure as possible.

The chief said that it made sense to do it while they were young; they would not remember the discomfort, and they would have their talents mastered before they got out of diapers. Camillia asked the chief if he would like to be there when the children got their vaccinations; the chief said absolutely. The couple needed to go home to let the nannies know to have the children ready to go to the hospital for their vaccinations then they could return to the chief's side of the castle for dinner. Andrew and Camillia excused themselves from the chief's presence to go to their side of the castle. The couple got their horses from the chief's stable boy and rode home. When they got there, they gave their horses to their stable boy to take to the barn. The couple rushed into their home and called on Bridgette and her parents. When Bridgette and her parents got to the family room, Andrew told them to have the children ready to go to the hospital for their anti human vaccine. They said they would show up with bells and whistles then return to their nurseries.

Andrew and Camillia left their home to go to the chief's home for dinner. The couple took a romantic walk from their side of the castle to the chief's side of the castle. They knocked on the chief's front door, and the butler answered it. He led the couple to the family room to wait for the chief. The chief got there within seconds and greeted them. Andrew and Camillia asked what the special occasion was, and the chief told them to remember what he said earlier that day. He said that he just wanted some personal time with his family, to share the love between them and enjoy a father, daughter, and son moment. Andrew and Camillia thought that it was a nice and sentimental gesture, and Camillia wanted to be a part of that experience. Andrew felt the same; he wanted to be a part of a quiet sentimental moment. The chief told Andrew and

Camillia to follow him to the castle's private dining hall and sit at the round table.

The couple did as they were asked, and the chief took a seat. After they did, the kitchen staff started to bring food out. It was a candlelight dinner with a beautiful floral centerpiece. As the kitchen staff brought out more and more food, the chief told the couple that he was a proud parent and grandparent.

The couple told the chief that they were proud children, and they respected him greatly. They told him that he was very kind and the wisest of all pale ones. They delicately ate their dinner, making sure to use their most proper manners. It took them the whole dinner hour to finish their meal. The kitchen crew was on their way out of the kitchen to gather up the dishes and clear the table when the chief stood up and said that they had better get moving to get the children to the hospital for their vaccinations. Andrew and Camillia stood up and agreed with the chief; they needed to get a move on it if they were going to reach the doctor before he went home for the evening. Andrew, Camillia, and the chief left the chief's castle and went to the couple's castle to pick up the children and their nannies.

By the time the chief and the couple got to the couple's castle, the nannies had the babies and were outside waiting for the stable boy to bring out the buggy. Just as the couple and the chief got side by side with the nannies and babies, the stable boy brought out the buggy. Everyone got on to the buggy, and Andrew let the driver take them instead of driving the team himself. They got to the hospital in a fair amount of time. They all got off the buggy and let the hospital's stable boy take the wagon to the hospital barn. The chief, Andrew, Camillia, the nannies, and the children all went into the hospital and approached the nurse's desk. Andrew told the head nurse that they needed the doctor's assistance. The charge nurse had them go to the waiting room while she went after the doctor. The doctor walked into the waiting room seven minutes later and asked what he could do for them.

The scientist had just walked into the waiting room on time to hear the doctor ask what he could do for them. The scientist answered the doctor and told him that they had brought the three children to get their anti human vaccinations. The doctor followed what the scientist had said so far, but he still failed to see why they needed him. The scientist knew through telepathy that the doctor was somewhat dumbfounded so he explained further. He told the doctor that the vaccine was a bit uncomfortable to go through, and it had an immediate side effect of depressing the respiratory drive to the extent that they stop breathing for about three minutes. The reason they wanted to have him there was if the children failed to start breathing again, he could step in and try to get them to breathe or put them on life support until they either recovered or he could find a solution. The doctor asked what the chances were of the children being harmed, and the scientist told the doctor that the vaccine had only been given once and that was to Andrew and Camillia. The scientist believed it was safe for the children because it did not harm Jaquelina who was intrauterine when Camillia got the vaccine and she turned out pure.

The doctor was not satisfied with the explanation given so he asked again what the chances were of the babies being harmed. The scientist told the doctor that the risk was essentially absent. The doctor agreed to be on standby so he led the group to the emergency department where there were several beds side by side. The scientist asked for the nannies to place their child on the bed and stand with them. He told Andrew and Camillia to stand back out of the way. Everyone did as they were asked, and the scientist pulled three injection needles out of his lab coat pocket. He went to Armellya and injected her then waited for her to stop breathing and called the doctor over to keep an eye on her. After three minutes, she started to breathe so Bridgette picked her up and soothed her. She was quiet again and snuggled into Bridgette's chest. The scientist then went to Kaylina and injected her; he waited for her to stop breathing then told the doctor to watch over her. After three minutes, she started to breathe so Bridgette's mother picked her up and let her nestle into her chest.

Finally, the scientist went to the last of the children, Kevin. The scientist gave Kevin his injection and waited for him to stop breathing; then like the other two, he told the doctor to watch him. Within three minutes, Kevin started breathing so Bridgette's father picked him up and cuddled him. All the babies were fine and were now pure. Camillia and Andrew could now relax; all their children were turned and safe. The scientist and the couple thanked the doctor for being on standby, and he said it was his pleasure.

The doctor walked out of the room so he could get ready to go home. The couple, the scientist, the nannies, and the children all went to get on the buggy. Everyone was relieved that the vaccinations were done. They got to the couple's side of the castle, and everyone got off the buggy to go inside the castle. The nannies took the children to their nurseries to be laid down for the night. The chief even stayed for a few moments to make sure that the couple was okay. The couple assured the chief that they were okay; it was during the time that the children were getting their vaccinations that they were on the edge. The couple gave the chief a hug and thanked him for his concern. The chief then left their home to go to his.

Andrew and Camillia went to their bedroom to spend some time together before it would be time to go to sleep. The couple changed into bedclothes and sat on the edge of the bed next to each other, and Camillia broke the silence. Camillia asked Andrew how soon he wanted another baby. Andrew looked at her with love and sincerity then told her he wanted as many children as they could have. He said how soon they got pregnant after having a baby was up to her body, but if her body was ready, he would leave it up to her as to whether to go ahead and get pregnant or abstain from lovemaking to avoid the pregnancy. Camillia was relieved to hear his answer because she wanted as many children as she could have and have the babies back to back. Andrew asked her why she asked the question that she asked. Camillia told him that she felt the same way but that she wanted to know his view on the subject because she was ovulating and that the present time was the perfect time to conceive. Andrew became aroused; he put his arms around Camillia and pulled her back on the bed then rolled on top of her. Camillia laughed as Andrew got playful, and she put her arms around him. They gazed deeply into each other's eyes, their faces drawn together; then they romantically kissed. They explored each other's bodies with their hands, and that led them into making love. When they were done, they lay in each other's arms, and Camillia told Andrew that they had conceived a baby boy and she would call him William. Then she asked him how William sounded for a boy's name. Andrew asked her if she was sure she conceived, and she said yes, she felt the union and she had already gotten the intuition that it was a boy. Andrew said that William sounded perfect, and he started to romantically kiss her. They lay together for a while then fell asleep in each other's arms.

The next morning arrived, and the couple woke up in a fabulous mood. They found out that the anti human vaccine did not make them sterile. After they said good morning to each other, they both started to suggest something so Andrew told Camillia she could speak first. She suggested that they go to the hospital to visit the doctor for a blood pregnancy test and ultrasound. Andrew told Camillia that he was going to suggest the same thing, not because he did not believe her but because they needed to have prenatal care.

They decided to go after breakfast, and when they got the doctor's confirmation, they would tell their friends. They changed into day clothes from their bedclothes then groomed themselves and went to the castle's private dining hall. Melanie was in the dining hall to oversee the kitchen crew; they brought out the couple's breakfast.

Right as Camillia was getting ready to take her first bite of breakfast, Melanie told Camillia that she had a mother's glow about her. Camillia simply thanked Melanie then took her first bite of breakfast. Melanie interrupted Camillia and told her that she thought Camillia was pregnant again. With that said, Andrew choked on his food; he could not believe that Melanie could tell that Camillia was pregnant already. Camillia was about to comment on Michelle's statement, but Andrew spoke up first to change the subject. Andrew told Michelle that he and Camillia wanted to do something special for their stable boy so he suggested that she make up a complete food basket for him to take home to share with his family. Michelle asked what he wanted in the basket, and Andrew told her a little bit of everything. Michelle told Andrew that she would have to visit some of the shops to get some supplies and, of course, the basket to put everything into. Camillia told her to go where she needed and get the items that she thought would be nice and, as Andrew said, to be sure to get a little bit of everything. Camillia said that it might be nice to do separate baskets for the distinct categories of food. The couple told her to be creative and fix the gift as if it were for her and her family. Michelle understood and verbalized that understanding to the couple.

CHAPTER THIRTY EIGHT

Michelle told Camillia that when she got everything prepared, she wanted Camillia to inspect it for her approval. Camillia said that she was sure it would be perfect but that she would like to see how it turned out. Michelle thanked Camillia for allowing her to be a part of the warm gesture, and Camillia thanked Michelle for helping her out with the warm gesture. Michelle left the dining area to go plan her shopping route and what items to pick up while the couple finished eating their breakfast in silence. It did not take long for Camillia and Andrew to finish their meal. The kitchen crew was starting to clear off the round table, and Michelle was leaving the castle at that moment. Andrew and Camillia were not far behind Michelle in leaving the castle for some errands. When the couple got outside to have the stable boy saddle up two horses, Andrew told him to see himself and Camillia in the evening before leaving the castle to go home. The stable boy was not sure what the whole ordeal was about, but he agreed to see them before going home. Then with a strange look on his face, he went to saddle up two horses so the couple could take care of their business. The stable boy got back to Andrew and Camillia with their horses, and Camillia took that opportunity to tell him that he was not in any trouble. He acknowledged her as she and Andrew were taking their horses from him. They told the boy that they would see him later then rode off. The couple had a few errands, and they were going to make the doctor's visit the first one because they were excited and could not wait another moment. They got to the hospital and gave their horses to the hospital stable boy and went directly to the nurse's desk. The charge nurse saw them coming, and before they could ask for the doctor, she said to let her guess, they needed to see the doctor as soon as possible. Andrew and Camillia chuckled and said yes. She chuckled as she walked away to get the doctor. When the charge nurse came back, she had the doctor in tow. The doctor took one look at Camillia and told her he believed that she had the mother's glow.

Andrew's jaw dropped open with disbelief; he did not see this mother's glow that everyone else seemed to see. Camillia giggled and told the doctor that she felt the conception and she already knew it was a boy, but she wanted to be seen to have the pregnancy officially confirmed. The doctor started to walk away and told the couple to follow him, and they did. He took them to their usual room. When they entered the room, the doctor jokingly said that he should put her name on the door and make it officially her room. Andrew laughed; Camillia just smirked. Camillia got on the bed and sat up while Andrew sat in a chair that was in the corner of the room. The doctor drew her blood this time and delivered it to the lab himself. The doctor left instructions to test the blood right away and to get the results to him pronto. The lab technician said he would do so and got right on it. When the doctor got back, he did an ultrasound and saw where they would be—a fetus embedded into the uterine wall. Then he put his equipment away and walked out of the room to wait for the lab result.

Fifteen minutes later, the doctor went back into the room and announced that they were going to be proud parents again. Camillia jumped off the bed and hugged the doctor and thanked him. He hugged her back and told her to thank her husband, that he had nothing to do with it. They all laughed and walked toward the doorway. The doctor told Camillia that he would see her in one week then congratulated the couple. They thanked him then said their farewells. Andrew and Camillia hugged and told each other that they were yet blessed again. Together they walked out of the hospital and got their horses from the hospital stable boy. They got on their horses and headed to the science hall to check on the status of the conception project and to tell the head scientist that the vaccine did not cause infertility because they had just found out that they were pregnant.

As they were leaving the hospital grounds, the couple ran into Melanie as she was riding by to get from one shop to the next. She noticed them and rode up to them and asked if everything was okay. Camillia told her that they were coming from seeing the doctor to get confirmation of another pregnancy. Andrew butted in and proudly told her that they were pregnant. Melanie was so happy for them; she squealed and bounced about on the buggy then asked if anyone else knew. Camillia told her that no one else knew, but they had planned to announce it during family time later that day. Melanie told Camillia that she still had a lot to do so she needed to get going. Camillia told her that they were supposed to be somewhere also so they said they would see each other back at the castle later. Michelle got the buggy moving and went on her way. Camillia and Andrew got their horses going and went on to the science hall.

When the couple went into the science hall, everyone was so busy concentrating and working that they did not notice them walk in. Andrew went to find the head scientist so they could discuss where they were with the conception project. The head scientist just happened to look up as Andrew was approaching him. He said hello to Andrew and started to walk around the desk to get to Andrew to shake his hand then together they would walk over to where Camillia was. Andrew asked how they were doing on the conception project, and the head scientist got a puzzled look on his face. He told Andrew that they had tested a lot of ingredients from the forest and so far, nothing seemed to target the reproductive system. The head scientist did say that there were many more ingredients to test so there was still a lot of hope. Camillia told the head scientist that she had good news for him; he just gave her a strange look and stayed silent. Camillia told him that they had just come from seeing the doctor, and they got confirmation that she was pregnant—that meant that the anti human vaccine was a success.

The head scientist hollered to the rest of the scientists that the anti human vaccine was a success. He added that Camillia was pregnant. The head scientist hugged Camillia and told her congratulations. All the other scientists jumped about, hugging one another and cheering. The head scientist told the other scientists to start working hard and get another successful vaccine. The chief scientist said that the success meant that they could turn the children into pure pale ones without negating their ability to reproduce. Andrew and Camillia said yes then told him that they just knew that he would be able to produce a vaccine for the community to awaken the community's reproductive systems. The head scientist now had more drive to find a successful reproductive vaccine than ever before; he told Camillia and Andrew so then thanked them for believing in him. Camillia told him that supporting other visions were what families were for, and the community was one big happy family. The head scientist agreed. The head scientist was in a rush to get back to work so he could find the special ingredients to replace the ones that were on the earth's surface. As Andrew and Camillia were ready to leave, Andrew reminded the head scientist that if nothing else would work, they would take the trip to the earth's surface. The head scientist thanked Andrew and said that hopefully they would be able to avoid going above ground. Andrew and Camillia walked out of the science hall and got their horses.

The couple wanted to walk from the science hall to their side of the castle just to observe the community at work and to greet others. They were always in such a hurry that they felt that they had lost touch with everyone. As they led their horses and moseyed home, Andrew and Camillia started to talk about how fortunate they were to be king and queen of the land of grandeur and being the only pale ones that could bear children. They realized that their children would be able to be active in the conception process, but without other children to conceive with, they were as well barren. They did not want their children reproducing with each other. Those thoughts made Andrew and Camillia desperate for the scientists to be successful in the conception project. Andrew told Camillia that he would go to the earth's surface a million times if that meant success for the conception project. Camillia was worried about that need coming to fruition. Andrew and Camillia's main concern now was in finding the means to protect their species from going extinct, and if the community could not reproduce, the species would die out in approximately four hundred years when their children finally perished. The couple decided not to overthink the situation because it was too premature now.

The couple found themselves walking close to where the stable boy was; they found it amazing how fast time flew when the mind was occupied. Andrew greeted the stable boy as he handed his horse's reins to him, and Camillia did the same. Then they both walked into the castle. Camillia told Andrew that she was going to check to see if Melanie had made it back. The butler informed her that Melanie had been back for a while now. Camillia wanted to see how far she had gotten on the basket for the stable boy and his immediate family. Camillia left Andrew to occupy his own self for a while.

With nothing at the castle to do, Andrew thought he would go visit the chief at his home. When Andrew got to the chief's side of the castle and knocked on the door, the butler answered. Andrew asked to see the chief so the butler took him to the chief. The chief asked Andrew if he could be of service, and Andrew told him that his visit was a social one. The chief was glad to see Andrew and told him that he needed to talk to him about something important, but that he also wanted Camillia present when he discussed the business on his mind. Andrew said very well and told the chief to have a social visit for now and that after family time, they would get together and talk about business. The chief agreed and sat with Andrew and discussed how much he and Camillia had done for the community so far.

Camillia went to the castle's private dining hall to see how far Melanie had gotten on the stable boy's basket. Melanie was at the round table with several large baskets that were almost full, and she still had many things to put into them. Camillia asked Melanie if she was going to have enough room in the baskets for the rest of the stuff. Melanie stood back and looked at the baskets then the food on the round table then back at the baskets and again at the food on the round table. She finally told Camillia that she could get it all to fit, but it would be a tight fit. Camillia asked if there was anything she could do to help, and Melanie told her if she could help get everything into the baskets neatly, then it would be a major help. Camillia started to help by putting things into the baskets, and finally, the food on the round table started to disappear.

All the baskets were complete in no time. There were six of them, and they were too heavy for the girls to pick up so Camillia went after Andrew. They needed the table cleared for the lunch hour so Melanie and Camillia wanted to have Andrew sneak the baskets out to the barn without the stable boy seeing him doing it. Camillia looked all over the castle for Andrew and failed to find him. She wondered where he could possibly be; then it suddenly dawned on her that he might be at the chief's side of the castle. Camillia told Melanie that she would be right back as she suspected that Andrew was visiting the chief.

Camillia got to the chief's front door and knocked; the butler answered the door. Camillia asked if Andrew was there, and he told her he was then invited her in. The butler told her that they were in the family room so that was where she went. Andrew and the chief were surprised to see Camillia; they figured she would be tied up with Melanie for a bit longer. Andrew asked Camillia how the basket was coming along. Camillia told him that there were six extra large baskets and that they were done, but they were too heavy for them to pick up so that was why she was there. Andrew and the chief both said that they would be happy to help move them wherever she wanted them. Camillia said thank you, and they all headed for the front door.

When they got into Andrew and Camillia's private dining hall, Melanie was there waiting. Camillia silently pointed at the baskets, and the men commented on how extravagant the baskets were. Camillia agreed and told them that Melanie had done a wonderful job. Andrew asked the girls where they wanted the baskets to be put. Camillia said that it would be best if they were put on the back of the buggy in the barn. That way, they would be ready for transport and they could take the stable boy home with his baskets. Andrew said okay then he and the chief went to pick up a basket each from the round table but were unable to pick them up alone. Andrew asked what was in the baskets that made them so heavy. Melanie told him that there were only food assortments in the baskets. The chief and Andrew teamed up and carried one basket together at a time; they had just realized that what they thought was going to be a breeze was going to take some time and be more like a chore, but they did not mind helping. When the chief and Andrew got the first basket outside, they had to put it down for a quick breather. The stable boy saw them having some difficulty with the basket and walked up to them and asked where they had to take the basket to. They told him that they were going to put that basket with five others in the back of the buggy until it was time to deliver them. The stable boy asked if he could suggest helping them, and both men welcomed it. He said that he could hitch the team and bring the buggy to them; then they would not have to walk nearly as far carrying the baskets. Andrew and the chief felt a bit silly for not thinking of that themselves. They told the stable boy that his suggestion was great and to do it. The stable boy had the team hitched and brought the buggy to the front door and kept the horses steady. Andrew and the chief put the first basket on the back of the buggy; now they had to do that five more times.

Camillia and Melanie were inside giggling at the chief and Andrew for how silly they looked trying to carry the baskets together and struggling to not drop them. The girls did not realize how heavy the baskets were going to be. Andrew and the chief finally got the last of the baskets on the buggy so the stable boy took the horses and buggy back to the barn until it would be time to deliver the baskets. He still had no idea that those baskets were for him and his immediate family. Andrew and the chief got back into the castle's private dining hall to talk with the girls.

When they got there, Melanie was not there and Camillia was on her way out. Camillia told them that Melanie had to check on things with the kitchen crew because it was almost time to serve lunch. Andrew told Camillia that he had not realized how late it was so the chief, Andrew, and Camillia stayed in the family room because family would start to arrive at any moment. The butler was on standby to answer the front door many times and, sure enough, he answered the front door many times, but the whole family was there and ready to move into the castle's private dining hall. Everyone got seated at the round table so Melanie had the kitchen staff start to serve everyone. Once everyone was served, it was time for individuals to start to share any current news, how their day had been so far, and what the day still held for them. Andrew, Camillia, and everyone else had shared what their day had been like so far and what their day still held in store for them so the couple decided that it was time to make their baby announcement. However, everyone was ready to go to the family room so they would tell of the new baby once everyone was settled.

Right as Melanie was going to get everyone's attention, Camillia asked for everyone's attention. Melanie was going to make way for the couple to make their announcement. Everybody got quiet and looked at Camillia; then she told her family that they were going to be welcoming in a new baby, that they were pregnant with little William. Everyone was happy and wanted the baby to get to know them before he was born just like they did with baby Jaquelina. Bridgette asked Camillia how she knew that the baby was a boy, and Camillia told her that she already had a telepathic link with him. They all thought that was special, and the female family members said that they wished they could experience that special bond. As once before, Camillia wished she could tell them about the conception project so that they at least had some hope, but it had to remain a secret. Everyone wanted to take turns loving on Camillia's stomach to talk to the new baby and let him get to know them so she let them rub her belly and talk to the baby.

Once everyone had their turn with the new baby and took their time letting him get to know them, family time was over so they all said that they would see each other later and everyone but the chief went their different directions. Melanie stayed behind to chat with Camillia quickly. Once everyone was gone, Melanie told Camillia that it was a good thing that she got everyone's attention when she did because it was exciting news and she wanted everyone to share it with her. Melanie got sentimental with Camillia and told her that she was special and a wonderful friend and excellent queen; she was proud to have her as family. Camillia gave Melanie a hug and told her that she loved her too. When Camillia and Melanie were done hugging, Melanie turned toward Andrew and told him that he was special to her also and that she loved him as her favorite brother. Andrew gave Melanie a hug and told her that he loved her also. Melanie told the chief that he was a father figure to her and that she loved him too then she gave him a hug. Then Melanie went to take care of her duties and left Camillia and Andrew to their business.

CHAPTER THIRTY NINE

It was time for Andrew and Camillia to have a private meeting with the chief so they went into Andrew's private office room. Everyone sat down, and Andrew asked the chief what the meeting could possibly be about because they were pretty much caught up on their business. The chief told the couple that the meeting was about needing to make some changes immediately to cover his position as the king's adviser. Andrew and Camillia were in shock to hear of that request; they could not imagine why. The chief could feel the couple's confusion and reluctance to accept him being replaced as the king's adviser. Andrew bluntly asked why he needed to be replaced immediately. The chief told them to calm down, that it was not because anyone did anything wrong, it was because he was dying. Just as Camillia could feel the conception of William, he could feel death approaching. Andrew and Camillia were at a loss for words. The chief told them that he was two hundred and thirty-five years old, and it was important that he train his replacement because there was a lot to the job. Camillia's emotions prevented her from speaking; all she could do was sit there with tears in her eyes and listen to what Andrew and the chief decided to do. Andrew told the chief that he felt apprehensive about having another adviser.

The chief told Andrew that they needed to at least have someone on standby. Andrew and Camillia knew what the job entailed and how time-consuming it was. Andrew suggested that Camillia take on that responsibility. The chief said that he knew she could handle it and that she would be easier to train than anyone else. Andrew asked the chief how much longer he planned on working. The chief said he would work up to his demise, but that it would be wise to get a replacement ready. Andrew said that he would accept having Camillia trained and on standby to take over at the time of the chief's demise but no sooner. The chief was happy with that arrangement. Camillia still had not said a word so Andrew asked her directly if she wanted to take the position when it was to be time. Camillia tried to compose herself, then told Andrew she would do what was asked of her, and she would always do what was best for the community. The chief stood up and said that it was settled then and that he would start training her the next day.

Andrew stood up, walked to Camillia, put his hand out to her, then told her to go with him. Camillia took Andrew's hand then stood up to go with him. The chief told her everything was going to be just fine while he rubbed her back. Suddenly, Camillia let go of Andrew's hand. She turned to the chief and threw her arms around his neck and hugged him. He hugged her back and told her that she was a wonderful daughter and a great leader. Camillia thanked the chief for his compliment and dried her eyes with her hands. Andrew, Camillia, and the chief were getting ready to walk out of the office room, but before Andrew could open the door, there was a knock on the door. Andrew answered the door, and it was a runner from the science hall. He had a note for Andrew to read. Andrew read the note quietly then passed it to Camillia for her and the chief to read. Andrew told the runner to tell the head scientist that he and Camillia would be there to talk with him before dinner. The runner said he would give the message to the head scientist then left abruptly. The chief told Andrew and Camillia that he would be going home so he could gather the items that they would need for the training so it could be done in Andrew's office room. Camillia and Andrew went out front to get the stable boy to saddle up two horses.

When the stable boy brought the horses, the couple left to go to the science hall and deal with the contents of the note that they had received. When Andrew and Camillia got to the science hall, the head scientist was watching and waiting for them. As soon as the couple walked into the science hall, the head scientist started to speak to them. Andrew boldly interrupted the head scientist and told him to quit talking, and he did. Andrew just simply wanted to know what was new with the conception project that he did not already know. Andrew told the scientist that he read the note that he sent over with the runner, and it was in his understanding that there were no ingredients from the forest that could be a substitution for the two ingredients that they isolated and found to target the female and male reproductive system.

The head scientist said that what he understood was correct. The head scientist told Andrew that the two ingredients that they needed were minerals and only produced where nuclear toxins were because the nuclear toxins changed the minerals' composition slightly, and that cannot be reproduced in a lab setting. Andrew asked the head scientist that what he was saying was that the pale ones would have to be indirectly exposed to radiation. The scientist simply replied yes. Andrew asked the head scientist if he understood what many people had risked besides their lives to protect the people from radiation because it killed many of them. The head scientist told Andrew that he had heard about it and that he was one of the humans who was rescued and turned. Andrew asked the head scientist if he knew what the radioactive minerals were going to do to the pale ones that he planned to give the vaccine to. The scientist said no but that was why they would ask for willful test subjects.

Camillia had not said a word. She just listened and processed the information, but she did not like what she was hearing. Camillia interrupted and told Andrew that she thought that the conception project should be put on hold until the two of them could discuss the situation with their adviser. Andrew agreed so he told the head scientist that the conception project was suspended until further notice. The head scientist tried to verbally fight for continuing the conception project, but Andrew and Camillia would not hear any of it. They silently turned around and walked out of the science hall. As the couple was mounting their horses, Andrew told Camillia that the two of them were going to have a meeting with themselves, the doctor, the chief, and the head scientist so everyone could get a clear picture of what had been going on with the project and what the next step would be, if any, with the suspected outcome. Camillia said that she was very comfortable with that idea, and she hoped that they could get to a solution easily that would not harm anyone.

Andrew and Camillia stopped by the hospital on their way home to let the doctor know that they needed him the next day for an important meeting. The doctor did not have anything important to do at that moment so he asked what the topic of the meeting was going to be. Andrew asked the doctor if they could go to his office room; he said yes then led them to his office room. Everyone entered the office room; then the doctor shut the door behind them. The three of them sat down then Andrew started to tell the doctor about the conception project. Andrew told the doctor that he had the science hall working on a vaccine to enable pale ones to reproduce. Andrew told him that there were problems with the project; for example, there had to be test subjects to find out how the vaccine would affect them, specifically if it worked or killed them due to radiation exposure, and that was not a gamble that he was willing to take. Then there was the fact that the two minerals only available on the earth's surface were altered by radiation exposure and had absorbed some of the radiation, the very thing that they had to be protected from by being turned. Andrew was about to go on with what was wrong with the project, but the doctor spoke up and told Andrew and Camillia that with the small amount of information he had heard so far, the project was a potential death sentence. Andrew told the doctor that he could get a full basic but direct written report on the conception project for him to review. The doctor said that he had heard enough and that he would see them the next day in their office room. Andrew thanked the doctor and told him that they would be seeing him the next day then turned and left to go home.

Andrew and Camillia made it back home before dinner, but they had to see the stable boy before going inside to eat dinner. It was time to give the six baskets to the stable boy then take him home. The stable boy greeted Andrew and Camillia as they rode up to the front door. The couple got off their horses and told the stable boy to hitch the horses to the buggy then bring the buggy out to them; he said okay then took their horses and headed for the barn. Nine minutes later, the stable boy brought the horses and buggy to Andrew and Camillia. The couple took the stable boy to the back of the buggy and showed him the baskets then told him that they were for him and his immediate family. The stable boy considered the baskets carefully; then with tears in his eyes, he grabbed Camillia and gave her a hug. After hugging Camillia, the stable boy grabbed Andrew and hugged him. The couple told the stable boy that he earned the baskets with the wonderful service that he had provided; he was quick to get his job done and took it very seriously. Andrew told him that he cared for their horses as though they were his own prized possessions, and that was very much appreciated.

The stable boy told the couple that the baskets would help his family greatly and that they did not have to give him anything because he was just doing his job the best way he knew how and that it was an honor to work for the king and queen of the land of grandeur. Camillia told him that he was like a son to her and Andrew. The stable boy told them that he did not know how to thank them, and they told him that he already had just by being appreciative. Andrew told the stable boy to get on the buggy and that he would take him home and help unload the baskets. The stable boy jumped onto the buggy and held the horse's reins while Camillia and Andrew got onto the buggy. The stable boy drove the buggy to his home, and when he got home, he jumped off the buggy with excitement and ran into his home yelling for his parents to go outside. His parents went to their front door quickly to see him and find out what the big fuss was about. The stable boy and his parents went to the back of the buggy with Andrew and Camillia.

Camillia told his parents that the six baskets were for them and that their son had earned them with his exemplary service. His parents were beside themselves; they could not believe how much food there was. Camillia told the stable boy's father that the baskets were extremely heavy and that it would take him and Andrew to pick up one of them and together get all six of the baskets into their home. The stable boy's mother was teary-eyed, and she thanked the couple again then gave her son a gentle hug. Andrew and the stable boy's father started to carry the baskets into the home; it took some time, but they finally got all six of them into their kitchen. Andrew and Camillia told the stable boy and his parents to enjoy the baskets and that they would see the boy on the next day.

The couple got back onto the buggy and headed home for their dinner. When Camillia and Andrew got home, Andrew unhitched the horses and got them taken care of then he and Camillia went into the castle. The couple was a bit late for dinner, but Melanie knew they might be so she had the kitchen keep their meal warm until they got there. Andrew and Camillia ate their dinner rapidly because they still had some business to deal with before it got too late. Melanie was surprised to see how fast the couple ate and that they both left quite a bit of food on their plates. She asked the couple if their dinner was okay, and they told her it was good but that they still had something to take care of before it got too late. Melanie understood then had the kitchen clear the table. Andrew and Camillia left their side of the castle to go to the chief's side of the castle. The couple knocked on the chief's front door, and the butler answered, then took them to the family room to wait for the chief. The butler went to get the chief and let him know that the couple was waiting in the family room to see him. The chief got to the family room and greeted Andrew and Camillia. Andrew told the chief that they needed to speak to him about something important. The chief took the couple to his office room and shut the door behind them.

Everyone sat down then the chief asked Andrew what he needed to discuss. Andrew told the chief that the next day, he wanted the three of them with the doctor and the head scientist to get together and talk about the conception project. The chief asked if there was something that went wrong with the research. Andrew reminded him of the note that was sent to them earlier that day by a runner then told him that they went to the science hall and got the details that the head scientist had for them. The chief commented that there must have been a major problem with what they were told to be wanting a large meeting with everyone that could be for or against the project. Andrew told him that the head scientist said that there were no ingredients from the forest that could be substituted for the minerals that targeted the male and female reproductive systems. Andrew told the chief that there was something else—the minerals were radioactive and that the radiation had changed the chemical composition of the minerals slightly and the radiation was a principal factor.

Andrew told the chief that the only way to produce the conception vaccine was to get more of the minerals from the earth's surface, which everyone knew that going above ground was dangerous. Andrew added that he did not like the idea that the vaccine would indirectly expose the community to radiation, the very thing that their people had worked so hard to be safe from. Andrew told the chief that the head scientist wanted to get volunteer test subjects to see what the vaccine would do; the scientists did not know if the vaccine would help, hurt, or even kill the test subjects. Andrew finished with his statement by telling the chief that he was not going to allow his people to be used like disposable Petri dishes. The chief understood what Andrew was saying and agreed with him. Andrew told the chief that he and Camillia were going to go home so they could get adequate rest for the meeting. Andrew told the chief that the meeting was going to be right after breakfast; he would send runners to get everyone and bring them to his office room. Andrew suggested that the chief get some good sleep for the morning meeting; the chief agreed. Everyone stood up and left the office room. The chief walked Andrew and Camillia out of his front door; then he went straight to his bedroom to change into bedclothes and climb into bed to go to sleep for the night. Andrew and Camillia walked to their side of the castle, went inside going straight to their bedroom, changed into bedclothes, and then got into bed to go to sleep for the night.

Andrew woke up very early so he lay in bed next to Camillia and watched her sleep peacefully. Eventually, Camillia woke up, and the first thing she saw when she opened her eyes was Andrew. They kissed and told each other that they loved each other. It was time to get out of bed, put day clothes on, and go to breakfast.

Andrew and Camillia went to the castle's private dining hall and sat down at the round table. Melanie walked out of the kitchen into the dining hall to see if the couple was there, and they were so Melanie had the kitchen staff bring out their breakfast. The couple leisurely ate their breakfast, enjoying every bite. Camillia reminded Andrew that after they were finished with the big meeting, she had an appointment with the doctor at the hospital for her prenatal checkup. Andrew acknowledged her, saying that he could not wait to see the baby on the ultrasound.

When breakfast was over, Andrew sent one of his runners to get the medical doctor, and he sent his other runner to get the head scientist. While Camillia waited for the medical doctor and the head scientist to show up, Andrew went to get the chief. Andrew and the chief got to Andrew's office room first, and Camillia was there with them. The medical doctor and head scientist showed up at Andrew's office room about the same time. Now that everyone was there, Andrew told the head scientist to explain the conception project in detail. The head scientist said that he was going to give the main details and make the project easier to understand. The head scientist told them that there were two minerals that were exposed to heavy radiation, which changed the chemical composition of the minerals a bit, and it was that change that allowed the minerals to target the male and female reproductive systems. He continued and told them that he was not certain that the radioactive minerals would work and allow pale ones to reproduce or if the minerals would kill them due to the radiation. The head scientist said that the only way to know for sure what the vaccine would do was to try it out on volunteer test subjects. The medical doctor told the group that radiation was what was killing the humans until they developed a serum to change themselves into pale ones. He told everyone that even though pale ones were immune to the effects of the earth's surface and diseases, that had been proven to be true so without testing the pale ones to find out how much radiation would be too much or if there was no such thing as too much, all they did know for sure was that the serum reversed the damage and made everyone sterile.

Andrew spoke up and told the group that it was not acceptable to use pale ones as test subjects because there was nothing with the test that gave the scientists any idea of what to expect, and it was wrong to have a test subject be blindly tested. Camillia spoke up and said that it would be amazing if they could come up with something to allow pale ones to reproduce so they did not have to worry about becoming an extinct species, but it was not worth killing anyone to find the cure for sterility. Andrew told everyone that they were going to vote on whether the conception project continued. Andrew called for a raising of the hands for those who thought the project should be terminated, and everyone but the scientist raised their hands. That was three of four individuals voting to terminate the conception project. With the vote over, Andrew informed the scientist that there would be a harsh punishment to anyone who tried to work on the conception project.

CHAPTER FORTY

The head scientist tried to tell everyone else that the project was a dire necessity to save and expand the species, and if they lost a few individuals in the process, then it would be for the better of the entire species. Andrew asked the head scientist if he would be willing to use himself or a close family member for the project's voluntary test subject. The head scientist told Andrew that he could not test the vaccine on himself because he needed to keep a fully functioning mind. He told Andrew that he would be willing to use his immediate family members as voluntary test subjects. The chief told the head scientist that he was sadistic and would be removed from the science hall as of immediately. Camillia seconded the motion, and the doctor moved for the third motion. Andrew told him that if there were going to be any real problems from him, he would be exiled to the earth's surface. Camillia told the head scientist that he was going to be watched very carefully. The head scientist excused himself from the meeting to go back to the science hall to gather his belongings and go home. The doctor asked the couple if they were ready for their prenatal checkup, or did they want to go to the hospital later that day? Andrew said that they could finish dealing with the late head scientist after their appointment. Andrew told the chief that they would need his help with reassigning the scientist's position to something relative to the science field but where he could not be of any threat to anyone. The chief said that he would be ready to work when they were ready for him. Camillia said that she had an idea—why not take the chief to their doctor's visit so he could see the baby also and then they could leave from there to finish dealing with the former scientist.

Andrew said that her idea was a good one; then he asked the chief what he thought about the idea. The chief told Andrew that he would love to go along and see his grandchild. The doctor told everyone that they had a plan for their appointment and finishing up with the science department so it was time to end the meeting and move on to the next thing on the agenda. Everyone else agreed so Andrew stood up and opened the office room door for everyone to exit. The doctor went out of the office room first and said that he would see them at the hospital and have everything ready for the exam. The chief and the couple went outside to get the stable boy to saddle up three horses for their travel. The stable boy got the horses ready then brought them out to them. The chief, Andrew, and Camillia got on their horses and headed for the hospital.

When the chief and the couple got to the hospital, they turned their horses over to the hospital stable boy then went inside the building. When they got close to the nurse's desk, the charge nurse told them to go to the same room they always got; the doctor was in there waiting for them. They went into the room, and Camillia get on the bed and got comfortable then lifted her shirt for the ultrasound to be done. Andrew and the chief stood out of the way but where they could see the ultrasound monitor. The doctor could get the baby on the screen easily. The doctor commented on how big the baby was; it was her largest baby yet, but he was definitely healthy. The doctor could tell the sex of the child so he asked if they wanted to know, and the couple said yes. Camillia told the doctor that she already knew that it was a boy, and the doctor confirmed it. The doctor finished the rest of the exam and said everything was great and going as expected. The chief told the couple that they were carrying a beautiful baby that he could see in the ultrasound. Andrew told the chief that he could not wait to hold his new baby in his arms. The doctor intervened and told them that it would not be long before it would be time to deliver him. Andrew and Camillia thanked the doctor for his services then got ready to leave with the chief.

As the couple and the chief walked out of the hospital to retrieve their horses, the chief asked Andrew if he knew what he was going to do with the former head scientist. Andrew said that he had thought about it, and he was going to make him the science hall's janitor and backup runner. Camillia said that the new position would help the other scientists because up to now, they did the cleaning, which took time away from their work. They were all three on their horses headed for the science hall when they noticed the former scientist heading for the science hall just in front of them. They decided to hang back and watch the man to see what he was up to because he was banned from the science hall until further notice. Sure enough, he got to the science hall, tied up his horse, and went inside the science hall; this was an offense, and the couple was willing to bet that he would commit another offense once inside. They gave the former scientist fifteen minutes before they walked into the science hall.

When Andrew, Camillia, and the chief walked in, the scientists all had guilty looks on their faces, and the former head scientist tried to make his way out of the science hall. The chief blocked the exit, and Andrew asked him what he was doing. Camillia was reading his thoughts and found that he was up to no good. The former scientist told Andrew that he was just saying his farewells to the rest of the team. Camillia told the chief to lock the science hall doors and to stand guard over them. Camillia told Andrew that the scientist was lying to them; he was there to get the rest of the scientists to continue the conception project, and he was saying that he would indirectly keep overseeing the project. Andrew reminded the former scientist that he was banned from the science hall until told differently or he would be exiled to the planet's surface. The chief spoke up and asked the scientist what he had to say for himself. He admitted that he did not want to see the conception project stopped because they were making some real progress with it. Andrew told him that the project was possibly harmful to their species, and he would not condone human sacrifices for anything.

Camillia asked the other scientists what their opinion of the project's progress was. They told her that it was true that they had made some progress, but it was headed for theory-based outcomes. There was not one thing that led them to believe that it would work; in fact, they believed that it had the potential to be deadly. Camillia asked the scientists what the former head scientist was wanting of them or if he was giving his farewell speech. They said that it was true that he was trying to talk them into continuing the project but that they told him no already and that was when everyone walked in. Andrew was reading their thoughts as they spoke to Camillia and could determine that they were telling the truth. Andrew told the former scientist that he was told not to push the limits because there was a zero-tolerance policy. The former scientist told Andrew that they had two injections ready for testing, one for a female and one for a male. He asked Andrew to authorize the male injection to be given to him; he had to know what the outcome would be. Andrew gave the authorization, and one of the other scientists gave him the injection.

Right after the injection, the former scientist lay on the ground and waited for the injection to do whatever it was going to do. Everyone watched intently; then suddenly the former scientist started to shake and froth at the mouth. The other scientists helped him the best that they could, but when he stopped shaking, he never started to breathe. The other scientists did rescue breathing, but finally his heart gave out also. They tried to revive him, but within seconds, his body stiffened and swelled up. Andrew instructed the science team to do an autopsy to determine what in the injection took his life. The rest of the scientists said that they would make the autopsy a priority duty and get back with him as soon as they find out anything. Andrew said he would appreciate that then he, Camillia, and the chief left.

It was nearing the lunch hour and family time so the chief, Andrew, and Camillia went to the couple's side of the castle to sit in the family room and wait for everyone to show up. While they were waiting, they discussed the incident at the science hall. Andrew suspected that the radioactive mineral killed him, not the other ingredients; those were just fillers for stabilizing the minerals' composition in going from a solid to a liquid. The chief told Andrew not to fret about it and that they would find out everything within twenty-four hours. Family started to show up so Andrew, Camillia, and the chief stopped talking about the science issue. It did not take long for everyone to arrive so they all went to the castle's private dining hall and took their seats at the round table. The kitchen crew brought out lunch, and it looked scrumptious as usual. Everyone shared their day while eating. There did not seem to be much for anyone to do that day, not even for Andrew and Camillia. Lunch ended and everyone already shared what there was to share, so when they all transferred to the family room, everyone wanted to know how the new baby was doing.

Camillia told them that she had just had an appointment with the doctor that morning and he said that the baby was very healthy. Andrew told them that the doctor even commented on how big the baby was right now. Camillia told everyone that the doctor confirmed the baby's sex, and it was a boy just like she had been saying all along. Andrew told everyone that his name was going to be William in case they had not heard. They all liked that name and asked if they could have some time with the baby. That meant that everyone wanted to rub her belly and talk to the baby; she told them that it was okay. Everyone lined up, and Camillia sat in her chair comfortably. They started to interact with the unborn child, and he seemed to like it; he was moving all over and pressing against people's hands. Camillia could feel a sense of joy coming from the baby.

By the time that family time was over, everyone was just finishing up with interacting with the baby. It was now time for the family members to go back to their duties; Andrew and Camillia even had things to do. The couple was supposed to meet with the chief for him to start training her for the job of the king's adviser; he had already gotten his things together to take to Andrew's office room. Andrew and Camillia wanted to go by the science hall to see how far things had gotten with the autopsy.

When the couple got to the science hall, all the scientists were buzzing around like busy bees. One of the scientists noticed that they were there and took a break to go over to greet the couple. Andrew asked how the autopsy was going, and the scientist told him that they had analyzed his blood and it appeared that he was consumed by radiation and, because the additional exposure was from the inside, it consumed him at top speed. They told Andrew that if he had been exposed to the same amount of radiation from the outside, he might have survived for a few years and would have been disease ridden. He would have been basically a walking dead individual. The scientist told Andrew that other than the radiation exposure, he was healthy and could have lived another two hundred years or so. He was ready to be placed into his grave so the science crew would get with the gardeners to get the hole dug, and the woodworkers were already building a casket for him so it would be final by the time dinner would be ready. Andrew thanked the scientist for the report and for being so prompt.

The community had an area to be used as a cemetery, but up to now it had been empty. The head scientist would be the first to be buried. It was a sad moment for the community, but everyone knew that they had to move on and keep up with their day-to-day duties. However, everyone was curious as to what killed the head scientist, buy Camillia and Andrew headed for the chief's side of the castle to discuss the training that he was going to provide Camillia with. When the couple knocked on the chief's front door, the butler answered and told them that the chief had left to go to their side of the castle to meet with them. Andrew thanked the butler; then he and Camillia rushed to get to their side of the castle to hopefully get to the chief before he left.

When the couple got home, they found the chief waiting for them in their family room with all his supplies to teach Camillia about the king's adviser job. The couple greeted the chief when they walked into their family room; then they transferred to the couple's office room. Andrew had the chief sit behind the desk, and Camillia sat in a chair in front of the desk. Andrew sat on the sofa seat behind Camillia, and he was just there to support Camillia's learning process. The chief told Camillia that her first job was going to be to be there to listen to the king's public troubles and offer as many solutions as possible along with the possible outcomes for each solution. Camillia said that she already did that on a regular basis. The couple had worked together on the community's issues since becoming king and queen of the land of grandeur.

The chief then picked up a large and very thick book to show to Camillia. The chief told her it was for logging major and minor daily events. The chief pointed to the rest of the books on the desk and told Camillia that there was a diary of sorts for each work hall as well as the religious hall. The chief said that he still had to do some entries in the science hall book about the failure of the conception project. Now that they have had a death in the community, the chief needed to get a book to record the community death of the chief scientist with the date, time, and details about the cause. The chief told Camillia that it seemed like a lot of work, but it really was easy. The worst thing about it was the time consumed. The chief told Andrew and Camillia that he would have all the books delivered the next day along with the bookshelves that they simply needed to figure out where they wanted them, and the movers would place everything in its place and that would give the chief enough time to catch up on the books. Andrew did not use his office room for much so he decided to give it to Camillia as her workroom. It was already set up for her with everything she would need to do the recordings of the community's business. The chief told Camillia that it would basically be her job to know everyone's business, which was no different from what she was already doing.

It was nearing the dinner hour, and the chief was still with Andrew and Camillia so they invited him to eat dinner with them and he accepted. Andrew, Camillia, and the chief left the office room to go to the castle's private dining hall. On the way to the dining hall, Camillia had a sharp pain shoot from her belly into her back so she had to stop and hold on to the hallway wall for a few seconds. Andrew and the chief were walking ahead of Camillia and conversing about what the chief would do with his time as of the morning so they did not notice that Camillia seemed to be in some minute discomfort. The men were exiting the hallway to enter the castle's foyer when they realized that Camillia was not with them. The two of them stopped, and Andrew called out to Camillia, but she did not answer him. He called out again but louder, and there was still no response.

The chief and Andrew went back into the hallway and followed it practically back to the office room before they saw Camillia leaning on the hallway wall. She had a look of alarm on her face, and through telepathy, Andrew sensed a feeling of panic coming from Camillia. Andrew and the chief rushed to Camillia's side and each one took a side and helped Camillia the rest of the way down the hall through the foyer and into the family room. They set her down on a couch and told her to lie down. As Camillia lay down, she told the chief and Andrew that she felt like she was in labor and it came on suddenly. The chief went outside to the stable boy and had him hitch up a buggy while Andrew picked up Camillia in his arms and carried her outside to the buggy.

Once the chief was on the buggy, Andrew got the horses going, and he headed straight for the hospital. When they all got to the hospital, the chief went inside to get a porter with a gurney. Andrew got Camillia out of the back of the buggy while the hospital stable boy held the horses steady. When the chief got outside with the gurney, Andrew placed Camillia onto the gurney gently. Camillia lay on her side almost in a fetal position with tears coming out of her eyes, but she remained calm. As the porter was wheeling Camillia into the hospital building, the chief walked ahead to try to locate the doctor, but the charge nurse stopped him and told him to stay at the nurse's desk. The porter was on the way into the hospital with Camillia and the charge nurse saw Camillia coming, so she told the porter to take Camillia to her usual room and she would find her doctor. As the nurse went around the back of the nurse's desk to go get the doctor, she told the chief to go to the hospital room with Andrew and Camillia and to be calm. The porter helped Camillia transfer from the gurney to the hospital bed. Again, Camillia curled into a fetal position on her side, and the tears continued to flow. Andrew was gravely concerned about Camillia and the pain she was in; he told her he wished he could take the pain for her. She gave a small smile that lasted only a few seconds and thanked Andrew for his concern.

Camillia asked Andrew what was taking the doctor so long to get to her when she needed him there because the baby was coming swiftly. Andrew asked the chief to peek out the doorway to see if the doctor was coming; he did and the doctor was on his way. The chief told Camillia that the doctor was just a few doors down and would be there in a few seconds. Andrew stood at Camillia's side and rubbed her back while telling her how much he loved her. The chief was now sitting in a chair that was in the corner of the room toward the head of Camillia's hospital bed. The doctor finally bounced around the corner and asked what was going on. Camillia told the doctor that little William was about to enter the world as they knew it to be. The doctor told Camillia and Andrew that he was going to check and see how dilated her cervix was. The doctor had Camillia roll over onto her back; then he put a drape over her from the waist down.

When the doctor checked to see how dilated Camillia was, he found that the baby's head was out and the shoulders were working their way out. The doctor told Camillia to give a good hearty push, so she did and baby William shot the rest of the way out. Suddenly, the pain stopped, and Camillia could stretch out her legs on the bed, and the doctor cared for little William as he had all the other newborns then he wrapped him tightly in a blanket and handed him to Camillia. Andrew and the chief huddled around her to admire the new baby. Although he was a month early, the doctor was not worried about him having any health problems. The doctor told Camillia that she and William could go home that evening, and everyone was overjoyed about that. A nurse went into the hospital room and took William from Camillia so she could finish cleaning him up and dress him; she would take William back to Camillia after he was clean, dry, and clothed.

After the nurse took William and left, another nurse went into the hospital room to get Camillia cleaned up, dressed, and into the chair next to the head of the hospital bed where the chief would have to stand up. Andrew and the chief went to the waiting room while the nurse was dealing with Camillia. A half hour later, the nurse was done with Camillia, and her nurse was going to let the baby nurse know that she was up and cleaned so she could get her baby back. On the way to the nursery, Camillia's nurse let Andrew and the chief know that Camillia was ready for them to return to her hospital room. Right after the chief and Andrew got to Camillia's hospital room, the nurse brought little William into the room and handed him to Camillia. After Camillia got William, a discharge nurse went into the hospital room and told Camillia, Andrew, and the chief that they could all leave and take William with them. Andrew thanked the nurse and helped Camillia up. They walked out of the hospital, and the hospital stable boy got their horses and buggy. The stable boy held the horses steady while the chief got onto the buggy; then Camillia handed William to the chief. Now empty-handed, Camillia got onto the buggy, sat down, and took William from the chief. Andrew finally got onto the buggy and drove them to their side of the castle.

CHAPTER FORTY ONE

Back at home, Andrew got down from the buggy then took the baby. The chief got down from the buggy then helped Camillia off. They all walked into the castle and sat in the family room and visited for a short while. During the visit between the chief, Andrew, and Camillia, their staff came along and fussed over how cute William was. Finally, William's nanny arrived to take him to his nursery room. Camillia, Andrew, and the chief still had to eat dinner, and Melanie had the kitchen crew keep dinner warm for them so when they went to the castle's private dining hall and sat at the round table, dinner was served. The chief really enjoyed having dinner with Andrew and Camillia, it sure beats eating alone.

Once dinner was over, the chief said his farewells to Andrew and Camillia telling them that he would see them the next day; then he left to go to his side of the castle. The couple went to their bedroom and changed into their night clothes then sat up for a few hours talking about Camillia's new position, the birth of William, and getting pregnant again as soon as possible. Andrew and Camillia decided that her having the job of the king's adviser would be nothing more than a wife supporting her husband's duties as king of the land of grandeur. Camillia already somewhat did the job; the only thing about it that she did not already do was to document everything big and small in books designated for all possible scenarios.

As for giving birth to William, he was another beautiful baby that would be gifted. He was intelligent and had a strong telepathic ability. There was no telling what his gifts would be; the other children did not show their abilities until they were about a year old, and their gifts varied. However, all the children had strong telepathic abilities that showed almost immediately following conception. Now for the topic of getting pregnant again as soon as possible, Andrew left it up to Camillia for only she knew how her body was doing and would handle another pregnancy right away. Now that they have had the anti human vaccination to get rid of the last of their human traits, they both were more aware of their bodies and were more sensitive to each other's bodies.

Camillia told Andrew that she was planning to have baby after baby until she could no longer conceive due to menopause. Andrew thought that was a good thing; however, they would soon need to expand their nursery rooms into the chief's side of the castle, taking up some of his spare rooms. The couple was sure that the chief would not mind them utilizing some of his spare rooms, but that was something that they needed to talk over with him, and soon. Andrew had planned to discuss the bedroom issue with the chief on the morrow because they only had four bedrooms left in their side of the castle. The chief had fourteen bedrooms on his side of the castle. The children would live at home until they were twenty-one years old unless they married first then they would move out to live with their new spouse, but that scenario was still a way away.

Now that those immediate thoughts were briefly discussed, the couple got into bed and nestled down to go to sleep. As they lay in bed, the couple could not get their minds to shut down so they could go to sleep. Camillia got out of bed as quietly as possible so she did not disturb Andrew, but it was too late because he was wide awake still. Andrew asked Camillia where she was going at eleven o'clock at night. Camillia told Andrew that she was going to the barn to get some fresh warm milk to help her go to sleep and asked him if he wanted some fresh warm milk or anything from the kitchen. Andrew got up with Camillia to go and get some fresh warm milk also.

When the couple got to the kitchen and opened the door that led to the barn, Melanie came around the corner of the dining hall into the kitchen and caught the couple before they went out of the door to the barn. Melanie asked if there was anything she could get for them. Camillia told her that they were on their way to the barn to get some fresh warm milk to help them get to sleep. Melanie told Camillia and Andrew to sit at the big roundtable in the private dining hall, and she would go out to the barn to get them some fresh warm milk. It took Melanie ten minutes to get three glasses of fresh warm milk from the milk cow and get back into the private dining hall with the couple. She sat with Camillia and Andrew and had a glass of fresh warm milk with them. Camillia asked Melanie why she was still awake at such a late hour, and she said that she just could not sleep; there was no reason. Melanie asked Camillia and Andrew what had made them awake so late at night. Camillia said that she was awake because she could not stop thinking about all the things that she had to do the next day. Andrew butted in and said he had the same reason.

After the small talk, the three of them sat quietly dind sipped on their fresh milk, hoping to finish it before it cooled off too much. Once everyone was finished with their milk, Melanie took the glasses into the kitchen to be washed later in the morning with breakfast dishes. When she came out of the kitchen and back into the private dining hall, she told Andrew and Camillia good night and to sleep well. The couple wished her the same, and the three of them went to their bedrooms to try to go to sleep again. When Melanie got back to bed, she fell asleep rather quickly; the warm milk did the job. Andrew and Camillia went back to their bedroom and climbed into bed, but they still could not fall asleep so they lay there and engaged in small talk, being very careful not to get into a big heavy conversation.

The couple talked about their children, how their personalities varied, how they each had extraordinary gifts that were unique to that child, how big they were getting and so fast, and even spoke to each other about having more children. Camillia told Andrew that she wanted as many children as her body would allow before going through menopause, she loved children and being pregnant. Andrew told Camillia that he too loved children and wanted as many of them as she could handle having. So far, they had five children, and they spent quality time with each one individually; eventually, they must take advantage of playtime to spend time with the children because there would be so many children. The couple spoke about needing to talk to the nannies to see how the children deal with their play dates with one another and to find out if there is anything the nannies need or desire for the children or themselves.

Andrew and Camillia exchanged words of love for each other and expressed their trust in each other. They felt that they were the perfect couple with a more-than-sufficient life; they had no needs or desires. They felt that they had a better life than anyone in the community; although their better life came with more responsibilities and expectations, there were no problems in meeting those expectations. The couple knew that they were blessed to be the king and queen of the land of grandeur and to be the only pale ones to be able to reproduce, and they felt that they owed the community their best efforts toward perfection as possible. All the thinking and conversing made time go by fast for now it was time to get up and start the new day even though they had not slept yet.

Andrew and Camillia got out of bed and changed into some day clothes and put themselves together then headed out of the bedroom for the castle's private dining hall. The couple sat at the large round table; then Melanie had the kitchen staff bring out their breakfast. Camillia told Melanie that they were going to eat dinner at the public dining hall so they could introduce William to the public after eating so she did not have to have anything fixed for them. She acknowledged Camillia and told her and Andrew to have a wonderful dinner. Once breakfast was over, Melanie had the kitchen staff clear the round table and start preparing for lunch.

Andrew and Camillia sent their runners to the nannies to call for an immediate meeting with themselves and all the other nannies for their house. It was a suitable time for the meeting with the nannies because the children had full tummies and had been cleaned up so they would not be fussy. Once everyone was there, Andrew told the nannies that the meeting was called to make sure that their needs and desires were met. Andrew went around to the nannies starting with the nanny of the first born, then second born, then third born, and so on. Andrew gave all five nannies a chance to say if they needed anything for the children or themselves or if there was any desire for themselves or the children, and all the nannies told Andrew that all their needs and desires for themselves and the children had been met. Camillia told the nannies that if a need or desire came up for them or the babies, they should let her or Andrew know and they would dmake sure that the need or desire was met as soon as possible. All the nannies agreed to keep up with the needs and desires for themselves and the babies that may arise. Andrew excused the nannies to go back to their duties. They all thanked Andrew and Camillia then went about their way with the baby that they were responsible for.

Now that the nannies were dealt with, it was time to deal with the chief about his extra fourteen bedrooms that were empty. Camillia and Andrew wanted to use them for baby nurseries after the four bedrooms they had left were occupied. The couple went outside of their front door to take a stroll over to the chief's side of the castle so they could speak to him about his extra bedrooms. Andrew and Camillia were being flirtatious with each other as they walked to the chief's side of the castle and spoke words of intense love for each other.

When the couple got to the chief's front door, they stood there for several minutes romantically kissing. Finally, Andrew knocked on the chief's front door, and his butler answered, let them in, then took them to the chief. The chief was in his office room directing the movers on how to pack up the various books that were to go to Camillia's office room. Andrew asked the chief if he and Camillia may pull him from the movers and discuss the usage of some of his rooms. The chief asked if they needed some privacy or if they could talk in the family room. Andrew told the chief that they could speak in the family room so they walked from the office room to the family room.

Andrew explained that he and Camillia had planned on having as many babies as her body would allow and basically getting pregnant as quickly as possible after the delivery of a child. As of the current moment, they had four empty nursery rooms; and if things were to work out the way they plan, they would need more nursery rooms. Andrew told the chief that he would like to know if they could get the usage of his extra empty bedrooms to utilize as nursery rooms for the upcoming children. The chief answered without hesitation and told the couple that what was his was theirs; he told them that he would be honored to help house their children and that if they needed more rooms, then the four they had plus the fourteen he had that they could build onto the castle would suffice.

The chief asked the couple where the nannies gathered to do play dates with the children. Camillia told the chief that they were currently using one of the empty bedrooms. The chief told Camillia that using a small empty bedroom was unacceptable for his grandchildren and that he wanted to convert his family room into a playroom for the nannies and babies to have their play dates in. Camillia told the chief that it was very gracious of him to offer to do that, but she asked him what he would do for an adult gathering place. The chief told Camillia that it was quite simple; he was no longer a working citizen in the land of grandeur so he did not need a meeting place for the adults to gather, and if there were ever a need for an adult gathering in his name, he would just use their family room if they did not mind. Andrew told the chief he would not mind at all, and he was right. As a retiree, he would no longer need to hold adult meetings, but Andrew told him that all meetings would include him to keep him up to date on the current events of the commune.

The chief told Andrew that it was settled then; the couple could have the fourteen empty bedrooms for the children, and he would have the use of their family room if needed. Andrew and Camillia told the chief that it sounded good to them as well. The conversation was at an end, which was good timing because the movers were ready to move the many books and 00000 bookshelves from the chief's office room to Camillia's office room. The movers told the chief that everything was loaded and they needed someone to take them to where the stuff was going. Andrew told the movers to follow him.

Andrew walked out of the chief's front door and to the walkway that joined the chief's side of the castle to the couple's side. It was not a direct route to the couple's front door from the chief's front door, but cutting through the yard would have made it difficult to wheel the books and shelves and they may end up accidentally dumping the books or shelves off the wheeled cart. As the movers were wheeling the carts to his and Camillia's home, he saw that the books and shelves were not going to all fit into the office room. Right next to the office room was an empty bedroom, and Andrew was considering making it into a work library for Camillia to keep all her record books in.

While the movers and the couple and the chief were all still walking to the couple's side of the castle, Andrew spoke to Camillia and shared his realization of the books and shelves being too much to fit into the office room. He told her about setting the shelves and books up in the empty bedroom next to the office room and making it a work library, and she agreed it would be the best way to get everything in one area. The couple had no worries about losing a bedroom for a library space because the chief already said that they could use any or all of his fourteen empty bedrooms as nursery rooms. It took a half hour to get the shelves and books into the new library room, but it got done. Now Camillia had to organize the books on the shelves as she wanted them. There was not enough time to organize the record books and have it done before the lunch hour and family time so Camillia decided to do it after the lunch hour and family time.

CHAPTER FORTY TWO

For now, Andrew, Camillia, and the chief would go to the family room and wait for everyone to show up and start family time. Once in the family room, the chief asked Camillia how many babies she would have if there were no limitations. Camillia looked at Andrew and thought about that for a moment then told the chief that if it were possible, there would be no limit. She said that she loved children and she loved being pregnant. Andrew told the chief he felt the same way, but in all reality, he was leaving the childbearing to Camillia because she was the one who had to go through all the changes and the pain that came with childbirth. The chief was somewhat surprised at their answer because he thought everyone would have a limit. Camillia's telepathic ability allowed her to perceive the chief's thought, and she told him that really, all she had to do was get pregnant, carry a healthy baby, and deliver the child; they had nannies that did the raising of the children. Andrew told the chief that although they could see the children at any time and participate in play time, Camillia was right; the nannies raised the children, and that was the hard part of parenting.

Camillia told the chief that between the children they already have and the empty bedrooms to turn into nursery rooms, they had enough room for twenty-two children. After that, they would have to build on the castle. The chief asked the couple if they were planning to have to build on to the castle, and they both immediately answered yes. The conversation was cut off with the arrival of family members. Everyone got there so they all transferred to the castle's private dining hall and sat at the round table. The kitchen staff served everyone, and everybody began to eat. Family members were sharing their day while eating; they were telling how their day had gone so far and what the day still had in store for them. Everyone finished telling about their day by the time the lunch hour was over, so they all went back to the family room where everyone would share their current short-term goals for themselves and how they plan to achieve the goals. This is also where if anyone can help another accomplish something they would speak up about how and when they could help; after all, they believed that everyone should be there for others when and where possible. That is in part why pale ones were known as loving and peaceful people. The family time was coming to an end and everyone would have to go back to their duties, but they all agreed that they would keep one another's goals in mind and help them if the opportunity arose. Everybody shared hugs then went their separate ways until the next day's family time.

Camillia asked for Andrew and the chief to help her organize the record books in the library room. She knew that with their help, she would get things done faster, and one of them may have a better idea than the other two on the organization of the record books. There were so many books that every wall in the library room had shelves up against it. Half of the books were full of history and information but still needed to be accessible. Andrew, Camillia, and the chief worked in the library room until it was time to go to the public dining hall and they had just finished shelving all the record books. They all three agreed that it was perfect timing; that meant that they would have the evening to visit the science hall and the rest of the night to themselves. Andrew sent a runner to get William and his nanny to go to the public dining hall so the people could welcome him into the community.

While the couple was waiting for the nanny and William, Andrew sent the chief to tell the stable boy to hitch up the horses to the buggy. The nanny and William got to the family room speedily; then everyone went out to the front yard to get on the buggy and go to the dining hall. The trip seemed to be a short one; when they all got to the public dining hall, the stable boy there held the horses steady while everyone got off the buggy. The stable boy took the horses and buggy to the stable; and Andrew, Camillia, the chief, William, and his nanny went into the public dining hall and took their seats up on the stage.

Everyone was staring at William and talking about how handsome he was and how much hair he already had. William smiled and cooed throughout dinner. Once everyone was done eating, the kitchen staff brought out a gigantic cake in honor of William's arrival into the community, and everyone got to have a piece of it. After having cake, the community lined up to take turns in seeing little William and rub his head; they all congratulated Camillia and Andrew. As the community took turns seeing the new baby, they asked one by one if there was anything the baby still needed or that they wanted for his nursery. Camillia gave the people an idea of things that they still needed and some things that they desired for his nursery to aid in his learning and comfort. Everyone said the same thing; they would bring their gift by their home on the morrow. Camillia and Andrew thanked everyone and gave them hugs and a kiss on the cheek. It took quite a bit of time, but the line did go down slowly and eventually ended. Now Andrew, Camillia, the chief, William, and his nanny could all go back to the couple's side of the castle. The nanny took William to his nursery room to get him bathed and ready for his snack then his bedtime story.

Andrew and Camillia had to go to the science hall, and they asked the chief if he wanted to go with them. The chief was more than willing to accompany the couple to the science hall. After letting the nanny and William off at the front door of their side of the castle and watching them go inside, the couple and the chief left to go to the science hall. They got to the science hall, got off the buggy, and tied the horses to the post provided; then all three of them went inside. The scientists were all busy doing their jobs, but it was awkward that when they suddenly saw Andrew and Camillia they practically jumped out of their shoes. That made Andrew curious about what they were working on so he asked. When it was time for the scientist to answer Andrew, the scientist got fidgety and started to stutter so Camillia used her telepathy to monitor his thoughts to tell if he was being honest or not with his answer. The scientist told Andrew that they were doing some routine testing of the soil and water supply along with some plant samples from the forest.

The answer was dishonest and Camillia knew that for sure, so she spoke up and asked the scientist to try to answer the question again and that she would appreciate an honest answer this time. The scientist said that he could not tell them what he was hoping to do, but at that moment, he was testing plant and soil samples from the forest. Andrew asked the scientist what he was ultimately hoping to find, and the scientist told Andrew the same thing he told Camillia, that he could not reveal his goal. Andrew informed the scientist that if he could not be honest and give a reasonable answer, then he could be banned from utilizing the science hall.

The scientist looked away and said that they were trying to find a plant that would mimic the effects of the radiation in the mineral that was obtained from above ground, and he just knew that he could come up with a vaccine to allow the pale ones to reproduce. Andrew thanked the scientist for finally being honest and told him to always be honest and he would get a lot further in life. Andrew asked the scientist why he was looking for a substitute in the forest because they had done that once before and said that they had no alternative. The scientist told Andrew that the head scientist that has since passed away did not test nearly half of what was gathered from the forest. The scientist admitted that he and the rest of the scientists were fearful of going against the former scientist because he was not open-minded and he was dangerous and had threatened them with death if they did not go along with him on how he was handling the conception project. The current scientist told Andrew that the former scientist knew that there was a 98 percent chance that the vaccination he took was going to kill him; he basically decided to commit suicide over having the community seeing him as a failure.

Andrew told the young scientist that the community would have only known what he would have told them because in a case such as that, he and Camillia were not free to comment. Andrew asked the scientist what research was done when the chief scientist was still in charge. The current scientist told Andrew that there was the breaking down of the mineral from the earth's surface to identify all the components then testing those components on lab rats to find out what targeted which body system. The current scientist continued and told Andrew that all the lab rats died because the radiation affected all the individual components; in other words, it was not the components that killed the rats, it was the copious amounts of radiation. Andrew asked the current scientist if they had tested any of the plant life from the forest, and if so, what did it reveal to them. The current scientist told Andrew that they had not been able to test any of the plants or soil; they had just gotten all their samples, and it took so long to get them because of the secrecy they were trying to keep. Andrew asked the current scientist if there was any hope of finding a vaccine to encourage reproduction in the pale ones. The current scientist told Andrew that at that point, there was no answer, but that they could provide more information as they tested the samples that they had and because there was no radiation and the plants were all nontoxic, the testing would be safe and controlled. Andrew asked the current scientist if his plans were to continue the conception project even though he and Camillia told them to drop the research and never pick it up again.

The scientist told Andrew that was correct, and he was willing to accept what punishment for his actions that they saw appropriate. Camillia asked to speak to the chief and Andrew in private before making any further decisions. The scientist showed Andrew, Camillia, and the chief to a private office room where they could go and shut the door for privacy and talk. The three of them did go into the office room and shut the door for privacy; then Camillia suggested that the scientist not be punished but to let him continue with the conception project under strict observation of the three of them, but have the chief ultimately in charge of observation and report back to them. The chief said he would be fine with that arrangement, and Andrew said that the project needed a fair trial and had not previously gotten one because the head scientist was biased and with that, he would only allow the project to get another chance if the scientists were going to be open-minded and non-biased.

Camillia suggested that they have a meeting with all the scientists and lay out the guidelines and see how they respond, keeping in mind that they need to be on alert for dishonesty by using their telepathic skills. Andrew agreed and so did the chief. The three of them exited the office room and told the scientist that they had been talking and he was to gather all the scientists immediately because they all needed to have a serious talk. The current head scientist sent his runners out to retrieve the scientists that were at home, and he pulled the scientists that were in the science hall over to the front of the science hall; then they waited for the rest of the scientists to arrive. The chief and Andrew sent their runners out to help get the scientists that were at home there quicker.

Fifteen minutes passed, and the scientists that were at home started to arrive. Within another ten minutes, all the community's scientists were in front of the science hall. Andrew spoke to everyone; he told them that it was unfortunate that the previous head scientist was biased with the reproduction project and that his death was uncalled for, but it was his decision. Andrew asked the scientists if there were any of them who may be biased to step forward at that time; no one stood forward. Andrew told them that he was if they were all open-minded; everyone shook their heads in a yes motion. Andrew told them that he would like to have a vaccine created that would allow pale ones to reproduce without any harmful effects.

Camillia intervened and told the scientists that becoming a parent was an important event in a couple's life, and it also helped to define who they were as far as shaping a young one to be an important part of the future society just as everyone in the current community was important; they all held a part of what made their society function. Camillia also told them that if the conception project could be a success, then their race could continue to thrive and not die out in three to four hundred years when their children passed. All the scientists were listening intently.

Andrew told the scientists that they would like to give the conception project a fair chance to succeed or fail; then he asked the scientists who wanted to give it an honest try to step over toward the back of the science hall and those who do not wish to give it a try to stay up front where they were. Within five minutes, all the scientists had made their way to the back of the science hall, with not one left up front. Andrew told them that it had been decided that the conception project is back, but that the chief would be there daily if not several times in one day. They were to report to him regularly and honestly, and if there was anything that the chief, Camillia, or he could do to assist them to just let the chief know and they would see what could be done.

Everyone agreed to be informative and truthful; they were so excited that the project was given another try that they said they were going to work in two shifts to keep things moving along starting that day. Andrew told them that they were done there for now; he congratulated them on the reinstatement of the conception project and wished them good luck. Andrew, Camillia, and the chief left the hall and got back on the buggy to go home. Andrew drove the horses to the chief's side of the castle to drop him off at home and make sure that he got inside okay; then they left the chief's side of the castle to go to their side. They gave their horses and buggy to the stable boy who took them to the stable to be unhitched and cared for. Andrew and Camillia went inside their home where they would stay for the rest of the night.

Andrew and Camillia went to their bedroom and changed into bedclothes. They both got into bed and propped themselves up so that they could discuss their day together. Andrew and Camillia were highlighting their day one situation at a time, and as they spoke, they kept moving closer and closer to each other. They were both feeling flirtatious toward each other. They fooled around for about an hour, then their flirting turned serious and suddenly Camillia asked Andrew if he was ready for another baby. He told her that he was always ready for whatever made her happy, and he knew she loved being pregnant and having children. Camillia told Andrew that she could feel that she was ovulating, and if they engaged in sex, she would surely get pregnant. Andrew told her he was ready for another baby. Camillia quit talking and resumed flirting with Andrew. The flirting turned into lovemaking, and when they were done, Camillia felt that familiar twinge in her abdomen; she knew she had conceived.

A few seconds later, Camillia felt another twinge in her abdomen, which was different from before. The twinges were the same, but the last time she got pregnant, she only had one twinge and one baby; now she had two twinges—could she just have conceived twins? Camillia told Andrew about having two twinges and the possibility of having twins; he was shocked by the fact that she could even feel the conception, but to know right away if it is one baby or two just astonished him. Andrew told Camillia that they would get the confirmation soon enough from the doctor. Camillia agreed that this was nothing to panic over; it would not be her first set of twins. Camillia told Andrew that having another set of twins would be a blessing; she said she even had a couple of names picked out already. Andrew and Camillia decided not to worry because this was a blessed event, and it did not matter if it was one baby or a bundle of babies, they would all be loved the same and get the same care.

The couple lay back on their pillows and cuddled; both were growing tired and eventually fell asleep in a halfway sitting-up position. They stayed in the same position throughout the whole night and into the morning and awoke in the same position. The couple knew that their day was going to be busy and they would have to stay home most of the day to greet the community with their baby gifts; it was welcomed and highly appreciated. Andrew and Camillia got out of bed and changed out of their bedclothes into some day clothes, and while they were changing, Camillia told Andrew that she hoped that the conception project was successful. He agreed. The couple finished grooming themselves then went to the castle's private dining hall for breakfast. Melanie had the couple's breakfast already on the round table so they sat down and started to eat. Melanie came out to see if there was anything they needed with their breakfast, but before she could ask them, she noticed the mother's glow on Camillia's face. Melanie told Camillia that she suspected that she was pregnant again, and Camillia smiled a big bright smile and told Melanie that she believed she conceived twins the past evening. But like usual, she was not going to announce anything of her own suspicion; she would announce it after the doctor confirmed it. She said that she and Andrew had to be home that day to receive guests so she would probably have to visit the doctor the next day. Melanie was excited for Camillia and Andrew. The couple finished breakfast, and the community breakfast hour was over so Camillia and Andrew went to the family room to wait for guests to arrive.

Camillia started to talk to Andrew, but they were interrupted by a knock at the door. The butler answered the door, and there were the people of the community lined up outside to give their gifts for William to the couple. The butler let one family at a time enter the family room to give their warm welcome gift for the new baby to the young couple. It took several hours, but the line of people finally dissipated and now the couple could go out of their home. Camillia suggested that because there was still a generous amount of time before family time, they ought to go see their doctor about the possible pregnancy. Andrew agreed. Camillia and Andrew went outside of the castle and had their stable boy saddle up two horses.

CHAPTER FORTY THREE

Once the horses were saddled and brought out to them, they mounted their horses and proceeded to ride to the hospital. Upon arrival at the hospital, the couple ran into the doctor outside of the emergency entrance. They started to chat while the hospital stable boy took their horses to the stable. The doctor asked Andrew and Camillia why they had come by the hospital, and after smiling at each other, the couple told the doctor that they believed they were pregnant with twins again and wanted him to check out Camillia to confirm or deny the suspicion. The doctor told them that it would be his pleasure to just follow him to their hospital room, and he would have the nurse take her blood sample and he would do an ultrasound.

Andrew and Camillia followed the doctor to their usual hospital room. Andrew sat in the chair at the head of the bed while Camillia sat on the edge of the hospital bed. The doctor called a nurse into the room and instructed her to take a vial of blood for a pregnancy test, and she did as he asked. After taking the blood sample, the nurse rushed it to the lab for testing with rush results. While waiting for the blood results to come back, the doctor went ahead and did an ultrasound to look for two embryos. The ultrasound took a while to do so. Right when the doctor got his ultrasound results, the blood test results came back. The blood test was positive and a bit high for a singleton for Camillia's timeline of conception, which correlated with the ultrasound. The ultrasound showed that Camillia had indeed conceived twins, but due to the conception being so recent, it was difficult to see so the doctor wanted to definitely do another ultrasound just to be certain.

The doctor congratulated Andrew and Camillia on the pregnancy of their twins then told them that he would see her in a week. The couple thanked the doctor for his time and concern. The appointment was now over so Camillia straightened her clothing, and the couple was ready to go home for family time. Andrew and Camillia got outside of the hospital and got their horses from the hospital stable boy. The couple mounted their horses and headed for home; they could not wait to tell everyone about the babies. Andrew and Camillia got to their side of the castle and gave their horses to their stable boy to take care of. The couple went inside their home and waited in the family room for everyone to show up since it was so close to family time.

Melanie was the first to show up, and she immediately asked how the doctor's appointment went. The couple smiled widely, and Andrew told her that she was going to be an aunt again, and this time, it was twins. Melanie got excited, and Camillia stood up to hug her. They hugged and while embracing jumped up and down several times. When Camillia and Melanie were done jumping, they broke their embrace and Camillia sat back down. Melanie sat next to Camillia and patted Camillia's tummy and talked to the babies; she made it a short encounter so no one else would know about the babies because she wanted the couple to make the announcement to everyone else. Others started to trickle into the family room slowly until finally everyone was there and it was time to go to the castle's private dining hall.

Everyone got seated at the big round table and started to share their day with everyone else. When it was Andrew and Camillia's turn to share, they told their friends that they were going to be aunts and uncles of twins, and everyone agreed that the news of the multiple pregnancy was cause for celebration. Melanie suggested that they all get together for dinner and have a celebratory dinner with a special meal, extravagant dessert, and gifts. The couple did not have a chance to say yes or no before everyone else concluded that it was a wonderful idea. Michelle offered for everyone to make the gift shopping a group trip to spend some quality time together while accomplishing a task, and everyone agreed that it was a splendid idea and they wanted to shop together. Michelle said that they would leave right after lunch if that's okay with Camillia and Andrew and use the two hours of family time to get the shopping done so that they could keep their work on schedule. The couple said that it was acceptable and that they appreciated their friends and their support and that they would not know what their lives would be like without them.

The lunch hour was almost over, and the couple needed to know if the chief had been to the science hall that day or not so they could be briefed on the progress of the conception project. Andrew briefly excused himself from the table and asked the chief to accompany him. Andrew asked the chief if he had been to the science hall that day and the chief had not so Andrew told the chief that he and Camillia would go to the science hall and fill him in on the progress of the conception project after the shopping trip. The chief thanked Andrew and said that would be great. Andrew let the chief get back to the group who were waiting for him to go shopping. The couple and friends all left the castle at the same time; the group of friends needed the stable boy to hitch a couple of horses to the buggy, and the couple needed a couple of horses saddled so they could run their errand. The stable boy got it all done, and everyone could leave at the same time. The group left for their shopping fun while Andrew and Camillia headed for the science hall.

Once at the science hall, Andrew and Camillia got off their horses, tied them up, then went inside the science hall. Everyone there was busy doing a task, but when the couple spoke up and announced their presence, one of the scientists stopped what he was doing and apologized for not acknowledging them before then greeted the couple. Andrew asked the scientist how the conception project was coming along, and he replied very slowly. The scientist told Andrew and Camillia that they were still collecting samples from the forest and had been testing what they already had and were coming up with nothing that would work for conception, but there were still a lot of things to test. The scientist did say that they may have found a few plants that could extend the life of a pale one further than the estimated two hundred and fifty years old. Andrew and Camillia were both surprised and quite interested, especially since the chief was expressing his assumption that he was close to death and was already two hundred and thirty-five years old. Andrew asked the scientist to expound on his explanation of the life-extending plants.

The scientist said that there were three plants that showed life-extending potential by their own quantity of weeks of survival potential after being picked. It appeared that the plants could produce chemical compounds due to being in a state of survival mode; all the scientists needed to do was to break down the plant chemistry to isolate the necessary chemical compounds to enable them to test it after breaking the compounds into an injectable form. Andrew asked the scientist if they could handle two projects at the same time, and the scientist told him absolutely. Andrew told the scientist that along with the conception project, he wanted them to work on the life-extension project, and the scientist told him and Camillia that they would. The scientist told Andrew that they would break up the group of scientists into four groups, two groups for the conception project and two groups for the life-extension project. By separating into four groups, both projects could be worked on around the clock.

Camillia and Andrew thanked the scientist for his time and told him that either they or the chief would check back with him on the morrow. The scientist told them that hopefully he would have some better news for them. Andrew told the scientist that his news on that day was great and that if they could extend lives, that would be near as good as reproduction. Andrew, Camillia, and the scientist said their goodbyes; then Andrew and Camillia left the science hall. Traveling back to their side of the castle, Andrew and Camillia spoke about how wonderful it would be if the life-extension project was a success; they could keep the chief around longer, but the question was for how long. They agreed that they had to find out if the project was a success first; then they could hope for the chief's life to be extended. It was time to quit discussing the life-extension project because they were back to their side of the castle, and they did not want anyone but them and the chief to know about the project. The couple dismounted their horses and gave them to the stable boy then went into their home to see if the chief had gotten back from his group shopping trip. Andrew and Camillia would know if he was back or not because if the rest of the staff was there, he would be back also.

Upon entering the castle, Andrew asked the butler if the group of friends had returned yet, and he told Andrew that they had just gotten back minutes before him and Camillia. Andrew thanked the butler for the information then went on to his family room to see if the chief was on their side of the castle waiting for them. The chief did not appear to be inside the couple's side of the castle so Andrew and Camillia left to go to his side of the castle to fill him in on what the science hall had come up with and to discuss the usage of the life-extension project on him if it proves to work after they explain what it is.

The couple knocked on the chief's front door, and his butler answered. Andrew asked if the chief was home, and the butler told him yes. Andrew asked if he was busy, and the butler told him that he did not believe that he was and took the couple to his family room to wait for him. The butler went to the chief and told him that Andrew and Camillia were there to see him, so he followed the butler to his family room. The chief happily greeted the couple and asked how things were coming along at the science hall, and Andrew told the chief that was why they were there.

Andrew told the chief that the conception project had not provided a way of conception yet, but there were still a lot of plants to gather and test; out of the plants they had already gathered, there were still a lot of them to test. Andrew told the chief that there was a new project that came out of the testing of the plants that had a promising potential of working. The chief was very interested in learning more so Andrew told him that it was the life-extension project and that the science hall had found three plants that may work to extend the lives of the pale ones. Camillia butted in and told Andrew and the chief that there was no telling how many more plants held the same potential or could assist the original plants to do the job, but that it would be nice if it worked and kept the chief around longer.

The chief told the couple that if it proved to work, then he would accept the vaccination so he could be there with them longer. He said he wanted to see all his grandchildren, new and older, grow into healthy young adults. Andrew and Camillia told the chief that as their father, they wanted him around for as long as possible. They could not fathom their lives without him; the chief told the couple that he loved them also and that they had made his life a wonderful and fulfilling one. The three of them shared a group hug; then Andrew mentioned that it was getting close to the dinner hour and invited the chief over to their side of the castle to converse while they waited the last fifteen minutes for everyone else to show up. The chief said he would love to go with them to sit in the family room to wait on everyone, but he had to show up with everyone else because he needed what time was left to wrap their gift.

Andrew and Camillia understood that the chief wanted the night to be special for him and Camillia so they said that they would see him over at their place when it was time and said goodbye for now. The chief said his goodbyes also and had the butler show them out while he went to his office room to wrap their new baby gift. Andrew and Camillia went back to their side of the castle and sat in the family room so they could greet everyone as they arrived. In the meantime, they held each other while sitting on the couch. Andrew and Camillia spoke words of love to each other, and when they started getting mushy, the chief showed up. While the couple and the chief were waiting on the rest of the crowd to arrive, they shared some fun times with each other and laughed about some of the silly things they had done with one another. It was great reminiscing about the great times. Everyone started to show up so the chief and the couple stopped reminiscing and expanded their conversation to involve those who were there. Everyone had gotten to the couple's home, and it was still too early to transfer to the castle's private dining hall so they all decided to do the gift giving before dinner.

The girls, Melanie, Michelle, and Bridgette got Camillia maternity dresses since it was way too early to tell the sex of the children, and the chief and Matthew got stuff for the babies such as bottles, fur blankets, and diapers; and each man paid to have a crib made by the wood hall, which would be delivered when they were finished. Andrew and Camillia were grateful and tearfully thanked their friends. Andrew and Camillia still needed to find nannies for the babies so they could get the babies' bedrooms ready for them. The new nannies could also see what the schedule was for the children and therefore could put the new babies on the same schedule.

Now that the excitement of gift giving was over, everyone noticed that they were feeling hungry so they all transferred to the castle's private dining hall and sat at the big round table. Melanie had dinner ready, and the kitchen brought it out and served everyone; it all looked so good and tasted even better. Dinner was scrumptious, and when the kitchen brought out dessert, it was tantalizing and extravagant that everyone wolfed down their dessert.

After the dinner hour, it was free time for everyone to do as they pleased until bedtime. If the in-house curfew was honored, it meant that no one was to be on the streets after ten at night unless they were needing to go to the hospital for an emergency. The chief said goodbye to everyone then went home to relax for a while.

CHAPTER FORTY FOUR

Everyone on the couple's side of the castle went to their bedrooms and relaxed. Andrew and Camillia went to their bedroom also and relaxed together on their bed. Andrew rubbed Camillia's tummy and spoke to the children for a while. Camillia felt that the babies were pleased with their father's interaction. The babies were still too small to feel their movement, but Camillia did already have a mental link with the babies. Andrew and Camillia got up out of bed and changed into their bed clothes then climbed back into bed to go to sleep. The couple slept soundly, and after a fulfilling night's sleep, they awoke refreshed and ready for the new day. Andrew and Camillia got out of bed and took off their bedclothes to put on their day clothes.

After dressing, Andrew and Camillia cleaned up their faces, brushed their teeth, and combed their hair; now they could go to the castle's private dining hall to sit at the big round table for breakfast. Melanie had breakfast ready for the couple and had the kitchen bring out their meal once they were sat down and comfortable. Andrew and Camillia ate their meal slowly so they could savor every bite; the couple only stopped eating long enough to compliment Melanie on a meal well done. Melanie enjoyed the compliment and thanked the couple for it.

The breakfast hour came to an end, so Camillia helped gather the dirty dishes off the table and handed them to the kitchen staff. They thanked Camillia, took the dishes, and took them to the kitchen to be washed, dried, and put away. It was not often that Camillia helped the kitchen staff with clearing off the big roundtable, but when she felt that she had enough time to help before needing to be somewhere, she would gladly help.

With breakfast being over, it was time to get the chief and visit the science hall again. Andrew and Camillia were running a bit late on getting the chief to visit the science hall so the chief went to the couple's side of the castle. The chief knocked on the couple's front door, and the butler answered it. He let the chief in and showed him to the family room then the butler told the chief that he would let the couple know that he was there waiting for them; the chief thanked him and patiently waited for Camillia and Andrew. The butler went into the private dining hall and told Andrew and Camillia that the chief was in the family room waiting for them, and they thanked the butler as they started to make their way into the family room. In the family room, the couple greeted the chief and asked him if he was ready to go to the science hall to check on the two projects'; he said absolutely.

The three of them went out of the front door together, and Andrew asked the stable boy to hitch up the buggy. With a quick "yes sir," the stable boy ran for the stable to do as he was asked. After just a few minutes, the stable boy came out of the stable with the horses hitched to the buggy. Andrew rubbed the top of his head and told him he was doing an excellent job. While the stable boy held the horses steady, Andrew helped Camillia into the buggy then got in followed by the chief. Andrew drove the team, and off they went to the science hall. It did not take long to get to the science hall, and once they got there, Andrew tied the horses up, then the three of them went into the science hall and asked to speak to someone who could fill them in on both projects.

There was one scientist that was walking around the hall looking over everyone's shoulder and talking to all the other scientists. He stopped what he was doing and approached the couple and the chief. Camillia, Andrew, and the chief greeted the scientist, and Andrew told him that it looked like he had things under control. He told Andrew absolutely and that he was the new head scientist by popular vote among all the scientists; and Andrew, Camillia, and the chief congratulated him. The new head scientist asked what he could do for the three of them, and Andrew spoke up and told him that he could fill them in on how they were coming along on the conception project and the life-extension project. The new head scientist said that it would not be a problem. He told Andrew, Camillia, and the chief that things were moving along slowly but well for both projects.

The new head scientist asked the group which project they would like to hear about first, and Andrew told him to start with whichever one he wanted and to just surprise him. The scientist said he would start with the life-extension project. The new scientist reminded the group that the last time they checked on the status of the project, they had three plants that showed life-extension components in them. Now they have three more plants that show some different components with the same outcome— life extension.

The new head scientist said that each plant had some differing qualities about them, but it may be possible to combine some of the plants for their individual specialties along with their common qualities to make the ultimate vaccine, but they were still in the process of breaking down the plant's individual components to assure that they knew exactly what they were dealing with.

The scientist told the group that they did not want to take any unnecessary chances with making the vaccine and that there were still a lot of plants to break down and test. He added that even though they were testing the vaccines on mice, they wanted to do so without killing the mice. So far, they have not killed any of the mice, and in taking blood samples from the mice and testing it, they have had satisfactory results and it has not had any effect on their reproducing capabilities.

In fact, they had given the vaccine to one mouse and she had become pregnant after receiving the vaccine by a male mouse that had also received the vaccine, so that was wonderful news. The scientists had samples of all the different plants in the forest so now it was up to them to just break the rest of them down for study and possible use. Camillia patted the scientist on the back and told him he was doing a splendid job and that she was very impressed with his work and felt safe with his disposition on ethics and morals. He thanked her and gave her a hug. The new head scientist told the group that they would now hear about the conception project's status. He told them first he could test it on the mice, but it would be difficult to know if it worked because it would not have any obvious signs of effectiveness like the serum to change humans to pale ones did, and there were no before and after blood samples of the changing of humans to compare for any possible clues on the vaccine's effectiveness. The new head scientist said he would have to figure out how they could go about testing for positive and detrimental changes in the mice.

So far, all the scientists came up with was to take blood samples before and after the vaccine was given and test the blood to look for any changes then investigate any changes found. The group felt that was a great idea and that there may very well be some changes in the blood composition. The new head scientist told the group that they had all the samples from the forest that they could possibly get because when they got the plant samples for the life-extension project, they took extra samples from the forest to use for the conception project since they were already there; it did not make any sense to go out there twice for the same task, and the group agreed. The new head scientist summed up the report on the conception project by telling the couple and the chief that so far, they were using the information from the life-extension project of the breakdown of the plants for the conception project also. It would shorten the gathering of information to completely break down the plants' composition once and document fully on what was found; then the two groups of scientists could take that information and focus on their specific project.

The new head scientist told Andrew, Camillia, and the chief that they found three elements that contributed to reproduction; two of them were male and female specific, but the third seemed to be universal. The new head scientist told the group that it would be difficult to know if it was effective because it would not have any obvious changes like the serum that they used to change humans into pale ones. The new scientist said that all they could do was to take blood samples before and after the vaccine from mice to compare for any changes that were indicative of the reproduction process. The new head scientist said that they could give the serum that was given to humans to turn them into pale ones to the mice and see if it had the same effect, hopefully so. Both groups of scientists would take before and after blood samples from the mice that would be given the serum and by comparing the subjects blood before any injection to their blood after the serum that changed humans into pale ones then again after receiving either the life-extension vaccine or the conception vaccine and then they would make complete comparisons and observations and make thorough notes.

With all that said, the head scientist wanted to give the group a tour and explain what they would be seeing, and the chief told him the tour was not necessary and that they did not want to be in the way of the scientists or make them nervous. The new head scientist told the chief that he felt it was necessary for them to have a greater understanding of what was said, and it would only make someone nervous if they were doing something purposefully wrong and that he really watches his staff for honesty and complete thoroughness. If anyone needed a second opinion on anything or help with something, he said he would be there right away to assist his workers. Andrew told the new scientist that he was impressed with his work and that they would love to have the tour, so the head scientist told them to follow him. Everyone followed the head scientist to the back of the hall to observe the mice in their habitats, and the new head scientist pointed out that they were kept as comfortably as possible and if one was to pay attention, the mice had tags around their necks. They were red for the conception project mice and yellow for the life-extension mice, and each tag had a number on it so the mice could be identified as to which project they were for and as individuals also to track what mouse got what vaccination, if any. Next to the mouse habitat was a refrigerator for serums, vaccines, and other scientific things that required a certain cold temperature. Next, they went to the wall next to the mice, which was behind an island-type table that contained jars with different plants in them. Across the hall was another island-type table that had the same jars on the wall behind it. One table was for the conception project, and the other table was for the life-extension project. On the tables were various tools that the scientists used to do their jobs.

As the head scientist walked through the hall, he introduced the other scientists to the group; and of course, all the scientists knew who Andrew, Camillia, and the chief were. The new head scientist showed the group that at the front of the hall was a second refrigerator where the staff could put their snacks and drinks, and there was another area where they could put their personal belongings in lockers. Above each locker was a hook for their laboratory coats, and if they wore regular coats to work, then they would take their laboratory coat off the hook to put on during work and put their regular coats on the hook until it was time to leave the science hall for some reason; then they would switch them out in the opposite way. The new head scientist told Andrew, Camillia, and the chief that the now-deceased head scientist did not have much organization or a natural type of environment for the mice; they were simply caged. Andrew told the new head scientist that it appeared that he had everything under control and that things were running better for all the scientists. The new head scientist said that was very true, and everyone was much happier. Andrew, Camillia, and the chief had been at the science hall for so long that the lunch hour was quickly approaching so they said their goodbyes to the science staff and thanked the new head scientist for his tour and challenging work; then Andrew told him that he or the chief would check back with him on the morrow. The group then excused themselves and walked out of the science hall front door.

Outside, Andrew helped Camillia onto the buggy, then the chief got on the buggy and Andrew untied the horses then went to the other side of the buggy and got on. With a quick smack of the reins, the horses started to go, and Andrew directed them in the direction of home. The small group would most likely make it home right as everyone began to gather in Andrew and Camillia's family room. Andrew, Camillia, and the chief knew that there was no urgency in getting to the castle so they simply strolled home. The trip was uneventful and lovely; it was a pleasant change from constantly rushing about. Andrew guided the horses to stop at the regular stopping point, right in front of the front door of his and Camillia's side of the castle. The stable boy had been waiting for them to return so he could take the horses and buggy to the stable and care for them.

After pulling up to the front door of the castle, Andrew immediately jumped off the buggy and approached their ten-year-old stable boy and told him to hurry with the horses and buggy then come into the castle to join them for lunch instead of going to the public dining hall because he was just as much a part of their family as the rest of the guests. The stable boy jumped up and down for a moment in excitement then grabbed the horses and ran with them to the stable, unhitched them, took care of them, and ran back to the castle's front door. Andrew, Camillia, and the chief were still out front since they were in no hurry to go in because there was still a bit of time before guests would start to gather in the family room. The couple and the chief were discussing nothing private so they brought their conversation to an end in front of the stable boy then Camillia took him by the hand and everyone went into the castle. Andrew and the chief sat on the couch to wait for the guests while Camillia took the stable boy on a tour of the inside of their side of the castle.

The stable boy asked if he could visit her children because he did not have any siblings and always wanted some to play with and love. Camillia told him that there was not enough time before family time, but after family time, he could spend some time with the children and that he was welcome to visit the children whenever he wanted during free time. Camillia told the stable boy that during family time, the children would be napping so all the nannies would be there with them. She would pull them aside together and request that they all go to the playroom together with the children so he could see all of them together and they could have their play time with him. Camillia also told the stable boy that he could go say goodbye to them in their individual bedrooms so he could see their bedrooms and thank the nannies.

The stable boy was amazed that Camillia and Andrew were so nice to him and have always been, but this was amazing to him that he was now a part of their personal family. The stable boy was anxious to go home to tell his parents all about his exciting day at the castle and how he was now a part of the king and queen's personal family.

The tour was not very long, but when it was done, Camillia took the stable boy back to the family room to greet guests that may be there already as well as those who were still arriving. Camillia introduced the stable boy as Jaden, the king and queen's godson. Jaden tugged on Camillia's skirt tail so she turned to him, bent down to his level, and asked what he needed. He innocently asked her what a godson was, and as she looked down to his large brown eyes and told Jaden that it meant if anything were to happen to his parents, she and Andrew would act on their behalf and finish raising him and providing for him, but while they were healthy and alive, it would be hers and Andrew's job to make sure he had everything he needed and to help his parents with his care and support their needs as well.

Jaden understood all this and thanked Camillia then gave her a peck on the cheek. Andrew heard what Camillia had said to Jaden so he walked over to Camillia and Jaden, and Andrew gave Jaden a big hug and told him that after family time, he wanted the boy to take one of the horses and go to get his parents and bring them to the castle for some tea and cookies so that he and Camillia could talk to them about his future. Jaden agreed to do as asked. Now that everyone was there, they left the family room and went to the castle's private dining hall and sat down in their chairs around the large round table. Jaden sat next to Camillia.

The lunch hour was as it usually was, everyone sharing their day and any updated news. When it became Andrew and

Camillia's turn to share, they formally introduced Jaden to the rest of the family, and each person said kind words and told him who they were and not to hesitate to ask for their assistance if it should be needed. Jaden greeted the group and told them thank you for their acceptance and kindness; then he said that if he needed help, he would be sure to ask. Family time had come to an end, and it seemed to go by fast because of the joy of getting a new family member and everyone participating in making the adjustment a smooth and positive experience. Jaden was out of the castle's front door and on the bare back of a horse heading for his parents before any of the other family members left the big round table.

CHAPTER FORTY FIVE

Everyone but Andrew and Camillia were surprised to see Jaden leave so fast and with such vigor. Everyone said that it would be nice to have his energy as they knew that they were not all that much older than Jaden, but they also knew that they no longer had his bursts of animation. Everybody chuckled then went their separate ways to get back to work, and right when everyone got to their designated areas, a horse and buggy came to the castle's front door; it was Jaden with his parents. They had closed their store early to go to the castle with their son. They got off the buggy, and with Jaden knocking on the castle door, the butler answered and let them in. Andrew and Camillia were nearby because they had expected them so the couple met the butler, Jaden, and his parents in the foyer of the castle and told the butler that they would take their company to the family room. Apparently, Jaden had enough time to tell his parents about being a part of the king and queen's personal family as a godson and that he could come and play with all the children in his free time. They saw his excitement and knew that he was in a special situation. Jaden's parents greeted the couple as their beloved leaders and thanked them for taking Jaden into their hearts and home. Camillia and Andrew told Jaden's parents that he was a special boy and a very hard worker, and it was their honor to be his godparents. They meant no disrespect to them;

in fact, they were special to them as well. Camillia told Jaden's mother that if she ever needed something to contact her and she would help; she said that she and Andrew wanted to make sure they were taken care of as well then finally told his parents to address them by their first names since as far as she was concerned, they were family too. Melanie brought out some tea and cookies for them to enjoy together, and they enjoyed the experience. They sat in the family room for several hours talking and getting to know one another while Jaden was in the playroom with all the children. The adults had a wonderful time.

It was getting near dinnertime, so Camillia asked Jaden's parents to stay for dinner and they accepted. Camillia called for Melanie to have her set three more places at the big round table. Melanie acknowledged Camillia and followed through with what was asked of her. Several minutes after having the big round table ready for everyone, Melanie announced that dinner was ready when they were ready, so everyone left the family room and the nannies and Jaden joined the others to go to the big roundtable in the castle's private dining hall

Once everyone was seated, Melanie signaled the cook to have the kitchen staff bring out the food. It looked wonderful and tasted even better. Jaden's parents commented on how tasty the meal was and that it was far better than the meals at the public dining hall. The chief told them that it was because Andrew and Camillia had a professional chef and baker while the public dining hall did not, but the public dining food was not too bad. It was just sort of bland so everyone could eat. As the group ate dinner, Jaden and his parents shared their hopes and dreams. The parents wanted to expand their store, they sold all the various food items available as well as furs and leather for clothing to be made. The only reason they had not expanded already was because it would take more money than they could put into it now. Jaden's parents had some extra money left over after taking some out for private living expenses and employee payments, and it was a good amount, which they had been saving. But there was still a long way to go. Jaden wanted to go to school and work, but the school hours were during his work hours and his parents did not have the money for a private tutor, and Jaden did not want to quit working for his beloved queen and king; they were his heroes.

Camillia interrupted and said she had some ideas on how to help and they would have a couple of different options to choose from, Jaden and his parents were eager to hear the options. The first option was that Camillia and Andrew could give the money to them as a gift from one family member to another to be able to afford the business expansion and schooling for Jaden. The second option was for Andrew to send some of the staff into the store and purchase some furs, leather, and other goods at a going price and a half and have their seamstresses make clothing for them with the purchased furs and leather. Jaden's mother came up with a proposition of her own. To have the couple pay for his tutoring, Jaden could do extra work daily and work on the weekends when he would normally be off since he loved working for them, and if the couple would pay for Jaden's tutoring up front, the money he would earn extra could go to her and Andrew and would repay them for the cost of the tutoring. Camillia said that was a grand idea, and if they wanted, he could receive his tutoring at the castle before dinner since he would already be there and they would come for dinner and go home together afterward. Jaden's mother said that was a great idea, but she would only do it if she could bring something to contribute to the dinner like dessert or something of the like. Camillia told her that would be better yet then her family would have a touch of home at the castle; they agreed on the tutoring issue.

Jaden's father stepped in and addressed Andrew to have a private discussion about the money for expanding the store so even though they were about to get dessert, the two men excused themselves from the big round table and went to Camillia's private office to talk. Andrew asked why the sudden privacy, and Jaden's father said it was because it did not involve his boy and his wife needed to be with their son and Camillia so he wanted to make the store expansion deal between the two of them and they could explain to their wives when no one who does not need to hear private business was not around. Andrew said very well that he would fill Camillia in on the deal in private after they came to some sort of understanding. Jaden's father thanked Andrew for humoring his desire to have privacy.

Andrew asked Jaden's father if he had something specific in mind for the store expansion deal, and he said first he would like to replace the family name of the store with the royal store in respect of receiving the royal family's help in the expansion of the store. Andrew told him that he did not need to do that but he insisted so Andrew said, "Okay, what next?" Jaden's father asked if they had some work there at the castle that he or his wife could do outside of business hours or both could do after business hours, and Andrew told him that he was sure there was but that he would have to discuss that with Camillia. Andrew suggested that once dinner was over, Jaden could visit with all their children and play with the toys in the playroom and while the nannies kept an eye on the children and Jaden, he, Camillia, Jaden's father and mother would meet to establish what the work would be and together come to an agreement that they would all be happy with. Jaden's father said okay, and the two of them went back out to the big roundtable where the women and Jaden were still eating dessert.

Melanie noticed that Andrew and Jaden's father had returned to the big round table before dessert time was over so she went to the big round table and asked them if they wanted dessert also. Camillia told them that there was more than enough time so Andrew and Jaden's father said okay, and Melanie brought it out to them. Once dessert was over, everyone went to the family room to relax for a moment and let their meal settle a little bit. Andrew decided that it was time to take care of business so he asked Jaden if he wanted to go to the playroom and play with all the children and the toys. Jaden looked at his father, and his father nodded his head in a yes motion so Jaden said yes and off he went.

Camillia and Jaden's mother were not sure of what to expect from Andrew and Jaden's father but knew that it was for the adults only and that was why Andrew sent Jaden to the playroom. Andrew spoke first and told Camillia that Jaden's father wanted to change the name of the store from their name to the royal store. Camillia was flattered, but she felt that the name of the store should stay as it was, and Jaden's mother said nothing for or against it. Andrew said that it might be best if the store kept the same name so people did not get the idea that the store was either owned or simply run by the couple. Jaden's mother saw Andrew's point and agreed so Jaden's father said, "Very well, it would stay the same."

The next task was to discuss how much money was needed to expand the store and how Jaden's parents would make up for it. Jaden's mother told the couple that the store was open seven days a week but that they would like to do some work for the couple after hours if they could. Camillia and Andrew both had some ideas of what they could do, but they had to find out what they could do first and what they were willing to do. Camillia and Andrew were aware of what each other was thinking through telepathy, and so they told Jaden's parents to let them talk between each other for a few minutes. They added that it was nothing private, but they wanted to combine their thoughts and come up with some appropriate ideas together. Andrew told Jaden's parents that they could do that in front of them or in private; it was their choice, and Jaden's parents said they would prefer to be with the couple while they discussed options because they may develop some ideas that the couple did not or they could even expand on an idea they came up with.

Camillia said she was ready to start brainstorming so Andrew said okay, and they went back and forth with ideas. Jaden's parents added some ideas, and they all four started to develop some of the ideas for their plausibility. In the end, they decided that they would have Jaden's mother tutor Armellya, and within the year she would also tutor the couple's first set of twins Kevin and Kaylina. Jaden's father would do some work on the two buggies that the couple had to make them more comfortable like putting pillow-type cushions on the seats for a softer seat, lining the back of the buggies with leather so there would be less chances of getting splinters and eventually their children could ride in the back.

Everyone finally came to an agreement on the expanding of the store and getting to tutor Jaden, and Jaden's parents were comfortable with that because they would be able to earn the money necessary for both projects and the couple would get something out of the deal also. On the eve of the morrow, Camillia and Jaden's mother would go together to get a tutor and pay the fees then get her to work so that after work was done, she could go to the castle to be able to start her tutoring with Armellya while Andrew and Jaden's father would go to the barn to get things started on the buggies. Jaden would have his first day of tutoring after working from early in the morning until his tutoring time and do some extra work in the barn like repainting it, making small repairs such as putting up hooks for gear that had come down, and taking inventory of all supplies to see what needs to be replaced or simply bought for the first time. They all thanked each other; then Camillia and Jaden's mother went to go get him from the children's playroom so they could go home and rest up for the busy new day.

Once Jaden and his parents left, Andrew and Camillia went to their bedroom and changed into bedclothes and climbed into bed. The couple lay on their sides with Andrew behind Camillia so he could put his arm around her and place his hand on her stomach. He talked to the babies, and Camillia could feel their contentment with their father's interaction. Camillia reminded Andrew that she had to see the doctor in the morning, and Andrew was excited to go with her. He could not wait to see the babies on the ultrasound monitor. It was getting late, and the couple had a busy day ahead of them so they lay the rest of the way down and went to sleep arm in arm.

When it was time to wake up, Andrew jumped right out of bed ready for the new day. Camillia was not so enthusiastic because she was up and down all night needing to use the restroom so she was exhausted and just rolled out of bed with Andrew's help to stay awake. They changed into their day clothes then washed their faces, brushed their teeth, and brushed their hair, and were as ready to meet the new day as they were going to be. Together, Andrew and Camillia went to the castle's private dining hall and sat at the big round table; and when Melanie came out with the couple's breakfast, she noticed Camillia sitting with her face in her hands and asked her if she was okay. Camillia did not look up, but she did answer Melanie and told her she was fine. Melanie set their food in front of each of them then went back into the kitchen to continue her tasks.

Suddenly, Camillia jumped up from her chair and raced down the castle's hallway toward her bedroom. Andrew went after her, uncertain of why she had burst out of the castle's private dining hall; he was not sure if she was upset by something or if it had something to do with the twins, but when he found her, she was in the bathroom vomiting violently. Andrew stood next to her and rubbed her back, trying to soothe her; and when she was done, he got a washcloth and wet it with cool water for her to wipe her face and neck with. Andrew asked Camillia if she was okay now, and she said sort of; she still felt nauseated, but she thought she was done vomiting. She turned toward Andrew and laid her head against his chest then thanked him for being there for her. Camillia told Andrew that they needed to go eat breakfast and get started on their errands; she did not want to be late for her prenatal checkup, and Andrew was very excited to go because he liked being able to see their children before they were born.

Back at the castle's private dining hall, Andrew and Camillia started to eat their breakfast and Camillia's nausea was getting worse so she stopped eating and asked Melanie for a fruit drink to try to get something in her since the food was obviously not going to sit well with her stomach. Melanie worked fast to get the fruit drink made and out to Camillia, and Andrew asked her if there was anything he could do for her, but there was nothing. Melanie brought the fruit drink out to Camillia and told her that she made it mild and as acid free as possible. Camillia thanked her and drank the drink down in practically one swig then apologized for her lack of manners, but if she had not drunk it down so fast she may not have gotten much down. Andrew and Melanie excused her lack of manners. Now that breakfast was over, it was time to go to the hospital to get Camillia's prenatal checkup so together the couple went outside, and Andrew asked Jaden to get the buggy since Camillia was not feeling well. He did not want her riding a horse; the buggy was going to be bad enough. Jaden brought the horse and buggy out to the couple from the barn, and Andrew helped Camillia get onto the buggy then onto the buggy and with a quick flick of the reins, the horse started to go. Andrew had the horse trotting so he and Camillia would get to the hospital quicker because Andrew was hoping that the doctor could give Camillia something to ease her nausea.

Now at the hospital, Andrew jumped off the buggy and gave the reins to the hospital stable boy then he went back to the buggy to help Camillia down. It was obvious that she still did not feel good because she was sweating, somewhat pale, and a little shaky. Andrew put his arm around Camillia's waist as they walked into the hospital, and upon approaching the nurse's desk, the charge nurse saw how weak and pale Camillia seemed to be so she went from behind the desk to approach the couple. Just before she could fully get to the couple, Camillia fainted.

Andrew helped ease her to the ground, but he could not prevent her from going down. The charge nurse knelt over Camillia and told Andrew to go get a wheelchair. While Andrew went to get a wheelchair, Camillia came to and wondered what had happened, so the charge nurse told her that she was okay, she had fainted, and that Andrew was coming with a wheelchair. It did not take Andrew long to get back to Camillia and the charge nurse with a wheelchair so with Andrew helping and Camillia doing what she could the charge nurse got her into the wheelchair. The charge nurse wheeled Camillia to her usual room and helped her onto the bed while Andrew stayed out of the way.

Before the charge nurse walked out, she told Andrew to stand next to Camillia so she would not fall off the bed and he did. The charge nurse said she was going to find the doctor to get him in the room as soon as possible; then with her ultraspeed Tas being a pale one, she darted out of the room and went up the hall looking for the doctor and asking everyone if they had seen him. She finally found him and told him that Camillia and Andrew were waiting on him, and as they were walking to her room, the charge nurse told him about Camillia fainting so he started to use his specialized skill of speed also and raced to Camillia's bedside. When the doctor got to Camillia's bedside, he asked her how she felt, and that was when she explained that her nausea was overbearing and that she had already vomited at home; she also told the doctor that she could not eat breakfast but that she did have a fruit drink.

CHAPTER FORTY SIX

The doctor noticed that Camillia was sweaty, pale, and tremulous, so without any further hesitation, the doctor examined Camillia and all was well there. Then he got the ultrasound and looked at the babies. Andrew was looking at the ultrasound monitor as well, and suddenly Andrew became sweaty, pale, and shaky also. The doctor hollered for a nurse to assist him immediately then instructed Andrew to sit down in the chair at the head of the bed, but he just stood there in a state of shock. Just as he became wobbly on his feet, a nurse walked into the room, and the doctor told her to grab Andrew and guide him to the chair behind him before he passed out and to stay with him.

The doctor went back to observing the ultrasound, and something caught his eye so he took a more detailed look and found that it was a baby. That meant that Camillia was not carrying twins; she was, in fact, carrying triplets, but the ultrasound before was clear and they only saw twins. The doctor finished up with the ultrasound then listened for the babies' heartbeats, and he could hear all of them. They sounded good so the doctor told Camillia she could put her shirt down and said that nausea could be very hard as she had experienced it already and sometimes required a hospital stay. Then the doctor called for the charge nurse and whatever other nurse was available. The charge nurse and several other nurses were at the nurse's desk and heard the doctor calling for help so the charge nurse grabbed the closest nurse to her by the arm and told her to go to Camillia's room.

When the nurses got to Camillia's hospital room, the doctor ordered the charge nurse to admit Camillia into the hospital for observation and told the other nurse to take six vials of blood in which types of tubes and what they were for. She said okay then went to gather the things she would need to follow through with the doctor's order. The charge nurse had come back into the room with papers for Camillia to sign for admission into the hospital, and Camillia would not sign the papers. She wanted to go home on bed rest and have the doctor go to the castle to see her; she was even willing to have a home nurse stay with her. The doctor thought about that for a minute or two then told her that if she could stay in bed, he would get home nursing set up and she could go home. Camillia said okay so the charge nurse made the appropriate arrangements and canceled the inpatient arrangement.

The doctor turned his attention to Andrew. The doctor tried to get Andrew's attention, but he was still spaced out so the doctor popped open an ammonia inhalant and put it under Andrew's nose then Andrew started to respond to the doctor. Andrew asked the doctor if he saw the other baby, and the doctor told him yes, that he and Camillia were having triplets and they were all healthy but he wanted Camillia on bed rest at home until he said otherwise. The nurse that went to get blood draw supplies was back and went ahead and drew Camillia's six tubes of blood then took them to the lab herself. The doctor told Camillia and Andrew that he was going to give her a medicine that would decrease if not stop the nausea so she could continue to eat and stay healthy and drink so she did not get dehydrated because dehydration could cause her to go into premature labor and they did not want that, as it was because she was carrying multiple babies that put her at risk of going into labor early.

Andrew and Camillia acknowledged the doctor's words; then a different nurse from whom they had been getting treatment walked into Camillia's hospital room. The doctor introduced her and said she was the home health nurse and would leave the hospital with them to go to the castle and begin her duties. Andrew and Camillia were pleased to meet the home health nurse, and they welcomed her cheerfully. While they were talking with the home health nurse, the doctor gave Camillia a shot to get her nausea under control. Now the doctor was ready to let the couple and home health nurse leave. He told the couple that he would visit them in the afternoon. The couple said okay then Camillia got off the hospital bed, and Andrew stood up from his chair. Together with the home health nurse, they left the hospital.

Outside the hospital, their buggy was ready for them so Andrew helped Camillia onto the buggy then climbed up himself. The home health nurse mounted her horse, and they left to go to their side of the castle. The ride home was not too very long, but Andrew kept the horse at a slow steady pace so Camillia was not jostled around so much. By now, Camillia's nausea was gone, and she let Andrew know and he was so happy for her and it even gave him some relief.

Now back at their side of the castle, Andrew jumped down from the buggy and gave the reins to Jaden then went to help Camillia down while the home health nurse got off her horse. Once she was off her horse, she gave her reins to Jaden also who took the horses and buggy to the stable to take care of while Andrew and Camillia showed the home health nurse around the castle. The home health nurse could not believe how spacious the inside of the castle was, and she loved the decor. After the short tour, she suggested that Camillia put on some bedclothes and get into bed; Camillia did as directed. Andrew told the home health nurse that if she needed or wanted anything to just let him or one of his staff know, and she said that she would and thanked him.

Just then the butler approached Andrew and told him that Jaden's mother was there to see Camillia. Andrew thanked the butler and told Camillia that he would take her to the tutoring hall and take care of the arrangements for Jaden's tutoring for her; then he was going to be with Jaden's father while he spoke to the building crew about expanding the store then deal with the building crew himself over the cost of the project and the approximation of the finishing date then he would be back to check on her and spend some time with her. Camillia asked Andrew to have Jaden's mother visit when she had some free time maybe before she started to tutor Armellya on that evening and Andrew said he would, he gave her a mushy kiss and quickly rubbed her belly then left the bedroom to take care of the day's duties.

As Andrew was leaving the bedroom, the home health nurse instructed Camillia to make her aware of any discomfort, nausea, needs, and desires; and she would love to chat if Camillia wanted to because it would help the time go by faster for both. Camillia assured the home health nurse that she would keep her completely updated on how she was doing and would let her know if she needed or desired anything, and the home health nurse thanked Camillia. The home health nurse got up from her seat and went over to Camillia's bed to fluff her pillows and help her get comfortable; then they started chatting as the home health nurse sat back down. Meanwhile, Andrew had already taken care of Jaden's tutoring; it was paid for in full and arranged for the instructor to go to the castle to teach Jaden. Now Andrew was taking Jaden's mother to their family's general store to run the store while he and Jaden's father dealt with the store-expansion project with the construction crew.

Upon arriving at the general store, it was apparent that it was busy so it was going to take some time to get Jaden's father freed up and have Jaden's mother take over. Fifteen minutes later, the general store's business lightened up a bit, and Jaden's mother had everything under control so Andrew and Jaden's father went to the back of the general store where there was an office room, and that was where the head of the construction crew was waiting for them so they could talk business. Jaden's father introduced himself and Andrew to the head of construction then they got right to business.

When the conversation was over, they decided to start on the expansion project the next day and work long hours to get the project done quicker but just as safe as if they were to work slowly. The head construction worker told Jaden's father it would just be a matter of days, and the general store would be everything that he and his wife expected it to be. Andrew intervened and wanted to discuss the cost of the project, and the head construction worker did talk with Andrew about the cost of the expansion project. It was not as pricey as Andrew thought it would be so Andrew took the money out of his pouch and paid the cost of the expansion project in full then Jaden's father thanked Andrew.

After the head construction worker left, Jaden's father took Andrew over to the section of the general store to pick the furs and leather that he would need to make the couple's buggy's more comfortable; then Jaden's father gathered the sewing materials and stuffing for the seats then put all the materials in a burlap sack so that at the end of the day for the general store, all he had to do was grab the burlap sack and head over to the castle to start working off the money that the couple advanced to him and his wife. Andrew told Jaden's parents that he would see them later and that he needed to go check on Camillia and spend a little bit of time with her. Jaden's mother asked Andrew if Camillia was okay, and Andrew told her that she was fine for now but that she was placed on bed rest by the doctor until further notice because he wanted to keep her from going into premature labor as they just found out that morning that Camillia was carrying triplets instead of twins as they had all thought. Jaden's parents congratulated him and told him to tell her that they send their love; then Andrew told Jaden's mother that Camillia wanted her to come and visit with her before starting the tutoring with Armellya, and she said she would most definitely.

Andrew and Jaden's parents said their farewells, and Andrew left the general store to go back to the castle. Andrew got on the buggy and ran the horse all the way home so he got back to the castle quite quickly. He was anxious to check on Camillia and make sure that she and the babies were okay and did not need anything. When Andrew got home, he jumped off the buggy and tossed the reins to Jaden then ran into the castle headed straight for his and Camillia's bedroom. When Andrew got to the bedroom, he found Camillia sound asleep. He asked the home health nurse how Camillia had been doing all day, and she said that Camillia and herself had a long chat that covered just about every subject known to them and then she felt a bit tired so she lay down and was asleep in no time. Andrew told the home health nurse to let him know when Camillia awoke so he could spend some time with her, and the home health nurse acknowledged Andrew positively.

It was getting close to family time so Andrew went ahead and went to the family room to rest for a few minutes before guests would start to arrive. He had a busy day with nonstop work; he felt like he could use a nap also, but before he could get any further thoughts, someone knocked at the castle door. The butler answered the door, and it was Jaden coming for family time. Right behind him was the rest of the family, and Andrew muttered something about how time was going by so fast, and Jaden heard Andrew but did not say anything. He just gave Andrew a hug and told him that he loved him. Now that everyone except Camillia was there, Andrew announced that it was time to go to the private dining hall. Bridgette asked why they were not waiting for Camillia, and Andrew said he would explain it and everything that went with it when it was his turn to share his day so everyone went ahead and went to the castle's private dining hall.

Once everybody was seated around the big roundtable, everyone voted for Andrew to share his day first because they were concerned about Camillia; she would never miss family time. Andrew told the group of friends about going to the hospital that morning for her prenatal checkup and being just coincidental that she had serious nausea and vomiting then when the doctor did the ultrasound and listened to the babies' heartbeats, they found out that they were not having twins after all, they were having triplets. Before Andrew could get another word in, everyone cheered and congratulated Andrew, then they settled down so Andrew could tell them that the doctor put her on bed rest so she hopefully would not go into labor early; however, Camillia and the babies were healthy.

Over the lunch hour while eating, everyone else shared their day including ten-year-old Jaden; then when the lunch hour was over, everyone wanted to go visit Camillia so Andrew went to see if she was awake yet and she was because the home health nurse woke her up so she could eat lunch. Andrew asked Camillia if she was up to receiving guests, and she said yes, she would love to see the family. The home health nurse let the family go into the bedroom two at a time with a fifteen-minute time limit, which was better than nothing, but they wanted to all go in together and have the whole two hours to spend with Camillia. By the time everyone got their fifteen minutes with Camillia, it was time for everyone to go back to their duties, and now Camillia felt that she was going to be bored for the rest of the day and she dreaded that bed rest was something that she had a challenging time doing because she was so used to being active and scheduling her day herself.

Andrew and Camillia were supposed to go to the science hall that day, but Andrew planned on letting the chief go alone so Andrew could spend some time with Camillia and the chief could give Andrew and Camillia an update on how the life-extension project and the conception project were coming along. Andrew called for a runner to go get the chief and bring him to Andrew so he could give the chief instructions to go to the science hall then get back to him. The runner left right away, and about fifteen minutes later, the runner was back with the chief who was then left alone with the couple. Camillia told the chief that if he had some spare time, she would like to spend some time just talking with him about nothing specific. Camillia only wanted to have company so the day would go by faster for her. Andrew said he had an idea, and that was for the chief to stay with Camillia while he went to the science hall and did a check on the two projects. Andrew told Camillia and the chief that they usually spend a lot of time at the science hall so he probably would not be back until dinnertime; then after dinner, Jaden's mother was going to visit before tutoring Armellya, and after Jaden and Armellya's tutoring was done, the couple would have the rest of the night to themselves and Camillia thought that was a good idea. Andrew bent over Camillia and gave her a kiss on the lips then told her he loved her and would be back as quickly as possible then left the bedroom. The chief pulled a chair up to Camilla's bedside and sat down; then he and Camillia started conversing.

Meanwhile, Andrew was on his way to the science hall; and when he got there, he got off his horse and tied it up to the post then went inside. The new head scientist saw Andrew walk into the science hall and greeted him right away. Andrew returned the greeting and then asked how things were going on the two projects. The new head scientist said he was sorry but there was not much to report because they were at the slow part of the research, and that was breaking down all the plants that they had gathered down to their individual basic components, documenting their findings, then moving on to the next plant specimen. The new head scientist told Andrew that although that step was so tedious in having to do the same step repeatedly, it was the most crucial step. Andrew asked the new head scientist if they had found any more specimens that may work for one of the projects, and the new head scientist said that there were two more plants that showed potential for the conception project. Andrew said that it was great that they found more to work with and that he was hoping they could successfully produce a conception vaccine and give the gift of childbearing back to the community so they would have the option of expanding their families if they wanted to. The new head scientist said he was counting on the project being successful because he wanted to start a family with his wife, but not at the expense of possibly hurting anyone. Andrew told the new head scientist good luck on the project, and he hoped that the new head scientist would be able to benefit from it as well, especially since he wanted children because Andrew could tell the new head scientist that children were a real blessing to each one in their own unique way.

CHAPTER FORTY SEVEN

Suddenly, one of the scientists hollered in excitement so Andrew and the new head scientist turned to see what was so wonderful, and it was one of the scientists working on the life-extension project. He requested that the new head scientist come to his side right away. The new head scientist and Andrew went over to the other scientist, and all the other scientists stopped what they were doing and watched because they wanted to know about what was so thrilling to holler about. When the new head scientist got to the other scientist, he was told to consider the microscope slide and asked if he saw what the other scientist had seen. The new head scientist exclaimed that they had finally found the secret to extending the lifespan of an individual, and Andrew asked the head scientist to explain the finding. The new head scientist took Andrew by the shoulder and walked him back to the office area and told him to sit down.

The new head scientist took a book off his bookshelf and turned to a specific page then tilted the book so Andrew could see the pictures in the book and then asked Andrew if he knew what the drawings were, and Andrew told him of course it was cellular division. The new head scientist told Andrew that he was correct and that was what the microscope showed, and Andrew jumped out of his chair and asked if he was sure he was seeing cellular division in the microscope. The new head scientist said yes and offered for Andrew to look. Andrew and the new head scientist went to the microscope, and Andrew considered the microscope and saw two cells dividing. When the new head scientist asked what he was seeing, he said two cells dividing. The new head scientist told Andrew that when he looked, it was only one cell dividing and, if left alone, the cells would continue to divide and who knew how many new cells would be produced. Andrew got inspired; he asked the new head scientist what the next step was, and he told Andrew that there was still a lot of research to do on the plant that could mimic human cells, plus there was the issue of replenishing what they would take from the forest if that plant was to be the solution to the pale ones' life expansion. That plant was scarce and known for eating flies and small bugs unlike any other plant known to be in the forest; that plant did have a lot of different qualities about it than any other plant.

The head scientist told Andrew that soon they would need pale one blood to compare to the plant cell and to possibly introduce the blood to the plant to see if it would still divide the cells, and Andrew told the new head scientist that he would be willing to donate some blood for the cause. The new head scientist thanked Andrew and told him when it was time, the science hall would let him know. The new head scientist said that he would need another two blood sample sources to be sure there was nothing different in the blood that made any cellular developments differ, and Andrew told the new head scientist that the chief would be willing to help and that he would check with the doctor to see if Camillia might be able to help also.

Andrew revealed that the life-extension project was to keep the chief around longer, and the new head scientist was surprised then asked if he was dying. Andrew told him that he was so they were on a time limit, but not to do anything rash to just do things with precision because they would not be helping the chief or anyone else by rushing that project or the other one. The new head scientist said he understood and that he would comply. With that, Andrew said he had to get back to Camillia and that he would be back the next day; then he left the science hall.

Andrew approached his side of the castle on time to have dinner so he left his horse with Jaden and told him to hurry with taking care of the horse because it was about dinnertime, and Jaden rushed off with the horse to finish his duties. When Andrew got into the castle, he went straight to his and Camillia's bedroom to check on her, and he found that the chief was still there and that pleased Andrew. Andrew told Camillia and the chief that he was glad that the chief was still there because he had some good news from the science hall and that they would discuss it after dinner since dinner was just minutes from being brought to Camillia and both Andrew and the chief had planned to dine with Camillia in her and Andrew's bedroom. Andrew did not want to discuss business during dinner; he wanted dinner to be a laid-back non intense experience, but he did tell the chief and Camillia that they would be overjoyous about the news from the science hall.

Camillia and the chief begged Andrew to tell them during dinner. Since it was so positive, it would not make dinner a negative experience; in fact, telling great news was a wonderful way to make dinner more of a positive experience so Andrew finally broke down and said okay, that he would tell of the latest news during dinner. With Andrew and the chief being in the bedroom with Camillia, the home health nurse could go to the castle's private dining hall and eat with everyone else as well as get a break from being confined in the bedroom. That would allow Andrew to tell the chief and Camillia the good news from the science hall and keep it a secret from the public and close friends.

Melanie popped into the couple's bedroom with three kitchen staff members to bring in dinner and serve Andrew, Camillia, and the chief. Melanie also wanted to see Camillia to check on her and to tell her she missed Camillia's presence during family time and that she wanted to visit with Camillia during some free time. Camillia thanked Melanie for her concern and service then told her that she would love to have her company, and if things were still getting done, she could pop in during nonfree time for a second or two. Melanie was happy to hear that and said that she would visit periodically and check to see if Camillia wanted anything that she could get for her. Andrew and the chief thanked Melanie for her concern, and Andrew told Melanie that she was such a devoted friend and family member and they would never trade her for any replacement because there was no one who could be as sentimental to them as she was. Melanie thanked Andrew and gave him a hug then went over to Camillia and gave her a hug and on the way out of the couple's bedroom she gave the chief a hug and then left the bedroom to go about her business.

Andrew, Camillia, and the chief started to eat their dinner while Andrew proceeded to tell Camillia and the chief about the surprise from the science hall. Andrew told them that the science hall had found a plant that had a cellular base that mimicked the human cell and could divide on its own and that was the secret to longevity because as individuals age, their bodies break down and fail to be as productive with cellular recomposition. With that plant being introduced into the pale ones' bodies, it may cause their bodies to start to rebuild what had been broken down. Andrew told Camillia and the chief that the science hall was not sure how the cells would react when being introduced into the bloodstream of an individual but that the science hall wanted to test their theory by getting three volunteers to donate blood so that it could be either proven a success or shown to be a failure. Andrew told them that he was one of their volunteers and that the science hall would contact him when they were ready to test their theory. Andrew then told the chief that he mentioned to the science hall that he would check with him to be a second source of blood, and the chief told Andrew that he would love to help especially since the project came about for his benefit. Andrew thanked the chief and said it was wonderful.

Camillia told Andrew that she would be willing to give blood if the doctor said it would be okay then the science hall would have their three volunteers, but if the doctor was not willing to allow her to give blood, she questioned Andrew about who would the science hall be able to get blood from without questions and having to reveal the reason. They had to keep the project under wraps until they could perfect the injection, and that was if the science hall was to be successful. Andrew had not thought that far in advance; he said he would deal with that one step at a time, and the chief agreed that it was the best way to handle things. He added that one should never get too far ahead of a situation because anything could change at any time and there was no reason to spend time planning for the inevitable or worrying over something that had not happened yet. Camillia saw his point and agreed. Andrew told the chief that the doctor would be visiting sometime soon after dinner so he would ask about a blood donation at that time and just let the doctor know it was not going to be needed right a Dinner went by so fast because they had such an interesting and delightful conversation while they ate, and right as Andrew finished discussing the life-extension project, Melanie and a few of the kitchen staff members returned to the couple's bedroom to gather their dishes and see if there was anything else that Melanie could get for them and to see if they were up to dessert. Andrew, Camillia, and the chief were all up for dessert even though they were all full from dinner. They were in such a good mood; they figured dessert was in order to celebrate the science hall's progress among themselves. The chief told Andrew and Camillia that the progress the science hall had made on the life-extension project was phenomenal, and he was really hoping that they would come up with an injection that could help him as well as any other pale one who needed it. He even said that he would be the first pale one to try it once they got to that phase because if it did not work, then he would be in no worse shape than he was already in; and if it should be harmful or even lethal, then since he was so close to death, even though it would be a loss, it would not take the life or harm someone who still had a lot of life in them or even had a wife, possibly a complete family. But that subject would not be discussed until the time came for the science hall to be ready for that phase. He was just mentioning his position on that step.

Andrew told the chief that his disposition was admirable, but that he did not believe in risking anyone's life, not even the chief's, and that was that. Camillia agreed and said that there was to be no more talk like that from the chief so the subject was dropped. The chief figured that he would secretly discuss that with the science hall and make sure that they did not reveal their conversation about it to Andrew or Camillia. Andrew, Camillia, and the chief somehow finished their desert and called for the kitchen staff to come and gather their dishes and also sent for Melanie to tell her how wonderful of a meal and dessert she had made. Melanie and the kitchen staff showed up at the couple's bedroom, and the kitchen staff took the dishes and left right away while the couple and the chief spoke to Melanie about her scrumptious meal and dessert. She thanked them for the compliment and told them she only wanted the best of meals and desserts for them, and she told them that if there was any specific meal or dessert that they wanted, they should just let her know. She knew that Camillia being pregnant may cause her to want certain things or make her unable to tolerate other things that otherwise she may have liked. Andrew, Camillia, and the chief thanked Melanie for her flexibility.

Since dinner was over and everyone was getting back to work, Andrew had to go and get Jaden's mother to bring her to the couple's bedroom to visit with Camillia for a few minutes before tutoring Armellya and get Jaden to his tutoring room until he could remember where it was and get there on his own. Andrew also had to get out to the barn to talk to Jaden's father about making the buggies more comfortable and making sure that he knew where everything was and where he could keep his own tools and supplies in the barn where they would not get in the way of Jaden's work. Andrew gave Camillia a kiss on the forehead and told her he would see her after his work was done. The chief had to go back to his side of the castle to tend to his own workers and get settled in for the night so he gave Camillia a hug and a kiss on the cheek then told her if she needed him for anything to just send a runner and he would be there promptly. Camillia thanked the chief then told him to have a good night and that she would see him the next day.

As the chief was walking out of the couple's bedroom, the home health nurse was walking in, and she sat in a chair right next to Camillia's bed. The home health nurse asked Camillia how her dinner and dessert was, and Camillia told her it was great and that she enjoyed her company. The home health nurse told Camillia that she was glad to hear that. Just then, the doctor walked into the bedroom. The doctor asked the home health nurse if there were any problems or concerns, and she told the doctor that Camillia had stayed in bed and that there were no issues to speak of. The doctor said good, then proceeded to walk closer to Camillia. The doctor asked Camillia how the nausea was coming along, and she told him that she had no nausea and that she was feeling fine, she had a lot of energy and really wanted to get off bed rest. The doctor said that he would see about that. The doctor examined Camillia and the three children she was carrying. He brought his portable ultrasound machine and his handheld machine that allowed him to listen to the babies' heartbeats and listened to the babies and looked at them then gave the babies and Camillia a good bill of health.

The doctor asked Camillia if she had been able to eat and drink freely without vomiting, and she said yes and it felt good. The doctor told Camillia that she may have felt ill due to a sudden surge of hormones and that it was possible that her body may not have been producing as much of the necessary hormones to sustain a third or even second child and that her body may have recognized the need for a surplus of hormones all of a sudden then gave a surge to defend the pregnancy, making her feel ill. The doctor told Camillia that her pregnancy hormones were not as high as he had hoped. Either she was producing only the absolute necessity or she was not as far in the pregnancy as they had thought, so the doctor told her that he wanted to redo the blood tests. If the tests came back as expected, then she would be able to get off bed rest; but if the tests came back as they did this time, then she would remain on bed rest.

Camillia did not like the idea of staying on bed rest, but she knew her body and it felt like it had compensated for the triplets and recovered to having the necessary hormones so she gladly let the doctor take her blood. While doing so, she told him that the test results were going to show that she could leave the bed and go back to her regular schedule of doing things and planning her day out and about. The doctor told Camillia that he certainly hoped she could get off the bed and be active again soon. He said that he was not punishing her; he was only looking out for the best interests of mother and babies. Camillia told the doctor that he was the best doctor ever and that she respected his opinions and knew that whatever he did no matter what it was, he was only looking out for her.

Camillia asked the doctor how soon she might know that she would be able to get up, and the doctor said that it would be about two hours and that no matter what the results, he would send a runner to let her know what the test results were either way. Camillia said she would be anxiously awaiting word from the runner, and then the doctor gathered all his equipment and left her bedroom to go back to the hospital. Right after the doctor left, Andrew came into the bedroom with Jaden's mother; it was good timing. Jaden's mother said she wanted to visit with Camillia before starting her tutoring session with Armellya. Jaden's mother brought a mixture of treats for Camillia to enjoy while being in bed. She thought the gesture would cheer up Camillia, and it did. When Camillia saw all the treats, she was surprised it was all her very favorites.

Camillia thanked Jaden's mother and told her that she appreciated all the vigorous work that she had put into preparing the treat plate. Jaden's mother said it was no problem, that it gave her something to do with her spare time; and because of making the treats for her, she could also have some for her husband and Jaden. Camillia told Jaden's mother that it worked out nice that everyone would get some treats, and Jaden's mother agreed. Jaden's mother asked Camillia how she was doing and when she might be off bed rest. Camillia replied that she was doing good and she could be off bed rest as soon as two hours from then. It was dependent upon the blood test that the doctor had just taken, and she was positive that the results were going to be such that the doctor would release her from bed rest. Jaden's mother said that would be great but warned her to make sure she did not overwork herself and to get plenty of rest. She then said that if there was anything she could do for her, just let her know. Camillia thanked Jaden's mother and said she would let her know if she needed anything, and Jaden's mother thanked Camillia. With that, Jaden's mother said it was time for her to go tutor Armellya but that when she was done, she would check on Camillia to see if there was anything she needed or could do for her. Camillia thanked her and told her how good of a friend she was to her. Jaden's mother worked her way to the bedroom door and waved goodbye, and Camillia waved back.

CHAPTER FORTY EIGHT

While Jaden's mother was tutoring Armellya, Jaden was receiving tutoring from a private instructor in another room in the castle. Andrew and Camillia had a room made up for Jaden right after taking him into their home as their godson. They had a sleeping area with a nice bed set up, a play area with lots of toys for a ten-year-old, a schooling area for him to receive his tutoring and a place for all his school work and books, and in the closet was clothing for Jaden for any event that may arise as well as bedclothes and work clothes. Jaden's parents had not seen the bedroom that the couple had made up for Jaden yet, and this was the first Jaden had seen of it. Camillia wanted to show the bedroom to Jaden's parents, but Camillia got on bed rest first so in her absence, Andrew would be showing Jaden's parents his new multifunctional room. In fact, when Jaden's parents were done with their work for the night, they were supposed to meet with Andrew in the couple's bedroom, and the tutor already knew to hold Jaden in the room until Andrew showed up with his parents. Jaden's mother was the first to finish her work, and she had told Camillia that she would check on her after working so she went to Camillia's bedroom.

Camillia greeted her and told her to come in and she did. Jaden's mother asked Camillia if there was anything she could get for her or do for her, and Camillia asked her to please sit down in one of the chairs next to the bed and that her husband and Andrew would be in soon. Not too long after having Jaden's mother take a seat, Andrew and Jaden's father showed up at the couple's bedroom, and Andrew asked Jaden's father to sit in the other chair that was by Camillia's bedside, which he did. Andrew said that he and Camillia did something for Jaden that before now he had not seen and still may not know was his and his only but that the tutor was holding him over so that Andrew could take them to see and together the family could look it over and let Andrew know if they like it or not and if there was anything to add or omit to let Andrew know and together Andrew, Camillia, and Jaden's parents could fix it to specifications that were acceptable. Jaden's parents told Andrew and Camillia that they had already done so much for their family that they just could not keep taking, and Camillia cut them off and told Jaden's parents that what they had done was nothing short of what they would and have done for their other children, and that as godparents, it was a pleasure.

Andrew asked Jaden's parents if they were ready to see the massive surprise, and they replied affirmatively so Andrew told them to follow him and he took them to his room where he was. When Jaden's parents walked into Jaden's room, they knew that Andrew and Camillia had made that room specially for Jaden, and Jaden's mother started to shed tears of sentiment and Jaden's father's eyes welled up, but as a man, he tried to suck it up and not shed any tears. Andrew told them it was just fine to let tears of joy flow. Jaden turned to see his parents standing behind him then jumped off his chair and ran to his parents and hugged them both. Andrew showed Jaden's parents the different areas and what they contained, and Andrew said that there was nothing personal of his in the room because everything was brand-new, but it would eventually get broken in and would be well loved just like his bedroom at home.

Jaden's parents thanked Andrew and said that they needed to stop by the couple's bedroom to thank Camillia also. They told Andrew that the room was simply beautiful and had everything that Jaden would need in it. Andrew told Jaden's parents that the bed was there in case he needed or wanted to stay a night over; then Andrew assured Jaden's parents that he and Camillia were not trying to get their son from them but that as godparents, they wanted to treat Jaden the same as they would their real children. Jaden heard Andrew and his parents talking, and he asked Andrew if the room was his. Andrew told him yes and so was everything in it. Jaden was just as excited as his parents were, and he gave Andrew a big hug and told him that he needed to go see Camillia to thank her also but that he also wanted to see her because he missed her a lot. Andrew thanked the tutor for keeping Jaden over so that Andrew could get his parents to the room before Jaden had left it, and the tutor told Andrew that it was not a big deal because Jaden was a wonderful student and a very bright boy. The tutor said that she saw a lot of potential in Jaden.

The tutor, Andrew, Jaden, and Jaden's parents left the room. The tutor walked to the castle's foyer to leave and go home while Andrew, Jaden, and Jaden's parents went to the couple's bedroom to see Camillia. When everyone got into the couple's bedroom, Jaden's parents thanked Camillia for the room she and Andrew had put together for Jaden, and Camillia told them that there was more than Jaden's room that they needed to know about. Andrew asked Jaden's parents to please take a seat in the two chairs by Camillia's bedside and Jaden could sit on the edge of Camillia's bed while Andrew stood. Camillia told Jaden's parents that they were in the process of putting together a room for them also with two areas in it, one for Jaden's mother and the other for Jaden's father so they had a place for work items such as store paperwork, tutoring schedules and materials, drafts and sketches for the buggy and barn work, and any other stuff they may want to put over there. Camillia told them that there would also be his-and-hers closets full of clothing for them for any occasion that may arise as well as bedclothes. There would also be a large bed in the room in case it was ever needed or wanted.

Jaden's parents were beside themselves. They thanked Andrew and Camillia and asked them why they were doing so much for them, and Camillia told them that family took care of family in ways that were beyond what a friend or stranger would do. Jaden's father asked Andrew what he and his wife could do to help him and Camillia. Andrew told Jaden's parents that all they had to do was appreciate what was done for them or given to them and that those things were gifts from the heart from himself and Camillia. Camillia told Jaden's parents that the rooms were just for nights when things ran over and it got too late to travel home due to the community curfew or if they just got too tired to travel, and Jaden was welcome to stay on the weekends if it was approved by them.

Andrew told Jaden's parents that the rooms were there as a backup also if things got too tight to stay in their home and that they could move into the castle and have a restricted area for multiuse and, if that ever did happen, their livestock could be taken in also. Andrew told Jaden's father that he would have another barn built for them if need be. Andrew told Jaden's parents that all their staff lived in the castle and had multipurpose rooms with balconies and that they had use of his and Camillia's horses and buggies when needed. Camillia said that every day at the lunch hour, they and the staff start what they call family time and carry it over to two hours so they can combine and discuss new business, old business, goals, hopes, dreams and support one another and function as one big unit called a family. Camillia told

Jaden's parents that they and Jaden had become a part of their small family unit. Jaden's parents told Camillia and Andrew that they were forever in their debt, and Camillia cut them off and told them that they were not in any kind of debt; they were forever family and that was that.

The home health nurse was amazed by the couple's generosity and at how close the couple was to their staff. She found it to be a grand arrangement and wished she had a family that was close like them. Jaden's parents, Jaden, Andrew, and Camillia all gave each other hugs and told one another that they loved them. Just then, the butler showed up at the couple's bedroom door and announced that a runner from the hospital had arrived. Camillia told the butler to send in the runner immediately and he did. The runner told Camillia that her blood test results had come back, and the doctor said that according to the extremely high amount of pregnancy hormones that were found, he believed that she was where they originally thought her to be in her pregnancy and that her bed rest was over.

Before the runner left, he told the home health nurse that he was also there to bring her back to the hospital. The home health nurse said her goodbyes to Camillia and Andrew and told them that she learned a lot from them that day and that she hoped that if they met again, it would be under positive circumstances and not for health concerns. As the home health nurse was leaving with the runner, she wished Andrew and Camillia a good pregnancy and said she looked forward to meeting the triplets when they were born. Camillia and Andrew thanked her for her service and told her that they would make sure she met the triplets once they were born. Jaden had the home health nurse's horse ready for her because the runner told him to get her horse ready on his way into the castle, so when the home health nurse and the runner got outside of the castle, they mounted their horses and rode off to go back to the hospital.

Camillia was thankful for her bed rest being over, and she got out of bed right away. As soon as she was upright, she told Andrew that she wanted to take a stroll in the chief's garden. Jaden's parents said that they were going to take Jaden and go home so that the couple could take their stroll in the chief's garden. Everyone said goodbye to everyone and then Jaden's parents took him and left to go home and settle down for the night. Andrew and Camillia went over to the chief's side of the castle and knocked on the door. The butler answered and took the couple to the chief's family room and told them that he would go get the chief for them. Several minutes later, the chief walked into the family room and was surprised to see Camillia out of bed. The chief told Camillia how great it was that her bed rest was over. He patted Camillia's belly and told her that the triplets must be okay, and Camillia told the chief that things were as they should be. Andrew told the chief that they were there to take a slow lovers' walk through his lovely garden and appreciate each other but that they would be back to their side of the castle by the time the community curfew came. The chief told Andrew that the garden was as much theirs as it was his and that they were welcome there without permission, and Andrew thanked him then the couple started to walk toward the door that led out to the garden.

Right as Andrew and Camillia got to the door that led to the outdoor garden, Camillia changed her mind and no longer wanted to go out to the garden because it was getting sort of late and Camillia was feeling a bit tired. She just wanted to spend time with Andrew alone in their bedroom. Andrew told Camillia that he was fine with staying in for the night as the day had been a long one and he even wanted to stay in, but he was willing to go to the outdoor garden for her because she had been inside on bed rest for a brief time past twenty-four hours. Andrew was relieved about Camillia's decision to stay in for the night. The couple got back to their side of the castle and went to their bedroom then changed into bedclothes and lay in the bed. Andrew and Camillia cuddled and engaged in some foreplay for a while then Andrew put one of his hands on Camillia's belly then spoke to the triplets.

As Andrew held a one-way conversation with Camillia's belly, Andrew and Camillia watched the triplets roll around in her belly, and Camillia could telepathically sense the babies' joy over hearing their father interact with them. Andrew was amazed at the ability to see Camillia's belly move slightly as the babies' arms and legs pressed against the front of her stomach. After an abbreviated time of interacting with the triplets, Andrew noticed that Camillia was ready to go to sleep so he quit talking to the babies and took his hand off her stomach then

The next morning, Andrew and Camillia woke up well rested, and they thought that it would be nice to have the chief over for breakfast so he did not have to eat alone in his side of the castle, so Andrew sent a runner over to him to relay the couple's invitation to breakfast. While the runner was gone, Andrew and Camillia changed into day clothes and put their bedclothes away, then went to their bathroom to wash their faces, brush their teeth, and brush their hair. As soon as the couple was ready to go to the big round table for breakfast, the butler stopped Andrew and Camillia in the long hallway and told them that the chief was in the family room waiting for them. Andrew thanked the butler then he and Camillia went to the family room to greet the chief.

When Andrew and Camillia got to the chief, he told them that he had a good night and that being invited over for breakfast made his day start even better because it was always nice to have company when one was used to being alone most of the time.

Camillia told the chief that he could eat with them any time he desired and all he had to do was show up at the big round table and find a place to sit, which was not a challenging thing to do, and the chief thanked her then told her that he would start to take her up on the offer. Andrew suggested that the chief just show up every day and join them for breakfast and then there would be no guessing as to whether the chief was going to join them on any day. Camillia told the chief and Andrew that it was an excellent idea. The chief told the couple that it was a generous offer, and he would like to be with them every morning. There was no better way to start the day than with your children. Andrew and Camillia said it was settled, and everyone ate their breakfast then sat at the big round table for a few minutes to let their food settle. Melanie had made a large breakfast with all the side dishes; there was even food left over so Andrew went to see if Jaden was hungry at all.

When Andrew got out to the barn, Jaden was already working hard, but Andrew interrupted him to see if he wanted anything to eat and he said he was full as his mother had made a big breakfast also. Andrew told Jaden that if he found himself hungry, he should take a break and let Melanie know. Jaden told Andrew that he would then thank him and go right back to work. Andrew went back into the castle and told Camillia and the chief that Jaden was such a good and hard worker that he was going to grow into a great young man; Camillia and the chief agreed.

Before leaving the big roundtable, Andrew, Camillia, and the chief shared the day's tasks for everyone to compare and see if any of them could use a hand or if there was something that they needed or could do together for the benefit of the task's well-being. The trio discussed the trip to the science hall for that day and decided to go altogether. Andrew and the chief would check on the construction of Jaden's parents' room in the castle while Camillia went to each of the children's rooms and checked with each nanny to see if there was anything that was needed for them or the children no matter what it was.

Once Andrew and the chief finished their morning duties, Camillia should be done with hers and everyone could meet back at the family room until family time then spend some time with everybody. After family time, the three of them could assess where they were with the previous tasks and make sure they knew the outcome of all the tasks in the event someone else had to deal with a task that they had not handled earlier that day. Andrew and Camillia wanted the chief to hear firsthand what the science hall had to say about the life-extension project since he was the reason it was originally brought about even though if it was a success it would be used on any pale one that needed it.

CHAPTER FORTY NINE

Andrew, Camillia, and the chief left the castle for the science hall first thing after getting happy tummies at the breakfast table and planning their day. Everyone rode in the buggy since after the science hall visit they would all have to go back to the castle to care for different things. Once they got to the science hall, they walked in and saw every scientist doing some sort of task; they had not even noticed that they were there so Andrew left Camillia and the chief next to the front door, and he went to the back of the science hall where the new head scientist was and said hello. The new head scientist looked up at Andrew and said hello then apologized for not acknowledging them upon entering the science hall. Andrew told him it was okay, that it looked like they were busy, and the scientist told Andrew that when they saw that he was working and not just supervising, yes, they were on to something and getting very busy.

Andrew and the new head scientist walked to the front of the science hall to meet with Camillia and the chief. The new head scientist said that they were ready for the blood samples because they had gotten to the point that they believed that since the plant could cause cellular regeneration in other plants, it may cause the several types of blood cells in a pale one to regenerate also. Camillia asked the new head scientist if he had said that the one plant caused other plants to regenerate, and he said yes; then Camillia asked him if they were aware of that the prior day. The new head scientist said that they were testing the plant variety the day before but that when they visited, they had just started to do the experiments so there was nothing to report at that time because then it was only a theory. The chief got excited and was suddenly fidgety; he said that he was ready for his blood to be taken, and the new head scientist told the three of them that he would send a scientist with them to the hospital to have their blood taken and that it had to be done at the hospital because they wanted a pint from everyone and it had to be handled quickly and carefully. The new head scientist said that some of the blood would be spinned down to separate the different cellular components and tested individually as well as test the whole blood product. Andrew said it was fine and that they were ready; he had told the new head scientist that they had not asked the doctor about Camillia donating blood so when they got to the hospital, they would ask then. The new head scientist asked Andrew who he had in mind to donate in Camillia's place if the doctor did not feel it was safe for her to give a whole pint of blood, and Andrew told him who better than a scientist and to pick one. The new head scientist called one of his subordinates over and instructed him to handle the transportation of the blood products and to give blood if Camillia's doctor said she was not in any position to give blood.

The scientist said okay and asked Andrew, Camillia, and the chief if they were ready. They all said they were ready when he was, so the scientist led the way out of the science hall door with the trio in tow. When they got to the hospital, the charge nurse saw Camillia headed her way and figured that she would need to see the doctor, so before anyone could say a word, she told Camillia she was on her way to go get the doctor. Camillia thanked her, and everyone waited there at the nurse's desk for the doctor.

A few minutes later, the charge nurse was back with the doctor and he asked Camillia how she was doing, and she told him she was doing great but that they needed to talk to him in private so he led the small group to his office room and shut the door behind them. The doctor offered everyone a seat on the sofa so they did sit. The doctor sat in his chair behind his desk then asked Camillia what he could do for them. Camillia told the doctor that what he was about to hear was top secret and it was a project being conducted by the science hall, so as far as he was concerned, he knew nothing but that they would keep him up to date because he could possibly be a resource for some of the research. The doctor told Camillia that what a patient was to discuss with him stayed between the two of them and that patient confidentiality was part of his oath. The only way he could reveal anything was with the patient's permission and if the life of the patient depended on it, and Camillia said very well.

Camillia told Andrew to fill the doctor in since she had missed some of the visits at the science hall, and she also told the scientist that if Andrew left out any information that may help the doctor understand what was being done, that information should be added; the scientist said very well. Andrew told the doctor that the science hall was working on a life-extension project and it was originally brought about for the chief since he was already two hundred and thirty-five years old, but if the project were to be a success, it would be used on any pale one that needed it. Andrew told the doctor that the scientists had found a specific plant that had a cellular composition that mimicked human cells and was able to undergo mitosis, and they wanted to introduce the plant cell to the whole blood cell as well as to separate blood components to see if it would cause the blood cell and or the individual blood component to multiply as well.

terested and willing to help in any way possible. He thanked Andrew, Camillia, and the chief for letting him know about the project. Andrew told the doctor that he had to be honest about something, and he got quiet and stared at Andrew so Andrew went on and told the doctor that the only reason he was brought into the loop was because Camillia wanted to give a pint of blood for the research because the science hall needed three or more blood samples to test out their theory, and they wanted to ask him but in doing so they felt that it was important for him to know the importance of the need for blood. The doctor apologized and told the scientist that he was not sure how the loss of blood would affect the triplets or if it were a singleton, and there was no issue with the pregnancy. He would consider it, but he told the scientist that they could have his blood as well if it would help. The scientist told the doctor that they would be happy to use his blood and that they would be getting a pint of blood from everyone there except Camillia, and the doctor said he would find four nurses to assist and they would be told nothing.

Andrew, Camillia, the chief, and the doctor left the doctor's office room and went to the nurse's station where the doctor requested four nurses to meet him in the waiting room area; then the doctor led the small group to the waiting room area and got everyone sat down comfortably then he also sat down. Four nurses walked into the waiting room area and reported to the doctor; then the doctor told the nurses to get a blood donation set up because all four of them would be giving a pint of blood. The nurses stood there for a few minutes with a look of curiosity on their faces, and the doctor told them no questions, just do it so they then left the waiting room area to go get their supplies.

Five minutes later, all the nurses were back and ready to start the blood collection process. The nurses got everything set up and prepped the group then started the collection of blood. The nurses stayed with the group just in case something went wrong; the nurses could address the situation without hesitation and hopefully save the collection. Everything went well for everyone, and now the nurses had their pints of blood so they labeled them and put them into a carrier and gave them to the scientist. The scientist left immediately to get the blood back to the science hall for the rest of the testing so in leaving right away, he rode hard back to the science hall.

When the scientist got back to the science hall, he rushed inside with the blood and gave it to the new head scientist and informed him that Camillia was not able to give blood but that the doctor gave blood in her place. He also told the new head scientist that he had given blood as instructed so that was how they got four samples. The new head scientist told the other scientist that he did an excellent job and that they needed to get started right away so all the scientists were pulled to work on the life-expansion project and the conception project was set aside for now.

Shortly after every scientist was at work and the new head scientist was supervising, Andrew, Camillia, and the chief showed up to watch and hopefully get some good news. They knew they may be stuck there for a while waiting for some sort of news. The trio sat in chairs to stay out of the way and kept quiet; they knew that if something good were to come up, they would know just by the reaction of the scientists. The group was almost ready to leave after forty-five minutes of waiting for some sort of reaction, good or bad, but just then, one of the scientists called out for the head scientist to assist him because he had found something promising. The new head scientist rushed over to his worker and asked what was happening then Andrew, Camillia, and the chief heard the scientists talking and saying that they had mitosis. The rare plant that ate bugs and could mimic a human cell was encouraging mitosis of the blood cell, but when looking at the blood sample under the microscope, it was also reproducing the individual blood components as well as the whole blood cell. The head scientist announced that to the whole group of scientists and everyone cheered.

Andrew asked what the next step would be, and the new head scientist said that now they have seen the plant do the same thing with all four blood samples, it was time to make an injection and test it on the mice. Camillia asked the new head scientist how they would know if it worked or not since the mice could live for quite some time and the scientist told her that they had some mice who were at their life expectancy, and the injection would either kill the mice or allow them to live longer. The chief asked the new head scientist, if the mice survived the injection, how long did they have to give them to know if the injection worked? The new head scientist told the chief that they would take blood samples and tissue samples from the mice to compare to current blood and tissue samples, and they would not have to worry about waiting for the mice that survived the injection to die of old age.

The new head scientist also wanted to test the injection for how many times it could be used on one subject before it would no longer work to extend the life of its subject and that was only if the mice survived the injection. The scientists would use the elderly mice for the project and continue to watch the effects microscopically. The chief told the scientist that he was willing to be the pale one subject, and the new head scientist said that the plant did show to be compatible with blood but that they would take tissue samples from him and test the injection under a microscope before giving it to him.

It was getting rather late in the morning, and Andrew needed to get to the castle to check and approve or disapprove of the building of Jaden's parents' room and Camillia had to return to the castle also to check on all the nannies to see if there was anything that they needed for themselves or the children. The chief was supposed to accompany Andrew, but he was not sure he was going to get the chief out of the science hall. Andrew told the new head scientist that he and Camillia needed to get back to the castle; then Andrew turned to the chief and asked him if he wanted to stay or go with him to the castle. The chief said he would go with Andrew and that if the science hall needed him, they could just send a runner. The new head scientist told the group goodbye and said that when they were needed and they were not there, he would send a runner for them, and they all said okay then left out of the front door. Everyone got onto the buggy and headed to Andrew and Camillia's side of the castle.

Once they got to the castle, Jaden came running out of the barn and held the horses steady while Andrew jumped off the buggy then helped Camillia off the buggy as the chief was getting off the buggy on the other side. Jaden took the horses and buggy back to the barn, and after tending the horses, he would go back to the work that he still had to do on the barn. Andrew and the chief went into the castle to go to the room that was being prepared for Jaden's parents while Camillia went into the castle to the oldest child's room where she would work her way down to the youngest of the children's rooms. Andrew and the chief both inspected Jaden's parents' room for how spacious it was, having two workstations, having a his-and-hers closet, and having a balcony with flowers, and so far, all of that was good.

The interior decorator wanted to speak with Andrew about the decor, which animal prints and which neutral colors were to be used, and what to stock the room with since they were not actually living there. Andrew told the interior decorator to use her imagination and that he wanted the room to feel cozy and warm by the sleeping area but stimulating by the work areas and for those two styles to come together in the neutral part of the room. She said she understood and knew just what to pick. Andrew was done with Jaden's parents' room for now. He would recheck it once it was complete and either approve of it or have some alterations done, but he had a lot of confidence in his interior decorator because she had done the rest of the castle as it was growing.

Now that the room had been taken care of for now, Andrew took the chief and they went to the barn to check on how Jaden was coming along with his small project. The inside of the barn looked completely different, all the tools and equipment had their own little cubby area, and he was starting to do the repairs. Jaden asked Andrew how he liked what had been done, and Andrew told him that he was doing a fantastic job. Jaden told him he wanted to paint the inside and outside of the barn. Andrew told him that they would discuss it. Meanwhile, Camillia was going room by room to speak with each of the children's nannies to see what they may need for themselves or the children and all the children needed more clothing because they were growing out of them so fast. Camillia decided to save the children's clothing that they outgrew and have new clothing made instead of handing them down where they would be able to. Camillia was hoping that the science hall would be able to successfully produce a conception vaccination and then she would give all her little ones' used clothing to Jaden's parents to sell at their store. Camillia figured that would be another way to help them with their business. The children were also starting to need various learning tools that were fun but educational. Andrew and Camillia had already put a bed into three of the toddler bedrooms because they had outgrown their cribs, but the cribs were going to go into the new babies' rooms. Camillia had the list of her babies' needs, and the nannies said they did not need anything so Camillia was ready to give the list and some money to the castle's baby shopper.

CHAPTER FIFTY

It was close to the lunch hour and family time so Camillia went to the family room to wait for everyone, and as she was getting comfortable on the couch, Andrew and the chief walked in from being out at the barn with Jaden. Andrew and the chief sat on the couch with Camillia, and the couple filed each other in on the things they had taken care of separately. Then Camillia told Andrew that she wanted him to go with her to see how far the workers had gotten with the triplet's rooms and Andrew said he would love to go with her to do that. Andrew told Camillia that after checking on the progress of the triplet's rooms, he needed to go out to the forest to check on its condition with the science hall plucking so many plants; he feared that there may be some barren spots, and Camillia said that she wanted to go with him. Andrew told her it would be okay.

Camillia leaned over Andrew to look at the chief and ask him if he wanted to go to the forest with them and he answered yes. Family members started to show up so Andrew, Camillia, and the chief stopped talking about business and started to greet family. Once everyone was there, they all went to the castle's private dining hall and sat around the big roundtable. As soon as the big family was seated, the kitchen staff brought out lunch and served everyone their drinks. As they all ate, they went around the table and shared their day and their plans for the rest of their day. When it got to Andrew and Camillia's turn, they took that opportunity to announce that Jaden's parents' room would be done the next day. Jaden's parents got excited; they could not wait to see it. Everyone asked how Camillia and the triplets were doing so Andrew let everyone know that they had a checkup and all was well, the babies were getting bigger, and it looked like they would all three be a good weight when they were born. Everyone was glad to hear that and relieved to know that all three babies were thriving equally and developing as they should.

At that point, the lunch hour was coming to an end so everyone got quiet and focused on finishing their meals and the kitchen staff was waiting to gather the dishes and clear off the big roundtable. After another ten minutes, everyone was full and ready to go to the family room to finish the two hours of family time left. When the family all got to the family room, they were pleasantly surprised to see all the nannies with the children there. Seeing the children was everyone's highlight of the day; everyone played with the children and passed them around. The nannies only kept the children in the family room for one of the two hours of the family time left so the family's attention turned from the children that were there with the nannies to the triplets that Camillia was still carrying. They were all rubbing her tummy and talking to the babies, and the babies pleased everyone by moving about for them to feel and that took the last hour of family time.

It was now time for everyone to get back to their duties, and Camillia, Andrew, and the chief still had a couple of things that they had to do before their day was done. The first of two things that Andrew and Camillia needed to do was to visit the triplet's rooms, and the chief tagged along since he was invited to go on the next errand. When Camillia got to the first baby's room, she was beside herself because it had been finished and it was perfect for what she had in mind. Camillia turned toward Andrew and the chief and told them to hurry to go to the other room to see how it was coming along. When Andrew, Camillia, and the chief got to the second of the three rooms, Camillia was even more surprised than before because that room was completed also. Camillia grabbed Andrew and the chief by the arms and pulled them swiftly to the third room to see if it was done also, and to her uttermost surprise, it was.

Camillia walked over to the crib and placed her hand flat on the made-up bedding then gingerly told Andrew that their baby would be lying there soon. Andrew walked over to Camillia and turned her body toward him then gave her a gentle hug and told her he loved her and all their children. The chief told them that they were the perfect couple and that they produced some beautiful children that he was proud to call his grandchildren. The chief asked Andrew if the workers were supposed to let them know when the rooms were done, and Andrew said yes but that it was possible that they just got finished that day. Camillia turned so as to be side by side with Andrew, and she looked up at him then told him that she was ready to go to the forest now. Going to the forest was Andrew, Camillia, and the chief's final thing that had to be done before the day was over so they left the baby's room and headed toward the castle's front door.

As the three of them got out the front door, Jaden asked Andrew if he wanted the buggy or horses, and Andrew told him thanks for asking and he needed three horses. Jaden ran into the barn as fast as his little legs could go. Twelve minutes later, Jaden shot out of the barn pulling three horses behind him. Jaden held on to Camillia's horse while she mounted and Andrew and the chief mounted their horses at the same time as Camillia. Andrew called Jaden over to his side then took a small amount of money from his satchel and gave it to Jaden. Andrew told Jaden that it was a tip for his prompt service with the horses and to get one of the horses and go to his parents' general store to give his parents a hug and get something for himself but to come straight back afterward. Jaden was very thankful, and he ran into the barn and got himself a horse and came riding out to thank the couple again. Camillia told him to be careful and that they would see him shortly.

Now it was time to go to the forest, which the chief had previously told the couple was off limits to everyone except the hunters; and if anyone had business out there like the scientists, they had to have special permission and take hunters with them due to some of the wildlife and poisonous plants. Andrew and Camillia told the chief that they recalled that then the chief told them that the general rule was to have two hunters per person going, so for the three of them, they would need six hunters. The chief explained that the hunters lived close to the great wall's doors due to their job taking them out there daily and in the event of an emergency, such as a wild animal sneaking past the great wall doors when they were open for a brief time.

Andrew and Camillia said they understood and so the chief led the way to the chief hunter's home. On the way, the chief told Andrew and Camillia if they ever did need some hunters to always go through the chief hunter because he had to know who was where and when as far as his hunters were concerned. Andrew and Camillia acknowledged the chief. They arrived at the chief hunter's home and got off their horses then tied them up and proceeded to go to the front door and knock. When the door opened, Camillia was shocked to see what the chief hunter looked like. He was gorgeous, very muscular with tanned-looking skin, and he wore only pants and had black shoulder-length wavy hair. The chief spoke with him and told him that they needed to go into the forest to scan the foliage looking for a specific plant area. The chief told the chief hunter that some plant specimens were needed, and they wanted to make sure that what was taken was replaced with seeds and starting to grow.

The chief hunter asked how many of them were going, and the chief told the chief hunter that all three of them would be going; then the chief hunter told the chief that he would gather six hunters for them to take along with them. The chief hunter invited Andrew, Camillia, and the chief into his home to wait for the hunters to arrive. He had already sent for the hunters. Eight minutes later, the hunters started to show up; and nineteen minutes later, all the hunters were there with their hunting gear. The chief hunter told them that the chief, Andrew, and Camillia were wanting to take a ride into the forest to check for damage to the plant life and find a specific plant area. The chief hunter asked the chief what the specific plant was that they were in search of, and Andrew answered the question and told him they did not know the name of it but that it was the only plant that ate bugs, flies, and things of that nature. The hunters said they knew exactly what plant they were looking for and where to find the patch.

The hunters, the chief, Andrew, and Camillia went out on their horses and headed to the great wall's gate. When they got there, the doors were opened and everyone headed for the forest line. Once inside the forest, the chief and the couple started scanning for bare areas that might imply there were a lot of plants taken from that area and not having been replaced. After an hour of riding through the forest, everything looked good; there were some places where it was obvious that some replanting had occurred but which was what the couple had an agreement with the scientists to do. The new plants were growing beautifully. One of the hunters called everyone over to his area, and he was pointing at a beautiful floral-like plant that he said was the eating plant. The group observed the area, and they could see where new eating plants were coming up out of the ground. They were pleased to see that the science hall had kept their word and that the plants were doing well.

Camillia had ridden off away but still stayed within sight of everyone else, and she noticed a strange glow that fluttered about in waves so she went on to investigate it. As she got closer and closer, the light seemed to be tiny individual lights dancing about, but they did not act or look like lightning bugs. Camillia did a huge no-no by getting off her horse, but she just had to take a closer look; there was something mesmerizing about the mini lights. From where she was, the pattern of lights looked like the dinosaur tail she remembered seeing on the earth's surface. She wondered if those lights were the miniangels that were above ground. Camillia got closer slowly so as to not startle the possible miniangels, and when she was just a couple of inches away, she was able to confirm that the lights were the miniangels. Camillia spoke softly and quietly to them, telling them not to fear her as she was a friend.

They understood her and spoke back. They told Camillia that they visited her daily while the community slept and that they were her protectors as well as her husband's and the children's protectors. Their voices were as angelic as their appearance. After their friendship was verbally established, several of the miniangels fluttered up to her belly and encircled her pregnant stomach; then they reached their tiny hands toward her belly and touched her. The babies moved about in joy and contentment. Camillia could tell through telepathy that the unborn children and the miniangels communicated back and forth. The miniangels told Camillia that they would always be with her and her family, and it was not because she and her family were the royal leaders but because her and her family were gifted in ways that no other pale one was and that they had not even discovered their full gifts yet, but the children would develop their additional gifts as they aged and be aware of those gifts.

The miniangel told Camillia that she and Andrew would be enlightened through dreams planted by them. Camillia sensed a great warmth filled with love from the miniangels so she put her hand to her lips and gently kissed her fingers and then put her hand forward as if to blow kisses to the angels, who sent kisses back in the same manner. Camillia told the miniangels that she would never forget their encounter and that if she could, she would visit again; but if not, she asked them if they could awaken her during the night so she could interact with them. One of the miniangels said that she could wake her in the night and that she would because it was too dangerous to visit in the forest, and at that point, only her and her children knew of their existence. The miniangel told Camillia that she would see her that night and that she needed to get back with her traveling party before she was missed or she found danger. The miniangel said that every part of nature was aware of them and was a friend; however, that was not so for pale ones.

As far as her people knew, they were mythological creatures that only existed in another realm that was unreachable for pale ones; and for their safety, they left their existence a secret. Camillia said that she understood and that she would not speak a word of their encounters to anyone, not even her children or husband. The miniangel told Camillia that she could talk to the children of them in stories but to wait for Andrew to come to her with his encounter because they knew he would, but their encounter had to be done when the time was right. Camillia said very well, and just then she could hear her traveling party calling for her so she told the miniangels she would see them another time then she mounted her horse and rode to meet up with everyone she had gone to the forest with.

When everyone saw Camillia, they asked her where she had run off to, and she said she was looking at the forest's beauty. A hunter warned her to stay close, and she agreed not to run off again. They were there to check on the plants that the science hall had taken to make sure that they had kept their word and replanted some more of the plants that they had taken, and that was confirmed so it was time to head back to the compound before any wild animals found them.

Once they got back to the compound, the hunters headed to the chief hunter's home to report back to him that they were done with the royal escort and ready for another assignment. As Andrew, Camillia, and the chief were separating from the hunters, Andrew thanked the hunters for their assistance; and they told Andrew no problem and that if he needed them again, not to hesitate to let them know. It was nearing dinnertime, and the couple had Jaden and his parents to meet with so they asked the chief if he just wanted to have dinner with them, and he said sure so everyone headed for the couple's side of the castle.

When they got to the castle, Jaden was waiting for their return so he could take care of the horses before going inside for dinner. The three of them got off their horses, and Jaden took the horses into the barn and took care of them then met the couple and the chief in the family room to wait for his parents to arrive. Shortly after Andrew, Camillia, Jaden, and the chief got settled in the family room, Jaden's parents showed up shortly after everyone got settled so then they all went to the castle's private dining hall and sat at the big round table. After everyone got settled there, Melanie had the kitchen staff bring out dinner, and then she joined them for dinner. Everyone ate and talked about their day since they had previously met that day and they all had a pleasant time.

CHAPTER FIFTY ONE

When dinner was over, it was time for Jaden's mother to tutor Armellya and for Jaden to go get his tutoring also. Jaden's father went out to work on the buggies in the barn. Right when everyone was separating to go do what they needed to do, Camillia felt a sharp pain in her back so she told Andrew and then said that she was going to lie down until it passed, and Andrew said he would take care of things and for her to just relax. She said okay. When Camillia got to hers and Andrew's bedroom, she changed into her bedclothes and lay down in the bed. When Camillia lay down in the bed, she expected that the sharp back pains would ease up, but they got worse and started to come around to her sides. Andrew had popped into the bedroom to check on Camillia, and she told him how the sharp pains were spreading and getting more intense as well as lasting longer and becoming more frequent.

Andrew asked Camillia if she felt that he needed to summon the doctor, and she said yes so Andrew sent a runner to retrieve the doctor from his home while he stayed in the bedroom with his wife. Melanie went to the couple's bedroom to make sure that Camillia was okay, and Camillia told Melanie that she feared she was in labor that Andrew had sent for the doctor. Melanie asked if she minded everyone being there to witness the birth of the triplets, and Camillia said she did not mind so Melanie went through the castle getting all their friends and telling them to go to the couple's bedroom as it was time for the triplets to be birthed. Everyone dropped what they were doing and went directly to the couple's bedroom.

About the time that everyone got to the couple's bedroom, the doctor showed up at the castle's front door so the butler took him to the couple's bedroom to see Camillia. When the doctor got to the bedroom, he asked Camillia to describe the pain, and she told him it was sharp pains in her back that wrapped around to her sides and that she had a dull pain in her stomach. The doctor took the blankets off Camillia, and she said it was happening again that the pain came in waves about every two minutes. The doctor could see Camillia's stomach tightening. The doctor told Camillia and everyone in the bedroom that he believed that it was about time to welcome the triplets into their world; everyone got excited. The doctor checked to see if Camillia's cervix was dilating, and he found that she was completely dilated.

Just as the doctor finished checking Camillia for dilation, she said another contraction was coming and the doctor noticed that one of the babies was crowning, and he said that it was showtime. Andrew went to the side of the bed and held Camillia's hand and told her to just keep breathing deeply. Two minutes later, the doctor was holding a baby girl. Camillia told everyone to welcome baby Clarissa. Camillia was delivering quickly. Right after Clarissa was delivered, the second baby was crowning so the doctor made sure Clarissa's airway was clean, cut the umbilical cord, wrapped her in a receiving blanket, then handed her to Andrew. Right away after handing Clarissa off to Andrew, the doctor prepared for the second baby. By then, the shoulders were delivered so the doctor helped the torso and legs to deliver; then he cleared that baby's airway, clipped the umbilical cord, and announced that it was a boy. Camillia said for everyone to welcome baby Troy while the doctor was wrapping him in a receiving blanket; then the doctor handed him to Melanie.

When the doctor looked back at Camillia, he was amazed to see another head crowning. It was not the number of deliveries that surprised the doctor; it was how fast she was delivering the babies. Andrew passed Clarissa to Matthew and got ready to receive the third baby. Within seconds, the third baby's shoulders delivered and the doctor told Camillia to give one more good push as it was all downhill from there, and Camillia gave another good push and the third baby was completely delivered. The doctor cleared the baby's airway, cut the umbilical cord, announced that it was another boy, then wrapped him in a receiving blanket and handed him to Andrew. Andrew told everyone to welcome baby Jeffrey. The pain was finally over, and Camillia was exhausted. She asked if the triplets were okay, and Andrew assured her that they were; then she went unconscious.

The doctor called her name loudly, but Camillia was not responding and everyone in the bedroom became concerned for Camillia's well-being. The doctor took his knuckles and rubbed Camillia's breastbone very hard to try to get her to respond, and she still did not come around. Andrew asked the doctor what was wrong with Camillia, why she was not coming around. The doctor said that he was not sure. The doctor checked her pulse and respiration, and they were fine so the doctor felt that Camillia's being unresponsive might be associated with her exhaustion and possibly a delayed reaction to the unbearable pain that she endured for such a long time. The doctor had one more thing to try so he pulled an ammonia inhalant out of his pocket, broke it open, then waved it under Camillia's nose, and finally she moved. Camillia had turned her head to get away from the pungent smell of the ammonia, so the doctor started to call out her name loudly and Camillia opened her eyes slightly. Andrew and everyone else was relieved; they all took a deep breath and let it out. Camillia continued to regain consciousness and finally could speak. Camillia's first concern was the babies; she asked if they were okay, and Andrew assured her that they were fine. The doctor told everyone that all Camillia needed was some rest and that she would be normal after several hours of sleep.

Before Camillia could fall back to sleep, Michelle's mother, Camillia's personal maid and caregiver, told everyone to leave the room except Andrew so she could get Camillia and the bedding cleaned up because she did not want Camillia sleeping until she and the bed were cleaned up so everyone piled out. Together, Andrew and Michelle's mother cleaned up Camillia and the bed and got Camillia back into the bed and let her sleep. Andrew made sure the triplets were with their new nannies and got cleaned up as well. Everyone was talking among themselves about how childbirth was such a miracle and how much demanding work went into it by the mother. This was the first time that they had seen a child birthed, and they were just beside themselves. They thanked Andrew for allowing them to witness the birth of the triplets, and he said it was a family event and that he was happy to share the experience with the family.

The doctor told Andrew that Camillia did very well and that she would most likely sleep until it was time to wake up the next day but that she was just fine. Jaden and his parents did not get much work done, and it was getting late. But they said they were willing to work late to make up for the work time that they had missed by being in the bedroom during the delivery of the triplets, and Andrew told them to take the rest of the night off to use the rest of the night for their family time. Jaden's parents were thankful, and Andrew told them that they would get the work done in due time and that he was not worried about them missing out on the work that night because they were participating in a family event. Jaden's parents were ready to go home and let Andrew go to be with Camillia and the children so they told Andrew that they would see him and Camillia the next day; then Andrew walked them to the castle's front door and bid them a farewell. Everyone in the castle was settling down so the chief told Andrew that it was time for him to leave and then congratulated Andrew on the birth of his triplets. Andrew thanked the chief and walked him to the front door of the castle then saw the chief off.

Now that everyone who needed to leave was gone and everyone that belonged in the castle was settled down in their quarters, Andrew went to his bedroom to be with Camillia. When Andrew got to his bedroom, Camillia woke up at the sound of the bedroom door closing, and Andrew apologized for waking her. Camillia told Andrew that she was feeling much better and that she loved him. Andrew walked up to the side of the bed by Camillia and bent over her and gave her tender kisses on the lips then told her he loved her too and that she produced some beautiful babies. Camillia chuckled and told Andrew that he helped make the babies and that they had some of his features. She said that if the boys grew up to look like him, they were going to be very handsome. Andrew told Camillia that she was beautiful, and he hoped the girls would have her features when they grew older. Then Andrew and Camillia agreed that they had beautiful children, and regardless of who they took after for their looks, it would be their personalities that would make them precious and that they were lucky to be parents. Andrew asked Camillia if she was looking forward to having more children, and she said yes but that she wanted to get back on her feet first; then Andrew said wonderful, as she wished.

After the small sentimental discussion, Andrew changed into bedclothes and climbed into bed and lay next to Camillia to cuddle with her. Andrew told Camillia that he did not want to keep her awake because she worked so hard to deliver the triplets and he knew she was still tired so he lay down behind her and put his arm around her then said good night. As Camillia closed her eyes to go to sleep, she remembered her encounter with the miniangels earlier that day and was more than ready to go to sleep because once everyone was sound asleep, the miniangels could visit and she could speak with them again. Camillia knew that the miniangels would be visiting the triplets, and she was hoping that they would wake Andrew for his first encounter so she could share that secret with him because keeping it from him as she promised until he went to her with their existence made her feel as though she was lying to him about something.

Camillia and Andrew had shared everything including discussions of their lives from before they met so they practically knew everything about each other. Shortly after lying down, Andrew fell asleep, but Camillia was looking forward to seeing the miniangels that she was unable to fall asleep even though she was exhausted. Camillia lay in bed for another two hours and was starting to get restless when it happened. A mini angel showed herself to Camillia. Camillia held her hand out with her palm up so that the miniangel could land on her hand and take a rest from her long flight. The miniangel did land on Camillia's hand and blew her a kiss then said hello. Camillia and the mini angel spoke for quite some time in very quiet tones, and Camillia enjoyed every minute of it.

Finally, the miniangel told Camillia that she had to go visit the children and that she would be back to visit with Andrew. Camillia told her she would see her shortly then lay her head back down and waited. Camillia was trying to stay awake to see the miniangel come back for Andrew, but it did not work. Camillia fell asleep, and before long, she was in a deep sleep. The miniangel finished visiting with the children without anyone but the children knowing she was there so it was time for her to go back to Camillia and Andrew's bedroom to visit with Andrew.

When the miniangel got back to Andrew and Camillia's bedroom, she heard someone get up and walk past the bedroom door so she hid under the bed and stopped glowing until she heard the footsteps go the opposite direction and knew for sure that it was safe to come out and visit with Andrew. The butler had awakened during the night and gone to the kitchen for a glass of milk from the refrigerator. He stayed in the kitchen and drank his milk down quickly then placed his glass in the kitchen sink and went directly back to bed; he fell back to sleep as soon as his head hit his pillow. Once the miniangel knew for sure that it was safe to come out from under the couple's bed, she did and flew to Andrew's side and used a song like that of a sailor's siren to wake Andrew. The miniangel used her special abilities to make sure that Andrew did not call out in fear or surprise, and she used another talent to keep Andrew from moving about. It was as though an invisible tight-fitting shield was around his body so he could not move about, and when he was awakened, he saw the miniangel immediately. Andrew did not feel fear because she was using telepathy to send feelings of compassion.

The miniangel started to talk to Andrew right away and started out by telling him that she was a friend, not a foe, and he welcomed her. At that point, they had established a mutual understanding that she was there for a positive reason so she took away the shield and gave him back his ability to speak. The miniangel explained to Andrew just like she did to Camillia that she was only to be seen by him, Camillia, and their children and that she and the other miniangels were their protectors and that no one else was to know of them. She explained that her duty to them was not due to them being the royal rulers but that it was because they were extremely gifted and that he and

Camillia did not know of the full extent of their gifts. The mini angel told Andrew that she would assist them in revealing their gifts and that their children would know of their gifts as they grew because they too were special. She said that their gifts were beyond what any other pale one had. The miniangel revealed that she had been visiting them and the children every night since they had been in the commune. She told Andrew that she would continue to visit every night. Andrew told her that he felt blessed to have such a beautiful and wondrous creature to protect him and help him develop his talents, and he promised to never speak of their existence to anyone. The mini angel told Andrew that Camillia knew, and it was safe for him to share his experiences with her and for her to share with him as well but that they had to be very careful to make sure that there was no way that anyone could hear them or read them telepathically.

Again, Andrew promised to keep the secret then the miniangel said it was time for her to leave so Andrew told her he was looking forward to seeing her again. The mini angel told Andrew that she would be back the next night to see the children, then she would see him and Camillia, and she would wake both him and Camillia at the same time. Andrew thanked her for her visit; then she told him to get his rest so he snuggled down into the bed. She told Andrew to have a good night and fluttered off. Andrew tried to fall asleep but found himself too excited about the encounter with the miniangel to stay still long enough for fatigue to affect him. Andrew was getting a bit frustrated that he could not fall asleep so he woke Camillia.

When Camillia was fully awake, Andrew whispered to her that the miniangel visited him, and Camillia's eyes got big and she smiled with relief that she could now share the experience with her husband. Camillia asked Andrew how the encounter was, and Andrew told her that he could not believe how beautiful the creature was and Camillia agreed. Camillia said that their voices were so lovely and mesmerizing that the miniangels had to be sent by God himself and Andrew agreed. Andrew and Camillia shared their experience of the night encounter with each other and were surprised to find out that they had abilities that no other pale one had, and they could not fathom what they might be but they could not wait to have the abilities revealed to them. Camillia told Andrew that she was happy that he finally found out for himself because until he found out on his own, she was instructed to keep the miniangels' existence to herself, and she felt like she was lying to him and she did not like how that felt.

Camillia said she was surprised that Andrew did not figure out what had been on her mind through telepathy, and Andrew told her that she hid it well because he did not realize that she was heavy in thought over anything. Camillia told Andrew that she would like to do something for or give something to the miniangels, something special, but that she did not have any clue what she could do or give. Andrew told Camillia that on the next night, they could ask the miniangel what they like as treats and if there was anything special that the couple could do for them besides keeping them a secret. Camillia said that was a clever idea and that she could not wait for the next night because she looked forward to seeing the miniangels. Camillia reminded Andrew about when they were in the forest and she had wandered off, and he said he remembered because all he could think about was that she was taken by a wild animal and how he had lost three children and a wife all at the same time. Camillia apologized to Andrew then told him that she was talking to some miniangels. Camillia told Andrew that she noticed a strange light that she could not help but check out; then she found another dinosaur tail and it was a bundle of miniangels. Camillia said they were so beautiful and welcoming so she interacted with them for a brief time then when everyone was calling for her, she knew she had to get back before anyone came looking for her and came upon the miniangels.

CHAPTER FIFTY TWO

Andrew told her that at first, he had been wondering where she was and what she had been doing, but like he already said after a brief period, he was concerned for her safety. Camillia told Andrew that it just occurred to her that they had far more abilities than any other pale one, and Andrew told her he was aware of that. Camillia made her point by telling Andrew that she wondered how that happened or why they were so special. Andrew thought about that for a few minutes then told Camillia that he had no clue either, but maybe the miniangels knew and that he was going to ask the miniangel when she returned the next night. Camillia told Andrew that she was going to have a tough time getting to sleep since the visit from the miniangel was so stimulating, and Andrew said he was having a tough time sleeping also so they both decided to wake Melanie to have her get some fresh warm milk from their cow. Andrew and Camillia got out of their bed and put on their robes then went to Melanie's bedroom and woke her up and asked if she would get them some fresh warm milk from the cow. She started to get out of bed and said certainly.

Together, they all three went to the kitchen area and Melanie told the couple to have a seat at the big round table while she went out to milk the cow, and she would put their milk in a cup and bring it to them. Andrew and Camillia said okay as they sat at the big round table. It took about fifteen minutes from the time Melanie left the dining area to the time she got back to the big roundtable with the milk, and she got some extra so she could sit with the couple and have some milk also. Melanie asked them if they were having trouble sleeping and added that she was expecting Camillia to be unwakeable until morning since she had just given birth to the triplets. Andrew said that it was just one of those nights and that he accidentally woke Camillia up by tossing and turning.

Jokingly, Melanie told Andrew shame for waking Camillia after she had just given him three babies; then the three of them giggled. Andrew, Camillia, and Melanie sipped on their hot milk and engaged in small talk while everyone else slept, and they were not worried about getting more sleep. Once the three of them finished their warm milk, they said good night to one another and went to their bedrooms to try to get some more sleep. Once Melanie got to her bedroom, she found that she was still tired and that she would not have a problem falling back to sleep; she figured that the warm milk did its job, and after she got back into her bed, she fell asleep without hesitation. Andrew and Camillia got back to their bedroom and sat on their bed then found that the warm milk trick did not work on them that time; they were still stimulated from the miniangel's visit. Andrew and Camillia spent some quality time together, and it had been a short while since they were able to do that because they had been pulling some late night hours with their duties, and by the time they had gotten to their bedroom, they were too tired to do anything but fall asleep so the inability to fall asleep at this time was actually acceptable to both of them. They knew that the next day might be hard to get through, but they figured they would sleep well the next night until the mini angel came to visit. They both agreed that they would need to figure out how they would get back to sleep after their nightly visits because if not, they would definitely have some issues getting through every day.

Camillia suggested that she and Andrew take a nap early in the day if there was nowhere they needed to be, and Andrew told her that it would be difficult because they always had so much going on that he could not see where they could shave off some time for a nap. Camillia said that she was aware of that and she must have been having a wishful thought that sort of popped out of her mouth without thought, and Andrew told her that was okay because if she had not popped out with a wishful thought, he probably would have. They both laughed at the thought being turned verbal then lightheartedly kissed each other. After the kiss, Andrew and Camillia stared into each other's eyes lovingly then at the same time told each other that they loved the other one. The couple lay down on their bed and engaged in some mild foreplay for quite some time, and the next thing they knew, it was morning time. Andrew and Camillia knew it was time to get their day clothes on and get themselves ready for a new day because they could hear the castle staff up and around. All the staff were getting to their posts for another day's work and play.

Andrew and Camillia got out of the bed slowly then changed into day clothes, washed their faces, brushed their teeth, then brushed their hair and headed for the bedroom door to go out and start a new day. The couple headed for the castle's private dining hall to sit at the big roundtable and have breakfast. When Andrew and Camillia got settled at the big round table, Melanie came out of the kitchen, and Camillia asked Melanie to join them for breakfast so she did. The kitchen staff served the three of them, and as they ate, they talked and laughed together. It was a terrific way to start the day off. When Andrew, Camillia, and Melanie finished eating, they told each other to have a wonderful day and that they would see each other at the lunch hour. Then Melanie continued her duties and the couple got ready to go to the chief's side of the castle.

Right when Andrew and Camillia got to the foyer of the castle, the castle's shopper found Camillia and told her that the list of things to purchase for the children and their rooms was done and that she got a little something for the nannies. Each nanny got a small gift of appreciation that was specific to everyone, and Camillia told the castle's shopper thank you as the castle's shopper was giving the leftover money to Andrew. Andrew and Camillia got outside, and Jaden was right there waiting to find out if Andrew wanted the buggy or if he wanted two horses saddled. He said good morning to Andrew and Camillia then asked Andrew how they were traveling that day; then Andrew told Jaden to saddle two horses and that there was no rush so Jaden did not run to the barn but walked.

As Andrew and Camillia were waiting for their horses, they noticed the science hall's runner heading to the chief's side of the castle. Camillia told Andrew that hopefully that was a good thing, and Andrew told Camillia that maybe the science hall was ready for the tissue sample. Camillia told Andrew that they should try to head the chief off when they got their horses and go to the science hall with him and Andrew agreed. Jaden got back with two horses saddled, and the couple mounted and had their horses going before they were completely settled in their saddles; they almost missed the chief. The chief had his horse going as fast as it could so Andrew had to holler for the chief twice for him to hear and stop.

After the chief stopped his horse, the couple rode up to him and asked him if he was on his way to the science hall, and he said yes. Andrew asked the chief if they were ready for their tissue sample, and the chief told Andrew yes and invited him and Camillia to go along so the couple went with the chief to the science hall. When Andrew, Camillia, and the chief got to the science hall, they all jumped off their horses and tied them up then rushed into the building. When the chief and the couple got inside, the new head scientist commented about how fast they all got there; in fact, the runner was walking into the science hall a couple of minutes behind them. The chief asked the new head scientist if he was ready for his tissue sample, and the new head scientist said yes. Andrew asked the new head scientist if he could fill them in on where they were with the research, and the new head scientist said yes, he would after getting the chief's tissue sample so that the other scientists could work on the project while he was speaking with them.

The new head scientist asked the chief to sit in a chair right outside of the office room at the back of the science hall, and the chief replied gladly as he sat. The new head scientist took the tissue sample and gave it to the other scientists; then they started to get to work with it. The new head scientist said that they may need another sample, but if all went well with that sample, then the one sample would be enough. The chief told the new head scientist that he would give and do whatever was needed for the benefit of the life-extension project, and the new head scientist said thank you. The new head scientist took Andrew, Camillia, and the chief into his office room and told everyone to take a seat so the three of them sat in the chairs in the office room then the new head scientist sat in a chair behind his desk. The new head scientist told Andrew, Camillia, and the chief that he would explain their findings as simply as possible since they may not be familiar with the science procedures and vocabulary.

The new head scientist said that the plant cells had been introduced into some of everyone's blood one at a time, and the plant cells combined with all the blood sample cells and started to go through mitosis. The new head scientist said that if everything went as theorized, the plant cell would cause the tissue sample to repair itself, and that was why they needed the chief's tissue sample. Camillia asked the new head scientist to elaborate on the tissue explanation. The new head scientist told them that his tissue sample would be degraded due to his age; the aging process had progressed and was degrading quickly so their theory was that the plant cell would combine with the tissue cell and start the process of meiosis and cause the tissue sample to repair its degradation and possibly grow. The chief said that was extraordinary, and Andrew and Camillia agreed.

The new head scientist told the small group that if that tissue sample was not repaired by the plant cell, they would have to get another tissue sample from a different source out of the chief and try again. The reason was because the first sample was skin and the plant cell may only work on vascular tissue, but the theory was that it could work on any living tissue because all living tissue had to have some sort of blood supply for nourishment to survive. Andrew, Camillia, and the chief understood what the new head scientist had told them. Camillia asked the new head scientist, if he was doing blood samples under the microscope, which did not take much blood, then why did he need a pint of blood from everyone? The new head scientist said that the rest of the blood had been injected with fluids that the plant gave off, which contained the cells necessary for meiosis, and they were considering producing a means for synthetic blood for the hospital to keep on hand for any necessary transfusions. It was a well-known fact that pale ones did not get sick, but they could get hurt on their jobs and those injuries were usually traumatic and required blood to be given to the patient.

Andrew, Camillia, and the chief were stunned by the possibility of synthetic blood and thought that was a great idea if it could be done and was safe for the community. The new head scientist said that the doctor was helping with some of the things that were more clinical in nature than scientific. One of the scientists asked for the new head scientist's assistance so he excused himself from Andrew, Camillia, and the chief to go over to the scientist, and he was asked to consider the microscope slide. He did and stood there watching something in the microscope; it was as though he was watching something intense.

After a few minutes of looking in the microscope, he kept his eye where it was and called out to the chief, Andrew, and Camillia to stay where they were so Camillia asked if it was good news or not. The new head scientist did not answer her right away; he still watched whatever was in the microscope; then after a few minutes, he slowly said that it looked like success. The chief looked at Camillia and Andrew with hope and despair in his eyes. Camillia and Andrew grabbed each other's hand and tightened the grip for a few seconds then held hands loosely.

Finally, the new head scientist stood upright and took his eye off the microscope lens and told the other scientist to document everything thoroughly. The other scientist said okay and quickly started to write. He would check the microscope periodically, and each time he checked the microscope, he would write faster and faster. It also seemed that not only was the scientist writing faster, but he was also writing more each time. The new head scientist went back over to Andrew, Camillia, and the chief and explained that what he saw in the microscope was what they had hoped to see; and so far, the plant fluid mixed with a small amount of the chief's blood was injected into the tissue sample and the tissue sample was regenerating and growing larger. The chief asked the new head scientist if the procedure was ready to try on a living thing, and the new head scientist said yes, so they were going to get one of their older mice and give it an injection of its blood mixed with some plant fluid. The new head scientist said the only catch was to find out if the plant fluid could be added to a blood type and given to anyone of that blood type or if it would only work on an individual with their own blood as part of the injection mixture.

Andrew asked if the new head scientist had any idea on how to find out what the blood source had to be, and the new head scientist said no but that it may be a situation where the injection would be made fresh when needed and done with the individual's blood that was in need just to be safe. The new head scientist said the other problem would be to keep the injection stored properly so that there were no dead cells or cellular components in the injection. The other scientist butted in and said that was why he was documenting everything in detail. The new head scientist said that even though it seemed that they had gotten close to being able to use the injection, there was still a long way to go; they were only a quarter of the way through the project because he did not want to make any mistakes that could take an individual's life. Andrew, Camillia, and the chief all agreed that he was definitely being responsible and that they had profound respect for his work. Andrew asked if there was anything else that they needed to know about, and the new head scientist said no, so the couple and the chief said they would be back the next day. The new head scientist said hopefully he would have some answers for their questions the next day and that if they needed the chief, they would send a runner for him. They all thanked the new head scientist and left the science hall so the scientists could work without interruptions.

Andrew, Camillia, and the chief got on their horses and headed for their side of the castle so they could be on time to meet everyone for the lunch hour after checking on the progress of Jaden's parents' room. When the couple and the chief got to the castle, they got off their horses, and Jaden took Camillia's and Andrew's horses to the barn to take care of, and the chief tied his horse to the pole in front of the castle door. The trio went into the castle, and the chief sat down on the couch in the family room while Andrew and Camillia went back to Jaden's parents' room to see how the construction and decor was going.

When the couple got to the room, they were surprised to see the castle's decorator packing up her work supplies outside the door of the room. Andrew and Camillia asked the castle decorator how the room was going, and she told them that she had just finished with it and was about to send it for them so they could inspect it. Camillia could not believe how fast the construction crew and the castle's decorator got the room done so she and Andrew went into the room and checked it out, and to their disbelief, it was done perfectly.

The bed area was cozy while the work areas were stimulating and the two styles met in the middle of the room and blended smoothly; the clothing was already made also and in the correct closets. Camillia told the castle decorator that once again she had done a spectacular job. Andrew and Camillia could not wait to show Jaden's parents their new room. Camillia and Andrew hoped that they would like their room. The couple went back to the family room to sit with the chief and wait for everyone to get there and start family time. The first guests to show up were Jaden and his parents, and in excitement, Andrew and Camillia asked the chief if he would keep Jaden company and greet the guests as they arrived so they could take Jaden's parents to see their new room, and the chief said that would not be a problem. Andrew and Camillia told Jaden's parents that their room was completed and that they wanted to show off the room. Jaden's parents said that they were anxious to see their new room so Andrew and Camillia took them back to their new room and showed it to them.

When Jaden's parents saw their new room, they were touched and said that it was much more elegant than anything they had ever seen. Andrew and Camillia told Jaden's parents that the room was theirs to use whenever they wanted and that they did not need to ask permission because that would be like asking for permission to utilize their own house. Jaden found his parents and went running to their side; then he checked out their room and told them that he liked his room too. Then he asked his parents if they could spend the night in the castle since their room was done. With that request, Jaden's parents looked at Camillia and Andrew as if they were waiting on them to say yes or no so Camillia told Jaden's parents that it was completely up to them. Jaden said please so his parents told him yes. Andrew and Camillia asked Jaden's parents to look around their entire room and check to see if they had everything that they needed and wanted in the room, and if there was something missing, they should just write it down and give the list to Camillia and on the next day she would correct the error. Jaden's parents told Camillia that she and Andrew were very thorough and felt that there was probably nothing left to need or desire but that they would check.

CHAPTER FIFTY THREE

Camillia and Andrew told Jaden's parents that they were pleased to have them overnight and they hoped that the experience would be a good one, and Jaden's parents told the couple that just sleeping in a castle was wonderful enough. Andrew said that he was sorry to cut the moment short, but it was the lunch hour and they needed to go out to the family room to join the other family members. Jaden, his parents, Andrew, and Camillia went to the family room, and everyone was there so they all went to the castle's private dining hall and got seated around the big roundtable. Once everyone was seated and ready to eat, Melanie summoned the kitchen staff to serve lunch. Everyone ate and shared their day so far and shared what their day still held for them.

When it got to be Jaden's parents' turn, they went on about how thankful they were for their space in the castle and how beautiful the room was. Jaden made sure everyone knew that he was going to spend the night at the castle in his very own room because he was so proud of that. Everyone told Jaden and his parents that if they needed them to just call on them and they would be happy to assist them at any time through the night, and they thanked everyone for their support. Now that the lunch hour was coming to an end, everyone went to the family room to spend some time with the couple's children and their nannies. The entire family got so wrapped up in playing with the children and admiring the triplets that they spent the whole two hours after the lunch hour with the children. One of the nannies announced that family time was over and she had to take the child she was responsible for to take a nap as it was important to keep the children on a schedule as well as possible.

Everyone was shocked that the time went by so fast so they all said quick farewells and darted off in different directions to get back to their duties. Before Melanie could get too far, Camillia and Andrew stopped her and asked her if she could make a child-friendly dinner for Jaden and serve a regular meal to the adults if it would not be too much trouble, and Melanie told the couple that she would enjoy that and it would be no problem. Melanie said she would have the kitchen staff make dinner for the adults and that she would make Jaden's dinner herself. The couple thanked her and let her go about her business. Camillia told Andrew that she needed to go by Jaden's parents' general store for a proposition, and he asked what the proposition was just so he could back her up. Camillia told Andrew that she felt it was likely that the science hall was going to successfully find a conception vaccine for their people, and once they did, she wanted to donate the gently used items from the storage showroom to their store for them to sell and get a little profit they were not counting on so they would have a little more money.

Andrew said that was an excellent idea but it would take some time, and Camillia told Andrew that they could have the construction crew build a storage room for them that was set up like a showroom so everything could be organized and look good. Andrew told Camillia to do as she wished and that it was a great idea for storing things until it could be given to whoever was to be the recipient. Before leaving for Jaden's parents' general store,

Camillia sent a runner for the head construction crew member and another runner for the castle decorator. While Andrew and Camillia were waiting in the family room for the runners to bring back their targets, Andrew told Camillia that he wanted to go by the science hall again because they only got news on the life-extension project and he wanted to find out where they were on the conception project as well. Camillia told Andrew that she was curious as well and that going by the science hall again was a clever idea.

Right then the runners both returned with their targets, and Andrew and Camillia greeted the head construction worker and the castle decorator, and they returned the greeting. Camillia asked them to have a seat because she wanted to talk to them about another project, so they sat down and were ready to listen. Camillia told the head construction worker that she needed a room built to use as storage but wanted it set up as a showroom so that it would be organized and attractive; she did not want a bunch of boxes lying around and having the room disorganized. The head construction worker told the couple that he understood what Camillia wanted and that he had the perfect layout in mind; Camillia said it was wonderful. Andrew asked the head construction worker when he would be able to start the project, and he told Andrew that he was not working on anything now so he could start immediately. Camillia got excited and said great.

Camillia turned to the castle decorator and told her that her expertise was needed to keep the room looking like a showroom and not just a room of boxes. The castle decorator told the couple that she would get with the head construction worker to get an idea of what he had in mind then she could put together a decor that would accentuate the idea of a showroom. Camillia told the castle decorator that she wanted to see the plans before the project was started to be sure it was what the couple had in mind, and the castle decorator said no problem. Andrew excused the workers to start their work, and they went straight back to the back of the castle hall to pick a room to be used while they kept in mind that there were probably going to be more children coming so they did not want the storage room in the middle of the children's rooms. The head construction worker decided to use the room closest to the chief's bedroom because the couple was out of rooms and any children that came along would have to be placed in one of the chief's bedrooms that met up with the other children's rooms.

While the head construction worker was working on a draft of the room to be done, the castle decorator found the chief to have the use of the room approved, and the chief told her that it was fine, the couple could have anything that was his because they were his children and he wanted to make sure that they had what they needed. The castle decorator told the chief thank you then went to find Camillia to have her approve the location of her new room, and when the decorator found Camillia and told her of the plans for the room location, Camillia first asked if the chief knew about the plan. The castle decorator told Camillia that he approved it so Camillia said that was a good plan, and she thanked the castle decorator for being mindful of the family dynamics. The castle decorator excused herself from Camillia's presence and went to the room that was going to be converted to a storage showroom and told the head construction worker that the use of that room was approved. He said very well and continued making his floor plans. While the head construction worker and the castle decorator were getting started on their plans and getting their supplies gathered to start the project, Camillia and Andrew got ready to go to the science hall to check on the progress of the conception project.

Camillia and Andrew got outside of the castle, and as usual, Jaden was right there waiting to serve them. Jaden asked the couple how they were traveling, and Andrew told Jaden to saddle up two horses. Jaden ran to the barn and within a matter of minutes was back with two saddled horses. Andrew and Camillia were very pleased with their godson; he was prompt and hardworking. As the couple mounted their horses, Camillia suggested that when they went to Jaden's parents' general store they buy some of Jaden's favorite goodies and make a treat basket to put in his room for him to find when he came over to spend the night, and Andrew told Camillia that was a clever idea and he was happy that she thought of those types of things because as a guy, he was not so sentimental in thought.

After that small conversation was done, the couple arrived at the science hall so they got off their horses and tied them to the pole in front of the building then went inside to see the new head scientist. When Andrew and Camillia got inside the science hall and looked around for the new head scientist, they quickly spotted him walking around behind all the other scientists and observing their work. The new head scientist finally looked up and noticed the couple at the front of the hall and started to walk over to them. When the new head scientist got to Andrew and Camillia, he gave them a hug and asked them how he could help them. Andrew told the new head scientist that when they were there earlier they were so wrapped up in the life-extension project that they forgot to find out where the scientists were with the conception project. The new head scientist told Andrew and Camillia that it was funny they should return to find out because the doctor was there in the office room; they were working together on the conception project.

The new head scientist told the couple that he was thankful that they told the doctor about the other project because the scientists had mentioned the conception project to the doctor and he was able to add some valuable input that was quite simple and had made the project more of a reality than just a theory. The couple questioned the new head scientist how the project had become more of a reality, and the new head scientist told the couple to follow him to the office room in the back of the hall and he would let the doctor explain what he had come up with. As they walked to the office room, the couple told the new head scientist that they had not told the doctor anything about the conception project, only the life-extension project. The new head scientist was surprised because when he mentioned it to the doctor, the doctor had ideas right away, almost without thought. The couple told the new head scientist that the doctor was brilliant and that they were glad that the science hall was teaming up with the doctor.

They all got to the office room, and the couple sat in the chairs in front of the new head scientist's desk and the new head scientist continued to stand. The couple greeted the doctor, and he greeted the couple right back. The new head scientist told the doctor that he had told the couple that the science hall had teamed up with him for the conception project and that he had some ideas on how to make the project a reality. The doctor told Andrew and Camillia that the plant that caused the blood and tissue sample to multiply for the use of longevity would also work on the conception project. He said that the problem for the pale ones to conceive was that they were producing underdeveloped sex cells and not releasing them and therefore the sex cells were unable to undergo meiosis since there was no chance of the union of spermatozoa and ovum; that was also why the females did not experience menses. The doctor felt that if the individuals were producing a sizable number of mature sex cells, some would be released for union at the proper timelines and the females would restart their menses so the couples would be able to have an educated guess when the women might be ripe. The big issue was how to introduce the plant serum to just the reproductive system and not affect the rest of the systems.

Andrew asked the doctor if he had any ideas of how to introduce the plant serum to the people's reproductive systems, and the doctor told them that if the plant serum were to be given to an individual through their vascular system, it would go throughout their entire body and that alone might introduce the plant serum to their reproductive system while the blood was being sent to all the other systems for oxygenation of the organs because the only way to introduce the plant serum to an individual who needed it for life-extension reasons would be to inject it into a main artery to be carried throughout the body. Andrew and Camillia were stunned with the doctor's explanation of how to reduce conception; they asked the doctor how safe the injection would be for a rather young and healthy individual, and the doctor told them that he was not sure. The doctor feared that if an individual got it for reproductive purposes and did not need much regeneration for their other systems, it might cause their body to produce extra organs and that they would develop much like that of an embryo—start underdeveloped then with time grow into a healthy full-term organ.

The new head scientist told Andrew and Camillia that they were going to test the plant serum on young healthy mice and watch them for any changes that may occur such as extra organ growth and any other mutations that they may not have thought about. Camillia and Andrew understood what the doctor was saying, but they felt that the science hall and the doctor had a bit of a mess to work through. Andrew told the new head scientist to keep them informed of the outcome of each step, and the new head scientist told the couple that depending on what came about, he or the doctor would make sure that they knew about it. Andrew told the new head scientist thank you then said that he and Camillia would leave them to work in peace. Andrew and Camillia left the science hall and got on their horses to head back to their side of the castle.

When the couple got to their front door and gave their horses to Jaden, Jaden asked if they were done with their horses and the couple said no so Jaden tied the horses to the pole. The chief came riding up, and he said he needed to talk to them so they told the chief to tie his horse up and join them in the family room unless it was a private matter, and the chief told them it was not a private matter. Andrew, Camillia, and the chief went to the family room and sat down. Andrew asked the chief what was on his mind, and the chief told Andrew and Camillia that he wanted to discuss the building of the storage showroom. Camillia asked the chief if there was a problem because the castle decorator said that it had been approved. The chief told Camillia that he had approved of it but that they were going to flip one room for the project and he felt that the head construction worker should have his men knock out the wall that separated that room from the room next to it and convert two rooms to be one space so there was enough space for them to store things in a show type of way. Camillia asked the chief if he was sure about what he had said, and the chief told Camillia that they would end up putting a lot of things in the room because the babies grew fast so not only would they have clothing but toys, educational things, possibly bedroom furniture, and various household items. Camillia told the chief that she knew there would be some things but that she had not looked at just how much there could really be.

The chief told Camillia that their staff could contribute to the storing of extra things also, and Camillia told the chief thank you for the idea and that she would make the announcement at family time for everyone to pass their unused things to the storage showroom for the benefit of Jaden's parents. The chief told Camillia that was a sensible idea. Andrew told the chief that he and Camillia needed to go to Jaden's parents' general store to do some shopping and to talk to them about gathering things for them to sell in due time, provided the science hall came through with the conception project, and he invited the chief to go with them. The chief said he would love to go; he loved to shop especially when it was for someone else. The three of them went outside of the castle, got on their horses, and we're off to Jaden's parents' general store.

When Andrew, Camillia, and the chief got to Jaden's parents' general store, they got off their horses, tied them up, then went inside to find Jaden's parents. Jaden's mother saw the trio first and went to them to see how she could help them, and Camillia asked Jaden's mother to find his father so she could talk to both at the same time. Jaden's mother walked to the back of the general store and got her husband then together they went back to see Camillia, Andrew, and the chief. Camillia told Jaden's parents that she wanted to make a treat basket for Jaden for him to find when he went to his room in the castle that night and that she wanted to fill the basket with his most favorite yum-yums. Andrew's parents showed Camillia Jaden's favorite things, and Camillia grabbed a little bit of everything. Jaden's parents saw how much Camillia was getting and that she was getting a bit of everything and they told Camillia that she did not have to put together anything elaborate. Camillia told Jaden's parents that she wanted the best she could come up with because he had earned it; he was a hard worker and always there when he was needed, plus he was doing much more in the barn than what was agreed on.

CHAPTER FIFTY FOUR

At that point, Jaden's parents helped Camillia gather all of Jaden's favorite things and picked out a masculine basket and wrapping. Andrew took some money from his satchel and paid Jaden's father for the things that Camillia had picked up. Andrew asked Jaden's parents if the chief could watch the store for a few minutes so that they could talk about something, and Jaden's parents said sure. Jaden's parents took Andrew and Camillia to the back of the general store to an office room, and they all sat down. Camillia told Jaden's parents that they were gathering some items to put into a storage showroom to eventually give to them to sell so that they could make some extra money that they were not counting on, and although it was going to be some time before they would get the items, she wanted to make sure they would be okay with the arrangement. Jaden's mother told Camillia that she had done so much for them already, and Camillia cut her off and told her that they would always help them in any way that she could. Andrew told Jaden's parents that he and Camillia were very family oriented and they did not just take care of them but they also took care of all their family members and they just did not know about it because they kept things with individuals between them and those individuals. Jaden's parents said that there was not really anything that they could do for them and it felt unfair, and

Andrew told them that if there were ever something that came up, he knew that they would act on it. Jaden's parents said that the arrangement was a wonderful idea and that they would use the extra money on necessities. Camillia told Jaden's parents that she was going to make an announcement at family time that they were collecting for the storage showroom but that they would not reveal why. Jaden's parents said they appreciated their help; then they got up and everyone hugged everyone and kissed one another on the cheek. Jaden's parents, Andrew, and Camillia went back out to the front of the store with the chief. Jaden's parents went back to what they were doing, and Andrew, Camillia, and the chief told Jaden's parents that they would see them at the lunch hour and they left the general store.

Outside the store, Camillia showed the chief the basket supplies and goodies that she and Andrew picked out for Jaden, and the chief told Camillia that it was going to be a beautiful basket for Jaden and that he knew Jaden would get excited over it. Finally, Andrew, Camillia, and the chief got on their horses and started to make their way to the couple's side of the castle. As they rode, Camillia told the chief that it was so close to family time that he might as well go to their side of the castle and hang out there. The chief told Camillia that he would like to watch her put the basket together so he was happy that she invited him to hang out. Andrew told the chief he was welcome any time to their side of the castle, and if he needed any of their staff for any reason, he was welcome to utilize their services as well because he was their father; they wanted to assure that he had everything he needed and wanted. The trio was getting very close to the castle so Camillia asked Andrew to ride ahead and take Jaden into the barn to check on his progress of the work he was doing in the barn so she could sneak the surprise gift supplies into the castle. Andrew told Camillia he would and that he would have Jaden take care of the horses after she and the chief got into the castle. Camillia told Andrew thank you and that she loved him then he rode ahead.

Meanwhile, Andrew was finishing up with Jaden and he told Jaden that he expected Jaden to do the work agreed upon but no more. And because he was doing so much more, he had earned a bonus, and the extent of the bonus would be decided on after the barn was completed. Jaden told Andrew that he did not expect anything extra; he was only doing what he felt needed to be done. Andrew told Jaden that he was a very special young man and that he had a lot of potential to be anything he wanted to be when he got to be an adult, and Jaden said he wanted to be an animal doctor while he helped his parents with the general store. Andrew told Jaden that he and Camillia would do everything possible with his parents to help him be what he wanted to be, Jaden told Andrew thank you.

Now that Jaden was finished showing Andrew his work, they walked out of the barn, and Jaden noticed Camillia and the chief's horses tied up to the pole. Jaden started to apologize to Andrew for not getting the horses right away and that he had not heard them ride up to the castle's front door. Andrew told Jaden not to worry about it and that he could take care of the horses now as it was no big offense. Without any more words, Jaden ran over to the horses and got to work. Andrew went into the castle to find Camillia, and the first place he looked was in the castle's private dining hall. Sure enough, Camillia was at the big roundtable with the chief. Camillia asked Andrew if Jaden had suspected anything, and Andrew told Camillia not a thing, but that he was doing an excellent job on the barn and she needed to go out there and let Jaden show her what he had done so far. Andrew told Camillia that he wanted to give Jaden a bonus when he finished with the barn, and once he was finished with the barn, he would decide what the bonus would be. Camillia told Andrew that after family time she would go out to the barn with

Jaden. Andrew told Camillia that he was so proud of Jaden's work and that it was a fabulous job. Camillia was just finishing up with putting the basket for Jaden together, and she asked Andrew what he thought of it. Andrew told Camillia that it was very elaborate and that Jaden was going to really like it. The chief said that it looked wonderful and that the basket had the appearance of being done by a professional basket maker. There was a shop for professional basket making, but Camillia liked to do them herself because it kept the individualized touch to it.

Now that the basket was done, Camillia took it to Jaden's room and set it on his bed and went back to the castle's private dining hall to meet back up with Andrew and the chief. Camillia checked the time and realized that she had finished the basket right on time for family members to start to show up; it was a close call. Andrew, Camillia, and the chief went to the family room to greet the family members as they arrived; and as soon as the three of them sat on the couch, Jaden and his parents showed up. Jaden always waited for his parents to get to the castle before entering the castle because he wanted to show his parents some respect by waiting for them and showing up as a smaller family unit. Right after Jaden and his parents sat down in the family room, the rest of the family members started to arrive one after the other; and within fifteen minutes, everyone was there so they all went to the castle's private dining hall and got seated around the big roundtable.

Melanie had lunch ready sooner than usual so the kitchen brought lunch out right away and everyone was extremely hungry that day so they ate without conversation. The family was going to sit in a big circle in the family room and share their day with one another, and Camillia figured that she would make sure that she and Andrew were first to share so she could make the announcement about gathering things for the storage showroom.

Everyone finished eating eight minutes before the lunch hour was over so they went ahead and left the big round table before the kitchen staff got out there to clear the table, and Melanie told everyone that it was acceptable to do that because it would make clearing the table easier for the kitchen staff because they would not have to work around people.

Once in the family room, Andrew spoke up and asked everyone if he and Camillia could share first, and everyone agreed to let the couple share first then they would go around the room from there. Camillia said she was going to start her sharing off with a family request; then she told everyone that she was having a storage showroom made to keep gently used things that were no longer needed by the owner, and she was going to donate the items to a charitable cause. Everyone commented in their own way that it was an innovative idea that Camillia had because there was a lot of individuals that could not afford to get some of the things that they needed because getting those items brand-new was expensive to them and that the gently used things that Camillia would donate would be at a reasonably lower price. Everyone said that they had quite a bit of things to give to Camillia for the storage showroom; then Camillia asked everyone to hold on to those items until the storage showroom was completed.

After that announcement, the sharing of everyone's day began, and it took the full two hours for everyone to be able to get a turn because everyone had a lot more going on than usual. Family time came to an end, and everyone said their goodbyes and went their own way to go on with their day. Before Jaden got out of the castle's front door, Camillia caught up with him and asked him to show her the barn so she could see the fantastic job he was doing, and he got excited and told Camillia he would love to and that he found a lot to do in the barn so he was doing some extra things that he felt needed to be done and he wanted the barn to be as beautiful as the castle was. Jaden took Camillia by the hand and led her out to the barn, and when he opened the door to the barn, Camillia was already amazed; she could see a lot of work had been done already. Jaden led Camillia around the barn and pointed out what was finished, what he wanted to do and how, and what he was in the middle of, and how it would be upon completion. Camillia told Jaden he was working so hard, and she was so proud to have him and now she understood why Andrew wanted to give him a bonus. Camillia told Jaden that he was her best worker. Jaden was finished showing off his completed work and his planned work so he led Camillia back to the castle's front door and told her he had to escort her to the door so he could be a gentleman then Camillia bent over and kissed Jaden's forehead and told him thank you. Jaden said he would see her later then ran off to the barn to get more work done, and Camillia went inside the castle to meet back with Andrew and the chief.

All the errands were done for the day so Andrew, Camillia, and the chief had nothing left to do that day except relax. The chief told Andrew and Camillia that he was going to go to his side of the castle so that the couple could spend some much-needed time together alone. Camillia and Andrew said goodbye to the chief, and he left the couple's side of the castle to go to his side. Once the chief was gone, Camillia asked Andrew to go to their bedroom with her because she wanted to talk to him in private, and Andrew said okay then took Camillia by the hand and led the way to their bedroom. When Andrew and Camillia got to their bedroom, they went in, and Andrew closed the door behind them. Camillia sat on the bed, and when Andrew got to the bed and sat down, Camillia told Andrew that it might be an excellent idea to take the free time that they had and take a nap so when the miniangel came to them in the night, they could interact with her without being fatigued. Andrew told Camillia that she had an excellent idea and added that if they should have a troublesome time falling back to sleep, they would not be as tired the next day and Camillia agreed. Andrew and Camillia changed out of their day clothes into their bed clothes then climbed into their bed and snuggled together; the couple fell asleep rather fast.

A few hours after falling asleep, the couple was awakened by a knock on their bedroom door so Andrew got out of bed and answered the door. It was Jaden wanting to thank them for the goody basket that he found on his bed. Camillia called out to Jaden telling him to enjoy his treats, and he told the couple that the basket had all his favorite snacks in it. Camillia told Jaden that he was very welcome. Suddenly, Jaden turned away from the couple's bedroom door and darted back to his room. Andrew stepped back into his and Camillia's bedroom and shut the door then went back to the bed and climbed back in. Andrew and Camillia snuggled back down and proceeded to go back to sleep; the rest of the family that was residing at the castle with the couple were getting ready to go to bed also. Andrew and Camillia knew that the next time that they were awakened it would be by the miniangel so they wanted to fall back to sleep fast to get well rested, and they did fall back to sleep fast.

Time flew and it was already the middle of the night. Andrew and Camillia were sleeping hard when it happened; the mini angel appeared and started to sing her siren song to wake the couple, and it worked. Andrew and Camillia were very pleased to see their miniangel back. Camillia blew kisses to the miniangel, and she blew kisses back. The couple told their miniangel that they had a couple of questions for her over a couple of things that they could not figure out, and she said that she would try to answer their questions and to go ahead and ask. Camillia told the miniangel that she had said that they had more abilities than any other pale one; what were they then, why had they not become aware of them yet, and why was it that they had the extra special abilities that no one else had?

The miniangel said that those questions were rather difficult to answer but that she would try. She said first they were the chosen ones, and no one or thing had control over that. It was something genetic that was rare and unheard of happening. Until the couple came along, the chosen ones were just a fairy tale; but once they came along and showed everyone that they could reproduce, it was obvious that the fairy tale came true because reproduction was the main sign of the chosen ones. The mini angel told Andrew and Camillia that they had all the abilities of a regular pale one but that they as the chosen ones had some extra special abilities such as the power to heal another pale one, an animal, and non animal parts of nature, for instance, plants and trees. The miniangel told the couple that they were unaware of their healing ability because they had not been in the position to need the gift. She told the couple that if there were to be some sort of tragedy in their presence, their ability would have shown itself as a natural reaction and that she could help them to develop the gift without having a tragedy.

The mini angel told Andrew and Camillia thatchers and the others' existence was because of them; they did not exist until both of them were turned and their essence combined released the miniangels from the petals of a flower after they finished maturing and that flower no longer existed because when they flew from within the flowers' petals, the flowers died due to the lack of contact with the many miniangels that provided them with specialized nutrients that they could not get any other way. Andrew and Camillia told the miniangel that it was kind of sad that they lost a species of flower. The miniangel told the couple that they could produce more special flowers from a seedling of any species of flower by using their gift of healing on the seedling, and the new flowers would only release more miniangels when the miniangels were mature but that the couple would have to continuously encourage the making of that flower due to its short lifespan.

The miniangel made sure to point out that the gift of bearing more miniangels should only be used to keep the miniangel population alive because they did not live forever. Andrew asked his miniangel how they would know when to produce more miniangels, and she told the couple that one of the miniangels would alert them to the need when it came time, and she would let them know how many angels were needed. The mini angel told Andrew and Camillia that they had enough to think about for now and that the next time she saw the couple, she would start to help them expand their abilities little by little. She told the couple that the morning hour was coming soon so she had to return to the dinosaur tail with her fellow miniangels. Camillia and Andrew told the miniangel that they were looking forward to their next encounter and that they loved her. The miniangel expressed her love and her devotion to them then she disappeared. Andrew and Camillia tried to see how she could have gotten out of their bedroom door so easily, but they failed to find any cracks for her to fit through.

The couple quit searching for an answer and decided to question her on the next visit.

Andrew and Camillia settled back down in their bed to try to go back to sleep, but they had so much on their minds that they could not go back to sleep. Andrew and Camillia sat up in bed and went over what the miniangel told them to make sure they both heard the same things because those things were so wondrous. The couple wondered what their extraordinary gifts were; they were told of only one and that was a healing power so the couple made the decision to specifically ask the miniangel to give them the whole list of their gifts so they would know what they were. Another question for the miniangel was what type of gifts their children were capable of since the miniangel said that the couple's genetics made them the chosen ones and their children had the couple's genes.

CHAPTER FIFTY FIVE

Andrew and Camillia did not get to discuss their miniangel or the things that they had spoken to her about anymore at that time because they could hear family members walking about the castle and starting to get to work. The couple knew it was time to get out of bed and prepare for the new day so they got out of bed and changed from their bedclothes to clean day clothes then they went to the bathroom to brush their teeth, wash their faces, and brush their hair. Andrew and Camillia were now ready to go out to the castle's private dining hall to join Jaden and his parents for breakfast so the couple left their bedroom and went to sit at the big roundtable in the castle's private dining hall.

When the couple got to the big roundtable, they met with Jaden and his parents. They were waiting on Andrew and Camillia to start eating breakfast. Now that everyone was at the castle's private dining hall and ready for breakfast, Melanie had the kitchen staff bring breakfast out to them, and everyone was very hungry so they ate without conversation. Breakfast ended after what seemed to be a brief time, and Jaden's parents left the castle together to go to their general store for the first half of their day until it would be time for Jaden and his parents to join in on family time. Jaden's mother would go to the back of the castle to tutor

Armellya, and Jaden's father would go out to the castle's barn to work on the buggies.

Andrew and Camillia went down the castle hallway to the rooms that the construction crew and castle decorator were working on, and to the couple's surprise, the construction crew had the wall between the two rooms that were going to be converted into one larger room knocked out already. The missing wall area was repaired, and the construction crew was working with the castle decorator to put in shelves and stands for show items; the area was really starting to come together well, and the couple was very impressed. The construction crew told Andrew that they would be done that day, and the castle decorator told Camillia that she was about to take over the storage show space and work her magic; then she concluded the update by telling Camillia that if everything went smoothly, she would finish her job on the storage showroom late that day. Camillia told the castle decorator that she was pleased with the progress of the project. The castle decorator said that she knew that she would have to work over her time to quit so the project would be finished that evening, but that when it was completed, she would send for the couple to inspect the storage showroom, and Camillia told her not to work over too late because she needed to have her evening time with her family just like everyone else.

The castle decorator told Camillia that she lived in another couple's extra bedroom and paid them rent because she had no husband or children to go home to and she could not afford to have her own home so working overtime was welcomed; then Camillia told her that she should join the royal family and spend some of her spare time with them. The castle decorator asked Camillia if she was sure that she would be welcomed, and Camillia told her that the royal family consisted of her, Andrew, the chief, and their entire staff. The castle decorator was surprised that the couple was so generous, and Camillia knew what she was thinking so she told the castle decorator that the family gatherings were not for generosity, they were wrapped around the family unit because everyone had a long history together from before they were turned into pale ones. Camillia told the castle decorator to think about what a family really was and let her know if she wanted to be a part of theirs; then Camillia walked away from her and rejoined Andrew.

Before Andrew and Camillia could leave the storage showroom area, the castle decorator called out to Camillia and told Camillia that she would be honored to experience what a family really was and that she meant no disrespect to the couple on the family subject, but she had no family since she was just a baby because before the tragedy above ground, she had been in an orphanage and the feeling of abandonment left her somewhat fearful of having a family. Camillia went over to the castle decorator and gave her a hearty hug and told her welcome to the family. Camillia told the castle decorator that they all met in the couple's family room and, once everyone was there, they would go to the castle's private dining hall for lunch, and everyone would share their day, share up-to-date news, ask for help with whatever they needed help with, and give support to the other family members.

The castle decorator said that it sounded like a very supportive experience, and Camillia told her that it did not end there and that after the lunch hour was done, they would all go back to the couple's family room for two hours to engage in fun activities, spend time with the royal children and their nannies, and continue conversation from the lunch hour if needed; then when the two hours was over, everyone would go back to their duties. The castle decorator said that she was thankful for the invitation and that she would give everyone her full love and support because that was what family was supposed to do. Now that both females understood each other, Camillia told the castle decorator that she would see her in the castle's family room as early as five minutes before the lunch hour, and the castle decorator told Camillia that she would be there and that she could not wait. Camillia and Andrew left the storage showroom to work on getting the chief.

When Andrew and Camillia got up the hall and right outside of the family room, they heard the chief engage in small talk with the butler so the couple stood outside of their family room to let the chief finish his conversation with the butler. Within a few minutes, the chief and the butler finished their conversation, and the butler started to walk out of the castle's family room so Andrew and Camillia went on into their family room and said hello to the chief. The chief returned the greeting and asked what the plan was for the day. Andrew and Camillia told the chief that the storage showroom was coming along well and should be done that evening, and the chief told the couple that the workers were working so fast and that he did not expect the project to be completed in such a short time; then Camillia told the chief that the castle decorator was going to have to work a little overtime to have the storage showroom done but that she did not mind because she did not have anyone to go home to. Camillia told the chief and Andrew that she invited the castle decorator to be a part of the royal family.

Andrew told Camillia that it was great that she invited the castle decorator to join the royal family and that he hoped she would feel comfortable with everyone, and Camillia told Andrew that before the tragedy above ground, she was an orphan so she never got the chance to experience what a family was. The chief told Camillia that it was unfortunate for the castle decorator to have had such an empty life but that they were going to change all that. The chief said that the couple should find out what her living conditions were because he doubted that she had a house of her own and he would be willing to give up one of his rooms for the castle decorator to move into rent free if she wanted. Camillia said that was generous and that she would talk to the castle decorator to see if she may be interested; then Andrew told Camillia and the chief that it made sense for the castle decorator to move into the castle because all their workers lived in the castle rent free. Camillia knew that she, Andrew, and the chief had a few things to do that day, but she wanted to talk to the castle decorator right away about moving into the castle so she could think about it and get back with the couple hopefully later that day. Andrew and the chief told Camillia to bring her to the family room and they would wait there for her and the castle decorator. Camillia left right away to go to the storage showroom to see if the castle decorator was still there and she was so Camillia asked her to go to the family room to speak with the couple and the chief, and the castle decorator said okay and followed Camillia down the long hallway.

When Camillia and the castle decorator got to the family room, she greeted the chief and Andrew in a very respectful way, and Andrew told her to just call him by his first name because that was how all his family addressed him. She said thank you then Camillia asked her to have a seat in a reclining chair so she sat down quietly. Camillia was very blunt but gentle in asking the castle decorator about her level of content with her living arrangements, and the castle decorator told Camillia that the couple that she lived with was very nice to her but they did not include her in anything; for instance, when they ate dinner, she had to eat separately. Camillia was heartbroken.

The chief butted in and told the castle decorator that he wanted to have one of his rooms converted to a room for her, and it would be for her to live there rent free just like the rest of the staff, and she asked if they were serious then Andrew told her that they would never joke about something like that. The castle decorator asked the couple and the chief why they were willing to have her live in the castle and rent free at that, then Camillia told her that all of their staff lived there rent free and not only were they the castle staff but they were family and that the couple believed that if anyone in their kingdom needed assistance and they found out about it, they would do their best to help because as king and queen, it was their responsibility to uphold the welfare of the community. The castle decorator told the couple that she would love to live in the castle as part of the family and that she could always feel the love and respect from the family, but she never dreamed that she would ever be a part of a family like theirs.

Then Andrew told her that later that day, they would go to the house that she was living in and let them know that her job had come to the point that she needed to be at the castle round the clock and that they would take the blame for her moving out and then she could thank the home owners and say whatever she felt she needed to say to them then Andrew and the chief would pack her belongings and put them in the buggy and bring her and her belongings back to the castle to get her settled. The castle decorator thanked Andrew, Camillia, and the chief. The castle decorator stood up from the reclining chair and told the couple and the chief that she needed to get back to work and that she would wait for them to call on her for the move; then Camillia stood up and walked over to her then gave her a hug and told her welcome to the family. She got teary-eyed and told Camillia that she would not let them down over anything and she was really feeling loved.

Andrew, Camillia, and the chief told her that they would see her later as they had some places to go but that they would try to take care of moving her before the dinner hour, but if their errands took too long, they would move her right after dinner and for now on she was to have dinner in the castle's private dining hall at the big round table with them and their other staff. The castle decorator said okay then left the couple's family room to go back to work on the storage showroom. The couple and the chief needed to visit the science hall sometime that day, but they knew that they would be there for quite a bit of time so they agreed to do that visit after the other things that they needed to do. Everyone was getting ready to leave the couple's family room when suddenly, Andrew firmly said wait then asked for everyone to sit back down because an idea came to him. The chief and Camillia sat back down in their seats. Andrew reminded Camillia and the chief that he mentioned giving Jaden a bonus for all the excellent extra work he was doing on the barn both inside and outside, and they both told Andrew that they remembered then asked if he had something in mind. Andrew told them that he had just thought of something and he wanted their opinion about the idea, and if it did not pass approval, he wanted them to make some suggestions. Andrew told them that not only did Jaden have a bonus coming to him but that he had his eleventh birthday coming too and that most of the kids in the community had their own horse except Jaden. Andrew wanted to talk to Jaden's parents about their finances to find out if they could support another horse and if not create some regular work for either Jaden or his parents to do to earn the money to care for another horse because when they need to go somewhere, they either had to hitch the buggy or Jaden had to ride double with his father.

Andrew told Camillia and the chief that Jaden was great with horses and knew everything there was to know about taking care of them, and he had a long-term goal of being an animal doctor so what could be better to get him than his very own horse. Camillia and the chief agreed with Andrew's idea, and everything Andrew said made sense so the couple and the chief decided to go out to the barn and bring Jaden's father into the castle's family room to talk to him about getting Jaden a horse. Andrew told Camillia and the chief to wait where they were and he would go get Jaden's father and bring him to the family room. Andrew jumped up out of his seat and briskly walked to the castle's front door.

When Andrew got to the barn, he noticed Jaden working hard then he went to Jaden's father and told him that he, Camillia, and the chief needed to discuss something with him so the two of them left the barn and went to the castle. Once Andrew and Jaden's father were in the castle, they headed for the family room and Andrew told Jaden's father when they got into the family room to take a seat. When they got there, Jaden's father did as asked then Andrew asked him if he remembered that Jaden had earned a bonus and Jaden's father told Andrew that he remembered, so Andrew told him that he also knew that Jaden had a birthday coming up and his father said that was true. Andrew told Jaden's father that they would like to get Jaden a horse of his own for the bonus and give it to him on his birthday but that they were not sure if their family could support another horse, and Jaden's father said that they could support another horse and the reason he did not have a horse already was because they had not been able to save the large amount of money that it cost to purchase the horse but that was one of the things they had planned to get with the money earned from the general store's donated funds.

Camillia asked Jaden's father if he would be offended if they bought the horse for him, and Jaden's father told the couple that if someone that they did not know well offered, they would refuse the offer but since it was close family and Jaden had definitely earned it, he would be much obliged. Andrew told Jaden's father it was a deal and they would get the horse that day and keep it in the couple's barn and not tell Jaden until it was time because his birthday was the next day. Jaden's father told Andrew that he would let his wife know without Jaden hearing him. Everyone stood up, and Jaden's father went back to the barn to do some more work on the couple's buggies while the chief, Andrew, and Camillia prepared to go to the science hall.

Andrew, Camillia, and the chief went out of the castle's front door and summoned Jaden for three horses to be saddled so they could get to the science hall, and Jaden brought the trio their horses. They all mounted their horses then off they went. When the couple and the chief got to the science hall, they got off their horses, tied them up, and went inside the science hall. The new head scientist heard the front door close behind the three visitors so he walked to the front of the science hall to greet his company. Andrew asked the new head scientist if they were working on both projects or just the life-extension project, and he told Andrew that they were working on both projects because one supported the other due to the plants' nondiscriminatory nectar. The chief asked the new head scientist if he had any good news for them that day, and he said he had some news but it was neither good nor bad because there were some results that they were monitoring for. So far, all was okay, but the observation period was not through yet.

The chief asked the new head scientist to elaborate on the situation so he told the chief and the couple that they did make an injection for the life-extension project and they had given it to several of the old mice that had severe cell degeneration due to their age, and the scientists were keeping a close eye on those mice for any changes positive or negative. The mice would also be getting daily examinations, and the scientists would be documenting every action and reaction that the mice exhibited with great detail. The chief asked the new head scientist if he knew how long the observation period would be, and if the mice survived with positive results, what would the next step be? The new head scientist told the chief that the observation period would go on until there were no more changes whatsoever over a reasonable period of time occurring in the mice so he could not give any estimate of how long that period would be then the new head scientist told the chief that if all the mice had all positive results with no side effects and they remained alive, then they would start to consider giving the injection to the chief.

The chief asked what the new head scientist meant by starting to consider giving the injection to him, and the new head scientist said that they would like to be sure that the injection would work on a pale one just like it did on a mouse. Because of the species' differences, they may not be able to find out without giving it to him, but they did not want to risk his life. The new head scientist told the chief that if the mice had a good response without side effects, they would send the chief to see the doctor to get documentation in detail of his health status to try to establish the full extent of his cellular degeneration. The new head scientist also told the chief that they would have the doctor do a biopsy, which meant that he would take a couple of small organ samples from the chief so that they could expose them to the plants' nectar to be sure that they regenerated like the chief's skin sample did.

CHAPTER FIFTY SIX

With the additional information the chief had received, he started to get nervous about having the biopsy done, and Andrew picked up on the chief's apprehension so he told the chief that the doctor would be gentle with him and there would not be any severe pain in the gathering of the tissue samples and that he may just feel some pressure where the doctor was working. The chief asked Andrew if he was sure that there would not be any real pain, and Andrew told him that on the way back to the castle, they could stop by the hospital and discuss the procedure with the doctor. The chief got a hold of himself and said okay. Andrew asked the new head scientist if there was anything more to be said about the life-extension project, and the new head scientist told Andrew that they were at the point where they could only wait and watch, but in due time, there would be a lot to be said and eventually they would hopefully be able to move forward with the project. Andrew said very well. The new head scientist told Andrew, Camillia, and the chief that they were stuck in the conception project because they knew that the plant nectar they were using for the life-extension project was almost sure to be the answer to boosting the ability to reproduce, but they were not getting anywhere on how to introduce the injection to just the reproductive system without introducing it to the rest of the body systems.

Another issue was if the injection could be introduced to just the reproductive system, there was no guarantee that it would create a gamete, which was the name of a mature sex cell. The injection may reproduce more immature sex cells, which would be ineffective because that would leave the pale ones with the same problem of being unable to reproduce. Camillia told the new head scientist that the project was not looking very hopeful, and the new head scientist agreed then he told the couple and the chief that there was not really anything to say about the conception project at that point so Andrew, Camillia, and the chief told the new head scientist that they would be back the next day to see how the life-extension project was going. Everyone said goodbye then the trio left the science hall and got on their horses to head out to get Jaden's horse. Andrew, Camillia, and the chief rode to the edge of the community where the horse corral was, and as soon as they got there, they were greeted kindly then Andrew told the ranch owner that they were there to buy a good horse that was no older than two years old. The ranch owner told Andrew that he had several two-year-olds for them to look at, and he took the couple and the chief to see them and immediately one of them caught Camillia's eye.

It was a beautiful buckskin, and Camillia walked very swiftly over to it then told Andrew to check that horse out so Andrew walked over to that horse and looked it over, and while he was checking the horse out, he could tell that Camillia had fallen in love with that horse so Andrew asked Camillia if she wanted the buckskin. She told Andrew that they were there to get Jaden a horse, not her. Andrew told Camillia that they would get Jaden one of the other two-year-olds, and Camillia got thrilled then the chief told the couple to go ahead and look for a horse for Jaden and he would go get the ranch owner to let him know that they wanted the buckskin then the chief walked off. There were two other horses to look at so Andrew looked at both and decided on which one to get for Jaden so by the time the ranch owner and the chief got to where Andrew and Camillia were, they were ready to tell the ranch owner which two horses they wanted.

By the time the chief and the ranch hand got to the corral, Camillia had been able to coax the buckskin over to her and was petting the horse. When the ranch hand saw that, he made a comment that the horse really liked her and he knew that because that horse was not fully broken and never went to any pale one. Camillia told the ranch hand that she wanted that horse so he told her as she wished and reminded her that the horse was not fully broken and Camillia told the ranch hand that she could ride that horse with no problem. The ranch hand gave Camillia the bridle and told her to put it on the horse because it would not let anyone else near so Camillia took the bridle and placed it on the horse; then Camillia told the chief to please take her saddle off the horse she rode there because she was going to ride the buckskin home.

As the chief was taking Camillia's saddle over to her, Andrew was telling the ranch owner which other horse he wanted, and the ranch owner went into the corral and got the horse for Andrew to give to Jaden. By the time the ranch owner got the horse that Andrew was asking for, Camillia had already saddled up the buckskin and was mounted. The ranch owner was surprised to see Camillia sitting on her horse's back. The couple and the chief were done at the horse ranch so Andrew took some money out of his satchel and paid the ranch owner; then the three of them left to go back to the castle. Once the couple and the chief was mounted, Andrew told the chief that they would have to go to the hospital after the lunch hour and family time because going straight to the castle from the corral would have them in the family room to meet for the lunch hour a little late so the chief told Andrew that they could just summon the doctor from the castle after their day was done and before he went back to his side of the castle, and Andrew said okay.

When Andrew, Camillia, and the chief rode up to the castle, Jaden was outside waiting for them to show up so he could take their horses to the barn and care for them before lunch. When Jaden saw the two new horses, he got excited because he loved horses and liked to care for them. When the couple and the chief stopped their horses at the castle's porch, they got off their horses and Jaden took all five horses into the barn to do what he had to do with them while Andrew, Camillia, and the chief went into the castle's family room and told everyone that Jaden would be in soon then they could all go to the castle's private dining hall. While everyone was waiting for Jaden, Camillia got everyone to be quiet so she could announce that Jaden's birthday was the next day and that they wanted to have a birthday party for him. Everyone thought that was a promising idea; they were all in agreement that every little boy should have their birthday celebrated so Camillia told Melanie to have her mother make a wonderful cake, and she said okay.

Eighteen minutes into the lunch hour, Jaden made it into the couple's family room and it was right after everyone finished talking about his birthday plans when Jaden came into the family room. He was bragging about how beautiful the new horses were and telling everyone how proud he was to be their caretaker. As family, all went to the castle's private dining hall. Camillia hugged Jaden and told him that she knew her horses were in good hands with him then patted him on the back and told him to catch up with his parents. Finally, everyone got seated in their places at the big round table; and as the kitchen brought out everyone's meals, Camillia said that she had an announcement so everyone gave her their undivided attention. She introduced the castle decorator and told them that she was a new family member for everyone to welcome her and that she was going to be moving into the castle that day.

Upon finishing her announcement, everyone clapped and whistled for the castle decorator. They all said that after the lunch hour, they wanted to spend what time was left getting to know the castle decorator. The castle decorator was touched and said thank you to everyone; then everyone started to eat and go around the table sharing their day. When the lunch hour was over, the kitchen got busy gathering the dirty dishes and clearing off the big roundtable in a hurry to try to catch up on their day's chores and get dinner prepared on time while the group of family members transferred to the couple's family room and got seated. Everyone decided that they would go around the room and tell something about themselves then ask the castle decorator a question about her so they could get to know her intimately, and she agreed that it was the easiest way for them and her versus her telling her story from a child to present; she felt that would be rather boring.

Once most of the family time was over, everyone felt as though they grew up with the castle decorator. Since there was still quite a bit of time left, Andrew suggested that they reverse the role and have the castle decorator go around the room consecutively and ask everyone a question or two about them so she could get to know everyone a little bit better. Everyone was happy to participate so that was what they did for the rest of family time. While everyone said their farewells and was going their own direction, the castle decorator pulled the couple aside and told them that she would be honored if she could meet the children. Andrew told her that they still had to go by the animal doctor's home, shop for a birthday gift for Jaden, and try to move her into the castle before dinner. The castle decorator asked if she could go with them to get a birthday gift for Jaden also, and the chief butted in and said certainly so they all four went out of the castle's front door to summon Jaden. When Andrew, Camillia, the chief, and the castle decorator got onto the front porch of the castle, Andrew hollered for Jaden, and he ran from the barn to Andrew's side. Andrew told him that they all needed their horses saddled up, and Camillia was sure to let Jaden know that the new buckskin was her new primary ride; then Jaden told Andrew and Camillia that there was no horse for the castle decorator. Andrew asked the castle decorator if she had a horse, and she told him no that she would walk everywhere she had to go and just leave extra early so Camillia told Jaden to saddle up her old horse for her. While he was saddling up the horses, Camillia told the castle decorator that she now had a horse of her own; Camillia was giving her old horse to her to have as her own possession. The couple no longer owned the horse, and the castle decorator told the couple that she felt that she needed to earn the horse. Andrew told her it was to be a welcoming gift and that all of their staff had their own horse, and the care of the horses was taken care of by him and Camillia as part of their pay and as a new member of the family, they had a right to give her personal gifts.

Now Jaden was back with all the horses, and the castle decorator told Andrew and Camillia thank you as they all mounted their horses and started off for Jaden's parents' general store to get his birthday gift for the next day. On the way to Jaden's parents' general store, the castle decorator asked Camillia if she would mind that after they got the birthday gift, she rode back to the castle to work on the storage showroom, and Camillia told her that would be fine because their next errand would just bore her. They arrived at Jaden's parents' general store, got off their horses, tied them up, and went inside where Jaden's parents greeted them by first name and gave them all a hug and asked if there was anything they could help them with.

Before answering Jaden's mother, Camillia noticed other shoppers from the community looking strangely at them. They were in shock that Jaden's parents were so brazen to address the king and queen so loosely so Camillia told them that Jaden's parents, the general store owners, were personal family members and then the shoppers relaxed. Camillia answered Jaden's mother and told her that the three of them were there to purchase a birthday gift for Jaden, and she told the couple that they had already gotten him a wonderful gift. Andrew told her that he had another great surprise for them and Jaden but that they would have to wait until Jaden got it to find out what it was. Camillia reminded Jaden's parents that the horse was his bonus for his hard work and he was just getting it on his birthday because that day came at a good time to present the horse.

CHAPTER FIFTY SEVEN

Jaden's parents changed the subject and asked the four of them if they were ready to look around for a gift, and they said yes then Andrew asked Jaden's parents if they had a saddle for Jaden and they said no so Andrew told his parents that he and Camillia were going to get him a saddle for his birthday and help them save a bit of money that they may not have to spare. Jaden's parents told Andrew that at that time, they could not afford the saddle so they really appreciated the saddle as a gift; then the castle decorator said she would get the saddle blanket and a grooming kit for Jaden so he would have his own accessories and be able to feel independent, and Jaden's mother hugged the castle decorator, thanking her then telling the castle decorator that the gift she was going to get Jaden would mean a lot to him and that although Jaden could use their grooming things for his horse, he would be thrilled to have his own and one day if he decided to have his own home he would have it. Camillia told Jaden's parents that they could not see Jaden moving out because he was so family oriented that he would help to expand their homestead and take care of them in their upper years. Jaden's mother told Camillia that she was right, he was a good and devoted young man.

The general store was starting to get busy so Jaden's father took his royal family to the back of the general store to look at saddles and saddle blankets as well as grooming kits while Jaden's mother stayed up front to make herself available for other shoppers. The castle decorator saw a couple of saddle blankets that she felt Jaden might like so she asked Camillia to help her pick the right one because she knew that Camillia would know exactly what Jaden's taste was as a young man. Camillia could not pick between two saddle blankets so she asked Andrew to help reduce the two options into one purchase, and he could not choose either so the castle decorator said she would take both of the saddle blankets for Jaden and let him pick his favorite one.

Andrew found a saddle that was Jaden's size, and he asked Jaden's father if Jaden would like that one. When his father saw it, he told Andrew that they had some cheaper ones and there would be some in Jaden's size. Andrew told Jaden's father that he was interested in that particular saddle because it was beautifully decorated and he knew that Jaden would like it and he wanted to do for Jaden just like he would do for the adult family members and get him the very best and that money was no option. Jaden's father told Andrew that Jaden would love that saddle, and he knew that because when Jaden came into the store, he always checked to see if it was still there. Jaden's father went on to tell Andrew that when Jaden would come into the store, he would sit on that saddle and pretend that it was on the back of a horse and he was riding so Andrew told him to ring it up with the grooming kit after the castle decorator picked one out.

Jaden's father took that saddle off the post and took it to where the cash register was and set it on the floor along with the two saddle blankets. He took the castle decorator over to where the grooming kits were and showed her the different colors and styles that they had, and she picked one out right away then said that was the perfect one, the handles were easy grip, and the kit had some extra things in it that the other grooming kits did not have; it was the deluxe kit and more expensive than the basic kits, but the castle decorator felt it was worth it because of the extras and the wood color was a deep brown, which was more masculine than the cherry red color of some of the other ones. Jaden's father took the deluxe kit off the shelf and then he, Andrew, Camillia, and the castle decorator went to the front of the store to ring up the purchases and pay for everything. Jaden's father rang up the castle decorator first and she paid for her saddle blankets and grooming kit; then he rang up the saddle for Andrew to pay for, and Andrew gave Jaden's father a generous tip for helping them through the store and helping them target Jaden's liking and desires. Jaden's father was very thankful and told the couple and the castle decorator that Jaden was going to love his birthday gifts and that this birthday was going to be the best one he had ever experienced.

Then out of excitement, Camillia revealed the other present they were getting for Jaden. Camillia told Jaden's father that they were going back to the castle to sneak Jaden's gifts into their bedrooms then she and Andrew were going to visit the community's veterinarian to pay for him to start tutoring Jaden to be as he called it an animal doctor, and Jaden's father started to weep in joy. He called his wife over to where they were so they could tell her about the special birthday gift. When Jaden's mother got over to join her husband, she noticed the tears in his eyes and asked if everything was okay then her husband told her that the couple was going to pay for Jaden's specialized tutoring to be an animal doctor and that the community's veterinarian was going to be at the birthday party to tell Jaden of the tutoring gift. Jaden's mother started to cry in joy, and she told the couple that being an animal doctor had been Jaden's dream ever since he could talk. Camillia told Jaden's parents that he had a gift with animals and that he already knew a lot of things beyond that of a normal ten-year-old boy; then she told Jaden's parents about her new buckskin being jumpy and not fully broke and how no one was able to get too close to it but that Jaden handled it like they had been best friends since it had been born. Jaden's parents were not surprised; they told the couple that he had the gift of dealing with animals ever since he could walk on his own. The chief told Jaden's parents that he was going to come back to their general store to get a gift for Jaden but that he needed to occupy Jaden so the couple and castle decorator could sneak in their gifts. The couple told the chief that they would look forward to seeing him later then the couple, the chief, and the castle decorator left the store.

Andrew, Camillia, the chief, and the castle decorator headed for the couple's side of the castle, and the chief rode ahead to have Jaden's attention when Andrew, Camillia, and the castle decorator got there so they could slip into the castle unseen by Jaden. The chief got to the castle, got off his horse, tied it up, then went to the barn where Jaden was and proceeded to have him show the chief around while the chief asked of his plans for the barn's overhaul and Jaden got so engrossed with telling the chief his plans for the king and queen's barn that he did not hear the couple and the castle decorator ride up so they got into the castle without Jaden knowing. The castle decorator asked Camillia where she could put the gifts so while Andrew went on to the couple's bedroom to put away the saddle, Camillia took the castle decorator to a room and told her that was going to be her new room and to put the gifts in there and she could start to work on redoing the room at her leisure and if there was anything she needed to just let the couple know, the castle decorator thanked Camillia then Camillia went to her bedroom to meet up with Andrew. The castle decorator went to check on the storage showroom to see if the construction was done, and it was so now the rest of the work was up to her so she got started with the decor right away to have the job done by the dinner hour.

Andrew and Camillia went out of the castle to rejoin the chief and go to see the community's veterinarian. When they got outside, the chief and Jaden were with the horses and Jaden was petting the new buckskin, which was loving the attention Jaden was giving her. The couple said hello to Jaden then they and the chief untied their horses and told Jaden as they mounted their horses that they would be back after a while. The chief told Andrew and Camillia that he was going to go shopping while they ran their errand, and the couple said okay and that they would see him after their errand because they still needed to see the doctor for a discussion on what a biopsy was and how it was done; the chief said okay then rode off. Andrew and Camillia waited for Jaden to move out of the way of the buckskin; then the couple headed the opposite direction from the chief.

It did not take long for the couple to get to the veterinarian's home and thankfully his horse was there tied up in front of his home so they knew he was home. Andrew and Camillia got off their horses, tied them up, walked to the front door, and knocked, then the veterinarian answered his door and greeted the king and queen appropriately and asked what he could do for them. The couple asked to enter his home and discuss a job opportunity so the veterinarian let the couple in and led them to his family room and offered them a seat to make themselves comfortable. Before Andrew or Camillia could start to speak, the veterinarian asked the couple if they would like to have something to drink or a snack, and they told him no thank you. Then Andrew told the veterinarian that they had a job opportunity for him that would occur in the evenings if he was interested. The veterinarian told the couple that if they needed him, he would make the time for them and Andrew told him that they had a ten-year-old boy as part of their family that had dreamed of being an animal doctor ever since he could walk and talk and that the boy had a notable talent with animals. Andrew continued and told the veterinarian that it was to be the boy's birthday the next day and they wanted to pay the veterinarian for tutoring services to teach the boy how to be an animal doctor so he could have a profession when he got to be a full-grown man and support himself and his parents.

The veterinarian told Andrew that it was a wonderful birthday gift and he was interested because he was the only animal doctor in the community and demand was high for visits and sometimes he had more calls than he could handle and because of that he had no home life. Andrew asked him how much the tutoring would be, and he said that he never thought about that but that he would teach the boy for free if it would give him the ability to have a home life and assurance that someone can take over when he was ready to retire. Camillia told the veterinarian that he was generous but that his time and knowledge was valuable and should not go unpaid that what he would be doing was a service, so Andrew cut into the brief conversation and made an offer of payment. The veterinarian told Andrew that his offer was too kind, then Camillia told him that they had an agreement then and the veterinarian asked when they wanted him to start. Camillia told the veterinarian that the next day during the lunch hour they were going to have an eleventh birthday party for the boy and they would like for him to be there to tell the boy himself who he was and that he was going to teach him and eventually certify him to be an animal doctor. The veterinarian told the couple that some of the instructions would require the boy to go out on calls with him, and Andrew told the veterinarian that they would make him available.

Andrew took a generous sum of money out of his satchel and gave it to the veterinarian, telling the veterinarian that he and Camillia had more errands so they needed to go about their business but that they would see him at their side of the castle on the next day's lunch hour. The veterinarian shook hands with the couple and told them he would be there if not a few minutes early he would at least be on time. Andrew and Camillia left the veterinarian's home to go back to the castle to try to catch the chief so they could talk to the medical doctor about the biopsy procedure and ease his mind.

As they were riding, Camillia told Andrew that since they were passing Jaden's parents' general store, they might check inside to see if the chief was there and if not they could ask if he had already been there and that way they could get an idea of where he was if they did not actually run into him. Andrew told Camillia that was the smart thing to do, and when they got to Jaden's parents' general store, they saw the chief's horse tied up outside. Andrew and Camillia waited several minutes for the chief to walk outside, but he did not so the couple got off their horses, tied them up, and went into Jaden's parents' general store to find the chief.

When the couple got inside, they spotted the chief right away and they walked over to him and asked him how the shopping was going. The chief told the couple that he was unsure of what to get Jaden because the main things he wanted were gotten already; then he asked Andrew and Camillia for ideas, and Camillia told the chief to check with his parents to see if there was anything else that he had been wanting or admiring. While Andrew and Camillia looked around, the chief walked over to where Jaden's mother was and told her that he wanted to speak to her and her husband together so Jaden's mother waved her hands at her husband. When he saw her, he walked over to her and the chief then asked what he could do for him. The chief said he was there to get Jaden a birthday gift but he did not know what to get him and asked if they could help him. Jaden's parents said sure, and they took the chief around the store and showed him Jaden's favorite treats, hobby items, and some items to redecorate his bedroom.

When Jaden's mother mentioned that Jaden wanted to redecorate his bedroom, the chief asked why he wanted to do that, and Jaden's mother said that it was because his bedroom decor was from when he was a toddler and looked cute but that he wanted it to look more grown up and educated so the chief told Jaden's parents that he was going to send the castle decorator over to them and with their help have her redecorate his bedroom at home so he needed them to spend the night at the castle and not tell him why just to make it a fun thing, and the chief would pay the redecorating cost. Jaden's parents said okay then the chief, Andrew, and Camillia left Jaden's parents' general store to go by the hospital to talk to the doctor.

When Andrew, Camillia, and the chief got to the hospital, they left their horses with the hospital stable boy and told him that they would not be very long, then they went into the hospital and walked up to the nurse's desk. The charge nurse asked Camillia if she needed the doctor, and Camillia told her that the chief needed the doctor for some information about a possible procedure so the charge nurse sent one of the other nurses that was standing at the nurse's desk to go get the doctor out of the break room. No more than five minutes later, the nurse was coming up the hall with the doctor next to her; and when he got close, he greeted Camillia and asked her how she was doing. She said she was doing great. After that, the doctor asked Andrew how he was doing, and he replied that he was doing fine. The doctor told the chief that he must be the one who needed to see him. The chief told the doctor that he was correct but it was not because he was ill; it was because he wanted to get some information about a procedure so the doctor told the three of them to follow him to his office room, and they followed the doctor.

When the doctor got to his office room, he opened the door and let Andrew, Camillia, and the chief go in. The doctor told them to take a seat and get comfortable then he walked into the office and shut the door behind him then sat in his chair behind his desk and asked what the chief needed to know. The chief told the doctor that the science hall was mentioning that they may need some organ tissue samples and that would require a biopsy. The chief asked what a biopsy was. The doctor told the chief that a biopsy was a procedure in which he would numb an area with a local anesthetic then put a long hollow needle into the center of the numb area and that the needle was not very big, just long, and that it was hollow so the doctor could take out a very small sample of the organ that they had the needle in. The doctor said it was an uncomfortable feeling, and some said it was just a feeling of pressure but that it was not actually painful and that he did not have to stay at the hospital afterward.

The doctor told Andrew, Camillia, and the chief that he was aware of the possibility that the science hall may ask for the samples if the injected mice showed positive results with the injection of the plant serum but that it would not be something they did right away because the monitoring of the mice may take a great deal of time, and if all was well, the scientists wanted to be sure that the plants' serum would be safe for a pale one and the only way to help determine that was to test the serum on organ tissues. Andrew, Camillia, and the chief told the doctor that was correct; then the chief told the doctor that he had been nervous about the biopsy procedure because the thought of giving a part of an organ sounded so painful. The doctor told the chief that he had done biopsies on a regular basis on the planet's surface right after the great disaster because everyone that had survived and did not come down with disease wanted to be sure that they had not had severe radiation exposure and that was how the healthy humans found out that their domes did protect them. The chief was satisfied with the doctor's explanation and felt like he could handle the procedure with ease so he told the couple he was ready to let the doctor get back to whatever he was doing before they got there so Andrew, Camillia, and the chief thanked the doctor for his time and told him it was nice to see him on a non emergency basis. The doctor agreed then asked Camillia if she was ready to get pregnant again.

Camillia told the doctor she was but they were not going to push their lovemaking to ensure that they conceived; they would make love when the mood hit and conceive whenever things happened to be timed just right. The doctor told Camillia and Andrew good luck conceiving and he looked forward to having her as a patient soon because it was a blessing to bring babies into the world and they made beautiful children. The couple thanked the doctor for the compliment and told him that when she felt that she was pregnant again, she would waste no time getting in to see him. The conversations were over so Andrew, Camillia, and the chief said goodbye to the doctor and the doctor said goodbye to all of them then everyone came out of the office room. The doctor went back to the break room to finish his snack, and the couple and the chief went out of the hospital to retrieve their horses and make their way back to the castle.

CHAPTER FIFTY EIGHT

On the way back to the castle, the chief told Andrew and Camillia that his gift to Jaden was to redecorate his bedroom at home because it had been the same since he was a toddler and Jaden had been wanting an educational big-boy bedroom so the chief asked Andrew and Camillia if he could get the castle decorator to redecorate Jaden's bedroom and have it done by the time they were ready to meet for the lunch hour. The couple told the chief that it would be no problem and they would get the castle decorator to get over to Jaden's parents' home right away. The chief thanked the couple, and with that, they were back at the couple's side of the castle. As everyone was getting off their horses, Camillia asked the chief to join them for dinner and the chief thanked them and accepted so they gave their horses to Jaden and went into the castle.

While the chief and Andrew sat in the family room to relax, Camillia went to the storage showroom to see if the castle decorator was there and she was. When she saw Camillia, she got excited and told Camillia that she had just finished with the storage showroom so Camillia went into the room and was amazed at how much room she had for storage and with all the showcase abilities that the room held. Camillia told the castle decorator that she did a wonderful job and that she finished just on time because she had an urgent project for her that needed to be finished by the lunch hour on the next day. The castle decorator asked Camillia what the project was. and Camillia told her that Jaden's bedroom at home was decorated nicely but it was for a toddler and Jaden had been wanting a bedroom that was educational and mature and that she and Andrew had spoken to Jaden's parents and they were going to spend the night at the castle with Jaden so the bedroom makeover could be a surprise.

The castle decorator told Camillia that since the storage show room was done ahead of schedule, she could start on Jaden's bedroom right away and have it done by her bedtime that evening. Camillia thanked the castle decorator and told her when she went to Jaden's parents' general store to get anything and everything that she needed and that Jaden desired and have Jaden's parents ring up the bill and have it sent to them so they could get the money to Jaden's parents right away. The castle decorator told the couple that she would do that, then the couple thanked her, and she went out of the castle's front door right away. Camillia went to the family room to join up with Andrew and the chief. While Andrew, Camillia, and the chief sat in the family room passing time with pleasurable conversation, the castle decorator left the castle with the couple's buggy to go to Jaden's parents' general store to find his mother. The castle decorator found Jaden's mother and told her that she needed her to take her through the store to pick up things to turn Jaden's bedroom into an educational and mature space and that they needed to get everything possible so there was no desire for additional objects and the bedroom would serve its purpose for a long time. Jaden's mother said okay that they would start in the back of the store and work their way to the front where the cash register was, and the castle decorator told her that was wise.

The castle decorator was instructed to redecorate Jaden's bedroom in a certain way and not to worry about the cost so she went through the store picking out every educational thing that had to do with veterinary work and a bundle of supplies that Jaden would need to do his schooling for his work area; then it was time to focus on the bed area so the castle decorator relied on Jaden's mother to show her the things that Jaden had been wanting and admiring so as they went through the general store, the castle decorator picked up everything that Jaden's mother pointed out and finally the castle decorator went through the general store one more time, picking up items that would tie Jaden's sleeping area to his study area so there would be a smooth transition between the two areas. Jaden's mother rang everything up; then her husband loaded everything on the buggy, and the castle decorator thanked Jaden's parents for their help and they thanked the castle decorator for redoing Jaden's bedroom, who rode off to go to Jaden's parents' home to get started on his bedroom. Jaden's parents gave the bill to the store runner to take to the chief.

The general store's runner went to the chief's side of the castle looking for the chief, and when the butler told the runner that the chief was not there, he went to the couple's side of the castle to try to find the chief. When the couple's butler answered the door, he did confirm that the chief was there so the butler led the runner to the family room where he gave the chief the bill then the chief took a large amount of money out of his satchel and gave the runner what he owed Jaden's parents. The runner left to go back to the general store to give the money to Jaden's parents.

The castle decorator got all the things she had picked up from Jaden's parents' general store into their home and set it down right outside of Jaden's bedroom. The next step was the easiest; it was to remove all the decor already in Jaden's bedroom and place it in the family room so she could load it onto the buggy and take it to the couple's castle and donate it all to the storage showroom. The chief told Camillia and Andrew that he could not wait to see

Jaden's bedroom when it was finished, and the couple agreed; the three of them sat there in the family room and talked some more about life in general since they had planned to stay there and relax until the dinner hour.

Finally, the dinner hour was there; and before Andrew, Camillia, and the chief could get up from their seats to go to the castle's private dining hall, the castle decorator came bursting into the family room and excitedly told the trio that Jaden's bedroom was finished and it looked wonderful. As soon as the castle decorator finished her statement, Jaden and his parents walked into the castle's front door so they all got quiet then Jaden and his parents greeted the couple, the chief, and the castle decorator then they returned the greeting and everyone went to the castle's private dining hall and sat down at the big round table. The kitchen staff brought dinner out to everyone, and they ate slowly while discussing their day. Jaden told everyone about the new horses and how he loved them then went on to discuss the progress that he had made in the barn. He was so proud of how things were going for him, and he thanked the couple, the chief, and his parents for their support and love. The adults practically ate without conversing because Jaden had so much that he was thankful for and the adults let Jaden express himself, which took the whole dinner hour.

Now that the dinner hour was over, it was time for Jaden to go get his tutoring and for Jaden's mother to tutor Armellya. Andrew and Camillia told the castle decorator that they were free to take her to her previous home to get all her belongings and bring them to the castle for her to be able to get settled into her new room, and she said okay. The chief offered to stay at the couple's side of the castle to be available in the couple's place if they should be needed, and Andrew thanked the chief then he, Camillia, and the castle decorator went out of the castle's front door and got two horses to hitch to the couple's big buggy; but before Andrew could hitch the horses, Jaden slipped outside to hitch the horses before his tutoring session so Andrew let him hitch the horses. With the horses hitched, Jaden went back into the castle to be with his tutor; and when he passed his parents while following his tutor to the education room, they quickly told him that they were going to spend the night at the castle. Jaden got excited then Jaden's mother went to Armellya's bedroom to follow through with tutoring her.

Since Jaden and his mother were busy, his father decided to go out to the barn to do more work on the buggy that was there. Meanwhile, Andrew, Camillia, and the castle decorator had gotten to her previous home and were talking to her former landlords and thanking them for all their help; then Andrew told her previous landlords that her job at the castle had come to the point that she needed to be there all the time. Her previous landlords were understanding and told her that if she ever needed anything to let them know and they would help if they could. The castle decorator told her previous landlords thank you then everyone helped to load her belongings onto the couple's buggy. With the buggy loaded and everyone ready to return to the castle, the castle decorator said her goodbyes then Andrew got the horses moving.

The trip back to the castle was short, and the castle decorator thanked the couple for their generosity several times and the couple told her that it was their pleasure and with that they were back at the couple's side of the castle. Jaden's father saw the buggy arrive so he went over to the buggy and asked if he could help get the castle decorator's belongings into her new room. Andrew told him that would be an immense help and that they appreciated his help. The chief even went outside to help bring things in. With Andrew, Camillia, the chief, Jaden's father, and the castle decorator bringing her things inside, they finished rather quickly and the castle decorator said she was going to spend the rest of the evening putting her new room together then she said that hopefully she would finish that night by bedtime. Camillia told the castle decorator that she had worked so hard that day so she should not overwork herself; she should take her time because there was always another day. The castle decorator thanked Camillia for her concern then started to work on her new room while everyone else left her to her new room and went back to the family room.

Jaden was finished with his tutoring for the night, and his mother had finished her tutoring session with Armellya so they went to the family room to wait for Jaden's father to come inside from the barn. Soon after Jaden and his mother got to the family room, he came in, then the three of them said good night and went to Jaden's room so his parents could tuck him in for the night. When Jaden's parents were finished tucking him in, they went to their room and settled down for bed also. It was getting late, and people were already going to bed so the chief said it was time for him to leave to go to his side of the castle and get himself ready for bed. The chief told Camillia and Andrew good night then the couple walked the chief to the front door and saw him off. Then they went to their own bedroom to get settled down and spend some time together. Andrew and Camillia changed from their day clothes into their bed clothes then went to their bed and lay down facing each other and looked deep into each other's eyes while they spoke of their love for each other. The couple started to caress each other's bodies, and after a while, the caresses led to long romantic kisses.

After a while of kissing and caressing, Andrew and Camillia made love then they redressed and lay together in the bed silently holding each other for the next fifteen minutes. Because of her telepathic abilities, Camillia knew that Andrew was about to ask her if their timing was just right for conception because he knew that she could feel the initial union of her ovum with his spermatozoa so she gave a guilty-like smile then took his hand

and placed it on her stomach. Andrew knew that meant she had conceived. Andrew was so excited that he scooped Camillia up in his arms and pulled her closer to him then told her about how overjoyed he was because it was a miracle that she could carry a part of him in her and he knew that she shared the same feelings. They were both moved by the conception, and they discussed the possible sex of the new baby. Camillia informed Andrew that the new baby was a girl so the two of them started to go through girl's names to pick one then Camillia came up with Lynndia, and Andrew thought it was perfect so they decided that Lynndia was going to be the name of their new baby. Andrew asked Camillia when she wanted to see the doctor to have the pregnancy officially confirmed so she could start getting her prenatal care. Camillia told Andrew that they could go in the morning and have the doctor take a blood test if it was not too early to tell. Andrew reminded Camillia that they had gone to the doctor on the first day of conception before and got the right results. Camillia told Andrew that he was right so they would go first thing after breakfast.

Now that the two of them had established when to visit the doctor, Camillia told Andrew that they had better get some sleep in case their mini angel showed up and woke them; they looked forward to it so they snuggled down into their bed and prepared to go to sleep. It only took about ten minutes for the couple to fall asleep; they had a full day that was exhausting and the next day was going to be somewhat busy also. Andrew and Camillia got a couple of hours of sleep when their mini angel appeared and sang her siren song to wake them, and when they woke up, they were pleased to see their miniangel. Like always, Camillia blew her kisses and told her how she loved her then the miniangel blew kisses back and told Camillia she loved her also. Camillia told the miniangel that she and Andrew had some questions for her, and she told the couple to go ahead and ask their questions so the first question Camillia asked was how she got out of their bedroom without there being any space in the bedroom door for her to get through. The miniangel told the couple that she was not actually there, that she had astral projected to their bedroom from the dinosaur tail in the forest. The couple knew what astral projection was and thought that was clever then the miniangel told them that they had the ability to do the same and that way they could be anywhere they desired without having to take their bodies but that they needed to assure that their bodies would not be disturbed while they were having their out-of-body experience.

The mini angel told Andrew and Camillia that they and their children had many talents that other pale ones lacked such as the ability to control nature, which included but was not limited to the beasts of the forest, plant life, the rainfalls, the winds, and they were able to move objects with their minds, they were able to see the future as well and the past of others and themselves. The miniangel told the couple that she knew about the conception project and that it was not going to be possible for the scientists to be successful but that the couple had healing powers and could induce the reproductive cycles of their fellow pale ones one at a time. The mini angel told Andrew and Camillia that all they needed to do was to focus on what they were trying to do, and they could use all their gifts but to be careful what they allowed others to know. It would be in their best interest to keep their gifts to themselves except for the healing power, and the couple said they would, then they thanked their miniangel for telling them of their abilities. Camillia asked the miniangel if she and Andrew could visit all the miniangels at the dinosaur tail through astral projection, and she said yes that they would love to see the couple. Camillia told the miniangel that whenever she and Andrew were able to catch a nap during the day, they would visit but that it was not very often they had the chance to nap during the day because as the king and queen, they had so much to take care of. The miniangel said that she understood and that she looked forward to seeing them during the day, but she would not expect their visit; it would be like a wonderful surprise, and Camillia thanked her for her understanding.

Once the couple and the miniangel got the necessary talk out of the way, the miniangel fluttered around Camillia's abdomen and told Camillia that she was with child and Camillia told the miniangel that she felt the conception and that she knew it would be a girl and that they had already agreed upon a name for her. Andrew told the miniangel that they were going to go see the doctor after the morning meal to start the prenatal care, and the miniangel was pleased. The miniangel told the couple that there was only three hours until they would need to wake for the new day and that she had better let them get some sleep so they would be able to get through their next day without being too tired, and the couple told her that they did not like to see her leave because they enjoyed her company but that they understood they had natural needs.

The mini angel blew kisses to Andrew and Camillia then told them that she loved them and that she would be back the next night. Andrew and Camillia blew kisses back and told her that they loved her and they would see her the next night; then the miniangel disappeared. Andrew and Camillia nestled down in bed, held each other then fell into a deep sleep. It did not seem long before the couple was roused by the noises of their staff wandering about the castle to go to their job postings to begin working for the day so Camillia and Andrew slowly finished waking up. Andrew and Camillia gave each other good morning kisses and hugs then crawled out of their bed to start their day also. The couple changed out of their bedclothes into clean day clothes then went to their bathroom to brush their teeth, wash their faces, and brush their hair. A half hour after waking, the couple went out of their bedroom to go to the castle's private dining hall and sit at the big roundtable to have breakfast. Melanie already had their breakfast ready for them so when they got seated, she had the kitchen staff bring their meal out to them.

Andrew and Camillia ate their breakfast speedily without conversation so that they could finish breakfast and get going on their day's errands starting with the doctor's visit to confirm the pregnancy. Melanie noticed that Andrew and Camillia were not speaking to each other as usual so she commented to them that they must be in a hurry. Camillia told Melanie that they were because they had quite a bit to do and they wanted to get as much of their errands done by the lunch hour as possible so they could relax during the birthday party and spend some extra time with Jaden after family time was over, and Melanie said that Jaden would be thrilled; after all, it was his day. Andrew and Camillia did not finish their meal, but their stomachs were satisfied so they told Melanie that they were finished eating, who told the couple to have a wonderful day and she would see them at the lunch hour. Melanie sent the kitchen crew out to clear the big round table while she got into the kitchen to help her mother with Jaden's birthday cake; they had planned to make it three tiers with a veterinary theme; however, Melanie still needed to go to Jaden's parents' general store to get the mini farm animals and other things to put on the cake, and she would run that errand while the cake was baking.

In the meantime, Melanie's father was planning his lunch menu to be made of a variety of kid-friendly finger foods so it matched the theme for that day's family time. Melanie sent the dietary runner to bring the castle decorator to her so she could get the big round table decorated in a masculine type of veterinary theme with some things that Jaden could take after the party to keep in his new bedroom and the runner found the castle decorator quite quickly and brought her to Melanie. Melanie explained to the castle decorator the theme that she wanted the castle's private dining hall to have then told her that she had to go to Jaden's parents' general store for the cake decorations and that they could go together and she would pay for the dining hall's decorations. The castle decorator told Melanie that she was ready to go when she was so Melanie told her they should go right away. Melanie and the castle decorator went outside of the castle's front door and told Jaden that they needed their horses saddled for an errand so Jaden ran to the barn and got their horses. Melanie and the castle decorator got to Jaden's parents' general store and found his parents; then Melanie asked Jaden's father if he had any idea on how to distract Jaden so they could get their packages into the castle without Jaden knowing, and his father said that he would send a runner after him and have him make a delivery to the community's public dining hall and then he would send Jaden back to the castle. Melanie told Jaden's father that was perfect and she and the castle decorator would take the long way back to the castle so they would not run into Jaden.

CHAPTER FIFTY NINE

Melanie and the castle decorator went through the entire general store looking for anything and everything they could find that would be appropriate for the cake and the private dining hall, and they found more than enough of things that they could use so they got everything that they found and took it all to the front of the store to have it all rung up on the cash register then Melanie paid Jaden's mother for the large purchase. Jaden's father told Melanie and the castle decorator to get on their horses and take their packages to the back of the store to wait until Jaden got there, got loaded, and left for the public dining hall then they could ride quickly back to the castle and take the direct route instead of leaving right away and taking the long way back to the castle because it would actually be quicker and he knew that they were on a tight timeline. Melanie and the castle decorator said okay and did as Jaden's father said.

While Melanie and the castle decorator were at Jaden's parents' general store, Camillia and Andrew were at the hospital telling the charge nurse that they needed to see the doctor because she was pregnant again and they needed him to officially declare the pregnancy so they could start their prenatal care. The nurse got worked up in a positive way then she ran down the hall to bring the doctor up to the nurse's desk so he could check out Camillia. The nurse came back to the nurse's desk without the doctor, but she told Andrew and Camillia that the doctor was on his way. While they waited for the doctor, the nurse asked the couple what they were hoping for, a boy or a girl, and Camillia told the nurse that the new baby was a girl and that they already had a name for her. The nurse was amazed that Camillia could tell when she conceived and even more mystified that she could tell the sex of the child right away and she told Andrew and Camillia that. Right then, the doctor came walking up and he cheerfully greeted Andrew and Camillia who returned the greeting. As the doctor walked next to Camillia, he patted her on the back and said that he heard someone was pregnant then Camillia smiled big and said yes. The doctor walked past Camillia and Andrew, saying to follow him, and they went to the hospital room that they always had. When they all got into the room, Camillia sat on the examination bed while Andrew sat in the chair at the head of the examination table and the doctor proceeded to get the ultrasound machine. While the doctor was getting his equipment, he called out for a nurse to come in and draw Camillia's blood. Then the doctor sat on his rolling chair and rolled over to Camillia's side and told her to pull up her shirt. Camillia rolled up her shirt, and the doctor squirted some gel on Camillia's lower belly then put the Doppler on the same; he was silently looking for something so small that he had to move the Doppler slowly. It took some time but he suddenly said "there it is," and Camillia asked the doctor if he found the point of implantation and he said yes.

A nurse finally made it into the hospital room and took six tubes of blood from Camillia then took the blood samples to the laboratory herself, and the doctor told the couple that it would take about a half hour to get the test results; then he asked Camillia and Andrew if they were going to wait for the test results, or did they want him to send a note by runner when the results came back. Andrew and Camillia told the doctor to send a note by runner because they had a lot to do before Jaden's birthday party so the doctor said very well and wished them a good day. Camillia straightened her clothes, got off the examination table, then she and Andrew walked out of the hospital room. On the way out of the hospital, Andrew and Camillia told the nurses that it was nice to see them and for them to have a good day; they wished the couple a good day and went back to work. Andrew and Camillia were on their way back to the castle to have Matthew and the other security individuals take on the extra task of unloading the things from Jaden's old room from their second buggy and put the items into the storage showroom anywhere, and when there was extra time, Camillia would straighten it up how she wanted it. She and Andrew ran into Melanie and the castle decorator; they were on their way back to the castle also with their party purchases so they rode the rest of the way back together.

When they all got back to the castle, Melanie and the castle decorator went to the private dining hall to separate their purchases on the big round table so that Melanie could take the cake-decorating things into the kitchen and the castle decorator could start to decorate the private dining hall while the couple spoke to Matthew about unloading their second buggy. Matthew said that he did not mind the extra task, and he gathered the rest of the security individuals and they got right to work putting the things into the storage showroom, and within twenty minutes, they were finished and back at their posts. Andrew and Camillia sat in the family room and discussed the rest of their errands to decide what to do first with the time that was left before it was to be family time. Andrew and Camillia had to visit the science hall with the chief to find out where they were with the two projects, and they needed to ride through the community to check with each business and the various halls to see how they were doing and if there were any concerns or needs that needed to be addressed.

Camillia also wanted to get the storage showroom organized before they started to put more things in there, and with that she wanted to announce that the room was done so everyone that had something to donate could now do so. Andrew suggested that she announce the donation status and the new pregnancy while everyone was still in the family room before going to the private dining hall. Camillia agreed to that, then asked Andrew about the two lengthy errands that were left, saying that they would not have either one done on time to show up for family time with everyone else.

Andrew told Camillia that he had an idea for each errand so she gave him her unswerving attention then told her that they had been to the science hall every day since they started the two projects and the science hall's progress was slowing down and that they could miss one day of visiting and catch up with them the next day, and Camillia agreed with that idea. Andrew continued with his next idea. He told Camillia that after the family time was over, they wanted to take Jaden out into the community to ride his own horse and show off his new saddle and saddle blanket, and Camillia said yes then Andrew told her to take Jaden out for a long ride through the community with her new horse and he would go through the community and check on the businesses and various halls by himself. Camillia agreed to that suggestion. Camillia told Andrew that there was still some time to occupy before family time, and Andrew told her that together they would get the storage showroom in order then Camillia jumped up from her seat and said okay as she reached her hand out for his hand. Andrew took Camillia's hand then stood up and said to go. Practically everything Jaden had was replaced during his bedroom makeover by the castle decorator so there were a lot of things to organize in the storage showroom, but between Camillia and Andrew, they got it done just in time to get to their family room and wait for everyone to show up.

Andrew and Camillia were in their family room waiting for their family members when Melanie and the castle decorator showed up because they wanted to let the couple know that the private dining hall was fully decorated and all of Jaden's gifts were in there except the horse and his new bedroom, of course. The castle decorator said she put a new lock on Jaden's bedroom so one of the boxes that was wrapped had the keys to his bedroom in it and they had planned to tell Jaden about his horse right away so his other gifts would make sense to him.

After the castle decorator said what she had to say, Melanie told the couple that the cake was finished and it had turned out beautifully; she had placed it on the big round table as a centerpiece; then she told Andrew and Camillia that her father had made kid-friendly finger foods to match the party theme and that the menu turned out well. As soon as Melanie and the castle decorator said what they had to say about the preparations, there was a knock at the castle's front door, and when the butler answered it, the couple recognized the guest's voice and told Melanie and the castle decorator that it was the veterinarian and that he was there to tell Jaden that he was going to start tutoring him to be a certified veterinarian and the schooling would start this evening and that it was a gift from Andrew and Camillia. Sure enough, when the butler came around the corner, the veterinarian greeted them and thanked them for inviting him to their family's party and he said that he could not wait to meet the special boy who wanted to be an animal doctor.

Andrew offered him a seat so he sat down and they waited for the rest of the family to show up. There was another knock on the castle's front door. Andrew and Camillia could not imagine who that would be because anyone else that was to show up would just walk in so Andrew stood up from his seat and went toward the front door, but before he got there, the butler met with him and had the hospitals runner with him; the runner had a note from the doctor saying that the blood test was positive and congratulations. Andrew thanked the runner and then the runner left so Andrew took the note over to Camillia and handed it over to her for her to read, and she told Andrew that she would make the announcement when everyone was there. Andrew bent over and kissed Camillia on the lips and told her how happy he was while the few individuals that were there already were wondering what the announcement could possibly be.

Andrew sat back down next to Camillia, and as soon as Andrew sat, the family started to show up and within minutes everyone was there. Camillia stood up and asked everyone to sit and give her their attention so everyone did as they were asked. Camillia announced that the storage showroom was complete and she would take any donations that anyone had then she paused a moment and looked down at Andrew. Andrew stood up next to Camillia and put his arm around her then told her to go ahead so Camillia made the announcement that they were pregnant again and it was a girl that would be named Lynndia. Everyone cheered for the couple and congratulated them. Andrew and Camillia remained standing than Andrew told everyone that he needed them to step outside for a moment. Camillia walked over to Jaden and took him by the hand as they walked outside.

When everyone was outside, Andrew headed for the barn while Camillia took Jaden to the front of the group then Andrew came walking up to the group with Jaden's new horse. When he got directly in front of Jaden, Andrew handed the lead to Jaden and told him that the horse was for all the extra work and for doing such a good job and even though the work was not finished, he and Camillia wanted to give the horse to him on his birthday. Jaden asked if the horse was his very own to have at home and everywhere he went, and Camillia chuckled then told him yes and gave him a big hug while telling him happy birthday. Jaden thanked Camillia and Andrew then went to Andrew and gave him a hug also. As soon as Jaden broke his embrace on Andrew, the veterinarian moved to the front of the group and said he had an important announcement also so everyone looked at him and got quiet. The veterinarian said that everyone knew who he was, and that as the only animal doctor in the community, he would need an assistant that could eventually take over his business so he was there to celebrate the birthday of the special young man who was going to be the next animal doctor. The veterinarian told the family members that he was hired by Andrew and Camillia to tutor Jaden to be the next certified veterinarian, and Jaden stood where he was in a state of shock for several minutes and then he started to cry tears of joy. Jaden told the veterinarian that it was his dream to be an animal doctor; then he asked Andrew and Camillia if the community's veterinarian was really going to make him a veterinarian also, and the veterinarian took Andrew by the shoulder then told Jaden that was a serious offer and the offer was for him if he wanted it that the tutoring would start that evening after his regular tutoring. The veterinarian added that some of the lessons would occur during house calls so he may be called on at any time including in the middle of the night, and Jaden asked his parents if it was okay for him to participate in house calls; his parents said he could do whatever it took to help him reach his dream and that they would help in every way possible. Camillia told Jaden that she and Andrew could handle things at the barn in his absence and that they already agreed with the veterinarian to always make him available and that his parents agreed also. Jaden looked back at the veterinarian and thanked him. The veterinarian said, "Welcome to medicine, birthday boy," and gave Jaden a hug then Andrew told Jaden to tie his horse up because there was a party inside waiting for him so Jaden tied his horse up and grabbed the veterinarian's hand then everyone went directly to the castle's private dining hall to start the party and eat lunch.

When everyone got to the castle's private dining hall, Jaden stopped at the entrance and looked the room over in its entirety, paying attention to everything in detail, then he turned to everyone and said he had an announcement of his own. He said that this would be a birthday he would never forget because this was the one that would change him from a boy into a man; then he told everyone as a group thank you. Jaden told Melanie and her mother specifically that the cake was so beautiful that it was a shame that they had to eat it; then Melanie told Jaden that there were things on the cake that after she had them washed he could keep in his room as a reminder of this day. Jaden told her how gifted she and her mother were to be able to make something that elaborate.

After dealing with Melanie, Jaden turned to the castle decorator and told her that he knew she was the one who decorated the private dining hall and that she did a spectacular job. Jaden thanked her specifically and then told him that just like the cake, there were some decorations that after the party he could keep in his bedroom. Jaden thanked her specifically. Camillia suggested that everyone go ahead and take their seats at the big round table so that was what they did and then Melanie's father stood back up and told Jaden that he had made lunch to be all his favorite lunch items; then he motioned for the kitchen staff to start bringing everything out.

There were so many different finger foods, all of them Jaden's favorites, and as the kitchen kept bringing things out, it seemed that the food would never stop coming but eventually it did and Jaden wanted a little bit of everything. As everyone ate, the conversation stayed focused on Jaden because this was his special day, and when they were all finished eating, the kitchen crew went out and cleared the big round table off then set it up for everyone to have some cake. The first piece of cake was to be cut by Jaden and put on his plate because the first piece also went to the birthday person so Melanie helped Jaden cut the first piece as everyone sang happy birthday to Jaden. As they finished singing, Melanie put his cake on his plate and put it in front of him. Jaden waited to take his first bite of cake until everyone had their piece, and as they ate, Jaden kept eyeballing all the wrapped gifts, some of which were big and some small, but there were so many of them and everyone knew that Jaden was getting anxious to see what he got.

Soon enough, everyone was finished eating their cake and Melanie had the kitchen staff clear off the big round table so Jaden could open his gifts right there. Jaden's parents were slowly giving Jaden his gifts one at a time starting with the smallest one and working up to the biggest one, and the smallest one was the set of keys to his new bedroom with a note telling him welcome to his new bedroom at home and after reading the note he looked up curiously then thought for a few minutes. After thinking, Jaden thanked the castle decorator and the couple for the new bedroom, saying that even though he had not seen it yet, he knew it would be perfect then he asked if he could ride his new horse home to see his new room, and Camillia told him absolutely and then she told Jaden that his parents had not seen it yet either so they would all go with him, and he was happy about that Before Jaden's next gift was given to him, he handed one of the two sets of keys to his new bedroom to his parents and told them that the key was theirs if they ever needed to get into his bedroom for any reason because he wanted to pretend that the bedroom was his house and everyone locked their front door; then he assured his parents that he would never have anything to hide from them. Jaden's parents told him that they would respect his bedroom as his personal space and that they would only use the key in the event of an emergency or if he requested that they go into his bedroom for some reason, and Jaden told them thank you then they moved onto another gift. After an hour and forty-five minutes, Jaden had received all his gifts then he requested that everyone line up in the private dining hall before leaving, which they did, then Jaden went to the beginning of the line and gave that individual a hug and a thank you working his way down the line to the last individual giving hugs and thank-yous to everyone one at a time, being sure not to leave anyone out. Then he told them that he was ready to move on to the next phase of the day. Jaden, his parents, Andrew, and Camillia went outside of the castle's front door and headed to the castle's barn to saddle up their horses; and once they did, they headed for Jaden's parents' home to go look at Jaden's new bedroom. They finally got to Jaden's parents' home, got off their horses, tied them up, then went into the house and headed straight to Jaden's new bedroom. When they got there, they had to wait for Jaden to unlock the bedroom door, which he did on the double. Everyone that was there including Jaden stepped into the new bedroom, and when they saw the new decor, they just stood there in awe. It took a few minutes to regroup, but everyone eventually did and they started to explore the new bedroom. Jaden was moving about the new bedroom methodically, intensely checking everything out detail by detail; and when he got to his study area, he noticed learning books for his veterinary tutoring as well as some fun books to relax with. Jaden finally finished searching his new bedroom to see everything there was to see so he turned toward everyone that was there with him and told them that his new bedroom could not get any better and that it was perfect for him. Everyone piled out of the new bedroom, and Jaden locked the door behind them.

CHAPTER SIXTY

Jaden, his parents, Andrew, and Camillia got outside and mounted their horses so Andrew could go visit all the shops and various halls to check for any needs or desires while Camillia took Jaden through the community for a leisure ride and his parents went back to work at the general store. Camillia and Jaden rode through the community until it was near dinnertime so by the time they got back to the castle, Andrew had just gotten there from finishing his rounds through the community checking with the shops and halls for issues and desires and Jaden's parents had just gotten there also from closing their general store. Everyone just happened to meet up outside of the castle's front door so they went inside the castle together and headed to the castle's private dining hall to eat dinner.

Now at the private dining hall, everyone sat in their seats at the big round table then the kitchen brought out their food. As they ate, Jaden was talking about his day and how wonderful it was, then he started to express his thankfulness for what everyone had gotten for him, and he was surprised that everyone got together and kept a veterinary theme. Jaden commented on how this birthday was celebrated in an educated way, and he was very impressed with that. Everyone finished eating so they had to interrupt Jaden to say goodbye for the evening because Andrew and Camillia were going to retire in their bedroom while Jaden got his schooling, his mother tutored Armellya, and his father worked in the barn on the buggies. The rest of the staff were gathering their donations and putting them into the storage showroom for Camillia before they turned in for the night so Camillia would have to organize that room on the next day.

Camillia and Andrew changed from their day clothes to their bedclothes and lay in their bed to talk while they embraced each other and they both knew what the other wanted to discuss and it just so happened that they both wanted to talk about their unique gifts that no other pale one had. The primary thing they wanted to talk about was astral projection because that would allow them to visit the miniangels when they wanted to, and if they ever needed to, the next thing they wanted to talk about was their ability to heal since their miniangel had told them that the conception project was not going to work and something had to be done, and their miniangel told them that they had the healing power which would work for enabling others to conceive; they just needed to know how to do that. Camillia suggested that instead of discussing something that they knew nothing about, they should simply spend some time together and go to sleep on time and when their miniangel showed up they could discuss those two things with her, and Andrew said okay.

As Andrew and Camillia lay in their bed holding each other and relaxing, they could hear that their staff was done putting the donations in the storage showroom and they were settling down in their rooms as well and that meant that Jaden was done with his two tutoring sessions and his mother was finished with tutoring Armellya and his father was stopping his work in the barn. By the time that Jaden and his parents made it home, the couple was already sleeping and it only took ten minutes for them to get home on horseback. Andrew and Camillia slept soundly until the middle of the night when their mini angel came and started to sing her siren song to wake them up; it did not take much of the singing to wake the couple, and when they realized she was there, the couple sat up in their bed to converse with her. Camillia did the routine thing and blew the mini angel kisses and told her she loved her then the mini angel blew Camillia kisses and told her that she loved her also. Once that was done, Andrew held out his hand to the miniangel and the miniangel reached out her hand and they appeared to touch, but it was impossible for Andrew to feel anything because she was not there in body, she was there in spirit through astral projection.

The miniangel's spirit landed on the couple's bed next to them and she told them that she knew they still had a lot of questions, and Camillia told her that they did then she told them to ask their questions. Camillia started out by asking the miniangel how to astral project and she said that it may take several tries before they accomplished it but all they had to do was to relax in a safe place where their bodies would not be disturbed and let their bodies feel the lightness of a feather while they focused on where they wanted to be, the miniangel added that it was quite simple and with practice they would successfully astral project faster and faster. The mini angel told Andrew and Camillia that her explanation was not very detailed but that astral projection was something that came natural to her and did not take any thought so trying to explain how to do it was difficult for her.

The couple thanked their miniangel for trying to help them with their question about astral projection then Andrew asked the miniangel if she would answer one more question for him and Camillia and she said yes. Andrew asked the miniangel if she could elaborate on how him and Camillia were able to heal others and their mini angel told them that just like the astral projection it would take some practice and all they had to do was to lay one of their hands on the injured part of the individual that needed healing then concentrate on the fact that they were healing and visualize the outcome of the healed individual or individuals part. The mini angel told Andrew and Camillia that when they were healing someone their hands would glow a very bright yellow color then Andrew and Camillia asked their miniangel if they should start healing couples that wanted children, she replied that it was their decision.

Andrew and Camillia decided to discuss that in more detail then make their decision later. Since Camillia was pregnant with her ninth child the miniangel felt it was important for her to get a good night's sleep so she told the couple that she was going to make her visits short but she would be watching over them. With that said, she told the couple good night and disappeared. Andrew and Camillia lay back down into their bed and slipped into a deep sleep. Five hours later it was time to wake up and start the day. Camillia and Andrew climbed out of bed and went to the bathroom to change out of their bedclothes into their day clothes, wash their faces, brush their hair, and brush their teeth.

Now it was time to go out to the castle's private dining hall for breakfast and as usual Melanie had their food and drink ready for them. The couple had some things to discuss and they wanted the chief with them while they had their discussion for his input since he was far wiser than them. Camillia needed to get the storage showroom straightened up and the couple needed to go to the science hall to put a halt on the conception project and try to come up with some sort of believable explanation for the scientists. Camillia started to think about the life extension project and if there was some way that her and Andrew could use their healing abilities to help the chief, that was something she wanted to talk to Andrew about before the day was over in case they needed to talk to their miniangel about it that evening. Camillia told Andrew that she wanted to have their meeting in the castle's office room about the chief's life extension project before getting the chief for the other business because she had an idea, Andrew agreed to cooperate. They both ate their breakfast quickly then headed for their office room together.

Camillia sat at her chair behind the desk and Andrew sat on the chair in front of the desk. Camillia started the conversation by telling Andrew that they may be able to use their healing powers to extend the chief's life. Andrew told her that it was definitely something to discuss with the miniangel. The chief was not going to die from any ailment, just old age and Andrew was not sure if that could be negated. Camillia agreed and said it was a good reason to try astral projection and if they were successful they would not have to wait until that night. Camillia told Andrew that they must explore the pros and cons of using their healing powers to allow others to conceive. She felt it would be safe to reveal their healing ability to the chief and get his opinion on using their gift for the conception of others. The last thing she wanted to discuss was the explanation they were going to give the science hall for stopping the conception project. Andrew told Camillia that they did not owe any explanation since they were the king and queen of the community. Camillia told Andrew that everyone was like family and always communicated fully so it would still be nice to give a reason for stopping the project. Andrew saw where Camillia was coming from then agreed that it was the civil way to be. Camillia suggested they attempt the astral projection first so they could hopefully get some good news for the chief, Andrew agreed.

The couple got comfortable in their chairs and closed their eyes then they began to associate their bodies with that of a feather, light and floating in the breeze. Within seconds they found themselves with the miniangels at the dinosaur tail in the woodlands. Their guardian mini angel spotted them so she went to them and asked what she could do for them. Camillia asked her if their healing abilities would allow them to extend the chief's life. The miniangel told Camillia that her healing power would give the chief another two-hundred year's but after that she did not know if it would work again, they would have to try and see. The mini angel told Camillia and Andrew that because they were the chosen ones, their lives would be extended by four-hundred-years or so beyond their average lifespan. That was good news for the couple because they would have a lot of time to train their replacements as rulers of the compound. Having other children for their children to marry and reproduce with was a good reason to help the other pale ones to reproduce.

Andrew and Camillia told their miniangel they would see her that evening when she came to visit and she said okay. The couple returned to their bodies, opened their eyes, looked around the office room, then realized they had successfully astral projected. The couple felt they had the answers to their immediate questions that they had originally asked their miniangel. Andrew and Camillia spoke to one another about helping other pale ones conceive and decided that it would not harm anything, it would be very welcomed and give their children the opportunity to take on spouses when they were old enough. The only thing they would have to do was to limit the children to two per family to keep the population under control. Now the couple needed to get the chief in their office room to let him know about their ability and how they planned to use it to help society. Andrew sent a runner to retrieve the chief while Camillia went on about helping the chief also.

While waiting on the chief's arrival, Andrew suggested that he and Camillia be honest with the science hall and just tell them that he and she can heal the people safely. Andrew suggested that he heal the men and she heal the women due to the area that needed contact with their hands, Camillia agreed. Now that the couple got that situation dealt with, the chief showed up with the runner. Andrew thanked the runner then excused him from their presence. The chief went into the office room and sat in the chair next to Andrew then asked what was going on. The chief knew there was something important the couple wanted to let him in on because the meeting was in the office room. When there was important personal business, the couple usually took the chief into the office room to let him know what was on their mind and get his input. Andrew took the initiative to tell the chief that he and Camillia had the gift of healing and not only would that ability allow them to heal injuries, it would allow them to help their fellow pale ones conceive. The chief thought that was great for their community and everyone involved. Camillia told the chief that there was more good news, they could use their healing gift to extend his life also. The couple told the chief that they would love to extend his life if he wanted his life to be extended. The chief said he was more than happy to receive the gift of life because he wanted to be with them and the children for as long as possible. The couple told the chief that they would do the procedure when he was ready. Knowing there were a few things that he and the couple needed to take care of that day, he told the couple that they could give him the gift of life that evening after dinner. The couple agreed that they would heal the chief's shortened life after dinner in their office room.

In the meantime, the couple and the chief needed to prepare for the dinner announcement at the public dining hall about the ability to conceive with the help of the king and queen. The chief will take on the chore of finding a way to do it with order. The chief will post a sign at the public dining hall's door so the community could prepare for a dinner meeting. While the chief took care of the dining hall sign, Andrew and Camillia went to the science hall to have the life expansion project and the conception project stopped. The couple would not give any explanation but would tell the scientists that their explanation would be given at the end of dinner when everyone was to be addressed over conception. The new head scientist asked if there would be an explanation about the longevity project and Andrew told him no. Camillia told the new head scientist that the explanation would come in due time. Andrew and Camillia said goodbye to the scientists then headed for home.

The couple met with the chief on the way home so the couple invited the chief over to wait for family time. Melanie came out of the dining area and asked Camillia if she minded Jaden coming inside to get his birthday party decorations now that they were clean. Camillia told Melanie she did not mind and that she would bring him inside. Camillia went directly to the barn to get Jaden and bring him inside. He was working hard on the barn to make it look good and be more functional. Camillia told Jaden that Melanie wanted him so together they went inside to go to the dining hall. Camillia rejoined the chief and Andrew while Jaden went to see Melanie. Melanie told Jaden that she had his birthday party decorations cleaned and they were now ready for him to take to his bedroom. Jaden got excited and took the party favors to his room in the castle so he could get his veterinary theme spread there.

As soon as Jaden finished placing his party toys where he wanted them, it was time to start family time so he went to the family room to join with everyone else. Once seated in the castle's private dining room Andrew announced that dinner was to be held in the public dining hall so some special business could be announced and tended to. The thought of the announcement excited everyone because they knew it had to be something special for the bettering of the community. Melanie had the kitchen staff bring out lunch and everyone started to tell about their day.

When it got to Andrew and Camillia's turn, Camillia announced that she wanted to have them help her move the contents of the storage showroom to Jaden's parent's shop so they could sell the items. Everyone got a look of dumbfoundedness as they had no idea why she would put things for sale that no one would benefit from. Everyone knew not to question Camillia's methods because there was always a good reason for her orders, the reason just was not always clear right away. Andrew asked Jaden's parents if they could make room for all the things that had been donated, they said yes. Andrew told Matthew that he needed him to load and drive one buggy and he needed Jaden's father to load and drive another buggy. Andrew said he would load and drive a buggy, then he asked the chief to load and drive a fourth buggy and the chief said okay. They would use the two buggies that Andrew and Camillia owned along with the two buggies that the chief owned. Jaden's father offered his buggy for a fifth transport in case they needed it and Andrew told him thank you. Andrew accepted Jaden's father's offer and told him to have it at the castle on standby. Camillia assured everyone that they would understand what that was all about after dinner at the community meeting. Camillia was so excited about the opportunity to allow others to have children that she wanted to tell her family with the assurance that they would not say anything until after the public announcement but she knew she had to wait.

Family time was now over, everyone spent the usual family room time at the big round table. Jaden's mother went to the shop to prepare it for receiving new products to sell while Jaden's father went home to trade his mount for the horse drawn buggy. The chief and Andrew went to his side of the castle to get the chief's two buggies. Jaden went to Andrew and Camillia's barn to get their two buggies ready and out front. Once all five buggies were out front of the castle, Andrew, Camillia, Jaden, his father,

Matthew, and the chief started to load the buggies. It took a half hour, but all the buggies were loaded and there was nothing left in the storage showroom. Everybody got on a buggy and like a wagon train headed for the shop. Camillia rode with Andrew, the castle decorator rode with Matthew, and Jaden rode with his father. Now at the shop, the drivers would unpack the wagon and those who rode along would help Jaden's mother put the things where they were going to be. It took two hours for the shop to be organized but it looked great. Jaden's father stayed at the shop to help his wife with their duties and Jaden rode back to the castle with the chief. Before anyone left the shop, Andrew told the chief that they still needed to talk with him over some important business. The chief told Andrew that he was going to put his buggy away and he would be at their office room immediately after. Andrew thanked him then everyone headed back to the castle with their buggies. Back at the castle, Jaden put the horses and buggies away while Andrew and Camillia went to their office room to await the chief's presence. The chief wasted no time getting to Camillia's office room, shutting the door behind himself, and taking a seat next to Andrew.

Camillia started the conversation by telling the chief that he knew she and Andrew had more abilities than the average pale one. The chief told her that he was aware of that, but he knew they had not found what they were yet. Camillia told the chief that they had in fact found some of their abilities but not all. Camillia told the chief that they had found what may be the most important one of all, the power to heal. The chief held a surprised look on his face and remained silent. Andrew told the chief that they had the ability to heal injuries, reverse barrenness, and prolong life. Camillia told the chief that she and Andrew wanted to prolong his life if he would allow them to. The chief told the couple that if they could expand his life, he would be in their debt. Andrew said very well, to meet him and Camillia at the science hall after the dinner hour and it would be done. Andrew and Camillia felt that the scientists needed to see the reason that they ordered the life expansion project to be stopped since they were given no explanation. They needed to know that the couple got information from a spiritual source that their project was not going to be fruitful but that the couple had the special gift of giving life amongst other things.

CHAPTER SIXTY ONE

With that said, Andrew sent a runner to the science hall to have the scientists meet them at the science hall after dinner. The chief questioned if he had heard right, they could reverse the barrenness of the pale ones. Camillia told the chief that was correct and that was what they were going to announce at the dinner meeting. The chief was ecstatic, that meant all the pale ones who wanted children could have them. Andrew asked the chief not to tell anyone that they would make the announcement at the dinner meeting along with the guidelines. The chief questioned what the guidelines were. Andrew said that the couples had to be married but they could not marry just to have children. They needed to be married for at least a year and could only have two children. They needed to control the population to some extent. The chief said that he now understood why all the storage showroom contents went to the shop for sale. The chief asked how the couple found out about their new ability and Camillia told the chief that they could not disclose that information at that time. The chief told the couple that it did not matter if they discovered their full potential and they were well on their way. The chief asked if their children had the same abilities and Camillia said yes, but there were stipulations as they reproduced. The further down the line of reproduction, the less the gifts would be passed down. Eventually, they would be like a normal pale one. Camillia said that she and Andrew with the help of the nannies would raise the children to control their reproduction rate to be able to keep the special abilities alive longer than if they were to quickly reproduce. The chief said that would be nice but questioned if that was fair to the children. Camillia told the chief that as the royal family, all duties came before personal desires. The chief agreed and said no more about the situation.

As soon as that conversation was settled, the runner returned from the science hall to tell the couple that the entire science team would be at the science hall after dinner to meet with them and the chief. Andrew thanked the runner and excused him to go about his way until he was needed again. Andrew stood up from his chair with the intent to exit the office room and the chief stopped him from leaving the room and asked about the couple's healing ability. Andrew sat back down in his chair and asked the chief what he wanted to know. The chief asked to what extent they could heal, for instance if another pale one had an amputation of a finger could the couple heal it. Andrew told the chief that they did not know how much their healing ability could benefit the community in tragedy but hopefully they would not need to find out. Camillia told the chief that they would need to make a mental note to ask their source and Andrew agreed.

It was nearing dinnertime and that excited the chief because that meant he was close to being given an extension on his life. Andrew, Camillia, and the chief went to the castle's family room to wait for the family to arrive for the dinner trip to the public dining hall. Jaden's father was the first to arrive and he had good news for the couple, the buggies were completed. Even though it was close to the dinner hour, Andrew and Camillia could not wait to see the buggies. Jaden's father had worked hard on both buggies to make them stylish and comfortable. When Andrew and Camillia saw the buggies, they were speechless at first. Camillia broke the silence when she commented on how lovely they were. Andrew told Jaden's father that he had done a fabulous job at making them comfortable, the padding was properly placed and seemed to be durable. Camillia gave Jaden's father a big hug and thanked him for a job well done. Andrew told Jaden's father that he was surprised at how quick the job was done. Jaden's father asked the couple if there were any other projects he could do for them and the couple said they would think about it then get back with him. The three of them hurried back to the castle's family room to prepare for the dinner trip.

When Andrew, Camillia, and Jaden's father got inside the castle's family room, they noticed that everyone was there and waiting for them to go to the public dining hall. Andrew got everyone quiet then announced that the buggies were completely done and offered for them to ride in the buggies to the dining hall. Andrew had Jaden's father drive the big buggy with most everyone in it and Jaden got to drive the smaller buggy with everyone that was left in it. Camillia, Andrew, the chief, and the other individuals from the castle got to the public dining hall before anyone else so the couple took their place on the podium and had the chief join them. Little by little the rest of the community arrived and took their seats.

Once everyone was there, the kitchen staff served dinner and beverages. Dinner seemed to go by fast and when the kitchen staff got the tables cleared, Andrew stood in front of everyone and made his announcements. Andrew told the community that he and Camillia had the ability to reverse barrenness through a healing ability. He continued by telling them that there were conditions that must be met prior to him and Camillia allowing a couple to conceive. Andrew told them that they must be married for at least a year so getting married just to have children was not acceptable. They were informed that there would be an interview to assure that the couple could afford to care for a child and that the child would be raised with good ethics and morals. Andrew said that the procedure may sound long and quite personal but that it was easy yet necessary. Andrew assured the community that the growth would be supported by the royal family and that there would be more job positions to fill so anyone interested must speak to him or Camillia. Andrew told the public that there would be a sign-up board at the spiritual hall and that he and Camillia would go down the list to address the public as they came along. Andrew finished addressing the community by telling them that the sign-up board was already set up and for the doctor to please go to the podium immediately. Upon finishing his address, the public clapped and cheered.

The doctor made his way to the podium and asked Andrew if everything was okay. Andrew told the doctor to ride to the castle that there was some business he and Camillia wanted to discuss with him, he said okay. Everyone that rode to the public dining hall on the couple's buggies made their way back to the buggies and headed for the castle. The doctor mounted his horse and followed the couple to the castle. On the way home, Camillia started to feel somewhat uncomfortable and her belly started to glow a bright yellow.

Right as everyone got to the castle, Andrew noticed Camillia's belly glowing and he became somewhat frightened. Between the look on Andrew's face and the telepathic link she had with him, she knew she had to explain but she did not have an explanation. Andrew asked Camillia if she was okay and she told him she felt uncomfortable. The doctor rode up beside the couple and noticed Camilla's belly glowing and he suddenly forgot what he was going to say, becoming speechless. Everyone but Jaden, the doctor, and the couple went into the castle. The doctor got off his horse and tied it to the post while Andrew got off the buggy and held out his hand to help Camillia down.

As Camillia got her feet to the ground, her water broke. Camillia knew her water had broken but neither the doctor nor Andrew knew. Camillia started having heavy contractions right away so she grabbed Andrew's arm and told him she was in labor. The doctor heard Camillia and he told Andrew to get her to their bedroom right away. Andrew picked up Camillia and took her directly to their bed while the doctor followed closely behind them. Andrew and Camillia's personal maid helped Camillia get out of her day clothes and into her bedclothes. Camillia got laid down in the bed as comfortably as possible then the doctor checked her to get an idea of when they might be seeing the new baby. Andrew stood at the head of the bed so he could hold Camillia's hand and to encourage her to push and breathe. Camillia's personal maid went to get the new baby's nanny, clean sheets, receiving blankets, and clean clothes for Camillia.

After the personal maid brought everything into the bedroom and placed the clean items on a chair in the room, she went to get the chief so he could witness the birth of his grandchild. As Camillia's belly became brighter, her labor pains decreased. Because of the connection Camillia had with the baby she knew that the baby had the ability to heal and was using that ability to make Camillia more comfortable during a painful time. Camillia realized that was why her belly was glowing so she told Andrew and the doctor so they would be at ease with the new event. Just a matter of seconds later the doctor told Andrew that the baby was coming. As the baby delivered, Camillia's belly glowed less.

Finally, the baby was delivered and crying and Camillia's belly no longer glowed. The doctor gave the baby to her nanny who would clean her up then give her to Camillia for her first feeding. Andrew hugged Camillia and told her that baby Lynndia was beautiful and looked just like her. The chief was shedding tears of joy and agreed that Lynndia looked just like Camillia. The doctor told the couple that Lynndia was a beautiful name for a beautiful baby girl then they thanked him. Lynndia's nanny had her cleaned up and wrapped in a clean receiving blanket so she handed her to Camillia for her first feeding. Camillia put the small child to her breast and she started to suckle. The doctor told the couple that the miracle of pregnancy and childbirth never ceased to amaze him; it was truly a gift from God. Andrew told the doctor that it was truly a blessing and he felt special that he could share the experience with his wife, he only wished he could contribute more to the miracle. The doctor told the couple that his part in the process was over and he was going to leave the proud parents to spend some precious time with Lynndia before Camillia had to give her to the nanny in exchange for some much-needed sleep. Andrew thanked the doctor and walked him to the bedroom door, the doctor said he could find his way the rest of the way out.

After Lynndia was finished nursing, Camillia handed her over to her nanny so Camillia's personal maid could get her and the bed cleaned up. The chief congratulated the couple and said he was going to leave them for now but would be back after Camillia got some rest, he said good bye to the couple then saw himself out. Andrew asked if there was anything he could do to help and Camillia's personal maid told him yes. She told Andrew to help Camillia with a shower and while they were doing that she would change their bedding, Andrew agreed. Camillia's personal maid had gotten the bedding changed and into the washroom for the castle's washing people before Andrew was finished giving Camillia a shower so the maid took over with the shower and told Andrew to get some clean bedclothes. Andrew did as he was asked and by the time he had the bedclothes in the bathroom, Camillia and the maid were ready for them. Andrew helped Camillia back to the bed and between Andrew and Camillia's personal maid, Camillia was tucked into bed and comfortable.

The maid excused herself to seek out the castle's hand washers to get the bedding and receiving blankets cleaned immediately. Camillia and Andrew's friends had already gone to visit Lynndia and were now going to visit the couple and see how Camillia was doing. Everyone piled into the couple's room and saw how great Camillia looked and commented that she had never looked so good after childbirth and questioned what was so different this time. Camillia told everyone that Lynndia had used her healing ability to make the delivery easier for both mom and infant, she said the delivery was essentially painless and fast.

Andrew had to interrupt the baby moment to remind Camillia that they were supposed to be at the science hall meeting with all the scientists. Camillia apologetically asked everyone to excuse them so they could discuss business and everyone understandingly left the couples bedroom. Camillia told Andrew to send a runner to the science hall to bring the scientists back to the castle's office room so they could heal the chief. Andrew told Camillia that it may not be a promising idea to perform a healing so soon after delivering a baby. Camillia told him that she was as strong now as she would have been if the baby had not been born that evening. Andrew double checked with her and she repeated herself with the same answer so Andrew summoned a runner to bring all the scientists to the castle's office room. Camillia told Andrew that they needed to get the chief back over to their side of the castle so he summoned another runner to retrieve the chief.

While waiting for everyone to arrive at the castle's office room, Andrew and Camillia went to the office room and sat in the chairs in front of the desk. It was not long before the runners returned with their targets and Andrew told them to pile into the room. As the chief walked by Andrew, he told the chief to sit next to Camillia and he did. Andrew stepped the rest of the way into the office room and shut the door behind himself. The scientists had no idea why they were at the castle but they sat quietly awaiting the explanation. The chief figured that since Camillia had just delivered Lynndia, the couple was still going to do the longevity healing but it was going to occur at the castle so Camillia would not have to travel. Andrew started to address the scientists by apologizing for not being at the science hall and told them it was because Camillia gave birth to the baby and her name was Lynndia. The scientists congratulated the couple and became more relaxed now that they knew why the meeting place had been changed at the last minute, but they were still curious what the meeting was about. Andrew wasted no time in telling the scientists what the meeting was about. He told the scientists that their projects were not going to work and that he and Camillia were made aware of that fact by a reliable source that they could not reveal at that time. All the scientists got a look of defeat and Andrew told them not to fret because he and Camillia had a simple solution. The scientists perked up and then looked at the couple with curiosity.

Without hesitation, Andrew told the scientists that he and Camillia had the ability to heal and that meant the ability to reverse barrenness, heal injuries, and extend life. The new head scientist asked Andrew if he and Camillia had that ability, then why were they working on the two projects? Andrew responded with full honesty when he told the scientists that they had only recently found out that they had the gift of healing and they were still trying to understand it. The new head scientist asked why the science department was there and Andrew told him it was to witness the elongation of life that was going to be done for the chief. With all that said, Andrew told everyone it was time to give the gift of life and everyone became silent. Andrew moved over to the chief and Camillia stood up then she moved over to the chief. The couple placed both of their hands on the chief's shoulders and concentrated on the extension of life, then suddenly their hands began to glow. The couple continued to concentrate and their hands began to glow brighter and brighter until the light from their hands was blinding. The chief's body began to glow all over and he began to shake slightly.

After a few moments, the chief stopped shaking and the glowing of his body began to diminish until he no longer glowed. The couple's hands started to lose their glow until there was no more light coming from them. The couple then told the science staff that the chief would have another two-hundred-year's or so. The scientists asked how the couple knew that the chief got his life extended. Andrew told them that he and Camillia could feel the transfer of energy, sort of like temporarily sharing a life source.

Suddenly, before anyone could say another word there was a continuous obnoxious banging on the office room door. Andrew answered the door and there before him was Jaden's mother in a panic, it was hard to understand what she was saying because she was speaking so fast. Andrew put his hands on her shoulders and told her to take a couple of deep breaths and speak slowly. Jaden's mother took a few deep breaths then slowly told Andrew that she needed him in the castle's family room because she believed her husband was having a heart attack. Andrew told her to take him to her husband and they quickly walked to the castle's family room.

When they got to her husband, he was on the floor grasping his chest. It was obvious he was not getting enough oxygen and he was mildly sweaty. Andrew quickly dashed up to him and placed his hands upon Jaden's father's chest then focused on healing his heart. Andrew's hands started to glow and Jaden's mother gasped, to her the sight was miraculous. Andrew continued to focus and his hands became brighter and brighter. A few minutes after Andrew's hands were so bright they were nearly blinding, they started to dim down. As Andrew's hands dimmed, Jaden's father showed signs of recovering.

CHAPTER SIXTY TWO

Finally, Andrew's hands stopped glowing and Jaden's father spoke to Andrew. He told Andrew that he felt normal again and started to stand up from the floor. Andrew stood up and extended his hand out to Jaden's father to help him up. He took Andrew's hand and bounced right up then he told Andrew that he felt great and he thanked Andrew for his help. Jaden's mother said Andrew's gift was very much appreciated, she would not know how to go on without her mate. She told Andrew that there did not appear to be enough time to retrieve the doctor and there was no guarantee that the doctor could have saved his life. Andrew told her he was happy he could help because they were special to him and Camillia, they would definitely grieve if one of them were to pass away. Jaden's mother hugged Andrew and told him she was in his debt. Andrew told her he only did what was the right thing to do then he asked them to go with him to see Camillia and they said okay. The three of them walked back to the castle's office room where they met up with Camillia and the scientists. Camillia knew all was well when she saw Jaden's father, she got up out of her chair and walked up to Jaden's father then gave him a warm hug. Camillia told him that she was glad to see he was okay because he was a part of her family and she was not ready for him to pass nor would she ever be ready for that. Camillia told Jaden's mother that she did the right thing by getting Andrew to help her husband and that if they could help anyone they would be happy to do so. Jaden's mother thanked Camillia then told her she had better sit back down because she still looked weak from childbirth, Camillia did as suggested.

Jaden's parents said they would go about their way and let them finish their business with the scientists then they walked out of the office room and closed the door behind themselves. The scientists were amazed and did not understand how the couple could have such gifts and Camillia told them that they did not question the gift they just thanked God and used it for the good of the community. The new head scientist told the couple that they now understood why the conception project and the life extension project were stopped but he asked how the couple knew that they would not be able to come up with a vaccine for either project. Andrew told him that he could not tell of his source but that it was divine, the new head scientist said he would not question it any further. The new head scientist said it was getting late and he felt it was time for him and the rest of the scientists to leave but he felt that him and the rest of the scientists were privileged to get an explanation on why the two projects were stopped and get to witness first-hand the healing properties that the couple were blessed with.

All the scientists left the castle to go to their homes and Andrew wanted to get Camillia back into bed to get some rest before their miniangel arrived for her nightly visit. On the way to their bedroom, the couple noticed that everyone else was already in their bedrooms to settle in for the night. Andrew got Camillia back into bed then he told her they needed to visit the doctor the next day to find out if he knew what happened to pale ones when it was their time to pass away because when he healed Jaden's father it felt like a life transfer not a healing. Camillia asked Andrew how he knew that and he told her it had the same feeling as when they elongated the chief's life. Camillia told Andrew that they had not done a healing yet so she questioned how he would know the difference and he replied that the feeling had to be different in some way, she agreed. The couple agreed to save any further deduction until after they see the doctor the next day then they could try to rationalize the healing of Jaden's father.

With that subject set aside, Andrew got changed into bedclothes and climbed into bed with Camillia. Andrew cradled Camillia and told her how much he loved her and that she had done wonderful delivering Lynndia. Camillia told Andrew she loved him also and that together they had produced some beautiful children. They fell asleep in a wink of an eye. After five hours of sleep, the couple's miniangel arrived and sang her wake up song. Andrew and Camillia woke up and were glad to see their miniangel. The couple sat up in their bed, Andrew held his hand out for her to appear to stand on while Camillia blew a kiss to her. She went to Andrew's hand and blew a kiss back to Camillia. She congratulated the couple on the birth of Lynndia and told them that she was a beautiful baby and that she was special, she carried the gift of healing which the other children had not. Camillia told the miniangel that she thought all the children had all their abilities and the miniangel told Camillia that the children had the abilities that she used during pregnancy as well as the basic pale one abilities. The miniangel told Camillia that her ability to heal had just developed enough to use it even though the ability was there the whole time she had been a pale one.

The miniangel told the couple they had other abilities they had not used but they would have to wait to use them until they developed. Camillia asked what those abilities were and how they would know they had developed. The miniangel told Camillia that when the extra abilities developed they would just know they had them as options, it would come to them as a dream came to them. She told Camillia she was not permitted to go into a detailed explanation at that time but to please trust her. The miniangel told the couple their other gifts would be to make things hot or cold with the use of their minds, they would be able to levitate and fly, and they would be able to move objects with their minds.

Camillia questioned the miniangel on what extra gifts the children would have since she only used the abilities that every pale one had during her pregnancies. The miniangel told her the children would have the abilities that were priming during her pregnancies that even though she had not used them, she had them. Andrew asked how they would know who had what and the miniangel told them to observe the children during their formative years and they would know. The miniangel told the couple that each child they had would have more abilities. At that point, Camillia asked if Armellya had any extra abilities since she was their first born and they had not had any extra abilities. The miniangel told them that Armellya would have some extra abilities but not as many as her siblings, the more children they had the more each child would possess. The couple said they understood but that did not seem fair to the children. The miniangel told the couple she understood what they felt but those gifts were God given and if they wanted any changes they should pray and have faith. Camillia said she was going to do just that and she would do whatever God deemed necessary for her children to be equals in that manner. The miniangel told the couple that they had enough of seriousness and Camillia needed extra sleep since she had given birth that day so she was leaving but would be back the following evening. The couple thanked their miniangel for her visit and in helping them to understand the children's gifts as they were. Camillia gently blew a kiss to the miniangel and she blew a kiss back.

The miniangel disappeared so Andrew and Camillia lay back down in their bed nestled together. Before the couple could fall back to sleep, a bright light appeared in the center of their bedroom. The light got bigger and brighter, the couple sat up in their bed and held one another tight. They were not afraid but they were curious about what could be happening. Finally, the light took the form of two male angels with griffins wearing harnesses with leashes. One angel spoke to the couple and he told them he and the other angel were their protectors, comforters, strength, and source of wisdom. The other angel told the couple that he knew they were happy with their lives and they demanded respect from others which was given by everyone but they were not pleased with the start of their children's lives. The first angel listed all the children's names with their gifts, then he told the couple that he received an understanding that they wanted all their children to have equality with their gifts. Camillia told the angels that it was correct to have the understanding that she and Andrew wanted their children to have equality with their gifts. The second angel responded that it shall be done, they would visit each child in their sleep on the next evening and bestow upon them the gifts that they lacked because God had smiled upon them as a faithful family. The couple thanked the angels and faster than they had appeared, they were gone. Andrew and Camillia got out of bed and knelt on the floor and said a prayer of thanks to God.

By the time the couple was finished praying, they could hear their staff starting to go to work around the castle. Andrew and Camillia realized it was time to get the day started for themselves.

Camillia and Andrew did their normal routine, go to the bathroom and change out of night clothes into day clothes, wash their face, brush their teeth, and brush their hair. The couple went to the castle's private dining hall for breakfast and Melanie did not have their breakfast waiting for them as usual. Andrew sat at the big round table while Camillia went into the kitchen to find out what was taking Melanie so long to get breakfast out to the big roundtable. Camillia found Melanie then asked her if she was okay that morning, she said she was fine just running late due to over sleeping. Melanie said she could not explain it but there seemed to be a disturbance about the castle. She said she was awakened by a bright light outside of her bedroom door, it was there for only a moment and she did not go to see what it was because she felt like she was in a state between sleep and awake. Camillia knew the light that Melanie said she thought she saw was the miniangel going into Lynndia's bedroom to see her for the first time and welcome her to this world. Camillia knew she and Andrew had to keep the miniangel's a secret so she did not say anything to Melanie about what the light was. Camillia simply told Melanie that maybe later she would get a chance to take a short nap to help her get through the day. Melanie said that sounded like an excellent idea then she turned away from Camillia to help her parent's get breakfast ready to serve. Camillia told Melanie she would get out of her way and go to the big round table and join Andrew.

Back at the table, Camillia told Andrew that Melanie saw their mini angel's glow through the cracks of her bedroom door but she did not check it out so she had no clue of what it was nor was she sure it was real. Andrew was surprised that it woke Melanie up from a dead sleep then he remembered that the two male angels with griffins had appeared after their miniangel left. Andrew asked Camillia if the bright light Melanie thought she saw was from the two male angels with the griffins that had appeared after their miniangel left and Camillia told him that was more likely because their miniangel never disturbed her before. Melanie came out of the kitchen with the couple's breakfast so they stopped discussing the source of the mystery light.

While Andrew and Camillia ate their food, Camillia told Andrew she wanted to go to the hospital right after breakfast to see the doctor about how pale ones die because it did not seem they would pass from an ailment since pale ones never got sick. Andrew agreed and told Camillia he figured pale ones would just fall asleep and go gently in their sleep, Camillia agreed. It was officially settled between the couple, they would make the hospital their first stop after breakfast then they could go to the spiritual hall to see if anyone had signed up for the conception interview and possible healing.

The couple was just about finished eating when Jaden went barreling into the castle's private dining hall. He was in search of Andrew and Camillia to tell them the barn was finished and have them go look at it to approve or disapprove of it. The couple told Jaden to go back to the barn and take a last look at it to make sure he had everything in order while they finished their breakfast and they would be there very soon. Jaden ran back to the barn to make sure he had everything where he wanted them, then he got the idea to put a big bow on the barn door to make it more like a present. Jaden got his horse, mounted, and took off like a streak of lightning to go to his parent's shop to get the bow that was most appropriate. Jaden got to the shop and jumped down from his horse before it was completely stopped, tied it up, then ran into the shop to find his mother.

When he found his mother near the bow section, he told her that he needed a big bow for the barn door so he could make the new barn like a present for the king and queen. Jaden's mother agreed that was a great idea so she picked out the perfect bow and gave it to him to take back. Jaden took the bow and ran out of the shop, untied his horse, mounted, then got back to the barn as quickly as his horse could go. Jaden got back to the barn before the couple got outside and he put the big bow on the barn door then stood there outside of the barn as though nothing was happening.

Finally, the couple went outside and saw Jaden standing right outside of the barn door. They noticed the big bow on the barn door and thought it was a nice topper for a job so carefully done. Jaden got excited and told the couple that he was going to give them a tour from one end of the barn to the other end and the couple separated and each one took one of Jaden's hands. Andrew opened the barn door so they could go inside and Camillia immediately noticed how much the barn had changed so she asked if the barn was the same barn they had some time ago. Jaden laughed and told Camillia that it was the same barn but it was special now. Andrew took a quick look around at what he could see from where he was and commented on how fabulous the barn looked so far. Jaden took the couple on the tour and showed them how he had painted the inside of the barn and found a special place for everything to be. The barn was organized in a functional manner and everything that was run down or broke was fixed like new. The couple was truly amazed at how much work went into fixing the barn and for all that was done, how fast Jaden got it done.

Back at the barn door, Jaden told the couple he wanted to fix up the stable also. Andrew told Jaden his debt was paid upon the completion of the barn. Jaden told the couple that the extra work kept him busy on down time and he just wanted to fix the stable for the benefit of the livestock as well as making it look like it belonged to a royal family, he said it needed to match the barn. Andrew looked at Camillia and she shook her head in a yes motion then Andrew told Jaden he could do the stable also. Jaden jumped in joy and hollered words of excitement then he told the couple he was going to get on the job right away. Andrew told Jaden he needed two horses for his and Camillia's errands for the day and Jaden went right away and saddled two horses then brought them out to Andrew and Camillia. The couple told Jaden not to work himself too hard and to let them know if he needed anything or any help then Jaden said he was going to do the stable like he did the barn. He would ask Andrew if he needed anything purchased and transported then Camillia told Jaden to have fun with his project and he promised he would. Jaden watched the couple ride away, then he went to the stable to plan what was going where, what needed fixing, and what kind of add-ons he could come up with.

Andrew and Camillia rode on to the hospital to see the doctor, bypassing the spiritual hall where they needed to get the fertility requests from the community. Once they got to the hospital they tied their horses to the post and entered the hospital together. The nurses at the nurse's desk saw Andrew and Camillia coming and they all waved to them. When the couple got to the nurse's desk, Camillia asked if the doctor was busy, and the charge nurse told them she was not sure but she could find him and let him know they were there. Camillia told the charge nurse that her getting the doctor for them would be great because she and Andrew had a quick question for him. The charge nurse told Andrew and Camillia to wait in the waiting room while she went to find the doctor, then she walked from behind the desk to go down one of the hallways. Andrew and Camillia went to the waiting room and sat in chairs side by side while the nurse ran through the halls looking for the doctor.

About a half hour later, the charge nurse popped in on the couple to apologize for taking so long to get back with them, the doctor was hard to find and it turned out that he was a bit busy. The charge nurse told the couple that if they wanted to wait another fifteen minutes or so, the doctor should be able to get away from his duties with others and see them. Camillia spoke up before Andrew had a chance to accept or decline waiting time and told the charge nurse they would be happy to wait on the doctor to have some free time. The charge nurse told Andrew and Camillia if they needed anything while waiting for the doctor to just let her know, the couple said okay and thank you. The charge nurse went back to her desk to finish gossiping with the other nurses while finishing paperwork.

Ten minutes after the charge nurse left, the doctor appeared in front of the couple. The doctor seemed to be in high spirits, he had an unusually big smile on his face and addressed the couple in a lighthearted voice. Instead of shaking hands, the doctor gave Andrew and Camillia each a big bear hug. When the doctor was greeting the couple, he asked what he could do for them and Andrew told him they needed a question answered that they felt only he could answer. The doctor quickly asked if the discussion needed to be in private or could it be held in the waiting room, Andrew told the doctor he was not sure then they both looked at Camillia for the answer. Camillia told the two men that it may be wise to take the discussion to the doctor's office room so that was what they did.

In the office room with the door shut, Camillia bluntly asked the doctor how pale ones died, if it was a matter of going in a state of sleep or was it an ailment that would take them. The doctor said he was not sure what type of question and answer they were seeking but if he understood correctly, they wanted to know what had to occur for a pale one to die. Camillia said that was essentially what she and Andrew needed to know. The doctor told the couple that some pale ones may be lucky enough to die in their sleep but majority of the time it was a serious ailment that had a sudden onset followed by a quick yet painful death.

Since pale ones did not get sick it was almost always a sickness that killed them even though the ailment for a regular human may be able to be managed it was a matter of the ailment striking a hundred times fold. Andrew told the doctor that the past evening he believed that Jaden's father suffered a heart attack and he had healed him because there did not appear to be enough time to get help. The doctor told Andrew that without the special healing ability to help, he would have died no matter what was done or how fast something could have been done. The doctor told Andrew that it sounded like he extended Jaden's father's life. Andrew told Camillia that was what he had told her that night but he was not one hundred percent sure. The doctor told the couple that so far, their community had lost only one member, the original head scientist and it was due to the faulty vaccine he insisted on giving himself because he was disillusioned. Camillia said that was a sad day and watching him die was very difficult. The doctor asked the couple if he had answered their question sufficiently or not and both said yes.

CHAPTER SIXTY THREE

The doctor told the couple he had a question for them and Camillia asked what it was. Then the doctor asked if they had anyone sign up for the conception interview for approval. Andrew told the doctor that they had not made it to the spiritual hall yet and that was their next stop. The doctor said it would be exciting to bring babies into their world for so many couples who have yearned for a child or two. Camillia told the doctor that she could keep him informed on the progress of that new miracle and the doctor told Camillia she was right to call it a miracle because conception and fetal growth were amazing, a work of God. Andrew told the doctor he and Camillia had to get going because it was getting close to the lunch hour which was their family time and the doctor understood the importance of family time so he bid them a farewell. The doctor stayed in his office thinking about all the things that had been happening since Andrew and Camillia came along while the couple went out to retrieve their horses and head home. Andrew told Camillia they would pick up the sign-up sheet for the conception request's then go straight to the castle for family time and they would deal with the list after the lunch hour. Camillia agreed and with that decision and off they went.

When the couple got to the spiritual hall, they were surprised to see so many names on the sign-up sheet, they left one page for the community thinking that would be a slow starting thing but someone added another paper that had more names on it. Seeing all the names was a bit exciting yet a bit overwhelming, at that point they knew they were going to need help with the interviews if the list continued to grow at that pace or faster. The ride home was faster than usual because the couple was focused on the conception subject, suddenly they were home and it was time to go inside for family time.

Now inside the family room waiting for all the family members to be there, the couple had a few moments to rest and catch their breath. Jaden's parents were the first to arrive and Camillia commented on how well Jaden's father looked. Jaden's father said he was feeling great and the heart incident was not affecting his work either. Shortly after Jaden's parents arrived, Jaden and the rest of the family trickled into the family room. Once everyone was there they went to the castle's private dining hall to eat and discuss their day so far. Everyone was asking to see baby Lynndia before family time was over so Camillia summoned the nanny to bring Lynndia out. Even though it was Lynndia's nap time, the nanny agreed to bring her out for everyone to see her. She said one day of veering off the schedule would not hurt things too badly.

When everyone was done eating their lunch and spoke of their day, they went back to the family room for the best part of their day, visiting with Lynndia. As soon as the group saw the baby, they all agreed that she looked just like Camillia; she did not have any features from Andrew. Andrew felt his wife was the most beautiful woman ever so he took the family's opinion of Lynndia's looks as a compliment. Lynndia started to get fussy so her nanny took her into her arms and started to rock her gently saying she was overdue for her nap and really needed to be laid down in her crib. The family all said good night to Lynndia as her nanny walked toward her bedroom with her. Family time was about over and everyone stood up to give one another hugs before going their separate ways then Jaden burst out vocally saying he could not wait to get started on the stable. Everyone chuckled and gave Jaden hugs then went on to giving one another hugs. Everyone except Bridgette and Matthew went their separate ways to get back to their duties. Bridgett pulled Matthew toward Andrew and Camillia because Bridgette wanted to discuss the chance of being healed for conception as soon as possible. Camillia noticed Bridgette and Matthew approaching them and assumed it might be about conceiving a child so Camillia grabbed Andrew's hand and walked toward them.

When the four of them met up, the two girls gave each other a big hug while Andrew and Matthew shook hands. Bridgette asked Andrew and Camillia if they could speak privately, and the couple said absolutely so they all four went the Camillia's office room. Once at the office room Camillia went in and sat on her chair behind the desk, Bridgette and Matthew sat in front of the desk, and Andrew shut the door behind them and stood by the door. Bridgette looked at Camillia and told her that they had signed up for an interview for conception and they would like to find out when their interview would be. Camillia told Bridgette that they had just gotten the list from the worship hall and had not had a chance to look it over yet. Andrew suggested that Camillia look at it quickly to be able to give an estimate of when Bridgette and Matthew's turn would be.

Before Camillia could look at the sign-up pages, Bridgett told Camillia that they were the first ones to sign the sheet. Camillia looked down at the sign-up paper and noticed Bridgette and Matthew's names on the sheet at the top of the first page. Camillia put the papers on her desk and with an ink pen she crossed off

Bridgette and Matthew's names then told them their interview was now. Bridgette and Matthew grabbed each other's hands and held on for positive support to one another. Camillia told the couple that they had met the first requirement by being married for at least a year; then she asked the couple how many children they wanted to have. Matthew said he wanted as many children that it took to make Bridgette happy then Bridgette said that since two children was the limit she would have to settle for only two children. Camillia made a note of that response on a separate paper that she had written their names on.

Andrew asked Bridgette and Matthew when they would be ready to start trying for the first child and the couple responded together saying as soon as possible. Camillia made a note of that response also; it was not the response that got Camillia's attention but the fact that they were in unison with the response. Andrew asked how they would support two children and Matthew replied that they both worked and made enough to not only support two children but to have two nannies as well. Bridgette was concerned about housing because they lived in the castle and had limited space. She felt they would have to have a house built and they would have to save for that. Camillia told Bridgette that housing was not a problem because as the royal staff it was the king and queen's responsibility to make sure housing was adequate. Andrew told the couple that it would take some work on the castle but it would be complete by the time the first baby was born. Matthew asked Andrew what kind of work was involved and Andrew told Matthew that he and Camillia would have their bedroom extended into a full house with two children's bedrooms. Camillia told the couple that the same arrangement would be made for all the staff that were to reproduce. Bridgette asked Camillia and Andrew if they passed the pre-process requirements and Andrew told them yes. Camillia told them that if they would not have passed they would not have gone on to discuss the housing arrangements. Andrew told the couple that he needed to explain how the healing process was going to work so they could relax and let it happen with ease. Andrew told them that they could stay seated and he would heal Matthew while Camillia healed Bridgette, this was due to the need to touch a sensitive area and the necessity to keep any wrong and uncomfortable situations from arising. Camillia told them that meant she would heal the women and Andrew would heal the men so they were not uncomfortable with being touched in the lower abdomen by the opposite sex and there was no way someone could say there was any foul play during the healing process. Camillia told them that when one leaves no way for error to occur, error was less likely to occur and everyone could be protected.

Camillia got up out of her chair and went around her desk then walked over to Bridgette while Andrew walked from the office room door over to Matthew. Bridgette and Matthew let go of each other's hands and Camillia told them that she and Andrew needed them to hold hands while the healing was occurring, they both said okay then took one another's hands again. Andrew put his hands upon Matthew's abdomen while Camillia put her hands upon Bridgette's abdomen then Camillia and Andrew started to concentrate on conception for their target. Andrew and Camillia's hands started to glow which made Bridgette and Matthew's abdomen and hands start to glow also. Andrew and Camillia's hands became brighter and brighter until the glow was blinding, the couple being healed had to close their eyes due to the brightness.

After a few minutes, the glow started to dim until the glowing stopped. Once the glow was gone, Andrew and Camillia took their hands from Bridgette and Matthew's lower abdomens. Camillia told her friends that the healing process was done and they were ready to start trying to conceive. Bridgette and Matthew thanked the king and queen for their help then everyone hugged. Bridgette and Matthew left the office room to get back to their duties but before separating they gave one another a romantic kiss. Andrew and Camillia stayed in the office room to discuss how the approval process needed to be carried out. Camillia told Andrew that it took about a half hour to do the interview and healing and they did not have enough time in the day to do the two steps before more individuals would be back for their second child. Andrew agreed and suggested that the chief do the interviews and send those who passed the requirements to them, Camillia said that was a great idea. Andrew and Camillia decided to go to the chief's side of the castle and discuss with him about doing the interviews. The couple knocked on the chief's front door and his butler answered, then took them to the family room to wait while he went to get the chief.

When the chief got to his family room, he asked the couple if everything was okay and they said yes. Andrew spoke up and told the chief that he and Camillia needed his help with the conception process. The chief said he would help in any way he could so Andrew asked him if he would be willing to do the interviews for the couples that signed-up for help. The chief told Andrew he would be glad to but he and Camillia needed to give guidelines for the ability to pass or fail a couple. Camillia told him they would and they would even let him know what types of notes he needed to take down. Camillia told the chief that they did not have enough time to do the interview and the healing along with the rest of their duties because each interview would be about twenty minutes if not more but the healing was just a few minutes. The couple knew they would be putting most of their days into healing for quite some time but by the time they got used to it the healing would come to an end and they would feel bored from lack of things to be done. The chief told Camillia and Andrew to give him the list and he would start on it right away, they said they would as they headed for the chief's front door. Andrew and Camillia headed for home to get the contraceptive list so they could go right back to the chief's home and get it to him.

When they got home, they were greeted by Matthew. He wanted to thank them for the healing saying he was so excited that he forgot to do that. Camillia gave him a hug and told him she and Andrew already knew that he and Bridgette were thankful. As they started to go their separate ways, Camillia told Matthew to give Bridgette hugs for her and he said he would. Andrew went back to the office room to get the sign-up list for the chief then met back up with Camillia in the castle's foyer. Andrew and Camillia went back to the chief's side of the castle to give him the list. The chief was waiting for the couple, and it was obvious because he answered his door himself when they knocked on the door; that was rare. The chief took the list and told the couple like he had already said, he would start on the interviews right away.

As the couple left the chief's side of the castle, he also left to go to the places he needed to go so he could meet with each couple that signed-up for healing. To put some order to the healing process, the chief decided to give a list to the couple of those who were approved for the conception healing and he would do about ten healings an evening and that way he would be able to tell each couple about when the king and queen would be doing their procedure. Andrew and Camillia did not have much to do that day so they decided to go home and tell Matthew they were going to take a nap and they did not want to be disturbed but they were really going to astral project so they could visit the miniangels in the forest.

When the couple got home, they did not have any problem finding Matthew so they were able to tell him about taking a nap and not wanting to be disturbed and Matthew told them no problem that he would guard their door himself. Andrew and Camillia thanked Matthew and went into their bedroom, shut the door behind themselves, and got out of their day clothes. Before the couple could get into their bedclothes, Camillia grabbed Andrew by the arm and whipped him toward her. He chuckled and pulled her body close to his body. Camillia told Andrew that even though they had planned to see their miniangels, they needed to choose what to do because she was ready to conceive again and they would not have time for both events. Andrew told Camillia that making love to her was like spending a moment in heaven, Camillia told Andrew that she knew he was her soulmate. The couple made their way over to their bed, folded down the sheet and blanket, then lay down together. They snuggled and spoke intimate words of love before stroking and kissing one another's erogenous areas, after some time of foreplay the couple made love. When the lovemaking ended, the couple cuddled and stayed in bed for a while discussing how special it was going to be for other couples to have children.

With no warning, the couple heard a gentle knock at their bedroom door. Andrew asked who it was, and there was a voice that said, "Me." Andrew asked, "Who is me?" Then the voice said Matthew. Andrew asked what he could do for him, and Matthew told Andrew that it was coming up on the dinner hour, then Matthew apologized for disturbing him and Camillia. Andrew thanked Matthew for letting him know what time it was. Andrew and Camillia got out of bed, went to the bathroom to clean up, got their day clothes back on, and went to the castle's private dining hall. They had made it just on time; Melanie was putting dinner on the big round table. As Melanie made it from Andrew's side of the big round table to the other side where Camillia was, Camillia started to get a subtle glow about her. Melanie was shocked to see Camillia start to glow right before her eyes and the sight was so startling that Melanie dropped Camillia's dinner on the floor. Melanie immediately apologized and knelt to start to pick up the spilled food and Camillia got up from her chair then knelt next to Melanie to help pick up the food. Melanie told Camillia it was okay she did not have to help pick up the mess and Camillia told her it was no problem.

Melanie's mother came out of the kitchen to find out what the commotion was and saw the two women picking the food up off the floor so she went back into the kitchen to get a broom and dust pan. Melanie's mother asked Melanie and Camillia to let her get the rest of the food up so the two women stood up and moved out of the way then Melanie's mother started to sweep the food up into the dustpan. Melanie's mother said she would go make another plate for Camillia and bring it to her right away. Camillia asked Melanie if she was okay and she told Camillia that she was but it startled her when she started to get a glow about her. Andrew just sat there at the big round table smiling, he did not say a word about Camillia glowing for a few seconds. Andrew saw Camillia glow and he knew why so it did not surprise him but it did make him feel happy and proud. Camillia told Melanie to sit down and she would explain so Melanie sat down and waited for the explanation. Camillia told Melanie that the glow did not come from her, it came from the new baby.

Melanie's mouth dropped open then she questioned Camillia with surprise if she was pregnant again. Camillia told Melanie that the glow was a sign of the union of the gametes and she knew that she had conceived a boy. Andrew told Melanie that the child would be called Connor and Camillia said that was the perfect name for him. Andrew asked Camillia if she wanted to visit the doctor on the next day or that day and she said on the next day because they would most likely have some conception healing to do that evening, Andrew acknowledged her then told her he loved her. Camillia said she loved him too then the two of them started to eat their dinner while Melanie got back to work.

As Melanie was walking back into the kitchen she hollered out to the couple congratulations and they hollered out thank you. As Andrew and Camillia finished eating their dinner, the chief showed up at their front door. The butler let him in and took him to the castle's private dining hall to see the couple. The chief told Andrew and Camillia he had a list of couples who passed the interview and were ready for the healing process and so far, there was no one who failed the interview. Andrew and Camillia agreed they would get on the list immediately and get as many of them done as possible. Andrew and Camillia knew they could heal ten couples but were not sure if they could do any more and if so how many so they got their two runners, gave them five couples each to retrieve, and prepared for their work. The butler would answer the front door and take the couples back to Camillia's office room one by one then see them out as they got finished. Andrew and Camillia had one concern about doing so many healing procedures at one time and that was an exhaustion factor because it did take a bit out of them to heal and with Camillia being pregnant again she needed her strength and could possibly tire easier. The couple made an agreement with one another that if they felt they needed to stop they would let the other one know and without question stop healing for the night.

Andrew and Camillia got most everything worked out then the first two couples arrived with the runners. The butler did not have to take one back to the office room because Andrew and Camillia were still in the family room with the chief so they took the first couple to the office room with them and the chief stayed in the family room to keep the other couple company. Now in the office room, Andrew told the couple to sit in the chairs as he closed the door behind them then he started to tell them how the healing worked and what he needed out of them. Each healing would be the same as what the couple did for Matthew and Bridgette, the couple to be healed would sit in the chairs and hold one another's hand while Andrew put his hand upon the man's lower abdomen and Camillia put her hand upon the woman's abdomen then they would focus of fertility. Eventually the glow would appear, get blindingly bright, then dim and the disappearance of the glow would mark the end of the healing process. The couple being healed would be told good luck and the butler would show them out and bring in the next pair to be healed. The process would go at least ten times a night before Andrew and Camillia would be done unless they were able to do more and that would depend on how Camillia was feeling.

On this night, being the first night of doing bulk healing, Andrew and Camillia only did ten procedures and they felt that they could do more but they did not want to put their strength to the test on the first night. Andrew and Camillia spoke about how they each felt the night went and they decided that they could do more than ten healings per night so they would add a couple procedures a night and work their way up to whatever their limit was. With the last of the couples gone, the chief asked Andrew and Camillia how they felt and they said they felt rather energized which was a great feeling and opposite to how they figured they would feel. Camillia told Andrew and the chief that it felt like the new baby was helping to heal.

All ten couples that were brought to the castle to get fertility healing had been done and were on their way home. The chief realized it was getting late and he wanted to turn in early so he could rise earlier than usual and take a walk through his private garden before starting his day. Andrew and Camillia knew they needed to get to bed as early as possible because they were going to be awakened during the night by their miniangel and they wanted to make sure that they got enough rest also. Everyone in the castle was wrapping up their duties for the night so they could go to their private quarters but Matthew and Bridgette wanted to catch Andrew and Camillia before bedtime to get a quick answer about their quarters being expanded. The chief said good night and gave his adopted children a hug then left to go to his side of the castle and as soon as the chief was gone Bridgette and Matthew asked the couple if they had a moment to talk. Andrew told them he and Camillia always had time for them then asked what was going on. Matthew asked when the construction would be started on their quarters then Andrew told him the next day and during that time he and Bridgette would stay in one of the chief's extra bedrooms. Matthew asked if they would have any access to their room during the construction or did they need to take everything they would need to the chief's extra bedroom and Andrew told him he would not have any access to the room until it was finished then Andrew advised him to take as much as possible to the extra bedroom and if he needed help they would get it for him. Camillia told Bridgette and Matthew she knew it was going to be a pain to move as much as possible from their room to the chief's room just to move it back to their room in the end but once everything was done they would have more than just quarters, they would have their own house with space for two children and when they could hear the pitter patter of small feet that would bring them joy.

Bridgette said that it all made sense and that they were blessed to get the ability to reproduce and she hoped she would conceive quickly but she was not going to stress on it rather she was going to enjoy trying and welcome the pregnancy when it occurred. Camillia told Bridgette that she had the right idea because sometimes if one stresses on conception it could delay it from occurring. Matthew told Andrew and Camillia that they would get up earlier than usual in the morning to pack their things then Andrew told Matthew he would help move their things and Camillia spoke up saying she would help also. Andrew said he needed to go to the chief immediately to find out which bedroom he wanted Bridgette and Matthew in so Andrew excused himself saying for them to stay with Camillia until he returned with the answer. Andrew left quickly to catch the chief before he got into his bed to rest for the night. When Andrew got to the chief's front door he knocked gently so he would only hear it if he was still awake.

Because the butler was in bed already, the chief answered the front door and asked Andrew to enter his home. Andrew apologized for showing up so late then told him that Bridgette and Matthew needed to know which bedroom the couple was to use until the construction of their home was completed. The chief said it was not a problem for arriving late because he was still awake due to all the excitement that the day had provided to him then the chief told Andrew that Bridgette and Matthew could use the room after Lynndia's then Andrew thanked the chief and excused himself to go home so he could go to bed also. Andrew got back to his side of the castle then told Bridgette and Matthew their temporary room was going to be the room next to Lynndia's and the couple said okay then turned toward the hallway and went down it to go to their original quarters for the night and make love before going to sleep to encourage conception. Now everyone was in their quarters so Andrew and Camillia headed for their quarters also.

In the privacy of their quarters, Camillia told Andrew that she hoped Bridgette would conceive soon because it was always her dream to someday have a family. Andrew replied that he believed when individuals were given the healing the woman would ovulate at that time making conception almost immediate. Andrew and Camillia changed from day clothes into bed clothes while they were talking. As Camillia and Andrew climbed into bed, Camillia continued about how Bridgette never gave up hope of being a mother even though she was a pale one and supposedly barren. Bridgette prayed every night for children and now her prayers have been answered. Andrew suggested giving a congratulations party for Bridgette when she could announce she was pregnant and Camillia agreed that was a great idea. Camillia started to talk about Bridgette again but Andrew cut her off and told her they needed to get some sleep before their mini angel came to visit them, Camillia told Andrew he was right then she nestled down in the bed and got comfortable. Andrew nestled down beside his wife and cuddled with her with his arm around her so he could sleep with his hand on their new baby. Andrew and Camillia fell into a deep sleep and were dreaming good dreams when their miniangel arrived and sang her wake up song. The miniangel's song was so beautiful that the couple awoke slowly so they could listen to more of the miniangel's song.

CHAPTER SIXTY FOUR

As Andrew and Camillia opened their eyes, they noticed a bright light peering through the cracks of their bedroom door, they knew it had to be the male angels that were to visit their children. Camillia and Andrew welcomed their miniangel like usual then asked her if she was aware of the male angel's that had visited them and she said yes. The miniangel told the couple that the male angels were of a divine nature and it was an act of God to see them and to receive the gifts they had brought with them. The couple agreed and said they were blessed that their children would still be individuals but have equality with their gifts, the miniangel concurred. As Camillia and Andrew spoke to their miniangel. The male angels made their way from the oldest child, Armellya, to the youngest child, Lynndia, and made sure each child had all the gifts possible then left them with a kiss from God. The children's nannies were not disturbed but the children did wake up and seemed to understand who the men were and why they were there. It was said by some individuals that babies still see the angels until a certain age. It amazed the couple that the bright light did not awaken the nannies but that must have been a divine intervention. It seemed that the male angels left as quickly as they came, leaving the couple with only their miniangel which was fine, the male angels did what they vowed to do.

Andrew and Camillia were relieved that all their children now had all the gifts possible. The miniangel did not stay long, she was just checking up on the couple and assuring them that she had not forgotten them by sticking to her promise to visit every night. The miniangel told the couple good bye then disappeared leaving the couple to go back to sleep. There was still a lot of the night left so Andrew and Camillia got a lot of sleep before having to wake up the next morning. Andrew and Camillia were woken up by the sound of violent vomiting so Camillia put her robe on and went to her bedroom door, opened it, then followed the sound to Bridgette's room. Camillia knocked on the door then she heard Matthew holler come in so she went in to make sure everything was okay and to see if there was anything she could do to help.

As it turned out, Bridgette was seemingly sick and Matthew was holding her hair back and trying to support her the best he knew how. Matthew said that Bridgette woke up extremely hungry so she went to the kitchen to get some food then she brought it back to their bedroom to eat it and right after eating she got nauseated and started to vomit, now she was just dry heaving. Camillia told Matthew that he needed to get Bridgette to the hospital to see the doctor for a pregnancy test because she and Andrew were discussing the healing process and deducted that the woman should ovulate within twenty-four hours of the healing process not to mention that pale ones never get sick so it so it seemed that Bridgette was not sick she was showing signs of early pregnancy and the blood test could pick up on the altered hormones earlier than a urine test. Matthew asked Camillia if she and Andrew would go with them to see the doctor and Camillia said absolutely. Camillia walked on into the bathroom to console Bridgette, Camillia told Bridgette that the nausea and vomiting would not last too very long. Camillia told Bridgette and Matthew that she had to see the doctor that day also because she knew she had conceived the night before but she had to make it official before telling the family. Matthew told Camillia congratulations then he told Camillia that he thought it would make her and Bridgette's pregnancies special because they could share the whole experience together through the entire nine months. Camillia told Matthew he was right because before becoming pale ones the girls had always dreamt of sharing so many of life's experiences and supporting one another, it was just a shame that some of the girls were not married yet to share the experience of pregnancy with her and Bridgette. Matthew told Camillia that the children would be their nieces or nephews and the other girls would share in the upbringing so it was as though they shared in the responsibility also, Camillia agreed. Bridgette was now feeling better but was concerned about how she would feel working around food all day because she realized the smell of her snack set her off before she even ate it. Camillia told Bridgette that she and Andrew could find something else for her to do for the nine months and put her back into her original position after the baby was born, she thanked Camillia as she started to recompose. Matthew let go of Bridgette's hair as she stood upright, she went to the sink, grabbed her toothbrush, put toothpaste on the brush, and started to brush her teeth.

After brushing her teeth, Bridgette gave Camillia a hug and thanked her for her support. Then she went to her husband and thanked him for his support also. Camillia told Bridgette and Matthew that she and Andrew were going to make the trip to the hospital their first errand of the day then she asked the couple if that would work for them and Bridgette said yes. Camillia told Bridgette she was going back to her bedroom to prepare for the new day and to let Andrew know that they were going to the hospital with them then she and Andrew would meet her in the castle's private dining hall. Matthew said he would dress for the day and get to work but he would see them when it was time to leave for the hospital then he gave Camillia a hug and thanked her for her support. Camillia left the couples room to go back to her room to tell Andrew what was going on and that they had an appointment with Bridgette and Matthew.

When Camillia entered her bedroom, she noticed that Andrew was already ready to start his day; he was just waiting for Camillia to return with details of what was going on and to get ready for the day so they could go eat breakfast. Camillia hugged Andrew with excitement and told him that Bridgette was probably pregnant and that Bridgette and Matthew were going to the hospital for a pregnancy work up with them and the doctor could do both together, Andrew said okay and that he was excited for Bridgette and Matthew. Camillia was changing into day clothes while she was talking to Andrew so all she had to do was brush her teeth and hair. Bridgette was already in the kitchen by the time Camillia and Andrew were ready to go to the castle's private dining hall and Bridgette's mother had breakfast ready for everyone by the time Bridgette got to the kitchen so it was not late. Bridgette's parents knew that there must be something important making Bridgette late to work because she was always the first one to the kitchen, this was the first time she was late.

When Bridgette got to the kitchen, her mother asked her if she was okay and Bridgette told her mother that she was vomiting and dry heaving, her mother asked if she was sick because Bridgette's mother did not know that Bridgette had been healed for conception so Bridgette told her mother to sit down at the big round table because she needed to tell her something. Bridgette's mother took a seat at the big round table with Camillia and Andrew then Bridgette told her mother that the couple had done the healing procedure on her and Matthew the night before and they had made love so she believed she may be pregnant. Bridgette's mother got excited and called out to her husband, he came running out of the kitchen and asked what the problem was then Bridgette's mother told him that Bridgette may be pregnant and that she was going to the doctor after breakfast to find out because Camillia and Andrew did the healing procedure the night before. Bridgette's father was extremely excited and he hugged his daughter then he told her it would be a dream come true to be grandparents. Bridgette told her father that she and Matthew were going to the hospital with Andrew and Camillia because they were pregnant also and they just wanted official confirmation before telling the family during family time. Bridgette's father went over to Camillia and gave her a big hug and told her how happy he was to have another baby in the house then he went to Andrew and hugged him also. Bridgette's parents said they had to get back to work because they had to replan lunch so they could have a celebratory lunch in honor of the two pregnancies.

Bridgette told her parents that they did not have to do a special meal just for the pregnancies but if they wanted they could plan a baby shower for later in the pregnancies. Bridgette's parents said they would do both and they would hear no more about what they need and need not do. With all the commotion Camillia remembered that she needed to talk to Andrew about finding another job for Bridgette during her pregnancy so she interrupted saying excuse the interruption but together they needed to find another job for Bridgette until she had the baby because the smell of food that slithered through the castle was making her nauseated and the last thing they needed was to have Armellya unattended due to her morning sickness. Andrew suggested that maybe she could be the secretary for Camillia and the chief about the healing procedures because they needed to keep a detailed log of the healings and the results and they could get another nanny for Armellya. Andrew said that Bridgette could take Camillia's notes and the chief's notes and combine what needed to be combined and make sense of it so there could be a specific document of all cases, Camillia said that was a brilliant idea. Matthew asked Bridgette if that suggestion sounded good to her and she said she would love to serve the king and queen in a project so important, it would also allow her to sit and be off her feet as she got bigger. Camillia said then let it be, the job was to start that day and Camillia would give her notes that she had so far to Bridgette and tell the chief to give his notes to Bridgette also. Andrew and Camillia were finished eating so the kitchen staff removed the dishes and cleaned the big round table and Camillia asked Bridgette and Matthew if they were ready to go to the hospital for a checkup and they said yes. The two couples went to the patio outside the castle to let Jaden know they needed the buggy and Jaden immediately ran to the stable to retrieve the horses and buggy. In a brief period, Jaden brought the horses and buggy to the two couples so the men helped the women up onto the buggy then they got up onto the buggy and off they went to the hospital.

At the hospital, Andrew turned the horses and buggy over to the hospital's stable boy, then the two couples went into the hospital and headed for the nurse's desk. At the nurse's desk, Andrew told the charge nurse that the two women needed a pregnancy check-up and the charge nurse said to follow her. The charge nurse put Camillia and Andrew into their usual hospital room then started to walk toward the door to take Bridgette and Matthew to another hospital room when Bridgette spoke up and asked Camillia if she would mind being in the same room. Camillia told Bridgette she did not mind being in the same hospital room at all, it would be something special to share their confirmations together. The charge nurse heard Camillia and Bridgette's conversation and said they did not usually allow two appointments to be held together but since it was for the king and queen they could overlook it.

As Bridgette and Matthew were sitting in the chairs at the head of the exam table, the charge nurse headed for the door saying she would fetch the doctor, Andrew stood by Camillia holding her hand. As the charge nurse entered the hallway the doctor was walking by so she grabbed him by the arm to stop him then told him Camillia and Bridgette were in the hospital room behind her for a pregnancy work-up. The doctor got excited because it was always a joy to monitor a new life and bring them into the world and it was especially superb that he would be busy with a lot of babies, he loved babies. The doctor thanked the charge nurse for letting him know that the two couples were in the hospital room waiting for him. The doctor went into the hospital room right away and greeted the two couples then said he understood they both needed a pregnancy checkup. Camillia and Bridgette said he was correct then the doctor jokingly said he assumed Camillia was first since she was the one on the exam table and she said yes. The doctor felt Camillia's belly as he hollered for a nurse to come into the room to take some blood samples. The charge nurse entered the room and told Camillia to give her an arm for the blood draw and Camillia gave her the arm that was closest to her. The charge nurse took six tubes of blood then told Camillia she knew the drill would take twenty to thirty minutes for the results to get back to her. The charge nurse went over to Bridgette and told her she needed six tubes of blood and it would take twenty to thirty minutes for the results to get back to her then she asked Bridgette for an arm. Bridgette gave her an arm and the nurse drew the blood and when she was finished she took both sets of bloods to the laboratory. The doctor checked Camillia's cervix then said everything pointed to a positive pregnancy so he wanted to do an ultrasound to make sure the point of embedment was in the correct place, and it was.

Now it was Bridgette's turn so Camillia got off the exam table and straightened herself up then sat in Bridgette's chair. Matthew switched places with Andrew and the doctor did the same thing to Bridgette that he did to Camillia and she showed signs of a positive pregnancy also. The doctor told the two couples to wait in the waiting room for the blood results and assured them that they would come back positive. Everyone was excited and before leaving the exam room they had a group hug then both couples congratulated the other then they went out of the exam room to go to the waiting room. While waiting for the blood results to come back the two girls were discussing how they could go shopping together for the baby's rooms and material for maternity clothes while the men were discussing how to support the women during their pregnancies. It was Andrew giving pointers to Matthew since Andrew had gone through the pregnancy phase with Camillia nine other times and Andrew warned Matthew that every pregnancy was different along with the deliveries, the babies even had different personalities from the very beginning. Matthew said he was a little fearful of not being able to get through the pregnancy so Andrew assured him he would do fine that his active part of the process did not begin until the baby was born but it was made a bit easier with having a nanny.

A half hour went by and the doctor got the test results so he retrieved the charge nurse and instructed her to go to Jaden's parents' shop to pick up a congratulation gift for both girls and to make it quick so she left right away. The charge nurse got to Jaden's parents' shop and got the girls a gift, had it wrapped nicely then rode hard to get back to the hospital so the gifts and test results could be presented to the two girls. The doctor was waiting for the charge nurse at the hospital's front doors and when the nurse arrived he took the gifts, said thank you then headed to the waiting room to tell the couples that they were in fact pregnant and give them their congratulatory gifts.

When the doctor walked into the waiting room, he held a sad look on his face as if the blood tests were negative and when the two couples saw his face their hearts dropped. Then the doctor got right up to them and smiled big, brought the gifts out from behind his back, and told them they were pregnant. Matthew stood silently in a state of shock, it was obvious this was his first baby so Andrew shook him gently as he told him he would get used to the idea half way through the pregnancy when he first felt the baby move while it was still the inner uterine, Matthew came around after Andrew shook him.

The doctor had things to do so he left the two couples and they needed to get back to the castle to move Bridgette and Matthew out of their bedroom into the chief's spare bedroom that sat next to Lynndia's bedroom so the construction of their home could get started. The two couples got out of the hospital and Andrew retrieved the horses and buggy from the hospital's stable boy then everyone got onto the buggy and they traveled back to the castle. Back at the castle, Andrew turned the horses and buggy over to Jaden to take care of while they went into the castle to start working on Bridgette and Matthew's bedroom. The construction crew was already there waiting for the go ahead to start building the home so the two couples went quickly to the bedroom, Bridgette and Matthew would pack while Andrew and Camillia would move everything to the other bedroom then when the packing was done if there were still things to move Bridgette and Matthew would help with that. Everything was flowing smoothly with the packing and moving of everything and Bridgette and Matthew did have everything packed before Camillia and Andrew could get the bags moved so at the end of the transition everyone was moving bags. The bedroom was empty so Andrew gave the construction crew the go ahead to start the construction of the new house. Bridgette told Camillia that day was certainly the mark for a new life because they were getting a house, a child, and had the opportunity to share it with family, it was so much to take in that it was almost unbelievable. Camillia told Bridgette she was very happy for her and she was glad that they wanted to share the experience with her and Andrew.

Matthew went back to work while Camillia took Bridgette to her office room to give her the notes she had for the conception healing and while Bridgette was looking over Camillia's notes Camillia sent for the chief with word to bring his notes. The chief showed up at Camillia and Andrew's side of the castle and the butler answered the door when he knocked so he took the chief to Camillia's office room to meet with her and Bridgette. Camillia welcomed the chief and offered him a seat so he sat down then Camillia told the chief that Bridgette was going to be their secretary for the conception healing project, she would put the proper notes together and keep a record of all the healings and their outcomes. The chief did not mind Bridgette being the secretary but did not understand how she was going to find the time to do the note taking and work as the nutritionist but he did not outwardly question it. The chief gave Bridgette his notes and she said she would start right away before the notes piled up and became too overwhelming because she already had ten couples to write about and keep track of and that night would bring at least ten more couples to write about and keep track of. Camillia told Bridgette if she needed anything to let her know.

Just then Jaden found his way to the office room because he was looking for Camillia and Andrew together and until he found them and spoke to them he could not do anymore work on the stable. Camillia stopped what she was saying to Bridgette and asked Jaden if she could be of some help and he told her he needed to speak to her and Andrew together so she asked him to give her a couple of minutes and she would be right with him, he said okay and waited in the family room. Bridgette told Camillia to go ahead and talk to Jaden that she knew what she had to do so Camillia thanked her then told the chief thank you for responding so quickly. The chief told Camillia that since she was finished with him he was going to the spiritual hall to see if anyone else had signed-up for the conception healing and make sure there was enough paper for the sign-up, Camillia told the chief she would see him at family time and he said he looked forward to seeing the family that day as every day. The chief and Camillia walked up the hallway together but Camillia stopped at the family room while the chief continued to walk for the front door. Camillia tells Jaden to go with her and together they would find Andrew so Jaden took Camilla by the hand and let her lead him around. They found Andrew in his and Camillia's bedroom and before Camillia could tell Andrew why they were there Jaden spoke up and told Andrew that he needed to talk to them about something and asked if they could find a place to sit together. Andrew asked Jaden if the topic of discussion was private and Jaden said no that they could talk in the family room so that was where they went.

Everyone got seated then Jaden told Andrew and Camillia he needed some supplies for the stable work but he wanted to tell them what he needed and the cost before just going down to the shop and getting the supplies. Andrew told Jaden that he had told him at the beginning of the project he could get what he needed and not to worry about the cost and Jaden said he would feel more comfortable if they knew what was being purchased and what the cost was for their approval as the job went along, he was not used to having money. Jaden was raised to have respect for others and to be as frugal as possible, Andrew and Camillia knew that so they decided to follow Jaden's work and approve things as they came along because they did not want to change the way the boy was taught to be. The couple took Jaden's list and total cost, looked it over thoroughly, approved it, then told Jaden he had better take their bigger buggy to fetch the things he needed and Jaden said okay and thank you. Jaden gave them both a hug then sprang out of his seat and ran for the front door, once outside he hitched up the horses to the big buggy and headed for his parents' shop.

When Jaden got to the shop, he hugged his parents then told his father what he needed to purchase and together they gathered up the items and got them onto the buggy then Jaden's father gave Jaden a receipt for the items they put into the buggy so Andrew and Camillia could pay the shop on their next visit. Jaden said he would see them at family time then got going back to the castle so he could get started back on the stable. Once Jaden had spent some time at the shop getting his supplies and traveling to and from the shop it was about family time but he had to unload the buggy and relieve the horses before he could go inside.

Bridgette and Camillia were the first one's in the family room to wait on the others to show up because they wanted to share their good news so badly and little by little the others did show up apart from Jaden. Andrew and Jaden's father volunteered to go and see what was keeping Jaden so long, maybe it was just that he was so engrossed in what he was doing in the stable that he lost track of time. When the two men got to Jaden, they found him unloading the buggy and he still had quite a bit to get off the buggy so his father and Andrew helped him finish unloading the buggy, he already had the horses unhitched and taken care of. When they were finished, Jaden thanked his father and Andrew for helping him then he told them he had some big plans for the stable that he had already drawn up and now with those supplies he could start the super-sized transformation. He was so excited to get it done so everyone could enjoy it, especially the animals.

When Jaden, his father, and Andrew entered the family room, Jaden announced that he was there lend apologized for his tardiness. Everyone told Jaden it was fine that he was late because he was never late so there must have been something important holding him back and they accepted his apology. With all the explanations and responses out of the way, everyone went on to the castle's private dining hall to sit at the big round table and share their day while they ate lunch. Just before the kitchen brought out lunch Bridgette's mother and father came out of the kitchen and got everyone's attention then her mother said there were two important announcements that needed to be made before lunch was brought out then she asked Bridgette and Camillia to stand up so they did and Bridgette's mother told everyone to congratulate the two girls because they would be bearing children. Everyone clapped and cheered, then the two girls sat back down as Bridgette's father told everyone that they had made a special meal for them to share and enjoy together in honor of the new babies.

At that point, the kitchen started bringing out plate after plate of food, it seemed like the serving platters would never end. The group ate themselves sick as they shared their day with one another, there was so much food left over that Bridgette stood up and asked for everyone's attention and when everyone got quiet she told them that she wanted a hand vote for who was for and against having left over food for dinner. Bridgette started with who was against having left over food for dinner and no one raised their hand, then she asked who was in favor of having left over food for dinner and everyone raised their hands, with the vote being done Bridgette announced that dinner was going to be left over lunch by popular vote then Bridgette thanked everyone for their participation and sat back down. There was still a lot of time for family time but everyone was so uncomfortable from eating too much that they just stayed in their chairs at the big round table and chose to talk. No one started a conversation for quite some time they all just sat there with looks of pain and suffering so Jaden started to share his plans for the stable with everyone and as he got to the intricate details no one could believe that a child as young as he was could be so brilliant, the construction crew along with the castle decorator could not have come up with anything so wondrous for a stable.

CHAPTER SIXTY FIVE

At that point, Andrew asked Jaden if there was anything that the construction crew and the castle decorator could help him with and he said yes, he could use their help now that the offer was made. Jaden said he was going to redo the design that he originally did so he could do what was best for the animals and helpful to the workers, that excited Jaden even more and he was not deterred by the fact that he would have to wait for the construction crew to finish with Bridgette and Matthew's home. Jaden said he would need that time to have everything properly planned and drawn up then he would have to go back and check his supplies and make sure he had everything he needed and return anything he did not need if that became the case.

The adults were impressed at how Jaden's mind worked but they knew he was more intelligent than most boys his age and unlike most people he liked a dramatic challenge, the stable project just went to prove that there was no stopping Jaden from doing anything he put his mind to and with that realization one could deduce that he would make a wonderful veterinarian. Jaden had proven to have much more energy that the adults, he worked all day as the castle's stable boy, before his stable boy job and after he worked on extra projects, he had general schooling after dinner, after general schooling he had veterinary training, and finally he was on call with the town's only veterinarian. Jaden seemed unstoppable but with his busy life he did not play like other kids did and he was not meeting other kids his age and that concerned his parents because they felt he may be growing up too fast and with his conditioning of being on the go all the time they were also worried that he would never take on a wife and have a family. Andrew and Camillia had listened to Jaden's parent's concerns and assured them that he would slow down after the schooling was done and eventually he would run out of projects to find then all he would have left was his job as the stable boy and family life which would force him to seek out other relationships to fill his voids because he would not be used to sitting around.

Family time was now over and everyone was still painfully full, it seemed more appealing to go take a nap than going back to work but they had responsibilities therefore they must go back to work and use that day as a learning experience to control their portions of food. Jaden went out to the stable and started to make new drafts for better ideas for the project than originally thought of. Bridgette went to Camillia's office room to finish with the documentation of the ten couples who were healed the previous night, Matthew went back to walking about the castle for security reasons and checking with each guard that had a post on how they were doing, the chief caught up with Andrew and Camillia to give some more names of couples who wanted to be healed to have children and he made sure to let them know he put another paper up for more people to sign if there were any. Everyone was back to work like there was no problem with the hope of working off lunch. Andrew and Camillia needed to go by the science hall to check on the scientists and let them know they were not forgotten about. Besides, the couple was curious if they had any new projects they were working on and if not it would be up to Andrew and Camillia to get them back to work again. Andrew and Camillia went outside and had Jaden saddle two horses so they could go to the science hall and he got the horses ready quickly then got them to the couple and off they went while Jaden went back to drawing up some blueprints.

At the science hall, the couple got off their horses and went inside to see what the scientists were up to, when they entered the building the new head scientist noticed them coming in and he greeted them immediately. They approached each other in the middle of the laboratory, they shook hands, then Andrew asked the new head scientist how things were going. The new head scientist told Andrew and Camillia that they were working on technological developments to make their society better without making them rely on science like the humans had done prior to the last war that ended up on making humans extinct, the only good thing that came out of that incident was the development of a new species which was the pale ones and that was nothing short of a miracle. Andrew asked what type of things he was speaking of and the scientist gave examples of their products such as some spindles and shears so they could use sheep's wool for material to lighten the need of animal hide for the leather and fur, tranquilizer medicine for the pickers so while they were outside the great wall picking fruits, vegetables, flowers, and more if they ran into wild animals they would not have to kill them unnecessarily, they could just put them into a short sleep in which they would awake from after twenty minutes or so.

Andrew cut the new head scientist short so he could ask him who was approving the items he was having the science hall produce and he said nobody then Andrew told him the two examples he heard were fine but they needed to construct a full list of their creations for his approval and from there on out products needed to be approved by him or the queen and the scientist asked forgiveness for his indiscretion, the king gave forgiveness and a twenty-four-hour period to get the already mentioned list to him and the new head scientist bowed his head and said yes sir. Camillia told the new head scientist that Andrew was not scolding him or trying to belittle him but science always has and will always tread in deep waters they were just there to keep history from repeating itself.

At that point, their visit was over and the couple left the science hall while the new head scientist ran to his office room to start the list for the king and queen. Andrew and Camillia mounted their horses and rode back to the castle when they got there they peeked in on Jaden to see how he was coming along on his project and he was so into it he did not realize the couple was there so Andrew simply asked how it was going, Jaden was startled and quickly turned toward the couple then giggled and said he had not heard them ride up. Andrew told him that he was fine but to remember his job came before his project and Jaden apologized, Andrew told him no apology was necessary then he gave the boy a hug. Jaden took the couple's horses and cared for them while they went into the castle.

As Andrew shut the front door of the castle after entering, he felt some resistance so he opened the door and looked out then he saw Jaden there trying to get in so Andrew opened the door wider so Jaden could fit through. The couple was not sure why Jaden was coming into the castle so early but came to find out it was not early at all, it was dinner time and the family was in the family room waiting for Andrew, Camillia, and Jaden. No one was hungry but they decided as a group that they would snack a little on the leftover lunch meal so they went to the castle's private dining hall to sit at the big round table again, the kitchen staff brought the food out and everyone served themselves small portions of everything. No one ate much and the conversation between the family members consisted of small talk. Everyone was tired and still stuffed from the lunch meal and just wanted the night to be over but there was still some work after dinner. Everyone got up from the big round table and went to do what they still needed to get done. Camillia and Andrew went to Camillia's office room to prepare for more conception healings, the chief went to the couples family room to run couples back to the office room and back to the front door until all the couples for that evening were done, Jaden went to his bedroom in the castle to prepare for his general tutoring and veterinary tutoring, Jaden's mother went to the couples children's play room to tutor the three of the couples oldest children, Bridgette was in Camillia's office room with the couple to take notes on the healing procedure, Andrew was posted in the family room for security reasons due to all the pale ones that would be going through there, and the rest of the castle's workers were doing what they needed to do to wrap up their chore for the night.

Five minutes after the couple entered Camillia's office room, the chief brought the first couple for healing and sat them in the chairs for the couple to take over while he would wait outside the door so he could show them to the front door then get the next couple to take them to the office room. Andrew and Camillia went through the same process with everyone, explaining what the couple needed to do, explaining what they were going to do to the couple, performing the procedure, then calling the chief for him to do his part. Andrew and Camillia did thirteen healings that night while Bridgette wrote as fast as she could then during the day on the next day she would record her notes into a book of records. The whole event for that night took an hour and a half.

By the time the couple finished their healings for the night, Jaden finished both of his schoolings and Jaden's mother finished tutoring the couple's three oldest children. The night was now over and everyone could go to their own quarters and wind down for the night; that was a relief for everyone. Jaden and his parents went home, the chief went to his side of the castle, everyone left in the castle was in their own quarters, and so Andrew and Camillia went to their bedroom. The couple changed from their day clothes into their bed clothes then went straight to their bed and lay down, they got into a cuddling position and Andrew placed his hand on Camillia's belly then they went to sleep.

Three hours later, the couple's mini angel was there singing her wake up song, it took a bit longer to wake them up than it usually took but they did wake up and greet her in the usual way. The miniangel congratulated the couple on the conception of the new baby then they told her thank you. She told the couple that their children had been visiting the miniangels in the forest through astral projection and they had also been keeping them up to date on what had been happening around the castle and with them, she then said that they need not go over thirteen healings per night and since Camillia was pregnant they should stay with only ten healings because when she healed the unborn child did too and it was too much for the child, Camillia thanked her miniangel for the warning and said she was happy to know the children were close to the miniangels. Camillia was having a challenging time staying awake so the miniangel told the couple that she should go so they could get some rest, Camillia did not want her to go but she was gone before Camillia could plead for her to stay and she did not have the strength to do astral projection. The couple lay back down in the positions they were in and fell asleep again.

When it was time to wake up again, the couple felt well rested and ready for the day, their stomach's even felt normal again. Andrew and Camillia got out of bed and changed from bedclothes into day clothes then they did their teeth and hair in the bathroom, once they were done Camillia left the bedroom and went to find Bridgette so she could find out how she was feeling, Andrew went to the castle's private dining hall while Camillia went to Bridgette's bedroom. Bridgette was in her bedroom sitting on her bed crying and Matthew was already out and about in the castle somewhere. Camillia asked Bridgette what was wrong and she said she did not know she just started crying for no reason, Camillia chuckled a bit then told her it was the pregnancy hormones and it would stabilize soon. Bridgette got up and dried her eyes then the two girls went to the castle's private dining hall for breakfast. When the girls got to the big roundtable, Andrew could tell that Bridgette had been crying so he softly asked her if she was okay and she told him she was. Andrew told Bridgette to sit on one side of him and for Camillia to sit on the other side of him so he would have both of his pregnant ladies with him and he would be able to help both if they should need it, the women thanked Andrew and sat where he had requested. Bridgette's mother brought breakfast out to the three of them and told them if they needed anything else to just let her know, they said okay then started to eat. When they were done eating, Andrew told the girls that he wanted to check on the progress of the house construction and invited them to go with him, they said they would be glad to go so off they went.

When the three of them got to the home, they found that it was nearly done and that excited Bridgette. The head construction worker told the trio that the home would be finished some time that day. Bridgette let out a squeal then wrapped her arms around the head construction worker's neck and hugged him tightly. He told her she was welcome as he peeled her arms from around his neck so he could breathe normally again. When Bridgette's excitement tapered down some, Andrew told the head constrction worker that he had another job for him to do as soon as the blueprints were done and the head construction worker told Andrew to let him know when it was time to start the job and he would have his crew ready then Andrew thanked him. Andrew, Camillia, and Bridgette were on their way to the family room when Bridgette asked Camillia if she would let the castle decorator work for her to decorate the house how she wanted it but to help make it flow like she had done with all the rooms in the castle and Camillia told Bridgette that she would do anything for her, her and the other girls were like sisters to her and she took that very seriously. Bridgette said thank you then got sentimental with Camillia and told her that she was like a sister to her also along with the other girls then Bridgette got an idea, she told Camillia that they should have a girl's night with just the sisterhood.

Andrew told the two of them that was a prime idea and they should do it because before becoming pale ones they were inseparable but since being pale ones they had not shared the same closeness and that was a shame. Camillia told Andrew and Bridgette that they would have to do it in the daytime because they had the healings in the evenings but it was a wonderful idea plus doing it in the day time they could visit some shops and do some girl shopping together and they could go to the women's shop and get pampered together, Bridgette asked Camillia if they could make it a once a week thing and Camillia told Bridgette that it sounded like a plan. Andrew suggested to Bridgette to make up some invitation cards for the girl's and to make sure the cards also said the girl's must make a reservation so they would be able to plan proper transportation, Bridgette said okay and dashed off to do the cards because she wanted to get them off as soon as possible. Andrew told Camillia that he would be the chauffeur and take them anywhere they wanted to go and wait outside for them, he added that they could take their time and make a full day of it. Camillia told Andrew he was so good to her and she really loved him and appreciated what he always did for her, he told her he loved her also and would do anything for her.

Andrew and Camillia's sentimental moment was shortened when Jaden came bursting into the family room calling out that he had done it, Andrew asked Jaden what he had done and Jaden rushed over to the couple and shoved a paper into Andrew's face again saying he had done it. The couple could see Jaden's excitement so Andrew quickly looked at the paper Jaden had pushed in his face then realized it was a schematic of the stable showing the changes to be made. When Andrew noticed what the paper was, he looked at it more carefully then he told Jaden he liked what he saw, there were some major changes and the stable would be larger than what it currently was. Andrew showed Camillia the paper and explained the changes to her then she told Jaden it was amazing how he managed to draw up the schematics from his imagination then Jaden asked the couple if they approved the changes and they said yes at the same time. Andrew took one last look at the schematics before he would give the paper back to Jaden then Andrew noticed there was to be a large area in the stable that did not seem to be necessary so he asked Jaden what the area was to be used for and Jaden told Andrew it was for veterinary use, Camillia intervened and told Jaden he had thought of everything. Andrew told Jaden he had some good news for him then Jaden got serious and asked what the good news was and Andrew told Jaden that the construction crew would be finished with the house that they were building on that day so they would be able to start the stable construction on the next day and better yet, they would be working for him.

Jaden was honored that Andrew and Camillia would let him head the stable project instead of an adult then Andrew told Jaden that even though he was still so young, he was more responsible and intelligent than most grown men and Jaden started to sob in sentiment then he fell into Andrew and hugged him. Camillia reached over and put her hand on Jaden's back, patted his back then told him they loved him dearly and that he was one of their children and they were very proud of him. Jaden left Andrew's arms to give Camillia a hug and as she hugged Jaden she caressed his head while telling him he was a very special boy and they were proud of him, Jaden said thank you and he loved them also. Jaden stood up and straightened himself up then said he had been away from his job post long enough and he had better get back out there, Andrew and Camillia told Jaden they would see him later and to have a good day.

Andrew turned to Camillia and told her they needed to change their daily schedule so they were not doing healing in the evenings and running themselves rugged, she agreed then asked what he had in mind. Andrew said he had a schedule in mind but wanted her to come up with a schedule that included girl time then they could compare schedule potentials and find one that worked for them and he reminded her to include the chief as a resource and she said okay and that she would write it down on paper. Andrew told Camillia that writing the potential schedule on paper was great because they could see the layout of their day and physically compare notes. The couple went to Camillia's office room so they could work out their own daily schedule and when they got there, Bridgette was just finishing up with the girl's invitations for their weekly time together. Bridgette had a few different invitation cards made up so Camillia could pick the one she liked the best or share some ideas to make them better, Bridgette handed Camillia the invitations and Camillia liked all of them but she told Bridgette what she liked most about each one so that Bridgette cold make one invitation that had the best qualities of each original card. Bridgette sat behind the desk in Camillia's seat while Andrew and Camillia sat in front of the desk and they all three were busy at work.

It did not take long for Bridgette to combine the favorite things from each card into one card; she was an excellent artist and had been since she was a youngster, and everyone used to go to her to do artwork for them before she had become a pale one.

Andrew had his idea of a daily schedule on paper rather quickly because he had been thinking about it for a few days so he was waiting for Camillia to get her thoughts on paper so they could find a compromise that worked to their benefit. Although it took a bit longer for Camillia to get her thoughts of a daily schedule on paper she had finally done it and was ready to show Andrew. Andrew and Camillia stayed in the office room to compare notes but before they got a chance to start, Bridgette asked for Camillia's attention to check out the final draft of the girl's day invitation and as Camillia was looking at the final invitation draft Andrew was looking over her shoulder and became amazed at how well the artwork was. Andrew told Bridgette the art was of professional quality. Bridgette thanked Andrew then Camillia told Bridgette she loved the outcome and it was perfect for the event then Bridgette thanked Camillia for the compliment and she said she was going to go to the copy shop then when she got back she would address the envelopes and get them off in the mail. Camillia told Bridgette to make sure the time to meet was left blank and to let the girls know that it would be announced when it got closer to their first date and Bridgette said okay then went on her way.

CHAPTER SIXTY SIX

In Bridgette's absence, the couple could compare notes they made for a new daily schedule that would suit their needs and still serve the community so they held the papers side by side and compared what they had. It was almost like seeing a mirror image while looking at the two papers, they both started by writing the meal times then working around them and of course family time stayed the same and kept the same amount of time. The couple had the same idea of doing healings after breakfast so they did not run into bedtime then they would have time for two errands before the lunch hour and family time.

After family time, they could do the errands that only occurred weekly or biweekly such as prenatal visits, girls' day out, and errands that just happen to come up and with that they would be finished with everything by the dinner hour and have the rest of the evenings to themselves. Andrew and Camillia laughed about having the same idea for their schedule but they were not surprised that they thought alike because the longer they were married the more they had thought the same and became able to finish each other's sentences without using telepathy which was the way healthy relationships were according to both of their parent's. Camillia rewrote the schedule neatly so they could post it in the office room in the event someone needed them they could look at the posted schedule and track them down easily because there was occasionally an emergency where someone needed the king and queen although, they were not true emergencies to Andrew and Camillia they were to the individuals who had the situation.

Now that the new schedule was made and posted the couple needed to retrieve the chief and make sure he knew of the changes and where to find the post in the event he needed them so they left their side of the castle to go to the chief's side of the castle. On the chief's side of the castle they knocked on the front door and greeted the chief's butler when he answered the door and he already knew the couple was there to see the chief so he took them to the chief's garden where he was. The chief was surprised to see the couple because he figured they would be busy with errands, the couple got straight to the point and informed the chief that they had a radical change to their schedule and it was posted in Camillia's office room in case he needed them then Andrew told the chief that night would be the last night they would be doing healings. The chief assumed that the couple would not be doing anymore healings but Andrew quickly told him they were but they were going to be after the breakfast hour because they were getting too run down doing them after the dinner hour, the chief was relieved and told the couple he wanted to see the new schedule so he could see where he fit in.

Andrew, Camillia, and the chief left that side of the castle to go to the other side so the chief could see the new schedule and on the way the chief told Andrew and Camillia he wanted a copy of the schedule to keep in his office room for quick access, Andrew said okay and Camillia said it was a smart idea. Now at the couple's side of the castle, Camillia walked ahead to her office room to copy the schedule for the chief while Andrew kept the chief company in the family room and while they were having a general conversation they could hear men's voices coming up the hallway so the two men became silent so they could listen to the voices and try to establish who they were and what was occurring. Only a couple of minutes passed, by then a crew of men walked around the corner and it was the construction crew on their way to report to Andrew that the house was completed and to find out what the next job was. Andrew informed the head of the construction crew that the next job was the stable, it was going to get a complete overhaul and the blueprints were finished for them to look at then the head worker told Andrew that they were ready to start the new job that day because the day was still early and they did not like to have empty time on their hands. Andrew said very well then stood up, told the chief to join them, and led everyone to the stable to find Jaden.

Jaden saw everyone coming so he met them outside of the stable and when they met up Andrew told the crew they were going to be working for the boy and the head crew member asked Andrew if he was joking and Andrew told the head crew man that he was serious that the boy drew up the blueprints and they would answer to him then Andrew asked the head crew man if he still wanted the job, he said yes. The head construction worker was sour about working for a child, he had never heard or done such a thing. Andrew told Jaden the construction crew was ready to get started on the stable work when he was ready and Jaden told them he was ready that moment so the head construction worker introduced himself to Jaden and Jaden returned the act then told him he had a blueprint of what he wanted done then Jaden went to the stable to get it.

The head construction worker waited for Jaden to return and when Jaden returned he gave the blueprint to the head construction worker and when he saw Jaden's work he was beside himself, the head construction worker finally realized he was not dealing with a typical kid. The head construction worker told Andrew and Jaden that he owed them an apology because he did not realize Jaden was a prodigy; he said the blueprints were very well done and he did not know any professional that could have done better. The head construction worker took Jaden's blueprint to the other workers to discuss what they would be doing and to assign each worker to a task While Andrew and Jaden observed the workers, Jaden thanked Andrew again and Jaden told Andrew he would not let him down then Andrew told Jaden he already knew that. The head construction worker approached Jaden then asked him what he was going to do with all the animals and Jaden told him that he and some of the other children in the community were going to take the livestock to his barn and just keep some of the horses tied in front because they were consistently needed then Andrew asked Jaden if the livestock would fit in his family's barn and he said it would be a tight fit but it was only a temporary housing because he knew the construction crew would finish the project quickly and Andrew said very well. The head construction worker told Jaden they were ready to work and since the project was for him they would not mind offering their services to herd the livestock to his barn and they would do it off the clock as an act of apology for treating him with disrespect in the beginning.

Jaden told him it would be appreciated and he would accept their apology and he understood that they thought they were dealing with an ordinary kid because until people got to know him they treated him the same way because they also thought the same thing then the worker told Jaden that he learned a valuable lesson of not judging others. Now that everybody understood everybody the worker told Jaden it was time to get the livestock transferred to the other barn and Jaden said okay then the worker told his subordinates to start on herding the animals for the transfer to Jaden's barn and they all complied. It took an hour for the animals to get transferred from one barn to the other but there was still a lot of time to get quite a bit done.

The head construction worker asked Jaden to stay with him and help keep the other workers in line and doing what they needed to be doing and Jaden said he would be honored then he took the head workers hand and asked him if they could be friends and the head worker told Jaden he would be honored. Now that the head worker and Jaden had a solid understanding of each other, Andrew felt comfortable leaving the two of them alone so he went back into the castle to be with Camillia and the chief, he could not wait to tell the two of them about what just happened. When Andrew got to the family room back to Camillia and the chief, they asked if everything was okay and Andrew told them what conspired with Jaden and the head worker then Camillia told Andrew how wonderful it was that Jaden was accepted for who he was because as far as Camillia was concerned Jaden was a special boy.

As soon as Andrew got comfortable in the couch, there was a knock at the front door so the butler answered the door and it was the veterinarian coming for Jaden because there was an emergency call and he was to have Jaden on calls so he could learn first-hand and help where he could so Andrew told the veterinarian that Jaden was out at the stable and he would fetch the boy while the veterinarian waited in the family room. When Andrew got to the stable, he told the head worker that Jaden was needed for an emergency veterinarian call and the head worker called out for Jaden because he was in the stable with the workers instructing them on what to do, Jaden came out of the stable and asked Andrew what he needed and Andrew told him the veterinarian was waiting for him to go on an emergency call then Jaden ran into the castle's family room. The veterinarian and Jaden left immediately to go to the home where the call was for a mare giving a breech birth when the veterinarian told Jaden what the call was for he knew they needed to move quickly, and they did.

In the meantime, Andrew, Camillia, and the chief were chatting in the family room when the other family members started to arrive, the trio had lost track of time so the lunch hour had crept up on them then suddenly everyone was there and ready to eat while sharing their day so everyone except Jaden went to the castle's private dining hall to take their places at the big roundtable. Jaden's parents noticed he was missing and questioned his whereabouts then Andrew told them he was out with the veterinarian on an emergency call and he did not know when he would return. Jaden's parents were happy that he was getting some hands-on experience and they knew the kitchen would save his lunch then feed him when he returned but it did not make them miss him any less.

When everyone was finished eating and sharing, family time was over so everyone said their until tomorrow then got up from the big roundtable to get back to their duties and just then Jaden walked into the castle's private dining hall. Everyone said hello to Jaden then left, including his parents. Jaden ate his lunch alone then got back out to the stable to work with the construction crew, they were anxious to see the final product because they had never seen a stable done how that one was designed because all the stables in the community were the same and this one was glamorous for housing animals. The stable was designed like an open house with quite a few rooms and most of the spaces were obvious what they were going to be used for but there were a few rooms that the crew could not figure out what they were going to be used for and the men did not want to appear stupid by asking Jaden what room was for what purpose.

Jaden could see the look of curiosity on the head workers face as he kept looking at the blueprint of the new stable so Jaden figured he would clarify what room was for what purpose in a non-threatening way as to not offend the head worker's intelligence. Jaden asked the head worker if he could point out some details on the blueprint that were important and could be easily missed but would help the construction go smoother for the guy's and the head worker welcomed Jaden's offer without hesitation. Jaden took a pencil to label each room on the blueprint as he told the head worker what they were going to be for and by the time Jaden finished, the head worker told Jaden that it all made sense at that time because before the explanation there were some questions about a few of the rooms designs then Jaden told the head worker not to hesitate to question or make comments about the work because he had never done a project like that and that it was a learning experience for him. Jaden could feel the discomfort that the head worker had in response to working for him so he told the head worker that he respected his experience and intelligence with projects such as that, the head worker just said thanks then they observed the rest of the workers and their work in silence.

Meanwhile, in the castle, Camillia caught up with Bridgette in the hallway and told her that she and Andrew's schedule had changed effectively the following day and she needed to be aware of that because it would affect her schedule also. Bridgette said she was fine with the schedule change then asked what she needed to change with her schedule then Camillia told her about the healings being changed to occur after the breakfast hour so they were not having to stay up so late and Bridgette said that was an innovative idea because that would allow her to stay up to date with the notes and not a day behind. Camillia also told Bridgette that they would be doing girls day right after the lunch hour and family time, she just needed the day of the week that she chose for it to be on and Bridgette said that she put a small note in the envelopes with the invitations for the girls to vote on a day so they would have some say in the plan and to assure that it was convenient for everyone involved and Camilla said that was a clever thing to do.

Bridgette told Camillia that she left an invitation for her on her desk in her office room And Camillia told her thank you then she asked Bridgette if she would mind if she used the castle decorator before she had the castle decorator do her house and Bridgette told Camilla it would be fine then Camillia asked Bridgette if she was interested in helping with a task that involved the castle decorator and redoing another room in the castle for the healings to be done in and she told Camillia it sounded fun then Bridgette asked Camillia when she was going to start working on the new room, Camillia told her as soon as she could get the decorator there. Camillia summoned one of her runners to retrieve the castle decorator and while the runner was gone Camillia told Bridgette what she wanted to do with the room and Bridgette said the room sounded like a place to go when one needed to relax then Camillia told Bridgette that was the whole idea.

The two girls started to plan some of the items they wanted the room to have in it and the pattern for the seats and pillows then Camillia asked Bridgette if putting a desk into the room would take away from the relaxed feel of the room and Bridgette told Camillia it would depend on where she put the desk and how it was placed then Bridgette told Camillia to explain in detail to the castle decorator what she wanted the room to offer anyone who was to be in there and the castle decorator would do a wonderful job to make it happen because she was a great decorator and had already worked wonders for other rooms in the castle, Camillia agreed then relaxed and right then the castle decorator appeared in the hallway. The castle decorator would have waited in the family room for the butler to tell Camillia she was there but the castle decorator could hear Camillia and Bridgette talking in the hallway so she followed the sound and found Camillia not far away. Camillia and Bridgette welcomed the castle decorator then Camillia led Bridgette and the castle decorator to the room that was going to be used for the healings so they could see what they had to work with.

The castle decorator looked the room over then told Camillia it was perfect for what she wanted it for and she had many ideas but she needed to know in detail what she expected of it and if she had anything specific she wanted in there now was the time to tell her so Camillia told the castle decorator what she had told Bridgette and she was impressed with the ideas Camillia had for the room. Camillia asked the castle decorator how soon she thought she could have the new room completed and she told Camillia she could have the room done that afternoon but before she started it she would need to make a trip to a few shops to get some things for the room then Camillia told the castle decorator to take her buggy so she could transport everything at one time, the castle decorator thanked Camillia then headed for the front door. Camillia told Bridgette she needed to catch up with Andrew and Bridgette told Camillia she needed to finish the healing notes from the night before but she did not have much to do so she would be caught up by the time they healed again then the two girls said until later and went their separate ways. By the time Bridgette was in Camillia's office room, Camillia realized Andrew was not in the castle so she went to the stable to see if he was with Jaden and the construction workers and he was so Camillia asked Andrew how things were going with the stable project then he told her Jaden was doing an excellent job at keeping things moving without offending the intelligence of the adults and that was important so they could keep the workers under the impression that they had control of the project so they would work at their normal pace and finish the project quickly and efficiently.

As Andrew and Camillia went back into the castle, the castle decorator had just returned from the few shops she needed to go to so she could get the things she needed for the new room of relaxation. She gathered the new things from the buggy and went into the castle to get started on the new room. While the castle decorator worked on the room of relaxation and Bridgette caught up on her healing notes in the office room, the chief was doing more interviews for couples who wanted to conceive and still no one failed to be acceptable which was good so Andrew and Camillia were in their bedroom spending some time together and talking about how much things had changed for them during their reign. Andrew and Camillia were going on an hour of having some down time when someone knocked on their bedroom door so Andrew got up off the bed to answer the door and it was a runner from the science hall with the list of things to be approved for production to improve their society. Andrew took the list from the runner, thanked him, then took the list over to the bed where Camillia was.

The list was long and Andrew wanted to approve as much of the objects as possible but he had to be careful that he did not approve anything that would have their society dependent on science, the objects had to be simple things the commoners could produce if necessary and there had to be enough materials to build the objects where they would not deplete anything. Andrew wanted the science hall to understand they were a tool for society not a necessity to the existence of society and with that in mind Andrew and Camillia agreed that they both had to approve an object before it was accepted and with that they started to go over the list slowly. After seeing the first few items, Andrew suggested to Camillia that they also include the chief with the science halls list since he helped found their society he would be able to keep in mind the vision that the community was based upon and they could learn a lot with the chief helping them.

Andrew and Camillia agreed that the chief's influence could help them to be better rulers of the land of grandeur by allowing them to gain the pre-set vision to rule under and pass down to their children. There were only four founders and the chief was the last of them. They knew the history of the founders and why the new society was brought about but they never knew of the guidelines that may have been set and now wondered why the chief never passed them down. The couple had been at their side of the castle for quite some time and needed to get away so instead of sending a runner for the chief to be brought over they decided to go together to the chief's side of the castle for a different view then Camillia said that while they were outside they might as well see how the stable was getting along and Andrew answered that it would be okay. When the couple got outside, the head construction worker saw them then waved his hands and called out to them to get their attention, his actions and boisterous tone did get the couple's attention so they changed their direction and walked toward him.

CHAPTER SIXTY SEVEN

When the head worker and the couple met up, the head worker asked the couple if they would mind them working through the night because they were so intrigued by the project that they could not wait to see the final product, Andrew looked at Camillia and she looked at him as though they were asking for one another's opinion then Andrew told the head worker it would be fine. The head worker told the couple not to go anywhere then he called Jaden over to them and when Jaden got to them he asked if everything was okay and the head worker told him everything was fine then the head worker asked Andrew and Camillia if Jaden was willing could he stay at the castle that night in case they needed him for something pertaining to the stable. Camillia told the head worker that Jaden had a bedroom with them and it was fine with them if he stayed over but they needed permission from his parents then the head worker said he would ask but he needed to know who they were and where they were. Jaden offered to take the head worker to his parents' shop and ask them to stay the night over at the castle and before anyone could say anything he added that he was sure they would allow him to stay over so the head worker told the crew to keep working while he was gone at Jaden's parents shop but if they became unsure of anything to stop and Jaden could clarify whatever needed to be clarified when they returned, the crew agreed and kept on working. Andrew told Jaden he and Camillia would be at the chief's side of the castle and to let them know what his parents say and Jaden said okay then he and the head worker saddled up their horses and rode off while the couple headed for the chief's side of the castle.

Andrew knocked on the chief's front door and the butler answered the door, he knew the couple was there to see the chief so he took them back to the chief's office room and told them to wait until the door opened then they could slip in between interviews then the couple told the butler thank you as he walked away and they waited for the interview to be over. After only a few minutes of waiting, the chief's office room door opened and a couple came out happily heading for the front door so Andrew and Camillia went into the office room and apologized to the chief for interrupting his interviews and he said it was fine then asked them what he could do for them, Andrew told the chief that he and Camillia wanted his help with the list the science hall gave them to get approval to make some products for the bettering of the colony's functionality. While the chief did seem interested to see the list he asked the couple what he could possibly do to help them approve or disapprove the items and that was when Camillia spoke up telling the chief that she and Andrew knew he was one of four founding members of the colony and the only one left of the founders so they wanted to learn of the vision that the colony was founded on so they could be better rulers and keep the colony thriving in innocence.

As the chief was ready to say something to Andrew and Camillia, Jaden rushed into the office room with excitement and told the couple that he and his parents were going to stay the night at the castle then Camillia told Jaden it was wonderful news and she looked forward to it. Jaden told the couple and the chief that the stable should be done the next day and the construction workers said they would help put everything back into the stable and help organize those things then the workers would help retrieve all the animals from his parent's barn. Camillia told Jaden that it sounded like he had everything under control and he said he did then he turned around and ran out of the chief's side of the castle to go back to the stable on the couple's side of the castle. The chief, Andrew, and Camillia went back to talking about the science hall's list and the chief understood why the couple wanted his guidance so he said he would contribute his time to helping them understand the guidelines that the colony was built on then they could work on the list without him. Andrew told the chief there was no hurry to get their lesson about the colony's guidelines done and he was not worried about dealing with the science hall's list once he and Camillia were fully educated by the chief then the chief told the couple that he had a couple more interviews to do then he could devote his time to them, the couple said okay and for him to send for them when he was ready to do the lesson then they left his side of the castle to go back to their side of the castle.

Once they got home, the couple found Bridgette looking for Camillia to let her know she was up to date with her healing notes and that she also got all the invitations from the other girls and they all picked the same afternoon to do girls day so Camillia told Bridgette to go ahead and plan for their chosen day and she would make herself available. Bridgette told Camillia the girls voted unanimously on Wednesday for girl's day then Camillia told Bridgette that Wednesday was perfect for her also and Bridgette said that would have been the day she would pick as well. Camillia asked Bridgette if anyone had reserved for girl's day yet and she said not yet but she was going to send out letters to everyone to let them know Wednesday was the chosen day and to remind them to reserve their attendance. Bridgette left the couple to go back to the office room to write the letters to the girl's so she could get them out on time for the upcoming Wednesday, Andrew and Camillia went to their family room to wait for the chief to summon them but it was getting close to the dinner hour so they realized that the chief may not be able to educate them until the next day because after the dinner hour the couple had conception healings to do and the chief was to assist with the couples while Bridgette took notes.

Finally, the dinner hour was upon the community so the chief was finished with conception interviews until the next day, Bridgette finished the notes for the girl's and their special day together and got them in the mail so she went to the castle's private dining hall to prepare for dinner then Matthew, Andrew, and Camillia entered the castle's private dining hall for the dinner hour. Everyone was waiting for Jaden and his parents to arrive then the kitchen crew could serve dinner, once everyone in the castle's private dining hall got into their seats Jaden and his parents got there and sat in their seats then the kitchen crew started to serve dinner. Everyone at the big round table ate and shared some more of their day since family time ended and it was a pleasant experience for everyone.

Dinner lasted a bit longer than usual because of the conversation and everyone there participating in it so when they were all done socializing and eating it was time for the adults to get back to work and for Jaden to go to his tutoring sessions. As the kitchen crew cleared the big round table, everyone said see you then went their separate ways, Andrew, Camillia, and Bridgette went to Camillia's office room, the chief went to the family room to wait on couples to show up for their conception healing, Matthew went to the family room to assure safety and organization amongst the couples that would be arriving, Jaden's mother went to tutor the couple's three oldest children, Jaden went to his bedroom in the castle to wait for his tutors, Jaden's father hung out in the family room entertaining couples while his wife and son were taking care of their business.

The chief told the Andrew and Camillia he only had ten couples in the family room waiting for a conception healing but if they felt they could do more he would send runners out to get more couples then Andrew told the chief he did not want Camillia doing more than ten healings while she was pregnant with Connor, the chief said that was fine and he would keep that in mind. The chief asked Camillia if she was ready to do healings and she said yes then the chief went to the family room to get the first couple and while the chief was getting the first couple, Bridgette prepared herself to take the notes. It took two and a half hours for Andrew and Camillia to finish the ten conception healings but the night still seemed to go by fast for everyone and by the time Andrew and Camillia were finished with the healings, Jaden's tutoring was done, the couple's three oldest children were finished with their tutoring, Bridgette decided to work on the healing notes the next day, and Matthew saw the last of the guests out of the front door. Most of the castle's staff were already in their quarters getting ready for bed and the chief left to go to his side of the castle and get in his bed, Andrew, Camillia, Bridgette, Matthew, Jaden and his parents were headed for their quarters so they could go to bed also.

Now the whole castle was asleep, two hours had passed then the couple's mini angel appeared in their bedroom and she sang her wake up song and the couple woke up with no problems. The miniangel and the couple greeted one another in the usual way then the miniangel told Camillia she was happy that she took her advice and did only ten healings due to her pregnancy and Camillia told the miniangel she knew what was best for the children whether they were intrauterine or already birthed. The miniangel asked the couple if they had used any of their special talents and they both said no, Camillia told her angel that their days had been so busy that her and Andrew had not had a chance to do anything extra but they had changed their schedule around so they would have extra together time starting the next day and the miniangel was happy to hear the news of a daily regimen change.

The miniangel told the couple she was worried about their schedule as it was because they were not getting enough down time to spend time with one another or sleep and Camillia told the miniangel that now they would be able to get all their tasks attended to, spend time with one another, see her and the other angels, and work on fine tuning their abilities that they had just found out about. The couple's miniangel told them it sounded like they finally got everything under control then Camillia told the miniangel that they just found out her and Andrew did not know a great deal of necessary information about their society and they talked the chief into educating them but they were concerned about why he had not told them in the beginning of their reign. The miniangel told Camillia that the angels were there long before the pale ones had come along and the founders knew of them, as the new race and the angels worked together to set up the compound and how it was to be ruled then she said that just as her and Andrew were to keep the angels a secret, so were the four founders and that may be why the chief had not educated them.

Andrew told the miniangel that if the chief kept that in mind he may not give them a full education which would hold him and Camillia back from making the best decisions possible for the community. The miniangel told the couple to go to the chief and tell him the three of you need to talk. Then she told the couple to reveal their knowledge of the mini angels and their dinosaur tail to him and she believed the chief would open-up to them and give them a full education. The miniangel told the couple to reveal their extraordinary gifts to the chief, let him know their children also had the gifts, then explain how the gifts would be affected every time the children reproduced with a regular pale one and the couple told the miniangel they would do as she had instructed them to do. The miniangel told the couple she had to go so they said goodbye and the miniangel disappeared, Andrew and Camillia nestled down in their bed and Andrew held onto Camillia like usual making sure he had a hand on her belly to make it like he was holding the unborn baby then they went to sleep.

An hour before it would be time to wake up, the miniangel woke the couple up again with her beautiful wake up song and the couple was surprised to see her so soon, they asked her if there was some sort of emergency then she quickly said no she was back because she needed to tell them a couple of things. Andrew and Camillia asked the miniangel what was so important that it could not wait until the following night then she told the couple they had two other abilities they did not know about but they needed to start doing with the community.

Without allowing the couple to question anything the mini angel told the couple they both had the ability to communicate with unborn children and if there were to be a problem with anyone's pregnancy they would need to do that for the safety of the mother and the baby. The miniangel told the couple the last thing she needed to let them know about was that they could enter anyone's dreams and by doing that they could communicate whatever was necessary and find out anything they wanted to know from the individual whose dream they were in without deception. Andrew asked the miniangel how she could forget to tell him and Camillia about those two gifts and she told the couple it was not that she forgot to tell them, it was telling them about their gifts as needed so they would not become overwhelmed with too much at one time. The miniangel made the couple aware that their children could also engage in the two gifts that she had just informed them of and the children had already been performing their gifts then she told the couple she would see them the next evening and disappeared. Andrew told Camillia they only had forty-five minutes before they had to wake up so he suggested that they stay awake and enjoy some conversation together then Camillia told Andrew she was going to get ready for the new day then she would be ready to give him her undivided attention and he told her that was fine and he would do the same.

Andrew and Camillia get themselves ready for the new day then they heard noise outside of their bedroom which was odd because nobody was usually up and about in the hallway that early, the only individuals that should be up and about were the kitchen staff but they could not be heard from the couple's bedroom so Andrew and Camillia went out of their bedroom to find out what was going on. When the couple got to the hallway, where they heard the disturbance they found out it was the castle decorator finishing up with the room of relaxation and that excited Camillia because now her and Andrew could do their healing work in an appropriate environment and the castle decorator could start working on Bridgette's home.

Ten minutes after the couple got into the hallway, the castle decorator finished with the room of relaxation and caught up with Andrew and Camillia to tell them it was finished and to find out if there was another project for her to do then Camillia told her Bridgette wanted to work with her to decorate her new house. Camillia told the castle decorator Bridgette knew what she wanted in each room she just needed help getting the transition from room to room to flow smoothly and the castle decorator told Camillia that would be no problem then said she would find Bridgette after breakfast and get started right away then Camillia told her it was a wonderful idea and thanked her as they started to walk away from one another. Andrew and Camillia went on to the castle's private dining hall for breakfast and Camillia knew she would be seeing Bridgette so she was going to inform Bridgette that the castle decorator would be looking for her after breakfast to start working on her house. The couple got to the castle's private dining hall and took their seats at the big round table then the kitchen staff brought their breakfast out to them.

As they were eating their meal Bridgette got to the big round table and took her seat so the kitchen staff brought her breakfast out to her also then Camillia told Bridgette that the castle decorator would be looking for her after breakfast to get started on her house and that excited Bridgette. While they were eating, Camillia told Bridgette the room of relaxation had been completed that morning and it was gorgeous then Bridgette said she would go to look at it before starting on her home decor. Camillia told Bridgette the room of relaxation was her office room for her to be able to keep the conception records and take notes during the healing procedures, Camillia told Bridgette that the desk was hers and when she got a chance she needed to stock it with the things she would need and organize it to be functional for her and if she needed help doing any of that to just let her or Andrew know then Bridgette said okay and thanked the couple for having her own area and keeping her in mind while getting the room done. Camillia told Bridgette that they were supposed to do healings right after breakfast but on that day, they would do the healings right after the lunch hour so they could have some things taken care of that was out of the ordinary but on the next day they would do the healings after the breakfast hour and Bridgette said okay.

Andrew, Camillia, and Bridgette were done eating and talking so it was time for Bridgette to meet with the castle decorator and for the couple to go to the stable area to check on how it was coming along on their way to the chief's side of the castle so they could talk to him about what their miniangel said then get educated on their community's founding rules and regulations. As Andrew, Camillia, and Bridgette got up from the big roundtable the castle decorator walked into the castle's private dining hall and told Bridgette to go with her and they were going to her home to start and finish the decor in one day. Andrew and Camillia went on to take care of their business.

CHAPTER SIXTY EIGHT

When the couple got outside and over to the stable area, the construction workers were packing up their equipment while the head worker and Jaden were inspecting the inside of the new building and the head worker was amazed with the structure as Jaden explained what each area was for. Andrew and Camillia waited outside the new stable for Jaden and the head worker so they could get the details on what was left to be done to get an idea of how much longer before things were back to normal. After fifteen minutes the head worker and Jaden walked out of the stable and when Jaden saw the couple he ran over to them to tell them that the construction crew was going to help him herd the animals from his parent's stable back to their stable and put them inside where they belonged then everyone would work together to put the stable equipment where it was going to go and they planned to be completely finished with the stable that day, Andrew and Camillia told Jaden he had done a wonderful job and they were proud of him then he told the couple that he wanted them to take a tour of the new stable with him when it was completed and they said they would. Jaden said goodbye to the couple and ran back over to the workers while the couple changed their walking direction to go to the chief's side of the castle instead of theirs.

When Andrew and Camillia got to the chief's side of the castle, the chief was on his way out so Andrew told him they needed to have a serious talk with him and he told Andrew he was on his way to see them but they could go into his side of the castle since they were already there and the couple said okay. The chief told the couple he assumed the conversation needed to be confidential and Andrew said yes so, they went into the chief's office room and shut the door behind them then they all took a seat. Andrew told the chief that they needed him to hear them out before saying anything then they would be free for conversation and the chief said okay. Andrew told Camillia he would do the talking but if he left anything out to speak up right away and she said okay then Andrew told the chief that he and Camillia were advised by their miniangel to tell him they knew of their existence as well as the dinosaur tail and their mini angel visited them nightly through astral projection and by the same means he and Camillia visit the dinosaur tail. Andrew went on to tell the chief that their children also visited the miniangels and had the same abilities as he and Camillia and those abilities were endless; for instance, astral projection, going into others' dreams, communicating with unborn babies, moving objects through mind control, heating and cooling things with their minds, the ability to fly and levitate, the ability to heal injuries and reverse barrenness, and to have double the life expectancy of others. Andrew finished by telling the chief that as their children reproduced with regular pale ones the gifts would be bred out until eventually only regular pale ones would be left so all they were doing by healing the community was making them happy and bringing them the joys of parenthood while prolonging the extinction of their race.

Andrew then told the chief he was finished with what he had to say then Camillia said she had nothing to add and the chief sat in his chair in silence for a short bit, it was obvious he was trying to absorb all that Andrew had said so the couple stayed quiet because they felt it was the chief's turn to talk. Finally, the chief spoke and told the couple he was amazed at what they and the children could do then he said he was glad that he now could speak of the history of the community freely because there were some things he was sworn to secrecy over but since the source of his swearing to secrecy had befriended them and given permission for them to speak of the secrete things with him he could truly tell them everything and he was relieved at last. The chief did not want to keep anything from the couple and he certainly did not want to take the secret information to his grave and have it die with him.

The chief told Andrew and Camillia that he could fully educate them now that he knew they knew of the dinosaur tail and that it was made up of many tiny angels. Camillia asked the chief why the miniangels did not fraternize with all pale ones then the chief told her and Andrew that in time they would but the tail needed to grow first so every individual had their own miniangel and up to then he was the only individual reproducing the miniangels but now that he knew the couple knew of them he could show them how to reproduce the miniangels with the warning that it did take a lot of physical strength out of the individual doing the reproducing. The chief told Andrew and Camillia he would also educate them on the full policies and procedures of what the community was originally built on so they could keep the community as it was originally meant to be but it would have to wait until after the ten healings that they were going to do after the lunch hour because the chief did not want interruptions during the education session and it was too close to the lunch hour to do it. The chief suggested that he and the couple go to their side of the castle and wait in the family room for everyone to arrive and the couple agreed to go to their side of the castle to wait for everyone.

On the way to the couple's side of the castle, Jaden saw Andrew, Camillia, and the chief walking so he hollered for the couple to come see the new stable so the chief told the couple to go ahead then Camillia told the chief to come along and he did, when they got to Jaden he told them the stable was completed and Jaden wanted to walk the couple through the stable so they said okay and with the chief followed Jaden through the stable. Andrew, Camillia, and the chief were amazed and excited about how the stable turned out, it was larger than before, more organized than before, it had a veterinary room, and everything in there had a place to be without being on the ground.

Now that the tour of the stable was done, it was close to the lunch hour and family time so the chief, the couple, and Jaden went to the family room inside of the couple's side of the castle to wait on the rest of the family members. Right after the couple, the chief, and Jaden got seated in the family room, Bridgette and the castle decorator came up the hallway from Bridgette's house and she was as happy as one could be because her home decor was finished and when she got into the family room she walked up to Camillia then grabbed her by the hand and dragged her to the house to show her how it turned out. Bridgette carried on about how well things turned out as she showed Camillia all the rooms and Camillia told Bridgette the house looked perfect for her and Matthew and the baby's bedroom was done in a way that it could be for a boy or a girl and Camillia thought that was wise. Now that Bridgette had shown her decorated home to Camillia she was ready to go on with the day's events so they went back to the family room to wait for the rest of the family members to get there.

Finally, all the family members were in the family room so Andrew led the whole group to the castle's private dining hall so they could get in their seats at the big round table and the kitchen staff could serve lunch. Everyone started to eat and take turns sharing their day so far, it seemed that nearly everyone had wound up a project or overcame something personal. Everyone was finished eating and sharing their day so it was time to get back to work and everyone was anxious to continue such a momentous day to see what other wonderful things were in store. The kitchen staff cleared the big round table while Andrew, Camillia, and Bridgette went to the room of relaxation, the chief and Matthew went to the family room to deal with the couples that were to be there for their conception healings, Jaden went outside to stand by as the stable boy since his stable project was complete and he would have a lot of visitors horses and buggies to deal with during the healings, Jaden's parents went back to their shop, and Melanie went to the kitchen to get dinner plans started.

Andrew and Camillia were ready to heal their first of ten couples when the chief brought the first couple back to the room of relaxation, Andrew explained the procedure to them and within fifteen minutes they were done and leaving. Bridgette was writing as fast as her fingers would let her then the chief brought in the second of the ten couples then Andrew and Camillia repeated the healing process and while Bridgette had no break in writing, the third of the ten couples were brought back by the chief while Matthew stayed in the family room with the other seven couples. The same routine occurred until all ten couples had been healed then Matthew went back to overlooking the rest of the security people in and around the castle, the chief went back to his side of the castle to wait for Andrew and Camillia to show up for their education talk, Bridgette stayed in the room of relaxation to finish then organize her notes so she could transfer the information into the book of healing, Andrew and Camillia had to go to the chief's side of the castle to have their education discussion but Andrew was going to get another tour of the new stable from Jaden on the way. Andrew and Camillia went outside and sitting on the porch next to the front door was Jaden so Andrew told Jaden he was ready for another tour of the new stable then Jaden jumped up from his chair with excitement and took Andrew by the hand then drug him to the stable. Camillia could keep up with Jaden and Andrew but as big as she was from the pregnancy, it was difficult.

When Jaden, Andrew, and Camillia got into the stable, Andrew was surprised this time at how much it looked like a house with many rooms and each room served a specific purpose then Andrew noticed for the first time two rooms that he could not figure out what they were for so he asked Jaden and Jaden told Andrew that one room was a veterinary room for when the animals were sick or giving birth then he told Andrew the other room was a spare room that had no purpose yet. Andrew told Jaden he had done a superb job in designing the stable and enlarging the space was a prime idea then Jaden told Andrew it was a pleasure doing the barn and the stable and if there were to be any more projects arise, he would love to take them on and Andrew told him it was a deal.

Once the three of them were out of the stable, Jaden went back to his seat by the castle's front door and the couple went to the chief's side of the castle to have their education discussion. The chief was only expecting Andrew and Camillia so when Andrew knocked on the chief's front door, the chief answered it himself and welcomed the couple then they went to the chief's office room for privacy from the castle's staff. The chief told Andrew and Camillia there was going to be a lot of information and it would be given to them quickly so if there was something they did not understand they needed to ask their questions immediately before he had a chance to move onto something else and the couple acknowledged the chief with a positive nodding of the head. The chief reached into his desk drawer and pulled out a long flat metal box with a lock on it then he used a key to open the box, the chief pulled out a small stack of papers from the box then handed them to Andrew telling him and Camillia to read the papers silently in their entirety so Andrew held the papers where he and Camillia could read them together in silence.

As it turned out the papers were the community's constitution of rules and regulations complete with consequences of wrong doing for anything that could possibly be done in the community and the declaration was signed by the forefounders. It took the couple an hour to read the whole document carefully, when they finished they told the chief the document was clear and concise that they had no questions or concerns over it then the chief told the couple he wanted them to sign it after the four founders since they were the current ruler's if they had no problem with anything in the document and the way it was worded. Andrew and Camillia both asked for an ink pen about the same time so the chief handed Andrew a pen to sign with and he could give the pen to his wife when he was done signing the constitution. The chief told the couple he was going to hand the document over to them now that they had signed it because as the new rulers of the land of grandeur, they may need to refer to it at some point in time as he and the other fore founders had.

Both Andrew and Camillia agreed that the document had outlined what to approve and disapprove on the science hall's list of products for bettering society for them to produce and put on the market then Andrew told the chief he had looked at the list briefly and he already knew there was going to be quite a few of their ideas that were going to be disapproved. The chief asked Andrew if he could make a suggestion and Andrew told him certainly so the chief mentioned how the science hall had already had an issue with the vaccine that the original head scientist killed himself with which went to show that there was some deception in the science hall then, next the scientists fought to keep the life extension project and the conception project alive after being told to fold them up and now they had presented a list of things to improve the community's functionality with, Andrew said correct then the chief told Andrew that it may be wise to keep a close eye on the science hall because he was in fear of having some kind of an uproar over turning down some of their ideas from the list and though they had not had anyone be deceptive in the community in its existence so far, there could always be a first time. Andrew told the chief he would heed his warning and Camillia said she would also then the chief told the couple to deal with the science hall's list and wait a brief time to assure no retaliation then they would discuss how to reproduce miniangels, the couple said okay then got ready to leave the chief's office room to go back to their side of the castle to deal with the science hall's list. The chief told Andrew and Camillia he would walk them out then he was going to go out into his personal garden and enjoy some quiet time alone then Camillia asked the chief if he would like to have dinner with her and Andrew so they could spend some non-business time together and the chief said he accepted her offer.

Andrew and Camillia left the chief's side of the castle, and when they got to the patio of their side of the castle, the veterinarian was just riding up to them saying he needed to speak with them in private and Andrew told him that he and Camillia could see him right away so he slid off his horse and they went to Camillia's office room.

Once they were sat down and comfortable, the veterinarian told the couple that the tutoring session they were to have that day was to be his last because Jaden worked at such a fast pace and kept his score at one hundred percent he was to graduate and become the youngest veterinarian he had ever known throughout history. Camillia said they should throw a party where Jaden's diploma could be presented to him in front of the entire family then the veterinarian told the couple that the idea was a fabulous one but Jaden was not getting just a diploma, he would be getting his own tools of the trade and he just needed a place to practice for the individuals who brought their animals to the office for minor things. Camillia told Andrew she had an idea, they could give Jaden the unused room in the new stable for his office and he could set it up himself all they would have to do was put doors on that room with a lock so his tools and medicines would be secure then Andrew said he liked the idea. Andrew made the decision to have the construction crew put doors on that room with a lock during the hours of sleep so Jaden would not know and they could give the key to the doors to Camillia in the morning and Camillia could create a project for Jaden inside the castle to keep him from discovering the doors, Camillia said she could do that and she would get with Melanie before dinner time and let her know they needed a party lunch with a cake and to dress up the castle's private dining hall. Andrew said he would make sure the whole family knew of the plan so they could participate also then the veterinarian told Andrew and Camillia it sounded wonderful.

Andrew, Camillia, and the veterinarian left Camillia's office room so the veterinarian could gather the tools and medicines for Jaden's gift from him while Andrew went to see the head construction worker to offer him double pay to have him put the doors in the stable with a lock and to give the key to Camillia when he was finished in the middle of the night and Camillia went to see Melanie to tell her of the graduation party so she could do a cake and special foods and decorate the castle's private dining hall.

As it turned out, the head construction worker said he would put the locking door in the stable in the middle of the night and he did not expect double pay, Melanie said she would bake a grand cake and do special foods for lunch then have the castle's private dining hall decorated nicely and finally, the veterinarian got all the things he needed to for Jaden to be a self-sufficient veterinarian. Andrew returned to the castle and got his runners to send the message to all the family members about the graduation party then report back to him so he could assure no one was left out. When Andrew got a free moment, Camillia asked him to help her come up with a project inside the castle that Jaden would be interested in and would take the entire day and Andrew said okay then the couple sat down together and thought long and hard for an appropriate project.

CHAPTER SIXTY NINE

Neither Andrew nor Camillia could come up with something for Jaden to do on their property, and right as they were telling each other that, there was a knock on their front door so Andrew answered it and it was the chief arriving for dinner; the couple had not realized it was so late in the day. Camillia led the way to the castle's private dining hall with Andrew and the chief in tow Camillia mentioned the dilemma of not being able to find something to keep Jaden busy all day the next day so he would not go into the new stable until family time then the chief asked if he could suggest something and the couple said please do. The chief said if they did not mind him borrowing Jaden for a project that he had an idea and the couple told the chief to go on then the chief told the couple that his barn could use an overhaul like theirs had gotten and the couple said that would be perfect. Camillia told the two men that she had better tell Jaden that evening to report to the chief in the morning and that they would saddle their own horses for the day then the chief told her that would be wise and Andrew agreed so Camillia told them to consider it done. Melanie brought dinner out to the trio and commented that it was nice to see the chief with Andrew and Camillia as his adopted children and not as his king and queen, Andrew told Melanie that things had been so busy lately that he and Camillia haven't even gotten the chance to spend time together as husband and wife and they slept together then Camillia told Melanie that if it was not for the fact they worked together they would have not seen each other at all lately then Melanie chuckled and agreed that things in the castle had been busier than normal. The chief, Andrew, and Camillia even had to eat their dinner rather quickly because there were still a lot of things to get done that evening so they finished up then the chief excused himself from the couple's presence and went back to his side of the castle while the couple waited on people to start showing up for their responsibilities.

Jaden entered the castle to go to his bedroom for tutoring, but before Jaden could get to his room, Camillia caught up to him in the hallway and asked to speak to him, Jaden stopped walking and asked Camillia what was on her mind then she told him that the chief would like to have his barn overhauled starting in the morning then Jaden told Camillia he would gladly do it so Camillia told Jaden not to come to her and Andrew's side of the castle the next morning because the chief would be expecting him there. Jaden confirmed he would go directly to the chief's side of the castle in the morning but then he questioned Camillia about who was going to be saddling their horses and taking care of them after hard rides, Camillia told Jaden that Andrew would care for the horses for the day then Jaden said okay and went on to his bedroom for tutoring. Camillia went back up the hallway to meet up with Andrew in the family room and when she got there she told Andrew that she got it arranged for Jaden to go to the chief's side of the castle in the morning and Andrew said great then he sent his runner to the chief with a note confirming the plan. Jaden's parents entered the castle so his mother could tutor the couple's three oldest children and his father could visit with Andrew then the veterinarian entered the couple's castle rather early and Camillia caught up with him to inform him of all the plans. He thought the plans were great.

Once Camillia finished talking to the veterinarian she went to talk with Jaden's mother to tell her of the graduation party for the next day and of the things that the veterinarian, the chief, and they were going to get for him then Camillia told her to make sure her husband knew of the plans even though she was sure Andrew was telling him at that moment, she said okay then hurried off to tutor the couple's three oldest children. All of the couple's family were workers in their side of the castle so they each went to Camillia to asked for a bit of time away from their posts on the next day so they could go shopping to get something for Jaden's graduation celebration and Camillia told each of them it was fine with her and that she would inform Andrew then she finally got to meet back up with Andrew in their family room to fill him in on what had happened with her in his absence then he advised her of what he had been doing in regards to the graduation party in her absence.

As soon as the couple caught up on what had been going on and making sure they had the next day planned, Jaden's tutoring hour for general education was over and he was being tutored by the veterinarian for the last time before he graduated the veterinarian program and the general education tutor asked Andrew and Camillia if she could speak to them so they said yes and gave her their attention, the tutor told the couple that Jaden had just completed his requirement for the entire kindergarten through twelve classes and she was not qualified to tutor for college level general credit classes or specialized program credits but that she would like to present to him a diploma for what he had earned, Camillia told the tutor Jaden had been receiving tutoring from the community's veterinarian because that was what he felt his calling as an adult was and that he was receiving a diploma for finishing that program on the next day.

The general education tutor was surprised Jaden was working on both diplomas together but it did not surprise her that he finished quickly or with perfect scores because he was a prodigy she told the couple Jaden was her most favorite student yet and she did not believe she would ever have another one as special as Jaden then the couple thanked her for the compliment and told her about the plans they had for Jaden the next day and invited her to be there also. The tutor was touched that she was asked to be a part of the family's gathering then Camillia spoke to her firmly telling her that the whole community was one big family composed of smaller family units and she and Andrew were there for everyone in the community just the same as they were for their immediate family. The general education tutor told Camillia that she had not told Jaden he had completed his requirements yet, and Camillia said that was a good thing because his other tutor had not told him either so the next day was going to be a giant surprise and now it would be doubled then the tutor said that Jaden worked hard. The tutor walked to the front door and left the couples side of the castle to go to her own home and right after the tutor left Jaden came walking from the hallway to sit with his father and the couple so they could wait for his mother to finish tutoring the couple's three oldest children and after only a few minutes Jaden's mother walked into the family room saying the children were back with their nannies then Jaden and his parents went home. As Andrew and Camillia were going down the hallway to their bedroom Matthew walked up on them and wished them a good night right before ditching into his and Bridgette's bedroom, the couple wished Mathew a good night right back and the couple were the last to get to their bedroom. Andrew and Camillia decided to astral project the dinosaur tail to see all the miniangels while they updated their miniangel of the day's events, especially about the shared knowledge of their existence with the chief.

Andrew and Camillia never turned the light on in their bedroom so they changed from their day clothes into their bedclothes in the dark then climbed into bed, got comfortable then focused on astral projection and before they knew it they were at the dinosaur tail together. The couple's miniangel approached their essence and greeted them then they greeted her and the couple got right to business by telling the miniangel that the chief now knew they had encountered the dinosaur tail and all the miniangels and when things got settled down in the community the chief would show them how to produce more miniangels so the community could share the blessings the angels brought. Andrew also told the miniangel about the science hall needing to be watched closely and about the community's constitution that they now had possession of as well as the list of items the science hall wanted to market then Andrew finished rushing the miniangel with information after telling her about the warning the chief left them with about someone in the science hall possibly being deceitful somewhere in their agenda. The miniangel said that the couple just brought a lot of heaviness on the miniangels in dealing with the science hall because she had been watching the new head scientist to determine if he was a loyal member of the community because the original head scientist was not loyal to the constitutional purpose of the science hall and the death of him at his own hands saved the community from having to go through the euthanizations of a community member without the ability to understand why then the mini angel told Andrew and Camillia to heed the chief's warning about the science hall.

Andrew came up with an idea to put the scientists on a paid leave of absence for about a week so that he, Camillia, and the chief could go to the science hall and search for anything out of the accepted norm by reading their documents, checking out all the laboratory animals, finding out what herbs and medicines were there and what they were supposed to be for, and finally checking their stock of chemicals against what was supposed to be there and how much. The mini angel told Andrew that would help them get familiar with the science hall's allowances and requirements and enable them to start to search for discrepancies but they would also need to look at each individual scientist's personal files to look for any red flags such as a psychological instability as well as what projects they were a part of and what their role was in the project. Andrew and Camillia told the miniangel they would make the safety check happen as soon as possible and they would have the chief, Matthew, and Bridgette help with sworn promises to keep the search a secret and to keep the scientists unaware of what they were checking for.

Camillia suggested they tell the scientists it would be a vacation to take a break from doing such tedious work all day and allow them to catch up on things at home, spend time with family if they had one, or go out on a trip. The miniangel told Camillia that was a smart cover-up tactic to get the scientists out of the science hall for an extended period without suspecting anything then Andrew told Camillia and the miniangel he would take care of that when it was time for them to go into the science hall and start the search, Camillia told Andrew thank you and the miniangel approved the plan. The miniangel told the couple not to wait too long because the sooner they did the plan the sooner their minds could be at ease and if there were to be a wolf in sheep's clothing the sooner they got that imposter out of there the safer the community would be, she concluded by telling the couple that it may be wise to do the search periodically but make it spontaneous and at irregular intervals so there was no pattern for the scientists to catch on to.

The couple told the miniangel they would brief Bridgette, Matthew, and the chief on the next day and plan when they would do the search and they said they would keep her informed. The miniangel told the couple she was glad to see them and thanked them for catching her up to date on what was happening then she told them they had better get back to their bodies so the couple told her okay then disappeared and returned to their bodies.

Andrew and Camillia discussed the search of the science hall and each scientist individually and saw why it was so important to follow through with the process and they knew the next day was not a good day because they would be busy with getting Jaden set up for his veterinary practice but they figured the following day they could brief the chief, Matthew, and Bridgette then start on that day. Camillia told Andrew they should brief everyone the next day then do the search the day after and everyone could meet at the big roundtable to eat breakfast together then go to the science hall from breakfast then Andrew responded with okay. Camillia said she would be responsible for letting everyone know right after breakfast and again Andrew told Camillia okay. The couple settled down in bed and went to sleep, they knew because they went to the dinosaur tail their miniangel would not visit that night so they would be able to get some good uninterrupted sleep and they should feel revived in the morning. They had forgotten that they told the head construction worker to wake them and give the key to Jaden's new office to them.

Morning arrived and the couple woke up to the sound of castle employees moving about the castle doing their duties and once the couple sat up in bed and realized what the noises were, they concluded they had overslept so they jumped out of bed to get ready for the day in a hurry. The couple went to their bathroom to change out of their bed clothes into new day clothes, brush their teeth, wash their faces, and brush their hair then they practically ran to the castle's private dining hall to get seated at the big roundtable. Melanie told the couple they were right on time for breakfast as the kitchen staff brought out their breakfast and while they were eating Andrew called for his runners to retrieve Matthew and Bridgette, Camillia got one of her runners to retrieve the chief then they quickly ate their breakfast and left the big round table to go to the family room. The kitchen staff cleared the big round table and got it cleaned then started on the cake and special lunch foods so everything would be ready by lunch time and once Melanie had made sure her staff knew who was to do what, she left the castle to shop for a gift for Jaden and to get the decorations for the castle's private dining hall. Andrew and Camillia waited for ten minutes for the runners to bring their targets to the family room and once they were all there Camillia led everyone to her office room then Andrew started to tell them why they were there before anyone could sit down.

Andrew told Matthew, Bridgette, and the chief that they needed to raid the science hall while the scientists were under the impression that they were on a paid vacation for one week then he told everyone what they would be looking for and into then how often they would be repeating the search and why, everyone was happy to serve the cause and they were sworn to secrecy and finally, Andrew told them they would gather for breakfast the next day and go from there. Now that business was over Matthew and Bridgette asked if it was okay to leave to go shopping for a gift for Jaden's graduation and Camillia spoke up saying yes. The chief was going to take the opportunity to get Jaden a small buggy right away before anything else could pop up so he left the couple's side of the castle to go to the buggy shop. The chief figured getting Jaden a buggy to transport animals was a fine idea because he had gotten his own horse with all the gear for his birthday not too long ago and when the chief got to the buggy shop he immediately found the perfect buggy so he gave the merchant the money then hitched his horse to it and went to the couple's side of the castle to park it in the new stable with a big bow on it.

As the chief went to knock on the couple's front door, the chief was approached by the head construction worker and he asked if Camillia was home and the chief said yes so, the two of them were let in by the butler then the head construction worker asked for Camillia and the chief said he would wait his turn. The butler got

Camillia and took her to the family room where the two men were waiting for her. When she got there, the head construction worker handed her the key to Jaden's office room in the new stable, saying there was a bow on the door and that he could not get himself to wake her in the middle of the night. Then she said thank you and invited him to the graduation party. The head construction worker was thrilled that he was invited to the party and he told Camillia he would be there then he left to go get a gift for Jaden and the chief told Camillia to get Andrew and go into the new stable to check out the new buggy for Jaden and she said okay then the chief left to go back to his side of the castle until the lunch hour and family time so he could keep track of Jaden.

As the two men were leaving, Matthew, Bridgette, and Melanie were returning from their shopping trips, they were going to prepare the gifts for giving but Bridgette stopped by Camillia first and told her that the conception journals were all caught up and that was why no one saw her yesterday, Camillia thanked her then Bridgette went on her way to prepare the gift to be given to Jaden. Melanie went to decorate the castle's private dining hall and supervise lunch and the cake while Matthew got back to his security work. Camillia went to the family room and found Andrew then told him she had the key to the door of Jaden's new office room and Andrew was glad, Camillia told Andrew the head construction worker said to go look at the new door and he even put a big bow on the door then Andrew said they could see it when they took Jaden out there and Camillia said okay. Andrew reminded Camillia she had a prenatal check-up that day with Bridgette so he was going to go get Bridgette and Matthew then get back with Camillia so she needed to wait in the family room for them and they would all go together, Camillia said okay. Camillia sat on the chair next to her and waited for Andrew to return with Bridgette and Matthew.

Andrew returned within ten minutes with the other couple so they all left to go to the hospital and when they got there it was very busy but they turned their horses and buggy over to the hospital's stable boy and went to find the doctor. As the two couples approached the nurses desk, the charge nurse told them the doctor was real busy because he was swarmed with pregnant women and it would take a couple of hours for the doctor to get to them then Camillia asked if they could make an appointment for their final prenatal checkup before their delivery date then the nurse told them that he was booked a month out so the couples decided they would see him on delivery day. The charge nurse tried to encourage the two couples to stay and wait but they had too much going on that day and they could not wait around so they left the hospital and got their ride from the hospital's stable boy to go back to Andrew and Camillia's side of the castle.

Time really flew by fast, it was time to sit in the family room to wait for the entire family to show up for the lunch hour and family time which had both couples excited because of the graduation party for Jaden and while they waited for family to gather Andrew commented that even if the doctor could have seen them right away, they would have been late for family time and everyone agreed. Shortly after Andrew made his observation known, family was showing up and within minutes everyone was there so Andrew had everyone but Jaden go to the castle's private dining hall, Andrew told Jaden he needed to speak to him in private.

At that point, Jaden wondered what he may have done wrong to attract the couple's attention for a private meeting because they wanted to talk in private he made a quick assessment of his duties then he knew for sure that he was not involved in anything that was of a private matter so Jaden sat down quickly to get his possible reprimanding over with. Andrew walked over to Jaden and put his hand on Jaden's shoulder then told him he was special to him and Camillia as their adopted child, very intelligent, reliable, hardworking, and a loyal citizen of the community then Andrew smiled at Jaden and told him not to be worried he was not in trouble. Camillia got up from her chair and walked over to Jaden and took him by the hand then pulled on him to stand up then she led him to the castle's private dining hall and pushed him in front of herself then everyone called out surprise.

Jaden was surprised when he saw the castle's private dining hall all decorated for him then he knew he had achieved something but he had no clue what it could be then his tutors stood up and walked over to him and stood on opposite sides of him then put their hands around him and announced that he had graduated their programs. Jaden got a look of shock on his face and became speechless. He hugged both tutors one at a time then everyone clapped and whistled and once everyone was quiet again Andrew instructed Jaden to take a seat at the head of the big round table which was Andrew's seat because he was the head of the household. Jaden sat down then the basic education tutor presented Jaden with her diploma of completion with honors and when she was finished the veterinarian presented Jaden with his diploma of completion for an occupation with honors and when that was complete the head construction worker startled everyone when he stood up and told Jaden he had something that he believed Jaden had earned for his honors and for being such a brilliant construction worker also then he brought a beautiful handcrafted porcelain statue of a veterinarian with various animals from behind his back and presented it to Jaden. Jaden started to sob tears of joy and he asked everyone to excuse the tears he was just so happy that his whole family was there and was sharing his successions with him then Jaden got out of his seat and went to the head construction worker then gave him a hug and thanked him for giving him a chance to work with the crew and that it was a learning experience he would never forget as well as a pleasure, the head worker told Jaden he was welcome to work with the crew anytime and if they had any issues with a job that he would consult with him and Jaden said he would be honored to help the crew any way he could then he sat back down.

The head construction worker sat back down then Jaden's parents stood up and gave Jaden his first gift to open and sat back down. The gift was from them and it was a few laboratory coats for him to wear during his work hours as a veterinarian then everyone else except the couple and the chief gave Jaden their gifts. Once all the gifts were opened, the chief announced that he had a gift for Jaden but they would have to go to the barn to see it so everyone went to the barn and the chief took Jaden by the hand and took him to a one-horse buggy with a big red bow on it then the chief told him it was his new buggy to transport whatever was necessary then Jaden gave the chief a big bear hug and said thank you.

Everyone started to walk out of the barn and Andrew announced that they needed to go to the new stable for another gift so Andrew led the crowd to the new stable and when they got just inside of it Andrew called for Jaden to come to the front of the group and when Jaden got to Andrew he took Jaden by the hand and walked to the extra room that now had doors on it then Jaden looked at the doors and noticed the big bow on the doors and said there were no doors before that day then Andrew handed Jaden the key for the doors and told him that was his new office room for his veterinary practice and it would not matter what time of day or night he needed to be at the castle or the new stable because animals did not make appointments to be sick. Jaden hugged Andrew and Camillia then told them thank you then the veterinarian told Jaden he had not seen the gift that he was giving to him so Jaden stood there in silence for a few minutes then Andrew told everyone that the gift from the veterinarian was back in the castle's private dining hall so everyone went back inside and took their seats at the big round table.

There was a medium-sized metal table with wheels in the corner covered with a blanket that the veterinarian wheeled over to where Jaden was sitting then the veterinarian took the blanket off the table and told Jaden all those things were his including the exam table then Jaden stood up to examine what was there then he realized he had everything necessary to be a veterinarian including all the medicines and he was beside himself. The veterinarian hugged Jaden and told him welcome to the practice boy then Jaden announced he had some things to say and he wanted everyone to remain in their seats until he was finished speaking. Jaden gave an impromptu speech of appreciation and gave a vow of duty to the community then he added that he would still work as the castle's stable boy and when Jaden finished his speech he sat back down saying it was time to have lunch and everyone could share their day so that was what the family did next.

CHAPTER SEVENTY

When everyone was finished eating and sharing their day, Melanie brought out an elaborate five-tier cake in honor of Jaden and everyone said how beautiful the cake was then Melanie told the family that the top of the cake was for Jaden to save for his one year anniversary as the community's veterinarian and on that day, he was to thaw out the cake topper and share it with whomever he wanted for a small celebration of success.

The party got wrapped up right after eating cake because family time was over and everyone needed to get back to their duties so the kitchen crew cleaned up the big round table but before they could take down the decorations Jaden told them he wanted the decorations for his new office and they said okay then got back to work. Jaden took his gifts to the new stable and put them in his new office room, he got everything organized for functionality then he wanted the veterinarian to see his office room so Andrew sent for him with a runner and the runner returned within five minutes so Jaden showed off his office room and asked the veterinarian if it looked right to him then he told Jaden it looked better than his office room. The veterinarian told Jaden he was going to send out letters to everyone in the community to make them aware that they now had both veterinarians to turn to and Jaden thanked him then the veterinarian told Jaden he had some house calls to make to follow up on previous calls then he asked Jaden if he wanted to go with him if the couple did not need his services.

Just then, Matthew was running out to the barn in a panic so Jaden asked what was wrong then Matthew told Jaden it appeared Bridgette was in heavy labor with the baby then the veterinarian told Jaden he had to leave because he was behind his schedule so Jaden told him farewell then he went into the castle to check on the situation with Bridgette. While Jaden was assessing the situation with Bridgette, Camillia was at Bridgette's head sitting in a chair holding her hand and telling her to breathe through the contractions and not to push yet, Andrew waited right outside the door and once Jaden got the situation assessed he called out to everyone that they were about to have a baby and right then Matthew returned and burst into the front door saying the doctor could not make it because he was busy at the hospital with multiple births there. Jaden told everyone not to worry because he could deliver the baby, it was no different than birthing an animal's young one because nature, the child, and the mother combined efforts to do everything necessary to deliver the young then Jaden said he was only there to assure everything went smoothly and he knew it would.

Sure enough, Bridgette started pushing with contractions as Jaden had told her to do and the baby was delivered with no problems then Jaden cut the umbilical cord, tied it off, then handed the infant to Bridgette telling her she did a wonderful job and Bridgette told Jaden thank you for helping because he was calm and did what no one else could have done. Camillia had not felt well throughout the delivery of Bridgette's baby so now that she knew all was well Camillia stood up from her seat and started to walk to the doorway of Bridgette's bedroom and she fell to the floor due to a major contraction and Jaden rushed to Camillia's side then asked her what was going on then Camillia told Jaden to get Andrew so he could put her in her bed because she felt like she was in labor also then Jaden said he would help her to her bed and get Andrew on the way so Camillia stood up with Jaden's help and when they got into the hallway Andrew saw what was going on so he went to help put Camillia in their bed.

Once Andrew and Jaden got Camillia in her bed Jaden checked Camillia then told Andrew the baby was coming fast then it was like a game of catch and Jaden had the crying Conner in his hands, he cut the umbilical cord, tied it off, then handed the child to Camillia saying he looked just like Andrew. Jaden left the bedroom to clean up and give the couple's some family time while the children's nannies took the babies from their mothers to get them cleaned up, dressed, and wrapped in clean receiving blankets while the personal maids got the girls cleaned up and changed their bedding. Both Andrew and Matthew were in the hallway staying out of the way and congratulating each other then once the nannies and personal maids were finished with their jobs both men went into their bedrooms with their wives. Jaden was on his way back out to the castle's patio where he was supposed to be when the chief walked up to him and asked if everything was all right because he sensed a lot of tension coming from that side of the castle then Jaden told the chief he may want to go see Bridgette and Camillia because he had just delivered both babies so the chief ran into the castle heading for the bedroom area.

The chief stopped by to see Bridgette and Matthew first because their bedroom was closest to the end of the hallway and when he saw Bridgette holding her new baby a feeling of sentiment overcame the chief and he was fighting back tears of sentiment as he went on inside of the bedroom to congratulate the new parents and once Bridgette saw the chief she offered for him to hold the baby and he declined saying he feared he would break her then he asked what the baby would be called and Andrew told the chief she was to be called Sheeba. The chief spent about fifteen minutes with the new family then he said he needed to go see Camillia and Andrew with their new bundle of joy and left Bridgette and Matthew's bedroom. The chief got to Andrew and Camillia's bedroom saying hello as he entered to make his presence known then Andrew told the chief to come right in and look at baby Connor and when the chief saw little Connor he told Andrew that he was an identical image of him. The chief spent fifteen minutes with Andrew, Camillia, and Connor then he left to let the couple be with their new baby alone before the nanny came to get him.

The two nannies showed up about the same time to get the newborns so Andrew and Camillia decided to go over the list of products to produce for the bettering of the community from the science hall, Matthew went back on duty as the head of the castle's security, and Bridgette stayed in her bed to rest. Andrew and Camillia went to her office room where the list was then Camillia sat in her chair behind the desk and Andrew sat in a chair in front of the desk, they both got comfortable then Andrew asked Camillia to give him the science hall's list so she did. Andrew was looking at the list to see if he could find the major project they were working on because even though the couple told them it was an innovative idea he was looking to see if it was up for official approval, and it was not.

Andrew asked Camillia if she remembered talking to the head scientist about a medicated arrow that would put animals to sleep for about twenty minutes that they wanted to use so they would not have to kill any animal unless it was for food and Camillia told him she had remembered then asked what about it then Andrew told Camillia it was not on the list for official approval even though they knew the scientists were working on it. Camillia said it made sense to put the aggressive animals to sleep long enough to escape them without unnecessarily killing them but she was concerned about the use of arrows because if they went too deep they may kill them anyway. Andrew thought about what Camilla said for a few minutes then agreed, then he came up with an idea of using small blow darts that even if they went in all the way would just administer the tranquilizer not kill the animals but the individual who put the animal to sleep would have to wait until the animal was asleep then remove the dart before fleeing.

Camillia agreed then said there would have to be different amounts of sleeping drug for different-sized animals because a dart for a large animal would be an overdose for a small animal then Andrew told Camillia the process was getting too complicated because by the time they could get the right dart for the size of aggressive animal before them, they could be attacked. Andrew mentioned to Camillia that there were not many animal attacks and that was only because the animals den was about to be compromised which was a natural response even for a human then Camillia spoke up and told Andrew that idea had to be denied and they had better get through the list before the science hall started to work on those things also.

As the couple started from the top of the list then there was a knock at the office room door, Andrew answered the door and it was Jaden he wanted to know if the couple could get a temporary stable boy until he finished the chief's barn and Andrew told Jaden he would to just have fun with the barn and let them know how it was going, Jaden thanked Andrew then told Andrew he would be back soon. Andrew immediately sent a runner for the chief so he could get the couple a good trustworthy stable boy then they got back to the science hall's list. As Andrew and Camillia went through the list they discussed the ways the items could help as well as the ways they could be harmful and if the harm was minute they would go over them again, the item had to have no negative effects on society to be passed for the science hall to work on. The couple got through two items when the chief arrived so the couple stopped going over the list long enough to deal with the chief, they told the chief that Jaden was going to be working on his barn and would not be able to do his job as the stable boy as he had for them because he was on the opposite side of the castle and he had requested a temporary stable boy for the couple and they had approved of it but they needed the chief to find a trustworthy boy since he knew more people personally than the couple did. The chief said he would do the stable job himself since he had no other real responsibilities then they would not have to worry about any breach of confidentialities and they would know their horses were being taken good care of so Andrew told the chief that was a good idea and he was honored that the chief would take the job and work for them. Andrew told the chief he would get Jaden's pay for the job as it was only fair and the chief told the couple that Jaden would not miss out on any pay because he was paying Jaden for the barn work and the couple was glad.

With the stable job squared away, the chief went outside to sit at his new post and the couple got back to the science hall's list to approve or disapprove the fourteen other projects in question. It took a few hours to finish the list but the couple had done it and just on time for the dinner hour so Andrew rushed outside to where the chief was and told him he was having dinner with them so the chief accepted and the two men met Camillia in the castle's private dining hall, when they all three got into their seats at the big roundtable Melanie had the kitchen staff bring out their dinner and while eating the couple discussed the science hall's list with the chief. Andrew was telling the chief of all the things the science hall had wanted approval for then he told the chief that they had no approvals for the list but that they were working on three items that they had mentioned to them but were not on the list and they had to put a stop to one of them and make sure they understood why so they would not hold a grudge against them.

The chief inquired about the two things that they were approving and Andrew told the chief that they wanted to produce spindles and sheep's shears to produce cotton based materials. The chief said the cotton based materials would be good because they could make lighter clothing that would be cooler also and the couple agreed then Andrew suggested that they remind Matthew and Bridgette of the closing of the science hall on the next morning, especially to make sure Bridgette would be up to the job so Andrew summoned a runner to go to Bridgette and Matthew to get their word of doing or not doing the raid. Five minutes later, the runner returned and told Andrew that both Bridgette and Matthew would be ready bright and early. Then Andrew apologized to the runner for having to interrupt his dinner and thanked him for his service. Then everyone resumed their dinner. Andrew, Camillia, and the chief finished their dinner so they went their separate ways, the chief went to his side of the castle to go to bed so he could rise earlier than usual and the couple went to their bedroom to get some sleep before their miniangel woke them and about the time the couple crawled into bed the rest of the individuals in the castle were heading for their bedroom's also.

An hour into their sleep, the mini angel woke Andrew and Camillia with her special song then the couple greeted the miniangel like usual, and she gave greetings back, the miniangel inquired about the day's events and what was in store for the next day so Andrew told her about shutting down the science hall for one week and why. The miniangel asked Andrew if he really believed someone in the science hall was truly going against the community's constitution, and Andrew told her he hoped not but that there were subtle signs of it being true. The miniangel asked what would happen to the scientists if they were to be found guilty, and Andrew told her it would fall under treason for which the punishment would be euthanization carried out by the doctor and observed by him and Camillia. The mini angel told Andrew and Camillia it looked like they had a busy day ahead, and they said yes then the miniangel told the couple she was going to go visit the new babies then return to the dinosaur tail. The couple said their farewells as she disappeared then lay back down to get some sleep before the long day ahead of them. Andrew and Camillia woke up a bit early due to the anxiety of what they might find at the science hall so they went ahead and got ready for their day, went to the castle's private dining hall, and sat at the big round table. Melanie put a rush on the couple's breakfast and took it out to them herself, and when they started to eat, they were approached by Bridgette and Matthew; they had a tough time sleeping also due to possible issues with the science hall so they got up early also and Melanie got their breakfast to them quickly.

Before the two couples could finish their meals, the chief walked into the castle's private dining hall, saying he could not sleep due to the job they had to do that day, which referred to the science hall raid, so Melanie asked the chief if he had breakfast yet and he said no. Melanie told the chief to take a seat at the big round table then had the kitchen staff bring out some breakfast for the chief, and like everyone else, he picked at his food. Melanie noticed everyone not eating well so she asked if the food was okay, and they all agreed that it was good but none of them had much of an appetite that morning. They agreed to leave at that time to go to the science hall to catch the scientists as they got to the science hall. Andrew told everyone he was going to wait until all the scientists were there to tell them that they were starting a weeklong paid vacation then watch them leave before going inside to search.

Since Jaden was on his way to the chief's barn, Andrew saddled up his and Camillia's horses while Andrew saddled up his and Bridgette's horses. The chief already had his horse ready to go then they mounted and rode off. Andrew and his crew got to the science hall at the same time the scientists got there, so as Andrew was getting off his horse, he told the scientists to stay on their horses. Of course, they questioned Andrew's request so Andrew politely told the scientists that he was giving them one week off with pay starting that day. The scientists were surprised and all but one seemed to be elated, and that was the new head scientist who asked if he could go inside the science hall to retrieve some paperwork to have something to do while he was home since he had no family. Everyone that was there for the raid looked at Andrew for an answer even though they knew it was going to be no, and it was. The new head scientist tried to argue with Andrew, but Andrew refused to argue and finally Andrew told him that he was about to have his one-week vacation without pay then the new head scientist rode off quickly without saying another word. The encounter with the new head scientist made Andrew suspicious of him so Andrew said he would consider the personnel files himself. Andrew said when they got inside that he would appoint each person a duty so there would be some organization in the raid; everyone agreed that Andrew would be the leader of the raid.

Not seeing any of the scientists anymore, Andrew used his skeleton key to open the doors of the science hall, and everyone went inside then Andrew locked the doors back. Andrew reminded everyone he was going to go through the personnel files, Bridgette was to go through the project recording books, Matthew was to use the official supply allotment books to compare equipment and chemicals that were there with what was allowed, the chief was to stand by as a lookout for the scientists to return and to help one of them if needed, and Camillia was to check into the life-expansion project and the conception project to assure the science hall had in fact stopped the projects. Everyone agreed to do as asked and got to work right away. Andrew started with the head scientist's personal file and was determined to read it page by page so far. The chief was just on the lookout because no one needed help yet. Andrew searched the head scientist's personal file and found he was favored by the previous head scientist and he was the lead scientist of the conception project and the life-extension project but no others, it seemed to Andrew that he only took on projects that would make headlines on a major newspaper if they still had them.

There was one thing that caught Andrew's attention—all the work the new head scientist did that was completed was marked complete, and all but two projects that were to be shut down were marked denied. It seemed that the conception project and the life-extension project were left active according to the personnel record. Andrew asked Camillia if she had gotten any suspicious information from the two project records, and Camillia told Andrew as far as she could see, both projects were active and had more information than they had been told about when they were active projects. Matthew told Andrew there were quite a few numbered vials of unidentified fluid that were not on the guide book's list of allotted supplies and they were sitting on the counter in between the two mice cages with used syringes. Andrew went to the cages and observed the mice in two small cages with either yellow or red tags on their ears; those were the mice being used for the two projects that had been rejected so it was odd that they were not in their mansion-type cage with all the other mice because that cage was prepared like a natural environment for the mice. Andrew asked the chief what his impression of what had been found so far was, and the chief told Andrew that it seemed that someone was still working on the conception project as well as the life-extension project, and Andrew said he concurred. Andrew asked Bridgette what she had found in the project records book, and she said there were entries dated just the day before on the two projects they had been discussing that were supposed to be shut down. Andrew asked the group to take note of who was involved in the wrongdoings because they would need to be tried and possibly punished but to be careful that they did not get innocent people involved, and everyone said okay then went back to work.

The chief abruptly announced that the new head scientist was on his way back, and from the way his horse looked, he rode hard then Andrew told everyone to go into the office room and be quiet so they did while Andrew stood behind the science hall's door. As soon as everyone was where they were told to be and Andrew got himself into place, the science hall's door opened and in stepped the new head scientist; he did not notice Andrew when he shut the door. Andrew stayed quiet and watched the new head scientist gather some documents and the numbered yet unlabeled vials of liquid that was in between the two mouse cages then walked toward the front door to exit. Before the new head scientist could grab the doorknob, Andrew stepped out from behind the door and asked the new head scientist what he was doing. The new head scientist held a look of surprise on his face and said nothing so Andrew hollered for everyone to come out of the office room. When everyone excited the office room, they walked over to Andrew to back him up if necessary.

CHAPTER SEVENTY ONE

The chief reached out and took the items that were in the hands of the new head scientist then handed them to Camillia. Andrew told Matthew to detain the new head scientist until they could find out what he was there for and why, so Matthew cuffed him and left with him to take him to the holding room. Andrew told Camillia and Bridgette to look through the things the new head scientist was trying to take from the science hall and try to find out why; both women said okay then got to work. Come to find out the files on the conception project and the life-extension project were there with what was assumed to be a trial vaccine for both that either had been or was going to be given to the mice. Andrew asked everyone if they had seen everything they needed to see, and they all said yes so Andrew said it was time to leave and they did. Bridgette and Camillia rode back to the castle while Andrew and the chief went to the hospital to get some medicine that had an effect of telling the truth so they could interrogate the new head scientist; they would only use the medicine if they had no other options.

When the chief and Andrew got to the hospital, the chief stayed with the horses while Andrew went to speak to the charge nurse. When the charge nurse saw Andrew, she congratulated him on the birth of baby Connor, and Andrew said thank you. Then she said she had heard an eleven-year-old boy delivered the baby, and Andrew said yes then he told the charge nurse he needed to talk to the hospital's anesthetist. The charge nurse went to get the anesthetist and brought him to Andrew. Then he asked Andrew what he could do for him, and Andrew told him to get the truth serum and go with him so he did. The anesthetist, the chief, and Andrew went to the holding room then Andrew asked the new head scientist what he wanted with the items he went back to the science hall for, and he said nothing. Andrew told the new head scientist that nothing from the science hall was to be removed from there, then he asked again what he was doing and again he said nothing. Andrew ordered the anesthetist to administer the drug so he did. Then Andrew asked the new head scientist what he wanted with the items he was taking from the science hall. The new head scientist told Andrew that the files he was trying to get were proof that he had not stopped the research for the conception project or the life-expansion project, and the vials were new vaccines to try and he was doing the projects because he knew that the ability to heal would be bred out of their children after many generations and without that ability or a vaccine, their species would eventually die out. Andrew asked the new head scientist who else was working on the projects, and he told Andrew that no one even knew what he was doing. Andrew told the new head scientist that what he did was treason and punishable by euthanization.

The new head scientist told Andrew to do what he had to do but the vaccines had to be made, and if it was not him who made it, someone else would do it. Andrew told the chief and Matthew that the new head scientist was to stay detained and they would hold a trial the next day with twelve of his peers and he would be defending himself since he had no family to do it. After dealing with the new head scientist and hearing his story about the two projects, Andrew was led to believe that at least one other scientist was aware of the projects' still being open and active so the chief and Andrew went back to the science hall to look at the rest of the scientist's personnel files. Andrew and the chief got through number one through five's file; then when Andrew came upon scientist number six's file he saw something that caught his eye so he asked the chief to go through the file, and the same thing caught the chief's eye so together the chief and Andrew looked at scientist number six's personnel file very carefully from beginning to end one more time and they found out he was favored by the new head scientist and that if anything were to happen to the new head scientist, number six was to take his place. It seemed then to the chief and Andrew that he probably knew of the two projects being active and it was unclear whether or not he was a part of the projects.

Now the chief and Andrew needed to get scientist number six and question him about his involvement in the two projects and ask him about the new head scientist's plans with the two projects, especially since that scientist was favored by the new head scientist and the new head scientist did specify that if he could not finish the two projects, another scientist would. Andrew apologized to the anesthesiologist for keeping him from his work at the hospital for so long then Andrew told him it was a matter of life and death for whoever the scientists got to volunteer as a test subject for two projects that were supposed to be shut down, and the anesthesiologist told Andrew that when he got into his profession he had to make a vow to save lives and for him it did not matter if it was for the hospital's use or for the royal family's use as a vow was a vow. Andrew thanked him again. The anesthesiologist, Andrew, and the chief waited at the holding room while Matthew went to retrieve scientist number six.

After twenty-three minutes, Matthew returned to the holding room with scientist number six and sat him down in the interrogation seat then Andrew asked him if he had any idea why he was there. He said yes, that it was about the new head scientist and he only knew that because he could see him in the holding room so he assumed it was work related, but other than that, he had no clue.

Andrew wasted no time getting to the point; he told scientist number six that they had evidence of the conception project and the life-extension project still being active after the science hall was told to close them down then they found evidence that he would be the next head scientist if something happened to the current head scientist. Scientist number six told Andrew that he did not know about the projects' still being active because he had not done any work on them since they were shut down and again he said that he was not aware that the new head scientist was working on them, so if he had any of the other scientists working with him, it was kept quiet. Andrew did not believe scientist number six's story about not knowing of the projects still being done so Andrew told the anesthesiologist to administer the medicine to scientist number six and he did so. Within seconds, it was obvious the medicine was ready to work.

Again, Andrew asked scientist number six if he was working on the two projects with the new head scientist and he said yes then Andrew asked him if there were any other scientists working with him and the new head scientist, and he said no but they felt they were real close to getting the vaccines ready for use and wanted to create what used to be called the black market so the two scientists could get some extra money for giving people children and extending people's lives. Andrew had never gotten angry since becoming a pale one, but the situation with the two scientists really upset Andrew because he knew the vaccines would never work no matter what combination of things the science hall was to come up with because his and Camillia's mini angel told them so and they were all-seeing and for the most part all-knowing. Andrew instructed the anesthesiologist to return to the hospital then told Matthew to put him in the holding room, and like the new head scientist, they would hold a trial for him also but he had a wife who could defend him unless she declined, then he would have to defend himself so it would be up to Andrew and Camillia to visit his wife and find out how she wanted to handle the situation. Matthew put scientist number six into the holding room then went out to summon twelve individuals to stand as a jury for two cases while Andrew and Camillia went to scientist number six's home to see his wife. The chief was asked to stand guard for the holding room, and he accepted the responsibility while Matthew resumed his duty of being head of the castle's security in seeking out a jury.

When Andrew and Camillia got to the home of scientist number six, his wife answered the front door and told them they were there for the things he had been bringing home from the science hall. Andrew asked to enter her home and she told him of course. Andrew acted as though he knew about the items being removed from the science hall and told the woman that they did want the items that her husband had been bringing home, so she went to get them and when she came back to the couple she had far more items than the couple could imagine. Scientist number six's wife handed everything to Camillia as she asked if they had him in the holding room; then Andrew told her yes and she had the right to defend him if she wanted because on the next day there was to be a trial with twelve of their peers to serve as a jury. She told Andrew that he was guilty of treason, and she wanted no part in it so he would have to defend himself. The woman told Andrew she knew what he was doing from the beginning but could not tell anyone and defy her husband but she knew it would be found out eventually and she had tried to keep him an honest man, but he would hear nothing from her so nothing from her he would continue to hear. Camillia told her to be strong and that she and Andrew were there for her so she should not hesitate to come to them for anything. She thanked the couple, and they took the items she had given to them and left.

Andrew and Camillia took the items from scientist number six and the items from the new head scientist to their side of the castle, and in Camillia's office room, they started to make their arguments as prosecuting attorneys, which they felt would be easy enough that it would not take long to do. It took Andrew and Camillia only three hours to prepare their deposition on both scientists, which was great timing because it was very near the lunch hour and family time so Andrew and Camillia went to their family room to wait on everyone to show up including the chief because Andrew was having a community guard watch the scientists in the holding room. Jaden was the first to show up, and he was excited, he could not wait to see the chief because he had just finished with the chief's barn.

Once everyone was in the family room, Jaden bounced up from his seat and called out that he had an announcement. Everyone got quiet and looked at Jaden then he announced that the chief's barn was complete and that when everyone had time he wanted them to see it because he did it differently from Andrew and Camillia's. Right then, Andrew told everyone that they should make a small trip before eating to go see it. Everyone kept together and walked over to the chief's barn, and when they saw it, they were speechless. It seemed that Jaden got better with each new building that he did, and everyone told Jaden so. Now that the barn had been seen by the family, they all walked back to the couple's side of the castle to go to the castle's private dining hall, and when they got there, everyone scrambled to get in their seats because they were so hungry since nearly everyone just picked at their breakfast that morning. Melanie did not have all the food out before everyone was ravaging their food so Melanie firmly told everyone to slow down and use their manners because they were acting like a pack of wild dogs; then everyone put their hands in their laps and waited for the rest of the food to be on the table so each person could pick up a dish, serve themselves, then pass the plate to the next individual and accept a plate from the person ahead of them. Everyone ate with manners while they shared their day with the others, and while that was happening, Melanie got up and went into the kitchen then returned with Jaden's graduation decorations that he was going to put up in his office room located in the new stable he had built for the royal couple. Jaden thanked Melanie, and she hugged Jaden then sat at her place and continued to eat. Everyone finished their meal and shared their day so it was time to return to their duties. Jaden was going to go decorate his office room, Matthew was going back on patrol, the chief was going back to the holding room to stay with the two scientists, and Bridgette was going to plan girls' day for that week and she wanted to talk to Camillia about having another baby and how soon would be safe as well as plausible, Andrew and Camillia were going to their bedroom to work on some of their gifts, Jaden's parents would return to their shop, and Melanie would oversee the kitchen staff and start working on dinner.

While Andrew and Camillia were working on fine-tuning a couple of their abilities, Camillia suggested that they each try to go into one of the scientists' dreams to get more answers about the two projects as well as any they had not known about, and Andrew told Camillia that they did not know anything about how to do that. Camillia told Andrew that they might not know, but their mini angel must know and they could astral project to her and find out. Andrew told Camillia they would do that, but they had to go to bed quite early. Camillia said they could use the morning trial as an excuse to get extra sleep and end up going to sleep at their normal time then Andrew said okay. Andrew and Camillia continued to try out their other abilities so they decided to try levitation, and little did they know, it came to them naturally so they knew they would be able to fly. Andrew and Camillia decided to visit the chief's private garden the next day and try to fly because they knew if levitation came easy, flying should also and there was enough room to fly without being seen by anyone but maybe the chief, and that was fine with the couple. Andrew and Camillia sat on the edge of their bed to talk about what gift to try next, but before they could choose one, there was a knock on their bedroom door so Andrew went and answered it. It was the butler saying a runner had left a message for him and Camillia and that they must go to the holding room immediately as there had been a situation that no one else could handle. Andrew and Camillia rushed out of the castle and rode hard to the holding room. Upon arrival, they saw the chief sitting in a chair outside of the holding room with his face in his hands. They could feel his distress so Andrew checked on the chief while Camillia spoke to the security person who was there with the chief, and he told Camillia that the new head scientist had hung himself with his clothing in the holding room and they needed to remove scientist number six so they could take the new head scientist's naked body down from the ceiling beam.

Meanwhile, Andrew was consulting the chief and trying to convince him that it was not his fault that the new head scientist had done what he did, and the chief kept saying it was his fault because he did not keep a close enough eye on the two prisoners or the new head scientist would not have had enough time between checks to hang himself to the point that it killed him because it was not as fast of a death as it had been thought to be. Matthew was patrolling near the holding room and saw the commotion so he went over to Andrew and asked what was going on, so Andrew asked him to get the new head scientist out of the holding room while he held onto scientist number six and Camillia could be with the chief. Matthew said okay so Andrew and Matthew went inside the holding room.

When Matthew got into the holding room, he stopped in his tracks and asked why he was not told what he was walking into; he said it was nothing he could not handle, but it was always nice to know about something like that so one could be prepared mentally. Andrew apologized then he took scientist number six out of the holding room and handed it over by the chief while Matthew told Andrew he accepted his apology, he was cutting the new head scientist down from the ceiling beam.

After Matthew got the new scientist's nude body down from the ceiling beam, he cut the rest of his clothing from the beam so Andrew could put scientist number six back into the holding room. Andrew walked scientist number six into the holding room then Andrew told him to strip down to his loincloth so he could not copy the now deceased new head scientist then Andrew exited the room with the clothing and locked the door behind himself. After locking the holding room door, Andrew asked scientist number six why he did not holler for help when the new head scientist was about to hang himself with his clothing, and scientist number six said it was his right to choose how he was to die because he knew his twelve peers were going to sentence him to euthanization and he believed he was working on two projects for the betterment of society and he believed he had not committed a crime, he just did not follow orders to stop the two projects. Andrew asked scientist number six if he felt that he was going to be sentenced to euthanization and his response was that his wife would represent him in court and jurors go easy on women. At that point, Andrew was disgusted by the scientist's way of thinking then he remembered that scientist number six's wife said she was always told to be quiet so she would remain quiet and he could defend himself. Andrew did not see any reason to hang around the holding room because he had six guards to keep an eye on scientist number six three shifts of two guards which would switch up watch so someone would have their eye on him constantly as a suicide precaution.

Andrew asked Camillia to take the chief to their side of the castle and wait for him in the family room and she said okay then took the chief by the hand and headed for her and Andrew's family room. When they got to the family room, Camillia sat next to the chief and called on Melanie to bring some tea for her, the chief, and Andrew. Before Melanie returned with the tea, Andrew walked into the family room and stood in front of Camillia and the chief, saying he had an idea that he and Camillia could try and possibly take the guilt from the chief and Camillia said she would try anything so Andrew suggested a healing session. The chief was so distraught that he had not heard anything the couple had said so they assumed their positions and did a healing session on the chief, and when they took their hands off the chief, they waited to see if the chief was going to speak.

The chief did speak, and he asked the couple what they were waiting for, then Andrew asked the chief if he was okay, and the chief told Andrew and Camillia he was fine. He realized the death of the new head scientist was not his fault even though it was a tragedy because he did not know for sure he was going to be euthanized because it was up to the jury what would happen, and what he was doing did not negate the love that the whole community had for him. The chief was aware of the healing the couple had just done on him so he thanked them for it. They told the chief that was why they had the gift, and they could not watch his anguish go on any longer so they had to try something. The chief said he would be glad to see the hearing for scientist number six be over.

That was when Andrew told the chief that he was going to have to defend himself, and the chief commented on the fact that he had a wife then Andrew told the chief that she was going to stand down. The chief asked Andrew if he knew why scientist number six's wife was standing down, and Andrew said yes then Andrew told the chief that according to his wife he always told her to be quiet so she decided that she had always been quiet so why change that now. The chief said that was unfortunate. Camillia suggested that the chief have dinner with them that evening, and he told Camillia he would love to, and at that moment Melanie came back to the family room with tea for Andrew, Camillia, and the chief. At that moment, Camillia asked Melanie to set a place at the big round table for the chief and she said no problem then walked away so the small group could finish talking in private. The chief asked Andrew and Camillia if they were ready for the trial, and they told the chief they had their deposition written that now it was a matter of showing up.

It was about dinnertime so the chief, Andrew, and Camillia were heading for the castle's private dining hall and suddenly a runner came bursting through the couple's front door talking so fast he was inaudible. Camillia took the runner by the shoulders and told him to settle down and talk slowly so they could understand him. The runner took a deep breath, swallowed hard, then slowly told Camillia that the number six scientist needed a doctor but the doctor was too busy to leave the hospital so no one knew what to do. Camillia asked why he needed a doctor, and the runner told her he had slit both of his wrists with a lunch knife but they got it from him. Andrew told the chief to ride hard and go get Jaden, and without question, the chief ran out of the castle, hopped on his horse, and off he went. Ten minutes later, the chief came back into the castle with Jaden. Jaden asked if an animal was sick, and Andrew told him they needed a doctor to do wound care and possibly stitches on a pale one but the doctor was too busy to leave and he was the next best thing. Andrew told Jaden to mount his horse and follow him so the two guys went outside and rode off to the holding room, and when they got there, Andrew and Jaden noticed a lot of blood everywhere but it did not bother either one of them. Jaden took his little black bag into the holding room and assessed the wounds on scientist number six's arms. Jaden called out for Andrew so Andrew stepped into the holding room and asked Jaden what he needed. Jaden asked Andrew if he could hold the scientist down while he put about thirty stitches in each arm. Scientist number six told Andrew and Jaden he would not allow them to close up his arms and he was not done injuring himself because it was his body and he could do what he wanted with it.

CHAPTER SEVENTY TWO

Andrew told scientist number six that he would not get any sympathy from the jury for what he had done to himself and that he and Jaden were not going to allow the arm injuries to go unattended and get infected; besides, all it would do if it got infected to the point that it got gangrene was that they would just remove the arms then what would he do for a living if he was not euthanized. Andrew told Jaden to stand down until he got help in there then Andrew went back to the castle to get Matthew to help him and Jaden because he did not want Jaden getting hurt doing a job for them that was not in his scope of practice; he just happened to know how to do the job because sewing up a pale one was the same as sewing up an animal.

Finally, Andrew found Matthew during his rounds in the castle, and Andrew stopped Matthew then asked Matthew to help him hold down scientist number six while Jaden sewed up his arms because he had taken the lunch knife and cut his arms badly. Matthew asked Andrew why the scientist would do something like that, and Andrew told Matthew maybe it was to get sympathy from his twelve peers during the trial. Besides, the scientist still thought his wife would be defending him; he would not find out that she was not defending him until the trial was ready to begin unless she was to visit him in the holding room. Matthew said he would help hold the scientist down for him and Jaden. Matthew asked Andrew if the two of them would be enough to hold the scientist down for Jaden to do a good sewing job because he could get other security to help and Andrew told Matthew to get two more guys just in case so Matthew called on his two largest men to help. Matthew briefed the two security individuals on the situation then off they went.

When Andrew, Matthew, and the two other guards got back to the scientist, Jaden told them that the scientist had been tearing at the wounds with his bare hands so they were still bleeding heavily and may possibly take more stitches because he may have to do two layers of sutures if he got to any veins or arteries, which it appeared that he did. Andrew and Matthew held the scientist's arms and lay across his upper body while the other two guards helped with holding the arms while lying across the scientist's legs. The scientist tried to fight everyone off but he was unsuccessful and Jaden did a prime job of sewing up the scientist's arms in two layers. Jaden told Andrew that the inner stitches would dissolve, but in seven to ten days, they would have to remove the outer stitches if he was not euthanized first. Andrew thanked Jaden for his services, and Jaden told Andrew he was at the service of the community. Jaden, the two extra guards, and Matthew were ready to leave and did so while Andrew went back to speak to scientist number six, but his wife walked up to speak to him first and she did not look happy at all. She approached Andrew asking if she could talk to her husband for a few minutes so Andrew told her she could speak with him for as long as she needed; she said it would not take long then she approached the holding room's window.

The scientist was happy to see his wife and told her so, but she boldly told him that he always told her to be quiet so that was all she knew and, as far as the trial was concerned, she was going to respect him and follow his consistent advice of keeping her mouth shut so he had to defend himself. Then she walked away from the holding room's window while the scientist stood there in shock. After a few minutes, he went to the bench inside the holding room and sat down. The scientist quickly got over the shock of his wife's actions and now had to think of what he was going to say on his behalf of the projects' being illegally continued, and after a few minutes he decided to put the blame on the new head scientist since he was not there to defend himself and he could use the new head scientist's suicide as a token of guilt for involving him in the continuation of both of the projects. Now it was a matter of finding a reason that was good enough for the jury to believe that he had to do the projects with the new head scientist or there would be some sort of personal issue that would go public and cause problems for him and his wife. Scientist number six decided that he would say the new head scientist used his name in the projects without him knowing then was told to take some documents home for safekeeping and told if he did not keep the documents he would be blackmailed as doing unlawful work on the two projects, and his wife knew of the things he was bringing home because he felt he had nothing to hide and he would attack his wife's testimony as it came during the trial.

Andrew telepathically detected some deliberate deceit from scientist number six so he decided to stay by the holding room and read the scientist's mind, and after two hours, Andrew got quite a bit of information from scientist number six's mind without him knowing it. It was now time for dinner so Andrew needed to go back to the castle, but before he left the holding room, he instructed the guards there that the scientist was not to have any silverware due to his poor state of mind, which became obvious when he used his previous silverware to injure himself. The guards acknowledged Andrew then served the scientist his meal without silverware.

As Andrew was leaving for his side of the castle, he could hear the scientist giving the guards a demanding time about having to eat with his hands and how uncivilized that was, but the guards ate their meals and paid the scientist no mind. Andrew made it back to his side of the castle a bit late for dinner so Camillia asked Andrew if everything was okay, and Andrew told Camillia everything he perceived from the scientist's mind and how the scientist was trying to get silverware to eat but the guards had already been advised not to give him any silverware. The couple were at the big roundtable discussing the scientist, and Melanie was bringing their dinner out to them so the couple ate slowly while they continued to discuss the scientist and his case. Camillia said it would be a promising idea to go into scientist number six's dreams that night if they could and get the whole true story about the projects and his involvement in them then Andrew agreed that they needed to try and hopefully succeed. Andrew told Camillia that the problem with only being able to read the scientist's mind and going into his dreams was that they could not prove anything; it was essentially their word against his. Camillia told Andrew if they were lucky with the information they could get from the scientist's mind they would know better what his contribution was to the projects and possibly be able to use the evidence of what was in his possession against him then Andrew told Camillia he hoped so.

The couple finished their dinner then went into their family room to relax and talk romantically to each other, but they were interrupted by Bridgette and Matthew. They asked if the couple had a moment to talk about babies, and Camillia told Bridgette and Matthew that she and Andrew always had time for them. Bridgette and Matthew were told by the couple to have a seat so they did. Bridgette asked Camillia how close was too close to having babies, and Camilla told Bridgette she could conceive when baby Sheeba reached ten months, but it would be better if she waited a bit longer. Camillia asked Bridgette why she was asking the type of questions she was asking, and Bridgette said she wanted another baby then Andrew told Bridgette and Matthew that they could do another healing whenever they were ready to just let them know. Bridgette asked if they could do a healing for them the next day because it was already sort of late, and Camillia told Bridgette that it would only take about ten minutes so they could do it right away. Matthew got excited so Andrew told Bridgette and Matthew to follow him and Camillia to the room of relaxation. Bridgette and Matthew took a seat then Camillia and Andrew took their positions, and it took about ten minutes for the royal couple to do the conception healing then when the healing was finished, Camillia told Bridgette and Matthew good luck then thanked Andrew and Camillia then they had a group hug. Bridgette and Matthew went to their quarters early to wind down and try to conceive their next child, Camillia and Andrew went back to their family room to relax until it was time to go to their own quarters.

Right after the royal couple got settled in their seats, Jaden burst through the castle's front door and headed straight for Andrew and Camillia. When he got in front of them, he asked if there was enough time to have a small conversation, and Andrew told Jaden they would always make time for him. Jaden got right to the point he told the royal couple that he was happy being a veterinarian and he wanted to continue to be at service to all the animals in the community, but he also wanted to be at service to the pale ones in the community because it seemed when the doctor was needed he was too busy to respond outside of the hospital so Jaden got the idea to be a home visiting doctor. Andrew and Camillia told Jaden that was a great idea and they would support him with that, but what was the problem that he needed to go to them. Jaden said he needed the funds; he was willing to work off the money or get a loan he could pay back, and Andrew interrupted Jaden then told him that he and Camillia would pay for the schooling and he owed them perfect scores and a graduation. Camillia told Jaden she would find a tutor and try to start the education the next day; then Jaden gave the royal couple big hugs and said he had better get home before his parents missed him then he told Andrew and Camillia he would see them the next day and to have a good night so Andrew and Camillia tells Jaden to have a good night and that they loved him.

It was now overtime for Andrew and Camillia to turn in for the night so they went to their bedroom, changed out of their day clothes, and into their bed clothes then got into their bed and cuddled as they usually did and fell asleep. Like every other night and every night to come, the royal couple's miniangel visited and sang her beautiful wake-up song then the couple greeted her and she greeted them back. The royal couple wasted no time in telling the miniangel about their day especially with the new head scientist and scientist number six and his plan to try to deceive the jury then Camillia told the miniangel that they wanted to go into the scientists dream to get the details of his involvement in the two projects that were being illegally continued and they wanted to know how he planned to blame the deceased new head scientist for as much as possible but they did not have a clue how to enter another individuals dreams.

Andrew asked the miniangel if she could help them to try to enter others' dreams and she said yes then explained the process to the royal couple; it was simple so they knew they would be able to do it within several tries. They just hoped those tries occurred within that night with the scientist because it would help in prosecuting him for his transgressions. The miniangel said she would cut her visit short so they would have more time to work and still get some peaceful sleep then she disappeared. The royal couple lay back down and assumed their positions then started to do as the miniangel had instructed.

It was not long before Andrew and Camillia were in the scientist's dream, and they greeted each other then went right to work on finding out the whole scam that he had planned about saying he was under the threat of a false blackmail and that was partially why he had the items from the science hall that he had then there was the plan to put as much of the blame on the new head scientist since he had committed suicide. Andrew and Camillia found out that it was scientist number six that would not stop working on the projects and when the new head scientist found out scientist number six told him about the profit they could get once the royal family could no longer perform the reproductive and life-extension procedures due to the abilities' being bred out of them, he also told the new head scientist that if they did not continue with the projects, their people would become extinct in time and it would be nice to be famous for saving their species. Scientist number six also spoke of creating other projects along the way but did not have anything in mind at the time; the new head scientist thought about what scientist number six had said and then he felt the projects would be for the better of the community and only wanted to do what was right.

Andrew and Camillia awoke from being in scientist number six's dream then Andrew told Camillia he had an idea for the trial, and Camillia told Andrew to continue on then he told her they could get the anesthesiologist to be at the trial with an injection of truth serum then Camillia told Andrew they had another problem so Andrew asked what the problem could possibly be and Camillia told him that the projects both were looking hopeful and they only put a stop on the projects because their miniangel advised them that the projects would never work, then Camillia asked Andrew how they were supposed to explain that they knew the projects would not work without giving up their source of information. Andrew said they would try to avoid that question by focusing on the scientists suddenly with the concern of how the royal couple could possibly know the projects would not work their mini angel appeared before them and told them that she could go to the trial then all that had to be said about the pre knowledge of the projects failing was divine intervention. Camillia told the miniangel that she thought no one was supposed to know of her and the dinosaur tail; then she said that it would be an opportunity to introduce the idea that everyone had an angel of their own but that would mean the chief and the royal couple had to reproduce the miniangels quickly and sooner than planned. The miniangel asked the royal couple if they were willing to do massive reproductions of miniangels in a brief period with the chief and they both said yes. The miniangel said she would go to the chief right away and let him know that reproductions were to start immediately, the couple said okay.

The miniangel left the royal couple then went to the chief's bedroom and sang her wake-up song for him, and he awoke quickly then greeted the miniangel and she greeted the chief. The miniangel explained the need for her to be at the scientist's hearing in the next morning but doing that would expose the dinosaur tail so everyone would be told they each had a miniangel and with that he and the royal couple would have to reproduce the miniangel's starting the next day and they would have to keep going until they had enough miniangels to go around then they could rest a few days before reproducing more miniangels. The chief said he could do as she was asking then he checked with her to make sure it was wise for them to be revealed at that time, and she said it was inevitable and there was not a better time than the trial then the chief said very well and she disappeared so the chief went back to sleep. Four hours later, it was time to wake up for a new day of events, and when the chief got out of bed he hurried to get ready for his day then raced to the royal couple's side of the castle and banged wildly on the front door, the butler answered the door and asked the chief to wait in the family room saying the royal couple would be out of their quarters any moment. Andrew and Camillia got out of bed and leisurely got themselves ready for the new day.

Andrew and Camillia were not aware that the chief was in their family room so when they went around the corner from the hallway toward the castle's private dining hall, the chief walked up behind them and surprised them then after Camillia recomposed herself she asked the chief if he was okay and he said the three of them needed to talk immediately. Andrew asked the chief if they needed to go to Camillia's office room and he said they could talk during breakfast at the big round table then he asked the royal couple if they would mind him eating with them. Camillia told the chief he was always welcome at their big round table; then everyone sat down and the chief waited for Melanie to bring out breakfast and leave before he spoke to Andrew and Camillia. The chief told the royal couple that a mini angel visited him the previous night and she was not his miniangel. Camillia cut him off, saying that it was hers and Andrew's mini angel that had visited him after seeing them and they knew why. The chief asked Camillia if she knew that her miniangel was talking about showing up at the trial and Camillia corrected the chief and told him she was going to be at the trial but because of that there would be an announcement that all pale ones had their own miniangel therefore Andrew, him, and she would have to do mass production of the miniangels then rest a couple of days and do it all over again.

Andrew asked the chief if they could produce enough miniangels for each pale one in one day and he told Andrew it was possible because there were three of them, but it would depend on how strong their gifts were. Andrew asked the chief what he meant by that, and the chief told Andrew that if he was underdeveloped in his gifts, he would not be able to produce many mini angels without tiring out quickly. Camillia spoke out and told the chief and Andrew that the three of them could do it and still have energy afterward; then she asked the chief if that was what he wanted to talk to them about and he said yes then they finished eating.

Before leaving the big roundtable, Camillia told Andrew and the chief that she needed their help finding a tutor for Jaden to be a home visiting medical doctor because he had spoken about it the evening before and she said she would take care of it and try to get the tutoring started that evening. The chief knew just who to get and told the royal couple to go with him. The chief headed out the front door and got on his horse so the royal couple saddled their horses and rode off with the chief who led them to the hospital and when they got there the chief jumped off his horse and told the royal couple to hurry up. Andrew and Camillia slid off their horses and turned their horses over to the hospital's stable boy then followed the chief into the hospital. They walked past the nurse's desk to a small office room right around the corner, and the chief just walked into the room and said hello without an escort or invitation.

There was an individual sitting behind a desk, and when he looked up from his reading, he jumped from his seat and flew around the desk to give the chief a big bear hug then respectfully greeted the royal couple and asked what he could do for them. The chief told Andrew and Camillia that the man was a close friend to him and a retired doctor with a license to teach, then the chief told the retired doctor that he had a prodigy boy who was a veterinarian and wanted to be a home visiting doctor as well. The retired doctor asked when did the boy want to start, and Camillia told the retired doctor that he wanted to start that day and the time was up to him. The retired doctor asked Camillia if she was familiar with the boy's schedule and she said yes, the boy was her godson as well as the stable boy for the castle and on occasion had to leave for a veterinary call, but his easiest time would be after breakfast then the retired doctor said very well and to have the boy in his office then, the royal couple thanked him then told him he would be paid handsomely. The retired doctor told the royal couple he was not in need of money just something to keep him busy so Andrew told the doctor he could donate the money to the hospital and he said no he was going to use the money to get the boy tools of the trade and a graduation gift as well as a little cash in his pocket for whatever he wanted to spend it on. The chief said he would send a runner to get the boy to him immediately because he could not do it due to needing to be at the trial of scientist number six then the retired doctor told the chief to take it easy and he told the royal couple to visit sometime. The chief, Andrew, and Camillia went to the nurse's desk and got a runner to bring Jaden to the retired doctor while they went to the trial. Andrew, Camillia, and the chief went out of the hospital and retrieved their horses from the hospital's stable boy and rode off to the hall of justice.

CHAPTER SEVENTY THREE

Andrew, Camillia, and the chief got to the hall of justice and left their horses with the hall of justice's stable boy then went inside of the building to take their places and after they were seated they all three looked for the miniangel but did not see her although, they knew she would be there when she felt the time was right. The chief and the royal couple did notice that the whole community was in the hall of justice except the twelve who were the jurors and the one who was the judge. After a brief time of arriving, Andrew asked that everyone be quiet unless they were on the stand; then the twelve jurors came out and sat in their area. Once they were settled, everyone rose to their feet silently as Matthew announced the presence of the judge and once the judge sat down everyone else sat down. The judge called the court to be in session then two guards brought scientist number six into the hall of justice, sat him in his seat, and stayed at his side for his protection as well as the protection of the public.

Now it was time for the judge to read the charge, which was two accounts of the continuation of a project found to be lethal to society. Then the judge said Andrew and Camillia were the prosecutors and the scientist was to defend himself. The judge called for the scientist to take the stand so he was escorted to the front of the room and offered a seat. Matthew stood in front of the scientist then asked him to stand and be sworn in so the scientist stood and went through the appropriate motions then sat back down then Andrew stood behind his table and asked the judge if he could use a nontraditional means of getting the truth out of the scientist and the judge asked for an explanation. Andrew explained that the scientist with-held information and tried to lie when originally questioned and because it was so obvious he had the anesthesiologist inject the scientist with truth serum and he would like to use the truth serum for the trial and the judge approved it. Andrew motioned for the anesthesiologist to go forward and give the scientist the injection and he did then once the medicine had a chance to get throughout his system Andrew started questioning the scientist about his involvement in the projects after they were supposed to be shut down.

The scientist told everything honestly and not only did he tell of his participation, but he also told of the deceased new head scientist's participation. Now there was only one question that Andrew had for the scientist and that was if there were any other scientists that knew about the project still being active and if so who then the scientist told the court that the whole department knew the projects were still active but only he and the new head scientist were working on them. While still on the stand, the scientist asked Andrew how he knew the projects would never work because as far as the science hall was concerned they were close to having the vaccines ready for public use.

Before Andrew or Camillia could answer the question, the courtroom door flew open and a bright yellow light shone in and everyone put their hands to their eyes trying to peek through their fingers. Slowly a figure started to emerge from the light; it was a beautiful iridescent angel, and she gave off a cool breeze as she floated by. When she got to Andrew and Camillia, she softly spoke to the court and said she told the royal couple of the projects being fatal and that there was nothing they could produce that would have the effect they were looking for. The judge asked the angel who she was and where she had come from so the angel told the judge she lived deep in the forest, and she was the royal couple's guardian angel then she said everyone had a guardian angel and now that they were being told of the angel's existence they would be meeting their angels soon then the angel and light just disappeared. The judge asked the jurors to deliberate for as long as they needed and to remember it was a life that was in their hands; then the jurors got up from their chairs and closed themselves off in a back room. They deliberated for only an hour when they came back out of the back room. Eleven of the twelve jurors sat down then the one left standing waited for the judge to ask for the verdict, and when the judge did ask for the verdict, the lone standing juror handed a folded piece of paper to the judge to read aloud; then the judge unfolded the paper and looked at it. The judge said that the scientist on trial was guilty of two counts of potential crimes against humanity punishable by the permanent closing of the science hall, then the judge went on to say that the other scientists were to be individually tried for accessory to potential crimes against humanity with the use of the truth serum. The judge then ordered each scientist to defend themselves against the royal couple, and the trials would start when the royal couple had enough time to get the information necessary and approached the court with a starting date. The judge also ordered the scientists all be held in the holding room on suicide watch with limited clothing and no eating utensils, the judge said there were to be no accidents this time. Andrew and his subordinates took all the scientists to the holding room, and once the scientists were locked up the public, jurors, royal couple, security, and judge could leave and go about their business.

Now that the trial for scientist number six was over, it left a half hour before the lunch hour so the royal couple went to their family room with the chief to wait for everyone to arrive and they spoke of their plans to go to the dinosaur tail to mass-produce the mini angels and Camillia told the chief that she did not know their miniangel had the ability to change her form then the chief told Camillia there were many things she did not know about the mini angels and their abilities. Camillia asked the chief what else the mini angels could do and the chief told her to ask her miniangel because it was not his place to say so she said she would the next time she and Andrew saw her. Camillia changed the subject of conversation and asked the chief if he minded her talking to Andrew about something sort of private in front of him and the chief told Camillia he did not mind as long as she was comfortable talking in front of him so Camilla turned to Andrew and asked him if he was ready for another pregnancy and baby then Andrew perked up and said really and Camillia told Andrew that day was perfect for conception and she could feel the ovulation occurring then Andrew asked Camillia how soon they needed to retire to their bedroom to catch the ovulation on time and she said it could wait until that night but if he wanted to avoid a pregnancy they had to abstain for a couple of days; then Andrew said he was ready when she was so she told Andrew that she was ready.

The chief told the royal couple that he was glad for them and he would keep it quiet until they announced it officially then Camillia thanked the chief and told him she did not mind him knowing because he was their father. The chief thanked her for the trust. Just then Jaden came in to wait for the rest of the family to arrive and he immediately went over to Andrew and Camillia then gave them both hugs and told them he loved them and thanked them for his tutoring to be a medical doctor. The couple told Jaden that they were doing nothing more than what parents do for their children when they could. Jaden told Andrew he knew it was expensive to pay the doctor for his tutoring service, and he wanted to earn his tutoring then Andrew told Jaden that the doctor did not want to be paid for his services but he was going to give the doctor money anyway and he said he was going to use the money for a wise purpose. Jaden told Andrew he was a veterinarian because of him and Camillia and he was going to be a medical doctor because of him and Camillia so he would be at their service when needed for free forever as a token of his appreciation and Andrew told Jaden that it would not be right to use him like that so Jaden told Andrew they would meet in the middle, he would charge them half price and Andrew said okay.

During Andrew and Jaden's talk, the rest of the family showed up in the family room so Andrew took Jaden by the hand then together they led the family into the castle's private dining hall for the lunch hour and family time. Everyone sat in their assigned seats at the big round table then Melanie had the kitchen staff bring the food out. Once everyone was served, they started to go around the table and share their day. It seemed that everyone wanted to talk about the trial and what might be in store for the other eight scientists. Andrew told everyone that he wanted to assure a fair trial so he, Camillia, Bridgette, the chief, and Matthew were going to consider all the documents possible and keep an open mind while looking at the documents from their perspective because the eight scientists left were not working on the projects and the two that were only wanted to help the community, they did not have divine intervention to guide them. Melanie made the comment that it seemed like he and Camillia were going to go easier on the scientists that were left than they did scientist number six; then Andrew told Melanie that no one was going to go easier on anyone but the important fact that the scientists left were not involved in the projects did need to be kept in mind, and truthfully, they really were not guilty of anything other than withholding information, which they did, because like the other two scientists, they felt they were contributing to society.

Camillia told Melanie that the scientists would most likely lose their licenses and struggle with their finances, which would affect their responsibilities for some time until they could get another job from someone, and that would be hard since no one would trust them to be honest and follow instructions. Jaden's parents asked how their community would come up with new things to better their society, and Camillia told her they would make an announcement after the trials and that she and Andrew would be open to anyone's ideas and they would be responsible for having accepted items made by the appropriate shop or a combination of shops if necessary. Jaden asked who would be responsible for producing the medicines that the doctors and veterinarians used then Andrew told Jaden that he and Camillia would make an extension on the hospital, which would include a wing for veterinary medicine and the sole purpose of the two areas would be for medication production then the royal couple would find the right people for the job and the chief would keep a close eye on what was going on in the wings. Jaden told the royal couple that their plan for medication production sounded good then he officially offered his service to replace the chief to supervise the two wings in the hospital especially since he had the necessary education and the chief did not. Andrew told Jaden that his schedule was becoming full, he had his doctor's education, veterinary practice, and stable boy job he may not be able to keep one of his obligations so Andrew told Jaden he would have to give up the stable boy job because the others were too important and he had worked so hard to achieve the status to get those positions.

Jaden told Andrew he was correct and he was setting himself up for adulthood and the ability to eventually sufficiently support a family because he was achieving his dream jobs and had his eye on a girl, but she did not know it and neither did anyone else. Andrew apologized to the chief telling him Jaden was going to be the medication-making supervisor then the chief told Andrew that was fine with him because he was not qualified for the job. The chief asked Andrew who he was going to get to replace Jaden as the stable boy, and Jaden interrupted, saying he knew a boy who had just come to the right age to work and did not have a job yet. Jaden went on to say that the boy he had in mind would find it an honor to work for the royal family so Andrew told Jaden to bring the boy to the castle after family time and they would make the switch immediately. That way, Jaden could draw up the blueprints for the medication rooms and get the construction crew on it immediately then Jaden said okay. Andrew made sure to tell Jaden that he wanted the construction crew cut into teams so they could work on the hospital's additions around the clock and get the rooms done quicker because he did not want the doctors or veterinarians running out of medications and Jaden concurred. Andrew instructed Camillia, Bridgette, Matthew, and the chief to go to the science hall and gather all the information there was and divide it into five piles so each one of them could go through a pile and that night would be to find all the documents and divide them up and the next day they could start going through them and everyone said okay.

Lunch and family time were over so Melanie went into the kitchen to supervise the kitchen staff cleaning the big round table and starting on the dinner meal. Jaden left the castle to go get the potentially new stable boy. Camillia, Bridgette, Matthew, and the chief went to the science hall to gather all the documents and notes there were to separate them into five piles to go through the next day. About the time everyone left, Jaden and a boy about his age walked into the castle's family room. Jaden told the boy to wait there while Jaden went to find Andrew so Jaden went toward the castle's private dining hall and ran into Andrew so Jaden told Andrew the new stable boy was in the family room waiting for his interview then Jaden and Andrew went to the family room. When they got there, the boy stood up and properly greeted his king.

Andrew told the boy to have a seat then started the interview and found out he had never had a job due to his age, but his parents knew he was at the castle to try to get the stable boy job and they approved of his decision to work for the king and queen.

After talking to the boy extensively, Andrew said he just needed to speak to the boy's parents as a courtesy to allow them to say anything they feel necessary; but as far as Andrew was concerned, the boy had the job and he told the boy and Jaden so. The boy asked Andrew how soon he would be ready to speak to his parents, and Andrew told the boy whenever they had the chance to get there so the boy told Andrew he could have both of his parents there in fifteen minutes then asked if that would be fine and Andrew said he would wait for them right there in the family room. The boy sprang out of his seat and ran out of the castle and rode hard to get to his parents' shop to get them to the castle to speak with the king, and as the boy said fifteen minutes later, there was a knock at the castle's front door. Andrew told the butler he would get the door so the butler stood down and Andrew opened the door.

As soon as the front door was opened all the way, the boy and his parents properly greeted the king, then Andrew invited them in and directed them to the family room where Jaden was. Everyone got seated then Andrew told the boy's parents that he would like to hire the boy as the castle's stable boy, and the boy's parents were elated that the king would want help from them so the parents said it was fine with them then proceeded to tell Andrew that the boy had just come of age to work and had never had a job before. Andrew told the parents that everyone had to start somewhere and he was delighted to be the boy's first employer then the parents thanked Andrew. Jaden offered to show the boy around and let him know the dos and don'ts of the job, and Andrew and the boy's parents thought that was a prime idea and a very cordial thing to do. The boy's parents went back to their shop to finish working for the day, Andrew went to the science hall to see if he could help with the day's project, and Jaden took the boy around the barn and stable. Jaden was very direct about how the boy was to care for the buildings and animals as well as making sure the boy knew the room with the doors was off limits due to the fact it was a veterinary office. Jaden told the boy if he did not keep things as he had done, he would fire the boy from his job himself; the boy said he would comply with everything. The boy started immediately so Jaden went to his parents' shop to let them know about the change in his schedule because it would be an immense help for Jaden to not be a stable boy with all the other things that required his attention; besides, soon enough, he would be taking on the new job of producing veterinary and medical medications and he was super excited over that.

Once Jaden left the new stable boy, Andrew was arriving at the science hall; and Camillia, Bridgette, Matthew, and the chief were coming out. When they saw Andrew, the chief told Andrew they were ready to start the investigation the next morning. Bridgette went back to the castle to plan the events for girl's day, Matthew went back on patrol to check on the other guards, then the chief suggested that he, Andrew, and Camillia get to the dinosaur tail and start reproducing miniangels before the public started complaining that they had not met their guardian angel yet. Andrew and Camillia agreed so off they went.

When Andrew, Camillia, and the chief got to the great wall's doors, the guards there initially told them that they could not pass without six hunters; but Andrew used his position in the community to convince the guard to let them pass for official business that was of a private nature. Andrew and the chief did not know where the dinosaur tail was, but Camillia had told them that she was there one time and found it by accident and assured them that she could find it again so Andrew and the chief followed Camillia. Camillia told Andrew and the chief that if they did not find the dinosaur tail in a reasonable amount of time, she had an idea of what they could do to assure they would find it. Andrew asked how, so Camillia explained that he and the chief would protect her body while she astroprojected to her miniangel and ask her to come to them and guide them then she could get back to her body.

The chief and Andrew agreed that was an innovative idea then asked Camillia why they did not just go ahead and do that, and Camillia told them that for one to help another, one must first try to help themselves. The chief said that was wise. Camillia had been seeing her landmarks, so she told the chief and Andrew she knew where she was and they were close. As soon as Camillia said they were close, they walked up to the dinosaur tail. Andrew and the chief were beside themselves; this was their first time to see the dinosaur tail, and they could not believe how beautiful it was, and Camillia told Andrew and the chief that the dinosaur tail was just as beautiful the second time as it was the first time. Andrew and Camillia's angel approached them and greeted them, they returned the greeting then she asked the royal couple why they were there and Camillia told her they were there to produce more miniangels so the community could meet their guardian angels and there would be enough of the angels to keep the dinosaur tail alive.

The miniangel asked the royal couple if the chief had taught them how to produce miniangels already, and Camillia said no. The miniangel told the couple that she could link minds with them and show them much quicker than the chief's way, so the couple asked her if she would link minds with them and show them how to produce more miniangels and she said yes. The miniangel told the couple to relax and said she was going to link minds with both together; then she positioned herself between the couple, put her hands on their temples, whispered something seemingly foreign, then the couple saw images in their mind's eye. At first, the images were unclear, but they quickly became clear and started to make sense. When they were finished, the miniangel gently broke the link between the three of them, and the chief was astonished at what he saw.

Once the miniangel got the link with the royal couple, they all started to glow then the couple lifted off the ground and slowly spun around; then when the link broke, they stopped spinning and glowing, but they landed in the same position they started in. Andrew and Camillia told the chief that they now knew how to produce miniangels and they were ready to start. The chief asked the couple if they could do the production in mass amounts and the couple said yes that they would be as energetic after the production as they currently were. Camillia told the chief that the miniangel showed her and Andrew a way that was different than how he produced miniangels, but their way was impossible to him because he did not have the healing ability, which was less stressful and quicker. Then Andrew told Camillia they needed to do less talking and get to the production of miniangels because they would be due to be back at the castle soon and the walk would take quite a bit of time then he told the chief to do the productions his way.

The chief watched as the miniangels arranged themselves into a single-file line then Andrew followed the line, touching each angel on the top of her head and moving on. Each angel he touched divided into two angels; then Camillia went behind Andrew doing the same thing, and each angel divided into two angels, and when they got at the end of the line, they went back to the beginning of the line and did it again until there was uncountable numbers of angels, from the looks of it there were many angels per person. When Andrew and Camillia were finished, they told the miniangels they would try to visit the dinosaur tail in person occasionally then they told their miniangel they would see her that night after everyone was asleep. Andrew, Camillia, and the chief started walking toward their compound. All the way back to the compound, the chief could not stop talking about how wonderful it was to see the couple produce so many miniangels without any effort. The chief spoke of the production as being miraculous; the chief just could not express how happy he was that everyone would have their own miniangel to consult with as he and the couple had been for quite some time.

Now as the chief, Andrew, and Camillia approached the compound doors, the chief stopped speaking of the production of the miniangels because that was their secret and had to stay that way for the safety of the miniangels and good of their society because if others knew of the dinosaur tail and found it deep in the forest, there could be devastating effects for the miniangels which could be the end of the relationship of the miniangels with the pale ones. The gate guard saw the chief, Andrew, and Camillia approaching so he called out to the other door guards to open the heavy doors for them so that when they were ready to enter the commune, they could do so without having to wait several minutes for the door to be opened. As the royal couple and the chief entered, they thanked the guards and proceeded to go to the couple's side of the castle. When the chief and the royal couple got in the couple's side of the castle, everyone was wrapping up their day in preparation for going into their quarters for the night and that was what made the chief, Andrew, and Camillia realize how late it was so the chief said he was going to his side of the castle so the couple could turn in for the night. The couple told the chief to have a good night and to come to their side of the castle for breakfast, then they could go to the science hall together to work, and the chief said okay. Camillia went to Bridgette and Matthew's bedroom and knocked on the door. Matthew answered the door then Camillia told him to bring Bridgette and join her and Andrew for breakfast in the morning then they could go to the science hall together. Matthew said okay.

CHAPTER SEVENTY FOUR

While Camillia was inviting Bridgette and Matthew to breakfast, Andrew went to the couple's bedroom and waited for Camillia to get there so they could spend some romantic time together and hopefully make a baby girl. It was not long before Camillia met up with Andrew in their bedroom and as she walked into the room. Andrew quickly went to her, grabbed her around the waist, picked her up off the floor, and spun around with her a few times then put her down and told her he loved her. Camillia wrapped her arms around Andrew's neck and kissed him passionately then pulled him to the bed and removed his clothing then he removed her clothing and they engaged in foreplay for an hour then they made long passionate love. When Camillia and Andrew were done making love, they lay together and cuddled while professing their love for each other and in the middle of speaking words of love Camillia told Andrew she could feel the union of the gametes and she felt that they had just conceived a girl. Andrew was elated that they had just conceived and he was wanting a girl so he was overjoyed over the fact that Camillia felt that the new baby was a girl and he knew she was right because she had never been wrong about her pregnancies yet.

Andrew and Camillia got out of bed and put their day clothes that they had taken off each other into the dirty clothes bin and put on their bed clothes then got back into bed and assumed their cuddling position to try to go to sleep so they could get a bit of rest before their miniangel was to arrive. The royal couple only got a couple of hours of sleep before their miniangel arrived due to their sexual encounter, Camillia's miniangel sang her beautiful wake up song that the couple woke up to every night and when they woke up this night Andrew and Camillia found that there were three miniangels instead of the usual one. With surprise, the couple greeted the three miniangels and they returned the greeting then Camillia said she was glad to see three mini angels but questioned why there were three instead of the usual one then the miniangel that had been coming told Camillia that she was her guardian angel then she pointed to the second mini angel saying that guardian angel was for Andrew and the third guardian angel was for the unborn child they had just conceived.

Camillia's guardian angel told her that thanks to her and Andrew, that night was a special night because the whole community would be meeting their guardian angels and it was an honor to serve the new breed. Andrew's guardian angel told the couple that they had tried to have a relationship with humans, but they were too fearful of the unfamiliar and they did not believe enough to take heed to their warnings and that was why it took the angels so long to attempt a relationship with the pale ones. Andrew told the miniangels that it was he and the rest of the pale ones who should be honored to have guardian angels and to be able to converse with them. Camillia concurred, and the three miniangels thanked the couple for their modesty. The unborn infant's guardian angel fluttered about Camillia's stomach touching it and softly sang a lullaby while Andrew's guardian angel spoke directly to him and Camillia's guardian angel spoke directly to her.

Both Andrew and Camillia's guardian angels spoke to them about the scientists who were going to be tried for possibly being accessories to two accounts of a crime against humanity. They advised the couple to tread lightly during the trial because they were not actually doing the work they only knew that the new head scientist and scientist number six were doing the work and it was questionable if they were actually guilty as charged because they truly thought they were working for the benefit of the people. The scientist did not try the vaccines they had on anyone and had not planned to; that was why they had the mice then the guardian angels told the couple that they had been told the science hall would not find a vaccine because there was no combination of anything available to them that would work but due to the lack of divine intervention for the scientist's they did not know that. The two guardian angels finished what they had to say about the matter by telling the couple that they just wanted to mention a couple of small facts for them to think about during the gathering of information and during the trial itself and the couple told their guardian angels they would think about what they said and try to be fair in not putting the eight scientists left as active participants. The three angels said their good nights and disappeared so Andrew and Camillia lay back down to try to get another couple of hours of sleep but their consciences would not allow their eyes to shut so the couple sat back up in bed and discussed the eight-scientists and some options of how to correct the wrong doing on their part since no true crime had been committed by them. Andrew and Camillia did agree that the case was a difficult one and by the time they agreed on that also it was time to get out of bed and prepare for the new day so the couple got up, went to the bathroom, took off their bedclothes, got their day clothes on, brushed their teeth, washed their faces, and brushed their hair then they hugged and kissed each other, said they loved each other and went out of the bedroom heading for the castle's private dining hall to meet up with the chief, Bridgette, and Matthew for breakfast together then they could head to the science hall together.

Andrew and Camillia were the first to arrive at the castle's private dining hall so they sat down and advised Melanie that the chief, Bridgette, and Matthew were going to be joining them for breakfast so Melanie set more places at the big round table then told the kitchen staff to make plates for three more people and they did. Bridgette and Matthew were next to arrive at the big round table, and Bridgette looked a bit peaked so Camillia asked Bridgette if she could ask a personal question, and Bridgette told Camillia there were no secrets between them and nothing was personal amongst their group so Camillia asked Bridgette if her and Matthew made love the night before and Bridgette told Camillia yes. Camillia asked Bridgette to remain standing as Matthew sat down then Camillia told Bridgette that one of the gifts her and Andrew had was to communicate with unborn children and at that point Camillia put her hand on Bridgette's stomach, closed her eyes, shook her head in a yes motion then told Bridgette that her unborn child was hungry and that she would feel better once she ate.

As Melanie brought everyone's breakfast to them, Bridgette asked Camillia if she said there was a hungry baby, and Camillia told Bridgette yes and congratulations at that point Matthew and Bridgette got excited then Matthew asked Camillia if she could tell if it was a boy or girl, and Camillia told Matthew yes then he asked Camillia if she would do that for them and Camillia told Bridgette to remain standing. As Camillia walked back to Bridgette, Matthew told everyone he was hoping for a boy since they could only have two babies and they already had a girl. Camillia felt Bridgette's belly, and after a couple of minutes, Camillia announced that Bridgette and Matthew were having a boy. Both Bridgette and Matthew were elated, and they sincerely thanked Camillia then Camillia told the expecting couple that she and Andrew were expecting also but not to tell the family until the doctor made it official. Bridgette asked for the same favor and everyone there agreed to wait for the doctor to make their pregnancies official then the couples could make their own announcements. The chief, Bridgette, Matthew, Andrew, and Camillia finished their breakfast then left the castle's private dining hall headed to the science hall.

When everyone got outside, the new stable boy asked the royal couple if they wanted two horses saddled or a buggy hitched, and Camillia told him two horses saddled then he ran to the stable and quickly got two horses saddled while Matthew got two horses saddled for him and Bridgette; the chief already had his horse there so everyone mounted and headed to the science hall. Everything the five of them needed was already gathered and split into five piles so they could all gather information then compare who found out what and try to make a fair case against the eight-scientists. Everyone was getting in front of a pile, but before anyone could start to go over their pile of papers, Andrew told everyone what his guardian angel had told him the night before about the scientists that they had not been working on the projects but did know the new head scientist and scientist number six were working on the projects but all ten scientists were working for the benefit of the community and did not know there was no combination of anything available to them that would work so it was a question of whether or not this was a crime against humanity for the two scientists that worked on the project therefore it was also a question as to whether or not the other eight scientists were an accessory to the crime against humanity. Camillia added that it was their duty to have a fair trial so everyone needed to tread lightly; then everyone realized that what Andrew and Camillia had said had not been taken into consideration before then everyone verbally agreed to keep those thoughts in mind while going through the information before them and with that everyone started reading page after page of information.

It was a long tiring process, but the group of five got the reading completed, and it was now the lunch hour and family time so the five of them left the science hall, agreeing to meet back at the science hall to discuss their findings so Andrew and Camillia could get the whole story before going to trial and changing eight people's lives forever. By the time the group of five got to the couple's side of the castle, everyone else was already there in the family room waiting for them so that when they stepped inside, Andrew immediately led the family to the castle's private dining hall to take their seats at the big round table and Melanie had the kitchen ready to bring their meal out to them.

While everyone ate their lunch, they went around the room sharing their day and what their day still held for them and by the time they went around the table sharing they were done eating and family time was over. Everyone got up from the big round table and went their separate ways except the five that were to meet at the science hall and once everyone was out of the castle's private dining hall the kitchen crew cleaned the big round table then focused on dinner preparations.

Back at the science hall, everyone that was supposed to be there was there and they got right to work starting with Bridgette explaining what she found in the documents and notes she read then Matthew explained what he read and got out of the documents and notes then the chief had his turn to do the same. As Bridgette, Matthew, and the chief spoke about their findings, Camillia took notes on what she felt would be important for the case; then it was Andrew's turn to share his findings about the case and Camillia took notes from his findings. Now it was Camillia's turn to share her findings, and hers was vocalized slowly because she was writing notes that she felt were important to the case. Finally, everyone heard everything so it was time to discuss the possible charges if any and if need be the suggested repercussions. Like the lunch hour, the group of five finished just on time for the dinner hour so they left the science hall to go to the royal couple's side of the castle to eat together and have some recreational conversations. Melanie had the kitchen cook extra food because she figured she would have the same five that were working late during the lunch hour at the dinner table because they were going back to the science hall to try to wrap up their business and they would definitely be hungry. Sure enough, the five Melanie was expecting at the big round table for dinner were there at the big round table; however, they were much less stressed and more talkative. Melanie had the kitchen bring everyone's dinner out to them and they carried on a light conversation with laughter. They ate so slowly that by the time they finished eating, it was nearly time to turn in for the night so everyone parted ways and worked on winding down after a stimulating day.

Within a half hour, everyone was in their quarters and getting ready for bed. Andrew and Camillia had a challenging time settling down due to the upcoming trial of the scientists so Andrew and Camillia discussed the way they were going to handle it and started to make proposals with one another for mild consequences since there were no natural consequences available. Camillia proposed to try the scientists together since they all had the same charges and would most likely have the same consequences; then Andrew thought about Camillia's proposal and agreed so together they decided to approach the judge with that proposal. The discussion and conclusion that Andrew and Camillia had just finished took three hours, and they were still wide awake but they were relaxing in their bed. Then their guardian angels arrived, and for the first time, they did not have to sing their wake-up song. The guardian angels knew the couple was still rattled by the upcoming trial and that was why they were still awake so they told the couple that they did a respectable job that day in telling the others about treading lightly then the angels told the couple that the trial would work out for the better of their society if they followed through with the way they were planning and it was an excellent idea to try them together and get the incident over with. The guardian angel told the couple that the judge would accept their suggestion of a single trial because the judge's guardian angel was going to request it. The guardian angels said they would not stay long so the couple could get some sleep then they disappeared so Andrew and Camillia lay back down and tried to sleep. But the anticipation of the trial kept them both awake so they lay there in silence for five hours then it was finally time to start the new day.

The royal couple got out of bed and prepared for the new day then went to the castle's private dining hall and right after they sat down Bridgette walked in and told Camillia she was looking for her. Camillia asked Bridgette what she could do for her, and Bridgette told Camillia she was going to go to the hospital and try to see the doctor and wanted to know if she wanted to go with her and get the official word of being pregnant. Camillia told Bridgette that she and Andrew needed to stop by the justice hall first to get a date for the scientist's trial then Bridgette said she would go with her then they could go to the hospital together. Andrew told Bridgette that was an excellent idea. Andrew told Bridgette to have Matthew come into the castle's private dining hall for the two of them to have breakfast with him and Camillia so Bridgette said okay then went to retrieve Matthew and as she left. Jaden was bouncing in with a chipper attitude he greeted Bridgette and she returned the greeting. Jaden approached Andrew and asked to talk to him and Camillia about something sort of personal then Andrew asked if they needed to go into the office room to talk and Jaden said no but that he needed the royal couple's permission for something. Andrew and Camillia had no idea what Jaden could possibly be asking for so Andrew told Jaden that whatever he had to say seemed rather important so he should go ahead and talk to him and Camillia. Jaden told the royal couple that he wanted to date their oldest daughter Armellya. Jaden told Andrew and Camillia that he knew she was a few years younger than him but she was dating age and he was attracted to her personality and she was also beautiful then Jaden told the royal couple that if things worked out after a long courtship he would make a good husband and provider to her. Camillia looked at Andrew, and Andrew told Jaden he had the royal couple's permission to date their daughter and if things worked out after an appropriate courtship, they would be honored to see them get married. Jaden relaxed from his nervousness and thanked the royal couple and went about his business.

As Jaden was leaving the castle's private dining hall, Bridgette and Matthew walked in and took a seat at the big round table. Matthew suggested that he and Andrew go to the justice hall while Camillia and Bridgette head to the hospital, and after he and Andrew spoke to the judge, they could go to the hospital to meet up with the girls because they would probably have to wait for the doctor to have time for them. Andrew agreed that was the best way to get two things done efficiently so the girls said okay. Everyone finished eating so they went outside to get their horses and go about their ways. Andrew and Matthew got to the justice hall and spoke to the judge about being ready for the trial against the eight scientists and having them tried as a group instead of individually. The judge said they could be tried as a group then asked when Andrew and Camillia would be ready for the trial, and Andrew said they were ready immediately so the judge asked how about after the lunch hour and that sounded good so Andrew said he and Camillia would be there so now that was taken care of it was time for the two men to get to the hospital with their wives. The girls had only been at the hospital for a brief time and checked in at the nurse's desk, they were told that the doctor was not really busy so he would be with them shortly and the girls were hoping their husbands would get there on time to hear what the doctor had to say.

Sure enough, the guys got there before the doctor walked into the exam room, and the girls were relieved. A few minutes behind the guys, the doctor walked into the room and asked what the nature of the visit was, and both guys told the doctor they believed they were dads again and that they needed him to make it official. The doctor poked his head out of the exam room and called for a nurse to draw blood from both girls then he went back to the girls and asked who was going to be first for an exam and Bridgette said Camillia would be first so Camillia got onto the exam table. The doctor had his equipment ready this time so he did not have to dig in his desk for the tools. After the doctor did his physical exam, he did an ultrasound and saw a vibrant fetus; then he said next so Camillia got off the exam table and the doctor checked Bridgette the same way and saw the same things so he told Bridgette she could get off the exam table. The nurse went into the hospital room and took blood from both girls then took the vials to the laboratory herself and put a rush on them and while the nurse was gone the doctor told both couples that he saw a viable fetus in both women. Everyone in the room got excited and hugged the doctor then the doctor told the girls to be back in one month for their prenatal checkup. They said okay and went into the waiting room to wait for their blood test results. The two couples went to the waiting room to wait for their blood test results then Andrew told Camillia that the trial for the eight scientists was going to be after the lunch hour and that the judge agreed to try them all at once. Camillia said good because she wanted the ordeal done and she was sure the scientists did too.

Forty-five minutes after getting to the waiting room the girls' blood tests came back so the doctor got the results then went to tell the two couples the good news, their blood tests were both positive and now that they got the official word they could make the announcement during family time and neither couple could wait. Now that they were done with the doctor and the judge, Bridgette was going to go back to the room of relaxation and plan what the girls were going to do on girls' day then make reservations at the various shops since there were more than one person going in for services at one time, Bridgette wanted to assure they could get their services at the same time to achieve the whole togetherness goal. While Bridgette was taking care of girl's day arrangements, Camillia went to make sure everything was ready for the trial, and Andrew joined her.

Jaden was back in the castle's family room talking to Armellya and enjoying her company as he was working up the confidence to ask her to go steady. The two kids were laughing and having an enjoyable time with light conversation, but the conversation turned serious and was about the adults' situations. Then Jaden told Armellya that he had something serious to speak to her about since they were being serious and it involved them. Armellya became concerned about Jaden because he had never been so nervous looking and Armellya noticed that Jaden was trembling a bit so she took his hands into hers and told him that he could tell her anything. Jaden asked her to let him speak his thoughts without interrupting him and he would let her know when he was finished speaking, and Armellya said okay. Jaden told Armellya that he had a suitable job and was receiving lessons to have another suitable job so he would be a good provider for someone special; then he told Armellya that they had been friends for many years and were able to speak and share openly with each other and he treasured that and never wanted to lose that but he had to risk losing her by asking for her hand as a steady girlfriend and potential wife after a proper courting time. Jaden told Armellya he respected her and that he was attracted to who she was and her beauty was beyond that of a perfect rose then he told her he found himself falling in love with her more and more each day.

Jaden told Armellya that he had already spoken to her parents about this, and they approved of them being as one then Jaden told Armellya he was finished talking that it was now her turn. Armellya kept Jaden's hands in hers as she leaned forward toward Jaden and kissed him gently on the cheek then told him to be at ease because he had won her heart long ago and she would be proud to be his girl and someday get married and have his children. Jaden jumped up from his seat and took Armellya by the hands and pulled her to her feet then picked her up in his arms then he told her he loved her and she kissed him again then told him she loved him too then he put her down. Armellya told Jaden that they could announce their courtship during family time and Jaden told her that was an excellent idea then Jaden said he needed to go take care of something but he would see her at family time if not before then they gave each other a simple kiss on the lips and Jaden walked away. Armellya went to her quarters to daydream about what their house would look like and how fabulous it would be to be married to Jaden while Jaden was on his way to the jewel shop to buy Armellya a promise ring and look at engagement and wedding rings.

It did not take long for Jaden to find the perfect wedding set and a beautiful engagement ring, but he was not seeing what he had in mind for a promise ring so he decided to buy the engagement ring and wedding set then instead of asking Armellya to wear his promise ring he would ask her to be engaged to him and give her the engagement ring to wear and a gift of some sort. Jaden decided to surprise Armellya with those plans during family time on that day but he did not know Armellya had plans for family time that involved him also, after some daydreaming she left the castle to go shopping for a gift for Jaden that would be romantic so right after Jaden left the jewel shop she entered and wanted to get a promise ring for Jaden and she saw three rings that she had to choose from and she finally did then she left the shop and went in search of a gift to go along with the ring. Jaden and Armellya were already showing signs of thinking alike and being one; they both got the other's bed clothes so it would be like they were together during the night hours when they would be alone. It was extremely close to family time so Armellya and Jaden rushed back to the castle with their gifts and prepared them to be given while Andrew and Camillia went to the family room to greet family as they arrived, Matthew headed for the family room from his security rounds, Bridgette finished with her last reservation for the girl's day out and the rest of the family trickled in until eventually they were all there. Andrew led the family to the castle's private dining hall for the lunch hour in which everyone shared their day after Bridgette had the kitchen serve the meal and she sat down with everyone at the big roundtable.

CHAPTER SEVENTY FIVE

Everyone started to eat and share, and it seemed everyone was having a good day. Then it was time for Bridgette and Matthew to share their day, and they announced they were pregnant and everyone clapped and cheered. When it got to Andrew and Camillia's turn, they announced they were pregnant also, and again everyone clapped and cheered. A couple of more individuals shared their day; then it was Jaden's turn to share so he got out of his seat and walked over to Armellya. Everyone got extremely quiet as Jaden knelt on one knee and asked Armellya to be his wife after an appropriate courting time, and she said yes then Jaden put the engagement ring on her ring finger and Armellya started to shed tears of joy then Jaden handed her a present and when she opened it she shed even more tears as she hugged Jaden and told him she loved him. Everyone was smitten with sentiment then Armellya took her turn to share and presented a ring to Jaden as a token of their love and friendship and she said it was a promise to be married after their courting days were to come to an end.

By this time, everyone was shedding enormous amounts of tears of joy for the new couple then Armellya gave Jaden her gift for him, and when he opened it and saw it was essentially the same gift he gave her, he took her into his arms and gave her a long romantic kiss and everyone cheered and wished them a long life together. Everyone finished eating and had to go to the justice hall for the trial against the eight scientists so the new stable boy saddled up the women's horses while the men saddled their own then they joined the rest of the community headed for the justice hall. Like before, the community took their seats in the arena, Andrew and Camillia took their seats at the prosecutors table, security brought out all eight scientists to the defense table, the twelve jurors were in the jury box, and the judge was at the desk at the head of the building. The judge announced the charges as two accounts of accessory to a crime against humanity then gave the floor to Andrew and Camillia then they sounded more like defense attorneys than prosecuting attorneys in saying that the scientists were not working on the two projects, they only knew that the other two scientists were working on them and the eight scientists like the previous two had good intentions to work for the bettering of the community with no knowledge of the inability to make a combination of ingredients to provide the desired outcome.

Andrew and Camillia reminded the court that the only reason they told the scientists to abandon the projects was because they had a divine intervention to make them aware of the lack of accessibility to ingredients that would benefit the project. The royal couple told the courts that they recommended the scientists be disbanded and lose their licenses then the science hall be made into a workshop for allowing several shops to come together at any given time to create items that the public put in to the king and queen for approval for the bettering of the community such as spindles and sheep's shears to produce cotton material to make lighter clothing. The judge told the scientists they just got lucky by having the prosecution defend them so all they needed from the jury was a yes or no vote with the majority taking precedence on whether to make the proposed changes with the mentioned consequences. The jury went to the back room as they did before and in ten minutes they were back out with their decision, eleven jurors sat down while one juror stood and when the judge asked for the ruling the standing juror handed a folded piece of paper over then sat.

The judge unfolded the paper then read it quietly while everyone's curiosity piqued especially the scientists and finally, the judge read the verdict which was a unanimous vote of twelve to zero for changing the science hall into a workshop, disbanding the scientists, and stripping the scientists of their licenses. Now the eight scientists must find a new way of supporting themselves within the community and although they were committed to their scientific vows to serve the community they could not be trusted to obey the rules and regulations that the king and queen had made clear to everyone and lived by themselves. With the trial over, everyone but the eight scientists left the justice hall because they wanted to talk among themselves in private over their chances of surviving because even though they were free, they had to find a way to feed themselves and their families if they had one, keep a roof over their heads, feed and house their horses and livestock, and several other things. The scientists were debating on going to the earth's surface and utilizing the safe houses that the humans used to live in and living like retirees because they felt that no one would employ them in the commune and they would rather live in exile than give the community the satisfaction of seeing them sleep on the streets and beg to survive. All eight scientists agreed to the idea they came up with, but like everything, they must get the king and queen's permission then they would need a guide to get them there who would have to travel back alone and be in harm's way just to escort them. The scientists also had to take into consideration the elevated levels of radiation on the earth's surface. They could deal with it because they were pale ones, but it would take several years off their lifespan though they decided it would still be better than staying in the commune as recently observed. The eight scientists went to the castle to speak to Andrew and Camillia about their decision to live on the earth's surface so the couple met with the scientists in their family room and heard what they had to say without interruption then Andrew told the scientists that living outside of the commune was not an option because they needed to stay where they belonged and face their consequences. The scientists tried to argue the matter with the royal couple then Andrew told them he and Camillia we're not going to entertain the subject any further and they needed to leave the castle then Andrew called for his and Camillia's personal guards and the guards were at the couple's side within seconds then the scientists decided to leave saying that was not the last time the couple would be seeing them.

Andrew told Camillia he wanted to speak to her in her office room so the two of them went quickly to the office room and closed the door behind themselves then Andrew told Camillia that he did not want her anywhere without her guard with her because the scientists were disgruntled and may become dangerous and Camillia agreed and Andrew would keep his guard at his side as well. As soon as the couple finished talking in the office room, they opened the door and their guards were there so Andrew told Camillia's guard that she was to stay with Camillia always and during hours of sleep stay aware of anything suspicious then Andrew told his guard that he was to stay with him and just like Camillia's guard, sleep with one eye open and both guards said okay then asked if there was something specific they needed to be aware of. Andrew told their personal guards that they needed to be cautious of the scientists because they had promised that they would be back and that could only mean trouble.

After the couple finished speaking to their personal guards, Andrew sent a runner to track down Jaden so Andrew could ask him if he would be interested in drawing up the floor plans for the science hall to be reconstructed as a multi use hall then Andrew called for the construction hall to transport the chemicals from the science hall to the hospital and discard by fire the files in the science hall and strip the innards of the hall so they could hopefully prepare the hall for reconstruction according to Jaden's floor plans. The first runner returned with Jaden and Andrew asked him to have a seat then Andrew told Jaden he wanted to discuss the science halls reconstruction then Jaden interrupted the king to tell him about having the blueprints for the hospitals two medication production rooms and Andrew was elated then he asked Jaden if he had the blueprints with him and he said yes then Andrew told Jaden the head construction worker was on his way so together they could discuss that project then Andrew told Jaden he wanted to talk to him about reconstructing the science hall into a multi use hall for several halls to come together and work on projects that required more than one specialty to produce Jaden said he could draw up a floorplan for the construction crew to build by and Andrew said please. Jaden told Andrew the floorplan would be ready before the night was out and he would get it to him then Andrew told Jaden thank you so Jaden asked Andrew if there was anything else he needed to talk to him about and Andrew told Jaden about the disgruntled scientists and how there might be a possibility that they could target Armellya to get to him and Camillia then Jaden cut him off and told him not on his watch. Andrew asked Jaden if he would mind having a personal guard be with them around the clock that way when the two of them separate the guard would go with Armellya and she would still have some protection and Jaden told Andrew he welcomed the idea.

Andrew was finished talking to Jaden so Jaden left to go work on the floor plans for the science hall, and as Jaden was leaving, the second runner returned with the head of construction. Andrew handed the blueprints for the two hospital rooms he needed to be built so they could be used for medication production and he asked the head construction worker how soon they could get started. The head construction worker told Andrew they could start that night then Andrew told him that he would have the blueprints for the reconstruction of the science hall before the night was out, and he wanted to know if the crew could divide into teams of four and work twelve hours at a time so they could have two teams on the science hall and two teams on the hospital's medication rooms. That way, the construction on both could go around the clock to get done quicker because both projects were equally important then the head construction worker told Andrew they could do as asked; then he looked the medication rooms blueprints over closely.

After looking at the blueprints, the head construction worker told Andrew they could have the rooms done in two day's maximum then he excused himself to get his men into teams and have two of them start on the medicine rooms immediately. As the head construction worker was leaving, Andrew reminded him that he would get the other blueprints to him as soon as he got them from Jaden and he said okay. After talking with the head construction worker, Andrew realized it was getting close to the dinner hour so Andrew got his and Camillia's runners and sent the first one after Jaden, the second one after Jaden's parents, the third one after Bridgette, and the fourth one after Matthew, and he sent Camillia after the chief. But Camillia had no idea what Andrew was doing with sending runners after people especially so close to the dinner hour, but she did not question it because she knew he would reveal his madness eventually.

Andrew did not say a thing about what was going on until everyone was there then he led everyone to the castle's private dining hall then got everyone seated, and when Melanie started to bring the food out for everyone, Andrew finally told everyone that was there that gathering for dinner was going to be every night. Andrew told Jaden that his son-in-law should eat at least one meal with his spouse because it was a valuable time to catch up with each other and Jaden was honored that Andrew already considered him his son-in-law. Andrew told the chief that he was their adoptive father and they needed some time with him to just enjoy one another. Then Andrew told Bridgette and Matthew they were there because Camillia and Bridgette were so close and they did not really get enough time together to just be friends. It was not fair that the only time the two girls were together was for work, and Matthew and Andrew were buddies and also needed time to be such. Finally, he could not leave out Jaden's parents because they needed time to be with their son and daughter-in-law without it being for business, and everyone agreed then thanked Andrew for the idea and followed through with it. Dinner went smoothly and everyone enjoyed themselves, but it was time to end because everyone was finished eating and the hour was over.

Jaden loved on Armellya then he went back to his room in the castle to finish the science hall blueprints and an hour later he had the blueprints ready and took them to Andrew so the head construction worker could get them and start the work that night then Jaden spent the rest of the evening with Armellya talking about their relationship and when they should get married because they grew up together they knew everything about each other already. Andrew and Camillia had been keeping an eye on the young lovers and felt they would marry very soon. Bridgette and Matthew were already in their quarters spending quality time together before going to bed and Jaden's parents were at home spending some alone time together then finally, the chief went home to relax from a busy day that was full of exciting news. Andrew sent for the head construction worker to give the science hall blueprints to him so they could start that night and when he showed up he took the blueprints then looked over them and told Andrew they could have it done that night and Andrew was in disbelief but happy.

Now that Andrew was finished working for the night, he got Camillia and wanted to speak to her about Armellya and Jaden getting married because he believed he was seeing signs of an imminent wedding and they would need the construction workers to expand Armellya's bedroom into a home for her and Jaden. Camillia said she saw the same thing then she told Andrew they needed to have a talk with the two of them about being next to having the king and queen's position eventually and they would need to receive their training as soon as they marry. It was almost time for everyone to turn in for the night so everyone that was not in their quarters yet went to their quarters and the castle got silent so Andrew and Camillia got out of their day clothes and into their bed clothes but before they could get into bed they heard some noises down the hallway so Andrew said he would check it out and he told Camillia to stay in the bedroom and she said okay.

When Andrew got into the hallway, he saw all eight scientists, and they were holding the couple's security guards hostage and said they had demands and they wanted the king and queen to be out in the hallway. Camillia heard what had been said so she fled up the hallway to the chief's side of the castle and got the chief out of bed by telling him what was happening on their side of the castle. The chief sent one of his runners to gather all the hunters and their hunting gear so they could surround the scientists and use lethal force on them if necessary but they did not know the scientists were armed with knives and one of them had the king with a knife at his throat and the other scientists had the security guards with knives at their throats. The scientists did not take into consideration that everyone else in the community would defend the king and queen so when the hunters got to the castle with their bows and arrows, the scientists were surprised especially since they were surrounded by an army of armed individuals. The chief instructed Camillia to stay on his side of the castle and protect the unborn child then he told all his guards to stay with Camillia and protect her and the baby with their lives if they had to then the chief went down the hallway to the royal couple's side of the castle.

When the chief got to the scene of the incident, he realized there may be a standoff so he tried to talk to the scientists about their demands. By then, they were not willing to talk; they just wanted revenge for the new head scientist's death even though he was not murdered or euthanized; they felt he would still have been alive if he was treated with more respect than he had received and given options to stay within his field of work. The scientists were also wanting revenge for scientist number six who they believed was traumatized by the whole incident and now could not be found so they felt the royal couple had something to do with his supposed disappearance. Andrew and the chief had heard enough so they looked at each other and used telepathy to communicate then the chief told the scientists that if they were going to do anything with the knives they were holding at individuals throats they had better attempt it immediately because he was two seconds away from telling the hunters to end the standoff. The scientists did nothing and said nothing so the chief ordered the hunters to put an end to the standoff and arrows started flying then Andrew raised his right hand and grabbed the knife blade against him then he took it away from his throat and fell to the floor to avoid being shot by arrows. Andrew's guards tried the same maneuver as Andrew and were successfully on the floor avoiding having their throats slit and being shot by arrows.

One by one the eight scientists fell to the floor with many arrows in their bodies, there was blood everywhere, and Andrew as well as the guards were covered by dead bodies. But the arrows stopped flying so Andrew and the guards knew it was safe to unbury themselves from beneath the dead bodies. The chief was not sure who was alive and who was dead until he saw Andrew stand up, and once he did, he was looking for all his guards hoping they were okay. Once the guards were erect again, Andrew was relieved about that but he was saddened by the deaths of the scientists but he knew there was no other way to handle the situation so Andrew told his guards to go clean up then return to the castle's family room and Andrew went to his bathroom to clean himself up then he and Camillia would go to the family room and wait for all the guards to get there. Andrew told the chief thank you for saving his and Camillia's lives then asked him to wait in his family room because it was more important to deal with the situation that had just occurred to keep everyone's psychological health in check than to go straight to bed and Andrew felt it needed to be dealt with immediately before it could become an unfixable issue. Andrew wanted to make sure all the hunters and guards would receive free help for the incident at any given time and they needed to be told not to be ashamed if it did become damaging to them in any way. The hunters were used to shooting animals for the community's well-being, but killing a peer could be very stressful to them. Andrew went into his quarters to clean up, and Camillia rushed into her quarters to see for herself that her husband was okay. When she did, she was very relieved and before Andrew was fully cleaned up he asked Camillia to get the traveling medical crew out of bed to come and remove the eight bodies then get their cleaning crew out of bed to clean the hallway and Camillia said she could so she did.

Finally, everyone that Andrew wanted in the family room was there so he had the chief debrief the security crew and offer counseling then he did the same for the hunters, everyone said the debriefing was enough but if they started showing signs of work related stress they would seek help just in case it was a case of regression to that night's situation. Andrew asked if anyone had anything to add to the night's talk and everyone said they were comfortable with how things went so Andrew released everyone to go to their quarters to go to bed. As Andrew released the hunters and security individuals, the cleaning crew went to Andrew and told him the area that needed cleaning was finished but to be careful going to his quarters because the floor might still be damp. Andrew thanked the cleaning crew and apologized for waking them and they said no problem then went to their quarters to go back to sleep.

Due to the situation with the scientists, no one in the castle got more than a couple of hours of sleep so when it was time to get ready for the next day everyone was slow moving and running late for the breakfast hour. When Jaden got to the castle and knocked on the door, the butler answered the door in his pajamas then had Jaden sit in the family room to wait for Armellya to come out and get him for the breakfast hour then he went back to his quarters to get dressed and do his daily getting ready routine before coming out to do his day. Armellya, Andrew, and Camillia were even running behind because they had overslept also; but they were on their way to the family room and were walking leisurely when suddenly Melanie went running by them so she could get into the kitchen and see if the kitchen staff were in there or not. She was worried that breakfast was just starting to be prepared.

When Melanie got to the kitchen, she was relieved because the kitchen staff had been on time and had breakfast already prepared. They were wondering where everyone was. Armellya, Andrew, and Camillia made it to the family room and greeted Jaden then after he returned the greeting he told them they looked tired then Andrew started to tell Jaden about the incident with the scientist's in the middle of the night as they walked to the castle's private dining hall and he said he was elated that they were all okay and that it was a shame that the scientists had to die. Right after they got to the castle's private dining hall Jaden grabbed Armellya around the waist and turned her toward him then he gave her a romantic kiss and told her he was especially glad that she was unharmed because he could not imagine life without her. Armellya gave Jaden a big long hug and told him she could not imagine her life without him either, then they kissed each other again.

CHAPTER SEVENTY SIX

As Armellya and Jaden sat, Bridgette and Matthew showed up in the castle's private dining hall and took their seats so now that everyone was there Melanie could have the kitchen staff bring their breakfast out. Andrew told Armellya and Jaden that he wanted to talk to them so while they ate Andrew asked the kids if they had discussed marriage and they told him yes then Andrew asked the couple if they had an estimate of how long they were going to court before getting married and they said that they were ready to marry immediately because they had grown up together and had been close since they could talk and walk and they knew everything about each other then Armellya asked her father why he was asking those types of questions. Andrew told the kids that he did not see why they should wait to get married due to a proper courting period because of the very reasons she and Jaden had just said but on the other hand he did not want to see them marrying before they were ready for the responsibilities. Jaden asked Andrew if the conversation was another way of giving the blessing to marry without having the proper courting period and Andrew told Jaden that if they wanted to marry immediately he would like for them to wait for the wedding to get planned and prepared for because she was a royal member of the community she needed a royal style wedding. Armellya got excited then the young couple kissed and both asked for the wedding plans to be started then Camillia said she would get on it then both children thanked the royal adults.

The breakfast hour was now over so Jaden had to get to the hospital for his medical training, Andrew was going to check on the construction crews progress, Camillia told Bridgette to get the girls together in the family room, Camillia sent a runner to retrieve Jaden's mother, and Camillia went to get the chief since he had to perform the ceremony. Andrew left the castle immediately hoping to see the science hall completely changed over for a multi use hall for all shops who needed to combine efforts to work there especially since there was the spindle and sheep's shears to be made. When Andrew got to the old science hall, no construction workers were there so he took it upon himself to look it over and when he did he was pleased because it was finished and named the multipurpose hall then Andrew left the new building to go to the hospital to check on the construction of the two medicine making rooms and when he got there he found all of the construction workers working very hard so Andrew found the head construction worker and asked him how the progress was going and he said the rooms would be finished before the dinner hour that day and that included getting the rooms set up for work by the next morning all Andrew had to do was staff the rooms and he already had the individuals ready to work they were just waiting on the rooms to be done.

Now that Andrew had found out that the construction workers had some spare time on their hands which they did not like he knew just where to have them go to do more work, build Jaden and Armellya's house so it would be ready by the time they were married. Andrew told the head construction worker that he needed a house as an extension from the castle built and the bedroom that was there could be turned into a foyer because he wanted the house to be elaborate, it was for his oldest daughter and soon-to-be son-in-law. The head construction worker told Andrew congratulations then he said he would start on the house in the morning so he could plan it that evening and the new couple could empty out the bedroom and Andrew said perfect. As Andrew was leaving the near finished construction area he ran into Jaden who just finished a double session of tutoring so they both rode to the castle together and Andrew told Jaden he needed to tell him and Armellya something exciting when they got back to the castle. When Andrew and Jaden got back to the castle, they left their horses with the new stable boy and went in quickly because they both were wanting to find Armellya so the three of them could talk and Armellya was in the family room with the girls and the chief, they had not started with their business yet so it was good timing to talk with her because they would not be interrupting anything. Andrew asked Camillia to come over next to him then he asked Jaden to sit next to Armellya then Andrew told the young couple that they needed to move everything out of Armellya's bedroom by that night because the construction workers were going to be starting construction to build them a beautiful house that would be an extension off the castle. Armellya and Jaden were excited and surprised that they were getting their home so soon they thanked and hugged Andrew and Camillia then ran to Armellya's bedroom to pack everything so they would know what was where in case Armellya needed something then when they were ready to move the items out of the current bedroom it occurred to them that they did not know where to put them.

Camillia went to the bedroom to see how they were getting along and when she realized they were finished packing she told the couple to put the items in her storage show room until the home was finished and that Armellya was going to be in the chief's extra bedroom two doors down from her sister Lynndia temporarily. Camillia went back out to the family room with the chief, Bridgette, Melanie, and Michelle to let Andrew know they would update him on the wedding plans and with who was going to be responsible for what when they knew and that he may get an assignment.

Right after Camillia finished telling Andrew about his involvement in the wedding planning, family started pouring into the family room then it occurred to the girls, the chief, and Andrew that it was coming up on the lunch hour and family time so Camillia told the wedding crew they would get together later when it was convenient for everyone. Once everyone was in the family room Andrew led everyone to the castle's private dining hall and everyone took their seats at the big round table then Melanie had the kitchen bring everyone their lunch and while everyone ate they went around the table to share their day. When it got to be Armellya and Jaden's turn to share, they announced that the wedding was being planned and their house was going to be started the next day with the construction and the royal wedding announcements would be sent out soon then everyone clapped. Jaden and Armellya were the last ones to share and family time was over so Matthew went back on patrol, the girls got back together to plan the wedding, the kitchen crew was left to do dinner without Melanie, Jaden and Armellya were moving her belongings to the storage showroom, and Andrew went to the new multi use hall to leave word with the unfamiliar staff to gather the proper halls together and make the spindles and sheep's shears while the chief went to take a nap.

Andrew did not leave the castle right away because he sent runners to gather the fresh staff for the medicine rooms to meet at the medicine rooms that they would be working at so he could see the rooms put together and talk to them individually. It was also important to lay down the ground rules and make the medicine people aware of the consequences of breaking the rules but most of all he wanted to welcome the workers and make sure they knew that if they needed anything to let him know.

Finally, Andrew left the castle to go to the medicine rooms and as he was leaving he saw the head construction worker riding up to him so he stopped his horse and the head construction worker rode up to him and asked to speak to Andrew about building the house and as soon as he mentioned the house to Andrew, Andrew told him to build two baby rooms also and that was just what the construction worker needed to know about. After giving the head construction worker the information he went for then he went to go plan the house and make a blueprint and Andrew rode off to go to the hospital to see the medicine rooms and it did not take long to get there.

When Andrew got into the medicine room for the medicine, he greeted the new workers for that department then they talked about what they would be producing and Andrew approved of it then Andrew told the workers about the general rules and regulations and of the consequences for breaking them then left them with the theory of when in doubt check it out as far as whether or not they would be breaking a rule and Andrew told the workers he would be at their service twenty-four hours a day seven days a week including holidays then they agreed to do what was right and Andrew left to go to the veterinary medicine making room and did the same thing he did with the medical room and they also agreed to keep things honest. Andrew suddenly got an idea as he was leaving the hospital and it involved Jaden so Andrew raced to the castle to catch Jaden before he left the castle and when he rode up to the castle's front porch Andrew slid off his horse before it had stopped and left the horse with the new stable boy then ran into the castle and hollered for Jaden and the girls told Andrew that Jaden was back at Armellya's bedroom putting the last bag into the storage showroom for Armellya. Andrew walked briskly to Armellya's bedroom and there was Jaden just like the girls said so Andrew called out his name to get his attention and Jaden stopped and turned asking Andrew what he needed and Andrew told Jaden he needed someone to oversee the two medicine rooms then Andrew asked Jaden if he had the time and was interested.

Jaden said he was interested and would make the time but once his medical tutoring was finished he would have the time easily then Jaden told Andrew he was doing double the hours for tutoring than what was initially planned so he could finish sooner and if things were timed right he would finish before he was to marry Armellya and Andrew were pleased. Now that everything was caught up for everyone, the girls got back together to plan Armellya's wedding they had Melanie and her mother making and decorating a cake and making individual edible fruit flowers, Melanie's father would be in charge of the wedding dinner, the chief would do the ceremony and buy the new couple a buggy as a wedding gift, Andrew would be in charge of the men's wardrobe, the castle decorator would decorate the public dining hall and the castle's private dining hall, Camillia would be with Armellya getting the wedding dress, Michelle would work with the guards and hunters for their placement along the isle, and Bridgette was in charge of the invitations.

Camillia had the flower pickers and the fruit pickers ready to go outside of the commune walls with hunters for protection to get the flowers and fruit needed for their wedding projects and Camillia told everyone they were going to do everything the next day so everything could be fresh but the regular shopping needed to be done right away so they would be done by the dine hour so those who had shopping to do left the castle right away. Camillia and Armellya went to the dress making shop and looked at the wedding dresses where they found two dresses that they both liked so Camillia had Armellya try on both dresses to see which one felt and looked better and after that they felt they picked out the right dress So Camillia paid for the dress and the two women went back to the castle.

While Armellya snuck the wedding dress into the storage showroom Camillia checked with those who needed to shop that day since everyone was in the family room she figured it had been completed, the chief got the buggy he felt was the right one to present to the new couple and had it in their barn with a giant bow on it, Andrew had the men's wardrobe arranged and their clothing was in the storage showroom and everyone else had theirs at their home, Jaden's mother had the items she needed to do the bouquet and head dress and she was at home making them while her husband manned their shop alone, Bridgette was making the invitations for the entire community to be at the wedding, and the castle decorator got all the things she would need to decorate the castle's private dining hall and the public dining hall but she was not going to do the work until the last minute.

While everyone was scurrying around the family room with wedding preparations, there was a knock at the front door of the castle so Andrew and Camillia let the butler get the door because they were busy then the butler called Andrew to come to the foyer and Andrew knew when the butler did that it meant something was very seriously negative but Andrew could not imagine what it could be but as soon as he got to the foyer and saw the guest was the cemetery's groundskeeper Andrew knew it was in reference to the eight scientists. Andrew kindly greeted the cemeteries groundskeeper then he returned the greeting and told Andrew that the eight scientists had been buried and there was a private service for immediately after the burial for family only so that had been completed then Andrew thanked the groundskeeper for letting him know then he left.

As Andrew was going back into the family room he realized it was getting close to the dinner hour so Andrew told everyone so they would have a chance to get their projects to an acceptable stopping point and all get to where they dined. Andrew caught

Jaden and his father before they got out of the castle's front door and invited them to dinner and they accepted so they sent a runner for Jaden's mother then followed Andrew, Camillia and Armellya to the castle's private dining hall and took their seats at the big round table then Jaden's mother arrived and Melanie got the kitchen to serve everyone's dinner. The dinner conversation was positively pleasant but it was not about the wedding, it was about Armellya and Jaden wanting children eventually and how they were hoping for a boy and a girl then Jaden found out he had to undergo the healing process but Armellya did not with that Jaden wondered what other gifts he was not aware of so Armellya told Jaden she could heal, move objects with her mind, heat or cool things with her mind, fly, levitate, go into others dreams, communicate with unborn children, and of course telepathy. Jaden was amazed at what Armellya could do so he asked Armellya if she could give him any of the abilities and she said no but the mini angels could which Andrew and Camillia did not know. Armellya told Jaden that after they were married, she would have the angel give him the abilities, and he said thank you.

Dinner was now over and it was time to wrap up the day so when it was time for everyone to go to their quarters there would be no unfinished business and no one would still be wound up from the day it was also time for Jaden and his parents to leave so Armellya gave her goodbyes to Jaden then he and his parents left to go to their home. Armellya told her parents she was going to her room to astral project the dinosaur tail then Andrew and Camillia told her it was fine and to have a good night then the royal couple went to their room also to work on levitation. While Armellya, Andrew, and Camillia were performing their gifts, the rest of the castle's employees were going to their quarters and getting in their beds and anxiously waited for their miniangels to visit them.

Armellya had to leave the dinosaur tail so the miniangels could astro project and visit their pale ones so she gave her loving farewells and returned to her body. Camillia and Andrew were still levitating when their miniangels arrived so they stopped levitating and sat on the edge of their bed to talk with their miniangels and the unborn bay, Desirae, had her miniangel there also and she fluttered around Camillia's belly, Camillia could feel the baby responding to her miniangel and this brought boundless joy to Camillia. The royal couple spoke to their miniangels about the events of the day and how it affected them then the miniangels did their best to ease the royal couples pain but the death of the eight scientists was still lurking in their minds so the miniangels healed the royal couple then the mental anguish was gone all that was left was the memory the royal couple thanked their mini angels then the mini angels told the royal couple to call on them any time then Andrew and Camillia told their miniangels that they would. Suddenly their miniangels disappeared then there was a knock at the royal couple's bedroom door so Andrew got up and answered the door and it was Bridgette she said she did not feel well and she wanted to talk to Camillia so Andrew invited Bridgette into the bedroom.

Camillia sensed that Bridgette's issue was with the pregnancy so Camillia got off the bed and told Bridgette to lie down then Camillia asked Bridgette to tell her what was going on. She asked Camillia how to tell if she was in preterm labor because she felt that she was having contractions, with that said Andrew left the bedroom to go get the doctor out of bed and come check Bridgette. Camilla knew what Andrew was doing so she stayed at Bridgette's side and distracted her from the possible contractions by talking to her about the wedding invitations she was making and how beautiful they were going to be as well as the challenge of making so many to be able to give every individual in the community one. Matthew was in his bedroom pacing the floor worried sick about Bridgette and the unborn baby then finally, the doctor and

Andrew were there so Andrew went to check on Matthew then bring him to Bridgette as he told Matthew things were fine and when the men got to the bedroom the doctor was giving Bridgette some medicine that was supposed to stop the contractions as he was telling her she had to do bed rest for a few days and he would check on her several times a day during her bed rest days.

Matthew picked Bridgette up and carried her to their bed then tucked her in while the doctor was speaking with Andrew and Camillia the doctor told Andrew to go wake Jaden and bring him to the castle so Andrew left right away and within eight minutes Andrew was back with Jaden who was still trying to wake up. The doctor apologized to Jaden for getting him up so late but since he only had another day of tutoring before he graduated with his doctorates in medicine he needed Jaden to treat Bridgette in his absence so Jaden asked for a report on the situation then he asked for the status at that moment so the doctor briefed Jaden then the doctor told Jaden he was going to leave the anti contraction medicine and some syringes with him to give Bridgett the medicine every four hours and a bolus dose if the contractions were not affected by the regular dose and Jaden said he could do that.

When Matthew heard what the doctor said, he made Jaden a bed in his bedroom so he could sleep and be close to Bridgette and Jaden asked Andrew if he would send a runner to the retired doctor to have his final tutoring session at the castle so he could stay close to Bridgette and Andrew told Jaden that would be the first thing he would do when he got out of bed in the morning and Jaden thanked Andrew then everyone went to their beds to try to get some sleep. Bridgette slept through the night so that allowed Matthew and Jaden to sleep through the night also.

CHAPTER SEVENTY SEVEN

Now the morning hour had arrived and it was time to wake up, Matthew and Jaden woke up but Bridgette was still sleeping so the two men prepared for their day as quietly as possible then got out of the room quickly to go to the castle's private dining hall for breakfast and when they got there the retired doctor for Jaden's tutoring was there at the big round table, he was going to have breakfast with them then go to Jaden's bedroom there in the castle to do the tutoring. Jaden shook the retired doctor's hand and told him he appreciated him working with him to still tutor him while he kept an eye on Bridgette knowing they could be interrupted at any time which would make the tutoring session longer than usual. Everyone ate breakfast while discussing what they had to start their day out with, Matthew was doing guard duty like usual, Camillia would help Bridgette with the wedding invitations, Jaden would have his last tutoring session then graduate his doctorate program and get his license to practice medical medicine, Armellya was going shopping with the castle decorator to get the decor that Armellya wanted for her new house, Andrew had to go to the multipurpose hall to check on the production of the spindles and sheep's shears, and while all this was happening the other castle staff would be doing their preparations for the royal wedding.

Everyone had just finished eating and sharing when the construction crew showed up to start building Armellya and Jaden's new house but first the head construction member wanted Jaden to look at the blueprint he had made for the house and see if there could be any improvements and Jaden looked them over as the head construction worker told Jaden that Andrew told him he wanted the house to be elaborate, Jaden told him he did a great job but there would be a few changes he would make so the two of them discussed it and the head construction worker agreed with Jaden and thanked Jaden for his advice made the changes to the blueprint then went to get the men working hard and steady. After dealing with the head construction worker, Jaden went to check on Bridgette and she was awake so he called for the kitchen to bring her breakfast in bed then he told her if she needed him not to hesitate to call on him then he left the bedroom to go to his bedroom and finish his tutoring. Camillia, Armellya, Matthew, and Andrew all went to start their day.

After eating breakfast, Bridgette was going to work on the wedding invitations with Camillia's help, all Bridgette had left to do was have the invitations approved or disapproved by Armellya then either make some corrections then make copies or just make the copies then have them distributed. When Camillia saw the wedding invitations, she was in awe they were so beautiful and well done that she told Bridgette she was certain Armellya would approve of them right away but it would be a short while before Armellya would be back because she was out shopping for home decor with the castle decorator. As Bridgette and Camillia were waiting on Armella to see the wedding invitations, Jaden had finished his tutoring so he and the retired doctor went to check on Bridgette and the unborn baby and they were doing well but Jaden still had to give Bridgette her medicine so the retired doctor watched as Jaden drew up the medicine and gave the injection then told him he did a good job then Jaden told the retired doctor he had a lot of experience giving injections because of his veterinary practice then the retired doctor asked Jaden how he was going to handle veterinarian medicine with medical medicine and Jaden said he already had that under control, he would work during the day as a medical doctor because that was when he would be needed the most then work nights as a veterinarian and the other veterinarian would work days then the medical night calls would be for the other medical doctor and he would work both jobs eight hours then he would have eight hours to sleep if he had no calls.

The retired doctor told Jaden that was a nice plan but it was more for a bachelor so how would he work in time for his new wife then Jaden told him it would be during his veterinary time because he would only be out if there was a sick animal during the night hours because the original veterinarian would keep his schedule and get sleep every night then the retired doctor said it was a good plan then he remembered that Jaden was also responsible for keeping a watch over the medical and veterinary medicine making rooms then Jaden said that would be easy because he would already be at the hospital where they were and he could do random checks so if there was anything going on that should not be he would be more likely to catch it occurring and if they were following the rules and being honest they would not care when the checks were and he would read the workers as well as observe the physical surroundings and the retired doctor said Jaden had a great plan for them and it seemed that his new life was well balanced and rewarding. Jaden thanked the retired doctor for his help and understanding then the retired doctor thanked Jaden for choosing him to be his tutor because it was a wonderful experience working with a prodigy and passing his skills down to a promising individual, he felt that after his passing he would still be around through Jaden since he had no children to carry on his legacy and Jaden told the retired doctor it was a pleasure and honor then they hugged each other.

The retired doctor left Jaden to find Andrew so they could plan a graduation ceremony and right about that time Andrew walked into the castle from checking on the production of the spindles and sheep's shears so the doctor got his attention and told him Jaden was now an official medical doctor and a graduation party was in order so Andrew told the retired doctor to see Melanie and tell her there is to be a graduation party and she was to be in charge of it so that was what the retired doctor did while Andrew went to check on the construction workers and their progress.

Finally, after so long of being gone Armellya got back to the castle with a buggy full of things for her new house and Camillia caught Armellya at the castle's front door and told her that the wedding invitations were ready for her to approve or disapprove and Armellya asked the castle decorator to bring everything in from the buggy so she could review the wedding invitations with Bridgette and the castle decorator was happy to do that so Armellya and Camillia went directly to Bridgette's bedroom to see how she and the baby were doing and see the wedding invitations. When Armellya got to Bridgette and greeted her, Bridgette lit up and welcomed her into her bedroom then Armellya asked to see the wedding invitations so Bridgette gave Armellya one of them and Armellya was very pleased she told Bridgette that she had done a fabulous job and they were perfect then she told Bridgette that she approved of them then she asked how the baby was doing then Bridgette jokingly told Armellya the baby was still cooking then Bridgette and Armellya chuckled. Camillia took the wedding invitation to go and get it duplicated and on the way out of the castle Camillia ran into Andrew so he stopped her for a few minutes to tell her that the multi use hall was still working on the sheep's shears and spindles but it looked promising that they would have the first set ready for use in a matter of hours and they would let one of the sheep herders use the shears then the individuals waiting for their new job as Spindler's get started and if things went well it would be a permanent thing in the community.

After seeing Bridgette, Armellya looked for Jaden to tell him about all the things she had bought for their new house and they ran into each other in the hallway because he was on his way to check on Bridgette and give her the next injection so Armellya told Jaden to meet her in the family room after seeing Bridgette and he said okay. Jaden gave Bridgette her injection and did a basic exam to assure the baby was doing good and all was well so he told Bridgette she was due to be seen in four hours unless she needed to see someone and the next visit would be done by the doctor and she said okay then Jaden headed to the castle's family room to see all the things Armellya had gotten for their new house.

While everyone was going about their day doing the things that needed to be done they had popped in on Bridgette to check on her and the unborn baby while Matthew was out patrolling the castle's property inside and out, he was on his way inside the castle to check on the security that was posted there so he slipped into his bedroom to see Bridgette and make sure the baby was okay, Bridgette assured him they were fine then they kissed and Matthew moved on to do his job. Camillia returned to Bridgette's bedroom to let her know the wedding invitation was at the copy hall to be duplicated in color and it would take some time because there were so many of them needed but when they were done the copy hall would deliver them to her and Bridgette said great then Camillia told Bridgette that there was going to be a graduation party for Jaden so she had to go see Melanie to find out what had been done and what still needed to be done so she could help then Bridgette told Camillia that even though she was placed on bed rest she was going to the graduation party and they could help her get to the castle's private dining hall or she would get there herself. Camillia told Bridgette they would help her get to the castle's private dining hall and Bridgette said thank you then Camillia went to the kitchen to see Melanie and Melanie told Camillia she had already designated the tasks to prepare for the graduation party and they should be about finished by now. Camillia told Melanie if she needed anything done she could call on her then Melanie said thank you and Camillia went to see Armellya in the family room where she was still showing Jaden the items she got from the shops for their home. Jaden seemed to be happy with the things Armellya got and they were both excited about their new house and could not wait to see the finished product. After seeing Melanie, Camillia went to look for Andrew and found him down the hallway of the castle with the construction workers and he seemed to be over pleased so she asked him how things with the construction were going and Andrew told Camillia that if things continued the way they were the house would be finished that evening and Camillia got excited then she told Andrew to go with her to tell the kids so the two of them went to the family room to tell the kids their home would be finished that evening.

When Andrew and Camillia got to the family room Armellya had just finished showing Jaden the things she bought for their home so Andrew and Camillia had just caught them at a suitable time and they told the kids to follow them to their new home then Armellya asked if it was finished and Andrew told her no then he told her it would most likely be finished that evening then they could get the castle decorator to do her miraculous work. When the four of them got to the new house, the young lovers were surprised at how fast it was getting done. After a few minutes of standing there, Armellya wanted to seek out the castle decorator to make a request for her to start decorating that evening. As Jaden and Armellya went after the castle decorator, Andrew and Camillia heard a knock at the front door so Andrew answered it and it was a runner from the copy hall with a giant box that contained the wedding invitations. Camillia asked Andrew if he would take the box to the distribution hall and he said he would be glad to then he took the box and left. Camillia went to the castle's private dining hall to see how things were coming along with the graduation party and to her surprise everything was ready and the party would be held during the lunch hour and family time which was very near, it was so close that Camillia headed for the castle's family room to wait on the family members to arrive. Andrew was the first to show up so Camillia asked him to find Matthew so he could get Bridgette to the castle's private dining hall because she was determined to be there for Jaden's graduation party so Andrew went in search of Matthew. Andrew found Matthew in the castle's foyer as he was going in the castle from outside and Andrew told Matthew that Bridgette demanded to go to Jaden's graduation party so Matthew said okay then went to get her while Andrew went back to the family room.

When Andrew got to the family room, everyone was there except Matthew and Bridgette so Andrew led everyone to the castle's dining hall while Matthew was bringing Bridgette and once everyone including Matthew and Bridgette was in the castle's private dining hall Melanie had the kitchen bring out the special meal that was prepared for Jaden and serve everyone and they all ate while sharing their day with one another then when the lunch meal was over the kitchen crew cleaned off the table and Melanie brought out the cake right as the retired doctor was walking into the room. The retired doctor stood at the front of the room and called Jaden up to stand with him then the retired doctor presented Jaden with a diploma and a medal for perfect scores throughout his entire schooling and test taking, the two of them shook hands while Jaden accepted his diploma then Jaden hugged the retired doctor and told him he would make him proud then the retired doctor told Jaden he knew and that was why he got a gift for him then the retired doctor left the room and came back a few minutes later wheeling a table tray with something on it but the retired doctor had it covered with a small sheet and when he got the table tray where he wanted it he told Jaden he could remove the blanket so he did and there were all the tools of the trade there, Jaden was moved then he thanked the retired doctor. Everyone clapped and cheered then it was time for Jaden to cut the first piece of cake and get the first serving for himself then Melanie would take over the cake cutting and serving and while Melanie was working with the cake Jaden told Bridgette he was pleased that she was there because the party would not be complete without everyone there then she told Jaden she was not going to miss his graduation for anything because the baby was just going to have to understand how important it was for her to be there and that it was not time to see the world yet.

After Bridgette spoke about the baby Jaden got an idea of the royal couple talking with the unborn baby and possibly being able to heal Bridgette and the baby and Armellya said it was worth a try so the royal couple agreed to do it after the party when Bridgette was back in bed and comfortable then everyone said why wait it would be better to do it as soon as possible because the party was still going and would take some time before being over and Jaden did not mind sharing his party time with Bridgette and the baby. Andrew and Camillia stood up out of their chairs and went over to Bridgette then put their hands on her belly to talk to the unborn child then five minutes later they smiled and took their hands off her belly saying that the baby was happy and the medicine made him sleepy and there would be no more problems so his mommy could move now but Andrew and Camillia decided to do a healing over Bridgette anyway. Andrew and Camillia placed their hands back on Bridgette's tummy and concentrated on health and full term pregnancy then after a couple of minutes they were done and Bridgette said she felt better then she had been then she thanked Andrew, Camillia, and Jaden then she told everyone to go on with the party, so they did and everyone had fun.

The party came to an end and everyone had to get back to work, the royal wedding was to be the next day so everyone was to do the last-minute preparations and make sure the big jobs were finished as well as taking care of their normal responsibilities, Jaden's mother finished the bouquet and head dress so she went to her shop with her husband to work because the next day the shop would be closed due to the wedding as well as all the shops, Armellya had her dress so her only worry was getting her and Jaden's house built and getting their belongings in there including the decor, Bridgette's invitations were being distributed so she was free to help anyone who needed help, Melanie had the cake done, Melanie's mother had the many single serving edible fruit arrangements made, and Melanie's father had the dinner menu planned. Everything else had to wait until the next day like getting the guards and hunters dressed, setting up the decorations in the castle's private dining hall after breakfast, setting up the decorations in the public dining hall after breakfast, separating the bride and groom for the day until the ceremony, getting all the newlyweds gifts on a separate table in the castle's private dining hall, and so on.

Having nothing more to do for the royal wedding until the next day Andrew, Camillia, Armellya, and Jaden went to see how the construction workers were doing and as they were walking down the castle's hallway the head construction worker met the two couples before the door to the new house and told them that the new house was finished and ready to be moved into and when Armellya heard that she squealed and jumped into Jaden's arms and gave him a wild hug and Jaden told Armellya to find the castle decorator to get her to work while he got their belongings into the house and she could put the belongings where she wanted them and supervise the decorator then when he was finished bringing their belongings in she could tell him what he could do to continue to help and Armellya said okay then ran off. Andrew and Camillia were so happy for the new couple so they stayed together and let everyone know that the house was completed then they went to Jaden's parents shop to buy them a house warming gift but Camillia could not figure out what to get because she did not know what Armellya and Jaden already had and what Armellya had bought and weather Jaden had bought anything so Andrew suggested leaving a generous sum of money with Jaden's parents so the couple would have a starting tab at the shop to get what they wanted and Camillia agreed that would be the best thing to do and when they were finished with that errand they went back toward the castle to visit the chief. On the way to see the chief the multi use halls overseer ran into Andrew and Camillia which was who he was looking for so he could tell Andrew and Camillia that the first spindle and sheep's shears were completed and ready for presentation so the royal couple rode to the multi use hall with the overseer.

When the three of them got to the hall, the royal couple noticed that the head Spindler and a sheep herder with one of his sheep was there to demonstrate how the two products worked so Andrew and Camillia sat in chairs and listened to what the overseer was saying as the sheep herder shaved his sheep then they continued to listen to the overseer as the head Spindler started to spin the wool the royal couple was very pleased with the demonstration so Andrew told the multi use hall overseer to make eleven more spindles and to make twenty-three more shears and the overseer told Andrew they would get on it right away then Camillia told the overseer that they had a dress makers hall and as they got the spindles made to have them placed there and to let her or Andrew know and they would have a Spindler start working because they already had the staff the overseer told the royal couple he would comply. Andrew and Camillia shook hands with the overseer, Spindler, and the sheep herder then left to go see the chief.

When Andrew and Camillia got to the chief's side of the castle, they knocked on the door and the chief's butler answered the door then took them to the chief's private garden where he was. They asked the chief how he had been that day since they had not seen him except at Jaden's party, and the chief told them he was fine. Andrew asked the chief if they could use his private garden to practice one of their gifts that required unlimited height and a good amount of width as well as privacy, which was the most important for now. The chief told them he had said before it was now as much theirs as his and they did not have to ask anymore; then Camillia told the chief they just wanted to be respectful and she gave him a tender hug and told him she loved him and called him father. The chief softened up after what Camillia said and did then he got to thinking about the gifts he knew about the couple having and to his recollection they did not need a lot of space so he asked them what gift they were going to be working on out there and Camillia told the chief that it was one that nobody knew of not even him then Andrew told the chief that they could levitate and that they had been doing it in their bedroom during the evening hours before bed but they could also fly which they had not practiced and that was what they needed the private garden for. The chief was stunned it seemed that the couple's gifts were unending so he asked if they wanted him to leave so they could focus on their ability more easily and they told the chief he could stay and he was happy because he really wanted to see his adopted children perform their ability.

Andrew and Camillia were not sure how to go about flying and they had just learned how to levitate but they knew if they could levitate they should be able to fly because the first step of both was to get off the ground in the first place so they decided to levitate for a few minutes then take it from there. The couple extended their arms out from their sides with palms up and off the ground they went the chief could not believe what he saw but he remained silent so he did not break Andrew and Camillia's concentration then the next thing the chief saw was even more jaw dropping the couple became horizontal in the air and started to move forward, it appeared that they had flying figured out and with a little practice it would be a natural thing for them. After a few minutes of being in the air the couple gained enough control over their bodies that they were flying in a circle together then they made a perfect landing and the chief ran to them telling them how wonderful it was to see them fly then he vowed to never speak about their gift that if anyone was to know it would be up to them to tell about it and the couple thanked the chief for his dedication to them.

Now that Andrew and Camillia finally got the chance to fly and found out it was not hard that it would just take some practice because it was as natural as walking which took practice when they were toddlers and now they did not have to think about walking they just do it and in time they would not have to think about flying they would just do it when they chose. Andrew and Camillia were so caught up in trying to fly that they did not realize how long they had been in the air and it was later than they had thought so they told the chief thank you for supporting their effort to fly then they had a group hug and the couple went back to their side of the castle when they got there they found out that everyone was looking for them but never thought to look at the chief's side of the castle so they asked what they were needed for then Armellya and Jaden spoke up telling the couple that they had gotten their house all put together and wanted them to go see it. Andrew, Camillia, Armellya, and Jaden went to see the new house and when Andrew and Camillia saw it they both commented on how beautiful it was inside and it had a lot of room, there was a station for Jaden's work and two extra bedrooms for their children when they had them. Camillia hugged Armellya and told her it was a job well done then it was time for Armellya to say goodbye to Jaden so he could go home and for the castle to settle down for bed especially since the next day was a big one, it was Armellya and Jaden's wedding day so Jaden left then everyone went to their bedrooms for the night. Everyone looked forward to seeing their miniangels during the night and this night was special because everyone in their invitation was told to invite their miniangel to the wedding but just in case someone was to forget, Andrew and Camillia astral projected to the dinosaur tail to tell the miniangels of the royal wedding and when the couple got to the dinosaur tail the miniangels congratulated them on the union of their daughter and Jaden then Camillia asked the miniangels to go to the wedding and they said they would then Andrew told them he wanted the aisle lined with the miniangels and they said they would love to assist in the ceremony then they told the couple to return to their bodies because it was time for them to astral project and visit their individuals so the couple blew kisses and thanked them then returned to their bodies and when they got back they cuddled and tried to get some rest.

The night went by quickly and the couple did not see their miniangel the previous night in their bedroom but they figured it was because they saw her and the rest of them before going to sleep and that was fine because they knew they would see her at the wedding. It was time for the castle to wake up and for everyone to start the new day and as Andrew and Camillia were getting out of bed a bit early they could hear that everyone in the castle was already stirring so before Andrew could put on his day clothes he rushed out to Armellya's bedroom to see if she was still in there and she was so Andrew reminded her that she was not to see Jaden until the ceremony and she remembered but told her father it would be hard to do because they were used to having the freedom of seeing each other throughout the day then Andrew told her she could do it for half of a day then he left his daughters bedroom to go back to his own bedroom. When Andrew got back with Camillia, she was in her day clothes and almost ready to go out to the castle's private dining hall, but she told Andrew she would wait for him. As he was changing into his day clothes, he told her that Armellya already missed Jaden so it might be a task keeping the two of them apart until the ceremony. Camillia told Andrew there would be no problem because they did not want to spoil their wedding day. Andrew was ready to go to the castle's private dining hall to have breakfast so he and Camillia went and when they got there Armellya was already there moping so Camillia went to her daughter and hugged her then told her that it would all be worth it in the end and Armellya smiled. Camillia took her seat next to Andrew at the big round table so now that everyone was seated Melanie had the kitchen staff bring out breakfast then everyone ate in silence which was unusual. Without conversation breakfast went by quickly so they were ahead of schedule for the wedding preparations because it was agreed that it would take from the end of breakfast to an hour before the lunch hour to have everything perfect then they would have the ceremony and when they would be ready for the reception dinner it would occur during the normal lunch hour. When everyone got up from the big round table to scramble to do what they needed to be doing in preparation for the wedding, there was a knock on the castle's front door so the butler answered the door, and it was the doctor, who told the butler he needed to see Camillia and Bridgette. The butler took the doctor to the castle's private dining hall.

CHAPTER SEVENTY EIGHT

Because nearly everyone was at the castle's private dining hall the butler announced the doctor's presence then called on Bridgette and Camillia so they stepped forward then asked the doctor what he needed then the doctor told the girls that they had missed their prenatal visits. The doctor was especially worried about Bridgette since her preterm labor had occurred even though it had stopped. The doctor told the girls that he was there to do a quick prenatal exam on both girls because they did not show up at the hospital for their appointments so the girls agreed to get their exams on the condition that the doctor made the exams quick because they had wedding preparations to do with Armellya and the doctor said he would make the exams as quick as he could but he had to do the exams right and there were certain things he could not skip. Camillia told the doctor okay then led him to the family room where the girls could stretch out on the couch one at a time, Andrew and Armellya went to the family room with them to see the babies and Camillia went first so the doctor measured her belly, did an ultrasound, sonogram, then asked certain questions then the doctor told Camillia and Andrew that things seemed to be going as they should and now it was Bridgette's turn so Camillia got off the couch with help sitting up because she was so big then Bridgette lay down and the doctor did the same things with Bridgette that he did with Camillia then the doctor needed to check Bridgette's cervix for any dilation so he asked for some privacy then everyone went to the castle's foyer so they could keep anyone from going into the family room except Matthew if he should show up. Matthew did not show up and neither did anyone else by the time the doctor hollered he was finished and everyone could return to the family room Andrew, Armellya, and Camillia went back to see how Bridgette was doing and the doctor told everyone that fortunately she had not dilated at all. Bridgette and Camillia thanked the doctor for the house call and they knew it was an inconvenience then the doctor told the girls that was what he had Jaden for but since he needed to not see Armellya until the ceremony he had to do it.

The doctor told the girls good luck getting everything done perfectly and he could not wait for the ceremony because even though Armellya was a beautiful girl he knew she would be an angelic bride then Armellya gave the doctor a hug and said thank you and that she would look for him in the audience then the doctor told Armellya he would be sure to be somewhere in front then he left. As the doctor left Matthew was coming in and he asked Bridgette if she was okay because he thought that something could possibly be wrong then she told him the doctor was there to check out her and Camillia because they had missed their appointments at the hospital then Matthew relaxed and asked how the home appointment went and Bridgette told Matthew that her and Camillia and both babies got a clean bill of health. Matthew was relieved then he kissed Bridgette and turned to leave her to go on his patrol because he made a personal vow that nothing would happen to the royal family or his friends on his watch and he figured if anything was going to happen it would be this day because of everyone rushing from here to there and being focused on the wedding instead of their surroundings and other people. Matthew was going around taking all the security and replacing them with hunters long enough to have a meeting in the castle's family room about being on high alert and using the hunters to their benefit and answering any questions as well as taking any advice into consideration and when Matthew was done with the security guards he was going to gather all the hunters and brief them too then take any advice they have to offer and an hour before the wedding event security, the hunters, Andrew, and Matthew would get together and get their wedding attire on and the hunters would put their floral bands on their arrow sacks while Matthew and the security guards would put their mini floral arrangements on their jackets.

Unbeknownst to Armellya, Jaden was in the far part of their side of the castle so he was close to the individuals who were getting everyone ready for the wedding; his mother and father stayed with him and Andrew was in and out of the room where Jaden was. Things were really getting exciting and fast paced and with that no one had the chance to get nervous in fact, Armellya and Jaden were so sure about them being soul mates that they were the only one's calm now. Back at the castle's private dining hall the castle decorator explained to a small decorating team what she expected then she rode to the public dining hall and met with a large decorating team and explained what she wanted done then she told them only perfection would be acceptable then they got started on the public dining hall while the castle decorator rode back to the castle to check on the private dining hall's decor and the castle decorator spent the entire time of the decorating process riding back and forth between both dining halls to assure the decorating teams were doing the job as she expected in fact, the castle decorator had four horses she had used due to multiple hard rides and she kept the castle's new stable boy busy.

While the castle's dining hall was being decorated, Melanie's mother was putting nonperishable treats in small crystal bowls on the table at each setting along with name cards and Melanie was putting the finishing touches on the wedding cake tiers and gathering the cake stairs with cherubs and edible flowers so she could transfer the parts to the big round table then put it all together. The cake was beautiful and the largest that Melanie had seen made the center was five tiers high with four side tiers stacked three layers high and forty cupcakes around it in the shape of angels which was unique. Melanie baked the cupcakes in long tubes then with a paring knife she shaved them down into shapes of angels and frosted them to look like statues. Melanie's father was preparing the reception dinner it was like a Christmas, and thanksgiving, and Easter, and birthday dinners all together there was probably just about as much food in the castle's private dining hall as there was in the public dining hall but the couple was having more company at the big round table than they usually had. They were going to have the chief who had dinner with the family occasionally, the doctor, the retired doctor, Jaden's parents, the veterinarian, and all the castle's help and their parents, along with the usual individuals who ate at the big round table and they had moved some individuals around now Armellya was to sit next to her mother with Jaden on the other side and his mother would sit on the other side of him then his father.

Camillia and the professional hairdressers worked on Armellya's hair then Armellya and the professional hairdressers worked on Camillia's hair then the two of them got into their dresses and Jaden's mother showed up with the bouquet and floral head dress for Armellya then she got dressed while she was with Camillia and Armellya and on the other side of the couples castle Jaden, his father, Andrew, and the chief got their wedding attire on and Matthew, the guards, and the hunters were all dressed then the nannies for the twins Kaylina and Kevin were dressed, Kaylina was the flower girl and Kevin was the ring bearer and Armellya's other brothers and sisters were dressed in wedding attire also.

Everyone and everything was ready for the wedding ceremony and reception dinner. Even the bride and groom's gifts were already on the extra table in the castle's private dining hall. All that was left was to get everyone in the community in the spiritual hall and seated before the bride and groom showed up. The spiritual hall was not decorated by the castle decorator for the wedding because there was already a spiritual decor there that was great for uniting two people and having the mini angels there would be the perfect accent to the decor. Armellya's parents and Jaden's parents already discussed how to get the couple to the spiritual hall without seeing each other, Armellya's parents would take her first on a route hardly traveled with a guard with them then Andrew would backtrack to tell Jaden and his parents it was time to go to the spiritual hall then Andrew, Jaden, his parents, and guard would leave the castle to go to the spiritual hall using the same route that was used in taking Armellya but the two would be in different rooms until the music started to play then the ceremony would begin and within five minutes the groom and bride would see each other as the groom stood at the altar and the bride did her walk up the aisle.

With everyone in their places the miniangels arrived and lined the aisle now it was time to transfer Armellya and Jaden so their parents did as planned and they both got to the spiritual hall safely and quickly then when both sets of parents were out of the rooms that their children were in the music started and Jaden took his place at the altar then seconds later Armellya started down the aisle and everyone gasped because she was so beautiful and one of Armellya's brother's and one of her sister's did an excellent job doing what they were supposed to do. As Armellya walked down the aisle her sister tossed rose petals on the aisle floor and her brother followed with the special ring pillow and once they got up to the altar Jaden took Armellya by the hands and smiled softly at her then she smiled softly back then they both looked up to the chief then he started to speak the words of holy matrimony. When it came time to exchange rings, Armellya's brother gave them the rings, and they put the rings on each other as they said their own short vows to each other. Then the chief told Andrew he could kiss Armellya, and while they were kissing, the chief announced the new couple and everyone cheered and clapped. The couple went up the aisle to exit the spiritual hall and go to their side of the castle for the reception after Armellya changed from her wedding gown into a less bulky formal gown.

Now the miniangels have left so the general community could go to the community dining hall while personal friends and family would go to the castle's private dining hall where they would wait on the newlyweds to join them after Jaden helped Armellya out of her wedding dress, Jaden as a doctor was not embarrassed by seeing Armellya in the near nude but Armellya was a bit shy and Jaden made Armellya realize that it was no different to him seeing bodies with clothing as it was seeing them without then he was telling her how beautiful she was and she had nothing to hide from him then Armellya loosened up as she told Jaden he was right and how silly it was for her to be ashamed of her body and only he would be seeing her anyway. Finally, Armellya was in her formal gown and the new couple went out to the castle's private dining hall and took their seats next to each other at the big round table then they thanked everyone for making their wedding and their day so special and perfect because without the family the whole thing could not have happened. Now that the last two individuals got to the big round table and got seated Melanie's father had the kitchen staff serve everyone there was rotisserie chickens, lamb, pig roasted under the ground, all the vegetables they had to offer, all the fruits they had to offer, and various beverages it seemed that Melanie's father had thought of everything. Once everyone ate and got stuffed beyond what they had gotten before it was time for the newlyweds to open their gifts and there were so many that they were practically stacked to the ceiling from the table then there were many gifts under the table and many more around the table on the floor it took two hours for the newlyweds to open their gifts and Armellya kept the gift tags that said who the gift was from and she wrote what the gift was on the tag while Jaden actually opened the gift and Andrew used his and Camillia's runners to run the gifts back to the new couples house since it was not far away and that would save a lot of time in the long run. All the new couple would have to do was take their time and put the items where they wanted them in their home and after that Armellya planned to have Bridgette make some thank you cards so she could send them out and make sure everyone knew she was thankful for their generosity. It appeared that all the gifts had been given but the chief stood up and announced that he had a gift for the new couple out in the barn so everyone went to the barn and the chief pointed at the big red bow and the new couple was surprised at what they saw then the chief asked if they could use it and Armellya said yes because Jaden needed his buggy for work and now Armellya would have one for her outings such as shopping or going out with the girls.

From the barn everyone separated and went their own way the guards got into their regular uniforms and so did the hunters then went back on duty Matthew and Bridgette went home to spend the rest of the afternoon together and so did Andrew and Camillia the rest of the castle's crew went back to work Armellya and Jaden went to their house to put gifts away and as they did that Jaden asked Armellya a lot of questions about all her parents abilities then he found out that she and all her siblings had the same abilities so Jaden asked Armellya if she could heal him when the time came for them to want children and she said yes then they discussed having children which they both knew would be in their future somewhere but until now had not been spoken of.

By the time the newlyweds got everything put away and had an in-depth conversation about their future together, they were about to sit down and relax until the dinner hour but there was a frantic knock at their door so Jaden quickly answered the door and it was Matthew talking so fast that no one could understand him so Jaden told him to slow down and speak again then Matthew blurted out that Bridgette was having the baby and the feet were already out. Jaden yelled for Armellya to grab his black bag and go to Bridgette's bedroom while he ran out of his house following Matthew and when Jaden got to Bridgette he knew she was in immense amounts of pain so he told Matthew to talk to Bridgette and try to distract her because he had to try to support the baby and its airway just then Armellya walked into Bridgette's bedroom and realized what was happening so she told Jaden to tell her what he needed done and she would help then he told Armellya to get the manual suction out of the bag for the baby by then the baby's buttocks were out and facing up. Bridgette was hysterically crying and it was not because of the pain it was out of concern for her baby who was two months early and Jaden knew that due to his telepathy so he assured her the baby was going to be fine then he told Bridgette to give one good push and as she pushed Jaden told her to push harder finally, the baby was completely out and Jaden asked Armellya for the manual suction then she gave it to him and he cleared out the baby's airway then he announced it was a boy as the newborn started to cry. Now that the immediate emergency was over it was time to cut the umbilical cord and clamp it then Armellya took the baby and cleaned him up while Bridgette got cleaned up and her bedding was changed. Jaden gave Bridgette a great bill of health and told her she did wonderful delivering the baby then Bridgette told Jaden the baby's name was to be Brandon then Jaden told her it was a good name and right then Armellya brought Brandon back to Bridgette then Bridgette and Matthew loved on their new baby for a short while before the nanny came for him. Armellya told Bridgette she was happy for her then Armellya went back home leaving Jaden with Bridgette and the baby but the whole time Jaden remained gone Armellya thought about the miracle of creating a life then carrying it for nine months and the chore of bringing that child into the world it made Armellya long to experience the whole process and she realized the many years of bringing up the child while providing for the child and giving him or her the best chance possible for a productive life was a chore in itself but she was up for it. Armellya decided she was going to speak to Jaden about the topic when he had the time and at that moment he came home to finish relaxing with Armellya and once he sat next to her on their couch she started to kiss him passionately then he pulled her as close as he could and caressed her body and she caressed his body then they started to remove their clothing. Armellya and Jaden continued to caress each other and kiss as they moved from the couch to their bed by then they were naked and once they got up against the bed Jaden softly laid Armellya onto the bed then he lay over her and they engaged in foreplay for quite some time then they started to make love and when they did Armellya's body started to glow and the glow started to surround Jaden. The glow surrounded the two lovers until they finished making love then it just disappeared quicker than it came leaving them both to feel energized then they realized it was nearing the dinner hour so they had to get out of bed and rush to get redressed to get out to the castle's private dining hall with everyone else.

As Armellya and Jaden were headed for their front door three mini angels appeared and the new couple was surprised to see them so Armellya asked the miniangels why they were there then one of them went to Armellya's belly and started to glow then she reached out to touch Armellya's belly and when she did Armellya felt weak and nearly fainted so Andrew caught Armellya from behind and held her up until the miniangel stopped glowing and moved away from her then Jaden sat Armellya in a nearby chair and the miniangel told the new couple that the child she carried was to be called Jadellya and she would have all the family gifts and become queen of the miniangels when she reached the age of accountability. One of the other two tiny angels went to Jaden's forehead and gave him a kiss then he started to glow while his body lifted off the ground and turned several times before he was back on the ground and the glow disappeared then that miniangel told Jaden that was the kiss of life and he asked her what that meant for him, and she told him that his life span was doubled over that of a regular pale one and he now had the gifts of the royal family. Jaden was told to practice his talents and develop them because he would be needing them in the future then the third miniangel told Armellya to help Jaden with his talents and Armellya said she would then the miniangel told her she too would need her talents in the near future, Armellya did not understand why it was so important to nurture their talents to be needed in the near future so she asked the miniangel about it and the miniangel told her the three of them would visit regularly and give them details as necessary then the three miniangels gave their farewells for now and disappeared. Armellya and Jaden hugged each other tightly and told each other they loved the other then Jaden congratulated Armellya and asked her if she wanted him to be her prenatal doctor or if she wanted the same doctor that Bridgette and her mother used and Armellya told Jaden he would be perfect and it would allow him to have more participation in the pregnancy plus it would be quite an experience to deliver one's own child. The new couple decided that the next day Jaden would take Armellya to the hospital for a blood test and get the official word then they could announce it at family time and with all of that the couple was quite late for the dinner hour so they rushed out to the castle's private dining hall to join the rest of the family.

When the new couple got to the big round table and got seated, the family joked with them about being late and starting their honeymoon early while Melanie had the kitchen staff serve dinner. There was a lot of talking during dinner and everyone had an enjoyable time. The dinner lasted more than an hour and everyone ate slowly so when everyone was finished it was time to wind things up in the castle for the night so everyone hugged everyone then went their separate ways. Everything in the castle got wound up rapidly and everyone went to their quarters, Camillia was feeling exhausted but not ready to go to sleep and Andrew became concerned about her and the baby he could not put his finger on what was bothering him but something had his attention so while Camillia lay on the bed he sat next to her and rubbed her pregnant belly and he kept feeling a sensation like her stomach was hardening and perking it was hard for him to describe and he did not know if that was normal so he asked Camillia if she was feeling well and she told Andrew that she was having some mild contractions then Andrew knew what had him concerned and what had caught his attention. Andrew asked Camillia if that was normal and she told him it was a little early to have the baby but early contractions were normal and after having some for a brief time they go away and that sometimes happens during the last month then Andrew told her she had more than one month to go. Camillia kept trying to convince Andrew that she was fine but he was nervous that she may end up having the baby before morning so Camillia told Andrew to change from his day clothes into his bed clothes then lay next to her and at least rest and she promised if it was necessary for the doctor to respond for her pregnancy she would let him know and he could go get Jaden then Andrew said okay and did what Camillia asked him to do.

Andrew was in bed and Camillia fell fast asleep but Andrew could not sleep so he watched Camillia sleep and an hour later their miniangels showed up so Andrew woke Camillia than the mini angels told them that she came to make Camillia's delivery an easy one then she flew in a circle three times around Camillia's belly and when she was done the three miniangels expressed their love for the king and queen of the commune and as they were fading out they told Andrew to get Jaden then they were gone. Andrew flew out of bed and ran to Armellya and Jaden's front door then banged on it, Jaden answered the door then Andrew told him it was time for the baby to be delivered so Jaden told Armellya he was going to deliver her mother's baby and she said she wanted to go along so Jaden grabbed his black bag as he told her to hurry then Armellya put her robe on and left with Jaden and Andrew.

When the three of them got to Camillia, Jaden observed that she was relaxed and breathing normally so he went to her side and put his hand on her belly to feel for the contractions and time them and sure enough she was in labor. The contractions were strong and only a minute apart Jaden was stunned at how calm Camillia was and it caused him to believe she was only at the beginning of her labor but he went ahead and checked her cervix and found that not only was she completely dilated but the baby's head was delivered so Jaden told Camillia he needed one good push so she gave a good push with the next contraction and she gave it all she had which was all it took the baby started to cry right away then Jaden told Andrew and Camillia that they had a beautiful baby girl as he cut the umbilical cord and clamped the stub then Jaden handed the new baby to Armellya and asked her to clean her up then give her to Camillia and while Armellya was cleaning up the baby Camillia's personal maid was cleaning her up and had her sit in the rocking chair by the bed while she changed the bedding then Armellya handed Camillia her new daughter. Camillia said the baby's name was to be Desirae then she and Andrew doted over her while they could but only for a brief time before the nanny came to get her. Camillia got back into bed and Andrew walked Armellya and Jaden out of their quarters then he returned to his quarters and got into bed with Camillia meanwhile, Armellya wanted to talk to Jaden about how mothers do with delivering babies because she saw examples of how every pregnancy was different and so were the deliveries she was feeling a bit of fear over delivering the baby she had just conceived but Jaden told her he would be there with her for everything and with the miniangels being involved he believed the delivery would be easy for her and the baby would deliver normally with low stress. Jaden told Armellya not to worry, just go to bed and get the rest that was needed for a healthy pregnancy so Armellya took off her robe and hung it up then crawled into bed. Jaden had put his black bag away while talking to Armellya so he got into bed next to Armellya and held her close then they fell asleep arm in arm. Since Armellya and Jaden's mini angels had already visited them earlier and took care of their business that had them needing to visit within the night hours they did not visit during the hours of sleep and the same went for Andrew and Camillia their mini angels had already made their visit to help with the delivery of Desirae.

Everyone else was getting visits from their miniangels because it was the midnight hour and they had not seen their angels since the night before but of course everyone fell back to sleep after seeing their miniangels. The night went by fast and before anyone knew it the time to awaken was upon them so everyone was up changing from their bedclothes into their day clothes and going to their bathrooms to wash their faces, brush their teeth, and brush their hair and everyone was exiting their quarters within a few minutes of each other and heading for the castle's private dining hall. Once everyone got seated at the big roundtable, they told one another about the things they had to do that day before the lunch hour but Armellya and Jaden did not say anything about going to the hospital for a blood pregnancy test because they wanted the results to be positive before saying anything. Discussing the day's agenda reminded Armellya that she wanted Bridgette to make a thank you card to be duplicated for the individuals who had given gifts to her and Jaden for their wedding and when she asked,

Bridgette said she would and they would be ready that afternoon for her to fill out and distribute.

The kitchen staff finally got breakfast cooked so Melanie had them serve everyone as she apologized for the tardiness but everyone enjoyed the time they had together and it was a good start to the day but breakfast had to be cut short so everyone could get to their errands. Everyone got up from the big roundtable to take care of their business, Bridgette went to work on the thankyou cards in the room of relaxation while Armellya and Jaden went to the hospital for a blood pregnancy test and when they got there they left their horses with the hospitals stable boy and hurried inside Jaden took Armellya to the laboratory where he had her sit on a chair then he drew six tubes of blood then told the technician to test the blood immediately and send the report to the charge nurse as he handed the blood to the technician. Jaden told Armellya that it would take about forty-five minutes for the test results to come back so they went to the charge nurse and told her they were waiting for some blood test results and they would be in the waiting room and to get the results to him as soon as possible then Armellya and Jaden walked down the hall and sat in the waiting room and in the meantime Andrew and Camilla were at the multiuse hall checking on the production of the eleven spindles and twenty-three sheep's shears. When the couple walked into the hall, they found everyone working hard and so far, they had three spindles and ten sheep's shears left to make and the equipment that was finished was already in use and more individuals that needed a job had just gotten employed and that was nine Spindler's and fourteen shavers and this arrangement provided a little compensation to the sheepherders also. Andrew told the workers they were doing a fantastic job and he could not wait for them to get their next job because he believed they would stay busy so working well with one another was important but it appeared they did work well together then they all told Andrew they were happy with their job and with each other.

While Andrew and Camillia were wrapping up things in the multi use hall, Armellya's test results were ready for Jaden to look them over so the charge nurse did as Jaden requested by getting them as soon as they were available and taking the report to Jaden immediately and when he got them he thanked the charge nurse then looked carefully at the blood test results and as they already knew Armellya's pregnancy hormones were elevated creating a positive pregnancy test result. Jaden explained the results to Armellya and they were both excited to have the official word and they could not wait to tell the good news during family time but for now they needed to get back to the castle so Armellya could see Bridgette and find out how the thankyou card was going. Andrew and Camillia had to ride by the hospital to get back to the castle and as Armellya and Jaden were leaving the hospital they were seen by Andrew and Camillia so they waited for the kids to catch up to them which was only one-hundred feet away then Andrew and Camillia asked them if everything was okay and they told their parents nothing could be better then they got ready to get their horses moving toward home when the charge nurse ran out of the hospital yelling for Jaden to return so he told Armellya, Camillia, and Andrew to go on home and he would see them shortly so they moved on.

Jaden jumped off his horse asking what the emergency was then as the charge nurse was running back into the hospital past the nurses desk she told Jaden the emergency was with the retired doctor then Jaden's heart fell to his stomach and when Jaden and the charge nurse got to the retired doctor's office he was laid out on the floor holding his chest so Jaden did a primary physical assessment, checked his airway, breathing, and circulation and from what he could tell the retired doctor was having a heart attack so Jaden decided to try out his new healing ability even though he had not been taught how to use it. Jaden put one hand over the retired doctor's heart then concentrated on it resetting and repairing then Jaden's hand started to glow until it was a blinding yellow light then the retired doctor became more alert and quit clenching his chest then after a minute Jaden's hand no longer glowed and the retired doctor sat up and began to tell Jaden thankyou and about how much better he felt. Jaden and the charge nurse helped the retired doctor off the floor and into his desk chair then Jaden did a complete cardiovascular work-up on the retired doctor but everything came back normal so Jaden believed it was due to the healing because without it the retired doctor should have died and everyone there knew that, patient and health care workers alike. Jaden advised the retired doctor to slow down on his work load and he said he would if Jaden could help pick up the slack and he said he would. With everything now stable the charge nurse went back to work at the nurse's desk while the retired doctor gathered his things to go home so he soon left then Jaden left the hospital to go to the castle to be with Armellya. When Jaden got back to the castle, he found Armellya in the room of relaxation with Bridgette who had the thank you card done and it looked great but there was not enough time before the the lunch hour and family time to run it to the shop to run it to the shop to have it duplicated When Armellya saw Jaden, she asked how his patient was doing then he told Armellya that the patient was the retired doctor and he was having a heart attack then Armellya became deeply concerned so before Armellya could say or think anything further Jaden told her he healed him and he was fine now. Jaden told Armellya he was relieved when he found he could instinctively heal because they had not had a chance to practice their abilities and before he knew it an emergency came about that without the healing would have killed the retired doctor then Armellya hugged Jaden in relief of the retired doctor's life being saved and she told him how proud of him she was then Jaden told Armellya it was due to the blessing from his miniangel and he could not take the credit so when she showed herself again he would thank her as he told her about the event. Armellya told Jaden he did not have to wait for her to visit because the two of them could astral project to the dinosaur tail but it would have to be after the lunch hour and family time for now because they needed to go to the family room to meet with the rest of the family for the lunch hour.

When Jaden and Armellya got to the family room, only the new stable boy, Andrew, and Camillia were in the family room but it did not take long for the rest of the family to get there then Andrew led the entire family to the castle's private dining hall where everyone got seated at the big round table. Melanie had lunch ready so she had the kitchen staff serve everyone then everyone started to go around the table and share their day Andrew and Camillia started things off by announcing the new jobs for quite a few individuals due to the spindles and sheep's shears being produced and Camillia reminded everyone that there would now be wool cloth that could be used for anything that they previously used furs for and it was a lighter material and easier to work with, then half of the other family members shared and now it was Armellya and Jaden's turn so Jaden stood up and declared he had some amazing news for everyone to be a part of then he took Armellya's hand and pulled lightly to ease her into a standing position next to himself and he put one of his hands on her belly and announced they were pregnant and for a few moments everyone was in a silent shock because it was so soon then they congratulated the couple then the couple sat back down in their seats and as everyone continued to eat their lunch the rest of the family shared their day then about the time they were done eating the last individual shared their day and it was now time to leave the castle's private dining hall and go about the rest of the day. Everyone stood up from the big round table and gave one another hugs then piled out of the room, Armellya followed Bridgette to the room of relaxation to retrieve the thankyou card to take it to the duplication hall then have them deliver the cards back to the castle so Armellya could fill them out and get them distributed in a timely manner. As everyone was exiting the castle's private dining hall Andrew caught Jaden and asked him to sit in the family room with himself and Camillia so when Armellya was finished dealing with the thankyou cards she would join them and the four of them would discuss training for the king and queen's job so they could fill in if necessary and take over when Andrew and Camillia got in their upper years.

Twenty minutes later Armellya returned to the castle from the duplicating hall so Camillia called out to Armellya to come to the family room and when she got there she was a bit alarmed when she saw Andrew and Jaden sitting there with Camillia, Armellya knew it was not going to be a social meeting so she sat down and waited for her mother to speak. Andrew told Armellya and Jaden that when they reached a certain age or if something were to happen to them or if for some reason, they needed someone to fill in for the king and queen they could do it because Armellya was next to rule and since she married Jaden that made him next to rule also. Armellya asked Andrew when, where, and how long the teaching would be then Andrew asked Jaden what time of day would fit into his schedule and Jaden told Andrew it would have to be sometime after the lunch hour because from the breakfast hour to the lunch hour he had to be at the hospital working. Armellya interrupted to tell Andrew that after the lunch hour would not work for her on Wednesdays because it was girl's day and she wanted to participate so Andrew suggested that they leave their schedules as they were and meet two hours before the breakfast hour each day so they could expedite the training.

Armellya and Jaden were okay with the suggestion that Andrew had then Jaden asked if he could tell Andrew and Camillia something confidentially then they told him yes then he revealed that his angel visited the day before and gave him the kiss of life so now he had the same gifts as them and their children then the miniangel told of the child Armellya was carrying to be the queen of the miniangels when she was at the age of accountability and the miniangel said her name was to be Jadellya. Andrew told Jaden that only the chosen ones would have the abilities they had and it seemed to him that Jaden was a chosen one the only difference was that Jaden's abilities were bestowed upon him where Andrew and Camilla's abilities were naturally occurring. Andrew told Jaden he was not royalty just because he was married to their daughter but he was chosen by God as well then Jaden told Andrew that being a chosen one was a blessing but blessings came with responsibility and Camillia agreed then they heard a knock at the castle's door so Andrew went to answer the door and it was a runner with a medium sized box from the duplication hall and he had the thankyou cards that Armellya had done so now she had to fill them all out then she could have them disbursed. Andrew told Armellya and Jaden that he and Camillia would meet on the next morning then Jaden carried the box to the office of relaxation for Armellya and she sat in the chair at the desk and started to fill out the cards for the individuals she remembered while she sent Jaden for the gift tags she had kept track of and he was back within a few minutes and handed the tags to her. Armellya had the cards ready to disburse an hour later so she had Jaden drop them off at the distribution hall and they got to work right away and everyone should have their cards by the dinner hour. Now that the cards were done Armellya had the rest of the day free and Jaden was on call as the veterinarian but it was rare for him to have to go anywhere so Armellya advised Jaden that they should use the spare time for working on their abilities starting with astral projection because they did have a reason to see the miniangels before their midnight visit because Jaden wanted to thank his miniangel for the kiss of life and try to find out why he and Armellya were going to need their gifts in the near future as she said. Armellya and Jaden got to their house then Armellya told Jaden how to astroproject and added that it would get easier as it was done more and more, then Jaden said he could do it and the two of them got into comfortable positions on their bed.

When Armellya successfully astral projected to the dinosaur tail, she looked for Jaden and quickly found him then they sought out their miniangels and found them then they greeted the couple and the couple gave greetings back then their miniangels told them they could feel some curiosity in them and Jaden told his miniangel that she had said something that had him concerned. The miniangel already knew what Jaden was referring to and she told him that she could not reveal the future but she could help prepare them for those events that she saw coming and if the couple would head her word everything would work out as it should then Jaden's mini angel told him to use his knowledge for his medical and veterinary practice and not to always rely on his healing ability. Armellya asked the miniangel why she could not share what she saw for their future with them because she had done it before with the pregnancy and child's name and it was kept a secret until it was confirmed by the tests then when the time came for family time they shared the good news and it worked out for the better because trying to hide a pregnancy would be very difficult. The miniangel told them that was not foresight that was simply detection besides the times would not come to pass until they were king and queen of the land of grandeur and their first child was the queen of the miniangels so it would be too premature to give the foresight at that time and that was why she said she would reveal the information when the time came. Jaden asked the miniangel if she could give them the ability to see the future as she saw it and the miniangel told him yes then Armellya asked why she never gave them the ability and the miniangel told her it was because no one ever asked for that gift so Armellya and Jaden said they were now asking for the gift. The miniangel told Armellya and Jaden to go back to their bodies and she would go to them to give the gift of foresight then the couple returned to their bodies and waited for their miniangels who showed up five minutes after the couples return then each one got a kiss on the forehead from their mini angel then the mini angels told the couple to use the gift wisely because what they would see may not always be what it would seem then Armellya and Jaden promised they would be cautious and respect the visions then the miniangels revealed that the foresight would come in waves of what was called a Deja Vou then she explained what that was and without warning she disappeared. At that point, the couple agreed to share their foresight with each other openly so when a situation came to pass they both could recognize it and with that the couple realized it was getting close to the dinner hour so they decided to discuss the matter later when they would have more private time.

Jaden and Armellya went out of their house and headed for the castle's family room to wait for everyone to get there for the dinner hour and because their arrival was a bit early only Andrew and Camillia were there and though Armellya and Jaden were so excited about their new unusual gift that they wanted to share it with their parents but they knew that they could only share it amongst themselves. The joy for Jaden was interrupted when he saw a horrific vision of a spindle maker getting a severe injury while building the last of the spindles Jaden quickly pulled Armellya aside and told her he had to get to the multi use hall to save a spindle maker's hand because he just saw the vision of a terrible injury then Armellya told him to go quickly and she would cover for him. Jaden raced out of the castle and ran to the barn to get his own horse then he jumped on the horses back and rode bareback going as fast as the horse would go then when he got to the multi use hall he jumped off the horses back before the horse was stopped and did not even tie the horse to a pole he just raced into the hall and quickly scanned the workers and what they were doing then he spotted the worker that he envisioned having an accident so Jaden cautiously walked up to him and asked him to move away from the spindle so the worker looked up then moved away from the spindle and asked what the problem was.

Jaden told the spindle worker that he sensed there would be an avoidable accident with a terrible outcome then the worker said he was nearly finished with the last spindle so Jaden asked him if he would mind him observing the last of the work and the spindle worker said he would not mind so Jaden observed the finishing touches carefully. Jaden told the spindle maker to work with extreme care so he did and in doing so the spindle maker found a small flaw in the spindles wheel and he admitted if he were to keep working at the pace he had been working at he would not have noticed the small flaw and it could have been detrimental to him as well as made the spindle unsafe to use if it were to stay in one piece which was not likely then the spindle maker took that spindle apart and discarded the flawed piece then started the spindle over with a new piece to replace the previous flawed one. The spindle maker worked slowly on the final spindle to assure there were no more flawed pieces and Jaden stayed with him until the spindle was completed then Jaden saw a vision of everything being fine with the spindle worker and spindle so Jaden told the spindle maker he was satisfied with the spindle and his work style then he said farewell to the spindle worker and the spindle worker thanked Jaden. Jaden was thankful for his vision because had it have come true the spindle worker would have amputated his hand and even though it would have been able to be reconnected it would have been more for appearance than function because the nerves would not have completely recovered even though the arteries and veins would have he would have had little use of his hand. When Jaden got outside, his horse was still where he left it so he got back on it and leisurely rode back to the castle to join everyone for the dinner hour. When he got back to the castle, he tied his horse out front to be taken care of by the new stable boy after the dinner hour, then Jaden went inside and sat at the big round table next to his wife. Andrew asked Jaden if everything was all right and he said yes then he telepathically told Armellya everything that occurred at the multi use hall then she gently took his head into her hands and leaned into him then gave him a kiss on the forehead and told him she loved him. Andrew and Camillia knew something had gone on but they could not read Armellya or Jaden's mind because they were blocking their thoughts and that made Andrew and Camillia more curious about why Jaden took off so quick from the dinner hour and came back so late then it was obvious that he and Armellya were communicating telepathically. Andrew and Camillia decided not to ask about their secrecy because it was obvious that if they wanted what they were keeping between themselves known to them or anyone else they would have been verbal about it.

Melanie helped break the silence by reminding Camillia, Armellya, Bridgette, and Michelle that the next day was their first girl's day then the girls started talking about it and how there had been so much going on around the castle that they had to keep postponing it and now they were finally going to get to do it. Armellya told the girls that they could use her buggy for girl's day since that was an event that would require pooling together for transportation and it would give her a chance to use her buggy for the first time then the girls said it would be perfect. Even though the dinner hour was over Jaden was still eating due to his emergency errand at the multi use hall so everyone stayed at the big round table to keep him company then when Jaden was finished eating he and everyone else got up and said their good nights then went their separate ways to wrap up their day's responsibilities so they could go to their quarters to wind down and go to bed. Having nothing to do, Andrew and Camillia were first to go to their home and Armellya and Jaden had nothing to do either so they went to their home also and the kitchen crew was finishing with the dishes and putting leftover food away while Melanie supervised and Bridgette and Matthew went to their baby's bedroom to spend a little bit of time with their little girl Sheeba and Michelle went to her quarters since her maid services were over for the night.

Now that the castle was quiet for the night the only thing to occur before getting up and starting another day was for everyone's mini angels to visit them so everyone went to bed right away because they were eager to see their miniangels. Sure enough, the midnight hour had arrived seemingly quickly and each miniangel had appeared in their pale one's home singing their beautiful wake-up song so now the entire castle and community was awake with their miniangels. Armellya and Jaden's mini angels told them they were proud of how the couple handled the emergency that Jaden foresaw at the multiuse hall and that was definitely an event to try to alter from what had been seen then they warned the couple that there would be some things that they would foresee that were not meant to stop from happening they would be seen only to save the life of the victim and that meant that though they could reach the victim before the incident occurred they were to allow the incident to occur anyway and they needed to learn the difference in the visions because they would always see the before, during, and after of each incident but the feelings would be different and they needed to heed those feelings no matter who the individual was or how awful the outcome would seem to be.

The miniangels reminded the couple in the incidences just described they needed to remember that the individuals would survive the tragedy but their job would be to help the victim to overcome the mental and physical anguish, Armellya and Jaden were not happy to hear that they needed to hold back in some instances where it would be possible to avoid the whole situation then the miniangel told the couple that if they did not heed the feelings the outcome could be death of the victim or even them. The miniangels told the couple that if the victim survived the incident the outcome would be worse than if they did not intervene like the intuition told them then the couple questioned how they would be able to tell when to intervene and when not to and the miniangel told the couple to listen to their intuition and that it would be strong and unmistakable then without warning and seemingly in the middle of conversation the miniangel disappeared. Armellya and Jaden discussed their gift of being able to see the future and they thought it odd that they would only be able to see negative situations because it would be nice to see some positive things such as upcoming pairing of pale ones, weddings, births, and so on. The two of them also spoke of why if they saw negative things before they happened they had to allow the situation to happen when they could intervene and stop the tragedy whether it be big or small it would seem intervention would be why they had the ability. They both agreed that if the victim were to be one of their parents it would be difficult to refuse help and with that observation the couple decided that the gift could be a curse at times and they hoped it never came down to that. Armellya and Jaden agreed to not put any more thought into the gift and just address it as it occurred. The couple lay back down in bed and tried to go back to sleep though it took a while they both did fall back to sleep but they also had nightmares of the gift revealing trauma and them being held back from helping it woke them both up several hours before it would be time to get up for the new day and they spoke about their dreams and how awful they were and established that they may have too much of a conscience to handle the foreshadowing ability.

Armellya and Jaden were beginning to understand why seeing clips of the future were not a regular gift like the others and they agreed that they did not know what they were asking for even though their miniangels tried to deter them from obtaining the gift the couple wondered if the miniangels could take the gift back so the couple decided to astral project to the dinosaur tail and find out. Armellya and Jaden got into comfortable positions on their bed and the next thing they knew they were meeting each other at the dinosaur tail then they looked for their miniangels and found them quickly it was as though they were expecting the couple to show up. The couple did not greet their miniangels as usual they got right to their question and asked their miniangels if they could take back the gift of seeing the future in small events and the angels said yes but it would be better for them to have it so when they become king and queen they could better protect their community and keep it running smoothly. The couple asked their miniangels what could be so important in the future to see that they had to have the horrible ability to see the future but not intervene at times and the miniangels told the couple they had already seen that far in the future and they could not reveal that information but they would always stand by them.

Armellya and Jaden's mini angels told them there was nothing else to talk about so they had better get back to their bodies and get ready for their day then the couple said their farewells and returned to their bodies then Jaden checked to see how much longer they had until it would be time to get out of bed for the day and to his surprise it was that time because they had to rise two hours earlier than usual for a while so they could meet with Andrew and Camillia for their lessons on being king and queen of the land of grandeur so he told Armellya it was time to get up and they headed for their bathroom to change out of bedclothes into day clothes, wash their faces, brush their teeth, and brush their hair. When Armellya and Jaden got to the family room, they found Andrew and Camillia already sitting there so Armellya and Jaden hurriedly sat down and said they were ready for their lesson then Andrew and Camillia started the lesson and the first hour went by fast because it quickly covered things they were already aware of. The second hour was well paced but not fast and it covered some basic responsibilities over those of the individuals in the community. At the end of the second hour of the day's lesson the castle started to have some signs of life so Andrew told the new couple they would meet early the next morning Armellya and Jaden acknowledged him then they went to the castle's private dining hall and sat at the big roundtable where they waited for Bridgette and Andrew.

Once everyone was there Melanie sat down at the big round table and had the kitchen staff serve breakfast while she spoke of how excited she was for girl's day to occur then Bridgette and Armellya started to express their joy about finally getting to have a girl's day also. The three girls discussed the activities that they would be engaging in while the men stayed quiet and focused on eating but everyone finished eating at the same time and now it was time for Jaden to kiss Armellya goodbye to go to the hospital for an eight-hour shift. Andrew and Camillia needed to go to the multi use hall to check on the status of the last of the spindles and sheep's shears while Armellya was going to go to her home and take a much-needed nap and Melanie was going to be in the kitchen planning lunch and overseeing the kitchen crew as they made what she planned while Bridgette was caring for Lynndia and Michelle was overseeing all the maids in the castle. It took the kitchen staff a half hour to clean up the kitchen then while planning lunch Melanie got the idea to see if there was anything special that Armellya wanted since most pregnant women tend to crave certain things so she left the kitchen and went to Armellya's home and knocked on the door but after several times of knocking and Armellya not answering Melanie became concerned so she checked the door knob and it was unlocked so she went inside and went to Armellya's bedroom and found her on her bed sleeping hard but Melanie really wanted to fix something for lunch for Armellya so she shook her and called out her name but she did not wake up so she kept trying to wake Armellya and still no response Melanie knew something was wrong because nothing was waking her so she sent one of the castle's runners for a doctor.

It took eighteen minutes for the runner to get back and the doctor was with him so Melanie told him she was unresponsive then he tried to wake Armellya and found she was facing some sort of medical crisis then he checked her pulse and he could barely feel it then he checked her breathing closely and realized she was breathing shallower than if she was just asleep. The doctor told Melanie to get help so he could get Armellya into a buggy and get her to the hospital so Melanie grabbed the castle's runners and between all of them they got Armellya into the doctor's buggy then he rode off as fast as his horse could go then when he got to the hospital he got some of the security guards to help and get Armellya onto a stretcher then they wheeled her into the hospital and transferred her to a bed. The doctor called out for several nurses to get in the room right away and when they got in the room he ordered one to hook Armellya to the cardiac monitor and a second nurse to hook her up to the general monitoring equipment and a third nurse to get intravenous access and draw blood for all the basic tests and while all this was going on the doctor ordered one of the security guards to find Jaden and get him in there immediately.

The security guard found Jaden in his office and told him there was an emergency with a patient and the patient was his wife so Jaden jumped out of his chair, knocking it backward as he ordered the security guard to take him to her so the guard turned from the office door and started to walk to where Armellya was but he was not moving fast enough for Jaden's liking so he told the guard to move it then the guard started to run and Jaden kept up then when they got to Armellya's hospital room Jaden shoved the guard out of the way and went to her side the other doctor gave Jaden a report of her status and what had been done for her up to that point but the other doctor did not know she was pregnant so Jaden ordered the other doctor to give him the hand held ultrasound machine so he did as he questioned Jaden on what he was going to do with it then Jaden told the doctor he was going to check on the unborn child the other doctor was speechless then Jaden said that the baby looked good and ordered a fetal monitor to be placed on Armellya to keep track on how the baby was doing so the other doctor got one and put it on her then he said he was going to go look for the test results to be back and while he was gone Jaden tried to get a telepathic link with her and it worked so Jaden asked how he could help her and she explained that she was having a nightmare about foreseeing an unspecified pale one being a serial killer of women that meet his or her criteria and she has been unable to wake up from it because it went from victim to victim and she would not be able to point out the victims because it never showed their faces. Jaden found himself feeling what Armellya was feeling so he knew he had to sever their link and come back in short bursts or he would end up stuck in the vision as Armellya was and as Jaden was severing the link Armellya was begging him not to go. The other doctor just happened to walk in at the time Jaden was fully alert so he tried to explain to the doctor that Armellya was in a dream state that was horrific and if they could not get her out of it she would die from fear due to how the body naturally reacted for a moment because her reaction would be much longer than a moment then the doctor said it might be an inventive idea to treat Armellya as though she were in shock for starters and Jaden agreed then asked to be alone with her. The other doctor left the room so Jaden got the telepathic link with Armellya again and asked her how to get her out of the vision and she said to get the miniangels because it would take a healing power beyond that of many pale ones so Jaden broke the telepathic link with Armellya then astroprojected to the dinosaur tail. Jaden found his and Armellya's mini angels and told them what was going on with her then asked them if they could heal her or pull her out of the vision and they said they would have to find the source of the vision then Jaden asked the miniangels what they meant and they told him that it was not Armellya's vision, she was being pulled into someone else's vision in the future and she may very well be the first victim so they had to find the culprit right away.

With no time to lose, Jaden returned to his body and each miniangel put herself in the position to meld minds with their pale one to try to see who could have the ability to have a gift that only Armellya and Jaden could have and realizing that the culprit would have to be one of the royal members most likely Armellya's own son whom she has not conceived yet. It took the miniangels a half hour to get to their pale one, meld minds, and return to the dinosaur tail then discuss what each one had found out then Jaden's mini angel went to him to give him all the information there was. Jaden's mini angel told him that the serial killer was not born yet and it was a male that would be a part of the royal family and that was all they had been able to find out then Jaden asked his miniangel if Armellya could be pulled out of the coma state she was in and the miniangel told Jaden that it would take all the miniangels to try but there were no guarantees. Jaden begged his miniangel to bring the rest of the angels to try to help Armellya so she said okay then left without warning then within five minutes all the miniangels were in the hospital room surrounding Armellya. The miniangels lit up brightly and soon Armellya started to light up then her body lifted off the bed and hovered for quite some time and it appeared that the miniangels were struggling to hold Armellya off the bed then after a bit more time Armellya's body was set back down on the bed and stopped glowing but the miniangels were still glowing for a fleeting time. The procedure seemed to be taking everything the miniangels had but they somehow kept trying to heal her then at the last minute when the miniangels were about to give up Armellya started to move her arms and legs then she moved her head back and forth. The miniangels were exhausted and did not know how much longer they would be able to continue to heal Armellya but she sat up and opened her eyes so the miniangels stopped glowing and disappeared to go back to the dinosaur tail and rest. Armellya told Jaden everything she experienced and some information he had not been able to tap into about the serial killer and the victims then Armellya told Jaden they needed to be aware of their surroundings always and travel in groups because she knew she was to be the first victim but there would be more women to follow but she did not know who however, she could say they were similar in appearance to her. Armellya told Jaden that the serial killer was a male of royal descent and not yet born but he would be easy to spot before he started to kill if those around him paid close attention to his behavior at an early age before he met the age of accountability because he would have abnormal behaviors and the only way to keep him from killing would be to keep him locked up and drugged or euthanize him.

CHAPTER SEVENTY NINE

Armellya had a painful thought that she shared with Jaden she told him what if they were to get pregnant and their next time was with a boy and he turned out to be the serial killer because now they had an extra ability that not even the rest of royal family had and it would be possible for their unborn children to get that gift along with all the rest of the abilities. Jaden took that into consideration then told Armellya that they would have to watch the baby they have now for the gift of seeing the future but they did not have to worry about that baby because they were already told by the miniangels that she would be the queen of the miniangels and to note the miniangels said the baby was a girl and even gave what her name was to be. Armellya told Jaden that maybe they should not have their second child after all and Jaden told Armellya there was no guarantee their second child would be a boy and if so there was also no guarantee he would be the serial killer.

Finally, the test results came back and the other doctor returned to the room and told Jaden all the tests were in normal range then he paused for a few seconds when he realized Armellya was awake and fully aware of her surroundings. The other doctor asked Jaden how Armellya was brought out of the state she was in and Jaden told the doctor it was like magic and said no more so the doctor felt he had better not pry due to the answer Jaden gave. The other doctor asked the charge nurse to print up some discharge papers and let Armellya go home and the charge nurse said okay then about twenty minutes later she had Armellya's paperwork ready although there were no real discharge instructions because there was no real diagnosis for what happened and the other doctor had no clue of what really happened in that hospital room between Armellya and Jaden and he had no knowledge that the miniangels were there, he only knew that his mini angel visited him. The other doctor told Armellya to stay healthy and congratulations on the pregnancy then he walked out of the hospital room and she was free to leave but Jaden wanted to be near her for the rest of the day just in case it was to happen again so even though he had not worked his entire eight hours, he went home with Armellya. Only Armellya, the other doctor, and Jaden knew of the vision incident so Armellya and Jaden were not going to let the family or friends know about it and the other doctor cannot speak of it without Armellya's permission and she would never give it because this incident would cause a community wide scare and it was not necessary.

When Jaden and Armellya got to the castle, it was near the lunch hour and family time which reminded the new couple that they needed to come up with something to tell Melanie since she did find Armellya in a comatose state and anyone she may have told so Armellya turned to Jaden for an explanation since he was a doctor. Jaden told Armellya that they would just tell everyone she woke up at the hospital before they could reach a diagnosis and all the tests that were done came back normal and leave it at that. When Jaden and Armellya entered the castle, they went to the family room and only Andrew and Camillia were there and they asked how Armellya was doing and Jaden told them she was doing great and as soon as

Jaden answered Andrew and Camillia the rest of the family started to arrive. It was not long before everyone was there so Andrew led everyone back to the castle's private dining hall where everyone took their sets at the big round table then Melanie had the kitchen serve everyone their lunch and as usual it was splendid so everyone was going around the room sharing their day and talking with food in their mouths because they could not stop putting the food in their mouths. Andrew and Camillia reported that the last of the spindles and sheep's shears had been completed and everyone else shared how laid-back their day had been and by the time everyone got to share the lunch hour and family time was over so Melanie left her parents in charge of the kitchen so she could go out for girl's day. All the girls were to meet in the family room and Melanie was the first one in there because she was so excited to finally get to do the activities that had been planned for so long and the rest of the girls arrived about the same time so once Michelle, Bridgette, Camillia, and Armellya were there they went out to tell the stable boy to hitch Armellya's horse to her buggy and he did quickly then he brought the horse and buggy out and helped the women onto the buggy and off they went. The shop they went to did manicures, pedicures, facials, and massages so all the girls got the whole treatment and they were gone for four hours experiencing luxury the whole time. In fact, it was so relaxing that they forgot about all their worries and responsibilities.

Finally, it was time to pay for the services and go shopping for fun so the girls started with Jaden's parents' shop to do the bulk of their shopping and to help support their store and they knew the shop had virtually everything in it. Armellya, Bridgette, and Camillia bought some items for their husbands and the girls without the girls knowing and Melanie and Michelle bought some things for the girls without them knowing it. All the girls thought alike when they were humans and it seemed they still thought alike as pale ones. The girls finished shopping at Jaden's parents shop then as they were heading out to the buggy the shop was being closed and that was when the girls realized how long they had been in the store because it was the dinner hour so the girls got on the buggy and pushed the horse to get them to the castle on time instead of late for meeting in the family room.

When the girls got to the castle, they left their goodies in the buggy for the butler to bring in after the dinner hour. They hurried into the family room and found that everyone had been waiting for them. Now that the girls had arrived Andrew led the family to the castle's private dining hall to sit at the big round table and when they were all seated Melanie had the kitchen staff bring dinner out to everyone and since lunch was so extravagant the dinner meal was a light one but no one minded because they were all still full of the lunch meal. Everyone was tired from all the excitement of girl's day and worry over Armellya so they were ready for bed so they could try to relax and there was no real conversation during the dinner hour but everyone did enjoy each other's company of just being there but by the time individuals finished eating they left the table and went to their quarters where usually everyone waited for everyone else to finish eating before leaving the big roundtable. The girls were still eating while the butler brought their treasures into the family room from the buggy for them to separate and when they did get done eating they all took their gifts and went to their quarters to prepare their gifts for giving before going to bed so they could give them out during the breakfast hour. The girls were hoping the gifts in the next morning would help the day start out well and that the day would be a productive one with no negative events for anyone.

Finally, everyone changed out of day clothes and into bed clothes and got into bed for the night so they could see their miniangels around the midnight hour. The castle was quiet and everyone was fast asleep, the midnight hour came quickly then the entire castle and community was awakened by their miniangel's beautiful wake up songs. Most pale ones spoke to their miniangels about how their day went and what to look forward to on the next like receiving their horoscope because the miniangels knew exactly what to expect but spoke in short phrases that could be interpreted how one would want. Armellya and Jaden spoke to their miniangels about the comatose state that Armellya experienced that day and asked if it could happen again and how to keep her from being over powered by the vision then the miniangel told the new couple that it could happen again and to keep from being over powered she must recognize the specific vision for what it was and block it from her mind so she would not be drawn in then the miniangel told Jaden that he could even have the vision as a loved one to a major victim by seeing her murder and not being able to do anything about it the miniangel told Jaden it would be a way of the murderer toying with him for fun then Armellya asked why no other women had the comatose vision since this was a case of a serial killer and the angel told her it was because they could not see the future but it was possible for the killer to enter their dreams and possibly put the other victims into a comatose state the miniangel told the new couple there had never been anything like that occur in their entire existence and they had been placed with the first humans by God himself and they foresaw the end of the human race but never expected the pale ones to emerge the miniangels told the new couple that Darren and Deanna were truly brilliant and they too were guided by their miniangels and only a select few humans had the guidance of their miniangels. Jaden asked the miniangels if it was possible to check every newborn for the harmful intent as soon as they were birthed since the killer has not been born yet, and the miniangel told Jaden absolutely then she asked what they would do to the child who was the serial killer once they found him. Armellya said they would allow him his freedom until the age of accountability and closely observe the child from his first day then address the child in whatever way was necessary and hopefully not anything rash.

Jaden added that they would consult his miniangel as well as their miniangels then the mini angels told the new couple it sounded like a fair proposal at the time but be aware things could be much different than planned and the new couple took heed.

All the other miniangels were back at the dinosaur tail and the new couple's miniangels had exceeded their time so they said they had to go until the next time so they shared expressions of love to each other then the miniangels left. Armellya and Jaden stayed awake for a short time discussing the serial killers ability to cause harm before even being born and the couple decided they must ask their miniangels about how that is possible for a soul to be so powerful then they got comfortable in their bed and astral projected to the dinosaur tail where they were happily greeted then they found their miniangels and asked them how the child who was to be the serial killer was able to cause such violent harm before even being conceived and the miniangel told the couple that they all had souls before being born they were just waiting for a physical body and those souls were angelic like and had the abilities already that they would have as a pale one and that was how it was deduced that the child had to be of royalty because only the royal family had the abilities no other pale one had the abilities and the reason it was a sure bet was because those souls were predestined to their parents. Armellya told the miniangel that only she and Jaden had the ability to see the future so could they find out if the soul was able to see the future and the miniangel told the new couple that it was very likely because he was using the future to terrorize her and Jaden then Jaden said it might be a good idea for him and Armellya to not have their second baby because it would be a boy and most likely be the serial killer and by avoiding the pregnancy they could avoid the murders from occurring then the miniangel told them that it was destiny for the souls pre destined to their parents to be born and they cannot change destiny. This saddened Armellya because she wholeheartedly believed it would be her son who would be the serial killer and she did not know how to mentally handle the dilemma although she knew she could follow through with whatever needed to be done with the child, it would be with regret and she would have to deal with that but she supposed it would be no different than mourning the loss of a loved one. The new couple thanked their miniangels for their honest insight even knowing it would be hard on them then expressed their love toward the miniangels and went back to their bodies and again discussed the serial killer but this time they had enough evidence to assume they would have a son next and he would be the criminal that they would have to stop and now the couple was starting to understand why the miniangels said to get complete control of their gifts because in the future they would really need them.

The new couple was feeling the effects of fatigue so they got comfortable in each other's arms and got what little sleep was left to get before having to get up two hours early for their lesson. Armellya and Jaden were awakened by the kitchen staff making their way through the halls of the castle and they knew it was time to wake up so they sprang out of bed and got themselves ready for the new day and went out to the family room and when they got there Andrew and Camillia were not there yet so they waited, and three minutes later, Andrew and Camillia showed up then they greeted each other and got right down to business. The lesson was getting more intricate and seemed to go slower than before but there was a lot more to being the king and queen over a land than the ordinary individual could fathom but the two-hour mark of the lesson was obvious when everyone else was stirring in the halls of the castle. Everyone was now in the family room waiting for Andrew to lead everyone to the castle's private dining hall but Armellya darted to her home to get her gifts and was back quickly then Andrew led everyone to the castle's private dining hall and once everyone was seated at the big roundtable Melanie told the kitchen staff to hold breakfast for a few minutes. All the girls disbursed their gifts and by that time everyone had a gift to open and it was a surprise for everyone to get a gift so everyone opened their gifts right away and loved what they got because everyone paid attention to what the others were looking at in the shops and dreaming of having but dared not buy for themselves. That was definitely a good start to the day then Melanie let the kitchen staff bring out breakfast and to everyone's second surprise she had the kitchen fix different meals for everyone so they all got their favorite breakfasts.

Everyone ate and talked about their gifts and how much they had wanted what they had gotten but did not want to seem selfish by getting a desire over a necessity even though they had more than enough money to afford anything they desired. After talking about the gifts everyone told the others what they would be doing that morning before the lunch hour and family time. Jaden was going to make a surprise visit to the veterinary and medical rooms in the hospital to make sure all was well and honest, Andrew and Camillia were going to the multi use hall to have them make some plantation tools for every household after visiting the census hall to get a count of how many households there were, Melanie was going to maintain her job in the kitchen, and Armellya had a doctor's visit for her prenatal check-up. Everyone ate slowly and savored their meal but they just finished eating so they told each other to have a good and productive day then went their separate ways while Melanie had the kitchen staff clean off the big round table and planned lunch. Armellya and Jaden headed for the hospital together so she could get her check- up while he was popping in on the two medicine rooms and when they did get to the hospital they walked in together then they kissed and said they would see each other during the check-up then they went their separate ways. Armellya went to the nurse's desk and told the charge nurse she was there for her check-up then the charge nurse took Armellya to a hospital room and told her she would get the doctor then she found out that Jaden was the doctor and he was busy so the charge nurse went back to Armellya and told her that when Jaden had a free moment he would be in there.

Jaden was in the medicine room checking all the products against a list of what they were allowed to have and how much then he looked at what they were producing to assure it was only approved medicines and the right doses and amounts as well as having things labeled correctly then Jaden popped into the veterinary medicine room to do the same to them as he had done to the medical medicine room and all was well for both rooms so he told the workers how wonderful they were doing and left. Jaden knew the employees of the medicine rooms were assuming that if he checked one room he would automatically check the other right away because that was what he did that day but that was not correct he only did so this time to get them to think that because next time he planned to only check one of the rooms but he had not decided on which one yet then on the next check he would check the other room but that would not be the pattern either because he needed to keep the workers on their toes. Jaden was thinking about the room checks as he was walking to the hospital room that Armellya was in and it did not take him long to get there and when he stepped into the room he greeted Armellya with love then gave her a quick kiss before doing her checkup.

Jaden measured Armellya's belly and felt around it then he did the ultrasound and listened to the baby's heartbeat and when he finished with all that he asked some basic questions about the baby and the pregnancy in general then after he wrote all his notes in Armellya's chart he told her everything was on track and that the baby had turned and dropped which was normal for the number of weeks she was. Armellya gave Jaden a kiss and thanked him for seeing her then she told him she would see him during the lunch hour and they both walked out of the hospital room and went opposite directions. Jaden was going to do some paperwork before his next patient was due to be there and Armellya was going back to the castle to practice her extraordinary skills when on the way back to the castle she ran into her parents they too were headed somewhere. Armellya asked them if they were going to the multi use hall and they said yes because they were already at the census hall for a house count then they exchanged greetings and kept about their way and Armellya made it back to her home while Andrew and Camillia had made it to the multi use hall. When Andrew and Camillia went into the multi use hall, they found that the workers were begging for a project, and Andrew told them that was why they were there. Andrew told the workers that he wanted them to work with whomever they needed to produce some gardening tools for each household then Andrew gave them the number of households and specified what tools he expected to see from them. The workers were so excited to have a job after not having anything since the spindles and sheep's shears then Camillia told the workers that they could always investigate the community for ideas of things that would make life easier on the people without being a product that qualified as being too complex because the commune was made up of a race of simple, non technological individuals and it was to stay that way.

The multi use hall workers were getting started on the drafts for the tools while Andrew and Camillia were on their way back to the castle and when they got there they went to Armellya's house and knocked on the door to talk to her and see how her check-up went. Armellya stopped practicing her skills and went to answer her door and was surprised to see her parents but immediately invited them into her home so they went inside then Armellya offered for them to have a seat and everyone sat down then Camillia asked Armellya how her prenatal visit was and Armellya told her parents that it went well because she got to see Jaden and the baby was doing good and that the baby was turned and moved down.

Camillia told Armellya that it would not be long before she had the baby then Armellya told her mother that the time had gone by so fast then she revealed to her mother that she wanted her there for the delivery because she was starting to get nervous about the delivery and maybe she would not be able to handle the pain.

Camillia told Armellya that the pain might seem like a lot at the time but it was more work than pain and it would be temporary because right after the birth one remembers there was pain but the actual intensity of the pain would be forgotten then Camillia told Armellya that every delivery would be different some deliveries were no pain at all then some may have one feeling like they would die from the extreme amounts of pain. Camillia did not say those things to scare her daughter but she felt it was the truth and she told her daughter that then she promised she would try to be there for the delivery and not to think about it until it was to be time then Armellya hugged her mother and told her she loved her very much then she leaned over her mother to hug her father and tell him she loved him too. Camillia and Andrew told Armellya they loved her also and that she was their special child being the first one and only one having the extra gift that no one else had and managing to get Jaden to have the same abilities.

Armellya was shocked that her parents knew of her and Jaden being able to see the future and that Jaden even had abilities so she asked her parents how they found out and Andrew told her that it was in the stars when she was born that she would marry another that would be different as she was so that was how they knew about Jaden receiving the gifts then Camillia told Armellya that she had a horoscope when she was pregnant with her that she would be more special than the rest of the royal ones and that was how her and Andrew knew she would have a gift beyond what she already had and no one but her and Andrew knew of that. Armellya asked Camillia and Andrew why they had never said anything before and they told Armellya that it never came up and that it was her and Jaden's secret Armellya told her parents that she was glad they knew because when her and Jaden would need an extra opinion she knew she could go to them then her parents told her absolutely. Right at that moment, Jaden walked into his and Armellya's family room and everyone stared at him then he asked if everything was okay and Armellya told Jaden that Camillia and Andrew knew he had the same gifts as her and that included the ability to see the future. Jaden asked Armellya if that was an undesirable thing and she told him no because they had not revealed their ability status her parents they figured it out then Jaden suggested that they work on their gifts together and maybe they could help each other master the gifts by sharing helpful suggestions and if one of them had mastered a gift they could help the others get the gift mastered.

Armellya told Andrew and Camillia that their mini angels told them to work on their gifts and get them completely under control because in the future they would really need them but the miniangel did not say why or exactly when. Armellya told Andrew and Camillia that she believed her and Jaden must use their gifts when she got pregnant with their second child because the child would be a boy and have the same gifts but the child would be a spawn of satan. Camillia asked Armellya how she could say a thing like that then Armellya told her she had to explain what happened on the day she was rushed to the hospital because it was not a medical crisis it was their preconceived son. Before Camillia and Andrew could say anything, Jaden cut in the conversation and told them to not say anything to just listen so they said okay and did as asked. Armellya told Andrew and Camillia that she was having visions in her dreams and she got pulled into it so deeply that she could not wake up and no one could wake her either then Jaden had the idea to summon the miniangels and they got her out of the comatose state and they had a troublesome time and it almost did not work. Armellya said that she had been having foresight of an unspecified young man murdering females with the likeness of her and she was to be the first to be murdered. Armellya told Andrew and Camillia that the young man had gifts just like her and Jaden and the only pale ones who could get the gift of seeing the future would be their offspring then Camillia asked how the child was able to affect her at that time because he was not even conceived yet. Armellya explained as her miniangel had and told Armellya that everyone waiting to be born had a soul that was predestined to a set of parents and they can only use the gift of going into their parents dreams that was why when a woman dreams she was pregnant soon after she became pregnant and of course it symbolized change. Andrew asked Armellya and Jaden how to handle the seemingly tragic event and Jaden told him that if they were to conceive a boy they would birth him and closely observe him and with that would see the warning signs before the age of accountability then there would be two choices the first would be to place him in lock down with tranquilizers or the second choice would be to euthanize him. Camillia asked Armellya if she would be able to follow through with either of those options knowing that would be her young son and Armellya told her she would do whatever it took to keep the community safe because it was better to lose one dangerous member than a sizeable number of innocent women.

Right as Armellya paused in her explanation to Camillia there was a knock on the front door so Jaden went to answer the door and it was Matthew doing a security check because he knew Armellya was in there but could not find Andrew and Camillia and never thought they would be in there and he had no clue Jaden had left the hospital but everyone else had been in the family room waiting on Andrew to lead them to the castle's private dining hall for the lunch hour and family time. Jaden told Matthew that Andrew, Camillia, and Armellya were in there with him everything was fine and they would be out in just a minute and Matthew told Jaden he would let everyone know that Andrew was on his way then Jaden closed the front door. Jaden went back to the family room and told everyone they were thirty minutes late for the lunch hour and family time so Andrew and Camillia decided they knew enough and that if there were any questions or information to share they would speak at that time then Jaden and Armellya agreed that if there was any additional information or a need to have another opinion that they would go to Andrew or Camillia. Now that everything was out in the open and settled for now everyone in the house went to the castle's family room and Andrew apologized for their tardiness then led everyone to the castle's private dining hall where they got settled at the big roundtable. Melanie had the kitchen staff bring out lunch and serve everyone and everyone went around the table sharing their day and everyone got to share without being rushed and by the time family time was over it was a surprise that everyone finished sharing since they all got started a half hour late. Everyone got up from the big round table and went their own way while Melanie supervised the kitchen crew to clear and clean the big round table then go to clean the dishes, straighten up the kitchen, put extra food away, and start on the dinner meal.

CHAPTER EIGHTY

Jaden's day at the hospital was over for the day and he had nothing else he needed to do except be on call for the veterinarian, Armellya had no obligations for the rest of the day, and Andrew and Camillia had finished what their day held for them so Andrew suggested to Camillia, Armellya, and Jaden that they get together in Jaden and Armellya's home where there would be privacy and a lot of room to be comfortable and do some more teaching of what was expected of a king and queen. Everyone said that was an effective way to use inactive time then Camillia suggested that Andrew go over the community constitution because the kids would have to have that practically memorized and Andrew told Camillia that was an innovative idea and that maybe they could go over it before all further instruction because repetition was an effective way to get something into memory so Andrew excused himself from the young couple's family room and went to get the community's constitution. Andrew was only gone a few minutes by the time he returned with the document then Jaden asked if they were still getting up early the next morning since they were having a second teaching and Andrew told him yes because they were going to teach every opportunity they had so it could be completed as soon as possible. Camillia told the young couple that it would not be long before they replace them with the way time flies when Armellya told Camillia that she and

Andrew were still young and had a lot of ruling in them and that her and Jaden did not want to rule until there was no other possible choice. Camillia and Andrew told their children that ruling the commune was a big responsibility but not hard because the rules were founded by the first pale ones who created the commune in response of being able to create a way for those of them that survived the nuclear war above ground to survive below ground as pale ones and they did the hard work the rest was simply following instruction left on paper and it addressed all situations that could possibly arise as long as the commune was kept as a simple non technological community. Andrew told the kids that it would all make sense after reading the community constitution so Armellya and Jaden told Andrew to start and they would ask any questions they may have along the way and if there were any comments they would add those too so Andrew started to slowly read the community constitution.

Andrew finally finished reading the community constitution and the kids were relieved because it seemed to be a never-ending code of conduct and action to a reaction, Camillia asked the kids if they understood everything that was read and they both said yes then they both agreed with their parents that it would take some time to get it into memory. Jaden asked if there was a copy of the document anywhere because that would be the smart thing to do and Andrew told the kids that there was a copy in a safe with other important documents and they would share those other documents with them next. Andrew told Armellya and Jaden that he would leave that copy of the community constitution with them to read over in their spare time to make sure they got as much exposure to it as possible then he said he was going to go get the other documents out of the safe for them to see what type of things needed to be made official and secured. Andrew left for a few minutes and got back quickly then he sat down and got comfortable again then he handed the other documents to Armellya for her and Jaden to look at together while he stayed silent and let the documents speak for themselves. After several minutes Armellya looked up and said that the papers were on the death of the original head scientist, the suicide of the new head scientist, and the deaths of the last eight scientists due to the stand-off then Andrew told her she was correct that there were to be official papers on any death that was not due to age such as murder, suicide, and self-defense killing then Andrew added that if they did conceive a son who turned out to be a serial killer and had to either imprison him with tranquilizers or euthanize him that would be another document to keep in the safe.

Andrew took the death reports back from the kids and left the room with the papers to go put them back into the safe and lock them up then he returned and sat back in the spot he previously sat in. There was still a lot of time before the dinner hour, but the lesson had been a shocking one so Andrew asked the young couple if they wanted to continue or have some private time with each other then Armellya and Jaden agreed to continue with the teaching because they felt it needed to get done as soon as possible then they could spend more time observing their parents ruling and recognize the obvious but not seen side of ruling. The young couple could also take advantage of watching so if there were any questions or concerns they could get them addressed. There were another two hours of teaching then it was close to the dinner hour so they stopped the lesson for the night and the four of them headed out for the castle's family room to wait on the rest of the family. Within five minutes the rest of the family had arrived so Andrew led everyone to the castle's private dining hall and everyone got seated in their spots at the big round table then Melanie had the kitchen staff bring out dinner and serve everyone. As everyone ate they engaged in some light conversation and to Armellya and Jaden the meal seemed to end quickly and everyone else must have thought so also because while the kitchen staff was clearing and cleaning the big round table they all remained sitting and continued the conversation. While everyone was relaxing and conversing, Armellya suddenly bounced out of her chair and ran to her home. It alerted everyone because that was not something Armellya would ordinarily do so Jaden respectfully left the big round table to find out what was going on with Armellya. When Jaden got to his and Armellya's home, he went inside and quickly scanned the inside looking for Armellya then he realized she was crying hysterically so he followed the sound of the cries and found Armellya in their bed curled up in a fetal position.

Jaden sat on the edge of the bed and asked Armellya what was wrong, and she would not answer him she just kept on crying so Jaden had no choice but to try to read her mind but when he tried he found there was something blocking him and at first, he thought it could be their unconceived son but she was awake so that was not probable. Jaden put his hand on Armellya's side and he could feel immense amounts of heat radiating off her then out of instinct he put his hand on her belly and he realized it was the intrauterine baby blocking his efforts to read Armellya's mind, but for the first time he was reading the baby's mind and with that he found out she was in premature labor. Jaden jumped up off the edge of the bed and ran for his black bag then he got a vial of medicine and a syringe then he drew up some of the medicine and went over to Armellya and told her he was going to try to stop the labor then he stuck the needle in her buttock and injected the medicine. Jaden discarded the syringe appropriately then ran out of his house to the castle's dining hall to get Camillia to help calm Armellya and when he got to the castle's private dining hall no one was there so Jaden started calling out for Camillia. It took a few minutes and a lot of loud calling out but Camillia finally heard Jaden then she went to where he was and asked if Armellya was okay then Jaden told Camillia to follow him quickly then he turned and ran back to his house. Camillia ran right behind Jaden and when they got back to Armellya Jaden could tell the medicine was starting to work but he needed to check her out so he needed Camillia's help getting her to lay on her back and relax a bit. Armellya was still crying but not as bad so Camillia tried to talk to Armellya but she could only hear her own crying so finally Jaden rolled her over from her side to her back and told Camillia to keep her on her back and Camillia told Jaden she would try but that Armellya was a strong girl. Camillia tells Jaden to give her a few minutes to get Armellya's attention and he said to make it quick then Camillia spoke loudly to Armellya and told her that if she did not cooperate with Jaden she could hurt the baby then Armellya looked up to her mother and told her it did not hurt but she felt strange and it scared her.

Armellya was sobbing and slightly shaking, and Jaden saw her shaking but could not understand why she was in no pain and the temperature in the house was around seventy-six, which was appropriate for living in a cool, damp, non changing climate with no air conditioners or fans. Jaden took Armellya's temperature to make sure she did not have a fever, and it was sixty-five, which was normal for a pale one. Camillia had gotten Armellya's attention when she said something about her hurting the baby if she did not listen so Armellya told Jaden she was sorry for acting like such a mischievous child then Jaden gave Armellya a kiss on the cheek and told her he needed her to lay on her back so he could check her and the baby out. Camillia helped Armellya roll onto her back and held her hand while Jaden checked for cervical dilation and any sign of the baby crowning.

As Jaden got ready to cover Armellya back up, she said she had a contraction coming and it also gave a sensation of groin pressure. Jaden checked again as he told Armellya not to push, but it was too late, the baby's head was crowning. Jaden announced that this was it they were going to have to birth the baby that day because she was coming and there was no safe way to stop it with the baby already in the birth canal then Jaden told Armellya to push long and hard with the contractions and Armellya said okay then Camillia told Armellya that she could squeeze her hand as hard as she needed to help herself do what she had to do. Armellya asked Camillia to send for her father and the chief because she wanted to share the miracle of childbirth with her immediate family so Camillia summoned two of the castle's runners and told them who to find and instructed them to find their targets as fast as possible and get them into Armellya's bedroom because the baby was on the way then the runners ran off because they knew the baby could be born quickly or slowly but they did not want to chance their targets missing out on the blessed event if it were to be a quick birth. The runner for the chief went to the chief's side of the castle and knocked on the front door and when the butler answered the runner told the butler he needed the chief as fast as he could get him because Armellya was having the baby and fortunately he was there so the butler told the chief that a runner from the other side of the castle needed to get him to the other side for Armellya's delivery and the chief responded as fast as he could then not knowing the butler told the chief Armellya was in labor the runner told the chief that Armellya was having the baby and she wanted him there then the chief took off with the speed that only a pale one had which was much faster than that of a human. When the chief got to the royal family's side of the castle, he did not knock as usual. He just walked in and went directly to Jaden and Armellya's home and walked in and did not even shut the door back then the chief went to the couple's bedroom. The chief told Armellya he was there then shortly after the chief got there, Andrew was on his way. It took a few minutes longer for the runner to find Andrew because he had to go through the entire castle looking for Andrew starting with the most likely place and when the runner found Andrew he was in the least likely place then he told Andrew that Armellya wanted him by her side and she was having the baby so Andrew ran to Armellya and Jaden's home and when he got there he just walked in and went straight to Armellya in the bedroom.

Everyone that Armellya wanted by her side to help bring the baby into their world was there so she relaxed a lot, and Jaden could tell so he was pleased with her physical and mental state because it would make the labor easier on her and the baby. However, there was a problem that arose; it seemed that the anti contraction medicine had started to work and the contractions stopped but the baby had already crowned. Jaden had to give Armellya another medicine to induce labor for the safety of the new baby and the comfort of Armellya. Jaden was concerned about getting the inducement medicine into Armellya as quick as possible so instead of giving her an injection in her buttock, he got intravenous access and pushed the medicine into Armellya's veins for an almost instant absorption to start her contractions as soon as possible. It took about fifteen minutes before the contractions started again but they did and Jaden was pleased. Jaden announced that the baby was on its way; then Armellya told Jaden she could feel the contractions but she was not in any pain, it was a different sensation that she could not describe and she could feel the baby progressing. It was a slow progression but everyone was helping by telling Armellya when to push and to push hard so she followed their instruction, they could tell when she had a contraction by observing her stomach peak and harden.

The labor lasted about forty-five minutes, but when the baby was delivered, she cried immediately so to Jaden that was a good sign and everyone was relieved then Jaden checked the baby over then handed her to Armellya to hold while he cut the umbilical cord and clamped the stump. Armellya told everyone the baby was to be called Jadellya; then she checked the baby over as all new moms did and found she was perfect and as soon as Armellya checked baby Jadellya her nanny arrived to clean her up while Armellya's personal maid arrived to clean her and her bedding.

After Armellya and her bedding was cleaned, Camillia, Andrew, the chief, and Jaden gave Armellya hugs and kisses and told her how great she did during the delivery and that she had a beautiful little girl then Armellya thanked everyone for being there to support her and Jadellya because it was a special event that she wanted to share with them and they were thankful. Camillia, Andrew, and the chief needed to get back to what they were doing so they gave Armellya farewell hugs and told her they would check back with her later then Armellya told them she planned to have dinner at the castle's private dining hall with everyone then they said they would see her there and they left her and Jaden's home. Jaden stayed with Armellya since he had nowhere to be and nothing to do and it was only a half hour until the dinner hour. Jaden and Armellya talked about how wonderful it would be to raise Jadellya and see her reach and overcome milestones then find something to do in the community when she got old enough to have a vocation. In the middle of conversation, the couple was interrupted by their miniangels; they told the new parents that they had put the nanny to sleep, and they all visited the new baby who was to be their queen. When they left, they woke the nanny and she never knew what happened. The miniangels said the infant was beautiful and more intelligent than anyone in the compound including her father who was the only prodigy in the commune. The miniangels expressed that she was more than a genius and beyond that of a prodigy, and she would become queen at the age of accountability, which would be earlier for her than other children.

Other children usually hit the age of accountability around eight years of age but Jadellya would be of the age of accountability around five years of age and every night at the midnight hour all the miniangels would visit her then go to visit their pale one. Armellya told her miniangel that she had a strong telepathic bond with the infant then Jaden said he did also it started during the delivery then the mini angels told the couple that alone was not heard of and that was part of the child's strength in abilities to come because she already had her abilities mastered and all other babies did not have their abilities strengthened until they were past their toddler years. Armellya and Jaden told their miniangels they were blessed with such a child and honored that she would be queen of the miniangels then Armellya asked her miniangel why they needed a queen shortly from that point because they had been around for all time and never had a queen or dominant miniangel and Armellya's miniangel told her it was due to the changing times and that was all she could say about that but they would see the dramatic changes and figure it out soon.

The miniangel told the new parents it was like having a king and queen for their own society because there needed to be an entity for general guidance and the troubles of the society to be addressed and quashed, it was simply a safety measure. Armellya told the miniangel that it had something to do with their unconceived son that because he was to be as a demon seed there had to be an opposing factor like an angelic sibling and Jadellya was that factor then the miniangel said she could not respond to that comment but again they would see and understand why there were going to be adjustments made. The miniangels told the new parents that it was the dinner hour so it was time for them to leave but they would be back during the midnight hour then they left. Jaden checked the time and found that their miniangels left them five minutes to get to the family room so they left their house immediately and walked to the castle's family room to wait for everyone to be there. When the new parents got to the family room, most of the family was there and the rest trickled in behind them so as usual Andrew led everyone to the castle's private dining hall then everyone found their seats and sat down. Melanie had the kitchen crew bring dinner out and serve everyone and when the kitchen crew finished but before anyone had a chance to start eating Jadellya's nanny brought her to the castle's private dining hall for everyone to see and pass around and there were far more individuals at the big round table than there was in Armellya's bedroom.

Jaden, Camillia, Bridgette, Melanie, Michelle, Matthew, all their parents, and the chief were at the big round table and everyone held Jadellya then kissed her little head before passing her to the next individual. Thirty minutes later, the baby was handed to the nanny who took the infant to her nursery and everyone at the big round table began to eat. The conversation during dinner was all about Jadellya and how beautiful she was; then when everyone finished eating and when they finished, they knew it was time to wrap up the day and go to their quarters to get ready for bed and see their miniangel at the midnight hour. Melanie had to supervise the kitchen staff for cleaning the kitchen up and storing the leftover food. The chief had nothing to do so he went to his side of the castle and prepared for bed. Andrew and Camillia were going to practice some of their gifts before turning in for the evening like telekinesis, Michelle's duties were finished for the day so she went to prepare for bed, Bridgette went back to her nanny duties, and Armellya and Jaden went to their home to practice their abilities also. By the time the castle was settled down and most everyone was in bed, Andrew, Camillia, Armellya, and Jaden got ready for bed and now everyone was working on going to sleep; and it did not take long for the entire castle to be asleep. When the midnight hour came, all the miniangels visited Jadellya, and she loved her miniangel friends. With her abilities already fully formed, she bestowed strength to gifts the miniangels already had that they were weak in and after a short while the miniangels left Jadellya to see their pale ones where the general population talked to their miniangels about their day and the day to come. Camillia and Andrew talked to their miniangels about personal and community issues, Armellya and Jaden talked to their miniangels about the community and personal issues, and now their children both the one they just birthed and the one not conceived yet.

On average, each miniangel spent about a half hour with their individual, but the group of miniangels spent twenty to forty-five minutes with Jadellya, and the other children only got fifteen minutes with their miniangels. The miniangels had finished their visits for the night so they all went back to the dinosaur tail, and with the exception of Jadellya, everyone else went to sleep but Jadellya astral projected to the dinosaur tail to speak to the miniangels about her unconceived brother because she knew everything that Camillia, Andrew, Armellya, Jaden, and the miniangels knew about him and she wanted to help protect the commune as well as help her parents out in dealing with him and controlling what he would be able to do prior to the age of accountability. Jadellya knew there would be a battle of good versus evil between her and her brother, and her parents would be involved as victims. The miniangels told Jadellya they could not speak of the future that far in advance, but they could guide her when the time was at hand then Jadellya told the miniangels that she could see into the future farther than her parents but not as far as them. Jadellya even knew when her brother would be conceived and that it would be a dark angel that would lie with her mother in the form of her father; she even knew what the child would be called. Jadellya understood the miniangels could say and do only so much but with her help not just her parents, but the miniangels would have their gifts become stronger, which was necessary to stand up to her brother because one cannot avoid destiny, and her brother's existence was an act of destiny for without bad, recognizing good would be impossible. Jadellya left the dinosaur tail and returned to her body then slept the rest of the night, but she did not get much sleep because the early morning hour came quickly. When her parents awoke, their telepathic link woke Jadellya. Most babies slept more than they were awake, but the link with her parents had her sleeping when they slept and awake when they were awake. Armellya and Jaden had to get up two hours earlier than usual so they could get their lesson about ruling the commune then it would be the breakfast hour followed by time to take care of responsibilities then the lunch hour and family time then free time and bedtime.

Most everyone had the same schedule every day unless there was a situation that arose. The chief had the easiest schedule now that he had retired from being the community ruler. Camillia and Andrew had some challenging days when there were uprising situations, but generally, things stayed the same for them as well. Bridgette was a nanny so she was definitely on a schedule with the child she had to take care of. Melanie was always in the kitchen supervising things there so her day always stayed the same and only got exciting when there was to be a party. Matthew, being head of security, did the same thing every day, but he often had an extra duty pop into his schedule, which consisted of assistance calls. Michelle was head of the maids so she supervised the rest of the maids and served Camillia once in a while when her maid needed help, but her schedule was pretty much the same daily. The community members were the same; it was a simple society made up of polite law-abiding individuals who escaped the trauma of the corrupt and over complex human lifestyle according to Camillia's viewpoint.

www.ingramcontent.com/pod-product-compliance
Lightning Source LLC
Chambersburg PA
CBHW051304190726
48290CB00001B/4